Daughters of Earth

DAUGHTERS OF EARTH

Feminist Science Fiction
in the Twentieth Century

Edited by Justine Larbalestier

WESLEYAN UNIVERSITY PRESS

MIDDLETOWN, CONNECTICUT

Published by Wesleyan University Press, Middletown, CT 06459
www.wesleyan.edu/wespress

Library of Congress Cataloging-in-Publication Data

Daughters of earth : feminist science fiction in the twentieth
century / edited by Justine Larbalestier.
    p. cm.
Includes bibliographical references.
ISBN–13: 978–0–8195–6675–1 (cloth : alk. paper)
ISBN–10: 0–8195–6675–6 (cloth : alk. paper)
ISBN–13: 978–0–8195–6676–8 (pbk. : alk. paper)
ISBN–10: 0–8195–6676–4 (pbk. : alk. paper)
1. Science fiction, American.   2. Feminist fiction, American.   3. American
fiction—20th century.   4. American fiction—Women authors.   5. Sex role—
Fiction.   I. Larbalestier, Justine.
PS648.S3D38   2006
813'.08762099287090904—dc22   2005030647

The editor and publisher gratefully acknowledge the following:

"And I Awoke and Found Me, Here on the Cold Hill's Side" by James Tiptree, Jr., copyright ©
1972, 2000 by James Tiptree, Jr.; first appeared in *The Magazine of Fantasy and Science Fiction*; reprinted by permission of the author's Estate and the Estate's agents, the Virginia Kidd Agency, Inc.

"Rachel in Love" by Pat Murphy, copyright ©1987 by Pat Murphy; first published in *Isaac Asimov's Science Fiction Magazine*. Reprinted by permission of the Jean V. Naggar Literary Agency.

"Created He Them" by Alice Eleanor Jones, copyright © 1955 by Fantasy house, Inc. First published in *The Magazine of Fantasy and Science Fiction*, June 1955. Reprinted by permission of the
Scott Meredith Literary Agency and Spilogale, Inc.

"What I didn't See" by Karen Joy Fowler, copyright © 2002 by Karen Joy Fowler. First published
on www.scifi.com in *scifiction*, July 2002. Reprinted by permission of the author.

"Balinese Dancer" by Gwyneth Jones, copyright © 1997 by Gwyneth Jones. First published in
Isaac Asimov's Science Fiction Magazine, September 1997. Reprinted by permission of the author.

"Wives" by Lisa Tuttle, copyright © 1983 by Lisa Tuttle. First published in *The Magazine of Fantasy and Science Fiction*, December 1979. Reprinted by permission of the author.

"No Light in the Window" by Kate Wilhelm, copyright © 1963 by Kate Wilhelm. First published
by Berkley Publishing Corp., 1963. Reprinted by permission of the author.

"Heat Death of the Universe" by Pamela Zoline, copyright © 1967 by Pamela Zoline. First published in *New Worlds*, July 1967. Reprinted by permission of the author.

"The Evening and The Morning and the Night" by Octavia E. Butler, copyright © 1987 by Octavia E. Butler. First published by Omni Publications International. Reprinted by permission of
the author.

For all the amazing science fiction feminists
who blazed a trail for the rest of us.

Contents

Editor's Acknowledgments

Because *Daughters of Earth* is both an anthology of short stories and a collection of essays, it owes a debt to all the previous anthologists of feminist sf as well as earlier feminist sf scholarship. The anthologies that have made this one possible include Pamela Sargent's groundbreaking *Women of Wonder* series, the first of which was published in 1975, as well as Susan Janice Anderson's and Vonda N. McIntyre's *Aurora Beyond Equality* (1976), and Jen Green and Sarah Lefanu's *Despatches from the Frontiers of the Female Mind* (1985).

It is no coincidence that some of these anthologists are sf writers (Pamela Sargent, Vonda McIntyre) or scholars (Pamela Sargent, Sarah Lefanu) themselves. At the time those anthologies appeared, many believed there was little interest in feminist science fiction. You had to be passionately interested in feminism *and* science fiction to want to put such a book together. As Pamela Sargent writes in *Women of Wonder, The Classic Years: Science Fiction by Women from the 1940s to the 1970s* (Orlando: Harcourt Brace, 1995):

> Twenty years ago, my first anthology, *Women of Wonder*, was published. It was the first anthology of its kind: science fiction stories by women about women. For over two years, I tried to find a publisher for *Women of Wonder*, and the reactions of editors were instructive. A few editors thought the idea was wonderful but decided not to do the book anyway. Some editors found the idea absurd, a couple doubted whether I could find enough good stories to fill the book, and one editor didn't think there was a large enough audience.(1)

As Sargent says, she was the first, and her anthologies are still the best known in the field, reprinting wonderful stories and, just as important, introducing each of her anthologies with long, informative, witty accounts of women writing science fiction. *Daughters of Earth* owes Sargent and her anthologies a huge debt.

This anthology also owes an enormous amount to the pioneering scholars of feminist science fiction: Joanna Russ, Ursula K. Le Guin, Susan Wood, Mary Badami, and Beverly Friend. Their tireless work from the early seventies onward brought attention to the present absence that dares not speak its name: women and feminism in science fiction. In the years since Joanna Russ first wrote her heartfelt plea for science fiction to begin seriously engaging with the feminist revolution of the sixties and seventies

("The Image of Women in Science Fiction," 1971), feminist science fiction has not only prospered, it is now a worldwide community that gathers once a year at WisCon in Madison, Wisconsin.

The most direct precursor to this collection is Helen Merrick and Tess Williams's *Women of Other Worlds: Excursions Through Science Fiction and Feminism* (1999). *Women of Other Worlds* included essays and stories and even the transcript of an online discussion about one of the stories it reprinted, Kelley Eskridge's "And Salome Danced." The focal point of that collection was the 20th WisCon, the world's first feminist science fiction convention. You will find mentions of that convention sprinkled across the pages of this anthology. Indeed, it is where I first met two of the contributors, Brian Attebery and L. Timmel Duchamp.

Putting together an anthology like this is a great deal of work and involves many people. I thank Samuel R. Delany for mentoring me. Without his scholarly work this book and *The Battle of the Sexes in Science Fiction* before it would have been much the poorer, and without his active support and encouragement, I doubt either book would have found its way into print. Thank you.

Suzanna Tamminen, whose idea this book was, thanks for your support and patience. Who knew how tricky it would be?

Thank you, Brian Atterbery, Jane Donawerth, L. Timmel Duchamp, Joan Haran, Andrea Hairston, Cathy Hawkins, Veronica Hollinger, Josh Lukin, Mary Papke, Wendy Pearson, and Lisa Yaszek. Without you there'd be no book. Not only did you write the essays contained herein from which I have learned so much, but your numerous suggestions and ideas have made this book vastly better than it otherwise would've been. I especially thank Andrea Hairston for her last-minute heroics. I still don't know how you did it!

All the living writers were amazingly generous and enthusiastic about this project. Thank you, Octavia Butler, Karen Joy Fowler, Gwyneth Jones, Pat Murphy, Lisa Tuttle, Kate Wilhelm, and Pamela Zoline.

Thanks also to Jeffrey Smith for providing the authorative version of James Tiptree Jr.'s "And I Awoke and Found Me Here on the Cold Hill's Side." And to Julie Phillips, Tiptree's brilliant biographer, for all her advice and information about Alice James Raccoona Tiptree Hastings Davey Bradley Sheldon Jr.

I also thank the following for their help with copyright and tracking texts and authors down: John Clute, Ellen Datlow, Nalo Hopkinson, Barry Malzberg, Nanci McClosky (Virginia Kidd Associates), Brian Pearce, Tim Pratt, Gordon Van Gelder, and Terri Windling.

Thanks also to Ellen Datlow, Gordon Van Gelder, and Terry Windling for their advice on the tricky art of editing an anthology, and for their answers to questions about *Omni, The Magazine of Fantasy and Science Fiction,* and the genre publishing scene generally.

Special thanks to Scott Westerfeld for all his help in the final days of preparing this manuscript and to Kelly Link for bailing me out at the last minute with her transcription skills. And to Eloise Flood for everything.

Thanks to Betty Waterhouse for her excellent copyediting and to the unflappable Ann Brash, the world's best production editor, for answering all my questions so quickly and so well.

I adore librarians and my very favoritest librarians work in the Rare Books department of Sydney Uni's Fisher Library. Thanks once again to Neil Boness, Sara Hilder, Julie Price, Richard Ratajczak, and Suzana Sukovic. You're all amazing.

Lastly, many thanks to John Bern, Niki Bern, Jan Larbalestier, and Scott Westerfeld for putting up with my whingeing.

Contributors' Acknowledgments

BRIAN ATTEBERY: Thanks to all those who have pushed me toward some understanding of feminist ways of thinking, including Ursula K. Le Guin, Veronica Hollinger, Karen Joy Fowler, Joan Gordon, Jennifer Eastman Attebery, and the whole Tiptree gang.

JANE DONAWERTH: For the pulp science fiction research, I thank the Azriel Rosenfeld Science Fiction Research Collection, Special Collections, Albin O. Kuhn Library, University of Maryland, Baltimore County, and the librarians who work there. For the idea to write about this story in the context of the contest, I thank Jenny Bonnevier, who was a Fullbright graduate student from Sweden studying with me when I was beginning the essay.

L. TIMMEL DUCHAMP: I would like to thank Karen Joy Fowler, who commented on an early draft of this essay, Justine Larbalestier, for providing excellent editorial direction, and Eileen Gunn, for bibliographical assistance.

ANDREA HAIRSTON: Thanks to Pan Welland and James Emery for reading several drafts and talking through ideas any time of the day or night. Thanks to John Hellweg, Ama Patterson, Kevin Quashie, and Sheree R. Thomas for great feedback, support, and insight. Thanks also to the students in my Speculative Theatre and Film class at Smith College for regular inspiration.

JOAN HARAN: Thanks to Pat Murphy for careful consideration of and thoughtful answers to my questions about her story. Thanks to the Economic and Social Research Council for supporting the Centre for Economic and Social Aspects of Genomics where I work as a Research Associate. Thanks to Niamh Moore for feedback on my writing, and to my partner, Gary Fleming, for taking up all the domestic slack and providing constant moral support.

CATHY HAWKINS: I extend my sincerest thanks to Lisa Tuttle for sharing her memories of writing "Wives" and a host of other fascinating background details. My gratitude also to Anne Cranny-Francis for her continued support and knowledge of women's sf.

VERONICA HOLLINGER: I thank Gwyneth Jones both for her fine story and for her very helpful comments as I was preparing my essay. I also thank Istvan Csicsery-Ronay Jr., Andrew M. Butler, and the Merril Collection of Science Fiction, Speculation and Fantasy for providing me with indispensable research materials.

JOSH LUKIN: I thank Austin Booth and the SUNY–Buffalo libraries for the resources that enabled me to study Kate Wilhelm. The Pink Curmudgeons effectively persuaded me to embark upon the project and coerced me into completing it. Ann Keefer provided indispensable comments on initial drafts of the piece; Betty Waterhouse gave invaluable aid in polishing the final draft. Dr. Vince Gugino expressed an inspiring faith in the essay's importance. Samuel R. Delany and Ray Davis helped to persuade me that it was important to essay a defense of Kate Wilhelm's short fiction and provided many hours of stimulating conversation when my brain was about to roll over and give up the ghost.

MARY PAPKE: I am most grateful to Pamela Zoline for offering me new perspectives on her past and future. I also thank my brother Paul for sharing his *War of the Worlds* Classics Comic with me so very long ago and opening the door for me into the other world of science fiction. And as always, profound thanks to Allen, the best interlocutor in all my worlds.

WENDY PEARSON: I thank Justine Larbalestier for her invaluable editing skills, Veronica Hollinger for her steadfast encouragement and friendship as well as for her insights into Tiptree's work, and Susan Knabe for everything.

LISA YASZEK: First and foremost, I thank Doug Davis for his good critical eye and steadfast support throughout this project. I also thank professor emeritus Irving F. "Bud" Foote for creating the Bud Foote Science Fiction Collection and passing its care on to me; the collection has been a true source of joy and inspiration for science fiction scholars at Georgia Tech and beyond. Finally, I dedicate my essay to Katharine Calhoun, Martha Saghini, and all the other women who work for Georgia Tech's Interlibrary Loan Program: it is your hard work and dedication that make all things possible for all scholars at Georgia Tech.

Introduction

Daughters of Earth is a complete introduction to twentieth-century feminist science fiction, bringing together eleven of the best short stories from the genre's beginnings to the early twenty-first century. Each story is accompanied by an essay that examines the story and its author, illuminating their place within the history of science fiction and feminism.

The earliest tale was first published in 1927 in *Amazing Stories*, the first English-language magazine dedicated to science fiction (or "scientifiction" as it was known then). *Amazing* is where the science fiction community and fandom were born.[1] The most recent story first appeared online in 2002 at *scifiction*,[2] scifi.com's fiction site. This change in venue echoes the changes in the science fiction community over this period: seventy years ago all the debates, conversations, arguments, and ranting that were (and are) such an important part of the community were found in the pages of science fiction magazines and fanzines; now that conversation is predominantly found online.

Some of these stories have been out of print and unavailable for years. Of the four earliest stories, only Leslie F. Stones's "Conquest of Gola" (1933) has been reprinted in the last twenty years. Clare Winger Harris's "The Fate of the Poseidonia" (1927) and Kate Wilhelm's "No Light in the Window" (1963) have never been reprinted, and Alice Eleanor Jones's "Created He Them" (1955) was reprinted only once in the year after its first appearance.[3]

Too many sf stories are published and then disappear,[4] and of the stories that are reprinted, too few have received any critical attention. I wanted to find a balance in this anthology between introducing people to long-out-of-print stories they would never otherwise read and reprinting better-known works that have never been the subject of study. Certainly, the eleven stories in *Daughters of Earth* have not had much (in most cases, *any*) scholarly work done on them.

Daughters of Earth includes essays by eleven scholars working within the academy in Australia, Canada, the United Kingdom, and the United States, as well as one by the independent critic and science fiction writer L. Timmel Duchamp. Pioneers of science fiction and fantasy scholarship such as Brian Attebery, Jane Donawerth, and Veronica Hollinger are represented, as are relative newbies Joan Haran, Cathy Hawkins, Josh Lukin, Wendy Pearson, and Lisa Yaszek, all of whom received their Ph.D.'s within the last five years.

While *Daughters* is aimed squarely at newcomers to feminist science fiction, there's still plenty here for connoisseurs of the field. I was unaware, until I read Lisa Yaszek's wonderful essay, that Alice Eleanor Jones had written romances as well as science fiction, as well as a great deal of commentary about writing for popular fiction magazines. Nor was I aware of how little I knew about the black history of science fiction until I read Andrea Hairston's extraordinary essay in praise of that prophetic artist, Octavia Butler.

Feminism

But what *is* feminism? Is a story feminist merely because it is about women? Or written by a woman? Can a story that has no women in it be feminist? Can a man write a feminist story? Are all the stories in this collection feminist?

I can imagine definitions that would not count Harris's "The Fate of the Poseidonia" as feminist or would reject Wilhelm's "No Light in the Window." Indeed, Josh Lukin's eloquent essay about the Wilhelm story addresses the feminism of the story in great detail. As does Lisa Yaszek in her discussion of Alice Eleanor Jones's "Created He Them." The feminism of those stories can be argued with, but no one can question the feminist perspectives of the essays about the stories. This is not a fine distinction. Feminism is as much a way of reading as it is a way of writing.

This is not to imply that each essay is informed by the same kind of feminism. Definitions of feminism are varied, as are understandings of feminist science fiction's history. Joan Haran's essay verges on utopian when she writes of the political possibilities for change presented by Pat Murphy's "Rachel in Love," while L. Timmel Duchamp's view of contemporary feminism in her essay on Karen Joy Fowler's "What I Didn't See" verges on the pessimistic.

Science Fiction

Perhaps even trickier than defining feminism is the question, What is science fiction? Long and detailed arguments about the genre's borders and historical precedents have been raging since the advent of science fiction magazines in the 1920s.

I have long believed, along with Damon Knight, that something that is published as science fiction and read as science fiction *is* science fiction. However, even sf readers with a less elastic understanding of the field will find that the stories in this collection meet most people's definitions. Many are set in outer space or involve interstellar travel ("The Fate of the Poseidonia," "Conquest of Gola," "No Light in the Window," "And I Awoke and Found Me Here on the Cold Hillside," and "Wives"); set in post-apocalyptic futures ("Created He Them" and "Balinese Dancer"); treat directly with scientific theory and practice ("Heat Death of the Universe," "Rachel in Love," "The Evening and the Morning and the Night," and "Balinese Dancer"); or first contact ("And I Awoke and Found Me Here on the Cold Hillside" and "What I Didn't See").

Two of the stories have had their science-fictionness questioned: "Heat Death of the Universe" and "What I Didn't See." The essays about them by Mary Papke and L. Timmel Duchamp make compelling cases for their inclusion within the genre of science fiction — and more precisely, within feminist science fiction.

The Twentieth Century

Even the question of how to define the twentieth century is not straight-forward. Did it end in 1999 or the year 2000? An astute reader will notice that the last story in this collection, Karen Joy Fowler's "What I Didn't See," was originally published in 2002, which is in the twenty-first century no matter where you place the millennium's edge. Why include it? As L. Timmel Duchamp demonstrates, "What I Didn't See" is a story *about* twentieth-century feminist science fiction, neatly bringing together many of the themes, ideas, and issues of the genre and that century. Most partic-ularly, of course, the story is shaped by and comments on the life and writ-ings of that quintessentially twentieth-century feminist sf figure: James Tip-tree Jr., whose shadow lies across many of the essays in this collection.

Omissions

I let my essayists decide which story they wanted to write about, which meant that some stories that I wish could have been included weren't. It also led to no story from the 1940s being included, the only decade miss-ing from these pages.[5] Of course, one of the advantages of allowing essay-ists to choose their own stories is being able to pass the buck when this an-thology is accused of terrible omissions. "Well," I can say, "they chose the stories, you know, not me." But in all honesty, even if I had selected each one, the end result would have been the same: many extraordinary, im-portant, brilliant feminist sf stories would still have been omitted. Stories like Joanna Russ's "When It Changed" (1972), Ursula K. Le Guin's "The Ones Who Walk Away from Omelas" (1973), and Suzy McKee Charnas's "Boobs" (1989).

Daughters of Earth was always going to leave out stories critical to shaping the genre, no matter who made the selections. As a result this anthology cannot possibly claim to represent twentieth-century feminist science fiction exhaustively. But it can lay claim to opening up new understandings of the stories assembled here and thus of feminist sf in its first century of existence.

The omission of stories by the three giants of feminist science fiction — Suzy McKee Charnas, Ursula K. Le Guin, and Joanna Russ — was particularly hard. The impact on the genre of Charnas's *Holdfast* series and of the stories, novels, and criticism of Le Guin and Russ was, and is, enormous. Quite simply, this book would not exist without them.

There are too many other omissions to list them all. There are writers who weren't included because I couldn't secure the rights, because they don't write short stories, because their work has been so thoroughly written about already, or simply because no matter how wonderful their stories, there was only ever going to be eleven in this collection. Some of the other extraordinary feminist science fiction writers of the twentieth century are Samuel R. Delany, Sonja Dorman, L. Timmel Duchamp, Carol Emshwiller, Nalo Hopkinson, Leigh Kennedy, Kelly Link, Anne McCaffrey, Katherine McLean, Judith Merril, C. L. Moore, Kit Reed, Margaret St Clair, and Connie Willis. I hope this book will give those of you have not read feminist science fiction before a taste for more. Hunt out the names I mention here, and others that are mentioned in the essays. Read them. You'll not regret it.

The collection's title comes from Judith Merril's superb 1952 novella, "Daughters of Earth," which serves as a reminder that women have written science fiction for as long as the genre has been around, and that science fiction is always about the here and now, about this place where humans live.

We are all children of earth.

NOTES

1. For the full story, see my *The Battle of the Sexes in Science Fiction*, 15–38.

2. That's right, "scientifiction" with the "enti" left out. Coincidence? Probably. But it's a cool one.

3. And by the same people. The story originally appeared in the June 1955 issue of *The Magazine of Fantasy and Science Fiction* and was then reprinted in *The Best*

from Fantasy and Science Fiction: Fifth Series, edited by Anthony Boucher (Double-day, 1956).

4. These disappearings happen because many sf stories were originally printed in sf magazines and have only rarely been reprinted. There are very few public collections of these magazines—and even if you can get hold of the magazines, many are in very bad shape: I have had the awful experience of carefully turning the page of a pulp magazine only to feel it crumble beneath my gloved hands. Heartbreaking. There is an urgent need for these stories to be preserved.

5. Several were suggested.

Daughters of Earth

𝌚 1

The Fate of the Poseidonia

CLARE WINGER HARRIS

First published in Amazing Stories, June 1927

Third Prize Winner in the $500 Prize Cover Contest
Third Prize of $100.00 awarded to Mrs. F. C. Harris, 1652 Lincoln Avenue, Lakewood, Ohio, for
"The Fate of the Poseidonia"

That the third prize winner should prove to be a woman was one of the surprises of the contest, for, as a rule, women do not make good scientifiction writers, because their education and general tendencies on scientific matters are usually limited. But the exception, as usual, proves the rule, the exception in this case being extraordinarily impressive. The story has a great deal of charm, chiefly because it is not overburdened with science, but whatever science is contained therein is not only quite palatable, but highly desirable, due to its plausibility. Not only this, but you will find that the author is a facile writer who keeps your interest unto [sic] the last line. We hope to see more of Mrs. Harris's scientifiction in Amazing Stories.

I

The first moment I laid eyes on Martell I took a great dislike to the man. There sprang up between us an antagonism that as far as he was concerned might have remained passive, but which circumstances forced into activity on my side.

How distinctly I recall the occasion of our meeting at the home of Professor Stearns, head of the Astronomy department of Austin College. The address which the professor proposed giving before the Mentor Club of which I was a member, was to be on the subject of the planet, Mars. The spacious front rooms of the Stearns home were crowded for the occasion with rows of chairs, and at the end of the double parlors a screen was erected for the purpose of presenting telescopic views of the ruddy planet in its various aspects.

As I entered the parlor after shaking hands with my hostess, I felt, rather than saw, an unfamiliar presence, and the impression I received involuntarily was that of antipathy. What I saw was the professor himself engaged in earnest conversation with a stranger. Intuitively I knew that from the latter emanated the hostility of which I was definitely conscious.

He was a man of slightly less than average height. At once I noticed that he did not appear exactly normal physically and yet I could not ascertain in what way he was deficient. It was not until I had passed the entire evening in his company that I was fully aware of his bodily peculiarities. Perhaps the most striking characteristic was the swarthy, coppery hue of his flesh that was not unlike that of an American Indian. His chest and shoulders seemed abnormally developed, his limbs and features extremely slender in proportion. Another peculiar individuality was the wearing of a skull-cap pulled well down over his forehead.

Professor Stearns caught my eye, and with a friendly nod indicated his desire that I meet the new arrival.

"Glad to see you, Mr. Gregory," he said warmly as he clasped my hand. "I want you to meet Mr. Martell, a stranger in our town, but a kindred spirit, in that he is interested in Astronomy and particularly in the subject of my lecture this evening."

I extended my hand to Mr. Martell and imagined that he responded to my salutation somewhat reluctantly. Immediately I knew why. The texture of the skin was most unusual. For want of a better simile, I shall say that it felt not unlike a fine dry sponge. I do not believe that I betrayed any visible surprise, though inwardly my whole being revolted. The deep, close-set eyes of the stranger seemed searching me for any manifestation of antipathy, but I congratulate myself that my outward poise was undisturbed by the strange encounter.

The guests assembled, and I discovered to my chagrin that I was seated next to the stranger, Martell. Suddenly the lights were extinguished preparatory to the presentation of the lantern-slides. The darkness that enveloped us was intense. Supreme horror gripped me when I presently became conscious of two faint phosphorescent lights to my right. There could be no mistaking their origin. They were the eyes of Martell and they were regarding me with an enigmatical stare. Fascinated, I gazed back into those diabolical orbs with an emotion akin to terror. I felt that I should shriek and then attack their owner. But at the precise moment when my usually steady nerves threatened to betray me, the twin lights vanished. A second later the lantern light flashed on the screen. I stole a furtive glance in the direction of Martell. He was sitting with his eyes closed.

"The planet Mars should be of particular interest to us," began Professor Stearns, "not only because of its relative proximity to us, but because of the fact that there are visible upon its surface undeniable evidences of the handiwork of man, and I am inclined to believe in the existence of mankind there not unlike the humanity of the earth."

The discourse proceeded uninterruptedly. The audience remained quiet and attentive, for Professor Stearns possessed the faculty of holding his listeners spell-bound. A large map of one hemisphere of Mars was thrown on the screen, and simultaneously the stranger Martell drew in his breath sharply with a faint whistling sound.

The professor continued, "Friends, do you observe that the outstanding physical difference between Mars and Terra appears to be in the relative distribution of land and water? On our own globe the terrestrial parts lie as distinct entities surrounded by the vast aqueous portions, whereas, on Mars the land and water are so intermingled by gulfs, bays, capes and peninsulas that it requires careful study to ascertain for a certainty which is which. It is my opinion, and I do not hold it alone, for much discussion with my worthy colleagues has made it obvious, that the peculiar land contours are due to the fact that water is becoming a very scarce commodity on our neighboring planet. Much, of what is now land is merely the exposed portions of the one-time ocean bed; the precious life-giving fluid now occupying only the lowest depressions. We may conclude that the telescopic eye, when turned on Mars, sees a waning world; the habitat of a people struggling desperately and vainly for existence, with inevitable extermination facing them in the not far distant future. What will they do? If they are no farther advanced in the evolutionary stage than a carrot or a jelly-fish, they will ultimately succumb to fate, but if they are men and women such as you and I, they will fight for the continuity of their race. I am inclined to the opinion that the Martians will not die without putting up a brave struggle, which will result in the prolongation of their existence, but not in their complete salvation."

Professor Stearns paused. "Are there any questions?" he asked.

I was about to speak when the voice of Martell boomed in my ear, startling me.

"In regard to the map, professor," he said, "I believe that gulf which lies farthest south is not a gulf at all but is a part of the land portion surrounding it. I think you credit the poor dying planet with even more water than it actually has!"

"It is possible and even probable that I have erred," replied the learned man, "and I am sorry indeed if that gulf is to be withdrawn from the credit of the Martians, for their future must look very black."

"Just suppose," resumed Martell, leaning toward the lecturer with interested mien, "that the Martians were the possessors of an intelligence equal to that of terrestrials, what might they do to save themselves from total extinction? In other words to bring it home to us more realistically, what would we do were we threatened with a like disaster?"

"That is a very difficult question to answer, and one upon which merely an opinion could be ventured," smiled Professor Stearns. "'Necessity is the mother of invention, and in our case without the likelihood of the existence of the mother, we can hardly hazard a guess as to the nature of the off-spring. But always, as Terra's resources have diminished, the mind of man has discovered substitutes. There has always been a way out, and let us hope our brave planetary neighbors will succeed in solving their problem."

"Let us hope so indeed," echoed the voice of Martell.

II

At the time of my story in the winter of [1994–1995]*, I was still unmarried and was living in a private hotel on E. Ferguson Ave., where I enjoyed the comforts of well furnished bachelor quarters. To my neighbors I paid little or no attention, absorbed in my work during the day and paying court to Margaret Landon in the evenings.

I was not a little surprised upon one occasion, as I stepped into the corridor, to see a strange yet familiar figure in the hotel locking the door of the apartment adjoining my own. Almost instantly I recognized Martell, on whom I had not laid eyes since the meeting some weeks previous at the home of Professor Stearns. He evinced no more pleasure at our meeting than I did, and after the exchange of a few cursory remarks from which I learned that he was my new neighbor, we went our respective ways.

I thought no more of the meeting, and as I am not blessed or cursed (as the case may be) with a natural curiosity concerning the affairs of those about me, I seldom met Martell, and upon the rare occasions when I did, we confined our remarks to that ever convenient topic, the weather.

Between Margaret and myself there seemed to be growing an inexplicable estrangement that increased as time went on, but it was not until after five repeated futile efforts to spend an evening in her company that I suspected the presence of a rival. Imagine my surprise and chagrin to discover that rival in the person of my neighbor Martell! I saw them together at the theatre and wondered, even with all due modesty, what there was in the ungainly figure and peculiar character of Martell to attract a beautiful and

*The story as originally published gave the dates here as "1894–1895." In light of the calendar change in 1938 (see p. 5), this appears to be a printing error.

refined girl of Margaret Landon's type. But attract her he did, for it was plainly evident, as I watched them with the eyes of a jealous lover, that Margaret was fascinated by the personality of her escort.

In sullen rage I went to Margaret a few days later, expressing my opinion of her new admirer in derogatory epithets. She gave me calm and dignified attention until I had exhausted my vocabulary, voicing my ideas of Martell, then she made reply in Martell's defense.

"Aside from personal appearance, Mr. Martell is a forceful and interesting character, and I refuse to allow you to dictate to me who my associates are to be. There is no reason why we three can not all be friends."

"Martell hates me as I hate him," I replied with smoldering resentment. "That is sufficient reason why we three can not all be friends."

"I think you must be mistaken," she replied curtly. "Mr. Martell praises your qualities as a neighbor and comments not infrequently on your excellent virtue of attending strictly to your own business."

I left Margaret's presence in a down-hearted mood.

"So Martell appreciates my lack of inquisitiveness, does he?" I mused as later I reviewed mentally the closing words of Margaret, and right then and there doubts and suspicions arose in my mind. If self-absorption was an appreciable quality as far as Martell was concerned, there was reason for his esteem of that phase of my character. I had discovered the presence of a mystery; Martell had something to conceal!

It was New Year's Day, not January 1st as they had it in the old days, but the extra New Year's Day that was sandwiched as a separate entity between two years. This new chronological reckoning had been put into use in 1938. The calendar had previously contained twelve months varying in length from twenty-eight to thirty-one days, but with the addition of a new month and the adoption of a uniformity of twenty-eight days for all months and the interpolation of an isolated New Year's Day, the world's system of chronology was greatly simplified. It was, as I say, on New Year's Day that I arose later than usual and dressed myself. The buzzing monotone of a voice from Martell's room annoyed me. Could he be talking over the telephone to Margaret? Right then and there I stooped to the performance of a deed of which I did not think myself capable. Ineffable curiosity converted me into a spy and an eavesdropper. I dropped to my knees and peered through the keyhole. I was rewarded with an unobstructed profile view of Martell seated at a low desk on which stood a peculiar cubical mechanism measuring on each edge six or seven inches. Above it hovered a tenuous vapor and from it issued strange sounds, occasionally interrupted by remarks from Martell uttered in an unknown tongue. Good heavens! Was this a new-fangled radio that communicated with the spirit-world? For only in such a way could I explain the peculiar vapor that enveloped the tiny machine. Television had been perfected and in use for a generation, but as yet no instrument had been invented which delivered messages from the "unknown bourne [sic]!"

I crouched in my undignified position until it was with difficulty that I arose, at the same time that Martell shut off the mysterious contrivance. Could Margaret be involved in any diabolical schemes? The very suggestion caused me to break out in a cold sweat. Surely, Margaret, the very personification of innocence and purity, could be no partner in any nefarious undertakings! I resolved to call her up. She answered the phone and I thought her voice showed agitation.

"Margaret, this is George," I said. "Are you all right?"

She answered faintly in the affirmative.

"May I come over at once?" I pled [sic]. "I have something important to tell you."

To my surprise she consented, and I lost no time in speeding my volplane to her home. With no introductory remarks, I plunged right into a narrative of the peculiar and suspicious actions of Martell, and ended by begging her to discontinue her association with him. Ever well poised and with a girlish dignity that was irresistibly charming, Margaret quietly thanked me for my solicitude for her well-being but assured me that there was nothing to fear from Martell. It was like beating against a brick wall to obtain any satisfaction from her, so I returned to my lonely rooms, there to brood in solitude over the unhappy change that Martell had brought into my life.

Once again I gazed through the tiny aperture. My neighbor was nowhere to be seen, but on the desk stood that which I mentally termed the devil-machine. The subtle mist that had previously hovered above it was wanting.

The next day upon arising I was drawn as by a magnet toward the keyhole, but my amazement knew no bounds when I discovered that it had been plugged from the other side, and my vision completely barred.

"Well I guess it serves me right," I muttered in my chagrin. "I ought to keep out of other people's private affairs. But," I added as an afterthought in feeble defense of my actions, "my motive is to save Margaret from that scoundrel." And such I wanted to prove him to be before it was too late!

III

The sixth of April, 1945, was a memorable day in the annals of history, especially to the inhabitants of Pacific coast cities throughout the world. Radios buzzed with the alarming and mystifying news that just over night the ocean line had receded several feet. What cataclysm of nature could have caused the disappearance of thousands of tons of water inside of twenty-four hours? Scientists ventured the explanation that internal disturbances must have resulted in the opening of vast submarine fissures into which the seas had poured.

This explanation, stupendous as it was, sounded plausible enough and was accepted by the world at large, which was too busy accumulating gold and silver to worry over the loss of nearly a million tons of water. How little we then realized that the relative importance of gold and water was destined to be reversed, and that man was to have forced upon him a new conception of values which would bring to him a complete realization of his former erroneous ideas.

May and June passed marking little change in the drab monotony that had settled into my life since Margaret Landon had ceased to care for me. One afternoon early in July I received a telephone call from Margaret. Her voice betrayed an agitated state of mind, and sorry though I was that she was troubled, it pleased me that she had turned to me in her despair. Hope sprang anew in my breast, and I told her I would be over at once.

I was admitted by the taciturn housekeeper and ushered into the library where Margaret rose to greet me as I entered. There were traces of tears in her lovely eyes. She extended both hands to me in a gesture of spontaneity that had been wholly lacking in her attitude toward me ever since the advent of Martell. In the role of protector and advisor, I felt that I was about to be reinstated in her regard.

But my joy was short-lived as I beheld a recumbent figure on the great davenport and recognized it instantly as that of Martell. So he was in the game after all! Margaret had summoned me because her lover was in danger! I turned to go but felt a restraining hand.

"Wait, George," the girl pled [*sic*]. "The doctor will be here any minute."

"Then let the doctor attend to him," I replied coldly. "I know nothing of the art of healing."

"I know, George," Margaret persisted, "but he mentioned you before he lost consciousness and I think he wants to speak to you. Won't you wait please?"

I paused, hesitant at the supplicating tones of her whom I loved, but at that moment the maid announced the doctor, and I made a hasty exit.

Needless to say I experienced a sense of guilt as I returned to my rooms.

"But," I argued as I seated myself comfortably before my radio, "a rejected lover would have to be a very magnanimous specimen of humanity to go running about doing favors for a rival. What do the pair of them take me for anyway—a fool?

I rather enjoyed a consciousness of righteous indignation, but disturbing visions of Margaret gave me an uncomfortable feeling that there was much about the affair that was incomprehensible to me.

"The transatlantic passenger-plane, *Pegasus*, has mysteriously disappeared," said the voice of the news announcer. "One member of her crew has been picked up who tells such a weird, fantastic tale that it has not received much credence. According to his story the Pegasus was winging its way across mid-ocean last night keeping an even elevation of three thousand feet, when, without any warning, the machine started straight up. Some force outside of itself was drawing it up, but whither? The rescued mechanic, the only one of all the fated ship's passengers, possessed the presence of mind to manipulate his parachute, and thus descended in safety before the air became too rare to breathe, and before he and the parachute could be attracted upwards. He stoutly maintains that the plane could not have fallen later without his knowledge. Scouting planes, boats and submarines sent out this morning verify his seemingly mad narration. Not a vestige of the *Pegasus* is to be found above, on the surface or below the water. Is this tragedy in any way connected with the lowering of the ocean level? Has some one a theory? In the face of such an inexplicable enigma the government will listen to the advancement of any theories, in the hope of solving the mystery. Too many times in the past have the so-called level-headed people failed to give ear to the warnings of theorists and dreamers, but now we know that the latter are often the possessors of a sixth sense that enables them to see that to which the bulk of mankind is blind."

I was awed by the fate of the *Pegasus*. I had had two flights in the wonderful machine myself three years ago, and I knew that it was the last word in luxuriant air-travel.

How long I sat listening to brief news bulletins and witnessing scenic flashes of worldly affairs I do not know, but there suddenly came to my mind and persisted in staying there, a very disquieting thought. Several times I dismissed it as unworthy of any consideration, but it continued with unmitigating [sic] tenacity.

After an hour of mental pros and cons I called up the hotel office.

"This is Mr. Gregory in suite 307," I strove to keep my voice steady. "Mr. Martell of 309 is ill at the house of a friend. He wishes me to have some of his belongings taken to him. May I have the key to his rooms?"

There was a pause that to me seemed interminable, then the voice of the clerk. "Certainly, Mr. Gregory, I'll send a boy up with it at once."

I felt like a culprit of the deepest dye as I entered Martell's suite a few moments later and gazed about me. I knew I might expect interference from any quarter at any moment so I wasted no time in a general survey of the apartment but proceeded at once to the object of my visit. The tiny machine which I now perceived was more intricate than I had supposed from my previous observations through the keyhole, stood in its accustomed place upon the desk. It had four levers and a dial, and I decided to manipulate each of these in turn. I commenced with the one at my extreme left. For a moment apparently nothing happened, then I realized that above the machine a mist was forming.

At first it was faint and cloudy but the haziness quickly cleared, and before my startled vision a scene presented itself. I seemed to be inside a bamboo hut looking toward an opening which afforded a glimpse of a wave-washed sandy beach and a few palm trees silhouetted against the horizon. I could imagine myself on a desert isle. I gasped in astonishment, but it was nothing to the shock which was to follow. While my fascinated gaze dwelt on the scene before me, a shadow fell athwart the hut's entrance and the figure of a man came toward me. I uttered a hoarse cry. For a moment I thought I had been transplanted chronologically to the discovery of America, for the being who approached me bore a general resemblance to an Indian chief. From his forehead tall, white feathers stood erect. He was without clothing and his skin had a reddish cast that glistened with a coppery sheen in the sunlight. Where had I seen those features or similar ones, recently? I had it! Martell! The Indian savage was a natural replica of the suave and civilized Martell, and yet was this man before me a savage? On the contrary, I noted that his features displayed a remarkably keen intelligence.

The stranger approached a table upon which I seemed to be, and raised his arms. A muffled cry escaped my lips! The feathers that I had supposed constituted his headdress were attached permanently along the upper portion of his arms to a point a little below each elbow. *They grew there.* This strange being had feathers instead of hair.

I do not know by what presence of mind I managed to return the lever to its original position, but I did, and sat weakly gazing vacantly at the air, where but a few seconds before a vivid tropic scene had been visible. Suddenly a low buzzing sound was heard. Only for an instant was I mystified, then I knew that the stranger of the desert-isle was endeavoring to summon Martell.

Weak and dazed I waited until the buzzing had ceased and then I resolutely pulled the second of the four levers. At the inception of the experiment the same phenomena were repeated, but when a correct perspective was effected a very different scene was presented before my startled vision. This time I seemed to be in a luxuriant room filled with costly furnishings, but I had time only for a most fleeting glance, for a section of newspaper that had intercepted part of my view, moved, and from behind its printed expanse emerged a being who bore a resemblance to Martell and the Indian of the desert island. It required but a second to turn off the mysterious connection, but that short time had been of sufficient duration to enable me to read the heading of the paper in the hands of a copper-hued man. It was *Die Münchener Zeitung.*

Still stupefied by the turn of events, it was with a certain degree of enjoyment that I continued to experiment with the devil-machine. I was startled when the same buzzing sound followed the disconnecting of the instrument.

I was about to manipulate the third lever when I became conscious of pacing footsteps in the outer hall. Was I arousing the suspicion of the hotel officials? Leaving my seat before the desk, I began to move about the room in semblance of gathering together, Martell's required articles. Apparently satisfied, the footsteps retreated down the corridor and were soon inaudible.

Feverishly now I fumbled with the third lever. There was no time to lose and I was madly desirous of investigating all the possibilities of this new kind of television-set. I had no doubt that I was on the track of a nefarious organization of spies, and I worked on in the self-termed capacity of a Sherlock Holmes.

The third lever revealed an apartment no less sumptuous than the German one had been. It appeared to be unoccupied for the present, and I had ample time to survey its expensive furnishings, which had an oriental appearance. Through an open window at the far end of the room I glimpsed a mosque with domes and minarets. I could not ascertain for a certainty whether this was Turkey or India. It might have been any one of many eastern lands, I could not know. The fact that the occupant of this oriental apartment was temporarily absent made me desirous of learning more about it, but time was precious to me now, and I disconnected. No buzzing followed upon this occasion, which strengthened my belief that my lever manipulation sounded a similar buzzing that was audible in the various stations connected for the purpose of accomplishing some wicked scheme.

The fourth handle invited me to further investigation. I determined to go through with my secret research though I died in the effort. Just before my hand dropped, the buzzing commenced, and I perceived for the first time a faint glow near the lever of No. 4. I dared not investigate 4 at this time, for I did not wish it known that another [*sic*] than Martell was at this station. I thought of going on to dial 5, but an innate love of system forced me to risk a loss of time rather than to take them out of order. The buzzing continued for the usual duration of time, but I waited until it had apparently ceased entirely before I moved No. 4.

My soul rebelled at that which took form from the emanating mist. A face, another duplicate of Martell's, but if possible more cruel, confronted me, completely filling up the vaporous space, and two phosphorescent eyes seared a warning into my own. A nauseating sensation crept over me as my hand crept to the connecting part of No. 4. When every vestige of the menacing face had vanished, I arose weakly and took a few faltering steps around the room. A bell was ringing with great persistance [*sic*] from some other room. It was mine! It would be wise to answer it. I fairly flew back to my room and was rewarded by the sound of Margaret's voice with a note of petulance in it.

"Why didn't you answer, George? The phone rang several times."

"Couldn't. Was taking a bath," I lied.

"Mr. Martell is better," continued Margaret. "The doctor says there's no immediate danger."

There was a pause and the sound of a rasping voice a little away from the vicinity of the phone, and then Margaret's voice came again.

"Mr. Martell wants you to come over, George. He wants to see you."

"Tell him I have to dress after my bath, then I'll come," I answered.

IV

There was not a moment to spare. I rushed back into Martell's room determined to see this thing through. I had never been subject to heart attacks, but certainly the suffocating sensation that possessed me could be attributed to no other cause.

A loud buzzing greeted my ears as soon as I had closed the door of Martell's suite. I looked toward the devil-machine. The four stations were buzzing at once! What was I to do? There was no light near dial 5, and that alone remained uninvestigated. My course of action was clear; try out No. 5 to my satisfaction, leave Martell's rooms and go to Margaret Landon's home as I had told her I would. They must not know what I had done. But it was inevitable that Martell would know when he got back to his infernal television and radio. *He must not get back!* Well, time enough to plan that later; now to the work of seeing No. 5.

When I turned the dial of No. 5 (for, as I have stated before, this was a dial instead of a lever) I was conscious of a peculiar sensation of distance.

It fairly took my breath away. What remote part of the earth's surface would the last position reveal to me?

A sharp hissing sound accompanied the manipulation of No. 5 and the vaporous shroud was very slow in taking definite shape. When it was finally at rest, and it was apparent that it would not change further, the scene depicted was at first, incomprehensible to me. I stared with bulging eyes and bated breath trying to read any meaning into the combinations of form and color that had taken shape before me.

In the light of what has since occurred, the facts of which are known throughout the world, I can lend my description a little intelligence borrowed, as it were, from the future. At the time of which I write, however, no such enlightenment was mine, and it must have been a matter of minutes before the slightest knowledge of the significance of the scene entered my uncomprehending brain.

My vantage-point seemed to be slightly aerial, for I was looking down upon a scene possibly fifty feet below me. Arid red cliffs and promontories jutted over dry ravines and crevices. In the immediate foreground and also across a deep gully, extended a comparatively level area which was the scene of some sort of activity. There was about it a vague suggestion of a shipyard, yet I saw no lumber, only great mountainous piles of dull metal, among which moved thousands of agile figures. They were men and women, but how strange they appeared! Their red bodies were minus clothing of any description and their heads and shoulders were covered with long white feathers that when folded, draped the upper portions of their bodies like shawls. They were unquestionably of the same race as the desert-island stranger and Martell! At times the feathers of these strange people stood erect and spread out like a peacock's tail. I noticed that when spread in this fan-like fashion they facilitated locomotion.

I glanced toward the sun far to my right and wondered if I had gone crazy. I rubbed my hands across my eyes and peered again. Yes, it was our luminary, but it was little more than half its customary size! I watched it sinking with fascinated gaze. It vanished quickly beyond the red horizon and darkness descended with scarcely a moment of intervening twilight. It was only by the closest observation that I could perceive that I was still in communication with No. 5.

Presently the gloom was dissipated by a shaft of light from the opposite horizon whither the sun had disappeared. So rapidly that I could follow its movement across the sky, the moon hove into view. But wait, was it the moon? Its surface looked strangely unfamiliar, and it too seemed to have shrunk in size.

Spellbound, I watched the tiny moon glide across the heavens the while I listened to the clang of metal tools from the workers below. Again a bright light appeared on the horizon beyond the great metal bulks below me. The scene was rapidly being rendered visible by an orb that exceeded the sun in diameter. Then I knew. Great God! There were two moons traversing the welkin! My heart was pounding so loudly that it drowned out the sound of the metal-workers. I watched on, unconscious of the passage of time.

Voices shouted from below in great excitement. Events were evidently working up to some important climax while the little satellite passed from my line of vision and only the second large moon occupied the sky. Straight before me and low on the horizon it hung with its lower margin touching the cliffs. It was low enough now so that a few of the larger stars were becoming visible. One in particular attracted my gaze and held it. It was a great bluish-green star and I noticed that the workers paused seemingly to gaze in silent admiration at its transcendent beauty. Then shout after shout arose from below and I gazed in bewilderment at the spectacle of the next few minutes, or was it hours?

A great spherical bulk hove in view from the right of my line of vision. It made me think of nothing so much as a gyroscope of gigantic proportions. It seemed to be made of the metal with which the workers were employed below, and as it gleamed in the deep blue of the sky it looked like a huge satellite. A band of red metal encircled it with points of the same at top and bottom. Numerous openings that resembled the port-holes of an ocean-liner appeared in the broad central band, from which extended metal points. I judged these were the "eyes" of the machine. But that which riveted my attention was an object that hung poised in the air below the mighty gyroscope, held in suspension by some mysterious force, probably magnetic in nature, evidently controlled in such a manner that at a certain point it was exactly counter-balanced by the gravitational pull. The lines of force apparently traveled from the poles of the mammoth sphere. But the object that depended [*sic*] in mid-air, as firm and rigid as though resting on terra-firma, was the missing *Pegasus*, the epitome of earthly scientific skill, but in the clutches of this unearthly looking marauder it looked like a fragile toy. Its wings were bent and twisted, giving it an uncanny resemblance to a bird in the claws of a cat.

In my spellbound contemplation of this new phenomenon I had temporarily forgotten the scene below, but suddenly a great cloud momentarily blotted out the moon, then another and another and another, in rapid succession. Huge bulks of air-craft were eclipsing the moon. Soon the scene was all but obliterated by the machines whose speed accelerated as they reached the upper air. On and on they sped in endless procession while the green star gazed serenely on! The green star, most sublime of the starry host! I loved its pale beauty though I knew not why. Darkness. The moon had set, but I knew that still those frightfully gigantic and ominous shapes still sped upward and onward. Whither?

The tiny moon again made its appearance, serving to reveal once more that endless aerial migration. Was it hours or days? I had lost all sense of the passage of time. The sound of rushing feet, succeeded by a pounding at the door brought me back to my immediate surroundings. I had the presence of mind to shut off the machine, then I arose and assumed a defensive attitude as the door opened and many figures confronted me. Foremost among them was Martell, his face white with rage, or was it fear?

"Officers, seize that man," he cried furiously. "I did not give him permission to spy in my room. He lied when he said that." Here Martell turned to the desk clerk who stood behind two policemen.

"Speaking of spying," I flung back at him, "Martell, you ought to know the meaning of that word. He's a spy himself," I cried to the two apparently unmoved officers, "why he — he — "

From their unsympathetic attitudes, I knew the odds were against me. I had lied, and I had been found in a man's private rooms without his permission. It would be a matter of time and patience before I could persuade the law that I had any justice on my side.

I was handcuffed and led toward the door just as a sharp pain like an icy clutch at my heart overcame me. I sank into oblivion.

V

When I regained consciousness two days later I discovered that I was the sole occupant of a cell in the State hospital for the insane. Mortified to the extreme, I pled [sic] with the keeper to bring about my release, assuring him that I was unimpaired mentally.

"Sure, that's what they all say," the fellow remarked with a wry smile.

"But I must be freed," I reiterated impatiently, "I have a message of importance for the world. I must get into immediate communication with the Secretary of War."

"Yes, yes," agreed the keeper affably. "We'll let you see the Secretary of War when that fellow over there," he jerked his thumb in the direction of the cell opposite mine, "dies from drinking hemlock. He says he's Socrates, and every time he drinks a cup of milk he flops over, but he always revives."

I looked across the narrow hall into a pair of eyes that mirrored a deranged mind, then my gaze turned to the guard who was watching me narrowly. I turned away with a shrug of despair.

Later in the day the man appeared again but I sat in sullen silence in a corner of my cell. Days passed in this manner until at last a plausible means of communication with the outside world occurred to me. I asked if my good friend Professor Stearns might be permitted to visit me. The guard replied that he believed it could be arranged for sometime the following week. It is a wonder I did not become demented, imprisoned as I was, in solitude, with the thoughts of the mysterious revelations haunting me continually.

One afternoon the keeper, passing by on one of his customary rounds, thrust a newspaper between the bars of my cell. I grabbed it eagerly and retired to read it.

The headlines smote my vision with an almost tactile force.

"Second Mysterious Recession of Ocean. The *Poseidonia* is Lost!"

I continued to read the entire article, the letters of which blazed before my eyes like so many pinpoints of light.

"Ocean waters have again receded, this time in the Atlantic. Seismologists are at a loss to explain the mysterious cataclysm as no earth tremors have been registered. It is a little over three months since the supposed submarine fissures lowered the level of the Pacific ocean several feet, and now the same calamity, only to a greater extent, has visited the Atlantic.

"The island of Madeira reports stranded fish upon her shores by the thousands, the decay of which threatens the health of the island's population. Two merchant vessels off the Azores, and one fifty miles out from Gibraltar, were found total wrecks. Another, the *Transatlantia*, reported a fearful agitation of the ocean depths, but seemed at a loss for a plausible explanation, as the sky was cloudless and no wind was blowing.

"'But despite this fact,' wired the *Transatlantia*, 'great waves all but capsized us. This marine disturbance lasted throughout the night.'

"The following wireless from the great ocean liner, *Poseidonia*, brings home to us the realization that Earth has been visited with a stupendous calamity. The *Poseidonia* was making her weekly transatlantic trip between Europe and America, and was in mid-ocean at the time her message was flashed to the world.

"'A great cloud of flying objects of enormous proportions has just appeared in the sky blotting out the light of the stars. No sound accompanies the approach of this strange fleet. In appearance the individual craft resemble mammoth balloons. The sky is black with them and in their vicinity the air is humid and oppressive as though the atmosphere were saturated to the point of condensation. Everything is orderly. There are no collisions. Our captain has given orders for us to turn back toward Europe — we have turned, but the dark dirigibles are pursuing us. Their speed is unthinkable. Can the *Poseidonia*, doing a mere hundred miles an hour, escape? A huge craft is bearing down upon us from above and behind. There is no escape. Pandemonium reigns. The enemy —'

"Thus ends the tragic message from the brave wireless operator of the *Poseidonia*."

I threw down the paper and called loudly for the keeper. Socrates across the hall eyed me suspiciously. I was beginning to feel that perhaps the poor demented fellow had nothing on me; that I should soon be in actuality a raving maniac.

The keeper came in response to my call, entered my cell and patted my shoulders reassuringly.

"Never mind, old top," he said, "it isn't so bad as it seems."

"Now look here," I burst forth angrily, "I tell you I am *not* insane!" How futile my words sounded! "If you will send Professor Mortimer Stearns, teacher of Astronomy at Austin, to me at once for an hour's talk, I'll prove to the world that I have not been demented."

"Professor Stearns is a very highly esteemed friend of mine," I continued, noting the suspicion depicted on his countenance. "If you wish, go to him first and find out his true opinion of me. I'll wager it will not be an uncomplimentary one!"

The man twisted his keys thoughtfully, and I uttered not a word, believing a silent demeanor most effective in the present crisis. After what seemed an eternity:

"All right," he said, "I'll see what can be done toward arranging a visit from Professor Mortimer Stearns as soon as possible."

I restrained my impulse toward a too effusive expression of gratitude as I realized that a quiet dignity prospered my cause more effectually.

The next morning at ten, after a constant vigil, I was rewarded with the most welcome sight of Professor Stearns striding down the hall in earnest conversation with the guard. He was the straw and I the drowning man, but would he prove a more substantial help than the proverbial straw? I surely hoped so.

A chair was brought for the professor and placed just outside my cell. I hastily drew my own near it.

"Well, this is indeed unfortunate," said Mortimer Stearns with some embarrassment, "and I sincerely hope you will soon be released."

"Unfortunate!" I echoed. "It is nothing short of a calamity."

My indignation voiced so vociferously startled the good professor and he shoved his chair almost imperceptibly away from the intervening bars. At the far end of the hall the keeper eyed me suspiciously. Hang it all, was my last resort going to fail me?

"Professor Stearns," I said earnestly, "will you try to give me an unbiased hearing? My situation is a desperate one, and it is necessary for some one [*sic*] to believe in me before I can render humanity the service it needs."

He responded to my appeal with something of his old sincerity, that always endeared him to his associates.

"I shall be glad to hear your story, Gregory, and if I can render any service, I'll not hesitate — "

"That's splendid of you," I interrupted with emotion, "and now to my weird tale."

I related from the beginning, omitting no details, however trivial they may have seemed, the series of events that had brought me to my present predicament.

"And your conclusion?" queried the professor in strange, hollow tones.

"That Martian spies, one of whom is Martell, are superintending [*sic*] by radio and television, an unbelieveably well-planned theft of Earth's water in order to replenish their own dry ocean beds!"

"Stupendous!" gasped Professor Stearns. "Something must be done to prevent another raid. Let's see," he mused, "the interval was three months before, was it not? Three months we shall have for bringing again into use the instruments of war that praise God! have lain idle for many generations. It is the only way to deal with a formidable foe from outside."

VI

Professor Stearns was gone, but there was hope in my heart in place of the former grim despair. When the guard handed the evening paper to me I amazed him with a grateful "thank you." But my joy was short-lived. Staring up at me from the printed passenger list of the ill-fated *Poseidonia* were the names of Mr. and Mrs. T. M. Landon and daughter Margaret!

I know the guard classed me as one of the worst cases on record, but I felt that surely Fate had been unkind.

"A package for Mr. George Gregory," bawled a voice in the corridor.

Thanks to the influence of Professor Stearns, I was permitted to receive mail. When the guard saw that I preferred unwrapping it myself, he discreetly left me to the mystery of the missive.

A card just inside bore the few but insignificant words, "For Gregory in remembrance of Martell."

I suppressed an impulse to dash the accursed thing to the floor when I saw that it was Martell's radio and television instrument. Placing it upon the table I drew a chair up to it and turned each of the levers, but not one functioned. I manipulated the dial No. 5. The action was accompanied by the same hissing sound that had so startled my overwrought nerves upon the previous occasion. Slowly the wraithlike mist commenced the process of Adjustment. Spellbound [sic] I watched the scene before my eyes.

Again I had the sensation of a lofty viewpoint. It was identical with the one I had previously held, but the scene — was it the same? It must be — and yet! The barren red soil was but faintly visible through a verdure. The towering rocky palisades that bordered the chasm were crowned with golden-roofed dwellings, or were they temples, for they were like the pure marble fanes of the ancient Greeks except in color. Down the steep slopes flowed streams of sparkling water that dashed with a merry sound to a canal below.

Gone were the thousands of beings and their metal aircraft, but seated on a grassy plot in the left foreground of the picture was a small group of the white-feathered, red-skinned inhabitants of this strange land. In the distance rose the temple-crowned crags. One figure alone stood, and with a magnificent gesture held arms aloft. The great corona of feathers spread following the line of the arms like the open wings of a great eagle. The superb figure stood and gazed into the deep velvety blue of the sky, the others following the direction of their leader's gaze.

Involuntarily I too watched the welkin where now not even a moon was visible. Then within the range of my vision there moved a great object — the huge aerial gyroscope — and beneath it, dwarfed by its far greater bulk, hung a modern ocean-liner, like a jewel from the neck of some gigantic ogre.

Great God — it was the *Poseidonia!* I knew now, in spite of the earthly appearance of the great ship, that it was no terrestrial scene upon which I gazed. I was beholding the victory of Martell, the Martian, who had filled his world's canals with water of Earth, and even borne away trophies of our civilization to exhibit to his fellow-beings.

I closed my eyes to shut out the awful scene, and thought of Margaret, dead and yet aboard the liner, frozen in the absolute cold of outer space!

How long I sat stunned and horrified I do not know, but when I looked back for another last glimpse of the Martian landscape, I uttered a gasp of incredulity. A face filled the entire vaporous screen, the beloved features of Margaret Landon. She was speaking and her voice came over the distance like the memory of a sound that is not quite audible and yet very real to the person in whose mind it exists. It was more as if time divided us instead of space, yet I knew it was the latter, for while a few minutes of time came between us, millions of miles of space intervened!

"George," came the sweet, far-away voice, "I loved you, but you were so suspicious and jealous that I accepted the companionship of Martell, hoping to bring you to your senses. I did not know what an agency for evil he had established upon the earth. Forgive me, dear."

She smiled wistfully. "My parents perished with hundreds of others in the transportation of the *Poseidonia*, but Martell took me from the ship to the ether-craft for the journey, so that I alone was saved."

Her eyes filled with tears. "Do not mourn for me, George, for I shall take up the thread of life anew among these strange but beautiful surroundings. Mars is indeed lovely, but I will tell you of it later for I cannot talk long now."

"I only want to say," she added hastily, "that Terra need fear Mars no more. There is a sufficiency of water now — and I will prevent any — "

She was gone, and in her stead was the leering, malevolent face of Martell. He was minus his skull-cap, and his clipped feathers stood up like the ruff of an angry turkey-gobbler.

I reached instinctively for the dial, but before my hand touched it there came a sound, not unlike that of escaping steam, and instantaneously the picture vanished. I did not object to the disappearance of the Martian, but another fact did cause me regret; from that moment, I was never able to view the ruddy planet through the agency of the little machine. All communication had been forever shut off by Martell.

Although many doubt the truth of my solution to the mystery of the disappearance of the *Pegasus* and of the *Poseidonia*, and are still searching beneath the ocean waves, I know that never will either of them be seen again on Earth.

Illicit Reproduction: Clare Winger Harris's "The Fate of the Poseidonia"

Jane Donawerth

The first short story by a woman in a science fiction pulp magazine came remarkably early: Clare Winger Harris's "The Fate of the Poseidonia" was published by Hugo Gernsback in *Amazing Stories* in June 1927.[1] Selected from more than three hundred stories, it was the third prize winner in a contest conducted by Gernsback, inviting short "scientifiction" stories. Harris was paid one hundred dollars for her story, a princely sum in 1927, and she went on to write many more for Gernsback and other editors in the next decade. A collection of her stories, *Away from the Here and Now*, was published in 1947.[2]

In this essay I set up several contexts for viewing her story: science fiction by women in the pulps, early science fiction fandom, 1920s racial ideology, and early twentieth-century communications technology. This story by Harris looks anxiously to the future, fearing illicit reproduction in the guise both of alien-human romance and interplanetary televisual communication.

Science Fiction by Women in the Pulps

A number of historians of science fiction have claimed that women did not write for the science fiction pulp magazines. Curtis Smith, for example, says that women were "present only as voluptuous and helpless objects on the lurid pulp covers."[3] In the last few decades, however, several scholars have traced the history of women and the early science fiction pulps to suggest that women were indeed present. Pamela Sargent recorded the contributions of Francis Stevens (a pseudonym of Gertrude Barrows Bennett) and of C. L. Moore to the early pulp magazines, and Susan Gubar and Sarah Gamble examined C. L. Moore's fiction in important essays.[4] None the less, these critics all viewed science fiction by women in the pulps as exceptional, rather than accepted.

In the introduction to Harris's story (fig. 2), Hugo Gernsback, the editor,

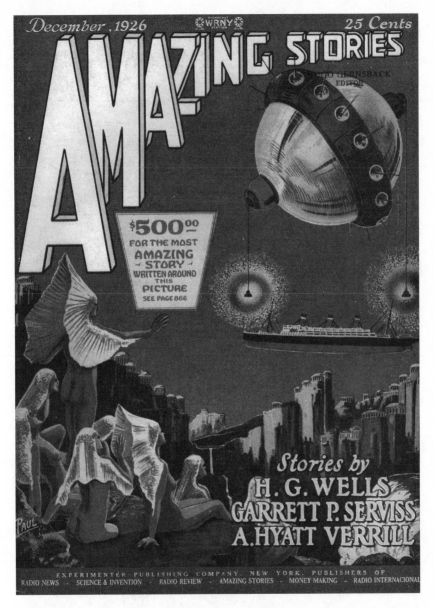

FIGURE 1. December 1926 cover of *Amazing Stories,* by Frank R. Paul

. . . and before my startled vision a scene presented itself. I seemed to be inside a bamboo hut looking toward an opening which afforded a glimpse of a wave-washed sandy beach and a few palm trees. . . . While my fascinated gaze dwelt on the scene before me, a shadow fell athwart the hut's entrance and the figure of a man came toward me.

The FATE of the POSEIDONIA
By CLARE WINGER HARRIS

I

THE first moment I laid eyes on Martell I took a great dislike to the man. There sprang up between us an antagonism that as far as he was concerned might have remained passive, but which circumstances forced into activity on my side.

How distinctly I recall the occasion of our meeting at the home of Professor Stearns, head of the Astronomy department of Austin College. The address which the professor proposed giving before the Mentor Club of which I was a member, was to be on the subject of the planet, Mars. The spacious front rooms of the Stearns home were crowded for the occasion

with rows of chairs, and at the end of the double parlors a screen was erected for the purpose of presenting telescopic views of the ruddy planet in its various aspects.

As I entered the parlor after shaking hands with my hostess, I felt, rather than saw, an unfamiliar presence, and the impression I received involuntarily was that of antipathy. What I saw was the professor himself engaged in earnest conversation with a stranger. Intuitively I knew that from the latter emanated the hostility of which I was definitely conscious.

He was a man of slightly less than average height. At once I noticed that he did not appear exactly normal physically and yet I could not

THAT the third prize winner should prove to be a woman was one of the surprises of the contest, for, as a rule, women do not make good scientifiction writers, because their education and general tendencies on scientific matters are usually limited. But the exception, as usual, proves the rule, the exception in this case being extraordinarily impressive. The story has a great deal of charm, chiefly because it is not overburdened with science, but whatever science is contained therein is not only quite palatable, but highly desirable, due to its plausibility. Not only this, but you will find that the author is a facile writer who keeps your interest unto the last line. We hope to see more of Mrs. Harris's scientifiction in AMAZING STORIES.

FIGURE 2. Title Page for "The Fate of the Poseidonia," *Amazing Stories,* June 1927

presents Clare Winger Harris as just such an exception: "That the third prize winner should prove to be a woman was one of the surprises of the contest, for, as a rule, women do not make good scientifiction writers, because their education and general tendencies on scientific matters are usually limited."[5] Gernsback himself welcomed many women writers into his periodicals, but he was not able to see their contributions without bias: "The story has a great deal of charm, chiefly because it is not overburdened with science, but whatever science is contained therein is not only quite palatable, but highly desirable, due to its plausibility."[6] While Gernsback praises both male winners for their "excellent science," he downplays the science that Harris interweaves in her story, a science that helps to make this story successful science fiction: it is televisual technology that enables Gregory to solve the problem of the disappearance of Earth's water.[7]

Gernsback's condescending support for Harris, then, helps us to see more clearly the limits that she overcame and the importance of her contributions: she was a woman writer in a genre generally written by men, she wrote stories that included portraits of feminine strength, and she offered visions of a science that was not solely the province of privileged white men.

In the last decade and a half, scholars have demonstrated that many women wrote science fiction for the pulp magazines, often under a female name. Robin Roberts has examined depictions of strong women aliens by men in the stories and illustrations of the pulp magazines.[8] I have argued that nineteenth-century feminist utopian fiction migrated to the pulp magazines in the 1920s, and I have explored the utopian science imagined by women writers, as well as women writers' appropriation of the figure of the alien monster-woman for political ends.[9] Justine Larbalestier has analyzed what the science fiction pulps made of gender through examining the genre of "battle of the sexes stories," not only in texts by both male and female writers, but also in fan responses to these stories.[10] And Brian Attebery has argued that science fiction is a code that intersects with gender as a code, so that, for example, the most popular story in the pulp magazines was a young man's initiation into science as an initiation into masculinity.[11] When I started teaching science fiction by women, students were often unable to find almost any biographical information on early female science fiction writers; fortunately, that has changed, as may be seen by comparing the number of women writers added to the second edition of John Clute and Peter Nicholl's *Encyclopedia of Science Fiction*.[12]

Harris fits into this context as the first woman to publish in the science fiction pulps and as one of many women writers who brought visions of feminine strength or alternative science to the pulps. Harris at first seems conservative. In "The Fifth Dimension," Harris's one story with a female narrator, the persona is a housewife, who uses her wits to save her husband's life but doesn't venture beyond her home.[13] In "The Artificial Man," Rosalind Nelson needs to be rescued from rape by the handsome doctor who is the hero of the story.[14] In "The Menace from Mars," however, Vivian Harley is a college-educated chemist and astronomer who assists her father, and later, her husband in their laboratories.[15]

In "The Fate of the Poseidonia," Margaret Landon is deceived by the alien Martell, while the male narrator, George Gregory, is rightfully suspicious. But in other ways, Margaret distinguishes herself. She does not fall apart when she is kidnapped by aliens and her parents are killed. Instead, she has the presence of mind to use the alien televisual communication system to contact George. She does not beg for rescue, but instead displays stoic control: "Do not mourn for me, George, for I shall take up the thread of life anew among these strange but beautiful surroundings. Mars is indeed lovely." Moreover, she heroically pledges herself to prevent any more predation by alien forces on Earth: "Terra need fear Mars no more. There is a sufficiency of water now — and I will prevent any — ." (Harris, 19) But her message is interrupted by the alien Martell.

Harris's conception of science is futuristic: she imagines personal aircraft, interplanetary travel, magnetic tractor beams, and interplanetary televisual communication. Harris's view of alien presence on Earth also belies the category of conservative; she imagines an invasion that causes relatively little harm to humans. The aliens steal a great deal of water but do not come to conquer Earth, returning instead to their home planet. They do take an airplane and an ocean liner, and consequently cause the death of hundreds of passengers. But they do not make war on Earth. Such a view of alien invasion is moderate for a majority-white nation fearing increased Eastern European immigration and a rise in nonwhite populations in the United States — as well as a nation recovering from a devastating world war.

Thus Harris brings to the science fiction pulps, in comparison to male writers, more attention to female characters and women's relationship to science, and a rationalism that is not utopian or radical, but yet responds with moderation to 1920s postwar anxieties.

Early Science Fiction Fandom: Permeable Boundaries

In Gernsback's 1927 contest, readers were invited to write a story to explain the cover of the December 1926 *Amazing Stories* (fig. 3). Gernsback described the cover (fig. 1) in this way:

VOLUME
1

DECEMBER, 1926
No. 9

THE
MAGAZINE
OF
SCIENTIFICTION

HUGO GERNSBACK, *Editor*
DR. T. O'CONOR SLOANE, Ph.D.; *Associate Editor*
WILBUR C. WHITEHEAD, *Literary Editor*
C. A. BRANDT, *Literary Editor*
Editorial and General Offices: 53 Park Place, New York, N. Y.

Extravagant Fiction Today - - - - - - - *Cold Fact Tomorrow*

$500.00 PRIZE STORY CONTEST

By HUGO GERNSBACK

SINCE the first appearance of AMAZING STORIES, we have received a great many manuscripts for publication in our magazine. We wish to state at this point that at present the magazine is not in the market for full length novels, because the editors have a great many on hand that await publication. They do, however, want short stories under 10,000 words, stories that would occupy nine or ten pages in AMAZING STORIES.

Furthermore, we receive an increasing number of letters, asking if we are in the market for short stories, and to these we wish to reply in the affirmative. We can not get too many real short scientifiction stories. To encourage this, we are starting a rather unique contest this month.

We have composed on our front cover a picture which illustrates a story to be written by our readers. We are frank to say that we haven't the slightest idea what the picture is supposed to show. The editors' ideas pertaining to the real solution,— if one there be,— based upon the picture, are necessarily vague.

There is for instance the strange race of people which you see in the left foreground, while in the distance there is an equally strange city which may or may not be on this planet, and there is the still stranger ball-like machine floating in space which apparently has captured a modern ocean greyhound in some amazing manner. What is going to happen to the ocean liner is the great secret. Does the ocean liner contain human beings, or have they been left behind? What force has lifted the steamship into space, in this incredible way, and where is it being transported? All these are vital questions that all of us should like to have answered.

Now, some one of our readers is going to write a *real* short story of less than 10,000 words, around this picture. He is going to study the picture from all perspectives and, knowing a bit about science, he will not have much trouble writing a most convincing story. We know it will be so convincing that we will actually believe it. And the author who is going to write the best story will be a good observer, because he will miss no detail of the picture, and will take cognizance of even the smallest detail.

It is in the very nature of this contest that there can not

be a great many prize winners. The editors have limited the prizes to three, and only three stories will be chosen, and only three will be printed. The reading of the three prize-winning stories will, we know be most interesting, because each will very likely be entirely different in plot and in treatment.

Here, then, is a great chance for you to become an author. It is a great opportunity to try your hand in an imaginative story of the scientifiction type. But before you jump to any conclusions, be sure that you read the rules carefully so as not to be disqualified.

1. The purpose of this contest is to have you write a story around the illustration on the front cover of this issue.

2. The story should be between 5,000 and 10,000 words.

3. The story must be of the scientifiction type and must contain correct scientific facts to make it appear plausible and within the realm of present-day knowledge of science.

4. The story must be typewritten or in pen and ink. No penciled matter will be considered.

5. All stories submitted to this contest must be received flat, not rolled.

6. Unused manuscripts will be returned if return postage has been enclosed.

7. AMAZING STORIES can not enter into any correspondence as to stories.

8. Three cash prizes will be awarded,—First Prize, $250.00; Second Prize, $150.00; Third Prize, $100.00.

9. This contest closes on January 5th at noon, at which time all manuscripts must be in.

10. In awarding the prizes, AMAZING STORIES acquires full rights of all kinds, including those of translation into foreign languages, second rights, as well as motion picture rights. The Editors will be the judges.

11. From this contest are excluded the employees of the Experimenter Publishing Company and their families.

12. Anyone may join this contest even though not a subscriber to the magazine.

Address all manuscripts to *Editor, Cover Contest*, AMAZING STORIES, New York City.

Mr. Hugo Gernsback speaks every Monday at 9 P. M. from WRNY on various scientific and radio subjects.

FIGURE 3. Editorial by Hugo Gernsback, *Amazing Stories*, December 1926

There is for instance the strange race of people which you see in the left fore-ground, while in the distance there is an equally strange city which may or may not be on this planet, and there is the still stranger ball-like machine floating in space which apparently has captured a modern ocean greyhound in some man-ner. What is going to happen to the ocean liner is the great secret. Does the ocean liner contain human beings, or have they been left behind? What force has lifted the steamship into space, in this incredible way, and where is it being transported?[16]

Up to this point, there had been no women writers in the sf pulps. But this announcement opened up possibilities. Writing about female spectatorship of film in "Pleasurable Negotiations" (1988), Christine Gledhill suggests that the meaning of texts is negotiated at three sites: institutional produc-tion, the text itself, and the text's reception. Multiple sites of intervention open opportunities for resistance to dominant ideologies.[17] The relation-ships between authors and fans in science fiction facilitates such inter-vention: authors may be fans, and fans may become authors. Thus, in terms of Gledhill's categories, resistance to dominant gender or political ideology is relatively easy in 1920s science fiction culture in all three areas: in textual content, because Gernsback promoted tolerance among races, for example, and welcomed women writers; in production, because mov-ing to a position of authorship was relatively easy; and in reception, be-cause fans were encouraged to write letters in response to stories, letters that were then published.[18] Women took advantage of this accessibility: Lilith Lorraine, for example, was both a published author and also a fan in one of the early science fiction fan clubs.[19] As Brian Attebery points out in this collection in his essay on Leslie Stone's 1931 story, women joined the conversation about science fiction in the early pulp magazines as both fans and authors, revising the tropes of science fiction narration to include women, and proclaiming the importance of female readership in the fan columns.

Indeed, the boundary between fan and author has remained remarkably permeable in science fiction and, under Gernsback's influence, readers of the early pulps frequently turned into authors. Gernsback himself initiated the term *fan*, referring to those who wrote letters to *Amazing Stories*.[20] The "Hugo," the award given by fans to science fiction practitioners each year, is aptly named for Gernsback. Gernsback promoted the interaction of fans and writers by idea contests, the story contest that Harris participated in, printing readers' letters, and asking readers to answer questionnaires. His sense of science fiction as a combination of romance adventure and accurate futuristic science influenced several generations of science fiction writers.[21] Certainly such an influence can be seen in Harris's story, which accurately extrapolates from 1920s communications and flight technologies, and overlays on the science a story of failed romance.

Although there existed collectors of science fiction materials before the 1920s, that decade saw the rise of the institution of fandom, largely due to the influence of Gernsback and his sf magazines. Gernsback added another fan column, called "Discussions," in January 1927.[22] Soon early fan correspondence clubs developed in California, Chicago, and New York, and some of the clubs began meeting in 1929.[23] The first fanzine was published through mimeographing in 1930, and later in the 1930s, Harris herself contributed to the Cleveland fanzine, *Science Fiction*.[24] Thus the fan who responded appreciatively to Clare Winger Harris's "The Fate of the Poseidonia," suggesting that it should have received second instead of third prize,[25] was part of this early, developing fan movement — as was Harris herself; she must have read the December 1926 issue of *Amazing Stories* that advertised the story contest.

What might be the effects on Harris's story of this permeable membrane between developing fandom and authorship? Harris's story, of course, wouldn't have been published unless Gernsback had called for his fan readers to become authors. Perhaps the opening scene of Harris's story also reflects the interests of early science fiction fans. In this scene, a group of people, mainly male (but the hostess is mentioned), are gathered to hear Professor Stearns, an astronomer, give a lecture with "lantern-slides" (an early form of a slide show) on the possibility of life on Mars. The audience is a gathering of the Mentor Club, and the narrator is a member. Professor Stearns concludes, from reviewing photographs of Mars, that "visible upon its surface [is] undeniable evidence of the handiwork of man." He also demonstrates that there is almost no water left on Mars, and that if people exist there, they would be waging "a brave struggle" for existence. The group focuses on the question, "what would *we* do were we threatened with a like disaster"? (Harris, 4) Thus the story opens at a lecture and discussion very like many that have occurred at science fiction club meetings and conventions since. Perhaps already in 1926 in Cleveland a group like those in California, New York, and Chicago was forming.

But there is another effect on the story of this permeable boundary between fan and author. Harris's story, as well as hundreds of others, were written in response to Gernsback's contest call: to write a story that would fit the cover illustration featured in the contest. Harris uses the cover illustration as her penultimate, climactic scene, the arrival of the ship carrying the Poseidonia at a Mars now possessing sufficient water and peopled by an alien, red, feathered race.

The writers who won first and second prize imagined quite different scenarios. In "The Visitation," which won first prize, Cyril Wates created a utopian society brought about by discovery of an isolated perfected race of humans hidden in South American coastal mountains: these humans are telepathic, without history since there is no suffering to record, healthy, nearly immortal, and possessing advanced technology (such as the gyroscopic air liner that helps to lift the ocean liner to safety after being blown off course during a hurricane).[26] In "The Electronic Wall," which won second prize, George Fox described World War I soldiers on a troop ship kidnapped by a superior female race from an asteroid that passes close to the Earth. This race, however, is not bent on conquering humans, but only on wooing male reproductive partners: they introduce the narrator to space travel, gravitation as an energy force, telepathic communication, vegetarianism, water conservation, and "pure freedom." The brave narrator tells his story only because he leaves paradise, returning to Earth to plead for worldwide peace and the development of similar powers for earth peoples.[27] In any case, all three of these prize winners were not only invited into the new activity of authorship, but also severely constrained by the limits of the illustration and Gernsback's direction.

Anxiety about Racial Mixing

The late 1920s and 1930s saw an increase in racial prejudice and concerted efforts against it. Because of the development over the fifty years since the Civil War of a prosperous black middle class, and because of the falling off of Northern European immigration and increase of Eastern European and Asian immigrants, white United States citizens felt threatened by new economic competition. The result was not only a rise in hate crimes, but also Congress's institution of strict anti-immigration quota laws and an avid interest in magazines and the book trade in eugenics, the science of genetically perfecting the human race (what Thomas Powell calls "scientific racism").[28] In *Eugenic Fantasies: Racial Ideology in the Literature and Popular Culture of the 1920s*, Betsy Nies argues that eugenics takes center stage because it is viewed as a science preserving white male privilege; white males in the United States were attempting to shore up the privilege and sense of power they had lost during the decade of devastation resulting from World War I.[29] Even in moderate 1920s magazines like the *Saturday Evening Post* and *Collier's*, eugenics was promoted, and Vice President

Coolidge was quoted in favor of excluding inferior immigrants in *Good Housekeeping*.[30]

Clearly, Harris's story reflects this racial anxiety.[31] George Gregory, the narrator, feels an immediate hostility to the alien Martell. When Gregory shakes Martell's hand, touching the skin that felt like "a fine, dry sponge," his "whole being revolted." The description of Martell follows the pattern of 1920s racial ideology, marking Martell as inferior: "He was a man of slightly less than average height. . . . he did not appear exactly normal physically and yet I could not ascertain in what way he was deficient," and his skin was a "swarthy, coppery hue." (Harris, 2) Martell's differences are automatically translated into deficiency by Gregory, reflecting the country's fears of the short, dark Eastern Europeans whose immigration had swelled in numbers from the 1890s on.[32] The immigrant of racist cartoons in the 1920s is also bearded, with long, unkempt hair;[33] the aliens of Harris's story have feathery crests on their heads and arms, and the last view that the narrator has of Martell suggests his animalistic status: "He was minus his skullcap, and his clipped feathers stood up like the ruff of an angry turkey-gobbler."(Harris, 19)

A main issue of 1920s racism was fear of miscegenation, mixture of races: men and women feared that they would lose their reproductive partners, that Caucasians would be a minority in a future, mixed race. In the story, this anxiety is worked out on a personal level as Gregory gradually loses his girlfriend, Margaret Landon, to Martell's courtship. George is confused to find that Margaret's interest in him has lessened, and is chagrined to discover that Martell is his rival. The reader is asked to side with Margaret as she defends Martell and argues for her own independence. In response to George's "derogatory epithets" for Martell, Landon judges him "a forceful and interesting character," and stipulates that she will not "allow you to dictate who my associates are to be." (Harris, 5)

The story asks the readers to change their sympathies to George when Margaret is deported. The success of Martell in deporting Margaret is handled very indirectly, however. George views himself as a "rejected lover," with Martell his rival. The audience does not see Margaret and Martell express physical intimacy, but the threat is implied in Margaret's final message. She is saved because "Martell took me from the ship to the ether-craft for the journey." And Margaret's final communication is cut off by "the leering, malevolent face of Martell." Margaret is thus represented as one of the "trophies of our civilization" that Martell has "borne away." (Harris, 18)

While many of Gernsback's writers in the 1920s science fiction pulps are radical promoters of racial tolerance, Harris is not. Margaret's strength undermines the stereotypes of women of Harris's generation, but Martell's villainy, associated with physical descriptions meant to arouse revulsion, reinforces 1920s fears of the mixing of races.

Anxiety about New Inventions: Television

While Hugo Gernsback was a science enthusiast who delighted in displaying technological advances in the stories of his magazines, his writers were often more ordinary citizens who, following in the footsteps of Mary Shelley's *Frankenstein*, expressed their anxieties about the effects of scientific advances on society. In Harris's "The Fate of the Poseidonia," it is the advent of television that triggers such anxiety. When George Gregory, the narrator, peers through the keyhole into his neighbor's apartment, George sees Martell seated in front of "a peculiar cubical mechanism" emitting "a tenuous vapor." Explaining to the 1927 audience, for whom television was yet fourteen years in the future, the narrator declares, "Television had been perfected and in use for a generation, but as yet no instrument had been invented which delivered messages from the 'unknown bourne!'" (Harris, 6) Anxiety about a communication device (in contrast to anxiety about the production of machines for human work, or technological warfare, for example) seems strange. But Harris juxtaposes anxiety about advances in communication technology with anxiety about miscegenation, and produces a tale where each anxiety about illicit reproduction is amplified by its association with the other.

Television, "the electrical transmission and reception of transient visual images" was predicted from early in the nineteenth century, and much effort, especially after the invention of the telegraph, telephone, and motion pictures, went into making it a reality.[34] The term *television* derives from a paper by Constantin Perskyi at the 1900 International Electricity Congress. Speculation about television made it into *Nature* magazine in 1908, and companies were working to achieve this goal in Britain, France, Germany, and the United States.[35] In June 1925, Charles Jenkins's success in transmitting a picture from Anacostia to Washington, D.C. (about five miles) was reported in newspapers across the United States.[36]

But there is also a personal connection to the publication of Harris's story. In December 1923, Charles Jenkins demonstrated a televisual apparatus to Hugo Gernsback, who was then editor of *Radio News*.[37] Through his editing, Gernsback may have suggested or reinforced the emphasis on television in Harris's story, or the emphasis on television may have been a reason that Gernsback chose Harris's story as a prizewinner. Harris's story is truly predictive, then, since there was no working system of televisual transmission in the United States until 1929. Moreover, in the 1920s, television was viewed not so much as a national or international entertainment medium (a purpose that develops in the 1930s) but mainly as a communication device — the goal just now being achieved with cell phones.

How can transmitting pictures be scary, especially to a people already devoted to motion pictures? In an important essay, Walter Benjamin theorized the effects on "The Work of Art in the Age of Mechanical Reproduction."[38] He argued that "the presence of the original is the prerequisite of the concept of authenticity," and that "the technique of reproduction detaches the reproduced object from the domain of tradition" so that "a plurality of copies" are substituted for "a unique existence," and tradition is shattered.[39] While Benjamin sees this process as potentially liberating, because it moves art from the realm of ritual into the realm of politics, Harris clearly sees this reproducibility as dangerous, and uses it to suggest how an alien invasion would shatter our sense of human tradition.

Harris's fears of such visual communication take several forms. First, when George sees Martell using the device, the alien is speaking "an unknown tongue." (Harris, 5) The phrasing is important, and reinforces George's description of messages sent from the "unknown bourne." A new form of communication demands learning new codes for communicating through it; the alien language represents the possibility that technology might outpace one's ability to learn. A second fear results from the reproducibility of television. When George risks everything to invade Martell's apartment, through the television he sees copies of Martell all over the world. When George pulls the first lever, "the Indian savage was a natural replica of the suave and civilized Martell," and when he uses the fourth lever, "another duplicate of Martell's" face appears. (Harris, 11) As he pulls other levers, George realizes that there is another copy of Martell in Munich, and another in Turkey or India. Here, the authenticity of the human being is called into question; these aliens all look alike to George, especially when distanced through televisual representation. They are somewhat like humans, but not really, with their attached crests of feathers. Moreover, while the physical description suggests American Indians, the geographical settings associate the aliens with peoples the United States in the 1920s viewed with suspicion: Germans, Turks, Asians. The multiple transmissions raise the possibility of countless reproductions: George is outnumbered even though he is alone in the room with the receiver.

Benjamin further suggests that there is a "shock effect" resulting from film because of its "constant, sudden change" of images.[40] Harris uses this aspect of television to arouse anxiety when George pulls the fifth lever and views an alien landscape. As in film, Harris quickly rotates through a sequence of visions, gradually building up the conviction that George is viewing an alien landscape on Mars: "Arid red cliffs," "two moons traversing the welkin!" and "a gyroscope of gigantic proportions"(Harris, 12–13). Thus setting the stage, Harris has George see that the gyroscope is carrying the Pegasus, a missing passenger plane. The constant, sudden change of images helps to magnify the alienation that George (and the reader) perceive at the idea of a race of intelligent nonhumans on Mars who have stolen an airplane full of people from Earth.

Indeed, Benjamin predicts that film and television will meld with modern "self-alienation" for the masses so that eventually only televised warfare will satiate their appetite for this technology, and humanity will be able to view "its own destruction as an aesthetic pleasure."[41] George's viewing of the final transmission from the television arouses and sensationalizes this fear. George is sent the television in an insane asylum where he has been incarcerated for breaking into Martell's apartment. He is "spellbound" as he watches humanity's fate. Tons of water stolen from Earth are now flowing down the gullies of Mars. Thousands of Martians stare at the sky as a gyroscope-vessel approaches bearing a missing ocean liner, the Poseidonia; the people in it perished because of the vacuum of space. George feels that he is watching "the victory of Martell, the Martian, . . . who has borne away trophies of our civilization to exhibit."(Harris, 18) Viewing the alien destruction of earthly property and peoples brings horror to George, but the description and the sf story in general bring horrific pleasure to the readers, as Benjamin warned.

When the screen fills with Margaret, the woman whom Martell stole from George, her story justifies George's fears: Martell has killed her parents and all the other passengers on the ship. But her final message to George is curious: "Do not mourn for me, George, for I shall take up the thread of life anew among these strange but beautiful surroundings." For the readers, this is the point where pleasure becomes anxiety: from thousands and thousands of miles across space, a beautiful young woman expresses self-alienation both through the reproducibility of her image, and also in her commitment to live without human (male) contact.

In "The Fate of the Poseidonia," Harris views with alarm the development of what Anthony Smith calls "a secondary environment of images," the development of modern communications technology.[42] Linking this anxiety about the uses of science to anxiety about racial mixing, Harris imagines a future very much in keeping with the lessons learned by the United

States in World War I, a future where technological expertise does not guarantee safety. Harris's story thus becomes a science fiction, where George and Margaret together rationally solve a problem based on science—the missing water. It is also, though, a story enmeshed in a particular historical context, a story in which each anxiety about illicit reproduction is amplified by its association with the other.

NOTES

1. Clare Winger Harris, "The Fate of the Poseidonia," *Amazing Stories* 2, no. 3 (June 1927): 245–252, and 267. The science fiction pulp magazines were the main forum for publishing science fiction from 1926 when they were established by Hugo Gernsback until the 1950s paperback explosion. The pulp magazines were generally on cheap wood-pulp paper, which deteriorates rapidly—hence the name—but often with slick paper covers and beautiful illustrations. Although some critics would argue that "Golden Age Science Fiction" refers only to the post–John Campbell editing era, I shall refer to this whole pulp period as "Golden Age."

2. Clare Winger Harris, *Away from the Here and Now: Stories in Pseudo-Science* (Philadelphia: Dorrance, 1947). This volume is not copyrighted by Harris, so may have been a pirated edition.

3. Curtis C. Smith, ed., *Twentieth-Century Science-Fiction Writers*, 2nd ed. (Chicago: St. James, 1986), viii. See also Peter Haining, ed., *The Fantastic Pulps* (New York: Vintage Books, 1975), 315, who calls science fiction "a man's literature"; even Lisa Tuttle, "Women SF Writers," in *The Encyclopedia of Science Fiction*, ed. John Clute and Peter Nicholls (New York: St. Martin's Griffin, 1993), 1344, claims that "women's contributions . . . were not substantial until the late 1960s."

4. See Pamela Sargent, ed., introduction to *Women of Wonder: Science Fiction Stories by Women about Women* (New York: Random House, 1974), xvi–xx; Susan Gubar, "C. L. Moore and the Conventions of Women's Science Fiction," *Science Fiction Studies* 7 (1980): 16–27; Sarah Gamble, "'Shambleau . . . and others': The Role of the Female in the Fiction of C. L. Moore," in *Where No Man Has Gone Before*, ed. Lucie Armitt (New York: Routledge, 1991), 29–49.

5. See Hugo Gernsback, inset introduction to "The Fate of the Poseidonia," *Amazing Stories* 2, no. 3 (June 1927): 245.

6. Ibid.

7. See Hugo Gernsback, inset introduction to Cyril G. Wates, "The Visitation," *Amazing Stories* 2, no. 3 (June 1927): 214; and inset introduction to George R. Fox, "The Electronic Wall," *Amazing Stories* 2, no. 3 (June 1927): 234.

8. See Robin Roberts, *A New Species: Gender and Science in Science Fiction* (Urbana: University of Illinois Press, 1993), esp. 40–65.

9. See Jane Donawerth, "Science Fiction by Women in the Early Pulps, 1926–1930," in *Utopian and Science Fiction by Women*, ed. Jane L. Donawerth and Carol A. Kolmerten (Syracuse: Syracuse University Press, 1994), 137–152; *Frankenstein's Daughters: Women Writing Science Fiction* (Urbana: University of Illinois Press, 1997); and "Science Fiction," in *The Oxford Companion to Women's Writing in the*

United States, ed. Cathy N. Davidson and Linda Wagner-Martin (New York: Oxford University Press, 1995), 780–782.

10. See Justine Larbalestier, *The Battle of the Sexes in Science Fiction* (Middletown, Conn.: Wesleyan University Press, 2002).

11. Brian Attebery, *Decoding Gender in Science Fiction* (New York: Routledge, 2002), esp. 43.

12. Compare Peter Nicholls, ed., *The Science Fiction Encyclopedia* (Garden City, N.Y.: Doubleday, 1979), with John Clute and Peter Nicholls, eds., *The Science Fiction Encyclopedia,* 2nd ed. (New York: St. Martin's, 1993).

13. "The Fifth Dimension," *Amazing Stories* 3, no. 9 (December 1928): 823–825, 850.

14. Clare Winger Harris, "The Artificial Man," *Science Wonder Quarterly* 1, no. 1 (Fall 1929): 78–83.

15. Clare Winger Harris, "The Menace from Mars," *Amazing Stories* 3, no. 7 (October 1928): 582–597.

16. Hugo Gernsback, "$500 Prize Story Contest," *Amazing Stories* 1, no. 9 (December 1926): 773.

17. Christine Gledhill, "Pleasurable Negotiations," in *Cultural Theory and Popular Culture,* ed. John Storey (New York: Harvester/Wheatsheaf, 1994), esp. 244–246.

18. Gernsback, for example, published Louise Rice and Tonjoroff-Roberts's "The Astounding Enemy," in *Amazing Stories Quarterly* 3, no. 1 (Winter 1930): 78–103, a story in which the heroes are a coalition of white, Asian, and women scientists who combat the villain's racism as well as an insect invasion to save the earth; Gernsback also published Lilith Lorraine's feminist utopia "Into the 28th Century," *Science Wonder Quarterly* 1, no. 2 (Winter 1930): 250–262 and 276; and works by several other women writers, including Louise Taylor Hansen, Minna Irving, and Leslie Stone.

19. See Lorraine, "Into the 28th Century." On Lorraine as a member of the Science Correspondence Club and her participation in their early fanzine *The Comet,* see Sam Moskowitz, "The Origins of Science Fiction Fandom: A Reconstruction," in *Science Fiction Fandom,* ed. Joe Sanders (Westport, Conn.: Greenwood, 1994), 30.

20. Moskowitz, "Origins," 27. See also Mark Siegel, *Hugo Gernsback: Father of Modern Science Fiction* (San Bernardino, Calif.: Borgo, 1988), 16; Siegel explains that Gernsback himself began writing science fiction when he read the scientific treatise *Mars as the Abode of Life* by Percival Lowell.

21. Siegel, *Hugo Gernsback,* 46.

22. Moskowitz, "Origins," 28.

23. See Moskowitz, *The Immortal Storm: A History of Science Fiction Fandom* (Westport, Conn.: Hyperion, 1974), 8–12; and "Origins," 29–30.

24. See Moskowitz, "Origins," 30, and *Immortal Storm,* 13–26, esp. 15 on Harris.

25. Alfred H. Richards of Flint, Michigan, fan letter, *Amazing Stories* 2, no. 6 (September 1927): 610. I thank Justine Larbalestier for this citation.

26. Cyril G. Wates, "The Visitation," *Amazing Stories* 2, no. 3 (June 1927): 214–233.

27. George R. Fox, "The Electronic Wall," *Amazing Stories* 2, no. 3 (June 1927): 234–244.

28. Thomas Powell, *The Persistence of Racism in America* (Lanham, Md.: University Press of America, 1992), 109. See Philip Dray, *At the Hands of Persons Unknown: The Lynching of Black Americans* (New York: Random House, 2002), 303, on the jump in lynchings from eleven in 1929 to twenty-two in 1930; see also Robert L. Zangrando, *The NAACP Campaign Against Lynching, 1909–1950* (Philadelphia: Temple University Press, 1980).

29. See Betsy Nies, *Eugenic Fantasies: Racial Ideology in the Literature and Popular Culture of the 1920s* (New York: Routledge, 2002), esp. xii–xiii and 3–13. In "The Artificial Man," Harris imagines that a crazed paraplegic tries to replace as many organs with mechanisms as possible, helped by a German scientist; such a story shows that eugenics as a science promoting racial superiority is already linked with German Nazis.

30. Nies, *Eugenic Fantasies*, 31–33.

31. We know that Clare Winger Harris was white because a sketch of her was published with her story "The Artificial Man," 79.

32. Nies, *Eugenic Fantasies*, 20.

33. Ibid., 24–25.

34. Albert Abramson, "The Invention of Television," in *Television: An International History*, 2nd ed., ed. Anthony Smith (Oxford: Oxford University Press, 1998), 9.

35. Ibid., 11.

36. Ibid., 14.

37. Ibid., 13.

38. Walter Benjamin, "The Work of Art in the Age of Mechanical Reproduction" (1936), in *The Critical Tradition: Classic Texts and Contemporary Trends*, ed. David H. Richter (New York: St. Martin's, 1989), 571–588.

39. Ibid., 573–574.

40. Ibid., 585.

41. Ibid., 588.

42. Anthony Smith, ed., *Television: An International History*, 2nd ed. (Oxford: Oxford University Press, 1998), 1.

2

The Conquest of Gola

LESLIE F. STONE

First published in Wonder Stories, *April 1931*

Hola, my daughters (sighed the Matriarch), it is true indeed, I am the only living one upon Gola who remembers the invasion from Detaxal. I alone of all my generation survive to recall vividly the sights and scenes of that past era. And well it is that you come to me to hear by free communication of mind to mind, face to face with each other.

Ah, well I remember the surprise of that hour when through the mists that enshroud our lovely world, there swam the first of the great smooth cylinders of the Detaxalans, fifty *tas** in length, as glistening and silvery as the soil of our land, propelled by the man-things that on Detaxal are supreme even as we women are supreme on Gola.

In those bygone days, as now, Gola was enwrapped by her cloud mists that keep from us the terrific glare of the great star that glows like a malignant spirit out there in the darkness of the void. Only occasionally when a particularly great storm parts the mist of heaven do we see the wonders of the vast universe, but that does not prevent us, with our marvelous telescopes handed down to us from thousands of generations before us, from learning what lies across the dark seas of the outside.

Therefore we knew of the nine planets that encircle the great star and are subject to its rule. And so are we familiar enough with the surfaces of these planets to know why Gola should appear as a haven to their inhabitants who see in our cloud-enclosed mantle a sweet release from the blasting heat and blinding glare of the great sun.

So it was not strange at all to us to find that the people of Detaxal, the third planet of the sun, had arrived on our globe with a wish in their hearts

---

* Since there is no means of translating the Golan measurements of either length or time we can but guess at these things. However, since the Detaxalan ships each carried a thousand men it can be seen that the ships were between five hundred and a thousand feet in length.

to migrate here, and end their days out of reach of the blistering warmth that had come to be their lot on their own world.

Long ago we, too, might have gone on exploring expeditions to other worlds, other universes, but for what? Are we not happy here? We who have attained the greatest of civilizations within the confines of our own silvery world. Powerfully strong with our mighty force rays, we could subjugate all the universe, but why?

Are we not content with life as it is, with our lovely cities, our homes, our daughters, our gentle consorts? Why spend physical energy in combative strife for something we do not wish, when our mental processes carry us further and beyond the conquest of mere terrestrial exploitation?

On Detaxal it is different, for there the peoples, the ignoble male creatures, breed for physical prowess, leaving the development of their sciences, their philosophies, and the contemplation of the abstract to a chosen few. The greater part of the race fares forth to conquer, to lay waste, to struggle and fight as the animals do over a morsel of worthless territory. Of course we can see why they desired Gola with all its treasures, but we can thank Providence and ourselves that they did not succeed in "commercializing" us as they have the remainder of the universe with their ignoble Federation.

Ah yes, well I recall the hour when first they came, pushing cautiously through the cloud mists, seeking that which lay beneath. We of Gola were unwarned until the two cylinders hung directly above Tola, the greatest city of that time, which still lies in its ruins since that memorable day. But they have paid for it — paid for it well in thousands and tens of thousands of their men.

We were first apprised of their coming when the alarm from Tola was sent from the great beam station there, advising all to stand in readiness for an emergency. Geble, my mother, was then Queen of all Gola, and I was by her side in Morka, that pleasant seaside resort, where I shall soon travel to partake of its rejuvenating waters.

With us were four of Geble's consorts, sweet gentle males, that gave Geble much pleasure in these free hours away from the worries of state. But when the word of the strangers' descent over our home city, Tola, came to us, all else was forgotten. With me at her side, Geble hastened to the beam station and there in the matter transmitter we dispatched our physical beings to the palace at Tola, and the next moment were staring upward at the two strange shapes etched against the clouds.

What the Detaxalan ships were waiting for we did not know then, but later we learned. Not grasping the meaning of our beam stations, the commandants of the ships considered the city below them entirely lacking in means of defense, and were conferring on the method of taking it without bloodshed on either side.

It was not long after our arrival in Tola that the first of the ships began to descend toward the great square before the palace. Geble watched without a word, her great mind already scanning the brains of those whom she found within the great machine. She transferred to my mind but a single thought as I stood there at her side and that with a sneer: "Barbarians!"

Now the ship was settling in the square and after a few moments of hesitation, a circular doorway appeared at the side and four of the Detaxalans came through the opening. The square was empty but for themselves and their flyer, and we saw them looking about surveying the beautiful buildings on all sides. They seemed to recognize the palace for what it was and in one accord moved in our direction.

Then Geble left the window at which we stood and strode to the doorway opening upon the balcony that faced the square. The Detaxalans halted in their tracks when they saw her slender graceful form appear and removing the strange coverings they wore on their heads they each made a bow.

Again Geble sneered, for only the male-things of our world bow their heads, and so she recognized these visitors for what they were, nothing more than the despicable males of the species! And what creatures they were!

Imagine a short almost flat body set high upon two slender legs, the body tapering in the middle, several times as broad across as it is through the center, with two arms almost as long as the legs attached to the upper part of the torso. A small column-like neck of only a few inches divides the head of oval shape from the body, and in this head only are set the organs of sight, hearing, and scent. Their bodies were like a patch work of a misguided nature.

Yes, strange as it is, my daughters, practically all of the creature's faculties had their base in the small ungainly head, and each organ was perforce pressed into serving for several functions. For instance, the breathing nostrils also served for scenting out odors, nor was this organ able to exclude any disagreeable odors that might come its way, but had to dispense to the brain both pleasant and unpleasant odors at the same time.

Then there was the mouth, set directly beneath the nose, and here again we had an example of one organ doing the work of two, for the creature not only used the mouth with which to take in the food for its body, but it also used the mouth to enunciate the excruciatingly ugly sounds of its language forthwith.

Guests From Detaxal

Never before have I seen such a poorly organized body, so unlike our own highly developed organisms. How much nicer it is to be able to call forth any organ at will, and dispense with it when its usefulness is over! Instead these poor Detaxalans had to carry theirs about in physical being all the time so that always was the surface of their bodies entirely marred.

Yet that was not the only part of their ugliness, and proof of the lowliness of their origin, for whereas our fine bodies support themselves by muscular development, these poor creatures were dependent entirely upon a strange structure to keep them in their proper shape.

Imagine if you can a bony skeleton somewhat like the foundations upon which we build our edifices, laying stone and cement over the steel framework. But this skeleton instead is inside a body which the flesh, muscle and skin overlay. Everywhere in their bodies are these cartilaginous structures — hard, heavy, bony structures developed by the chemicals of the being for its use. Even the hands, feet and head of the creatures were underlaid with these bones, ugh, it was terrible when we dissected one of the fellows for study. I shudder to think of it.

Yet again there was still another feature of the Detaxalans that was equally as horrifying as the rest, namely their outer covering. As we viewed them for the first time out there in the square we discovered that parts of the body, that is the part of the head which they called the face, and the bony hands were entirely naked without any sort of covering, neither fur nor feathers, just the raw, pinkish-brown skin looking as if it had been recently plucked.

Later we found a few specimens that had a type of fur on the lower part of the face, but these were rare. And when they doffed the head coverings which we had first taken for some sort of natural covering, we saw that the top of the head was overlaid with a very fine fuzz of fur several inches long.

We did not know in the beginning that the strange covering on the bodies of the four men, green in color, was not a natural growth, but later discovered that such was the truth, and not only the face and hands were bare of fur, but the entire body, except for a fine sprinkling of hair that was scarcely visible except on the chest, was also bare. No wonder the poor things covered themselves with their awkward clothing. We arrived at the conclusion that their lack of fur had been brought about by the fact that always they had been exposed to the bright rays of the sun so that without the dampness of our own planet the fur had dried up and fallen away from the flesh!

Now thinking it over I suppose that we of Gola presented strange forms to the people of Detaxal with our fine circular bodies, rounded at the top, our short beautiful lower limbs with the circular foot pads, and our short round arms and hand pads, flexible and muscularlike [*sic*] rubber.

But how envious they must have been of our beautiful golden coats, our movable eyes, our power to scent, hear and touch with any part of the body, to absorb food and drink through any part of the body most convenient to us at any time. Oh yes, laugh though you may, without a doubt we were also freaks to those freakish Detaxalans. But no matter, let us return to the tale.

On recognizing our visitors for what they were, simple-minded males, Geble was chagrined at them for taking up her time, but they were strangers to our world and we Golans are always courteous. Geble began of course to try to communicate by thought transference, but strangely enough the fellows below did not catch a single thought. Instead, entirely unaware of Geble's overture to friendship, the leader commenced to speak to her in most outlandish manner, contorting the red lips of his mouth into various uncouth shapes and making sounds that fell upon our hearing so unpleasantly that we immediately closed our senses to them. And without a word Geble turned her back upon them, calling for Tanka, her personal secretary.

Tanka was instructed to welcome the Detaxalans while she herself turned to her own chambers to summon a half dozen of her council. When the council arrived she began to discuss with them the problem of extracting more of the precious tenix from the waters of the great inland lake of No-tauch. Nothing whatever was said of the advent of the Detaxalans for Geble had dismissed them from her mind as creatures not worthy of her thought.

In the meantime Tanka had gone forth to meet the four who of course could not converse with her. In accordance with the Queen's orders she led them indoors to the most informal receiving chamber and there had them served with food and drink which by the looks of the remains in the dishes they did not relish at all.

Leading them through the rooms of the lower floor of the palace she made a pretence of showing them everything which they duly surveyed. But they appeared to chafe at the manner in which they were being entertained.

The creatures even made an attempt through the primitive method of conversing by their arms to learn something of what they had seen, but Tanka was as supercilious as her mistress. When she thought they had had enough, she led them to the square and back to the door of their flyer, giving them their dismissal.

But the men were not ready to accept it. Instead they tried to express to Tanka their desire to meet the ruling head of Gola. Although their hand motions were perfectly inane and incomprehensible, Tanka could read what passed through their brains, and understood more fully than they what lay in their minds. She shook her head and motioned that they were to embark in their flyer and be on their way back to their planet.

Again and again Detaxalans tried to explain what they wished, thinking Tanka did not understand. At last she impressed upon their savage minds that there was nothing for them but to depart, and disgruntled by her treatment they reentered their machine, closed its ponderous door and raised their ship to the level of its sister flyer. Several minutes passed and then, with thanksgiving, we saw them pass over the city.

Told of this, Geble laughed. "To think of mere man-things daring to attempt to force themselves upon us. What is the universe coming to? What are their women back home considering when they sent them to us? Have they developed too many males and think that we can find use for them?" she wanted to know.

"It is strange indeed," observed Yabo, one of the council members. "What did you find in the minds of these ignoble creatures, O August One?"

"Nothing of particular interest, a very low grade of intelligence, to be sure. There was no need of looking below the surface."

"It must have taken intelligence to build those ships."

"None aboard them did that. I don't question it but that their mothers built the ships for them as playthings, even as we give toys to our 'little ones,' you know. I recall that the ancients of our world perfected several types of space-flyers many ages ago!"

"Maybe those males do not have 'mothers' but instead they build the ships themselves, maybe they are the stronger sex on their world!" This last was said by Suiki, the fifth consort of Geble, a pretty little male, rather young in years. No one had noticed his coming into the chamber, but now everyone showed their surprise at his words.

"Impossible!" ejaculated Yabo.

Geble however laughed at the little chap's expression. "Suiki is a profound thinker," she observed, still laughing, and she drew him to her gently hugging him.

A Nice Business Deal

And with that the subject of the men from Detaxal was closed. It was reopened, however, several hours later when it was learned that instead of leaving Gola altogether the ships were seen one after another by the various cities of the planet as they circumnavigated it.

It was rather annoying, for everywhere the cities' routines were broken up as the people dropped their work and studies to gaze at the cylinders. Too, it was upsetting the morale of the males, for on learning that the two ships contained only creatures of their own sex they were becoming envious, wishing for the same type of playthings for themselves.

Shut in, as they are, unable to grasp the profundities of our science and thought, the gentle, fun-loving males were always glad for a new diversion, and this new method developed by the Detaxalans had intrigued them.

It was then that Geble decided it high time to take matters into her own hands. Not knowing where the two ships were at the moment it was not difficult with the object-finder beam to discover their whereabouts, and then with the attractor to draw them to Tola magnetically. An *ous* later we had the pleasure of seeing the two ships rushing toward our city. When they arrived about [*sic*] it, power brought them down to the square again.

Again Tanka was sent out, and directed the commanders of the two ships to follow her in to the Queen. Knowing the futility of attempting to converse with them without mechanical aid, Geble caused to be brought her three of the ancient mechanical thought transformers that are only museum pieces to us but still workable. The two men were directed to place them on their heads while she donned the third. When this was done she ordered the creatures to depart immediately from Gola, telling them that she was tired of their play.

Watching the faces of the two I saw them frowning and shaking their heads. Of course I could read their thoughts as well as Geble without need of the transformers, since it was only for their benefit that these were used, so I heard the whole conversation, though I need only to give you the gist of it.

"We have no wish to leave your world as yet," the two had argued.

"You are disrupting the routine of our lives here," Geble told them, "and now that you've seen all that you can there is no need for you to stay longer. I insist that you leave immediately."

I saw one of the men smile, and thereupon he was the one who did all the talking (I say "talking" for this he was actually doing, mouthing each one of his words although we understood his thoughts as they formed in his queer brain, so different from ours).

"Listen here," he laughed, "I don't get the hang of you people at all. We came to Gola (he used some outlandish name of his own, but I use our name of course) with the express purpose of exploration and exploitation. We come as friends. Already we are in alliance with Damin (again the name for the fourth planet of our system was different, but I give the correct appellation), established commerce and trade, and now we are ready to offer you the chance to join our federation peaceably.

"What we have seen of this world is very favorable, there are good prospects for business here. There is no reason why you people as those of Damin and Detaxal can not enter into a nice business arrangement congenially. You have far more here to offer tourists, more than Damin. Why, except for your clouds this would be an ideal paradise for every man, woman and child on Detaxal and Damin to visit, and of course with our new cloud dispensers we could clear your atmosphere for you in short order and keep it that way. Why, you'll make millions in the first year of your trade.

"Come now, allow us to discuss this with your ruler — king or whatever you call him. Women are all right in their place, but it takes the men to see the profit of a thing like this — er — you are a woman, aren't you?"

The first of his long speech, of course, was so much gibberish to us, with his prate of business arrangements, commerce and trade, tourists, profits, cloud dispensers and what not, but it was the last part of what he said that took my breath away, and you can imagine how it affected Geble. I could see straightway that she was intensely angered, and good reason too. By the looks of the silly fellow's face I could guess that he was getting the full purport of her thoughts. He began to shuffle his funny feet and a foolish grin pervaded his face.

"Sorry," he said, "if I insulted you — I didn't intend that, but I believed that man holds the same place here as he does on Detaxal and Damin, but I suppose it is just as possible for woman to be the ruling factor of a world as man is elsewhere."

That speech naturally made Geble more irate, and tearing off her thought transformer she left the room without another word. In a moment, however, Yabo appeared wearing the transformer in her place. Yabo had none of the beauty of my mother, for whereas Geble was slender and as straight as a rod Yabo was obese, and her fat body overflowed until she looked like a large dumpy bundle of *yat* held together in her furry skin. She had very little dignity as she waddled toward the Detaxalans, but there was determination in her whole manner and without preliminaries she began to scold the two as though they were her own consorts.

"There has been enough of this, my fine young men," she shot at them. "You've had your fun, and now it is time for you to return to your mothers and consorts. Shame on you for making up such miserable tales about yourselves. I have a good mind to take you home with me for a couple of days, and I'd put you in your places quick enough. The idea of men acting like you are!"

For a moment I thought the Detaxalans were going to cry by the faces they made, but instead they broke into laughter, such heathenish sounds as had never before been heard on Gola, and I listened in wonder instead of excluding it from my hearing, but the fellows sobered quickly enough at that, and the spokesman addressed the shocked Yabo.

"I see," said he, "it's impossible for your people and mine to arrive at an understanding peaceably. I'm sorry that you take us for children out on a spree, that you are accustomed to such a low type of men as is evidently your lot here.

"I have given you your chance to accept our terms without force, but since you refuse, under the orders of the Federation I will have to take you forcibly, for we are determined that Gola become one of us, if you like it or not. Then you will learn that we are not the children you believe us to be.

"You may go to your supercilious Queen now and advise her that we give you exactly ten hours in which to evacuate this city, for precisely on the hour we will lay this city in ruins. And if that does not suffice you we will do the same with every other city on the planet! Remember ten hours!"

And with that he took the mechanical thought transformer from his head and tossed it on the table. His companion did the same and the two of them strode out of the room and to their flyers which arose several thousand feet above Tola and remained there.

The Triumph of Gola

Hurrying into Geble, Yabo told her what the Detaxalan had said. Geble was reclining on her couch and did not bother to raise herself.

"Childish prattle," she conceded and withdrew her red eyes on their movable stems into their pockets, paying no more heed to the threats of the men from Detaxal.

I, however, could not be as calm as my mother, and I was fearful that it was not childish prattle after all. Not knowing how long ten hours might be I did not wait, but crept up to the palace's beam station and set its dials so that the entire building and as much of the surrounding territory as it could cover were protected in the force zone.

Alas that the same beam was not greater. But it had not been put there for defense, only for matter transference and whatever other peacetime methods we used. It was the means of proving just the same that it was also a very good defensive instrument, for just two ous later the hovering ships above let loose their powers of destruction, heavy explosives that entirely demolished all of Gola and its millions of people and only the palace royal of all that beauty was left standing!

Awakened from her nap by the terrific detonation, Geble came hurriedly to a window to view the ruin, and she was wild with grief at what she saw. Geble, however, saw that there was urgent need for action. She knew without my telling her what I had done to protect the palace. And though she showed no sign of appreciation, I knew that I had won a greater place in her regard than any other of her many daughters and would henceforth be her favorite as well as her successor as the case tuned out.

Now, with me behind her, she hurried to the beam station and in a twinkling we were both in Tubia, the second greatest city of that time. Nor were we to be caught napping again, for Geble ordered all beam stations to throw out their zone forces while she herself manipulated one of Tubia's greatest power beams, attuning it to the emanations of the two Detaxalan flyers. In less than an ous the two ships were seen through the mists heading for Tubia. For a moment I grew fearful, but on realizing that they were after all in our grip, and the attractors held every living thing powerless against movement, I grew calm and watched them come over the city and the beam pull them to the ground.

With the beam still upon them, they lay supine on the ground without motion. Descending to the square Geble called for Ray C, and when the machine arrived she herself directed the cutting of the hole in the side of the flyer and was the first to enter it with me immediately behind, as usual.

We were both astounded by what we saw of the great array of machinery within. But a glance told Geble all she wanted to know of their principles. She interested herself only in the men standing rigidly in whatever position our beam had caught them. Only the eyes of the creatures expressed their fright, poor things, unable to move so much as a hair while we moved among them untouched by the power of the beam because of the strength of our own minds.

They could have fought against it if they had known how, but their simple minds were too weak for such exercise.

Now glancing about among the stiff forms around us, of which there were one thousand, Geble picked out those of the males she desired for observation, choosing those she judged to be their finest specimens, those with much hair on their faces and having more girth than the others.

These she ordered removed by several workers who followed us, and then we emerged again to the outdoors.

Using hand beam torches the picked specimens were kept immobile after they were out of reach of the greater beam and were borne into the laboratory of the building Geble had converted into her new palace. Geble and I followed, and she gave the order for the complete annihilation of the two powerless ships.

Thus ended the first foray of the people of Detaxal. And for the next two *tels* there was peace upon our globe again. In the laboratory the thirty who had been rescued from their ships were given thorough examinations both physically and mentally and we learned all there was to know about them. Hearing of the destruction of their ships, most of the creatures had become frightened and were quite docile in our hands. Those that were unruly were used in the dissecting room for the advancement of Golan knowledge.

After a complete study of them which yielded little we lost interest in them scientifically. Geble, however found some pleasure in having the poor creatures around her and kept three of them in her own chambers so she could delve into their brains as she pleased. The others she doled out to her favorites as she saw fit.

One she gave to me to act as a slave or in what capacity I desired him, but my interest in him soon waned, especially since I had now come of age and was allowed to have two consorts of my own, and go about the business of bringing my daughters into the world.

My slave I called Jon and gave him complete freedom of my house. If only we had foreseen what was coming we would have annihilated every one of them immediately! It did please me later to find that Jon was learning our language and finding a place in my household, making friends with my two shut-in consorts. But as I have said I paid little attention to him.

So life went on smoothly with scarcely a change after the destruction of the ships of Detaxal. But that did not mean we were unprepared for more. Geble reasoned that there would be more ships forthcoming when the Detaxalans found that their first two did not return. So, although it was sometimes inconvenient, the zones of force were kept upon our cities.

And Geble was right, for the day came when dozens of flyers descended upon Gola from Detaxal. But this time the zones of force did not hold them since the zones were not in operation!

And we were unwarned, for when they descended upon us, our world was sleeping, confident that our zones were our protection. The first indication that I had of trouble brewing was when awakening I found the ugly form of Jon bending over me. Surprised, for it was not his habit to arouse me, I started up only to find his arms about me, embracing me. And how strong he was! For the moment a new emotion swept me, for the first time I knew the pleasure to be had in the arms of a strong man, but that emotion was short lived for I saw in the blue eyes of my slave that he had recognized the look in my eyes for what it was, and for the moment he was tender.

Later I was to grow angry when I thought of that expression of his, for his eyes filled with pity, pity for me! But pity did not stay, instead he grinned and the next instant he was binding me down to my couch with strong rope. Geble, I learned later, had been treated as I, as were the members of the council and every other woman in Gola!

That was what came of allowing our men to meet on common ground with the creatures from Detaxal, for a weak mind is open to seeds of rebellion and the Detaxalans had sown it well, promising dominance to the lesser creatures of Gola.

That, however, was only part of the plot on the part of the Detaxalans. They were determined not only to revenge those we had murdered, but also to gain mastery of our planet. Unnoticed by us they had constructed a machine which transmits sound as we transmit thought and by this means had communicated with their own world, advising them of the very hour to strike when all of Gola was slumbering. It was a masterful stroke, only they did not know the power of the mind of Gola — so much more ancient then theirs.

Lying there bound on my couch I was able to see out the window and trembling with terror I watched a half dozen Detaxalan flyers descend into Tubia, guessing that the same was happening in our other cities. I was truly frightened, for I did not have the brain of a Geble. I was young yet, and in fear I watched the hordes march out of their machines, saw the thousands of our men join them.

Free from restraint, the shut-ins were having their holiday and how they cavorted out in the open, most of the time getting in the way of the freakish Detaxalans who were certainly taking over our city.

A half *ous* passed while I lay there watching, waiting in fear at what the Detaxalans planned to do with us. I remembered the pleasant life we had led up to the present and trembled over what the future might be when the Detaxalans had infested us with commerce and trade, business propositions, tourists and all of their evil practices. It was then that I received the message from Geble, clear and definite, just as all the women of the globe received it, and hope returned to my heart.

There began that titanic struggle, the fight for supremacy, the fight that won us victory over the simple-minded weaklings below who had presumptuously dared to conquer us. The first indication that the power of our combined mental concentration at Geble's orders was taking effect was when we saw the first of our males halt in their wild dance of freedom. They tried to shake us off, but we knew we could bring them back to us.

At first the Detaxalans paid them no heed. They knew not what was happening until there came the wholesale retreat of the Golan men back to the buildings, back to the chambers from which they had escaped. Then grasping something of what was happening the already defeated invaders sought to retain their hold on our little people. Our erstwhile captives sought to hold them with oratorical gestures, but of course we won. We saw our creatures return to us and unbind us.

Only the Detaxalans did not guess the significance of that, did not realize that inasmuch as we had conquered our own men, we could conquer them also. As they went about their work of making our city their own, establishing already their autocratic bureaus wherever they pleased, we began to concentrate upon them, hypnotizing them to the flyers that had disgorged them.

And soon they began to feel of our power, the weakest ones first, feeling the mental bewilderment creeping upon them. Their leaders, stronger in mind, knew nothing of this at first, but soon our terrible combined mental power was forced upon them also and they realized that their men were deserting them, crawling back to their ships! The leaders began to exhort them into new action, driving them physically. But our power gained on them and now we began to concentrate upon the leaders themselves. They were strong of will and they defied us, fought us, mind against mind, but of course it was useless. Their minds were not suited to the test they put themselves to, and after almost three *ous* of struggle, we of Gola were able to see victory ahead.

At last the leaders succumbed. Not a single Detaxalan was abroad in the avenues. They were within their flyers, held there by our combined wills, unable to act for themselves. It was then as easy for us to switch the zones of force upon them, subjugate them more securely and with the annihilator beam to disintegrate completely every ship and man into nothingness! Thousands upon thousands died that day and Gola was indeed revenged.

Thus, my daughters, ended the second invasion of Gola.

Oh yes, more came from their planet to discover what had happened to their ships and their men, but we of Gola no longer hesitated, and they no sooner appeared beneath the mists than they too were annihilated until at last Detaxal gave up the thought of conquering our cloud-laden world. Perhaps in the future they will attempt it again, but we are always in readiness for them now, and our men — well, they are still the same ineffectual weaklings, my daughters . . .

The Conquest of Gernsback: Leslie F. Stone and the Subversion of Science Fiction Tropes

Brian Attebery

By now it has become a cliché: manly explorers invade a world run by women and shake up its presumably backward and inverted social arrangements. Variations on this theme have appeared in countless stories and novels and even some laughably bad sci-fi movies. However, in 1931, when Leslie F. Stone published "The Conquest of Gola,"[1] the scenario that Joanna Russ has called "the battle of the sexes in science fiction" was a striking new idea, and Stone's story was not only one of the earliest but also one of the most intriguing uses of the theme.

The First Female Star

Leslie F. Stone was not the first woman to write for the science fiction pulp magazines but she was one of the genre's first female stars. Of her contemporaries, who also included Clare Winger Harris, A. R. (Amanda Reynolds) Long, L. (Louise) Taylor Hansen, and Helen Weinbaum, only C. L. Moore eventually became better known than Stone, and that was partly because Moore continued to write (and to develop) after Stone left the field in 1940.

The contributions of these women have not always been acknowledged, either by male writers and critics or by later feminist scholars. For instance, of the list above, only C. L. Moore is mentioned in Sarah Lefanu's *In the Chinks of the World Machine*, and not even Moore appears in Robin Roberts's *A New Species: Gender and Science in Science Fiction* — even though the former book has a chapter on science fiction dealing with societies ruled by women and the latter has one on the pulp era.[2] Only recently has the history of women's contributions to science fiction been pushed back to the early magazine era. It is hard to tell to what degree the sex of these pulp writers was even noted at the time they were writing, as many either used their initials as a byline or had ambiguously gendered names. Henry Kuttner, who eventually married and collaborated with Catherine L. Moore, first introduced himself with a fan letter to "Mr. C. L. Moore."[3]

There were undoubtedly readers who similarly read "Leslie" as a masculine name. Stone herself said that "at the time my first name had decidedly masculine connotations . . . so by using just a middle initial I put myself on the masculine side of the ledger and thus 'passed.'"[4] Even the drawing of Stone that appeared with the first publication of "Gola" depicts her as short-haired and androgynous (fig. 4). Yet her sex was not a complete secret: a letter from one fan acknowledges her as "our very excellent authoress, Leslie F. Stone."[5] Another lists "Miss L. Stone" as one of his favorite writers.[6] Stone's identity as a pioneering woman writer of SF is one reason that "The Conquest of Gola" continues to be reprinted (at least four times to date) and read.[7]

When Stone's work is read today, it is usually in the context of her explorations of gender roles. Her 1929 story "Out of the Void," for instance, features a brave spaceman hero who is revealed to be a woman in disguise. The very titles of paired stories about "Men with Wings" (1929) and "Women with Wings" (1930) have obvious gender implications. A late story called "The Great Ones" (1937) describes a race of cavemen among whom the women play a far more active role than usual in such prehistorical romances: "The women left the meager, rock-bound slope of the tor, their few rough tools left between the furrows. . . . The weavers and the skinworkers threw down their handiwork and grabbed at their sleeping babies. . . ."[8]

Stone's best-known story, "The Conquest of Gola," is perhaps her most important statement on gender roles, but it is also an experiment in science fictional storytelling and a commentary on other issues of Stone's day.

Science Fiction as Jazz

"Well it is," says the storyteller in the first paragraph of the story, "that you come to hear me by free communication of mind to mind, face to face with each other." But who is this narrator telling us about "the conquest of Gola," which actually turns out to be an unsuccessful invasion of the planet of Gola by its neighbors? More importantly, who are we, the listeners? The answers to these questions anticipate some of the exploration of identities and narrative conventions that opened up the genre of science fiction in the 1970s.

By agreeing to stand in, as they read the story, for the Golan natives who are listening to an elder tell about the invasion, many readers end up looking at themselves from the outside. It is not the Golans but the Detaxalan

LESLIE F. STONE

FIGURE 4. Sketch of Leslie F. Stone, *Wonder Stories*, April 1931

invaders who match up more closely with the core readership of science fiction, which sociologist William Sims Bainbridge once summed up as "young men interested in engineering and the physical sciences."[9] The Detaxalans are human, gadget-crazy, aggressive, profit-minded, and male. The Golans are telepathic, low-tech, alien in form, and female — yet Stone's storytelling framework invites the reader to identify with them, even across boundaries of sex or species. Positioning ourselves not only as readers of the story but as listeners to its spoken narration, we become, for the moment, "we Golans." As a reward, we can think of ourselves as victors, for the Golans finally win out, even though the outcome seems in doubt for much of the story.

In the early 1930s, readers of science fiction magazines such as *Wonder Stories*, in which "The Conquest of Gola" first appeared, would have recognized several elements of its basic plot. The early magazines functioned as a sort of discussion group or pre-Internet bulletin board for writers. One writer would publish a story; another would find an intriguing detail in that story and develop it; a third would write a story that reversed everything in the first piece; a fourth would find a way to turn the whole thing into comedy. Robots are a good example: introduced as a metaphor for oppressed workers in Karel Čapek's play *R.U.R.* (1921), the robot evolved into a potential threat in stories like Isaac Asimov's "Liar!" (1941) and then into a comic foil in Henry Kuttner's "The Proud Robot" (1943).

Like jazz, SF is a collaborative art. Together, the pulp magazine writers and editors of the 1920s through the 1940s created not only a genre but also a consensus about what sorts of settings, objects, stories, and characters belonged in that genre. Writers still make use of that collective future, though sometimes the use they make is to contradict or critique it.

Leslie F. Stone played an important part in the development of several characteristic SF scenarios, or tropes, as they are sometimes called. At least four of these tropes show up in "Gola": the alien invasion, the planetary romance, the race of telepaths, and the gender-reversed society. A fifth is not so much a plot scenario as a pervasive technique: what might be called "the Martian astronomer's perspective." H. G. Wells was one of the first writers to explore this technique. At the end of his 1899 story "The Star," after describing the terrible devastation wreaked upon the earth by a star passing through the solar system, Wells shifts the viewpoint to that of an observer on Mars:

> The Martian astronomers — for there are astronomers on Mars, although they are very different beings from men — were naturally profoundly interested by these things. They saw them from their own standpoint of course. "Considering the mass and temperature of the missile that was flung through our solar system into the sun," one wrote, "it is astonishing what a little damage the earth, which it missed so narrowly, has sustained. All the familiar continental markings and the masses of the seas remain intact, and indeed the only difference seems to be a shrinking of the white discoloration (supposed to be frozen water) around either pole." Which only shows how small the vastest of human catastrophes may seem, at a distance of a few million miles.[10]

Stone's Golans are a variety of Martian astronomer; that is, they are distant and detached observers of human life. By adopting their perspective, Stone is able to point out ironies, absurdities, and injustices that might not show up closer at hand. Her story, like Wells's, helped pave the way for later writers who have turned a Martian astronomer's eye on everything from advertising to religion.

Stone does not introduce all four SF tropes at once, but develops them through a series of scenes that also gradually pull the reader away from habitual ways of seeing earthly society. The opening scene is that in which the storyteller and her audience are introduced, but the reader does not yet know what sort of beings they are nor what their relationship to humanity might be. All the opening reveals is that the narrator is a matriarch, a senior female ruler, and that she is not only recounting an event from her youth but also issuing a warning to her listeners. The reader learns, through a series of asides and rhetorical questions, that Gola is a planet wrapped in clouds, that the Golans possess a high degree of technology, represented by "our mighty force rays," that they could leave their world to explore and even conquer others, but that they choose not to. This opening sequence is important in laying the groundwork for what is to follow, especially in inviting sympathy for an understanding of the Golan natives — before their adversaries are introduced.

In subsequent scenes, the balance of power shifts back and forth betwen Detaxalan invaders and Golan defenders. It is finally tipped toward the Golans by virtue of their superior mental development. Seemingly helpless, they work in concert first to win over the minds of the Golan men and then to attack the Detaxalans:

> And soon they began to feel of our power, the weakest ones first, feeling the mental bewilderment creeping upon them. Their leaders, stronger in mind, knew nothing of this at first, but soon our terrible combined mental power was forced upon them also, and they realized that their men were deserting them, crawling back to their ships! (Stone, 48)

After this psychological battle, the Golan ships are disintegrated, and Gola is left in peace once again. Afterward, however, the narrator and other Golan leaders vow to remain "always in readiness for them."

Who Are the Aliens?

The title and opening remarks of the story both place it within the tradition of alien invasion stories, a tradition that can be traced back primarily to H. G. Wells's *The War of the Worlds* (1897). The outlines of this scenario usually involve an early warning from space, a first small engagement, a wholesale attack and spreading devastation, a seeming defeat of the defending forces by the invaders, and then an unexpected development (such as Wells's earthly microbes, to which the Martians are not immune) leading to victory.

Stone follows this format quite closely, but she complicates it by introducing such elements as a group of Golan sympathizers who join forces with the invading Detaxalans. The trope of the alien invasion can be played out as a story of horror, tragedy, heroic victory, desperate underground resistance, or even — as in the film *Mars Attacks!* (1996) — grotesque comedy. The impact, however, is almost always the same: the story invokes our sympathies for the besieged world and our admiration for its defenders. Stone makes use of this sympathy to create several reversals in the story's other tropes.

Planetary Romance

The planetary romance scenario is called to mind when the narrator describes her home world. Readers in 1931 would have recognized the elements of this description: they knew a watery, cloud-wrapped world not under the name Gola but Venus. Before astronomers were able to determine just how hot and inhospitable Venus really is, its cloudy atmosphere led to a general consensus (at least within SF circles) that it must be a planet of jungles, oceans, and mists. Similarly, Mars was "known" to be crisscrossed by ancient canals and dotted with ruined or decadent cities. Both planets were used by writers — such as Edgar Rice Burroughs, in *A Princess of Mars* (1912) — as the settings for stories of adventure and discovery, usually with a beautiful imperiled princess thrown in for added spice.

Behind Burroughs there is a whole tradition of similar romances set in exotic locales on earth, going back at least to John Smith's famous anecdote (invented or deliberately exaggerated) about his rescue by Pocahontas, the Indian princess. The best-known novelistic treatment of the theme was H. Rider Haggard's *She* (1887). Such adventure stories can be read as defenses of European colonial exploits. They portray profit-seeking white men as heroic figures bringing civilization to the savages of Africa or South America.

Robert Dixon has analyzed these stories as attempts at dealing with a central dilemma: how can the adventurer "go native" and fully immerse himself in the exotic locale and culture while at the same time retaining a British schoolboy sort of innocence?[11] How could the hero be both white and native, brutal and naive? Burroughs solved the problem by displacing it to Mars. He wrote about "bad" natives by making them green Martians and turned the "friendlies" into red Martians. He provided his earthborn hero with superior strength and intelligence, so that it seemed only natural for him to defeat the bad guys, marry a Martian maiden, and start to rule over the grateful natives, all the while remaining a proper Southern gentleman. This solution to colonial problems proved enormously popular. After *A Princess of Mars*, dozens of writers (including Burroughs himself) produced scores of imitations.

Stone makes several gestures toward a Burroughs-style planetary romance in "Gola." For instance, the Detaxalan men refer to their earlier exploits on Damin, or Mars, where things evidently went according to expectation. The men are clearly operating by the rules for such a romance, and they seem offended that the Golan women do not play their proper part.

The most explicit reference to the romance trope is the moment when the narrator is thrown into the part of alien princess, caught in the embrace of the manly Jon. Her appointed role at this point is to fall in love and join with the adventurers, and Stone teases the reader with hints that this is indeed going to happen: "I started up only to find his arms about me, embracing me. And how strong he was!" (Stone, 47) But no, this princess is no romance heroine, and she is not about to throw out the values and customs of her race for one hero, no matter how strong. Once again, Stone calls up the familiar trope only to reinvent it along unfamiliar lines. In this case the natives do not welcome their would-be colonizers with open arms, and they aren't pushovers.

Telepaths and Eggheads

The reader knows from the opening that the Golans are able to communicate directly from mind to mind. The usual scenario that goes along with such a race of psychically gifted beings is a contest between them and ordinary humanity. The telepaths can be aliens, usually monstrous in form but occasionally seductively quasi-human, as in C. L. Moore's first story "Shambleau" (1933). Or they can be mutated humans, as in Edmond Hamilton's "The Man Who Evolved" (the lead story in the very issue of *Wonder Tales* where "Gola" first appeared).

In either case, most instances of the trope in the early pulps treated telepaths as grotesque villains. Hamilton's superevolved man, for instance, is "thin and shriveled" with a bald head that looks like "an immense, bulging balloon."[12] Stanley Weinbaum, in *The New Adam* (1939), is not quite so odd looking, but he is just as menacing, with snakelike hands and hypnotic powers. In these early superman stories, normal humans are the good guys who are ultimately successful in defeating their mind-manipulating rivals.

Stone sets up the usual opposition between telepaths and ordinary humans but reassigns both empathy and success. We want the Golans to win (or at least we do if we go along with the narrator) and they do so.

Other writers were to follow Stone in this reversal. In John W. Campbell's story "Forgetfulness" (1937), for example, a similar group of arrogant, manly invaders arrives on an apparently backward world only to discover that its primitive appearance masks a highly evolved society dependent not on gadgets but on mental powers.

In Campbell's story, however, this telepathic and pastoral world turns out be a future earth, and so the reader gets the emotional payoff of being on the right side after all. Stone's story remains more daring than Campbell's in its reversal of sympathies. Her Golans are neither ordinary nor human. Gola is not a future earth, but its enemies might well be our descendents.

When Women are Men and Men are Absent

Boldest of all is Stone's treatment of the gender-reversal trope. The idea of a society dominated by women goes back at least to Greek folklore and its tribe of Amazon warriors, and it has been used satirically by writers from Aristophanes to Thomas Berger.

In the late nineteenth century, a few women writers began to explore the idea of a matriarchal society as something potentially utopian, or at least as offering a critical perspective on existing societies. A good example of the latter use is Annie Denton Cridge's *Man's Rights; or, How Would You Like It?*, published as a pamphlet in 1870.

Cridge frames her story as a dream, in which the narrator has visions of a society with gender roles precisely reversed. In the world of these dreams (eventually revealed to be Mars), men get the drudgery of housework, are denied educations, and are expected to console themselves with fashion. Cridge has fun with the reversals even while making her point:

> "I would like to go to the lecture on 'men's rights,'" I heard one man say to his wife very timidly.
>
> "I shall go to no such place," replied his wife loftily; "neither will you. 'Man's rights,' indeed!"[13]

The trope of gender reversal can also be traced back to works such as Charlotte Perkins Gilman's utopian *Herland* (1915). In this and related stories, men are not simply relegated to traditional feminine spheres, but are eliminated altogether. Yet these too are stories of gender reversal. The disappearance of males from the represented world is, in effect, a mirror image of the all-male societies depicted in stories by men, including Melville's *Moby-Dick*, Jules Verne's *Twenty-Thousand Leagues under the Sea*, and countless science fiction adventures.

Readers generally fail to notice the absence of women from such stories because of social conventions that identify most occupations and narrative niches with men. As Joanna Russ wryly comments in *The Female Man*, "I think it's a legend that half the population of the world is female; where on earth are they keeping them all?"[14]

Leslie F. Stone draws on the traditions of gender-reversed and single-sex societies in both their satirical and utopian modes. She lets her narrator express Golan attitudes about males, clearly modeled on men's comments about women: they are "intellectual weaklings," however "sweet" and "gentle" they may be. At the same time, the narrator lets contrary information slip through: the reader learns that at least some Golan men are able to think for themselves and that they are not content with their sheltered lives. The Detaxalans, on the other hand, represent a "normal" society so dominated by males that no Detaxalan women appear in the story, ever. Without the contrast with Gola, such an arrangement would not even be noteworthy. Stone makes the absence a glaring one.

There is a clear line of historical continuity between the reversals imagined by Gilman, Cridge, and Stone and the development of a feminist SF tradition in the 1970s, spearheaded by Joanna Russ and Alice Sheldon. Soon after publishing *The Female Man*, Russ wrote an essay called *"Amor Vincit Fœminam:* The Battle of the Sexes in Science Fiction," in which she discussed earlier gender-reversal stories by women and by men.

In the men's stories, frequently, the inverted or all-female societies are portrayed as backward, repressive places. The appearance of one "real man" is usually enough to undo hundreds of years of tradition: at the hero's touch, the erstwhile Amazon typically rejects her "unnatural" society to melt in his arms. This is the "amor vincit fœminam" of Russ's title: love conquers the woman.

Russ's essay does not mention Leslie F. Stone: she drew most of her examples from an anthology titled *When Women Rule*, and the editor of that anthology, Sam Moskowitz, did not include Stone's story. He did, however, include other stories that helped constitute the gender-reversal trope, stories to which Stone was responding and stories that responded to hers.

Framing The Story

In her book *The Battle of the Sexes in Science Fiction*, Justine Larbalestier has further analyzed Russ's article, Moskowitz's anthology, and the ongoing dialogue that both represent. Much of the early stage of that dialogue took place in the pulp magazines, but not solely in the stories. Instead, editorial introductions and fan letters to the editors constitute a surrounding text — a frame — that was intended to govern the way the stories themselves were read.

The editorial introduction to the issue of *Wonder Stories* in which "The Conquest of Gola" appeared, for instance, invited readers to read the fiction in terms of its scientific content. Extolling "The Wonders of Creation," editor Hugo Gernsback called attention to Einstein's theories, the magnitude of the universe, and the possibility of universes outside our own.[15] He said nothing about the emotional basis of the stories or about their representation of social issues.

Most of the fans followed his lead in praising or condemning stories primarily on the basis of their astronomical accuracy. Their favorite authors were the ones who got the orbits right. A few, however, raised the issues that Gernsback avoids. Writer and fan Jack Williamson, for instance, commented in 1937 that the *fiction* part of SF is as important as the *science*: "Its purpose, I think—like that of any art—is to create a unified emotional response to its material. It deals, in other words, not so much with science itself as with the *human reaction* to science."[16] Many of those who agreed with Williamson were women readers, such as Carmen McCable, who, just the year before "Gola" appeared, wrote to the magazine's editor that in reading about any space voyager, "What I am interested in and crave to occupy my interest is what kind of adventure he goes through after he gets there. What kick do you get out of reading a lot of numbers? We want the description. The emotions the character goes through."[17]

Discussions of emotional content within SF often came down to arguments for or against the presence of women characters. An infamous case is a letter by a teenaged Isaac Asimov, protesting the presence of "swooning dames" within SF stories.[18] In these letters, overt emotional content is often equated with the female sex, as if there were no emotional payoff in stories of masculine courage or loyalty. The presence or absence of female characters also tended to slip over into the question of whether women were or should be readers of SF. One of those who wrote to *Amazing Stories* to protest that, indeed, women readers did exist was a Mrs. L. Silberberg—who was most probably Leslie Stone, writing under her real name.[19]

The male fans' response to Stone's own use of female characters was one of anxiety: "And did I get a berating from readers," says Stone, "for putting females in the driver's seat, females that dared to regard their gentle consorts as playthings! Male chauvenism [*sic*] just couldn't take that!"[20] One of her milder critics was Harry R. Panscoat, who wrote, "I sympathize with Leslie F. Stone in her right to uphold the importance of women, yet I feel she has overdone the thing."[21]

A much more blatant form of male chauvinism was demonstrated in stories that followed Stone's. In them, such females were defeated, their pretensions to superiority mocked, their powers belittled. Both Nelson S. Bond's "The Priestess Who Rebelled" (1939) and Edmund Cooper's *Who Needs Men?* (1972), for instance, include scenes directly parallel to the one in which the narrator of "Gola" briefly considers and then rejects the masculine strength of the Detaxalan Jon. In those later texts, however, women succumb to the he-man. After one kiss from him, as Russ points out, "friends, family, her lifelong loyalties, her own traditions and her religion, count as nothing."[22]

Changing Covers

In its initial publication, "The Conquest of Gola" was part of a dialogue but it was also a voice of resistance within that dialogue. It drew upon prior stories for its repertoire of storytelling tropes, while at the same time challenging their uses of some of those tropes. The very fact that its author was a woman invited women readers to see the field of science fiction as something they had a claim to, something that could express their interests and viewpoints, even though that invitation was simultaneously denied by a noisy group of male fans. It was not fans who eventually silenced Leslie F. Stone, however, but editors. Her presence within the field was largely due to Hugo Gernsback, who, according to Stone, "liked the idea of a woman invading the field he had opened."[23] As Gernsback's influence waned, that of John W. Campbell increased, and Campbell was as hostile as Gernsback was welcoming. Stone recalled an appointment with Campbell: "Mr. Campbell said in a rather acid tone, 'I am returning your story, Miss Stone. I do not believe that women are capable of writing science-fiction — nor do I approve of it!' I grabbed my story from his hand and fled."[24]

Stone mentions other unwelcoming editors, such as *Galaxy*'s Horace Gold and anthologist Groff Conklin. Ironically, Conklin reprinted "The Conquest of Gola" in his 1946 anthology without knowing that its author was a woman.[25]

When stories are reprinted, they acquire new contexts that can shift their perceived meaning. In Conklin's *The Best of Science Fiction*, Stone's story appears without illustration, stripped of its surrounding ads and fan letters, and divorced from its original context of related stories. It becomes not so much a story about gender as one about alienness: Conklin puts it in a section that he calls "From Outer Space" along with stories of exploration and first contact.

The story is also made to serve a project of Conklin's to rid the genre of "stories as are usually to be found between lurid magazine covers showing luxuriantly-fleshed females scantily clad in either a leopard's skin or a two-piece female Buck Rogers outfit with a bare twelve inches of midriff, struggling (always valiantly struggling!) with an octopus-like monster or an other-world hellion with horns and a leer."[26] This description is oddly

FIGURE 5. April 1931 cover of *Wonder Stories*, by Frank R. Paul

inappropriate to most of the magazines from which Conklin gleaned his stories. The cover on the issue of *Wonder Stories* in which "Gola" appeared has no monstrous molluscs and no females, leopard-skinned or otherwise (fig. 5). Instead, it features a comically eggheaded "Man Who Evolved," illustrating Edmond Hamilton's lead story. Throughout the magazine, the visual emphasis is not on sensationalism or even manly adventure but on sober intellectual activity. The title page has an illustration of a draped woman (perhaps the goddess of Science) presiding over four readers of the magazine: a cosy married couple and a pair of men who might be coworkers.

The tone of the publication is best represented by an ad reading "Get into a Dignified Profession! Become a full-fledged chemist!" (fig. 6). The ad features a drawing of a young man in his shirt sleeves working in a laboratory while moonlight streams in the window; he is either studying or working late. A small photo shows what the young man hopes to become: a dignified (i.e., bearded) scientist identified as T. O'Conor Sloane, A.B., A.M., Ph.D., LL.D. The ad does not point out that Sloane was not only a scientist but also editor of the magazine *Amazing Stories*. The message comes through regardless: reading science fiction makes you smarter, and being smart is the way to achieve status, financial security (even during the Great Depression), and perhaps love (if you share your SF magazines with a sympathetic woman and if you don't overdo the intelligence to the point of becoming Hamilton's egghead).

Reframing the Story

If this ivory tower was what the magazines looked like, then what did Conklin really want to get rid of in his anthologies? In his introduction, Conklin indicates that his main objection to such stories is their wretched prose, but his examples hint that he is also trying to get rid of females and the sexuality with which he equates them. He certainly removed women from his roster of authors: Stone — included inadvertently — is the only woman writer of any of the forty stories he selected. (In a later anthology, the 1952 *Omnibus of Science Fiction*, he upped the number of stories by women to a whopping two out of forty-three.)

The next reprint of "Gola" has precisely the opposite project: it is in an anthology designed to remind readers of the presence of women in the genre. In Janrae Frank, Jean Stine, and Forrest J. Ackerman's anthology from 1994, Stone's becomes yet another story of a "new Eve," and its writer becomes part of a tradition of rebellious women who "challenged the sta-

FIGURE 6. Advertisement from *Wonder Stories*, April 1931

tus quo, and challenged people to imagine" other ways of organizing the world.[27]

This current reprinting also places Stone in the company of other women writers; by now, however, the range of SF by women is broad enough that stories can be seen as expressing more than simple discontent about gender roles. "The Conquest of Gola" examines not only roles but also body images (does Golan anatomy represent male views of women's bodies?), planetary environments, and colonialism, topics that thus come under the scrutiny of a feminist critique. In this volume, Jane Donawerth's essay on Clare Winger Harris's "The Fate of the Poseidonia" suggests that Harris, like Stone, used science fiction to address contemporary concerns about race, sexuality, and the threat of invasion. It would be interesting to read the story in conjunction with more recent stories by Octavia Butler, Gwyneth Jones (such as those included in this volume) or Nalo Hopkinson in which cultural difference, ecology, and the body are similarly linked.

The historical nature of this anthology also invites reading the story in conjunction with world events. The 1930s are now strongly identified with the Great Depression; however, Stone makes no obvious reference to hardships or heartless plutocrats. Yet there were several other current events to which she may have been responding. To name only two possible historical contexts, the year 1931 saw developments in U.S. colonialism and in the growth of anti-Semitism in Europe. In that year, the U. S.-backed government of Panama was overthrown but Marines remained in charge in Nicaragua, where they had exercised direct control since 1912 and were to continue to do so for two more years, until 1933. Stone's Detaxalans strongly resemble the long line of American adventurers in Latin America who similarly defended their interventions in the name of free trade and commercial development.

On the other side of the Atlantic, in 1931, anti-Semitic gangs attacked worshipers coming out of a synagogue in Berlin, and the National Socialist party consolidated its power in Bavaria. Leslie Stone, who was Jewish, may be referring indirectly to Nazi attempts to define some races as more fully human than others. Interestingly, though Stone mentions "passing" as male by making deliberate use of her first name and middle initial, she does not acknowledge another sort of passing: the adoption of a surname less ethnically marked than Silberberg. Biographical studies of Stone might indicate the degree to which her political awareness was linked to traditions of Jewish radicalism and reform.

"The Conquest of Gola" invites readers to look at many such issues from the outside, as if we were Martian astronomers looking at earth. It is an outstanding early example of science fiction's power to make familiar things strange, including patterns of thought and society that we usually take for granted.

NOTES

1. Leslie F. Stone, "The Conquest of Gola," *Wonder Stories* (April 1931): 1278–1287.

2. Sarah Lefanu, *In the Chinks of the World Machine: Feminism and Science Fiction* (London: The Women's Press, 1988); Robin Roberts, *A New Species: Gender and Science in Science Fiction* (Urbana: University of Illinois Press, 1993).

3. William P. Kelly, "Catherine L. Moore," in *Twentieth-Century American Science Fiction Writers, Part 2: M–Z,* ed. David Cowart and Thomas L. Wymer, vol. 8 of *Dictionary of Literary Biography* (Detroit, Mich.: Gale Research, 1981), 31.

4. Leslie F. Stone, "Day of the Pulps," *Fantasy Commentator* 9, no. 50, part 2 (Fall 1997): 100–101.

5. Robert A. Madle, letter to the editor, *Amazing Stories* (February 1937): 137.

6. Alan Britt, letter to the editor, *Amazing Stories* (February 1937): 135.

7. "The Conquest of Gola" has appeared in *The Best of Science Fiction,* ed. Groff Conklin (New York: Crown, 1946); Janrae Frank, Jean Stine, and Forrest J. Ackerman, eds., *New Eves: Science Fiction about the Extraordinary Women of Today and Tomorrow* (Stamford, Conn.: Longmeadow, 1994); Garyn G. Roberts, ed., *The Prentice Hall Anthology of Science Fiction and Fantasy* (Upper Saddle River, N.J.: Prentice Hall, 2001); and the present volume.

8. Leslie F. Stone, "The Great Ones," *Astonishing Stories* (July 1937): 75–76.

9. William Sims Bainbridge, *Dimensions of Science Fiction* (Cambridge, Mass.: Harvard University Press, 1986), 172–173.

10. H. G. Wells, "The Star," in *Science Fiction: A Historical Anthology,* edited by Eric S. Rabkin (New York: Oxford University Press, 1983), 233.

11. Robert Dixon, *Writing the Colonial Adventure: Gender, Race, and Nation in Anglo-Australian Popular Fiction, 1875–1914* (New York: Cambridge University Press, 1995), 11.

12. Edmond Hamilton, "The Man Who Evolved," *Wonder Stories* (April 1931): 31.

13. Annie Denton Cridge, excerpt from *Man's Rights; or, How Would You Like It?* in *Future Perfect: American Science Fiction of the Nineteenth Century,* revised and expanded edition, ed. Bruce Franklin (New Brunswick: Rutgers University Press, 1995), 338.

14. Joanna Russ, *The Female Man* (New York: Bantam, 1975), 204.

15. Hugo Gernsback, "The Wonders of Creation," *Wonder Stories* (April 1931): 1209.

16. Jack Williamson, letter to the editor, *Astounding Stories* (June 1937): 157.

17. Batya Weinbaum, "Leslie F. Stone as a Case of Author-Reader Responding," *Foundation* 80 (Autumn 2000): 47.

18. Justine Larbalestier, *The Battle of the Sexes in Science Fiction* (Middletown, Conn.: Wesleyan University Press, 2002), 119.

19. Ibid. 244, n. 14.

20. Stone, "Day," 100.

21. Cited in Batya Weinbaum, "Sex-Role Reversal in the Thirties: Leslie F. Stone's 'The Conquest of Gola,'" *Science-Fiction Studies* 73 (November 1997): 479 n. 9.

22. Joanna Russ, "*Amor Vincit Fœminam:* The Battle of the Sexes in Science Fiction." In *To Write Like a Woman: Essays in Feminism and Science Fiction* (Bloomington: Indiana University Press, 1995), 47.

23. Stone, "Day,"101.

24. Ibid.

25. Ibid.

26. Groff Conklin, introduction to *The Best of Science Fiction*, ed. Groff Conklin (New York: Crown, 1946), xxvi.

27. Frank, Stine, and Ackerman, introduction to *New Eves*, vii.

✪ 3

Created He Them

ALICE ELEANOR JONES

First published in The Magazine of Fantasy and Science Fiction, *June 1955*

Ann Crothers looked at the clock and frowned and turned the fire lower under the bacon. She had already poured his coffee; he liked it cooled to a certain degree; but if he did not get up soon it would be too cool and the bacon too crisp and he would be angry and sulk the rest of the day. She had better call him.

She walked to the foot of the stairs, a blond woman nearing thirty, big but not fat, and rather plain, with a tired sad face. She called, "Henry! Are you up?" She had calculated to a decibel how loud her voice must be. If it were too soft he did not hear and maintained that she had not called him, and was angry later; if it were too loud he was angry immediately and stayed in bed longer, to punish her, and then he grew angrier because breakfast was spoiled.

"All *right!* Pipe down, can't you?"

She listened a minute. She thought it was a normal response, but perhaps her voice had been a shade too loud. No, he was getting up. She heard the thump of his feet on the floor. She went back to the kitchen and took his orange juice and his prunes out of the icebox, and got out his bread but did not begin to toast it yet, and opened a glass of jelly.

She frowned. Grape. He did not like grape, but the co-op had been out of apple, and she had been lucky to get anything. He would not be pleased.

She sat down briefly at the table to wait for him and glanced at the clock. Ten five. Wearily, she leaned forward and rested her forehead on the back of her hand. She was not feeling well this morning and had eaten no breakfast. She was almost sure she was pregnant again.

She thought of the children. There were only two at home, and they had been bathed and fed long ago and put down in the basement playpen so that the noise they made would not disturb their father. She would have time for a quick look at them before Henry came down. And the house was chilly; she would have to look at the heater.

They were playing quietly with the rag doll she had made, and the battered rubber ball. Lennie, who was two and a half, was far too big for a playpen, but he was a good child, considerate, and allowed himself to be put there for short periods and did not climb out. He seemed to feel a responsibility for his brother. Robbie was fourteen months old and a small terror, but he loved Lennie, and even, Ann thought, tried to mind him.

As Ann poked her head over the banister, both children turned and gave her radiant smiles. Lennie said, "Hi, Mommy," and Robbie said experimentally, "Ma?"

She went down quickly and gave each of them a hug and said, "You're good boys. You can come upstairs and play soon." She felt their hands. The basement was damp, but the small mended sweaters were warm enough.

She looked at the feeble fire and rattled the grate hopefully and put on more coal. There was plenty of coal in the bin, but it was inferior grade, filled with slate, and did not burn well. It was not an efficient heater, either. It was old, second-hand, but they had been lucky to get it. The useless oil heater stood in the corner.

The children chuckled at the fire, and Robbie reached out his hands toward it. Lennie said gravely, "No, no, bad."

Ann heard Henry coming downstairs, and she raced up the cellar steps and beat him to the kitchen by two seconds. When he came in she was draining the bacon. She put a slice of bread on the long fork and began to toast it over the gas flame. The gas, at least, was fairly dependable, and the water. The electricity was not working again. It seemed such a long time since the electricity had always worked. Well, it was a long time. Ten years.

Henry sat down at the table and looked peevishly at his orange juice. He was not a tall man, not quite so tall as his wife, and he walked and sat tall, making the most of every inch. He was inclined to be chubby, and he had a roll of fat under his chin and at the back of his neck, and a little bulge at the waist. His face might have been handsome, but the expression spoiled it — discontented, bad-tempered. He said, "You didn't strain the orange juice."

"Yes, I strained it." She was intent on the toast.

He drank the orange juice without enjoyment and said, "I have a touch of liver this morning. Can't think what it could be." His face brightened. "I told you that sauce was too greasy. That was it."

She did not answer. She brought over his plate with the bacon on it and the toast, nicely browned, and put margarine on the toast for him. He was eating the prunes. He stopped and looked at the bacon. "No eggs?"

"They were all out."

His face flushed a little. "Then why'd you cook bacon? You know I can't eat bacon without eggs." He was working himself up into a passion. "If I weren't such an easy-going man — ! And the prunes are hard — you didn't cook them long enough — and the coffee's cold, and the toast's burnt, and where's the apple jelly?"

"They didn't have any."

He laughed scornfully. "I bet they didn't. I bet you fooled around the house and didn't even get there till everything was gone." He flung down his fork. "This garbage! — why should you care, you don't have to eat it!"

She looked at him, "Shall I make you something else?"

He laughed again. "You'd ruin it. Never mind." He slammed out of the kitchen and went upstairs to sulk in the bathroom for an hour.

Ann sat down at the table. All that bacon, and it was hard to get. Well, the children would like it. She ought to clear the table and wash the dishes, but she sat still and took out a cigarette. She ought to save it, her ration was only three a day, but she lit it.

The children were getting a little noisier. Perhaps she could take them out for a while, till Henry went to work. It was cold but clear; she could bundle them up.

The cigarette was making her lightheaded, and she stubbed it out and put the butt in the box she kept over the sink. She said softly, "I hate him. I wish he would die."

She dressed the children — their snowsuits were faded and patched from much use, but they were clean and warm — and put them in the battered carriage, looping her old string shopping bag over the handle, and took them out. They were delighted with themselves and with her. They loved the outdoors. Robbie bounced and drooled and made noises, and Lennie sat quiet, his little face smiling and content.

Ann wheeled them slowly down the walk, detouring around the broken places. It was a fine day, crisp, much too cold for September, but the seasons were not entirely reliable any more. There were no other baby carriages out; there were no children at all; the street was very quiet. There were no cars. Only the highest officials had cars, and no high officials lived in this neighborhood.

The children were enchanted by the street. Shabby as it was, with the broken houses as neatly mended as they could be, and the broken paving that the patches never caught up with, it was beautiful to them. Lennie said, "Hi, Mommy," and Robbie bounced.

The women were beginning to come, as they always came, timidly out of the drab houses, to look at the children, and Ann walked straighter and tried not to smile. It was not kind to smile, but sometimes she could not help it. Suddenly she was not tired any more, and her clothes were not shabby, and her face was not plain.

The first woman said, "Please stop a minute," and Ann stopped, and the women gathered around the carriage silently and looked. Their faces were hungry and seeking, and a few had tears in their eyes.

The first woman asked, "Do they stay well?"

Ann said, "Pretty well. They both had colds last week," and murmurs of commiseration went around the circle.

Another women said, "I noticed you didn't come out, and I wondered. I almost knocked at your door to inquire, but then — " She stopped and blushed violently, and the others considerately looked away from her, ignoring her blunder. One did not call on one's neighbors; one lived to oneself.

The first woman said wistfully, "If I could hold them — either of them — I have dates; my cousin sent them all the way from California."

Ann blushed, too. She disliked this part of it very much, but things were so hard to get now, and Henry was difficult about what he liked to eat, though he denied that. He would say, "I'd eat anything, if you could only learn to cook it right, but you can't." Henry liked dates. Ann said, "Well . . ."

Another woman said eagerly, "I have eggs. I could spare you three." One for each of the boys and one for Henry.

"Oranges — for the children."

"And I have butter — imagine, butter!"

"Sugar — all children like sugar. Best grade — no sand in it."

"And I have tea." Henry does not like tea. But you shall hold the children anyway.

Somebody said, "Cigarettes," and somebody else whispered, "I even have *sleeping pills!*"

The children were passed around and fondled and caressed. Robbie enjoyed it and flirted with everybody, under his long eyelashes, but Lennie regarded the entire transaction with distaste.

When the children began to grow restless Ann put them back into the carriage and walked on. Her shopping bag was full.

The women went slowly back into their houses, all but one, a stranger. She must have moved into the neighborhood recently, perhaps from one of the spreading waste places. They were coming in, the people, as if they had been called, moving in closer, a little closer every year.

The woman was tall and older than Ann, with a worn plain face. She kept pace with the carriage and looked at the children and said, "Forgive me, I know it is bad form, but are they — do you have more?"

Ann said proudly, "I have had seven."

The woman looked at her and whispered, "Seven! And were they all — surely they were not all — "

Ann said more proudly still, "All. Every one."

The woman looked as if she might cry and said, "But seven! And the rest, are they — "

Ann's face clouded. "Yes, at the Center. One of my boys and all my girls. When Lennie goes, Robbie will miss him. Lennie missed Kate so, until he forgot her."

The woman said in a broken voice, "I had three, and none of them was — none." She thrust something into Ann's shopping bag and said, "For the children," and walked quickly away.

Ann looked, and it was a Hershey bar. The co-op had not had chocolate for over two years. Neither of the boys had ever tasted it.

She brought the children home after a while and gave them their lunch — Henry's bacon crumbled into two scrambled eggs, and bread and butter and milk. She had been lucky at the co-op yesterday; they had had milk. She made herself a cup of coffee, feeling extravagant, and ate a piece of toast, and smoked the butt of this morning's cigarette.

For dessert she gave them each an orange; the rest she saved for Henry. She got out the Hershey bar and gave them all of it; Henry should not have their chocolate! The Hershey bar was hard and pale, as stale chocolate gets, and she had to make sawing motions with the knife to divide it evenly. The boys were enchanted. Robbie chewed his half and swallowed it quickly, but Lennie sucked blissfully and made it last, and then took pity on his brother and let Robbie suck, too. Ann did not interfere. Germs, little hearts, are the least of what I fear for you.

While the children took their naps she straightened the house a little and tinkered with the heater and cleaned all the kerosene lamps. She had time to take a bath, and enjoyed it, though the laundry soap she had to use was harsh against her skin. She even washed her hair, pretty hair, long and fine, and put on one of the few dresses that was not mended.

The children slept longer than usual. The fresh air had done them good. Just at dusk the electric lights came on for the first time in three days, and she woke them up to see them — they loved the electric lights. She gave them each a piece of bread and butter and took them with her to the basement and put them in the playpen. She was able to run a full load of clothes through the old washing machine before the current went off again. The children loved the washing machine and watched it, fascinated by the whirling clothes in the little window.

Afterward she took them upstairs again and tried to use the vacuum cleaner, but the machine was old and balky and by the time she had coaxed it to work the current was gone.

She gave the children their supper and played with them a while and put them to bed. Henry was still at the laboratory. He left late in the morning, but sometimes he had to stay late at night. The children were asleep before he came home, and Ann was glad. Sometimes they got on his nerves and he swore at them.

She turned the oven low to keep dinner hot and went into the living room. She sat beside the lamp and mended Robbie's shirt and Lennie's overalls. She turned on the battery radio to the one station that was broadcasting these days, the one at the Center. The news report was the usual thing. The Director was in good health and bearing the burden of his duties with fortitude. Conditions throughout the country were normal. Crops had not been quite so good as hoped, but there was no cause for alarm. Quotas in light and heavy industry were good — Ann smiled wryly — but could be improved if every worker did his duty. Road repairs were picking up — Ann wondered when they would get around to the street again — and electrical service was normal, except for a few scattered areas where there might be small temporary difficulties. The lamp had begun to smoke again, and Ann turned it lower. The stock market had closed irregular, with rails down an average of two points and stocks off three.

And now — the newscaster's voice grew solemn — there was news of grave import, the Director had asked him to talk seriously to all citizens about the dangers of rumor-mongering. Did they not realize what harm could be done by it? For example, the rumor that the Western Reservoir was contaminated. That was entirely false, of course, and the malicious and irresponsible persons who had started it would be severely dealt with.

The wastelands were not spreading, either. Some other malicious and irresponsible persons had started that rumor, and would be dealt with. The wastelands were under control. They were not spreading, repeat, *not*. Certain areas were being evacuated, it was true, but the measure was only temporary.

Calling them in, are you, calling them in!

The weather was normal. The seasons were definitely not changing, and here were the statistics to prove it. In 1961 . . . and in '62 . . . and that was *before*, so you see . . .

The newscaster's voice changed, growing less grave. And now for news of the children. Ann put down her mending and listened, not breathing. They always closed with news of the children, and it was always reassuring.

If any child were ever unhappy, or were taken ill, or died, nobody knew it. One was never told anything, and of course one never saw the children again. It would upset them, one quite understood that.

The children, the newscaster said, were all well and happy. They had good beds and warm clothes and the best food and plenty of it. They even had cod-liver oil twice a week whether they needed it or not. They had toys and games, carefully supervised according to their age groups, and they were being educated by the best teachers. The children were all well and happy, repeat, *well and happy*. Ann hoped it was true.

They played the national anthem and went off the air, and just then Henry came in. He looked pale and tired — he did work hard — and his greeting was, "I suppose dinner's spoiled."

She looked up. "No, I don't think so."

She served it and they ate silently except for Henry's complaints about the food and his liver. He looked at the dates and said, "They're small. You let them stick you with anything," but she thought he enjoyed them because he ate them all.

Afterward he grew almost mellow. He lit a cigarette and told her about his day, while she washed the dishes. Henry's job at the laboratory was a responsible one, and Ann was sure he did it well. Henry was not stupid. But Henry could not get along with anybody. He said that he himself was very easy to get along with, but they were all against him. Today he had had a dispute with one of his superiors and reported that he had told the old — where to go.

He said with gloomy relish, "They'll probably fire me, and we'll all be out in the street. Then you'll find out what it's like to live on Subsistence. You won't be able to throw my money around the way you do now."

Ann rinsed out the dish towel and hung it over the rack to dry. She said, "They won't fire you. They never do."

He laughed. "I'm good and they know it. I do twice as much work as anybody else."

Ann thought that was probably true. She turned away from the sink and said, "Henry, I think I'm pregnant."

He looked at her and frowned. "Are you sure?"

"I said I *think*. But I'm practically sure."

He said, "Oh God, now you'll be sick all the time, and there's no living with you when you're sick."

Ann sat down at the table and lit a cigarette. "Maybe I won't be sick."

He said darkly, "You always are. Sweet prospect!"

Ann said, "We'll get another bonus, Henry."

He brightened a little. "Say, we will, at that. I'll buy some more stock."

Ann said, "Henry, we need so many things — "

He was immediately angry. "I said I'll buy stock! Somebody in this house has to think of the future. We can't all hide our heads in the sand and hope for the best."

She stood up, trembling. It was not a new argument. "What future? Our children — children like ours are taken away from us when they're three years old and given to the state to rear. When we're old the state will take care of us. Nobody lives well any more, except — but nobody starves. And that stock — it all goes down. Don't talk to me about the future, Henry Crothers! I want my future now."

He laughed unpleasantly. "What do you want? A car?"

She said, "I want a new washing machine and a vacuum cleaner, when the quotas come — the electricity isn't so bad. I want a new chair for the living room. I want to fix up the boys' room, paint, and — "

He said brutally, "They're too little to notice. By the time they get old enough — "

She sat down again, sobbing a little. Her cigarette burned forgotten in the ashtray, and Henry thriftily stubbed it out. She said, "I know, the Center takes them. The Center takes children like ours."

"And the Center's good to them. They give them more than we could. Don't you go talking against the Center." Though a malcontent in his personal life, Henry was a staunch government man.

Ann said, "I'm not, Henry, I'm — "

He said disgustedly, "Being a woman again. Tears! Oh, God, why do women always turn them on?"

She made herself stop crying. Anger was beginning to rise in her, and that helped a good deal. "I didn't mean to start an argument. I was just telling you what we need. We do need things, Henry. Clothes — "

He looked at her. "You mean for you? Clothes would do you a lot of good, wouldn't they?"

She was stung. "I don't mean maternity clothes. I won't be needing them for — "

He laughed. "I don't mean maternity clothes either. Have you looked at yourself in a mirror lately? God, you're a big horse! I always liked little women."

She said tightly, "And I always liked tall men."

He half rose, and she thought he was going to hit her. She sat still, trembling with a fierce exhilaration, her eyes bright, color in her cheeks, a little smile on her mouth. She said softly, "I'll hit you back, I'm bigger than you are. I'll kill you."

Suddenly Henry sat down and began to laugh. When he laughed he was quite handsome. He said in a deep, chuckling voice, "You're almost pretty when you get mad enough. You hair's pretty tonight, you must have washed it." His eyes were beginning to shine, and he reached across the table and put his hand on hers. "Ann . . . old girl . . ."

She drew her hand away. "I'm tired. I'm going to bed."

He said good-humoredly, "Sure, I'll be right up."

She looked at him. "I said I'm tired."

"And I said I'll be right up."

If I had something in my hands I'd kill you. "I don't want to."

He scowled, and his mouth grew petulant again, and he was no longer handsome. "But I want to."

She stood up. All at once she felt as tired as she had told Henry she was, as tired as he had been for ten years.

I cannot kill you, Henry, or myself. I cannot even wish us dead. In this desolate, dying, bombed-out world, with its creeping wastelands and its freakish seasons, with its limping economy and its arrogant Center in the country that takes our children — children like ours; the others it destroys — we have to live, and we have to live together.

Because by some twist of providence, or radiation, or genes, we are among the tiny percentage of the people in this world who can have normal children. We hate each other, but we breed true.

She said, "Come up, Henry." I can take a sleeping pill afterward.

Come up, Henry, we have to live. Till we are all called in, or our children, or our children's children. Till there is nowhere else to go.

From *Ladies' Home Journal* to *The Magazine of Fantasy and Science Fiction*: 1950s SF, the Offbeat Romance Story, and the Case of Alice Eleanor Jones

Lisa Yaszek

Alice Eleanor Jones's 1955 near-future nuclear war story "Created He Them" ends with protagonist Ann Crothers caught in a terrible dilemma: she must either act on her personal desire to kill her selfish, abusive husband, or she can do her patriotic duty and submit to his nightly embraces. For the reader who opened this particular issue of *The Magazine of Fantasy and Science Fiction* expecting to read about sleek new technologies, heroic engineers, and exotic alien worlds, "Created He Them" must have come as something of a shock: how did Ann end up in this situation? What happened to the American dream of life, liberty, and the pursuit of happiness? And perhaps most urgently: why tell a story about nuclear war—usually the province of male scientists, soldiers, and politicians—from a housewife's point of view in the first place?

"Created He Them" is a classic example of a new kind of women's science fiction (SF) that emerged in the 1940s and flourished throughout the 1950s. Much like other SF, this particular form of midcentury women's SF provided readers with visions of brave new worlds extrapolated from current trends in science and technology. Rather than exploring the impact of new sciences and technologies on entire societies or civilizations, it invited readers to think more specifically about how science and technology might impact women and their families in the private space of the home. Because this fiction seemed to focus exclusively on traditionally feminine concerns including emotional reactions and interpersonal relations (rather than objective reasoning and outward-bound exploration), it was quickly—and somewhat unkindly—labeled "diaper" or "housewife heroine" SF.[1]

Such labels were very much part and parcel of the times. The 1950s are usually understood as a low point in feminist history, a time when women were encouraged to exchange education and paid work for housekeeping and childrearing in the newly developed suburbs.[2] For the most part, feminist and other literary critics have assumed that women's popular fiction from this era largely reiterated the postwar glorification of motherhood and domesticity at the expense of all other political investments.[3] Midcentury women's SF has been dismissed as an especially disappointing variation on this theme, as clever but silly tales about "galactic suburbia" where women tend their high-tech homes while their husbands are off solving interstellar crises.[4]

In the past decade scholars have become interested in revisiting galactic suburbia and putting housewife heroine SF in dialogue with postwar literary and cultural forces.[5] Midcentury authors such as Jones produced this new kind of SF by merging the conventions of women's "slick" romantic magazine fiction with those of science fiction. Housewife heroine SF was not overtly feminist SF, but it was a complex, politically charged mode of fiction that engaged the values of 1950s America in critical and creative ways.

Like other popular women writers in the 1950s, Jones published in both mainstream magazines and their science fictional counterparts.[6] For Jones, women's magazine fiction was a potentially rich literary form that could be used to write something other than the conventional, "happily ever after" romance story that ended at the altar on the heroine's wedding day. Tropes including "marriage," "motherhood," and even "the home" served as lenses through which she explored otherwise taboo sex and gender issues.

Jones extended this philosophy to her SF writing as well, using stories about domestic life in the future to interrogate the pressing scientific and technological issues of her day. In "Created He Them" Jones invokes some of 1950s America's most dearly held beliefs about hearth and home to critique the cold war militarization of everyday life, especially as it required soldiers and civilians alike to sacrifice individual rights in the name of national security. In this story, nuclear weapons do little or nothing to preserve the American way of life. Instead, they engender a rage for order and conformity that threatens to destroy the nuclear family itself, pitting parent against child and husband against wife in tragic but inevitable ways.

Housewife Heroine Stories in SF History and Criticism

By the 1950s American SF had fully entered what Edward James calls its "Golden Age," a period when the genre reached new levels of mainstream popularity.[7] Before this time SF was published primarily in short-story pulp magazines; after World War II, innovations in mass media manufacture and distribution led to the development of cheap, easily distributed paperback books. These innovations also led to a temporary boom in SF magazine production itself. Indeed, at least thirty-five new SF magazines appeared during the first half of the 1950s alone, paving the way for an ever greater number of authors to try their hand at this increasingly popular literary form.[8]

SF also reached new levels of stylistic and thematic maturity in this period. Throughout the 1940s *Astounding Science-Fiction* editor John W. Campbell insisted that authors exchange the wildly speculative and often uncritically celebratory tone of earlier science fiction for more scientifically accurate depictions of science and technology. Even more significantly, he encouraged writers to think through the *social* implications of science and technology: in essence, to put a human face on the sometimes overwhelmingly abstract issues attending new inventions ranging from television to the atomic bomb.[9]

By the 1950s these dictates had become the standard by which most written SF was measured. Indeed, new publications such as *The Magazine of Fantasy and Science Fiction* (which quickly developed a reputation for literary quality) and *Galaxy* (which encouraged authors to question the social and moral conventions of cold war America) provided homes for a whole new generation of authors dedicated to producing more thoughtful and socially engaged forms of SF.[10]

Women were active in the development of this new SF style. Well over 250 new women authors made their debut in the SF magazines of the 1950s; although some of these authors only published one or two stories, others including Judith Merril and Anne McCaffrey went on to have long and distinguished careers as authors, editors, and all-around spokespersons for the genre.[11]

This new generation wrote about the same diverse range of topics as their male counterparts, extrapolating from the forces shaping their own time to build new worlds and test the limits of the social and moral orders that might attend these possible worlds. At the same time, they went beyond their male counterparts by examining how these hypothetical new world orders might specifically impact women's lives, especially as they were connected to the home.

This socially conscious, domestically oriented SF sparked a great deal of debate within the SF community. On the one hand, powerful editors such as *The Magazine of Fantasy and Science Fiction*'s Anthony Boucher valued housewife heroine SF for its high literary quality and expansion of conventional areas of SF inquiry. Indeed, Boucher specifically praised the women of this generation as the first group of authors to produce "sensitive" stories depicting "the future from a woman's point of view."[12]

At the same time, conservative members of the SF community (male and female alike) disparaged housewife heroine fiction as "heartthrob-and-diaper" storytelling produced by a "gaggle of housewives" out to spoil SF for everyone.[13] As the references to romance and child-rearing suggest, such fans were convinced that housewife heroine SF was bad SF precisely because it wasn't really SF at all; instead, it was merely a variation on a seemingly far more mundane kind of prose: women's magazine fiction.

Similar convictions led the next generation of SF critics and historians to all but eliminate housewife heroine storytelling from the genre's canon.[14] Recently, however, scholars have begun to reassess both housewife heroine SF in particular and midcentury women's magazine fiction in general. Authors including Brian Attebery, Jane Donawerth, and Justine Larbalestier have all proposed new literary histories that position 1950s women's SF in relation to both the utopian writing of first-wave feminists at the turn of the twentieth century and the science fiction that second-wave feminists began writing in the 1970s.[15]

Elsewhere, Joanne Meyerowitz has persuasively demonstrated that mid-century women's magazine writing is more complex than feminist cultural historians have typically assumed, balancing fictional paeans to marriage and motherhood with nonfiction essays that championed women's wage work and political service.[16] Alice Eleanor Jones strikes a similar balance in her own writing. By telling stories about unusual romantic or domestic situations that do not necessarily have simple, happy endings, Jones encourages her readers to think about how those seemingly private situations might be shaped by very public social and political forces.

Offbeat Stories: Revising the Romance Narrative
in Midcentury Women's Magazine Fiction

Given the trajectory of her career, it is not surprising that Alice Eleanor Jones emphasizes her slick magazine writing over its speculative counterpart. Although SF was becoming increasingly important to American mass culture at this time, it was still not necessarily the first genre that a writer turned to when she set out to make a name or earn a living for herself; after all, midcentury SF editors typically paid authors just two or three cents per word. Publications such as *Cosmopolitan* and *Good Housekeeping* paid freelance writers anywhere between 60 cents and a dollar per word.[17] The women's magazine industry had been an important and highly profitable part of the mass culture landscape for nearly a century.

When Jones entered this industry in the 1950s, women's magazine fiction was predominantly romance fiction.[18] Feminist scholars generally agree that romance fiction is a broad category that encompasses a variety of story types, ranging from the sentimental and domestic novels of the nineteenth century to today's soap operas and Harlequin romances.[19] Whatever form romance fiction takes it is almost always characterized by certain perils and promises for the thoughtful woman author. As Anne Cranny-Francis points out, romance stories (like all forms of genre fiction) are written and distributed within patriarchal and capitalistic systems of production. Therefore, "if writers are not aware of the ideological significance of generic conventions," they run the risk of merely writing "bourgeois fairy tales" in which social and political differences are overcome by the natural and irresistible power of love.[20]

At the same time Cranny-Francis notes that politically progressive authors have long used romance stories to explore feminist concerns including "the nature of female/male relations in a patriarchal society and the constitution of the gendered subject."[21] Stories about love and marriage can, in the hands of an adept author, be used to do more than just reaffirm the natural order of social and sexual relations; they can also be used to demonstrate how certain kinds of gendered relations are valued over others in specific cultural and historical moments.

Although Jones never explicitly positioned herself as a feminist author, her essays about women's magazines for *The Writer* suggest that she was aware of the relations between specific modes of storytelling and dominant cultural understandings of sex and gender relations. At first, Jones's essays seem to focus almost exclusively on the first half of this equation, providing readers with very general, commonsense advice about how to become a successful commercial writer: don't ask friends for their opinions about your work unless you are prepared to take the bad with the good; be sure to talk with an expert first if you want to write about something you've never experienced, like plumbing or nursing; and don't worry too much about rejection slips because all writing, good or bad, is part of the creative experience.[22]

At the same time, Jones insists this advice has a very specific source: it comes from her experience as a commercial magazine writer who has enjoyed a relatively successful career by "writing against the odds;" that is, by identifying and carefully negotiating those "subjects considered taboo" by most magazine editors.[23] Jones encourages her readers to think about how commercial fiction is bound by narrative conventions (such as the belief that crime stories should conclude with the identification and capture of the villain, or that romance stories should inevitably end with marriage), and how these conventions are themselves determined by specific social and market forces.

This understanding appears most clearly in her 1962 essay "How to Sell an Offbeat Story," which is specifically directed at potential women's magazine fiction authors. Jones elaborates on the art of "writing against the odds" by carefully distinguishing between two kinds of romance stories. On the one hand, women's magazine editors tend to prefer "sweet, fluffy, boy-girl stories" that end at the altar.[24] On the other hand, she notes, many slick writers such as herself are drawn to a different type of romance story: "Suppose you simply aren't interested in the events that end with a wedding, but rather in what comes afterward: the problems of adjustment; the children; the troubles, the quarrels, and the crises; the accidents, the illnesses, even the deaths. Suppose your mind leans more to the dark than to the bright. What if your stories are offbeat, because *you* are offbeat?"[25]

Jones make an important point often missed by scholars who dismiss romance narratives as an undifferentiated mass of fairy tales about bourgeois love.[26] For Jones, the dominant romance narrative — the "sweet, fluffy, boy-girl story" — is indeed that kind of happily-ever-after tale. In contrast, the offbeat romance narrative quite literally writes, as Rachel Blau DuPlessis puts it, "beyond the ending" of both the boy-girl story that ends at the wedding and the patriarchal ideology that this story entails.[27]

Although these offbeat stories can, of course, also have happy endings, they operate in a relatively uncharted narrative space that enables the offbeat author to explore how the gendered identities and relations that seem to be fixed by certain archetypal events (a first kiss, a wedding, the birth of a child) might actually continue to develop and change over time. It is precisely by mapping these possible changes (and revealing the limits of conventional or "fluffy" romance stories) that women writers take the first important step toward a more radical feminist consciousness. In essence, authors like Jones who chose to write about "the dark" rather than "the bright" side of midcentury womanhood took the first important step toward identifying those social and sexual inequities that fueled the women's movement of the following decades.

Jones's advice about how to sell an offbeat romance story also anticipates the kind of critical literary awareness that later feminists attribute to successful feminist genre fiction. Simply put, the authors of such fiction provide readers with "a new and stimulating perspective" on both the ideological content of the conventional genre story and the way that this ideology is encoded in the story's narrative structure.[28]

Jones suggests a similar strategy in her explanation of how to get around editorial prejudices about forbidden, socially (or politically) charged subjects:

> After you have been around a while you will learn to get around the taboos in many subtle ways without . . . compromising yourself. You do it by giving your story a switch. . . . Do you want to write about a forty-three year old heroine? Do it. Despite what editors profess to believe, women do not stop reading at the age of thirty-five. . . . To get past the editor, make her a young-looking forty-three, and give her charm, wit, and style. Maybe the editor is forty-three himself and has a wife the same age, who he still finds charming. . . . The first editor [I tried this on] didn't fall for my [forty-three-year-old character], but the second, third, or fourth one did.[29]

Although the switch that Jones advocates is not identical to the shift in perspective associated with more overtly feminist authors, it is an important first step toward a more radical form of popular fiction.

Jones clearly identifies what Cranny-Francis calls "the ideological significance of generic conventions" — at least as they impact an author's ability to get her story published. Her advice about how to sell an editor on an offbeat story closely resembles Cranny-Francis's claim that successful feminist authors are those who carefully manipulate "the text's explicit description of a (displaced but clearly contemporary) social formation."[30] The offbeat story, when handled in the manner described by Jones, has the potential to become socially charged, politically progressive fiction.

The cultural significance of the offbeat romance story becomes clear when it is considered in relation to the larger tradition of twentieth-century women's magazine fiction. As Betty Friedan contends in her classic feminist treatise, *The Feminine Mystique* (1963), the decades following first-wave feminism and the establishment of universal suffrage in 1920 marked the emergence of a new heroine in the pages of women's magazines. This New Woman actively pursued an independent identity for herself through education, adventure, and paid work. She also pursued egalitarian sex and gender relations with the New Man who admired and courted her because "individuality was something to be admired . . . men were drawn to [the New Woman] as much for [her] spirit and character as for [her] looks."[31]

After World War II, Friedan then argues, the New Woman was gradually replaced by the Housewife Heroine, a woman who, through the miracles of modern capitalism, could free herself from the burdens of education and career in order to embrace the feminine mystique: that is, her mysterious, intuitive, and biologically determined identity as wife and mother.[32]

By 1958, the three oldest and largest women's magazines (*Ladies' Home Journal, McCall's,* and *Good Housekeeping*) had banished the New Woman from their pages altogether. As Friedan puts it, by the end of the domestic decade not a single one of these magazines featured "a single heroine who had a career, a commitment to any work, art, profession, or mission in the world, other than 'Occupation: housewife.' Only one in a hundred heroines had a job; even the young unmarried heroines no longer worked except at snaring a husband."[33] Magazine fiction of the 1950s assumed that women wanted to subsume themselves in their families rather than focusing on how women might pursue new personal identities and social relations. "Togetherness," as Friedan puts it, seemed to have completely replaced individuality.[34]

At first, Alice Eleanor Jones's slick magazine stories seem to be part and parcel of this conservative midcentury romance tradition. Without exception, every one of her stories revolves around domestic affairs, ranging from a teenage girl's first kiss to a young couple's wedding night to the trials and tribulations of parenthood. Most of the women in her stories are wives and mothers; those who are single are usually high school or college girls who have just begun dating and are likely to be married soon if not by the end of the story.

A different pattern emerged when I read these stories closely: much as she indicates in her *Writer* essays, Jones's stories about domestic life tend toward the dark more than the bright: newlywed couples finds that they are too overcome with sexual anxiety to consummate their marriage; men find that they must be both father and mother to their children after their wives die in childbirth; and women learn that their husbands, much as they themselves, secretly resent the demands of modern parenthood.[35]

Although many of these stories revolve around the efforts of wives (and sometimes husbands) to adjust to the togetherness of married life, Jones often suggests that togetherness is itself best achieved by women who actively pursue interests and identities outside the home. Her stories echo the tradition of New Woman magazine fiction while also anticipating the concerns of the 1960s women's movement.

Consider, for instance, Jones's first slick publication, "Jenny Kissed Me," which appeared in the November 1955 issue of *Ladies' Home Journal.* The story depicts two days in the life of Jenny Adams, a tall, gawky teenager who (much to her socialite parents' dismay) prefers poetry to dancing. Rather than choosing between the two, Jenny realizes that she can have both the life of the mind and body when she meets Paul, an old friend of her parents who, in the tradition of the New Man, admires her independent mind.

This admiration infuses Jenny with a new physical confidence, and by the end of the story it seems that she is well on her way to becoming a New Woman in her own right; indeed, even her parents admit that they have been "very stupid" in treating their daughter as a failed example of the feminine ideal.[36]

Much like the stories described by Friedan, "Jenny Kissed Me" is not strictly feminist literature; after all, attracting boys is as important as reading poetry for Jenny, and Jones never suggests that it should be otherwise. Yet the story departs from the tradition of housewife heroine fiction as Friedan describes it: Jenny is *not* asked to give up her intellectual interests or to subsume her unique personality to the expected social standards of the day. Jones's story echoes the tradition of New Woman magazine fiction as it was inspired by first-wave feminism, even extending this tradition, in however muted a form, well into the antifeminist climate of the 1950s.

Conversely, Jones's later stories look forward to the concerns of second-wave feminists — especially as Betty Friedan herself articulated them. For instance, "Real Me" (*Redbook*, October 1962) follows the story of Patricia Cameron, the wife of a university professor at a women's college who, in the course of her duties as a faculty spouse, attends a guest lecture by the unabashed feminist Miss Kent.

Miss Kent exhorts her listeners to remember the history of women's emancipation and to extend that tradition in even the most conventional aspects of their own lives: "when you marry, keep your own individuality, you own intellectual interests. Don't be 'just a housewife,' be a complete person."[37] Inspired by this lecture, Patricia decides to reorganize her domestic duties so she can resume the writing career she gave up when she first married and had children. In the end, she concludes, "I am a better wife and mother for being a private person, too. I am 'Mom' and 'Honey,' but I am also me. So thank you, Miss Kent."[38]

Just one year later, Friedan concluded *The Feminine Mystique* on a very similar note, arguing that the modern American woman "does not have to choose between marriage and career; that was the mistaken choice of the feminine mystique. [She can] combine marriage and motherhood and even the kind of lifelong personal purpose that was once called 'career.' It merely takes a new life plan."[39] Surprising as it may seem, at least some midcentury women's magazine fiction celebrated values that were compatible with those of a certain kind of liberal feminism.

Offbeat stories that explored romantic ideals in relation to the reality of women's daily lives did indeed critically engage many of 1950s America's most dearly held beliefs about sex and gender relations. Furthermore, the techniques of offbeat storytelling that worked so well for Jones as a slick writer could be put to good use in other literary forums as well. Specifically, when the offbeat romance story unfolds against the backdrop of a science fictional landscape, it invites readers to rethink their assumptions about both appropriate sex and gender relations, and, perhaps even more urgently, about how those relations are informed — and transformed — by larger scientific and social forces as well.

Housewife Heroine SF: Using The Offbeat Romance to Put a Human Face on Scientific and Social Issues

Although Alice Eleanor Jones's career as an SF author was relatively brief — she published just five SF pieces, all in 1955 — her stories are highly representative of the thematic concerns and literary techniques characterizing Golden Age SF, especially in its socially oriented form. For instance, her two stories that feature male protagonists provide readers with a biting condemnation of 1950s commodity culture.

"Life, Incorporated" (*Fantastic Universe*, April 1955) follows the misadventures of the human con man Baxter, who tries to exploit the Kryl, a gentle, highly advanced race who have learned how to control their lifespans and create a social and ecological utopia. After insinuating himself into Kryl society Baxter attempts to set up a black market for that most precious commodity: life itself. Inevitably, the aliens catch on to his scheme and banish Baxter from their world. In the end, the con man is "strangely bereft" by this turn of events, recognizing that his desire for money and power has denied him the chance to live out his years in a truly good society.[40]

Conversely, "The Happy Clown" (*If*, December 1955) explores a "perfect" twenty-first century where antisocial behavior has been eliminated through the perfection of advertising and consumerism.[41] When Steven Russell rejects the marketing forces that rule his world, he is treated with what his peers see as the pinnacle of compassion: he is lobotomized and released back into the care of his parents, who rejoice "because now he was irrevocably just like them."[42] Much like Frederik Pohl and C. M. Kornbluth in *The Space Merchants* (1952) or Fritz Leiber in *The Green Millennium* (1953), Jones extrapolates from the midcentury fascination with advertising and consumerism to imagine worlds that satirically comment upon that fascination itself.

Elsewhere Jones participates in the Golden Age tradition established by women authors like Leigh Brackett and C. L. Moore in the 1930s and 1940s. Both Brackett and Moore are remembered for writing interplanetary romances and heroic fantasies populated by characters that defy the simple gender stereotyping typical of much early SF. Indeed, Moore's Jirel of Joiry — a ferocious woman warrior from ancient France who battled invaders, gods, and male chauvinists alike — is often cited as the inspiration for later fantasy heroines such as Red Sonja and Xena. These Golden Age woman warriors stand in sharp contrast to dominant postwar depictions of women as creatures defined solely in terms of their biological function as wives and mothers.[43]

The first of Jones's woman warrior stories, "Miss Quatro," revolves around a shy, colorless governess who only comes alive around her small charges; indeed, she is so good with children — and so willing to care for all children, whether or not she is paid to do so — that her employers are convinced she cannot be of this earth. And they are right to think so: as Jones reveals to her readers toward the end of her story, Miss Quatro is actually the slave-scout of an alien race who feed on human children. Touched by the friendship of the human women who treat her as an equal rather than as a servant, Miss Quatro valiantly throws off her conditioning and nobly destroys herself to save her friends and foil her masters' plans.

"Recruiting Officer" recounts the adventures of Mrs. Quimby, a high-ranking officer from an all-female alien world who disguises herself as a helpless little old lady in order to make contact with young men from Earth and "recruit" them into service as the prized sexual playthings of her race. After a long and successful run, Mrs. Quimby encounters a series of mishaps that force her to withdraw from Earth without the one boy she wants for herself. Although she is saddened by this personal loss, she takes comfort in the social prestige she has already earned in her own world — and in the arms of one of her other conquests because, "as is the custom, they had saved one of the best for me."[44]

In addition to challenging dominant midcentury assumptions about the uselessness and frustration of "redundant" single women, these stories provide readers — however briefly — with glimpses of alternative social orders marked by strong bonds between women as affectionate and competent individuals.

Jones's fifth SF story, "Created He Them," is a nuclear holocaust narrative. As Edward James notes, this narrative form provides authors with an ideal way to explore "how societies decline into tribalism or barbarism . . . or develop from barbarism to civilization."[45] Given the very real devastation that occurred during the atomic bombing of Hiroshima and Nagasaki at the end of World War II — and the subsequent nightmare of total nuclear war that haunted much of the world throughout the postwar era — it is hardly surprising that this narrative became one of the most prevalent story types in midcentury SF.

This story type became particularly popular with housewife heroine authors. Judith Merril recalls feeling a tremendous urgency to tell this kind of story because

> in 1946, 1947, and 1948, a great deal was being published about [the effects of atomic radiation]. One read *The Smythe Report* and *No Place to Hide* and *The Bulletin of Atomic Scientists* and World Federalist Publications and the daily newspapers; and if one read the SF magazines, the total amount of information available was staggering, unarguable, and terrifying. . . . [But it was] not widely understood by many people, including ordinary families and even heads of government.[46]

Merril believed it was the job of the SF writer to convey this "staggering, unarguable, and terrifying" information to the public as imaginatively but accurately as possible.

Authors including Merril, Carol Emshwiller, and Alice Eleanor Jones herself took on this task specifically by merging the conventions of the nuclear holocaust narrative with that of the offbeat romance. In doing so, they performed both social and gender critique, demonstrating how technological disaster in the public realm of the nation would inevitably lead to familial disaster in the private realm of the home.

Although housewife heroine authors imagined a range of different outcomes for World War III, their nuclear holocaust narratives tend to present strikingly similar assessments of how this war will affect parents' ability to care for their children. For instance, in Carol Emshwiller's "Day at the Beach" (1959), nuclear war leads to the destruction of the nation-state and the collapse of law and order. Here, family life continues, but only as a grim parody of itself: men "go to work" to fight one another for the scarce resources they need to feed their families, and good family outings are those where husbands and wives successfully defend their children against marauding strangers.

Analogous patterns inform Jones's "Created He Them." The United States does survive World War III, but parents are faced with chronic food and medical supply shortages as well as the dreadful knowledge that if their children survive past the age of three, they will be taken away to mysterious government centers where "if any child were ever unhappy, or were taken ill, or died, nobody knew it." (Jones, 73).

The fate of the family is also compromised in housewife heroine stories because nuclear war never remains at a safe distance; instead, it ultimately invades the home and turns husbands and wives against one another. For instance, in one of her most famous stories, "That Only a Mother" (1948), Judith Merril imagines a near future where extended nuclear war results in both increasing levels of radiation and increasing numbers of physically mutated infants. In this world, war is waged not just between nations, but between the mothers who love their children unconditionally and the horrified fathers who wish to kill their mutated offspring.

Jones's protagonist Ann Crothers finds herself trapped in a loveless marriage to Henry, a petty tyrant who neglects his children because he knows they will be taken away from him anyway. Enraged by Henry's casual disregard for family, Ann spends her days dreaming about ways to kill her husband. Authors like Emshwiller, Merril, and Jones takes the offbeat romance to its logical extremes, amplifying all the problems that are left out of conventional "happily ever after" romance stories until they become something else: anti-romance tales.

Because these offbeat anti-romances take place within the narrative framework of a science fiction story, readers cannot simply dismiss protagonists such as Ann as hysterical women trying to adjust to the difficulties of married life. Instead, there are specific scientific and technological explanations for their difficulties: in the postholocaust world, all life — including domestic life — has been irrevocably altered by nuclear war.

Created He Them — But for What? Alice Eleanor Jones's Offbeat Nuclear Holocaust Narrative

Jones's "Created He Them" presents a particularly chilling depiction of this changed state. The story takes place in a near future where America has somehow survived World War III only to find that its fate remains in jeopardy because most of the population has been genetically damaged by radiation. The postwar government tries to ensure the country's survival by forcing strictly regulated marriages onto those few men and women who still "breed true." (Jones, 75).

By setting her offbeat romance story in a future specifically extrapolated from the cold war present of 1950s America, Jones makes clear the very real connections between public institutions and private lives, demonstrating how certain kinds of gender relations might be produced by the militarization of civil society. "Created He Them" implicitly enacts the project of feminist critique identified by Anne Cranny-Francis, using the conventions of SF to explore, in however allegorical a form, how gendered subjects and gendered subject relations are constituted in a patriarchal society.

Consider, for instance, Henry Crothers's behavior toward his family. When Ann tells him that she is pregnant with their eighth child, Henry moans, "Oh God, now you'll be sick all the time, and there's no living with you when you're sick." (Jones, 73). He eventually perks up when he remembers that another child equals "another bonus" from the government — one that, significantly, he plans to invest in the stock market rather than in the renovations that his children's nursery so desperately needs. (Jones, 74)

Henry could just be a bad and even unnatural father, but his behavior makes sense in the context of his world: by the time their children are old enough to notice their surroundings, they are taken away by the government. (Jones, 74). The logic of a war-oriented culture reproduces itself at every level of society: just as the government treats its adult citizens as objects of genetic manipulation so, too, do individual citizens like Henry Crothers treat their own children as dehumanized objects or commodities.

It is not just objectionable men like Henry Crothers who replicate the social and moral orders of public institutions in their private lives. Even the most seemingly angelic and caring of women are subject to these terrible new forces. Ann Crothers distinguishes herself from her husband in the most conventional of all ways: despite everything else, she loves her babies. This does not stop Ann from using her children as barter in even more literal ways than her husband.

Noting in despair that "things [are] so hard now, and Henry [is] difficult about what he likes to eat," Anne spends much of her day on the street with her childless neighbors, trading quality time with her children for black market goods including eggs, cigarettes, and sleeping pills. (Jones, 70). Although Ann loathes these "transactions," she seems helpless to stop them, only allowing herself to return home after her shopping bag is full. (Jones, 71)

Here then Jones suggests that motherhood — much like fatherhood — is defined not just by natural instinct but also by social forces that channel instinct in sometimes shocking ways. Of course, "Created He Them" provides readers with a specific, logical explanation for this seemingly unnatural, unhealthy maternal behavior: it is the product of an unnatural, unhealthy, war-oriented culture.

Jones makes what is perhaps her strongest case against nuclear weapons and the cultural logic they entail in the final scenes of her story, where she suggests that total war between nations will inevitably lead to total war between the sexes as well. From almost the beginning of "Created He Them" it is clear that Ann is actually a great deal less saintly than she might appear to her husband; indeed, she admits to herself, that "I hate him. I wish he would die." (Jones, 69). At the end of the story Ann almost makes good on this wish when she responds to Henry's bullying behavior with the threat "I'll hit you back, I'm bigger than you, I'll kill you!" (Jones, 74).

Although Ann's defiance stops Henry in his tracks—and leaves the reader hoping that somehow individual will can triumph over social convention and that Ann really will follow through with her threat—it is not to be. Perversely excited by his wife's words, Henry begins to laugh—and promptly orders Ann to have sex with him. Deflated by her failure to change anything, Ann tells Henry she is simply too tired. When that fails, she glumly follows Henry up the stairs, telling herself that, if nothing else, she can always ease the horror of her husband's embrace with the sleeping pills bartered earlier that day over the bodies of her unwitting children. (Jones, 75).

In the end, Jones seems to suggest that although some divine being may have originally "created he them" to go forth and multiply in joy and sorrow alike, in the brave new world wrought by atomic-age man the best a woman can hope for is to go forth and multiply in a Seconal-induced haze.

Conclusion: Housewife Heroine SF, Golden Age SF, and Feminist SF Revisited

The problem of whether or not women's housewife heroine SF from the 1950s can be either good Golden Age SF or good feminist SF typically revolves around two assumptions: that housewife heroine SF is inextricably bound up with midcentury women's magazine fiction, and that this fiction is itself inevitably conservative.

Midcentury women's SF is better understood when it is discussed in relation to other kinds of genre fiction. But not all of this fiction was created equal: for every story that uncritically celebrated the feminine mystique, another offbeat one called the totality of such stories into question by exploring what comes after courtship and the wedding day. Offbeat romance stories held the potential to perform socially conscious and even potentially feminist analyses of dominant gender ideologies; if nothing else, stories about the darker aspects of "happily ever after" certainly highlighted the limits of these ideologies.

This potential was fully exploited by Jones, who mobilized the romance narrative in the estranging landscape of the science fiction story. SF tropes of other worlds and times enabled Jones to explore, however allegorically, gender issues that could not be directly addressed in an era marked by political paranoia and cultural conformity. The tropes of the romance story provided her with a specific set of tools for interrogating cold war culture. By telling offbeat romance stories in science fictional futures extrapolated from then-current events (including the explosion of nuclear fear and the emergence of a militarized civil society), midcentury authors like Jones helped consolidate the new dictates of Golden Age SF as elucidated by editors like John Campbell: that SF writers should create stories putting a human face on the otherwise abstract changes wrought by new sciences and technologies. After all, what can be more human than a woman's concern for her children's future in the nuclear age?

Although I would not claim that housewife heroine SF was feminist SF as it came to be defined by authors such as Joanna Russ a generation later, it was a more important precursor than Russ and her peers acknowledged. Of course, stories about galactic suburbia and its inhabitants did have limits: while they may have enabled authors like Jones to speculate about the impact of new public institutions on the private sphere, such stories — defined as they were by the four walls of the home — restricted their creators' ability to imagine any kind of social or communal change beyond that which might occur in the home itself. Housewife heroine SF, much like the women's magazine fiction it was so closely bound to, always ran the risk of mystifying the social issues it engaged by reducing them to personal problems of psychological adjustment.

At the same time midcentury women writers — especially SF writers — *were* quick to identify the gendered implications of both public and private institutions. By demonstrating the connections between the two, women writing SF in the 1950s anticipated one of the major insights of the women's movement of the 1960s and 1970s: that the personal is always already political. Whatever their own gender politics might have been, authors like Alice Eleanor Jones were well aware of the possibilities inherent in deploying culturally specific ideas about sex and gender to create a mode of SF storytelling that anticipates Russ's own vision of a politically progressive speculative fiction that will "explore (and explode) our assumptions about 'innate' values and 'natural' social arrangements." [47]

NOTES

1. The term "diaper fiction" first appeared in the SF community of the 1940s and 1950s, where male and female fans alike used it to disparage those domestic-oriented SF stories that they believed would ruin the real imaginative fun of the genre for everyone. Two decades later, feminist SF author and critic Pamela Sar-

gent coined the term "housewife heroine SF" in her introductory essay for *Women of Wonder: Science Fiction Stories by Women about Women* (New York: Vintage Press, 1975) to describe what she perceived to be a "silly" kind of midcentury women's SF that was diametrically opposed to the politically progressive feminist storytelling of Sargent and her peers. For further discussion of these terms and their various histories, see Justine Larbalestier, *The Battle of the Sexes in Science Fiction* (Middletown, Conn.: Wesleyan University Press, 2002) and Lisa Yaszek, "Unhappy Housewife Heroines, Galactic Suburbia, and Nuclear War: A New History of Midcentury Women's Science Fiction," *Extrapolation* 44, no. 1 (2003): 97–111.

2. For one of the most influential discussions of this trend in 1950s political and cultural discourse, see Elaine Tyler May, *Homeward Bound: American Families in the Cold War Era* (New York: Basic Books, 1988).

3. Betty Friedan put forth one of the first and most eloquent arguments about the conservative nature of midcentury women's fiction in her classic feminist treatise, *The Feminine Mystique* (New York: Dell, 1963, 1984). Such arguments flourished for the next two decades, culminating in Eugenia Kaledin's scholarly monograph *Mothers and More: American Women in the 1950s* (Boston: Twayne, 1984). In that work, Kaledin concludes that women made important aesthetic contributions to midcentury culture, but that ultimately, "few women writers attempted . . . to translate personal dilemmas into ideology. And few attempted in any fictional way to comment on the real political anxieties of the time" (136).

Since the 1980s, however, scholars have largely been silent on the topic of midcentury women's popular fiction, especially as it appeared in the pages of mass-circulation magazines. Joanne Meyerowitz suggests that this silence stems from the enduring legacy of Friedan's work, which has led historiographers of all stripes to assume that women's popular fiction was wholeheartedly conservative. For further discussion, see Joanne Meyerowitz, "Beyond the Feminine Mystique: A Reassessment of Postwar Mass Culture, 1946–1958," in *Not June Cleaver: Women and Gender in Postwar America, 1945–1960*, ed. Joanne Meyerowitz, (Philadelphia: Temple University Press, 1994), 229–262.

4. Joanna Russ, "The Image of Women in Science Fiction," in *Images of Women in Fiction: Feminist Perspectives*, ed. Susan Koppleman Cornillion (Bowling Green: Bowling Green University Popular Press, [1971] 1972), 88.

5. Recent scholarly explorations of midcentury women's SF have taken a variety of forms. For discussions of how individual authors mobilized midcentury beliefs about gender relations to critique cold war politics, see Farah Mendlesohn, "Gender, Power, and Conflict Resolution: 'Subcommittee' by Zenna Henderson," *Extrapolation* 35, no. 2 (1994): 120–129; and David Seed, *American Science Fiction and the Cold War: Literature and Film* (Chicago: Fitzroy Dearborn, 1999). For an exploration of how these strategies circulated throughout a range of women's SF texts, see my essays "Media Landscapes and Social Satire in Postwar Women's Science Fiction," *Foundation* (November 2005); and "Unhappy Housewife Heroines, Galactic Suburbia, and Nuclear War: A New History of Midcentury Women's Science Fiction," *Extrapolation* 44, no. 1 (2003): 97–111. For an examination of how women revised midcentury SF conventions to present readers with female-friendly futures, see Brian Attebery, *Decoding Gender in Science Fiction* (New York: Routledge, 2002). For arguments concerning the relationship between midcentury

women's SF and its relation to feminist narrative strategies, especially in the works of Judith Merril, see Jane Donawerth, *Frankenstein's Daughters: Women Writing Science Fiction* (Syracuse, N.J.: Syracuse University Press, 1997). And finally, for discussion of how midcentury women's "sweet little domestic stories" marked the emergence of a literary sensibility that would inform the feminist SF community of the 1970s, see Justine Larbalestier, *Battle of the Sexes.*

6. Such authors include Shirley Jackson (who wrote for periodicals ranging from *Good Housekeeping* to *Collier's* to *The Magazine of Fantasy and Science Fiction*) and Mildred Clingerman (whose stories appeared in magazines including *Atlantic Monthly, Woman's Home Journal,* and *The Magazine of Fantasy and Science Fiction*). In addition to writing for the mainstream or "slick" magazines, women associated with midcentury SF also established names for themselves in other genres of popular fiction. The most notable of these are Margaret St. Clair (who wrote suspense stories under her own name and jungle tales under the name Wilton Hazzard) and, of course, Leigh Brackett, who wrote screenplays for films including *The Big Sleep* (1956), *Rio Bravo* (1959), and, just before she died, *The Empire Strikes Back* (1979).

For further reading on Alice Eleanor Jones's SF, see my essays "Unhappy Housewife Heroines, Galactic Suburbia, and Nuclear War: A New History of Midcentury Women's Science Fiction," *Extrapolation* 44, no. 1 (2003) and "The Women History Doesn't See: Recovering Midcentury Women's SF as a Literature of Social Critique," *Extrapolation* 45, no. 1 (2004). In "Unhappy Housewife Heroines" I consider Jones as one of several postwar women authors who wrote nuclear holocaust narratives; in "The Women History Doesn't See," I examine her in relation to a larger group of midcentury women writers who used SF to critique a variety of cold war social and political arrangements. This current chapter extends the arguments proposed in my earlier essays by specifically considering how Jones's SF developed in relation to her mainstream popular fiction.

7. More specifically, James defines the Golden Age of SF as a period that stretches from 1938 to about 1960. According to James, many of the themes and techniques commonly associated with Golden Age SF were actually established by the end of the 1940s, but it was not until the publishing boom of the 1950s that authors were able to explore these themes and techniques in the greater detail and length typically associated with "mature" SF. For further discussion, see Edward James, *Science Fiction in the Twentieth Century* (Oxford: Oxford University Press, 1994), 87–88.

Although it is not immediately relevant to this essay, it is worth noting that other members of the SF community define the Golden Age somewhat differently. As John Clute and Peter Nicholls note, older SF fans traditionally define the genre's Golden Age in relatively narrow terms, as SF published between 1938 (when John Campbell first began editing *Astounding Stories*) and 1946 (which marked the publication of the first two major hardbound SF anthologies: Raymond J. Healy and J. Francis McComas's *Adventures in Time and Space* and Groff Conklin's *The Best of Science Fiction*). For further discussion, see John Clute and Peter Nicholls, "The Golden Age of SF," in *The Encyclopedia of Science Fiction*, ed. John Clute and Peter Nicholls (New York: St. Martin's, 1995), 506–507.

8. James, *Science Fiction in the Twentieth Century*, 85–86.

9. Gary Westfahl, *The Mechanics of Wonder: The Creation of the Idea of Science Fiction* (Liverpool: Liverpool University Press, 1998), 184.

10. James, *Science Fiction in the Twentieth Century*, 86.

11. Figures provided in this essay regarding the number of women SF authors who began publishing in the postwar era are derived from my own personal count of those listed in Stephen T. Miller and William G. Contento, *The Locus Index to Science Fiction, Fantasy, and Weird Magazine Index (1890–2001)* (Oakland, Calif.: Locus, 2002). As such, these numbers only include those authors who published short stories rather than full-length novels (of course, the paperback industry was still quite new in the 1950s, so it is likely that authors who published novels also wrote short stories). My estimates are also conservative in that I did not count authors with gender-neutral names who were not specifically known to the SF community as women, nor did I include women who primarily worked in writing teams with their husbands.

12. Anthony Boucher, ed., *Best from Fantasy & Science Fiction, Fifth Series* (New York: Doubleday, 1956), 125.

13. Quoted in Justine Larbalestier, *Battle of the Sexes*, 172–173.

14. In the 1970s feminist SF authors and critics including Joanna Russ and Pamela Sargent dismissed housewife heroine SF as a kind of "ladies' magazine fiction" that failed to adequately imagine how new sciences and technologies might bring about new social and sexual relations; as late as 1995, editors John Clute and Peter Nicholls made similar arguments in the *Encyclopedia of Science Fiction*.

In retrospect, however, it is worth noting that these dismissals are not quite so sweeping as they might first appear. After all, Sargent includes several housewife heroine stories in her *Women of Wonder* anthologies, and Clute and Nicholls go to great pains to put housewife heroine SF in the context of its cultural moment — a move that mitigates whatever other criticisms they might offer regarding this particular kind of SF. And indeed, as I hope to demonstrate in this essay, these contradictory attitudes should come as no surprise to the discerning reader because the best housewife heroine SF itself strikes a compromise between celebrating midcentury gender ideals and using these ideals to critique other scientific and social developments. For a more detailed discussion, see my "Unhappy Housewife Heroines."

15. For a more general discussion of the need to revisit midcentury women's SF as an important part of the feminist literary tradition, see Helen Merrick, "'Fantastic Dialogues': Critical Stories About Feminism and Science Fiction," in *Speaking Science Fiction: Dialogues and Interpretations*, ed. Andy Walker and David Seed (Liverpool: Liverpool University Press, 2000), 52–68.

16. Meyerowitz, "Beyond the Feminine Mystique," 231.

17. For further discussion of pay rates for midcentury SF authors, see especially chapter 8 of Frederik Pohl, *The Way the Future Was: A Memoir* (New York: Del Rey, 1978). For further discussion of freelance journalist rates at major magazines in the 1950s and 1960s, see the National Writers' Union, *Report on Pay Rates for Freelance Journalists* (2002, <http://www.nwu.org/journ/minrate.htm>, 7 July 2004).

18. See especially chapter 2 of Betty Friedan, *Feminine Mystique*. Here, Friedan focuses primarily on the domestic aspects of midcentury romance fiction, demon-

strating the links between conventional gender roles, romantic love, and family "togetherness" that she saw as characteristic of this fiction.

19. For the many kinds of storytelling encompassed by the genre term "romance," see Janice A. Radway, *Reading the Romance: Women, Patriarchy, and Popular Literature* (Chapel Hill: University of North Carolina Press, [1984] 1991); and Tania Modleski, *Loving with a Vengeance: Mass-Produced Fantasies for Women* (New York: Routledge, 1996).

20. Anne Cranny-Francis, *Feminist Fiction: Feminist Uses of Generic Fiction* (New York: St. Martin's Press, 1990), 9 and 192.

21. Ibid., 178.

22. See, respectively, Alice Eleanor Jones, "How to Give Advice and Take It," *The Writer* 71 (December 1958): 12–13; Alice Eleanor Jones, "If You Want to Know, Ask," *The Writer* 73 (August 1960): 16–18; and Alice Eleanor Jones, "Ones That Got Away," *The Writer* 78 (May 1965): 17–18, 46.

23. Jones, "Ones That Got Away," 17.

24. Alice Eleanor Jones, "How to Sell an Offbeat Story," *The Writer* 75 (March 1962): 18.

25. Ibid., 18.

26. Scholarly assumptions about the conservative nature of romance fiction — and indeed, all mass culture — derive from two primary sources: Marxist critics of the 1940s and 1950s (most notably, Max Horkheimer, T. W. Adorno, and Herbert Marcuse) and feminist critics of the 1970s and early 1980s (such as Ann Douglas and Germaine Greer). For further discussion of this critical legacy and how contemporary scholars have challenged it, see Modleski, *Loving with a Vengeance*.

27. Rachel Blau DuPlessis, *Writing Beyond the Ending: Narrative Strategies of Twentieth-Century Women Writers* (Bloomington: Indiana University Press, 1985).

28. Cranny-Francis, *Feminist Fiction*, 2.

29. Jones, "Offbeat Story," 20.

30. Cranny-Francis, *Feminist Fiction*, 9.

31. Friedan, *Feminine Mystique*, 38.

32. Ibid., 43.

33. Ibid., 44.

34. Ibid., 48.

35. See, respectively, Alice Eleanor Jones, "The Honeymoon," *Redbook* (June 1957): 31, 88–91; Alice Eleanor Jones, "Morning Watch," *Redbook* (November 1958): 42–43, 111–115; and Alice Eleanor Jones, "One Shattering Weekend," *Redbook* (July 1960): 40, 72–76.

36. Alice Eleanor Jones, "Jenny Kissed Me," *Ladies' Home Journal* (November 1955): 170.

37. Alice Eleanor Jones, "The Real Me," *Redbook* (October 1962): 137.

38. Ibid., 140.

39. Friedan, *Feminine Mystique*, 342.

40. Alice Eleanor Jones, "Life, Incorporated," *Fantastic Universe* (April 1955): 74.

41. Alice Eleanor Jones, "The Happy Clown," *If* (December 1955): 105.

42. Ibid., 114.

43. Cranny-Francis, *Feminist Fiction*, 72.

44. Alice Eleanor Jones, "Recruiting Officer," *Fantastic* (October 1955): 101.

45. James, *Science Fiction in the Twentieth Century*, 90.

46. Judith Merril and Emily Pohl-Weary, *Better to Have Loved: the Life of Judith Merril* (Toronto, Canada: Between the Lines, 2002), 154–155.

47. Russ, "Image of Women in Science Fiction," 80.

No Light in the Window

KATE WILHELM

First published in her collection The Mile-Long Spaceship, 1963

The dust started blowing before the chaplain finished and when Connie said, "I do," she tasted the grit and knew her words had gone unheard. Hank's hand squeezed hers a bit and the rest went by in a blur of swirling sand and heat and wind-swept-away words heard only in her heart, not with her ears. They turned afterwards and looked up at the ship rising bluntly behind them, its snub nose obscured in the dust cloud that had pitted and torn and shot through and through Connie's extravagant lace and satin gown.

Someone yelled, "Come on, kids, or we'll be buried alive. Let's get the party rolling."

Hank and Connie stood hand in hand before the ship and slowly turned toward one another, searching in the obliterating sand and dust, the taste of sand on their mouths when they kissed. Then they too ran after the others toward the mess hall where the party was awaiting them.

They went to Tucson for the weekend honeymoon and in the predawn of Monday morning they were driving again toward the base, fulfilled, happy. Connie looked at Hank's thin face, deeply tanned, but too drawn for perfect health, the result of the three years of tension. His narrow hand rested on her leg just above the knee and she stroked it lightly watching the lines of his face come into bolder relief as the day hurried as if eager for the burning sun to be born anew. They didn't speak, only occasionally smiling into each other's eyes, too content for the utterance of mere words that could say only so much, none of it vital as their love was vital.

Connie closed her eyes dreamily and relived the weekend minute by minute, not knowing how or when the conversation with Phylis intruded and gained preponderance over her thoughts.

"Look, Connie, you're letting yourself in for more grief than you can take. You and Hank are happy now, aren't you? What if you are separated at take-off? It will be seven years before he can be declared legally dead and until then you'll be a married woman. Honey, in seven years you'll be pushing thirty."

"We won't be separated. Hank is sure of the astrophysicist post and I'll keep up in the bio-chemistry lab," Connie laughed at her.

"All right, suppose you both do get selected. Do you think life aboard the ship will conform to Earth's morality, laws and customs? There'll be five or six men for every woman aboard. How long do you think Hank could stand a situation like the one that will necessarily develop?"

"Oh, Phylis, shut up!" Connie retorted indignantly. "We are both adults and are both going into this thing with our eyes open. If that happens, it just will and we'll be able to stand it. First and foremost I'll be Mrs. Hank Quenton."

"Take-off smoke will automatically make that Mrs. Eligible," Phylis said maliciously. She softened immediately however and put her arms around the other girl. "You poor little goose," she said soberly. "Since I couldn't talk you out of it, let me be your maid of honor."

There was a smile on Connie's face when Hank shook her awake and they were before their barrack's one-room apartment, home for the next year until take-off of Earth's first star ship.

The days settled to the routine again quickly and it was almost as if they hadn't even married. She had problems to settle concerning biology, and problems about chemistry and problems that had nothing to do with either. And there were tests and classes and homework and physical exercise to be done. They ate together, when they could, in the mess hall and slept together when they could arrange the same hours in the small one-room home. Connie was deliriously happy.

She knew she would beat him home by at least an hour on their second month's anniversary, and she hurried, planning what to wear to celebrate. She opened the door quickly and was thankful for the air conditioned coolness that greeted her. Her eyes widened as she saw a figure rising from the chair by the window.

"Don!" she exclaimed and her hand stayed at the button she was undoing. Without realizing it she had gone pale and the other hand was clenched tightly. Don worked with Hank. Immediately she knew one of the tests had gone wrong. The centrifuge? The altitude chamber?

"Get hold of yourself, Connie," Don said quickly. "He's okay. They took out his appendix. That's all."

"His appendix!" Relief flooded through her, washing the strength from her legs and she sank into the other chair. "But there wasn't anything wrong with him. He's never had a bit of stomach trouble."

"The doc said it had to go. Preventive medicine. He wanted me to tell you about it and tell you not to do anything rash. He'll be able to see you tomorrow."

During the next hour she tried to get to Hank, but the night nurse at the infirmary was adamant and told her to return in the morning between ten and eleven.

"But just let me look at him! I won't even go inside his room. I have to know he's all right," she begged.

"Sorry, ma'am. Orders," he said courteously and escorted her to the door, standing there watching until she finally turned and walked away, shoulders sagging, tears threatening to spill over at a word.

She found Phylis in the general lounge.

"Honey, what can you do about it?" she asked callously. "So they took out his appendix. Everyone out here has to have it done to qualify. Last week it was your wisdom teeth. As routine as inspecting for t.b."

"But they should have told me! I'm his wife. I had a right to know. What if something had gone wrong? What if he'd called for me?"

"Well, nothing did, and even if he had called for you, he didn't need you. Now you'd better get some dinner and some sleep. For all you know this could be part of your testing. Someone could be recording your every action to see how you bear up under strain and surprise."

Connie felt something freeze within her and she thought distantly, two rabbits with one snare. She was sure they were studying her reaction. Raising her voice slightly she said quite clearly, "I hope they get it down right. I'm furious with them. At the whole scheming set-up. What right do they have to take people and manipulate them like so many animated puppets? They don't own my soul and if they make me mad, there's nothing I signed yet that says I have to grin and turn the other cheek."

Later she wondered what the psychologists thought when they studied that. Hank had been given the opportunity to contact her, she learned with indignation, and he had turned it down. "Don't you see, darling. Everything they do has a reason. They had to be sure I wasn't too dependent on you. I suspected it as soon as I saw Zorin there watching me."

The psychologists were the worst, and of them Zorin was the one she feared the most. They pounced on them at all hours, presenting problems that had no solutions, asking questions that made no sense, trying to tear out their very minds and dissect them into tiny cross sections so they could know exactly what was thought, what was felt. Connie was proud of Hank for outguessing them, but the little voice within her still protested that it was unnatural for a man's wife not to know about his surgery. He was so self-sufficient, she thought, that actually he didn't need her. She'd been of no use to him that other time when Zorin had got under his skin. He had returned at three in the morning, stiff and cold and hard, so icily controlled that she had been almost afraid of him.

"Darling, what happened? What did they do to you?"

"Go to sleep, Connie. It's nothing."

"But Hank . . ."

"I said it's nothing! Steve's flunked out. He left half an hour ago. They let me take him to town." And then it came out. "Zorin wanted to know how I felt seeing my best friend leave."

Connie had become silent with the awakened memory of that other night and the nameless fear, fear that couldn't be identified and examined, was smothering her, making breathing difficult. They had taken Steve's appendix out too. The thoughts Phylis had planted in her mind came back with overpowering force. What if she didn't make it? With thought giving the idea an identity, it came back repeatedly, each time stronger and with more urgency. What would she do without him? She knew that she had promised herself for life that day when they tasted sand saying the magic words, regardless of what happened after take-off. The feeling persisted for days and finally she knew what she must do.

"Hank, I think we should go to the sperm bank." She lay with his arm about her shoulders and felt him become taut with her words.

"Don't be ridiculous, Connie. It's either both of us or neither of us. Either way there's plenty of time."

"But Hank . . ." There was so much she wanted to say. She couldn't let him stay because of her. She had known that from the beginning. She knew she would die before she let it happen. Better that one of them should live the dream they both shared than neither of them. From the original four thousand, six hundred would be chosen, and if he were one of them, no power existed that could deny him. She said, "Darling, be reasonable. There are inheritance laws for one thing. Without children I wouldn't be able to touch your bank account, and that would be a hardship. Think of all those thousands of dollars sitting there and me drooling about them and not able to get even a peek."

She shushed his protest with a quick kiss and continued hurriedly, "And I just sort of figure a little-long-lanky-tow-headed junior edition of you would be better than all the memories I could conjure. And besides, think of all the other women who might want to conceive a child by you, and this way you could refer them to the dispensary with an indifferent wave of your hand."

He wasn't amused and it got worse. The next day neither of them was speaking and they might have continued that way until take-off if Dr. Zorin hadn't called for Connie that afternoon.

"Mrs. Quenton," he asked mildly, "what do you think of marriage?"

He knew. Connie didn't question how; it was enough that he did. Cautiously she answered, "I think it's fine, Doctor."

"Naturally," he smiled and she found herself stiffening her guard even more. "But in the broader sense, speaking in general terms, not subjectively, what function do you consider marriage to satisfy?"

"I think," she hedged, "that would depend entirely on the couple concerned. There are probably as many answers to that as there are married people."

"Um. And your own? What did you hope to accomplish by legalizing what was already an acceptable condition? Did you think it would give you a better chance to make the trip together?"

"Of course not! Actually I was afraid it might cause a great big minus ten to be put by our names," she cried. "I love Hank, Doctor. Can't you understand that? I love him and I wanted to marry him."

"And you want to bear his children, don't you?"

"Yes!" she flung out recklessly. "Isn't that the natural thing for a woman to want? Doesn't every woman want to bear the child of the man she loves?"

"Is that why you wanted to be married?"

"I don't know! I don't know!" She fought down her rebellion at the questions and the talk went on for almost another hour without bringing it down any closer than that. Before she left he told her all the men would be required to visit the sperm bank, for the protection of the unborn generations of children.

She walked back to her own room dejectedly not even noticing the heat or the eternally swirling dust that clogged her nose and caused her eyes to smart. Hank was waiting for her, his arms outstretched, drinks standing on the dresser steaming slightly.

"Hank," she moaned and buried her face against him blurting out an incoherent account of the interview. "I'll be flunked out too. I know I will. No more blow-ups. I swear!"

She did try, but weekly the tension mounted. People they were accustomed to seeing about would drop from sight and they'd think they had been eliminated only to find them present once more. And the problems became more and more complex, the heat more intense, and the hours longer. Sleep was interrupted countless times so that reactions could be tested. Their most intimate hours together, hours growing harder and harder to find, were most often the ones broken into with the hateful message to report to the department on the double.

Connie made a magnificent attempt to keep cool and controlled, but despite her effort, she blew up completely several times during the next few months, once weeping uncontrollably on Dr. Zorin's shoulder, unable to stop although she knew he was making clinical notes of her behavior all the while.

She envied and loved and hated Hank alternately during those last months. He was what she couldn't be, no matter how hard she tried, and she came to realize she was living only for him, pretending for his sake, when in her heart she knew she had long since been eliminated. Hank never mentioned the subject and for him she pretended and the talk never again drifted toward the agonizing possibility of his going alone.

The group was decreased gradually from four thousand to two thousand. They only became aware of what was happening during the briefing sessions when the auditorium suddenly seemed bare and the fact was brought home that over half of the seats were empty. Supplies kept coming to be checked and stored aboard the ship. Time was the worst, ever pressing enemy now, as the tentative date for departure drew nearer and nearer. Connie was becoming as thin as a dieting adolescent, and not only she alone, but also Hank and Phylis and nearly everyone else. Nerves were nearly visible, so close to the surface did they lay. Connie caught herself watching Hank with smouldering eyes as he chewed his food methodically or examined a new magazine with the same casual air of preoccupation he had always maintained.

"Why doesn't he break just once?" she asked herself in resentment. "How can he stay so calm and sure?" But he did and her fury with him mounted and was disguised as nervousness or tiredness or anything else so that he wouldn't suspect.

It would be a matter of weeks, they knew, when the last briefing was held. Less than a fourth of the seats were filled. Connie's wrath vanished as she swelled with pride, realizing that Hank was making it. She exulted and closed her eyes in a brief prayer that she would have the kind of strength she knew it would take to keep up the pretence of believing she would also go. He might need her now during these last weeks even if he hadn't before. Indeed it might be that because he was so sure she would go he was able to maintain his implacable calm.

She felt him nudging her and he was grinning and she listened to the remainder of the words being said from the stage. They were to have a holiday. After two months of being on call for twenty-four hours a day, seven days a week, they were to have a holiday.

"We'll go to town and we'll swim at the club and we'll have lunch at the Rancho and . . . and dance . . . and . . ." she began counting off on her fingers as she talked excitedly.

"And I'll get a horse and buggy and we'll have a ride right out of a history book," Hank laughed back at her.

"And I'll take the veiling off my tiara and wear my wedding gown to our last formal dinner, Earth style."

"And . . ."

The day passed by swiftly, leaving only momentary intervals for the pure joy of it to register. The old mare Hank had found somewhere jogged along slowly and Connie snuggled her head against Hank's shoulder contentedly. "It was a gorgeous day, every minute of it," she murmured happily.

"How can you be sure?" Hank yawned. "I don't seem to be able to remember taking time out to ask myself if I was having fun."

"That's the beauty of a day like this. For the rest of your life you can keep scraping and always come up with something new to remember. Darling," she whispered, "I have the feeling that everything will be all right. It's just a feeling of rightness. Know what I mean?"

Hank squeezed her shoulders and planted a kiss on the end of her nose. "I never stopped having it," he said.

They drew up to the first check point where they had to leave the horse and buggy for the farmer to collect in the morning. Before them stretching endlessly lay more of the desert, fenced off and patrolled and studded with concrete bunkers that gleamed whitely under the watchful moon, and only in the far distance was there a glow of light, reflecting back from the luminous sky, where the barracks were and where the ship stood waiting impassively.

"Home again," Hank said, and the lightness of his tone seemed to dissipate as he unconsciously erected the shield he wasn't even aware existed.

Connie felt the tenseness return and knew the holiday hadn't done anything to ease the burdensome pangs of anxiety. She sighed and stepped from the buggy and suddenly she was falling and couldn't stop herself. In the instant it took before she hit the ground she knew her heel had caught in the unaccustomed floor length gown and she even had the wild thought, "So this is how I'll end it all."

Somehow they got to her to the infirmary and her mind was as numb as her arm when they administered the local anesthetic. "Broken," the doctor said cryptically and put into motion the actions that would culminate in a cast. Connie couldn't even cry and when Hank tried to comfort her, she turned her head from him and stared dry eyed at the wall.

Dr. Zorin was the first visitor of the morning and his cheery grin had the effect of changing Connie's self pity into all encompassing fury at the events that had led to her failure. "In the army," Dr. Zorin said, "they call it gold-bricking."

"How dare you come in here and insult me now?" Connie flared back at him. He was going through his pockets and automatically she handed him her pen. "Go ahead and put your name on it! Makes you feel smug and superior, I suppose."

Hank entered while she was still railing at his imperturbable bent head as he signed his name with a flourish. "Connie," Hank said and for once there was a quality of near desperation in his voice, "you've had a rough night. Don't take it out on the doctor."

"Oh, shut up!" she snapped at him and handed the pen over without another glance at Zorin who was grinning at Hank.

"Well, I'll leave you two to point the bitter finger of accusation at one another," he said blithely. At the door he stopped again however and added meditatively, "She did furnish the pen, Hank."

The next day the ship got its first static firing test. On her narrow, antiseptic bed Connie felt the building shake and by closing her eyes she could imagine the huge ship quivering like a dog on a leash. It was self-sustaining. Nothing else was to be taken aboard or taken from it. To enter now, one first had to enter the air lock and wait for the exchange of air from outside with air from inside. They brought her news of it daily and it seemed in the week she spent in the infirmary more changes were wrought than in the entire four previous years. The surgery necessary for the urethrane [*sic*] treatment of her arm healed and the heavy cast was exchanged for a light-weight support. They said it wouldn't give her any more trouble and she was released. Again she was playing out the fantasy of pretending to believe she was going. Did Hank really believe it, she wondered. He acted so sure of it, never yielding, never indicating he'd ever had even the slightest doubt.

They were living aboard the ship in contingents of six hundred now. Never the same six hundred, but always a full crew aboard. Whole departments went through the routine of on-board living for days at a time, doing their work, eating, sleeping, occupying spare time with the ship's facilities for play as if in actual flight through space. It was impossible even to try to guess which ones would finally be eliminated now. Everyone seemed completely indispensable for the project. Connie tried not to think of the time immediately following take-off. There would still be some work to do on base, but she knew she wouldn't be able to stay and help with it. It would be a long time before she would be able to do work of any sort.

They weren't to be told when take-off would come. Connie heard the news with stunned disbelief. But she had counted so much on the last night together. Another small lifetime of memories had yet to be gathered. She put aside the plans for champagne and candle light and perhaps a few of her tears on his shoulder and went dazedly into the air lock to report for duty. She might go to sleep and awake to hear the roar of take-off. What if they didn't even have a chance for a last kiss. She was unaware of the others in the air lock with her and began planning for their every second together until the end. Every instant must have awareness, every word a deeper significance than its apparent meaning. There had to be enough memories to last a lifetime alone. She had to have more of him than she now possessed.

"Connie, report to Dr. Zorin," Phylis called to her and she turned impatiently and headed down a corridor to the doctor's office aboard the ship.

"Connie, sit down. Here." Dr. Zorin sat opposite her and removed his glasses, carefully placing them inside their case and returning it to his pocket. He leaned back comfortably in his chair. "I wanted to talk to you before you got too busy for me. How's your arm?"

"Fine. Just about as strong as it ever was."

"Good. Confirms the report I got from the infirmary. Connie," he said quizzically, "why you remained so unsure of your place aboard will always be a mystery to me. I can see part of the reason in your continual comparison of yourself with Hank, but your interpretation was so wrong. You're strong and resilient. You have natural outlets for worry and anxiety and you use them — tears once in awhile, anger, but anger that subsides quickly, the ability to reason and see justice, and while conditions may disturb you, you can accept them with good humor once you've made your gesture of rebellion. Don't you see, my dear, that these things aren't faults? You're very easy to get along with, have many friends . . ."

"Dr. Zorin," Connie interrupted breathlessly, "are you telling me I will go?"

"That's what I'm saying," he admitted soberly.

"Dr. Zorin! It's . . . it's . . . I could hug you!" she sprang from her chair, but at the look on his face she sank back into it. "What else? What is it?"

"You will go, Connie. But Hank will stay."

Only much later did she remember the rest of his words. Much later after the ship was a silently moving speck among the myriad star points. "He's the very things you are not. He's brittle and inflexible and unyielding. He can't accept occasional failure and being human he must fail. He has never faced the possibility that one of you might not be selected. What will such a man do when he does erupt? We can never know, only guess. Having no smaller safety valves to release the pressure before it becomes unbearable, he is powerless to stem it if the break does come."

They felt the tug, the impatient, searching, straining of the ship as the mighty engines roared defiance at the confining gantries. Automatically the seats accepted their bodies, conforming to their shapes and with the pressure came the blankness of sleep for Connie.

Cold War Masculinity In The Early Work Of Kate Wilhelm

Josh Lukin

Those who try to live by rationality alone, who cannot explore their inner realities, are not fully human; they are "brittle and inflexible and unyielding." . . . Many of these characters are men, portrayed with sympathetic understanding of how conformity to North America's ideal of the strong, silent male warps the individual." — SUSAN WOOD[1]

The control of emotions is closely linked to the control of women. — CAROLINE NEW[2]

Kate Wilhelm occupies an ambiguous space in the canon of feminist science fiction. Although one or two of her works appear in many of the genre's "Top 100" lists, very few critical analyses of her work have been published.[3] SF writers of the generation succeeding hers are more likely to claim Russ, Le Guin, and Tiptree as their feminist inspirations. Disagreements recur as to whether she belongs on lists of "feminist SF writers" or only on lists of "women in SF," whose importance to feminism lies in the fact that they wrote as women in oppressive times, or focused on female protagonists, rather than emphasizing antipatriarchal themes in their work. In the face of Wilhelm's achievement, this treatment constitutes unjust neglect. Wilhelm embarked upon a serious critique of gender norms early in her career and tied it to a more general suspicion of authority, one that deepened in her radical work of subsequent years and remains relevant in the present day.

"No Light in the Window" may seem an inauspicious beginning for such a celebration of Wilhelm's feminism or radicalism. On the surface, it is a largely conventional and formulaic SF story. The idea of the protagonist subjected to a series of ordeals (*épreuves*) that she thinks she's failed but that in fact establish her distinctiveness is a long-standing theme in SF, exemplified in Isaac Asimov's 1957 novella, "Profession,"[4] in which the protagonist discovers that the "Home for the Feeble-Minded" where he's been incarcerated is an institute from which society's most creative intellects direct the course of human development. Science fiction, long marketed to nerdy adolescents, thrives on the Ugly Duckling (or Cinderella or Young King Arthur) tale of a formerly despised hero achieving his or her rightful destiny.

The story's gender politics may not appear impressive. The device of a female protagonist who surpasses her male partner was not new: in Asimov's "The Mule" (1945)[5] and H. Beam Piper's "Omnilingual" (1957),[6] shrewd women solve problems that elude their husbands; and in Kit Reed's "To Lift a Ship" (1962),[7] the heroine discovers that, contrary to scientific wisdom, she can telekinetically launch a spacecraft without the help of her abusive male copilot. A heroine such as Wilhelm's Connie, who says, "Doesn't every woman want to bear the child of the man she loves?" and accepts 1950s-style marital property laws ("Without children I wouldn't be able to touch your bank account") cannot be seen today as a feminist role model. The somber tone of the story's title and conclusion seem to validate Brett Harvey's generalization about the convictions of 1950s women: "It was their own profound belief, internalized from a lifetime of messages, that achievement and autonomy were simply incompatible with love and family. The equation was inescapable: independence equaled loneliness."[8] In short, "No Light in the Window" lacks the affect of most famous feminist literature: it doesn't *feel* like what today's readers think of as a feminist story.

To appreciate the story's strengths, one may have to return to 1963.

Before The Second Wave

The years 1962-63 are commonly thought of as having marked the end of the era that academic humanists have come to call the "long 1950s."[9] In the earlier year, the oppressive effects of the Red Scare upon what Americans could do and say had been challenged: John Henry Faulk successfully sued to break the entertainment-industry blacklist, and Michael Harrington legitimized the discussion of poverty in America. But the changes of 1963 were even more dramatic. The assassinations of Medgar Evers and John Kennedy, the rise of the Beatles, the NAACP sit-ins, the report of the President's Commission on the Status of Women, and *The Feminine Mystique* began to establish political violence, youth culture, and liberal feminism as lasting societal forces that could not easily be ignored.

But such an overview is only possible years after the fact; zeitgeists tend to be created in retrospect, once history has sorted out burgeoning trends from passing crazes. It was not clear to every observer at the time that Betty Friedan's work would end up having the historical impact that it did, or that the Equal Pay Act would be taken seriously by hordes of workers demanding that it be enforced. Indeed, Title VII of the following year's Civil Rights Act, outlawing what would later be dubbed sex discrimination, was proposed in jest by a Congressman who thought he was exposing the absurdity of extending governmental protections to African Americans.[10] Even as women reversed 1950s trends by completing college and entering professions in greater numbers, the public discourse on gender issues in the early 1960s sometimes felt like the fifties with less red-baiting and more rock 'n' roll.

Ruth Rosen has described the 1950s as "an age of cognitive dissonance [during which] millions of people believed in ideals that poorly described their own experience."[11] She elaborates that in the early to mid-1950s, Americans believed in the ideal of suburban domestic consumerist bliss even as racial tensions, cold war terrors, and emergent forms of social activism increasingly belied such sitcom utopias. By the late fifties and early sixties, the dissonance remained, but the individual notes were somewhat different. As fear of acknowledging inequality in the domains of race, gender, and wealth receded, the mainstream discourse noted that such problems existed but assured people that they were being solved by good old American stick-to-it-iveness. Hence Arthur Schlesinger Jr. could write in 1958: "Women seem an expanding, aggressive force, seizing new domains like a conquering army, while men, more and more on the defensive, are hardly able to hold their own and gratefully accept assignments from their new rulers."[12] And in 1964, Dr. Lena Levine and David Loth explained in *The Emotional Sex: Why Women Are the Way They Are Today* that

> only a few decades ago a woman's role was precisely defined and her person protected. . . . She was a submissive helpmeet whose province was her home and children. . . . Now that is changed. Not that women burst out of their old restricted life by their own efforts. Men brought them out and are still bringing them out.[13]

It would perhaps be more accurate, with respect to confining and restricting women, that men had put them in and were still putting them in. Stephanie Coontz, an adept documenter of the 1950s gender gulag, reports on the extent to which widespread resistance to female autonomy was codified in law and institutional policy:

> All women, even seemingly docile ones, were deeply mistrusted. They were frequently denied the right to serve on juries, convey property, make contracts, take

out credit cards in their own name, or establish residence. A 1954 article in *Esquire* called working wives a "menace"; a *Life* author termed married women's employment a "disease." Women were excluded from several professions, and some states even gave husbands control over their wives' finances.[14]

Furthermore, most commercial and educational establishments refused to admit women wearing pants. The fight against such oppression in subsequent decades required more than goodwill, and men, *pace* Levine and Loth, did not lead the battle; nor, by and large, did they concede it gracefully.

The spectacle of Lena Levine, a female physician practicing at a time when no medical school even conceived of fairness in its hiring and admissions, promoting a sexist canard ("Men brought them out . . .") illustrates the strange bind that social norms imposed upon women in positions of authority. Rosen says of the fifties:

> Caught between the myth of the happy housewife and the reality of their working lives, some working women refused to acknowledge that they worked . . . career women downplayed their independence. . . . Journalist Dorothy Thompson argued that women who engaged in demanding intellectual work cheated their husbands and children. . . . A few former suffragists — like the repentant ex-Communists of the time — publicly recanted their youthful ways, belatedly took their husbands' last names, and dutifully bowed to the idea of man's natural superiority.[15]

The Communist analogy is particularly apt, as Rosen paints a picture of women who, under deep cover, went out and engaged in professional labor while using Aesopic language to conceal their transgressions from those close to them or while paying lip-service to conservative ideals while subverting them from within. Even though the 1963 *Presidential Report on American Women*

> reaffirmed [women's] roles as wives, housekeepers, and rearers of children, while documenting the inequalities they faced as workers . . . anthropologist Margaret Mead [nevertheless] worried that the report had not sufficiently praised full-time mothers and wives and asked, "Who will be there to bandage the child's knee and listen to the husband's troubles and give the human element to the world?"[16]

It is important to remember that being an active and intelligent woman did not enable many people to transcend near ubiquitous ideological pressures, or embolden them to speak out against the gender order.

The odd dissonance that arises when one contrasts the small gains made by women in the late 1950s and early 1960s with the alarm that Schlesinger claims to see among men suggests a kind of premature backlash, in which men, glimpsing the possibility of women's liberation, cast off their restrained, polite, and chivalrous 1950s demeanor to fight a desperate battle against the loss of their children's knee-bandagers. But it is as likely that the reverse occurred: as Barbara Ehrenreich has suggested, "male defection from family obligations in the 1950s preceded and in part inspired feminists' protests against their domestic role."[17] In the literature of the time, more and more men acted in accord with the fantasy that Schlesinger attributes to them, treating women as a newly empowered threat to their lives and liberty. The years 1958–1963 see an explosion of brutal misogyny, in the works of the Beats, the Black Humorists (prior to and excepting Thomas Pynchon), and more somber novelists such as John Updike. Women are not merely absent, or adjuncts to men, or passive characters: they are scapegoated, raped, and killed with unprecedented frequency, sometimes for comic relief.

The era's writers did not confine themselves to mistreating fictional women. In 1961, Donald Westlake (who has since shown himself to be a vastly talented novelist) published an over-the-top, self-congratulatory denunciation of the science fiction field, ostensibly to explain his abandonment of it in favor of crime novels. The strangest gratuitous snipes in the piece are directed at Cele Goldsmith, then editor of *Amazing* and *Fantastic*. It seems that she does not publish stories "in sensible English." Moreover, "Cele Goldsmith is a third grade teacher and I bet she wonders what in the world she's doing over at *Amazing*. (I know I do.)"[18] I queried one of Westlake's contemporaries: "His other characterizations make sense, but why does he say that about the Cele Goldsmith who first published Keith Laumer, Roger Zelazny, Thomas Disch, Ursula Le Guin, Sonya Dorman, and Phyllis Gotleib?"

"Everybody said such things," I was told. "It was *de rigeur* whenever possible to drop a remark about how this-or-that proved that women couldn't write, or edit, or whatever. You were allowed to charitably introduce one exception — at that time it would usually have been Harper Lee." In the context in which Westlake was operating, the exception that the man charitably introduced would have been — and was — Judith Merril. But my interlocutor's point was that the gender attitudes in evaluative criticism that I had thought peculiar to Norman Mailer were in fact standard for the era.

Nonetheless, the fact that Goldsmith was editing those magazines and publishing those authors speaks well of the treatment of women in the science fiction field, as far as visibility is concerned. And it has long been a commonplace that, notwithstanding the sexism of mainstream literature and of the national discourse, things were better for *characters* in science fiction. Chandler Davis in his 1949 article decrying ethnic stereotypes in SF explains that he feels a less urgent need to protest gender stereotypes because

> here s-f (or at least [*Astounding*]) is way ahead of most pulps, & still improving. Women in s-f are frequently educated (even the stock hero-marrying daughters of professors); they're also frequently dominant characters, important to the story as more than love-objects . . . on the whole s-f authors invent women who are people almost half as often as they invent men who are people, which is more than you can say for mystery writers.[19]

Luise White, in the 1975 Symposium on Women in Science Fiction, cites Bester and Kornbluth in support of her thesis that "for a male-dominated field, SF had an astonishing range of active, vigorous women characters."[20] The 1963 blurb for a Margaret St. Clair novel demonstrates a clumsy attempt to celebrate the presence of women's perspectives in SF:

> Women are writing SCIENCE-FICTION! Original! Brilliant!! Dazzling!!! Women are closer to the primitive than men. They are conscious of the moon-pulls, the earth-tides. They possess a buried memory of humankind's obscure and ancient past which can emerge to uniquely color and flavor an novel.[21]

This is an eccentric brand of feminism at best, but it's more empowering to have a "buried memory of humankind's obscure and ancient past" than to be suited for no job but that of a third-grade teacher, regardless of your accomplishments.

Still, despite the field's tradition of being friendlier toward women than other discourses, much early-1960s SF, including that of the field's most prominent authors, tended to posit distant or ideal societies with 1950s U.S. gender politics. Particularly unsettling are the novels of America's most prominent SF writer of the time, Robert Heinlein, who a few years earlier had been writing novels in which women occupied positions of authority on planets and starships: *Stranger in a Strange Land* (1961) and *Podkayne of Mars* (1963) — the former with its team of submissive women who "did not chatter, did not intrude into sober talk of men, but were quick with food and drink in warm hospitality"; the latter with its heroine who abandons her adolescent dream of becoming a spaceship captain upon realizing that she's far better suited for bearing and tending children. Podkayne's accidental death at the end of the novel, catalyzed by her incompetent brother, is used by Heinlein to illustrate the destruction wreaked by their mother's having been a "career woman" who subordinated her children's needs to her engineering profession.[22]

Challenging The Cult Of Toughness

Hence Connie Quenton in "No Light in the Window" is a somewhat distinctive woman even in the science fiction field of 1963, and an extremely distinctive woman in the broader literary and social scene. A skilled biochemist at twenty-two, Connie first defies peer pressure to marry Hank and then continually questions the rules and surveillance that she and her husband are made to live under, while he resentfully submits to authority and derides her rebellious attitude. Convinced that her conduct will disqualify her for space travel, she tries hard to conform to the standard live-through-your-husband-and-children ideal so common in 1963 America: "Connie's wrath vanished as she swelled with pride, realizing that Hank was making it. A part of her would make it, she exulted and closed her eyes in a brief prayer that she would have the kind of strength she knew it would take to keep up the pretence of believing she would also go. He might need her now during these last weeks even if he hadn't before." (Wilhelm, 102). Of all the virtues she has to be proud of, Connie here focuses on her ability to perform a role that might fulfill her husband's needs. Twenty years later, Arlie Hochschild was to describe that state of affairs, pointing out that women are most valued for doing "emotion work that affirms, enhances, and celebrates the well-being and status of others."[23]

Connie has not been reduced to this condition solely by internalizing abstract societal forces: Hank has taken an active role in casting her attempts at self-assertion as invalid and feeding her self-doubt. His repeated insistence that she is showing weakness by criticizing the rigors of their training and the arbitrary conduct of authority manifests his belief that, as Hochschild observes,

> The feelings of the lower-status party may be discounted . . . by considering them rational but unimportant or by considering them irrational and therefore dismissable. . . . It is believed that women are more emotional, and this very belief is used to invalidate their feelings . . . the lower our status, the more our manner of seeing and feeling is subject to being discredited.[24]

The stereotypical belief in the husband's greater competence, which persists in many marriages,[25] is continually reinforced by Hank's attempts to correct Connie's emotional responses: "Everything they do has a reason. . . . Don't be ridiculous. . . . You have to learn to control yourself better. . . . Don't take it out in the doctor." (Wilhelm, 99, 100, 104). Ultimately, her attempts to feel valued by swelling with pride and exulting in his success fail: she is unable to remain swollen and exulting, finally responding to Hank's anxious insistence on submission to authority with "Oh, shut up!" (Wilhelm, 104).

The story's fairy-tale denouement, with the authority figure of Zorin revealing that Connie's attributes make her the ideal space explorer while Hank's disqualify him, attributes a fascinating hierarchy of values to the space program in the story's world. Connie has assumed that Hank was the more qualified partner because, in his effort to second-guess the psychologists observing them, he presented a facade of stoicism and control: "He was so self-sufficient, she thought, that actually he didn't need her . . . so icily controlled that she had been almost afraid of him." (Wilhelm, 100). He has infuriated her with "the same casual air of preoccupation he had always maintained . . . he was able to maintain his implacable calm." (Wilhelm, 102). She, on the other hand, is acutely aware of her every emotional response, not only articulating it but manifesting it corporeally:

> Her eyes widened . . . she had gone pale and the other hand was clenched tightly. . . . Relief flooded through her, washing the strength from her legs. . . . Connie felt something freeze within her . . . fear . . . was smothering her, making breathing difficult. (Wilhelm, 98–99)

Attention to the somatic is not necessarily a feminist gesture: Podkayne of Mars concludes after contemplating her body, "You might say we were designed for having babies." But as an aspect of Connie's mode of response to the world, it is endorsed as superior to Hank's inhuman self-discipline.

Connie is ultimately rewarded for having "natural outlets for worry and anxiety," which somehow combine with her "ability to reason and to see justice" in making her "strong and resilient." Hank, however, is "brittle and inflexible and unyielding. He can't accept occasional failure and being human he must fail. . . . What will such a man do when he does erupt? We can never know, only guess. Having no smaller safety valves to release the pressure before it becomes unbearable, he is powerless to stem it if the break does come." (Wilhelm, 105–106) The very attributes that Connie envied in Hank and hoped in vain to be able to emulate are those that disqualify him for a stress-filled space mission.

Susan Wood, a founding mother of feminist science fiction criticism, remarked in the sole critical essay that mentions "No Light in the Window" that Connie and Hank are types that will reappear throughout Wilhelm's fiction: Hank is the first exemplar of how men are warped by "conformity to North America's ideal of the strong, silent male."[26] Recalling the pervasiveness of that ideal at the time the story was written demonstrates the story's powerfully utopian qualities: the hierarchy of values that dominated U.S.

political and literary discourse at the time was the inverse of that which Zorin maintains. K. A. Cuordileone has argued that in the years following World War II, there arose "a political culture that put a new premium on hard masculine toughness and rendered anything less than that soft and feminine, and as such a potential threat to the security of the nation."[27] Cuordileone analyses how the rhetoric of gender crisis pervades Arthur Schlesinger's 1949 cold war manifesto, *The Vital Center*. The threats to Schlesinger's America are the "hysteria-prone capitalists" on the Right who demand that the State facilitate their profit-making and the "sentimentalists" on the Left, who are "soft, not hard" and suffer from "feminine fascination with the rude and muscular power of the proletariat."[28]

By the time of his 1958 article, "The Crisis of American Masculinity," Schlesinger was no longer opposing manliness to feminine softness or submissiveness: "It is good for men as well as women that women have been set free." Immaturity, conformism, and homosexuality were more pernicious foes, all susceptible to defeat through the creation of "a virile political life."[29] He warned two years later: "By the early '60s the Soviet Union . . . will have a superiority in the thrust of its missiles and in the penetration of outer space."[30] Cuordileone explains how, in the 1960 election season,

> in the able hands of such men as Schlesinger, Mailer, and Alsop, John F. Kennedy became . . . the answer to the nation's crisis in masculinity. . . . The Kennedy administration's much-commented-upon cult of toughness did not arise in a vacuum, but amid a political culture that turned muscularity into a prerequisite for Democrats, style into a commodity, and failure to act boldly and decisively into another Munich, another failure of nerve, another *male character defect.*[31]

Hence a presidential candidate who accused the United States of having "gone soft — physically, mentally, spiritually soft"[32] and who, as president, defended America against the threat of the penetrating thrust of those Soviet missiles.

Of course, the idea that the Cuban missile crisis was resolved by America's standing firm and tall was a public-relations invention. But sexualized language such as that of Schlesinger and Mailer was more than a propaganda tool or even a reflection of mainstream ideologies: it informed and constrained the narrative by which policymakers defined their tactics and purposes. It is not only a case of goals in a male-dominated culture being *represented* in terms of themes significant to men, but of the possibilities for conceptualizing those goals being limited by a few predominant, gender-based tropes. Historian Robert Dean has traced how such factors as "fear of the consequences of being judged 'unmanly' influenced the reckoning [of] political costs or benefits associated with possible responses to [international] threats." He concludes that "gender must be understood not as an independent *cause* of policy decisions, but as part of the very fabric of reasoning employed by officeholders."[33]

Among the attributes of Kennedy-era masculinity that Dean identifies are a suspicion of women and a consequent insistence on male domination in the domestic sphere. *The Ugly American*, a novel that greatly influenced administration policy, "warned [that] women could subvert the imperial project from two directions: from within, as indigent luxury-loving 'Moms,' and from without, as alien sexual temptresses."[34] Kennedy, in denouncing his opponent, placed the feminization of the home in opposition to austerity and military strength:

> And in the Soviet Union, [Nixon] argued with Mr. Khruschev in the kitchen, pointing out that while we might be behind in space, we were certainly ahead in color television. Mr. Nixon may be very experienced in kitchen debates. So are a great many other married men I know. But . . . I would rather take my television black and white and have the largest rockets in the world.[35]

Hence, Dean observes, "Kennedy managed to construe Nixon as an emasculated husband."[36]

The sitcom cliché of the henpecked husband, although comparatively new as an instrument of political persuasion, was an instance of Kennedy's using a universally recognized trope of the private sphere to describe the realm of public policy. More specific to his own experience was his idealization of hazing as a key to manhood:

> Kennedy, and many of the men of his administration, were brought up in the tradition of the American upper class that forged manhood out of a specific pattern of "ordeals." . . . At boarding school . . . [boys were] taught the utility of conformity [and learned] that it was the responsibility of men with a legitimate claim to social power to harden their bodies and discipline their minds to realize their own destiny as men while serving the state.[37]

Discussing the strategies used by Sargent Shriver and William Sloane Coffin to promote the Peace Corps, Dean emphasizes that the corps members' "compulsory immersion in the strenuous life" was a central factor in framing the organization as part of a policy emphasizing "American male virtues."[38]

A subtle thug in the home who keeps his wife on the defensive and always agrees with her self-deprecation ("You have to learn to control yourself better"), a man incapable of complaint or of the thought of failure, a good soldier who submits unquestioningly to the ordeals his superiors put him through without admitting his dependency on others, Hank Quenton is as much an ideal American for Kennedy's era as he is a misfit in Wilhelm's world.[39] Even the uncertainty over whether he might lose his stoicism and "erupt" is a feature of cold war masculinity: the era's machismo depended to a great extent on the threat of a no-more-Mister-Nice-Guy moment, when the formerly patient and accommodating man is pushed beyond his limit and goes on a rampage: R. W. Connell has observed that "loss of control at the frontier is a recurring theme in the history of empires, and is closely connected with the making of masculine exemplars."[40] Connie, however, as a woman who survives the physical ordeals of the training base and whose emotional lability, mental flexibility, and anti-authoritarian streak are among her strengths, is inconceivable in the Kennedy worldview.

The Limits Of Expert Wisdom

The utopianism evident in the story's inversion of its era's gender ideals is complemented by another striking divergence from the realities of 1963, one that requires an intense suspension of disbelief. This factor is the role of "the psychologists," led by Zorin, as arbiters of value. The fairy-tale form requires a Prince Charming or a Merlin to anoint the hero; but for such a character to be a psychologist and a man and an agent of the State in a story that has hitherto encouraged skepticism of authority stretches the story's credibility and imposes limits upon my celebration of its feminist aspects. Although liberal feminism has a successful tradition of making appeals to male psychologists — Friedan's use of Maslow and Bettelheim to discuss human potential is effective and unexceptionable[41] — Zorin, as the ultimate authority who has the final word on the story's value-system, is something different.

Zorin's role in the story is to some extent simply another inversion of the 1963 status quo. Just as the ideals of cold war masculinity would in fact have endorsed Hank's personality rather than Connie's as ideal for the frontier, a psychologist of the time, confronted with a couple at odds over the appropriateness of each partner's behavior, would have sided with the husband. Women were pathologized in far more one-sided conflicts, as Coontz notes:

> Psychiatrists in the 1950s, following Helene Deutsch, "regarded the battered woman as a masochist who provoked her husband into beating her." . . . Mrs. K came to the [Family Service] Association because her husband was an alcoholic who abused her both physically and sexually . . . [but ultimately the Associa-

tion's] counselors . . . decided they had found a deeper difficulty: Mrs. K needed therapy to "bring out some of her anxiety about sex activities."[42]

Within the science fiction field, accounts of marital conflicts more realistic than Hank and Connie's were being written. Around the time *No Light in the Window* was published, Philip K. Dick—who, like Heinlein, had written a few novels with well-rounded female characters in earlier years—was composing his rollicking farce, *Clans of the Alphane Moon.* This novel's resolution features the protagonist's discovery that his anxieties about his mental health have been unfounded, and that it's his domineering wife who suffers a debilitating neurosis, a symptom of which had been her insistence that he was an underachiever who could be earning more money by fulfilling his potential: "My continual pressing of you regarding your income—that was certainly due to my depression, my delusional sense that everything had gone wrong, that something *had* to be done or we were doomed."[43] Her realization that *she's* the mentally ill partner saves their marriage.

It is difficult to avoid a flip tone in recounting such a preposterous and self-serving plot device, but the humor in it is black indeed. For, although Dick's novel must be read as satire, it was inspired by fact: in mid-1963, the increasingly paranoid Phil Dick had decided that his third wife was "a pseudo-demonic creature, the destructive feminine principle of the world"[44] and begun uncontrollably filling himself with amphetamines and antidepressants. Naturally, given the temper of the times, Dick's physician noted his marital problems and diagnosed Mrs. Dick with bipolar depression. Dr. A., with the local sheriff, had her committed for three weeks to a psychiatric hospital, where an attending physician recorded the observation: "Mr. Dick is unable to control his wife."[45] Upon her release, Phil forced Anne to spend three months taking Stelazine, an antipsychotic drug that he enjoyed but that can have permanent deleterious effects if administered to mentally healthy patients. A passage in Coontz's *The Way We Really Were* establishes that Dr. A.'s attitudes were not unique among physicians:

> Women who could not walk the line between nurturing motherhood and castrating "momism," or who had trouble adjusting to creative homemaking, were labeled neurotic, perverted, or schizophrenic. A recent study of hospitalized "schizophrenic" women in the San Francisco Bay Area during the 1950s concludes that institutionalization and sometimes electric shock treatments were used to force women to accept their domestic roles and their husbands' dictates.[46]

Anne Dick's experience illustrates that such practices persisted after the 1950s officially ended.

Given the realities of 1963, then, the use of Zorin as an authority who validates Connie is, on the one hand, just another aspect of the story's utopian reversal of conditions in the United States; on the other hand, it is a more superficial reversal than the story's acceptance of Connie's competence and condemnation of Hank's brand of masculinity. Whereas the story in celebrating Connie's emotional style and professional competence depicts a desirable state of affairs, the 1950s mindset that revered expert wisdom remains unchallenged, as does the assumption that agents of the State can serve as paternalistic arbiters of what's best.[47] Connie and Hank's individual psychologies and personal interactions are subjected to a more searching critique than is the institution in which they're enmeshed. Moreover, Connie is, in a strange way, domesticated; her protests against the authorities and against Hank's submission to what he thinks they want are no longer valid; indeed, she does not speak again after Zorin completes his Rhadamanthian judgment on who will go into space and who will remain earthbound. Even before she falls silent, Zorin minimizes her tendency to bridle at the unjust exercise of authority: "while conditions may disturb you, you can accept them with good humor once you've made your gesture of rebellion." (Wilhelm, 105). Hochschild's insights as to how the feelings of low-status people are treated still apply: whereas Hank regarded her feelings as a failure of rational control, Zorin sees her criticism of his methods as "rational but unimportant." Having survived her ordeal, then, Connie discovers that she is just what her superiors need and can set about working for The Man, like most of the powerful women who appeared in the science fiction of earlier years.[48]

But Connie's silence, and the somber tone that I have noted in the story's ending, suggest that having experienced a hazing of the sort favored by the Kennedy administration does not have the effect on Connie that such ordeals are meant to have in our world. R. W. Connell has observed that the presence of "a lot of stress, a lot of negative feedback, and a sense of being selected as an elite" are used in "a vigorous induction process designed to press [men] into an institutional mould."[49] The successful implementation of such a process would create a sense of shared purpose and solidarity among the inductees. "No Light in the Window," by contrast, concludes with a feeling of extreme isolation. Not only is Connie's separation from her husband emphasized, the image of "a silently moving speck among the myriad star points" is associated with her having received the news that he'd be left behind — which Zorin gave her just as she was about to hug that patronizing psychologist. While this sense of isolation could be interpreted as the story's internalization of its era's antifeminist dogma that "independence equaled loneliness," it also has a more critical connotation: a system that reduces human beings to servants of a technological agenda informs the space program and Zorin's authority over its participants and is inadequate for human happiness. This suggestion that there is something very wrong with the system will be explored in horrific detail in Wilhelm's more radical works of the late sixties.

Wilhelm's critique of masculine norms will also develop. That critique seems to have begun in 1960 with Cele Goldsmith's publication of Wilhelm's non-sf story, "When the Moon Was Red": the tale features a volatile domineering adulterous father who scapegoats his wife for his own faults and treats his young son as an extension of himself.[50] It continues in 1962's "The Last Days of the Captain," in which the title character is taught the limits of stoical and impersonal rationalism by a civilian woman. Her taunt, "What happened to that perfect Control training, Captain?" is a question one can imagine being addressed to Hank Quenton, were he to erupt.[51] In each story, the tactics of domination perpetrated by the overbearing male authority are defeated.

The years 1968–1971 saw the publication of twenty-one Kate Wilhelm stories, many of which address the problems of autonomous women in isolation or depict the pathologies of masculinity that were encouraged and exploited by the U.S. military-industrial complex in the 1960s and beyond.[52] In addition to stories with military or governmental settings, there are "Baby, You Were Great" (1967) about the treatment of women in the entertainment media; "How Many Miles to Babylon?" depicting the struggles of a battered wife; "The Most Beautiful Woman in the World," addressing aging and body image; "The Downstairs Room" (1968), in which a beleaguered housewife loses her sense of reality; and "The Infinity Box" (1971), which can be read as an extension of "Baby, You Were Great"'s indictment of men's exercising technological control over women's bodies.

The most harrowing of these stories include those that explore the bleak and fragmented inner lives of men who work for ruthless commercial or governmental enterprises. The intervention of a benignant psychologist who can validate the autonomous women or recognize and condemn what's wrong with the conformist men is no longer conceivable. The protagonist of "Windsong" (1968), a government employee in anguish over having been unable to control or understand his brilliant and independent childhood sweetheart, determines that the Department of Defense must remove her brain and use it to pilot their unprecedentedly powerful new killing machine; his DoD-employed psychiatrist facilitates his reaching this conclusion, although the doctor is grieved once the transplant is complete.[53] Dr. Doyle in "The Chosen" (1970) — a story in which a husband is punished for nonconformity while his wife proves to be well-adjusted to her world — institutionalizes those citizens in whom he finds an unconscious aversion to the suffocating overpopulation of his near-future Earth.[54]

Most of these stories illustrate the values expressed in Connie Quenton's "What right have they to take people and manipulate them like so many animated puppets? They don't own my soul." (Wilhelm, 99). Agents of the state or corporation in such stories are trapped by the impulse to own the souls, perceptions, actions, and lives of others. Wilhelm creates a gallery of male characters who cause immense damage while adhering to ideals of masculinity that require them to control emotions, nature, and women, and to erupt sadistically when their fantasies of what women should be are challenged. Like the New Frontiersmen of the Kennedy administration, these men simultaneously believe in their right to dominate others and in submission to ordeals developed by their superiors. Their better impulses are vanquished by a social order that threatens them with anguish and isolation for not maintaining their position in the hierarchy, a position from which they may dominate women but are in turn subjugated by the social elites who benefit from maintaining the status quo.

The use of traditionally masculine qualities as tools of domination does not appear in Wilhelm's work as part of an essentialist worldview: Susan Wood has pointed out that there are several nonauthoritarian men and a few cold or dominating women even in stories that highlight gender (*The Nevermore Affair*, "The Funeral").[55] Masculine attributes are not innate, but socially conditioned; and those institutions most in need of masculine overseers to dominate others naturally select for men possessed of such attributes. The women in these stories come with a wide range of personalities, from the free-spirited poet in "Windsong," whose autonomy so frustrated that story's protagonist, to the aged character in "The Most Beautiful Woman in the World," who has completely internalized society's message that her worth depends on her physical appearance, to the victorious and resilient wife of "The Infinity Box." While anatomizing the traits that prompt men to dominate, Wilhelm never falls into the trap of suggesting that it takes a certain personality-type on the part of women for them to suffer domination. No victims are blamed.

Recovering Wilhelm

Given the quality and intensity of Wilhelm's explorations of gender-related themes, one naturally wonders why that aspect of her work did not begin receiving attention so early and often as that of her near contemporaries in feminist SF. One likely reason is the attention to male subjectivity that I have made a focus of this essay. U.S. feminists of thirty years ago understandably had other priorities than reading more tales of beleaguered organization men, even for the purpose of understanding the psyches of men reified by the State; to some, even raising the issue smacked of an attempt to minimize women's distinct and catastrophic suffering under patriarchy. This was the era that elicited Robin Morgan's famous lines:

> Oppression is something that one group of people commits against another group specifically because of a "threatening" characteristic shared by the latter group — skin color or sex or age, etc. The oppressors are indeed FUCKED UP by being masters (racism hurts whites, sexual stereotypes are harmful to men) but those masters are not OPPRESSED.[56]

The passage, following an assertion that men are not oppressed by sexism, seems to end by insisting that men — although harmed and fucked up — are not oppressed period.

On the one hand, Morgan's formulation is compatible with Caroline New's recent claim that "the very practices which construct men's capacity to oppress women and interest in doing so, work by harming men."[57] But Morgan, and other radical feminists who traced all social ills to the institution of patriarchy, would recoil from New's argument that "men's agency is part of the explanation of women's oppression only in the context of a sex-gender system which also involves the oppression of men."[58] Like New, Wilhelm would probably

> find the ecofeminist idea that the military-industrial complex is in men's interests extraordinary, given the brutalization, abuse, wounding, and killing of men in war. This idea rests on a deficit model of human health and thriving, which assumes that, since to be oppressed is bad for women, to be the agents of oppression must be good for men.[59]

Such assertions may seem inoffensive today, but could not easily find a sympathetic ear thirty years ago. In their urgent need to overturn the gynocidal discourse of earlier years, radical feminists tended to dismiss arguments that focused upon how men were constricted and subjugated by the practices, styles, and attitudes of traditional masculinity.[60]

Feminists in the 1970s were engaged in an urgent struggle to alter legislation and popular consciousness so that women's oppression could be recognized and fought. They had to promote and institutionalize the view that rape was a crime of violence for which its victims were not responsible; they had to invent the terms "sexual harassment" and "sex discrimination" and encode them into the legal and popular discourse; they had to find strategies for asserting control over their own health and bodily integrity. Any analysis of society that included talk of male subjectivity smacked unpleasantly of the widespread attitude that male subjectivity was the only subjectivity; any talk of the suffering undergone by men had unpleasant associations with Norman Mailer's claim that men were *more* exploited than women:

> men have to work through their lives; just being a man they have to stand up in all the situations where a woman can lie down. Just on the simplest level, where a woman can cry, a man has to stand. And for that reason, men are often used more completely than women. They have more rights and powers, and also they are used more.[61]

Mailer, writing of his endless, anguished, unrewarded struggle to be sure that he was a man, left little doubt as to whom he was struggling against. Hence the suspicion that any arguments about the conflicts in men's inner lives could degenerate into tales of male self-pity that drew attention away from political struggles to spotlight and obliterate sources of female suffering. In 1980, Deidre English, implicitly acknowledging that the point had to be argued, wrote, "Whether we love men or hate them, we — as feminists — have no task more necessary than understanding them." In fact, however, a more urgent task had been to *stop* them; it is only in the past twenty years that scholars and activists have begun to make headway in forging a profeminist discipline of masculinity studies.

Further interesting evidence that Wilhelm was at odds with the feminist discourse of the mid-1970s appears in that milestone of feminist SF criticism, the 1975 Symposium on Women in Science Fiction. Samuel Delany here gives prescriptions for creating strong, believable female characters, one requirement of which is that

> women characters must have central-to-the-plot, strong, developing, positive relationships with other women characters. The commercial/art novel would be impossible without such relationships between men: from Ishmael and Quee-

queg . . . to Huck and Jim . . . to Nick and Gatsby. . . . I would pause here to
state . . . that any novel that does *not*, in this day and age, have a strong, central,
positive relationship between women can be dismissed as sexist (no matter the
sex of the author) from the start.[62]

It may be tempting to dismiss such a constricting pronouncement: De-
lany's list of examples suggests that he's unthinkingly paying tribute to
Leslie Fiedler; Nick Carraway's relationship with Jay Gatsby is not terribly
positive; and there are many counterexamples that could support D. H.
Lawrence's characterization of the American novelistic hero as isolated:
Wise Blood, A Hell of a Woman, Invisible Man.[63]

Nevertheless, Delany's prescription concerning women characters is of
interest because it came at a time when alliances among women were
starting to be celebrated in fiction. Excitement about the possibilities of
community created by second-wave feminism was generating many novels
of female community, and not only in the science fiction medium. That is
the context in which Wilhelm was producing her hard-boiled tales of
women in isolation whose attempts at connecting with others usually failed
(the first Wilhelm heroine I have found who has female supporters appears
in 1979's *Juniper Time*). Zorin observes that Connie has many friends, but
Wilhelm does not show her interacting positively with them; indeed, many
Wilhelm heroines have very conflicted relations with their mothers, sisters,
and female friends.

It seems as though Delany views an absence of "strong, developing, positive relationships" as dishonest. But plenty of women's lives were not filled
with community and positive interactions. Literature that models societal
problems without showing solutions to them is not an endorsement of in-
action in the face of those problems: Arthur Miller does not think the suicide of salesmen desirable or inevitable. Similarly, to create a canon of
work with female hard-boiled isolates rather than one with female Huck-
and-Jim homosocial bonds need not be sexist. Shirley Jackson created such
a canon in the 1950s; and Tony Tanner has written of Brontë's Lucy Snowe,
"If she thinks monadically instead of socially that is because that is the situation which, as an isolated female outsider, she finds herself in."[64]

In discussing Wilhelm's relationship to the symposium, one cannot
avoid mentioning her revelation that, at the time of its occurrence, she herself didn't quite grasp what was meant by "feminism." She characterizes
"the problems of women's lib" as "very serious, but secondary" to human
rights, anti-poverty efforts, and environmental justice, and she decries the
essentialist view that "women are more noble, more intelligent, more en-

lightened." After having thrown down that gauntlet, Wilhelm goes on to explain that she's having difficulty getting *The Clewiston Test* published because its heroine stands up to her husband after he's raped her and adds, "But this is not a feminist book, it is not a polemic for anything except the right to be an individual human being with certain inherent needs, the most important of which is to be free to choose."[65] In response, Joanna Russ rolls her eyes with such vigor that their angular momentum measurably affects the Earth's orbit and points out that Wilhelm is taking a feminist stand whether she acknowledges it or not: "It's funny, really: having disclaimed feminism, you go on to *define* it."[66]

The conversation with Russ, Delany, and others probably helped to give Wilhelm a better sense of the fact that what she'd been doing in her fiction was consistent with the agenda of writers and activists who accepted the feminist label. In the 1993 edition of the symposium, she takes aggressive stands on issues of gender and gives some indication of how her consciousness was raised a few years after the original exchange. Three years later, *The Clewiston Test* was shortlisted for a retrospective James Tiptree, Jr. Memorial Award—an accolade given to SF that "explores or expands our understanding of gender"[67]—on the grounds that it "shows that personal autonomy and sexual heroism are the same thing" and by virtue of its "respectful and intelligent description of a woman who practices science."[68]

Thus, Wilhelm's work seems to have gained recognition for its importance to feminist SF in spite of her early resistance to that movement, and her pessimism with regard to the possibilities of community, and her interest in male subjectivity, which made the radical nature of her work's gender critique difficult to recognize when it was first written. Four decades after the publication of "No Light in the Window," critics have a wide array of tools for appreciating Wilhelm's early fiction, with its analyses of how cold war culture and masculine ideals fostered lethal distortions of personality.

In fact, one of the story's central premises has been addressed by social scientists: in 1991, a study at Concordia University[69] suggested that, when falsely informed that their emotional response to distressing stimuli was unusually negative (subjects had to fill out questionnaires about their feelings after reading sad stories and were then told that nobody else was as grieved as they), masculine test subjects adjusted their emotional responses to conform better to what they thought was expected of them while feminine subjects brooded over what was wrong with them. These results not only recall Hank's and Connie's personalities but demonstrate that it is now possible to make claims about masculine conformism and emotional dishonesty that were barely conceivable forty years ago, when few coherent critiques of masculinity could be heard.

The outdated aspects of "No Light in the Window," then, cannot obscure the continued relevance of the story inasmuch as it favors Connie's emotional honesty and her "ability to reason and see justice" over Hank's "brittle" perfectionist domination in the service of authority. People in the United States and elsewhere are still being conditioned by rigorous military cultures to believe that their precarious material and psychic safety require controlling and obliterating an autonomous Other. "No Light in the Window" encourages readers to imagine a system in which Hank Quenton, who has succumbed to a version of that conditioning, is seen as pathological, while Connie's every "gesture of rebellion" testifies to her stability. Its critique of masculine domination is not so bleak and scathing as that in "Baby, You Were Great" or "Windsong," but it manifests a stubborn dissatisfaction with the social and political order of 1963 America, presenting a humble protest in favor of equality, authenticity, and autonomy.

NOTES

1. Susan Wood, "Kate Wilhelm is a Writer," *Starship* 17, no. 4 (Fall 1980): 9.

2. Caroline New, "Oppressed and Oppressors? The Systematic Mistreatment of Men," *Sociology* 35, no. 3 (2001): 739.

3. The current MLA bibliography lists 8 articles on Wilhelm, contrasting with 28 on Tiptree, 59 on Russ, and 348 on Le Guin.

4. Isaac Asimov, "Profession," *Astounding Science Fiction* (July 1957).

5. Isaac Asimov, "The Mule," *Astounding Science Fiction* (November–December 1945).

6. H. Beam Piper, "Omnilingual," *Astounding Science Fiction* (February 1957).

7. Kit Reed, "To Lift a Ship," *The Magazine of Fantasy and Science Fiction* (April 1962).

8. Brett Harvey, *The Fifties: A Women's Oral History* (New York: HarperCollins, 1993), xviii.

9. See Brian McHale, "Review of *Monsters, Mushroom Clouds, and the Cold War*" and Andrew Hoberek, "Sociology as Science Fiction," *Paradoxa* 18 (2003): 366–372, 81–98.

10. Flora Davis, *Moving the Mountain: The Women's Movement in America Since 1960* (New York: Simon & Schuster, 1991), 45.

11. Ruth Rosen, *The World Split Open: How the Modern Women's Movement Changed America* (New York: Viking Penguin, 2000), 8.

12. Arthur M. Schlesinger Jr., "The Crisis of American Masculinity." (November 1958), in *The Politics of Hope* (Cambridge, Mass.: Riverside, 1962), 238.

13. Lena Levine and David Loth, *The Emotional Sex: Why Women Are the Way They Are Today* (New York: Morrow, 1964), 10.

14. Stephanie Coontz, *The Way We Never Were: American Families and the Nostalgia Trap* (New York, BasicBooks, 1992), 32.

15. Rosen, *The World Split Open*, 26–27.

16. Ibid., 67.

17. Ann Douglas, "Periodizing the American Century: Modernism, Post-modernism, and Postcolonialism in the Cold War Context," *Modernism/Modernity* 5, no. 3 (1998): 86.

18. Donald Westlake,"Don't Call Me, I'll Call You," 1961. Reprinted in *Mystery Scene* 78 (Winter 2003): 33–34.

19. Chandler Davis, "Critique and Notes — 1949," Reprinted on Ray Davis, ed. Pseudopodium: Repress, <http://www.pseudopodium.org/repress/chandler-davis/critique-1949.html>.

20. Samuel R. Delany, *Silent Interviews: On Language, Race, Sex, Science Fiction, and Some Comics* (Hanover, N.H.: Wesleyan University Press, 1994), 167.

21. Unknown blurbist on Margaret St. Clair, *Signs of the Labrys* (New York: Bantam, 1963), back cover.

22. H. Bruce Franklin, *Robert A. Heinlein: America as Science Fiction* (New York: Oxford University Press, 1980), 142–144.

23. Arlie Russell Hochschild, *The Managed Heart: Commercialization of Human Feeling* (Berkeley and Los Angeles: University of California Press, 1983), 172–173.

24. Ibid., 165.

25. See Aafke Komter, "Hidden Power in Marriage," *Gender and Society* 13, no. 2 (1989): 187–216.

26. Wood, "Kate Wilhelm is a Writer," 9.

27. K. A. Cuordileone, "'Politics in an Age of Anxiety': Cold War Political Culture and the Crisis in American Masculinity, 1949–1960," *Journal of American History* 87, no. 2 (Fall 2000): 516.

28. Arthur M. Schlesinger Jr., *The Vital Center: Our Purposes and Perils on the Tightrope of American Liberalism* (Boston: Houghton Mifflin, 1949), 35–50, 159–161.

29. Schlesinger, "The Crisis of American Masculinity," 241, 246.

30. Schlesinger, "The New Mood in Politics" (January 1960), in *The Politics of Hope* (Cambridge, Mass.: Riverside, 1962) 86.

31. Cuordileone, "Politics in an Age of Anxiety": 538.

32. Robert D. Dean, "Masculinity as Ideology: John F. Kennedy and the Domestic Politics of Foreign Policy," *Diplomatic History* 22, no. 1 (Winter 1998): 29.

33. Ibid., 30.

34. Ibid., 42

35. John F. Kennedy, Freedom of Communications: Final Report on the Committee of Commerce, United States Senate: Part 1, The Speeches, Remarks, Pres Conferences, and Statements of Senator John F. Kennedy, August 1 through November 7, 1960 (Washington, D.C., 1961): 43, 810.

36. Dean, "Masculinity as Ideology," 45.

37. Ibid., 32.

38. Ibid., 56, 62.

39. It says much about the gender politics of the era that Hank is also an ideal American for its counterculture. Stoicism of the sort that Hank aspires to, and

chides his wife for lacking, was of course a hallmark of the hipsters and Beats, of whom Joyce Johnson long ago noted that "[t]hey seemed to believe they had a mission in life, from which they could easily be deflected by being exposed to too much emotion" (quoted in Rosen, *The World Split Open* 50).

40. R. W. Connell, *Masculinities* (Berkeley and Los Angeles: University of California Press, 1995), 187.

41. Betty Friedan, *The Feminine Mystique* (New York: Dell, [1963] 1984), 306, 309, 316–329.

42. Coontz, *The Way We Never Were*, 35.

43. Philip K. Dick, *Clans of the Alphane Moon* (1964); (New York, Carroll & Graf, 1988), 244.

44. Lawrence Sutin, *Divine Invasions: A Life of Philip K. Dick* (1989) (New York: Citadel, 1991), 122.

45. Ibid., 124.

46. Coontz, *The Way We Never Were*, 32.

47. Ibid.

48. Delany, in *Silent Interviews*, summarizing Luise White's insight: "active, vigorous women characters [in SF] invariably worked either directly for the state, or for some male-run institution that controlled so much power and revenue, it might as well be the state itself" 167.

49. Connell, *Masculinities*, 170.

50. Kate Wilhelm, "When the Moon Was Red" (1960), in *The Downstairs Room and Other Speculative Fiction* (New York: Doubleday, 1968).

51. Kate Wilhelm, "The Last Days of the Captain" (1962), in *The Mile-Long Spaceship* (New York: Berkley, 1963).

52. In 1968, Wilhelm also wrote "The Village," a prophetic parable of sexual violence and mass murder on the part of U.S. forces in Vietnam; no one would publish it until 1973. See H. Bruce Franklin, *Vietnam and Other American Fantasies* (Amherst: University of Massachusetts Press, 2000), 162.

53. Kate Wilhelm, "Windsong," in *The Downstairs Room and Other Speculative Fiction* (New York: Doubleday, 1968).

54. Kate Wilhelm, "The Chosen," in *Orbi,t* 6 ed. Damon Knight (New York: Putman, 1970).

55. Wood, "Kate Wilhelm is a Writer," 13.

56. Robin Morgan, "Goodbye to All That" (1970); reprinted in *Going Too Far: The Personal Chronicle of a Feminist* (New York: Vintage, 1978).

57. New, "Oppressed and Oppressors?" 730.

58. Ibid., 734.

59. Caroline New, "Man Bad, Woman Good? Essentialisms and Ecofeminisms," *New Left Review* 219 (March–April 1996): 93.

60. New quotes feminist authors who see claims of oppressive masculinities as a strategy on men's part for "donning the mantle of victimhood while maintaining hegemony" ("Oppressed and Oppressors," 743). One such author holds up to ridicule the claims that men suffer because they are drafted into wars, made to repress their emotions, and encouraged to tie their sense of self-worth to their earning power.

61. Norman Mailer. *The Presidential Papers* (New York: Putnam, 1963), 144.

62. In Jeffrey D. Smith, ed., "Symposium: Women in Science Fiction," *Khatru* 3 & 4 (1975); expanded ed., ed. Jeanne Gomoll (May 1993): 32.

63. Ibid., 32.

64. Tony Tanner, introduction to *Villette* by Charloltte Brontë (London: Penguin, 1979), 49.

65. In Smith, "Symposium," 72.

66. "Symposium," 89.

67. "The James Tiptree, Jr. Award," <http://www.tiptree.org> (accessed July 3, 2004).

68. Sherry Coldsmith and Eleanor Arnason, in "The Retrospective James Tiptree, Jr. Award: Short List," <http://www.tiptree.org/retro/short.html> (accessed July 3, 2004).

69. Michael Conway, Roberto DiFazio, and Francois Bonneville, "Sex, Sex Roles, and Response Styles for Negative Affect: Selectivity in a Free Recall Task," *Sex Roles* 25, nos. 11–12 (1991): 687–700.

۵ 5

The Heat Death of the Universe

Pamela Zoline

First published in New Worlds, *July 1967*

(1) Ontology
That branch of metaphysics which concerns itself with the problems of the nature of existence or being.

(2) Imagine a pale blue morning sky, almost green, with clouds only at the rims. The earth rolls and the sun appears to mount, mountains erode, fruits decay, the Foraminifera adds another chamber to its shell, babies' fingernails grow as does the hair of the dead in their graves, and in egg timers the sands fall and the eggs cook on.

(3) Sarah Boyle thinks of her nose as too large, though several men have cherished it. The nose is generous and performs a well-calculated geometric curve, at the arch of which the skin is drawn very tight and a faint whiteness of bone can be seen showing through, it has much the same architectural tension and sense of mathematical calculation as the day after Thanksgiving breastbone on the carcass of a turkey; her maiden name was Sloss, mixed German, English and Irish descent; in grade school she was very bad at playing softball and, besides being chosen last for the team, was always made to play centre field, no one could ever hit to centre field; she loves music best of all the arts, and of music, Bach, J.S; she lives in California, though she grew up in Boston and Toledo.

(4) Breakfast Time at the Boyles' House on La Florida Street, Alameda, California, The Children Demand Sugar Frosted Flakes. With some reluctance Sarah Boyle dishes out Sugar Frosted Flakes to her children, already hearing the decay set in upon the little white milk teeth, the bony whine of the dentist's drill. The dentist is a short, gentle man with a moustache who sometimes reminds Sarah of an uncle who lives in Ohio. One bowl per child.

(5) If one can imagine it considered as an abstract object, by members of a totally separate culture, one can see that the cereal box might seem a beautiful thing. The solid rectangle is neatly joined and classical in proportions, on it are squandered wealths of richest colours, virgin blues, crimsons, dense ochres, precious pigments once reserved for sacred paintings and as cosmetics for the blind faces of marble gods. Giant size. Net Weight 16 ounces, 250 grams. "They're tigeriffic!" says Tony the Tiger. The box blatts promises. Energy, Nature's Own Goodness, an endless pubescence. On its back is a mask of William Shakespeare to be cut out, folded, worn by thousands of tiny Shakespeares in Kansas City, Detroit, Tucson, San Diego, Tampa. He appears at once more kindly and somewhat more vacant than we are used to seeing him. Two or more of the children lay claim to the mask, but Sarah puts off that Solomon's decision until such time as the box is empty.

(6) A notice in orange flourishes states that a Surprise Gift is to be found somewhere in the packet, nestled amongst the golden flakes. So far it has not been unearthed, and the children request more cereal than they wish to eat, great yellow heaps of it, to hurry the discovery. Even so, at the end of the meal, some layers of flakes remain in the box and the Gift must still be among them.

(7) There is even a Special Offer of a secret membership, code and magic ring; these to be obtained by sending in the box top with 50 cents.

(8) Three offers on one cereal box. To Sarah Boyle this seems to be oversell. Perhaps something is terribly wrong with the cereal and it must be sold quickly, got off the shelves before the news breaks. Perhaps it causes a special, cruel cancer in little children. As Sarah Boyle collects the bowls printed with bunnies and baseball statistics, still slopping half full of milk and wilted flakes, she imagines *in her mind's eye* the headlines, "Nation's Small Fry Stricken, Fate's Finger Sugar Coated, Lethal Sweetness Socks Tots."

(9) Sarah Boyle is a vivacious and intelligent young wife and mother, educated at a fine Eastern college, proud of her growing family which keeps her busy and happy around the house.

(10) BIRTHDAY
Today is the birthday of one of the children. There will be a party in the late afternoon.

(11) CLEANING UP THE HOUSE. (ONE.)
Cleaning up the kitchen. Sarah Boyle puts the bowls, plates, glasses and silverware into the sink. She scrubs at the stickiness on the yellow-marbled formica table with a blue synthetic sponge, a special blue which we shall see again. There are marks of children's hands in various sizes printed with sugar and grime on all the table's surfaces. The marks catch the light, they appear and disappear according to the position of the observing eye. The floor sweepings include a triangular half of toast spread with grape jelly, bobby pins, a green Band-Aid, flakes, a doll's eye, dust, dog's hair and a button.

(12) Until we reach the statistically likely planet and begin to converse with whatever green-faced teleporting denizens thereof — considering only this shrunk and communication-ravaged world — can we any more postulate a separate culture? Viewing the metastasis of Western Culture it seems progressively less likely. Sarah Boyle imagines a whole world which has become like California, all topographical imperfections sanded away with the sweet-smelling burr of the plastic surgeon's cosmetic polisher, a world populace dieting, leisured, similar in pink and mauve hair and rhinestone shades. A land Cunt Pink and Avocado Green, brassiered and girdled by monstrous complexities of Super Highways, a California endless and unceasing, embracing and transforming the entire globe, California, California!

(13) INSERT ONE. ON ENTROPY.
ENTROPY: A quantity introduced in the first place to facilitate the calculation, and to give clear expressions to the results of thermodynamics. Changes of entropy can be calculated only for a reversible process, and may then be defined as the ratio of the amount of heat taken up to the absolute temperature at which the heat is absorbed. Entropy changes for actual irreversible processes are calculated by postulating equivalent theoretical reversible changes. The entropy of a system is a measure of its degree of disorder. The total entropy of any isolated system can never decrease in any change; it must either increase (irreversible process) or remain constant (reversible process). The total entropy of the Universe therefore is increasing, tending towards a maximum, corresponding to complete disorder of the particles in it (assuming that it may be regarded as an isolated system.) See *Heat Death of the Universe*.

(14) CLEANING UP THE HOUSE. (TWO.)
Washing the baby's diapers. Sarah Boyle writes notes to herself all over the house; a mazed wild script larded with arrows, diagrams, pictures, graffiti

on every available surface in a desperate/heroic attempt to index, record, bluff, invoke, order and placate. On the fluted and flowered white plastic lid of the diaper bin she has written in Blushing Pink Nitetime lipstick a phrase to ward off fumey ammoniac despair. "The nitrogen cycle is the vital round of organic and inorganic exchange on earth. The sweet breath of the Universe." On the wall by the washing machine are Yin and Yang signs, mandalas, and the words, "Many young wives feel trapped. It is a contemporary sociological phenomenon which may be explained in part by a gap between changing living patterns and the accommodation of social services to these patterns." Over the stove she had written "Help, Help, Help, Help, Help."

(15) Sometimes she numbers or letters the things in a room, writing the assigned character on each object. There are 819 separate movable objects in the living-room, counting books. Sometimes she labels objects with their names, or with false names, thus on her bureau the hair brush is labelled HAIR BRUSH, the cologne, COLOGNE, the hand cream, CAT. She is passionately fond of children's dictionaries, encyclopedias, ABCs and all reference books, transfixed and comforted at their simulacra of a complete listing and ordering.

(16) On the door of a bedroom are written two definitions from reference books. "GOD: An object of worship"; "HOMEOSTASIS: Maintenance of constancy of internal environment."

(17) Sarah Boyle washes the diapers, washes the linen, Oh Saint Veronica, changes the sheets on the baby's crib. She begins to put away some of the toys, stepping over and around the organizations of playthings which still seem inhabited. There are various vehicles, and articles of medicine, domesticity and war: whole zoos of stuffed animals, bruised and odorous with years of love; hundreds of small figures, plastic animals, cowboys, cars, spacemen, with which the children make sub and supra worlds in their play. One of Sarah's favourite toys is the Baba, the wooden Russian doll which, opened, reveals a smaller but otherwise identical doll which opens to reveal, etc., a lesson in infinity at least to the number of seven dolls.

(18) Sarah Boyle's mother has been dead for two years. Sarah Boyle thinks of music as the formal articulation of the passage of time, and of Bach as the most poignant rendering of this. Her eyes are sometimes the colour of the aforementioned kitchen sponge. Her hair is natural spaniel-brown; months

ago on an hysterical day she dyed it red, so now it is two-toned with a stripe in the middle, like the painted walls of slum buildings or old schools.

(19) INSERT TWO. THE HEAT DEATH OF THE UNIVERSE.
The second law of thermodynamics can be interpreted to mean that the ENTROPY of a closed system tends towards a maximum and that its available ENERGY tends towards a minimum. It has been held that the Universe constitutes a thermodynamically closed system, and if this were true it would mean that a time must finally come when the Universe "unwinds" itself, no energy being available for use. This state is referred to as the "heat death of the Universe." It is by no means certain, however, that the Universe can be considered as a closed system in this sense.

(20) Sarah Boyle pours out a Coke from the refrigerator and lights a cigarette. The coldness and sweetness of the thick brown liquid make her throat ache and her teeth sting briefly, sweet juice of my youth, her eyes glass with the carbonation, she thinks of the Heat Death of the Universe. A logarithmic of those late summer days, endless as the Irish serpent twisting through jewelled manuscripts forever, tail in mouth, the heat pressing, bloating, doing violence. The Los Angeles sky becomes so filled and bleached with detritus that it loses all colours and silvers like a mirror, reflecting back the fricasseeing earth. Everything becomes warmer and warmer, each particle of matter becoming more agitated, more excited until the bonds shatter, the glues fail, the deodorants lose their seals. She imagines the whole of New York City melting like a Dali into a great chocolate mass, a great soup, the Great Soup of New York.

(21) CLEANING UP THE HOUSE. (THREE.)
Beds made. Vacuuming the hall, a carpet of faded flowers, vines and leaves which endlessly wind and twist into each other in a fevered and permanent ecstasy. Suddenly the vacuum blows instead of sucks, spewing marbles, dolls' eyes, dust, crackers. An old trick. "Oh my god," says Sarah. The baby yells on cue for attention/changing/food. Sarah kicks the vacuum cleaner and it retches and begins working again.

(22) AT LUNCH ONLY ONE GLASS OF MILK IS SPILLED.
At lunch only one glass of milk is spilled.

(23) The plants need watering, Geranium, Hyacinth, Lavender, Avocado,

Cyclamen. Feed the fish, happy fish with china castles and mermaids in the bowl. The turtle looks more and more unwell and is probably dying.

(24) Sarah Boyle's blue eyes, how blue? Bluer far and of a different quality than the Nature metaphors which were both engine and fuel to so much of precedent literature. A fine, modern, acid, synthetic blue; the shiny cerulean of the skies on postcards sent from lush subtropics, the natives grinning ivory ambivalent grins in their dark faces; the promising fat, un- natural blue of the heavy tranquilizer capsule; the cool mean blue of that fake kitchen sponge; the deepest, most unbelievable azure of the tiled and mossless interiors of California swimming pools. The chemists in their kitchens cooked, cooled and distilled this blue from thousands of colorless and wonderfully constructed crystals, each one unique and nonpareil; and now that color, hisses, bubbles, burns in Sarah's eyes.

(25) Insert Three. On Light.
Light: Name given to the agency by means of which a viewed object influ- ences the observer's eyes. Consists of electromagnetic radiation within the wave-length range 4×10^{-5} cm to 7×10^{-5} cm approximately; variations in the wave-length produce different sensations in the eye, corresponding to different colors. See color vision.

(26) Light and Cleaning the Living Room.
All the objects (819) and surfaces in the living room are dusty, gray com- mon dust as though this were the den of a giant molting mouse. Suddenly quantities of waves or particles of very strong sunlight speed in through the window, and everything incandesces, multiple rainbows. Poised in what has become a solid cube of light, like an ancient insect trapped in amber, Sarah Boyle realizes that the dust is indeed the most beautiful stuff in the room, a manna for the eyes. Duchamp, that father of thought, has set with fixative some dust which fell on one of his sculptures, counting it as part of the work. "That way madness lies, says Sarah," says Sarah. The thought of ordering a household on Dada principles balloons again. All the rooms would fill up with objects, newspapers and magazines would compost, the potatoes in the rack, the canned green beans in the garbage pail would take new heart and come to life again, reaching out green shoots towards the sun. The plants would grow wild and wind into a jungle around the house, splitting plaster, tearing shingles, the garden would enter in at the door. The goldfish would die, the birds would die, we'd have them stuffed;

the dog would die from lack of care, and probably the children — all stuffed and sitting around the house, covered with dust.

(27) INSERT FOUR. DADA.
DADA (Fr., hobby-horse) was a nihilistic precursor of Surrealism, invented in Zurich during World War I, a product of hysteria and shock lasting from about 1915 to 1922. It was deliberately anti-art and anti-sense, intended to outrage and scandalize and its most characteristic production was the re-production of the *Mona Lisa* decorated with a moustache and the obscene caption LHOOQ (read: *elle a chaud au cul*) "by" Duchamp. Other mani-festations included Arp's collages of colored paper cut out at random and shuffled, ready-made objects such as the bottle drier and the bicycle wheel "signed" by Duchamp, Picabia's drawings of bits of machinery with in-congruous titles, incoherent poetry, a lecture given by 38 lecturers in uni-son, and an exhibition in Cologne in 1920, held in an annexe to a café lava-tory, at which a chopper was provided for spectators to smash the exhibits with — which they did.

(28) TIME-PIECES AND OTHER MEASURING DEVICES.
In the Boyle house there are four clocks; three watches (one a Mickey Mouse watch which does not work); two calendars and two engagement books; three rulers, a yardstick; a measuring cup; a set of red plastic mea-suring spoons which includes a tablespoon, a teaspoon, a one-half teaspoon, one-fourth teaspoon and one-eighth teaspoon; an egg timer; an oral ther-mometer and a rectal thermometer, a Boy Scout compass; a barometer in the shape of a house, in and out of which an old woman and an old man chase each other forever without fulfillment; a bathroom scale; an infant scale; a tape measure which can be pulled out of a stuffed felt strawberry; a wall on which the children's heights are marked; a metronome.

(29) Sarah Boyle finds a new line in her face after lunch while cleaning the bathroom. It is as yet barely visible, running from the midpoint of her fore-head to the bridge of her nose. By inward curling of her eyebrows she can etch it clearly as it will come to appear in the future. She marks another mark on the wall where she has drawn out a scoring area. FACE LINES AND OTHER INTIMATIONS OF MORTALITY, the heading says. There are thirty-two marks, counting this latest one.

(30) Sarah Boyle is a vivacious and witty young wife and mother, educated at a fine Eastern college, proud of her growing family which keeps her

happy and busy around the house, involved in many hobbies and community activities, and only occasionally given to obsessions concerning Time/Entropy/Chaos and Death.

(31) Sarah Boyle is never quite sure how many children she has.

(32) Sarah thinks from time to time; Sarah is occasionally visited with this thought; at times this thought comes upon Sarah, that there are things to be hoped for, accomplishments to be desired beyond the mere reproductions, mirror reproduction of one's kind. The babies. Lying in bed at night sometimes the memory of the act of birth, always the hue and texture of red plush theatre seats, washes up; the rending which always, at a certain intensity of pain, slipped into landscapes, the sweet breath of the sweating nurse. The wooden Russian doll has bright, perfectly round red spots on her cheeks, she splits in the centre to reveal a doll smaller but in all other respects identical with round bright red spots on her cheeks, etc.

(33) How fortunate for the species, Sarah muses or is mused, that children are as ingratiating as we know them. Otherwise they would soon be salted off for the leeches they are, and the race would extinguish itself in a fair sweet flowering, the last generations' massive achievement in the arts and pursuits of high civilization. The finest women would have their tubes tied off at the age of twelve, or perhaps refrain altogether from the Act of Love? All interests would be bent to a refining and perfecting of each febrile sense, each fluid hour, with no more cowardly investment in immortality via the patchy and too often disappointing vegetables of one's own womb.

(34) INSERT FIVE. LOVE.
LOVE: a typical sentiment involving fondness for, or attachment to, an object, the idea of which is emotionally colored whenever it arises in the mind, and capable, as Shand has pointed out, of evoking any one of a whole gamut of primary emotions, according to the situation in which the object is placed, or represented; often, and by psychoanalysts always, used in the sense of *sex-love* or even *lust* (q.v.)

(35) Sarah Boyle has at times felt a unity with her body, at other times a complete separation. The mind/body duality considered. The time/space duality considered. The male/female duality considered. The matter/energy duality considered. Sometimes, at extremes, her Body seems to her an animal on a leash, taken for walks in the park by her Mind. The lamp posts

of experience. Her arms are lightly freckled and when she gets very tired the places under her eyes become violet.

(36) Housework is never completed, the chaos always lurks ready to encroach on any area left unweeded, a jungle filled with dirty pans and the roaring giant stuffed toy animals suddenly turned savage. Terrible glass eyes.

(37) SHOPPING FOR THE BIRTHDAY CAKE.
Shopping in the supermarket with the baby in front of the cart and a larger child holding on. The light from the ice-cube-tray-shaped fluorescent lights is mixed blue and pink and brighter, colder, and cheaper than daylight. The doors swing open just as you reach out your hand for them, Tantalus, moving with a ghastly quiet swing. Hot dogs for the party. Potato chips, gum drops, a paper tablecloth with birthday designs, hot dog buns, catsup, mustard, picalilli, balloons, instant coffee Continental style, dog food, frozen peas, ice cream, frozen lima beans, frozen broccoli in butter sauce, paper birthday hats, paper napkins in three colors, a box of Sugar Frosted Flakes with a Wolfgang Amadeus Mozart mask on the back, bread, pizza mix. The notes of a just-graspable music filter through the giant store, for the most part by-passing the brain and acting directly on the liver, blood and lymph. The air is delicately scented with aluminum. Half and half cream, tea bags, bacon, sandwich meat, strawberry jam. Sarah is in front of the shelves of cleaning products now, and the baby is beginning to whine. Around her are whole libraries of objects, offering themselves. Some of that same old hysteria that had incarnadined her hair rises up again, and she does not refuse it. There is one moment when she can choose direction, like standing on a chalk-drawn X, a hot cross bun, and she does not choose calm and measure. Sarah Boyle begins to pick out, methodically, deliberately and with a careful ecstasy, one of every cleaning product which the store sells. Window Cleaner, Glass Cleaner, Brass Polish, Silver Polish, Steel Wool, eighteen different brands of Detergent, Disinfectant, Toilet Cleanser, Water Softener, Fabric Softener, Drain Cleanser, Spot Remover, Floor Wax, Furniture Wax, Car Wax, Carpet Shampoo, Dog Shampoo, Shampoo for people with dry, oily and normal hair, for people with dandruff, for people with grey hair. Tooth Paste, Tooth Powder, Denture Cleaner, Deodorants, Antiperspirants, Antiseptics, Soaps, Cleansers, Abrasives, Oven Cleansers, Makeup Removers. When the same products appear in different sizes Sarah takes one of each size. For some products she accumulates whole little families of containers: a giant Father bottle of shampoo, a Mother bottle, an Older Sister bottle just smaller than the

Mother bottle, and a very tiny Baby Brother bottle. Sarah fills three shopping carts and has to have help wheeling them all down the aisles. At the checkout counter her laughter and hysteria keep threatening to overflow as the pale blonde clerk with no eyebrows like the *Mona Lisa* pretends normality and disinterest. The bill comes to $57.53 and Sarah has to write a check. Driving home, the baby strapped in the drive-a-cot and the paper bags bulging in the back seat, she cries.

(38) BEFORE THE PARTY.
Mrs David Boyle, mother-in-law of Sarah Boyle, is coming to the party of her grandchild. She brings a toy, a yellow wooden duck on a string, made in Austria: the duck quacks as it is pulled along the floor. Sarah is filling paper cups with gum drops and chocolates, and Mrs David Boyle sits at the kitchen table and talks to her. She is talking about several things, she is talking about her garden which is flourishing except for a plague of rare black beetles, thought to have come from Hong Kong, which are undermining some of the most delicate growths at the roots, and feasting on the leaves of other plants. She is talking about a sale of household linens which she plans to attend on the following Tuesday. She is talking about her neighbor who has cancer and is wasting away. The neighbor is a Catholic woman who had never had a day's illness in her life until the cancer struck, and now she is, apparently, failing with dizzying speed. The doctor says her body's chaos, chaos, cells running wild all over, says Mrs David Boyle. When I visited her she hardly *knew* me, can hardly *speak*, can't keep herself *clean*, says Mrs David Boyle.

(39) Sometimes Sarah can hardly remember how many cute chubby little children she has.

(40) When she used to stand out in centre field far away from the other players, she used to make up songs and sing them to herself.

(41) She thinks of the end of the world by ice.

(42) She thinks of the end of the world by water.

(43) She thinks of the end of the world by nuclear war.

(44) There must be more than this, Sarah Boyle thinks, from time to time. What could one do to justify one's passage? Or less ambitiously, to change,

even in the motion of the smallest mote, the course and circulation of the world? Sometimes Sarah's dreams are of heroic girth, a new symphony using laboratories of machinery and all invented instruments, at once giant in scope and intelligible to all, to heal the bloody breach; a series of paintings which would transfigure and astonish and calm the frenzied art world in its panting race; a new novel that would refurbish language. Sometimes she considers the mystical, the streaky and random, and it seems that one change, no matter how small, would be enough. Turtles are supposed to live for many years. To carve a name, date and perhaps a word of hope upon a turtle's shell, then set him free to wend the world, surely this one act might cancel out absurdity?

(45) Mrs David Boyle has a faint moustache, like Duchamp's *Mona Lisa*.

(46) THE BIRTHDAY PARTY.
Many children, dressed in pastels, sit around the long table. They are exhausted and overexcited from games fiercely played, some are flushed and wet, others unnaturally pale. This general agitation, and the paper party hats they wear, combine to make them appear a dinner party of debauched midgets. It is time for the cake. A huge chocolate cake in the shape of a rocket and launching pad and covered with blue and pink icing is carried in. In the hush the birthday child begins to cry. He stops crying, makes a wish and blows out the candles.

(47) One child will not eat hot dogs, ice cream or cake, and asks for cereal. Sarah pours him out a bowl of Sugar Frosted Flakes, and a moment later he chokes. Sarah pounds him on the back, and out spits a tiny green plastic snake with red glassy eyes, the Surprise Gift. All the children want it.

(48) AFTER THE PARTY THE CHILDREN ARE PUT TO BED.
Bath time. Observing the nakedness of children, pink and slippery as seals, squealing as seals, now the splashing, grunting and smacking of cherry flesh on raspberry flesh reverberate in the pearl tiled steamy cubicle. The nakedness of children is so much more absolute than that of the mature. No musky curling hair to indicate the target points, no knobbly clutch of plane and fat and curvature to ennoble this prince of beasts. All well-fed naked children appear edible, Sarah's teeth hum in her head with memory of bloody feastings, prehistory. Young humans appear too like the young of other species for smugness, and the comparison is not even in their

favor, they are much the most peeled and unsupple of those young. Such pinkness, such utter nuded pinkness; the orifices neatly incised, rimmed with a slightly deeper rose, the incessant demands for breast, time, milks of many sorts.

(49) INSERT SIX. WEINER ON ENTROPY.
In Gibb's Universe order is least probable, chaos most probable. But while the Universe as a whole, if indeed there is a whole Universe, tends to run down, there are local enclaves whose direction seems opposed to that of the Universe at large and in which there is a limited and temporary tendency for organization to increase. Life finds its home in some of these enclaves.

(50) Sarah Boyle imagines, in her mind's eye, cleaning, and ordering the great world, even the Universe. Filling the great spaces of Space with a marvellous sweet smelling, deep cleansing foam. Deodorizing rank caves and volcanoes. Scrubbing rocks.

(51) INSERT SEVEN. TURTLES.
Many different species of carnivorous Turtles live in the fresh waters of the tropical and temperate zones of various continents. Most northerly of the European Turtles (extending as far as Holland and Lithuania) is the European Pond Turtle (*Emys orbicularis*). It is from eight to ten inches long and may live a hundred years.

(52) CLEANING UP AFTER THE PARTY.
Sarah is cleaning up after the party. Gum drops and melted ice cream surge off paper plates, making holes in the paper tablecloth through the printed roses. A fly has died a splendid death in a pool of strawberry ice cream. Wet jelly beans stain all they touch, finally becoming themselves colorless, opaque white flocks of tame or sleeping maggots. Plastic favors mount half-eaten pieces of blue cake. Strewn about are thin strips of fortune papers from the Japanese poppers. Upon them are printed strangely assorted phrases selected by apparently unilingual Japanese. Crowds of delicate yellow people spending great chunks of their lives in producing these most ephemeral of objects, and inscribing thousands of fine papers with absurd and incomprehensible messages. "The very hairs of your head are all numbered," reads one. Most of the balloons have popped. Someone has planted a hot dog in the daffodil pot. A few of the helium balloons have escaped

their owners and now ride the ceiling. Another fortune paper reads, "Emperor's horses meet death worse, numbers, numbers."

(53) She is very tired, violet under the eyes, mauve beneath the eyes. Her uncle in Ohio used to get the same marks under his eyes. She goes to the kitchen to lay the table for tomorrow's breakfast, then she sees that in the turtle's bowl the turtle is floating, still, on the surface of the water. Sarah Boyle pokes at it with a pencil but it does not move. She stands for several minutes looking at the dead turtle on the surface of the water. She is crying again.

(54) She begins to cry. She goes to the refrigerator and takes out a carton of eggs, white eggs, extra large. She throws them one by one onto the kitchen floor which is patterned with strawberries in squares. They break beautifully. There is a Secret Society of Dentists, all moustached, with Special Code and Magic Rings. She begins to cry. She takes up three bunny dishes and throws them against the refrigerator; they shatter, and then the floor is covered with shards, chunks of partial bunnies, an ear, an eye here, a paw; Stockton, California, Acton, California, Chico, California, Redding, California Glen Ellen, California, Cadix, California, Angels Camp, California, Half Moon Bay. The total ENTROPY of the Universe therefore is increasing, tending towards a maximum, corresponding to complete disorder of the particles in it. She is crying, her mouth is open. She throws a jar of grape jelly and it smashes the window over the sink. It has been held that the Universe constitutes a thermodynamically closed system, and if this were true it would mean that a time must finally come when the Universe "unwinds" itself, no energy being available for use. This state is referred to as the "heat death of the Universe." Sarah Boyle begins to cry. She throws a jar of strawberry jam against the stove, enamel chips off and the stove begins to bleed. Bach had twenty children, how many children has Sarah Boyle? Her mouth is open. Her mouth is opening. She turns on the water and fills the sink with detergent. She writes on the kitchen wall, "William Shakespeare has Cancer and lives in California." She writes, "Sugar Frosted Flakes are the Food of the Gods." The water foams up in the sink, overflowing, bubbling onto the strawberry floor. She is about to begin to cry. Her mouth is opening. She is crying. She cries. How can one ever tell whether there are one or many fish? She begins to break glasses and dishes, she throws cups and cooking pots and jars of food, which shatter and break, and spread over the kitchen. The sand keeps falling, very quietly, in the egg timer. The old man and woman in the barometer never catch each other. She picks up eggs

and throws them into the air. She begins to cry. She opens her mouth. The eggs arch slowly through the kitchen, like a baseball, hit high against the spring sky, seen from far away. They go higher and higher in the stillness, hesitate at the zenith, then begin to fall away slowly, slowly, through the fine clear air.

A Space of Her Own: Pamela Zoline's "The Heat Death of the Universe"

Mary E. Papke

Pamela Zoline exploded onto the science fiction scene in 1967 with the publication of "The Heat Death of the Universe" in *New Worlds*, a well-known science fiction magazine then under the editorship of Michael Moorcock. An American living in London, Zoline was a twenty-six-year-old student interested in radical art and agit-prop who quickly became a part of Moorcock's Notting Hill artist circle. Moorcock had just then taken over the financially strapped magazine and had rallied a group of distinguished writers and critics to help him win support from the prestigious Arts Council to help finance publication. Along with many other artists, Zoline contributed illustrations for this very new *New Worlds*, reborn as a venue for highly experimental extrapolative fiction that decidedly pushed the envelope on science fiction expectations.

"Heat Death" was the first story Zoline had written since high school and appeared in the same month that one of her paintings was exhibited in the Tate Gallery.[1] While she would go on to write only a few more new-wave science fiction stories, published in *The New SF*, *Likely Stories*, and *Interzone*, all her works are noteworthy for their refusal of straightforward realistic narratives. In "Sheep" (1981) she ingeniously deconstructs particular Western cultural genres — the pastoral, the spy story, the western, and science fiction itself — exposing, as it were, the Wizard behind the curtain putting on a show to keep the audience entranced and docile.

Her works are highly experimental in form and content, intensely provocative, and deeply felt. Moorcock himself said that upon first reading "Heat Death" it struck him so forcibly that it made him cry.[2] In the twenty years following its first appearance, "Heat Death" was reprinted in at least nine science fiction anthologies.[3] Because of her limited output of fiction, however, Zoline remains relatively unknown and underappreciated by both general readers and literary critics.[4]

"Heat Death" might not at first reading strike the reader as science fiction at all. It contains no bug-eyed monsters, interplanetary flights, post-apocalyptic worlds, or technological marvels. It focuses not on outer space as much as it does inner space (notably, that of a woman) and the geography of the mundane (that of the home and the supermarket) rather than the fantastic or extraordinary. Like some of the work that Kate Wilhelm, Judith Merril, Marion Zimmer Bradley, and Anne McCaffrey produced around the same time, Zoline's story explores relational spaces, those shared by mothers and children, husbands and wives, domestic economy and the public sphere.[5]

The story does so by extrapolating from the everyday reality of a middle-class American wife and mother a nightmare vision of endless meaningless routine, demands, and expectations, focusing intently on issues of gender, the ethics of care, and the promise of the future. Within this domestic space, "aliens" appear in the guise of children, the mother-in-law, high and low cultural figures such as Shakespeare and Tony the Tiger, and even, in the most disturbing scenes for the female protagonist, the central character herself.

The majority of women characters in male-authored science fiction originally served as receptacles for male valor, scientific expertise, or, literally, for out-of-this-world sex.[6] As the essays in this volume argue, women writers early on broke from this science fiction expectation in which women characters were merely instrumental, played upon by superior male protagonists for the pleasure of the readership, the vast majority of it male.[7] For these women writers, women characters are active subjects and not simply objects of lust or passive helpmates, even though the extraordinary dilemmas they face are not always easily resolved nor their worlds redeemed. While the women characters in these works often fail in their quests, the works draw attention to the writing of science fiction as a political act. That is, as we shall see in Zoline's story, while the main character cannot alone succeed in saving the world, Zoline's writing of her plight foregrounds the absolute necessity of Zoline's readers doing so.

Written shortly after the publication of Betty Friedan's 1963 *The Feminine Mystique*, a book quickly recognized as a groundbreaking feminist text, and novels such as Sue Kaufmann's 1967 *The Diary of a Mad Housewife*, Zoline's story was perhaps influenced by second-wave feminism. First-wave feminism focused on women's suffrage at the turn of the twentieth century; this new second wave focused its attention in turn on the social devaluation of women and the work they do. The issues of sex, gender, race, and class addressed by the feminist movement of the 1960s and 1970s were certainly taken up in several major science fiction novels of that period:

Joanna Russ's *Picnic on Paradise* (1968) and *The Female Man* (1975), Marge Piercy's *Woman on the Edge of Time* (1976), and, perhaps most famously, Ursula K. LeGuin's *The Left Hand of Darkness* (1969), to name a few.

At the same time, Zoline's work shows clear affinities with the avant-garde and frequently confrontational extrapolative fiction appearing at the time, of which J. G. Ballard's "The Assassination of John Fitzgerald Kennedy Considered as a Downhill Motor Race" is the most infamous example. Not surprisingly, in view of her attitude toward literary genres, Zoline herself considers the strict boundaries between types and subtypes of fiction as much more fluid than do most critics, and she suggests that much art and literature is more productively viewed as "cohort-based." She says, "in my case, the fact that I was lucky enough to run with a bad crowd in London including Tom Disch, John Clute, Mike Moorcock, John Sladek, Jimmy Ballard, etc. certainly gave a certain neighborhood for my stories."[8] Further, she happily acknowledges being influenced by and owing debts to "a very big library of writers, among whom are Nabokov, DeLillo, Pynchon, Disch, Ed Abbey, Crowley, Clute, Wallace Stegner, Gary Snyder, E. O. Wilson, John LeCarre, Robert Lowell, Louise Erdrich," and the reader can see those multiple influences mirrored in her venues of publication.[9]

Pamela Zoline

Besides "Heat Death," Zoline wrote four other stories between 1967 and 1985, all available in the collection entitled *The Heat Death of the Universe and Other Stories* published by McPherson in 1988. The cover illustration is by Zoline as is that of the 1988 British edition entitled *Busy About the Tree of Life* published by The Women's Press. In addition, she wrote and illustrated a children's book, *Annika and the Wolves*, published by Coffee House Press in 1985, a tale that bears striking commonalities with Angela Carter's reimagined fairy tales.

Zoline lived in the United Kingdom for eighteen years, mostly in London; there, she says, "my work consisted of writing, painting, constructing some installations, activism and practical politics as part of the group founding the first Arts Labs, studying art at the Slade School, studying philosophy, also at University College, London, where its founder Jeremy Bentham holds court, his body preserved and stuffed and sitting in a glass cage in the main rotunda."[10]

Zoline has lived in Telluride, Colorado, for the last three decades where she continues her work as a social activist and artist, most recently helping to write scripts for the MuddButt children's theater and with others the opera libretti for *Harry Houdini and the False and True Occult* and *Decreation: An Opera in 3 Parts: The Forbidden Experiment*. She is currently working on a novel "set one hundred years in the future in the Four Corners region on a planet much like our own. . . . It will be heavily illustrated with drawings, photos, charts and maps. Jeremy Bentham is featured, as are the local rivers and mountains, and there is a focus on opera, on bees, on fountains, on tribes, and much more."[11]

Like the artist Joseph Beuys, Zoline believes art to be "a radicalizing modality" that if "properly deployed" is "the pivot point for major progressive change."[12] "As to my agenda," she writes, "I believe that we bonny clever humans have outsmarted ourselves into a massive downward spiral, into the Age of Drastic Simplification as to the loss of species and of human languages and cultures, and that this means that we're living in a burning building, and that our works and actions have to do with how to survive, how to sustain, what to save, how to start building in the ruins."[13] For her, "art as action, huge, subtle, the irresistible seed," remains an enclave wherein or a venue through which one might envision this world, our home, as something other than a vale of tears.[14]

"Heat Death of the Universe" and Science Fiction

Zoline's fiction, notably "Heat Death," can be found in several science fiction anthologies such as *Decade The 1960s* alongside pieces by Philip K. Dick, J. G. Ballard, Brian Aldiss, Roger Zelazny, and Kurt Vonnegut Jr. Hers is often the only work included by a woman writer.[15] Her second story, "The Holland of the Mind," after first publication in a science fiction venue, was reprinted in *Strangeness*, sharing space with works by Virginia Woolf, Italo Calvino, Graham Greene, Thomas Mann, and Jorge Luis Borges.[16] While stories by these authors vary greatly in terms of aesthetic agendas, they consistently seek to defamiliarize what is accepted as the real and to make us question the most common assumptions we have about human affiliations and desires. Attacking "middlebrow well-made meretricious" high art, "those dreary bedroom/boardroom dramas," as useless, Zoline insists that "whatever the corpse of the Great Tradition (*sic*) is doing to our culturescape, it's not useful, as the real, messy, whirling world is under closer analysis and more profound exploration in the best of the Science Fiction, Speculative, Experimental, Extrapolative etc. etc. fictions."[17]

Michael Moorcock relates "Heat Death" to the other works in his *Best SF Stories from New Worlds 3* through the common link of mythology. While some stories in the collection are built upon the heroic myths of

Western culture or the human need for mythmaking, Zoline's work illustrates for him a striking connection between "the modern myths of science (entropy, etc.) as they are understood by the layman [sic] with that great myth figure of modern fiction, the Victimized Domestic Woman."[18] The story marries science to fiction, all for the purpose of detailing one day in the life of Sarah Boyle and her mental disintegration. It effects this marriage through the inclusion of scientific explanations but also in its presentation of all information through a series of axioms, hypotheses, definitions, narrative fragments and summaries that instantiate the scientific principles inserted into the story. The story thus literally embodies a new form of science fiction, one that in both form and content questions relentlessly the truth of science and the blandishments of fiction.

Not surprisingly, many conservative critics of science fiction dismiss such new-wave writing for what they see as its too facile, manipulative but inconsequential gestures toward science; they, bracket it off as not science fiction. David Ketterer, for instance, in his New Worlds for Old, insists that like the work of J. G. Ballard, Zoline's story merely borrows "a science-fictional conception only for its metaphoric appropriateness." While her description of one woman's ennui in relation to universal entropy is perhaps "apocalyptic in a psychedelic or surrealist sense," he argues, "because the reality is grounded in a housewife and her kitchen and because of the lack of plausible scientific rationale connecting the end of the material universe with her state, Zoline's piece cannot legitimately be classified as science fiction."[19]

Ketterer's reading suggests why many women writers have been denied admission to the science fiction camp: woman's work simply doesn't merit attention, exactly the sort of devaluation that Friedan, Lisa Yaszek, Justine Larbalestier and other feminists have argued against so vociferously. Of particular importance here is Lisa Yaszek's discussion of Alice Eleanor Jones's "Created He Them" and the 1940s/1950s development of housewife heroine science fiction. As Moorcock's remarks above suggest, Zoline's story clearly fits within this subgenre and thus extends its lifeline into another decade. Further, as becomes quickly apparent in comparing Jones's and Zoline's stories, Zoline's work is more overtly committed to radical political activism, and in that sense underlines the powerful way an author's times are reflected in her work. One clear connection between Jones and Zoline is that until very recently housewife heroine science fiction did not garner much critical respect. As Yaszek points out in her essay, even some early feminist critics such as Pamela Sargeant at first seemed to dismiss housewife heroine science fiction as a negative development in the genre.

Sargeant would, however, include Zoline's story in her 1978 *The New Women of Wonder: Recent Science Fiction Stories by Women about Women*, perhaps privileging its experimental nature over popular fiction like Jones's story. That the issues housewife heroine science fiction raised were important can perhaps best be illustrated by the appearance of Ira Levin's reactionary *Stepford Wives* in 1972. While the housewives in all these science fiction works are extremely limited in agency, they are nevertheless threatening. These stories' power lies precisely in their threat of disturbing the status quo of male-female relations and the future of the worlds science fiction investigates. Indeed, Zoline's story subtly insists through its meticulous elaboration of the relation between Sarah Boyle's increasing angst and her reflections on entropy that there is deep social value in defamiliarizing the "real" world of a woman who seems to have it made. Not to acknowledge this is to have a very skewed worldview, for, as Brian Aldiss points out, "the center of the galaxy lies in Sarah Boyle's kitchen."[20]

The debate about whether or not Zoline's story is science fiction is particularly puzzling in that "Heat Death" is imbued throughout with science fiction thinking. As Brooks Landon defines this term in his *Science Fiction after 1900*, science fiction thinking is not simply genre specific but, instead, is "a set of attitudes and expectations about the future," including particular protocols of both writing and reading, that now permeates and at times determines modern consciousness. "Most broadly," he writes, "science fiction thinking is a sense of common enterprise that underlies the discussion of science fiction, a belief that better thinking is a desirable goal for humanity."[21] Whether we consciously realize it or not, science fiction itself fosters one type of epistemology or way of knowing; and, as Zoline's story illustrates, it is a most curious mix of rationalism and humanism, the objective and the subjective, the here and the now and the future.

In "Heat Death," Sarah Boyle's life is presented as if it were a science experiment focusing on what she knows and what that knowledge means to her, thus explicitly focusing both on ontology, or ways of being, and implicitly on epistemology, ways of knowing. As Brooks Landon points out, "Heat Death" thus "has one foot in the camp of 'hard' SF with its traditional interest in physics, astronomy, and chemistry, and the other foot in the camp of 'soft' SF with its traditional interest in psychology, sociology, and anthropology."[22]

More importantly, science fiction itself demands "new ways of seeing from its readers."[23] Readers do not simply extract a moral from a science fiction text but must work at a constant decoding of each paragraph, phrase, and even each word to construct and thus come to understand the text's world and what it might mean to this world. Zoline's experimental style and subject thus require an experimental way of reading, one comfortable with observation, hypothesis, indeterminacy, and ethical adjudication. That is, it demands an ability to speculate not only about "*what has not yet happened*" but about what "will not happen and events that might happen" as well.[24]

Writing outside the American market and within the radical British art scene, Zoline extrapolates in her work the dark view of a post-Enlightenment rejection of the myth of inevitable social and technological progress. Scientific knowledge is not always a comforter, as Sarah Boyle discovers; the quest for knowledge of the future, the preeminent subject of science fiction, can lead as easily to quotidian despair as to extraordinary triumph. In Zoline's work, Landon asserts, "science and technology enter SF through the back door, stripped of wonder, submerged in the details of mundane life, offering neither pleasure nor horror."[25] No wonder few science fiction traditionalists, like Ketterer, could recognize Zoline's way of thinking for what it is: the cutting edge of a very different apocalyptic vision.

This is not to say that Ketterer's critique hides a simplistic sexist agenda of exclusion; as Ketterer's extended praise of Ursula Le Guin's *The Left Hand of Darkness* intimates, as well as his overall rejection of virtually all new-wave writers (most of whom were male), it is the style of writing — how one presents the science fiction narrative — that may be the major problem. Le Guin's work, however radical in its intent, is still easily recognizable as science fiction. That is, there is a clearly sequential story, extraterrestrial worlds and people, the usual elements brilliantly manipulated to forward a feminist/humanist message. Zoline's story, on the other hand, simply refuses to conform to or to satisfy those expectations.

"Heat Death" and Postmodernism

While women in kitchens were not at first favored in science fiction, the main reason conservative science fiction aficionados such as Ketterer find new-wave writing off-putting is its highly experimental nature. Zoline's story is roughly chronological, interrupted at times by scientific inserts, the story's action confined to a home and a supermarket. But the narrative is also fragmented (literally so on the page) and the "story" comprises a puzzling mixture of scientific discourse, domestic fiction, and direct address to the reader; in short, it refuses easy interpretation. It is an early taste of what became known as postmodern writing, the roots of which, as Ketterer and many others point out, lie in the surreal assaults of Alfred Jarry and Marcel

Duchamp, the modernist mind journeys of James Joyce and Virginia Woolf, the effect of stream-of-consciousness and magic realism on fiction, as well as the acceleration of world disasters since the bombing of Hiroshima and Nagasaki — including, most notably, the assassination of John F. Kennedy and simultaneously, for many, the end of believing in innocence, in the democratic process, and in a positive future. At the same time, this period saw the rise of suburbia and the megacities, intense commercialization touching every aspect of a person's life, and the mass production of goods and a new mass society taught to want those goods.

Postmodern writing focuses in particular on the failure of grand narratives, stories the majority in a particular place or time believe or buy into, such as the utopian promise of Marxism or the Christian originary tale of the Garden of Eden, stories that sustain and console through their ostensible explanation of why we are here and what we should do. Even though these stories have failed, postmodernists argue, many people still crave some sort of consoling fictions, since post–World War II culture has become both atomized and, in strange ways, hyperindividualized. That is, the rise of Western mass culture depends upon a certain conformity of desires with the products (including the human) of the moment; as people become lost in the mass, they also become more and more alienated from others as they move to protect home turfs and to satisfy just those desires that they are programmed to have.

Postmodern theory also posits that as the cityscapes take over the natural world and the remaining natural sites become centers of tourism, people are pressed into the position of voyeurs instead of actors, passive spectators rather than active agents, unable to distinguish the simulacra of the real from the real (watch any episode of "reality" TV to experience vicariously one's own desires performed by others). And while everyone is engaged in this endless process of buying and consuming, of attending to appearances above all else, the world is going to hell in a handbasket.

It is exceedingly strange that traditionalists dismiss experimental writing as incapable of sustaining or transforming science fiction's multiple agendas in productive ways; science fiction's capacity for embracing the newly imagined and socially relevant is unparalleled. Feminist and leftist criticism, in turn, often fault science fiction for not living up to its own goal: critiquing and challenging the status quo. Zoline's story, however, does precisely that. In Zoline's work, housewife heroine science fiction is both centered and then fragmented, instantly recognized and then estranged, radicalized, politicized, and made deadly serious play. As Brooks Landon argues of "Heat Death": "despite its ostensibly microcosmic view of Sarah's life, her thinking tends ever toward the macrocosmic, particularly as she repeatedly considers her children not in sentimental terms but in terms of the species implications of their bodies and manners."[26] Zoline, then, challenges the greatest status quo of all, our belief in our species' superiority and future.

The marriage of postmodernism and science fiction should, then, be cause for cautious rejoicing. Postmodernism refuses passive voyeurism and so transgresses against readerly expectations, often relying on eccentric juxtapositions, the blurring of fact and fiction, the inclusion of pornography, even, in some works, plagiarism of other well-known texts to shock the reader awake and to make the reader work, to engage passionately with the text. While many critics of all stripes fault postmodernism for its supposedly nihilist stance or apolitical making of art for art's sake, the most provocative postmodernist writers — very often women — promote social activism even in the face of despair. As decades of science fiction writing illustrates, the future is ours to make — or not. Zoline's story demonstrates how very hard it is for those living now to imagine a future at all.

Considering "Heat Death of the Universe"

Zoline's story, presented in fifty-four separate entries, begins with a definition of ontology — "That branch of metaphysics which concerns itself with the problems of the nature of existence or being" — calling attention to what constitutes experience and who is privileged enough to engage in the quest for knowledge. The second entry sets the scene for the "experiment" of our observing Sarah Boyle. This experiment concerns her particular "problems of the nature of existence or being," its setting an idyllic landscape in which there is both continual birth and growth (babies' fingernails) and death and decay (the eroding mountains, rotting fruit, the hair of the dead). There is still time for both even as time is running out.

The story reads something like a lab report, chronologically linear, highly descriptive, objective. The ostensible subject is the well-educated, financially secure, privileged Sarah Boyle, mother and wife, everywoman in a mass society. She is troubled: her nose is too large; her appearance doesn't fit the norm as she perceives it or has been taught to perceive. The scope then narrows to the particular place and time in which she exists: California, Alameda, La Florida Street, her house, breakfast time.

This is her closed system in which she continually expends energy, at the moment reluctantly serving her children sugary cereal that will, she believes, rot their teeth, just as mothers across America do in endless replication. She is called upon to adjudicate which of her children will own the secret gift inside the cereal box, who will win the Shakespeare mask on the back. High culture here meets low culture: Shakespeare and Tony the Tiger are equalized figures of everyday consumption, both rendered mundane by their mechanical reproduction. Sarah withholds having to decide until the box is emptied, and the secret gift in the (Pandora's) box of cereal remains concealed. The aggressive oversell of the cereal company's special offers makes Sarah wonder if the contents are poisonous, if she is being complicit in the slow murder of her children, but entry 9 assures us that she is really a happy and proud mother, dismissing the concerns of entries 4 and 8 as momentary aberrations of thought. Entry 10 puts Sarah on track again, planning a birthday party that afternoon, a celebration of birth and growing.

Entry 11 clearly positions the reader as participant in this experiment; "we" the readers are directly addressed by the unknown narrator (the primary investigator? a teacher?) and introduced to the kitchen, the central space of Sarah's closed system. The narrator up to this point seemed to be simply the omniscient "know-it-all" voice typical of much fiction, giving us access to all pertinent facts, even to the protagonist's thoughts. The narrator in this entry pointedly reflects Zoline's commitment to agit-prop activism. That is, "we" the readers are presented not only with a detailed description of a particular situation but are now positioned within the story itself and then lectured at by the narrator. We are told by this *"professor"* that as yet we all live in a larger closed system — "this shrunk and communication-ravaged world" — and that there is little chance for us or Sarah to escape "the metastasis of Western Culture," the phrase recalling Sarah's fears about the cereal's carcinogenic potential now transmogrified to the level of overall social dis-ease caused by a cancer that as it is transmitted throughout a body or system ravages and kills. The narrator's inclusion of such analysis (*prop*aganda) is meant to *agit*ate us. We are both invited to be spectators of Sarah's particular suffering and made to realize our own suffering, or passive acceptance, of this dying world, our complicity, then, in this "metastasis." Zoline thus destabilizes our comfortable position as perhaps sympathetic but nevertheless distanced readers. As the narrator will continue to insist through inclusion of readers through the use of "we" or (the supposedly universal) "one," even as we are privileged enough to be voyeurs into Sarah's inner space, we are each, just as she is, also an agent in that world. Fittingly, we now see, the narrator is an agent provocateur. And, as the story has suggested from the first, we are far from knowing it all. Our future depends on our decoding the story's address to us and its message: that the "aliens" destroying this world are us.

Surrounded by grime and the detritus of the everyday (bobby pins, a doll's eye, dust, a dog's hair), Sarah cannot be faulted, the narrator tells us, for imagining that all the world simply replicates her supposedly ideal setting; everywhere for her is the same, but it is grotesque. Mother Nature herself has been forcibly and obscenely transformed into "a land Cunt Pink and Avocado Green, brassiered and girdled by monstrous complexities of Super Highways." It is at this point in the experiment that the reader is offered its guiding principle and Sarah's principal obsession: the theory of the heat death of the universe.

As entries 13 and 19 inform us, the universe is a closed system subject to the second law of thermodynamics. As the entropy or disorder of particles (a doll's eye, a dog's hair) increases, we shall approach the end of the universe as we know it as its energy is used up and time "unwinds." The juxtaposition of these entries to those describing Sarah's work in her house foregrounds the similarity between the two closed systems. Sarah's work is never done; while she maintains the fiction of the possibility of homeostasis, of maintaining some sense of constancy, she is overwhelmed by the ever-increasing chaos of her home space. She attempts to use language and numbers to control disorder, carefully annotating, naming, or counting the things that constitute her world, but the arbitrariness of language's and enumeration's relation to real objects renders her attempts at ordering futile.

Such ordering is always provisional, as entry 15 states, an experiment itself having little relation to lived experience (what does it mean, after all, to know that you have 819 movable objects in your living room?). Indeed, such ordering actions, like encyclopedias and dictionaries, serve only to give a false sense of control. They are an unreal "simulacra of a complete listing and ordering." While Sarah is "transfixed" by ordering texts such as reference books and children's ABCs, concrete meanings, indisputable facts, ultimate order always remain beyond her reach (the hand cream is labeled CAT).

Sarah finds similar reassurance in the Baba, a toy that depends upon identical reproduction except for matters of size, all the various dolls fitting one into the other in a neat, harmonious closed system. Of course, it bears no resemblance to Sarah's own reproduction — she cannot, for example, remember, or count, how many children she has — and her system most assuredly does not offer the promise of infinite reproduction if one just had a large enough Baba or womb to contain all. Infinite reproduction of the same would, in any case, lead one to endless self-reflection, what literary theorists call the *mise-en-abyme*, a fall into sameness with no possibility of escape or change; crawling back into the womb is not an option either. Sarah is, instead, living on the edge of the abyss, though she hasn't yet accepted this.

Impotent in her attempts at ordering chaos, Sarah tries to imagine space as freed from sameness, sometimes to positive and sometimes to negative effects. She invokes surrealist and dadaist spectacles of riot and suffocating fecundity: New York will melt like a Dali watch, her house will go wild, its dust recognized as aesthetic perfection, and she will be freed of work, of pets, and of children. However, while these transgressive visions offer her momentary mental respite, time, as entry 2 reminded us, is running out (or, perhaps, is already broken): the sand in the egg timer falls, only some of the four clocks tick away, her life is measured and calibrated to the last degree of heat/energy (entry 28). A wrinkle in time — imagining an unclosed system — gives way to an all too real wrinkle on Sarah's face. As she gazes into the mirror at her own simulacra, her future is foreseeable in her present, and though she is, entry 30 insists again, a proud and happy wife and mother, chaos and death are prefigured in the increasing chaos around/ on/in her.

By entry 35, Sarah is being described as fragmenting herself into mind-body dualities. Already in entry 33, agency was seeping out of her as she is constructed by language instead of constructing it ("Sarah muses or is mused"). Something, she feels, is being done to her by inexplicable un-nameable forces, so she continually acts out in frenzied animation trying to hold off the state of becoming inanimate (those "terrible glass eyes"; her dead mother, her Baba in whom she was once safely enclosed).

The larger landscape serves only to intensify her disquietude. The sky is bleached of color; the blue of her contact lenses, her tranquilizers, the swimming pools of California have an acidic and synthetic tint bearing no relation to anything in nature as it once existed. The supermarket offers too many choices of the same thing in different sizes, again recalling the Baba, about which products Sarah cannot decide and so must buy (into) every-thing. In entry 38, her mother-in-law reinvokes the constant menace of a cancer metastasizing wildly, chaos vitiating the system, any system. Per-haps Sarah cannot recall how many children she has because she is ob-sessed with apocalyptic visions of world destruction, both natural and man-made; she cannot bear, that is, to remember how many children she has as they might be fated to die in a worldwide catastrophe. Art, she imagines, in entry 44, might offer salvation from such cruel absurdities, but she has no time for it, and nothing, in any case, will last forever. Even the turtle, sym-bol of placid longevity, will soon die.

The birthday party is both a momentary stay against Sarah's obsession and another scene of increasing chaos. The future promise it celebrates — another year, a cake in the shape of a rocket, an escape to an unclosed system — is undermined by the animality and unnaturalness of the children. One child, refusing to eat the food of the others, chokes on the cereal's surprise gift, a little green plastic snake that, once coughed up, becomes the prize all the children want. The child's seemingly individual act of refusal is thus readily transformed into and co-opted back into mass conformity and desire. Further, the snake — a debased mechanical reproduction of the natural — recalls Western culture's originary grand narrative, that of the Garden of Eden and Eve's quest for the knowledge of good and evil. The promise of experiencing knowledge, reinvoking the need to understand the reason for one's existence that opens this experiment/story, is most tempting, most seductive; as we see throughout, however, for Sarah knowledge is also a very dangerous thing.

Sarah knows from the outset that home life, like the birthday party, is only a temporary stay against confusion and chaos and in fact breeds even more chaos and fragmentation. Tellingly, Zoline's own illustration for the first appearance in print of the story emphasizes this: it was a montage consisting of pieces of Duchamp's *Mona Lisa*, an ad for a bathroom cleaner, and maps of California.[27]

Every momentary attempt at order is undone by visions of profound disease. She bathes and puts to bed her children; she also imagines eating them. She dreams of cleaning and ordering the entire universe but breaks down when she finds the turtle's dead body, a pathetic reminder that death will come, that no amount of cleaning will wash away that eventuality. She has cried before, as entry 53 informs us; she will cry again and again and again. And there is no one to respond to her cry for "Help, help, help, help, help." Her husband is strangely absent, her mother is dead, her mother-in-law a surreal intrusion into her space, her children "debauched midgets." Although grievously fatigued, in a last surge of energy before entropy is reached, she destroys the kitchen, hurling her eggs (and the promise of future life) into space only to watch them fall. An end to reproduction, an end to sameness, the sands have run out. She comes full circle, then, madly burdened with the problems of the nature of existence and being.

What, finally, does the experiment of "Heat Death" achieve? To mimic Zoline's countdown or piling-up of facts:

1. Her story is not simply a decadent exercise in despair or madness but has meaning beyond the personal world of Sarah Boyle, the object of observation.

2. It suggests that perhaps this world is not, despite all the material evidence available, a closed system or, at least, that there might exist enclaves where life might be experienced without repeated surrender to despair.

3. Art, even a science fiction short story, may be a means of salvation, although language is always tricky, easily ignored or misread, far from transparent.
4. The revolt against entropy must begin in the smallest of closed systems: your own body, the home, your family must be an opening out of that closed system.
5. Women, slandered in Western culture's originary grand narrative of Eden, have always been set up for a fall, fortunate or otherwise, and know only too well what is good and what is evil.
6. Perhaps a woman will lead humanity (again) into a new world and new narratives, not necessarily grand but nevertheless life-sustaining ones.

Zoline does so in this and her other short stories, particularly in her 1985 "Instructions for Exiting this Building in Case of Fire," in which the Mothers of a later time than Sarah Boyle's act in shockingly outrageous ways in their attempt to save this world from man-made destruction. Even the very depressing conclusion of Sarah Boyle's story rejects annihilation: the eggs fall, but they do not break; that closure is denied or, at least, postponed.

As Brian Aldiss writes, "the fatal error of much science fiction has been to subscribe to an optimism based on the idea that revolution, or a new gimmick, or a bunch of strong men, or an invasion of aliens, or the conquest of other planets, or the annihilation of half the world — in short, pretty nearly anything but the facing up to the integral and irredeemable nature of mankind — can bring about utopian situations. It is the old error of the externalization of evil." He continues by stating decisively that "'Heat Death makes no such error."[28]

Zoline's story is, in her own words, "an attempt to 'make sense' of things, of general data, by organizing the private to the public, the public to the private, by making the analogies between entropy and personal chaos, the end of the universe and our own ageing and death." She captures the unreal real world as she experiences it; the experimental form of her story, what she describes "as an arrow, an energy flow," challenges readers to be more than passive consumers of yet another useless fiction.[29] We have to put the pieces together, to study the data, and, unlike Sarah, to make careful ethical adjudications about what matters, what stories to create and consume.

Rose Flores Harris writes of Zoline's stories that "the alienation of Zoline's characters seems to be offset by their intelligence and desire to survive in a world not of their creation, which they do not understand yet struggle to cope with. This common dilemma of human beings of all eras and the tenacious frailty of the author's heroes unite the reader sympathetically with them and with their creator."[30] Thomas M. Disch, in turn, extols "Heat Death" as "the most technically accomplished and humane mosaic fiction produced by the New Wave." It is, most importantly, he says, a piece written not simply for personal fame and glory but "for an Other," for you, for me, for another mode of being with each other.[31]

NOTES

1. There is very little material available on Zoline. I have gleaned biographical facts from the following sources: Brian W. Aldiss's foreword to "The Heat Death of the Universe," in *The Mirror of Infinity: A Critics' Anthology of Science Fiction*, ed. Robert Silverberg (New York: Harper & Row, 1973), 267–273; "P. A. Zoline . . ." in *England Swings SF*, ed. Judith Merril (Garden City, N.Y.: Doubleday, 1968), 329–330; and "Michael Moorcock" in the same volume, 343–349. The last source also gives an interesting account of Moorcock's takeover of *New Worlds* and Zoline's involvement with the magazine. I have also been in correspondence with Zoline.

2. See Michael Moorcock's introduction to his *Best SF Stories from New Worlds 3* (New York: Berkley, 1968), 7.

3. "The Heat Death of the Universe" was reprinted in *England Swings SF* (1968), ed. Judith Merril; *Best SF Stories from New Worlds 3* (1968), ed. Michael Moorcock; *Decade The 1960s* (1976), ed. Brian W. Aldiss and Harry Harrison; *The Mirror of Infinity* (1970), ed. Robert Silverberg; *Voyages: Scenarios for a Ship Called Earth* (1971), ed. Rob Sauer; *The New Women of Wonder* (1978), ed. Pamela Sargeant; *The Road to Science Fiction #4* (1982), ed. James E. Gunn; *New Worlds: An Anthology* (1983), ed. Michael Moorcock; and *The Heat Death of the Universe and Other Stories* (1988). The best source for print bibliography information on Zoline's stories is <http://www.isfdb.org/cgi-bin/p1.cgi?Pamela_Zoline>. See also <http://www.isfdb.org/cgi-bin/pw.cgi?528853> for "Heat Death" in particular, as well as <http://www.scifi.com/scifiction/classics/classics_archive/zoline> and *Index to Science Fiction Anthologies and Collections* by William Contento (Boston: G. K. Hall, 1978), 257.

4. Besides the works cited in this essay, see also my "What Do Women Want?" *Context: A Forum for Literary Arts and Culture* 11 (Fall 2002): 12–13.

5. See, for instance, Merril's "That Only a Mother" (1948), Zimmer Bradley's "The Wind People" (1958), and McCaffrey's "The Ship Who Sang" (1961).

6. See Eric S. Rabkin's "Science Fiction Women Before Liberation" and Scott Sanders's "Woman As Nature in Science Fiction," in Marleen S. Barr's *Future Females: A Critical Anthology* (Bowling Green, Ohio: Bowling Green State University Popular Press, 1981), 9–25 and 42–59, for examples of vacuous women characters in early science fiction.

7. See Lisa Yaszek's essay on Alice Eleanor Jones's story in this volume for an overview of housewife heroine science fiction as well as Justine Larbalestier's *The Battle of the Sexes in Science Fiction* (Middletown, Conn.: Wesleyan University Press, 2002) for a detailed account of "the evolving relationship between men and women in sf" (1).

8. E-mail correspondence with Pamela Zoline, 24 March 2004.

9. Ibid.

10. Ibid.

11. Ibid.

12. See the website at <http://www.scifi.com/scifiction/classics/classics_archive/ zoline/ zoline_bio.html>.

13. E-mail correspondence with Pamela Zoline, 24 March 2004.

14. See the website at <http://www.scifi.com/scifiction/classic_archive/zoline/ zoline_bio.html>.

15. See, for example, Brian W. Aldiss and Harry Harrison, eds., *Decade The 1960s* (London: Macmillan London, 1977); Silverberg, ed., *The Mirror of Infinity*; and Moorcock, ed., *Best SF Stories from New Worlds 3*.

16. *Strangeness: A Collection of Curious Tales*, ed. Thomas M. Disch and Charles Naylor (New York: Scribner, 1977).

17. E-mail correspondence with Pamela Zoline, 24 March 2004.

18. Introduction to *Best SF Stories from New Worlds 3*, ed. Moorcock.

19. *New Worlds for Old: The Apocalyptic Imagination, Science Fiction, and American Literature* (Garden City, N.Y.: Anchor, 1974), 187.

20. Foreword to "the Heat Death of the Universe," 270.

21. Brooks Landon, *Science Fiction after 1900: From the Steam Man to the Stars* (New York: Twayne, 1997), 4, 7.

22. Ibid., 27.

23. Ibid., 7.

24. Ibid., 8–9.

25. Ibid., 27.

26. Ibid., 29.

27. The illustration is described by Aldiss in his foreword to "The Heat Death of the Universe," 269.

28. Ibid., 267–268.

29. Ibid., 268.

30. "Zoline, Pamela A." in *Twentieth-Century Science-Fiction Writers*, ed. Curtis C. Smith (New York: St. Martin's, 1981), 610.

31. Thomas Disch in "The Astonishing Pamela Zoline," in *The Heat Death of the Universe and Other Stories* (Kingston, N.Y.: McPherson, 1988), 8.

6

And I Awoke and Found Me Here on the Cold Hill's Side

JAMES TIPTREE, JR.

First published in The Magazine of Fantasy and Science Fiction, *March* 1972

He was standing absolutely still by a service port, staring out at the belly of the *Orion* docking above us. He had on a gray uniform and his rusty hair was cut short. I took him for a station engineer.

That was bad for me. Newsmen strictly don't belong in the bowels of Big Junction. But in my first twenty hours I hadn't found any place to get a shot of an alien ship.

I turned my holocam to show its big World Media insigne and started my bit about What It Meant to the People Back Home who were paying for it all.

"— it may be routine work to you, sir, but we owe it to them to share —"

His face came around slow and tight, and his gaze passed over me from a peculiar distance.

"The wonders, the drama," he repeated dispassionately. His eyes focused on me. "You consummated fool."

"Could you tell me what races are coming in, sir? If I could even get a view —"

He waved me to the port. Greedily I angled my lenses up at the long blue hull blocking out the starfield. Beyond her I could see the bulge of a black and gold ship.

"That's a Foramen," he said. "There's a freighter from Belye on the other side, you'd call it Arcturus. Not much traffic right now."

"You're the first person who's said two sentences to me since I've been here, sir. What are those colorful little craft?"

"Procya," he shrugged. "They're always around. Like us."

I squashed my face on the vitrite, peering. The walls clanked. Somewhere overhead aliens were off-loading into their private sector of Big Junction. The man glanced at his wrist.

"Are you waiting to go out, sir?"

His grunt could have meant anything.

"Where are you from on Earth?" he asked me in his hard tone.

I started to tell him and suddenly saw that he had forgotten my existence. His eyes were on nowhere, and his head was slowly bowing forward onto the port frame.

"Go home," he said thickly. I caught a strong smell of tallow.

"Hey, sir!" I grabbed his arm; he was in rigid tremor. "Steady, man."

"I'm waiting . . . waiting for my wife. My loving wife." He gave a short ugly laugh. "Where are you from?"

I told him again.

"Go home," he mumbled. "Go home and make babies. While you still can."

One of the early GR casualties, I thought.

"Is that all you know?" His voice rose stridently. "Fools. Dressing in their styles. Gnivo suits, Aoleelee music. Oh, I see your newscasts," he sneered. "Nixi parties. A year's salary for a floater. Gamma radiation? Go home, read history. *Ballpoint pens and bicycles —*"

He started a slow slide downward in the half gee. My only informant. We struggled confusedly; he wouldn't take one of my sobertabs but I finally got him along the service corridor to a bench in an empty loading bay. He fumbled out a little vacuum cartridge. As I was helping him unscrew it, a figure in starched whites put his head in the bay.

"I can be of assistance, yes?" His eyes popped, his face was covered with brindled fur. An alien, a Procya! I started to thank him but the red-haired man cut me off.

"Get lost. Out."

The creature withdrew, its big eyes moist. The man stuck his pinky in the cartridge and then put it up his nose, gasping deep in his diaphragm. He looked toward his wrist.

"What time is it?"

I told him.

"News," he said. "A message for the eager, hopeful human race. A word about those lovely, lovable aliens we all love so much." He looked at me. "Shocked, aren't you, newsboy?"

I had him figured now. A xenophobe. Aliens plot to take over Earth.

"Ah, Christ, they couldn't care less." He took another deep gasp, shuddered and straightened. "The hell with generalities. What time d'you say it was? All right, I'll tell you how I learned it. The hard way. While we wait for my loving wife. You can bring that little recorder out of your sleeve, too. Play it over to yourself some time . . . when it's too late." He chuckled. His tone had become chatty — an educated voice. "You ever hear of supernormal stimuli?"

"No," I said. "Wait a minute. White sugar?"

"Near enough. Y'know Little Junction bar in D.C.? No, you're an Aussie, you said. Well, I'm from Burned Barn, Nebraska."

He took a breath, consulting some vast disarray of the soul.

"I accidentally drifted into Little Junction Bar when I was eighteen. No. Correct that. You don't go into Little Junction by accident, any more than you first shoot skag by accident.

"You go into Little Junction because you've been craving it, dreaming about it, feeding on every hint and clue about it, back there in Burned Barn, since before you had hair in your pants. Whether you know it or not. Once you're out of Burned Barn, you can no more help going into Little Junction than a sea-worm can help rising to the moon.

"I had a brand-new liquor I.D. in my pocket. It was early; there was an empty spot beside some humans at the bar. Little Junction isn't an embassy bar, y'know. I found out later where the high-caste aliens go — when they go out. The New Rive, the Curtain by the Georgetown Marina.

"And they go by themselves. Oh, once in a while they do the cultural exchange bit with a few frosty couples of other aliens and some stuffed humans. Galactic Amity with a ten-foot pole.

"Little Junction was the place where the lower orders went, the clerks and drivers out for kicks. Including, my friend, the perverts. The ones who can take humans. Into their beds, that is."

He chuckled and sniffed his finger again, not looking at me.

"Ah, yes. Little Junction is Galactic Amity night, every night. I ordered . . . what? A margarita. I didn't have the nerve to ask the snotty spade bartender for one of the alien liquors behind the bar. It was dim. I was trying to stare everywhere at once without showing it. I remember those white boneheads — Lyrans, that is. And a mess of green veiling I decided was a multiple being from some place. I caught a couple of human glances in the bar mirror. Hostile flicks. I didn't get the message, then.

"Suddenly an alien pushed right in beside me. Before I could get over my paralysis, I heard this blurry voice:

"'You air a futeball enthusiash?'

"An alien had spoken to me. An *alien*, a being from the stars. Had spoken. To me.

"Oh, god, I had no time for football, but I would have claimed a passion for paper-folding, for dumb crambo — anything to keep him talking. I asked him about his home planet sports, I insisted on buying his drinks. I listened raptly while he spluttered out a play-by-play account of a game I wouldn't have turned a dial for. The 'Grain Bay Pashkers.' Yeah. And I was dimly aware of trouble among the humans on my other side.

"Suddenly this woman — I'd call her a girl now — this girl said something in a high nasty voice and swung her stool into the arm I was holding my drink with. We both turned around together.

"Christ, I can see her now. The first thing that hit me was *discrepancy*. She was a nothing — but terrific. Transfigured. Oozing it, radiating it.

"The next thing was I had a horrifying hard-on just looking at her. I scrooched over so my tunic hid it, and my spilled drink trickled down, making everything worse. She pawed vaguely at the spill, muttering.

"I just stared at her trying to figure out what had hit me. An ordinary figure, a soft avidness in the face. Eyes heavy, satiated-looking. She was totally sexualized. I remember her throat pulsed. She had one hand up touching her scarf, which had slipped off her shoulder. I saw angry bruises there. That really tore it, I understood at once those bruises had some sexual meaning.

"She was looking past my head with her face like a radar dish. Then she made an 'ahhhhh' sound that had nothing to do with me and grabbed my forearm as if it were a railing. One of the men behind her laughed. The woman said, 'Excuse me,' in a ridiculous voice and slipped out behind me. I wheeled around after her, nearly upsetting my football friend, and saw that some Sirians had come in.

"That was my first look at Sirians in the flesh, if that's the word. God knows I'd memorized every news shot, but I wasn't prepared. That tallness, that cruel thinness. That appalling alien arrogance. Ivory-blue, these were. Two males in immaculate metallic gear. Then I saw there was a female with them. An ivory-indigo exquisite with a permanent faint smile on those bone-hard lips.

"The girl who'd left me was ushering them to a table. She reminded me of a goddamn dog that wants you to follow it. Just as the crowd hid them, I saw a man join them too. A big man, expensively dressed, with something wrecked about his face.

"Then the music started and I had to apologize to my furry friend. And the Sellice dancer came out and my personal introduction to hell began."

The red-haired man fell silent for a minute enduring self-pity. Something wrecked about the face, I thought; it fit.

He pulled his face together.

"First I'll give you the only coherent observation of my entire evening. You can see it here at Big Junction, always the same. Outside of the Procya, it's humans with aliens, right? Very seldom aliens with other aliens. Never aliens with humans. It's the humans who want in."

I nodded, but he wasn't talking to me. His voice had a druggy fluency.

"Ah, yes, my Sellice. My first Sellice.

"They aren't really well-built, y'know, under those cloaks. No waist to speak of and short-legged. But they flow when they walk.

"This one flowed out into the spotlight, cloaked to the ground in violet silk. You could only see a fall of black hair and tassels over a narrow face like a vole. She was a mole-gray. They come in all colors. Their fur is like a flexible velvet all over; only the color changes startlingly around their eyes and lips and other places. Erogenous zones? Ah, man, with them it's not zones.

"She began to do what we'd call a dance, but it's no dance, it's their natural movement. Like smiling, say, with us. The music built up, and her arms undulated toward me, letting the cloak fall apart little by little. She was naked under it. The spotlight started to pick up her body markings moving in the slit of the cloak. Her arms floated apart and I saw more and more.

"She was fantastically marked and the markings were writhing. Not like body paint — alive. Smiling, that's a good word for it. As if her whole body was smiling sexually, beckoning, winking, urging, pouting, speaking to me. You've seen a classic Egyptian belly dance? Forget it — a sorry stiff thing compared to what any Sellice can do. This one was ripe, near term.

"Her arms went up and those blazing lemon-colored curves pulsed, waved, everted, contracted, throbbed, evolved unbelievably welcoming, inciting permutations. *Come do it to me, do it, do it here and here and here and now.* You couldn't see the rest of her, only a wicked flash of mouth. Every human male in the room was aching to ram himself into that incredible body. I mean it was *pain.* Even the other aliens were quiet, except one of the Sirians who was chewing out a waiter.

"I was a basket case before she was halfway through. . . . I won't bore you with what happened next; before it was over there were several fights and I got cut. My money ran out on the third night. She was gone next day.

"I didn't have time to find out about the Sellice cycle then, mercifully. That came after I went back to campus and discovered you had to have a degree in solid-state electronics to apply for off-planet work. I was a pre-med but I got that degree. It only took me as far as First Junction then.

"Oh, god, First Junction. I thought I was in heaven — the alien ships coming in and our freighters going out. I saw them all, all but the real exotics, the tankies. You only see a few of those a cycle, even here. And the Yyeire. You've never seen that.

"Go home, boy. Go home to your version of Burned Barn . . .

"The first Yyeir I saw, I dropped everything and started walking after it like a starving hound, just breathing. You've seen the pix of course. Like lost dreams. *Man is in love and loves what vanishes. . . .* It's the scent, you can't guess that. I followed until I ran into a slammed port. I spent half a cycle's credits sending the creature the wine they call stars' tears. . . . Later I found out it was a male. That made no difference at all.

"You can't have sex with them, y'know. No way. They breed by light or something, no one knows exactly. There's a story about a man who got hold of a Yyeir woman and tried. They had him skinned. Stories—"

He was starting to wander.

"What about that girl in the bar, did you see her again?"

He came back from somewhere.

"Oh, yes. I saw her. She'd been making it with the two Sirians, y'know. The males do it in pairs. Said to be the total sexual thing for a woman, if she can stand the damage from those beaks. I wouldn't know. She talked to me a couple of times after they finished with her. No use for men whatever. She drove off the P Street bridge. . . . The man, poor bastard, he was trying to keep that Sirian bitch happy single-handed. Money helps, for a while. I don't know where he ended."

He glanced at his wrist watch again. I saw the pale bare place where a watch had been and told him the time.

"Is that the message you want to give Earth? Never love an alien?"

"Never love an alien—" He shrugged. "Yeah. No. Ah, Jesus, don't you see? Everything going out, nothing coming back. Like the poor damned Polynesians. We're gutting Earth, to begin with. Swapping raw resources for junk. Alien status symbols. Tape decks, Coca-Cola, Mickey Mouse watches."

"Well, there is concern over the balance of trade. Is that your message?"

"The balance of trade." He rolled it sardonically. "Did the Polynesians have a word for it, I wonder? You don't see, do you? All right, why are you here? I mean *you*, personally. How many guys did you climb over—"

He went rigid, hearing footsteps outside. The Procya's hopeful face appeared around the corner. The red-haired man snarled at him and he backed out. I started to protest.

"Ah, the silly reamer loves it. It's the only pleasure we have left. . . . Can't you see, man? That's *us*. That's the way we look to them, to the real ones."

"But—"

"And now we're getting the cheap C-drive, we'll be all over just like the Procya. For the pleasure of serving as freight monkeys and junction crews.

Oh, they appreciate our ingenious little service stations, the beautiful star folk. They don't *need* them, y'know. Just an amusing convenience. D'you know what I do here with my two degrees? What I did at First Junction. Tube cleaning. A swab. Sometimes I get to replace a fitting."

I muttered something; the self-pity was getting heavy.

"Bitter? Man, it's a *good* job. Sometimes I get to talk to one of them." His face twisted. "My wife works as a — oh, hell, you wouldn't know. I'd trade — correction, I have traded — everything Earth offered me for just that chance. To see them. To speak to them. Once in a while to touch one. Once in a great while to find one low enough, perverted enough to want to touch me. . ."

His voice trailed off and suddenly came back strong.

"And so will you!" He glared at me. "Go home! Go home and tell them to quit it. Close the ports. Burn every god-lost alien thing before it's too late! That's what the Polynesians didn't do."

"But surely —"

"But surely be damned! Balance of trade — balance of *life*, man. I don't know if our birth rate is going, that's not the point. Our soul is leaking out. We're bleeding to death!"

He took a breath and lowered his tone.

"What I'm trying to tell you, this is a trap. We've hit the supernormal stimulus. Man is exogamous — all our history is one long drive to find and impregnate the stranger. Or get impregnated by him; it works for women too. Anything different-colored, different nose, ass, anything, man *has* to fuck it or die trying. That's a drive, y'know, it's built in. Because it works fine as long as the stranger is human. For millions of years that kept the genes circulating. But now we've met aliens we can't screw, and we're about to die trying. . . . Do you think I can touch my wife?"

"But —"

"Look. Y'know, if you give a bird a fake egg like its own but bigger and brighter-marked, it'll roll its own egg out of the nest and sit on the fake? That's what we're doing."

"We've been talking about sex so far." I was trying to conceal my impatience. "Which is great, but the kind of story I'd hoped —"

"Sex? No, it's deeper." He rubbed his head, trying to clear the drug. "Sex is only part of it — there's more. I've seen Earth missionaries, teachers, sexless people. Teachers — they end cycling waste or pushing floaters, but they're hooked. They stay. I saw one fine-looking old woman, she was servant to a Cu'ushbar kid. A defective — his own people would have let him die. That wretch was swabbing up its vomit as if it was holy water. Man, it's deep . . . some cargo-cult of the soul. We're built to dream outwards. They laugh at us. They don't have it."

There were sounds of movement in the next corridor The dinner crowd was starting. I had to get rid of him and get there; maybe I could find the Procya.

A side door opened and a figure started towards us. At first I thought it was an alien and then I saw it was a woman wearing an awkward body-shell. She seemed to be limping slightly. Behind her I could glimpse the dinner-bound throng passing the open door.

The man got up as she turned into the bay. They didn't greet each other.

"The station employs only happily wedded couples," he told me with that ugly laugh. "We give each other . . . comfort."

He took one of her hands. She flinched as he drew it over his arm and let him turn her passively, not looking at me. "Forgive me if I don't intro-duce you. My wife appears fatigued."

I saw that one of her shoulders was grotesquely scarred.

"Tell them," he said, turning to go. "Go home and tell them." Then his head snapped back toward me and he added quietly, "And stay away from the Syrtis desk or I'll kill you."

They went away up the corridor.

I changed tapes hurriedly with one eye on the figures passing that open door. Suddenly among the humans I caught a glimpse of two sleek scarlet shapes. My first real aliens! I snapped the recorder shut and ran to squeeze in behind them.

(Re)Reading James Tiptree Jr.'s "And I Awoke and Found Me Here on the Cold Hill Side"

Wendy Pearson

Gender is kind, syntax, relation, genre; gender is not the transubstantiation of biological difference. — DONNA HARAWAY, *PRIMATE VISIONS*

Sf is an expansionist myth. It's about *reproductive success.* The gadgets and the
spaceships are all very fine and dandy, but what we're *always, really* talking about
is how Man gets out there to the edge of the known, grabs hold of a chunk of that
alien dark, and pumps it full of his seed. We feminist fans and writers . . . decided
that we did not like being cast as *the alien dark.* We set about to give ourselves a
different costume and a little more variety. — GWYNETH JONES, "KAIROS"

James Tiptree Jr. and Feminist SF

Most readers of this collection will by now have noticed the apparent
anomaly of including a male science fiction writer, James Tiptree Jr., in a
collection of classic feminist sf. This is not to say that men cannot be feminists nor that there are not and have not been men with feminist beliefs
writing sf; the obvious examples are Samuel R. Delany and John Varley.
However, a quick perusal of any of the books and anthologies dealing with
feminist sf will reveal that the normal subject of study for scholars of the
field is science fiction written by women. Again, this classification does not
include all women; there are women writers of science fiction whose work
is, for varying reasons, unlikely to be understood by readers or critics — or
by the writer herself — as approaching science fiction from any sort of feminist perspective.

James Tiptree was an important and much-lauded writer of science
fiction short stories, as well as one novel, from 1968 until the early 1980s.
His work won two Hugo and three Nebula awards and received ten nominations for the Hugo and nine for the Nebula. "And I Awoke and Found

Me Here on the Cold Hill Side" was nominated for both the Hugo and the Nebula in 1973; the winner of the Nebula short story award that year was the more overtly feminist "When It Changed," by Joanna Russ.

SF writer and editor Robert Silverberg compared Tiptree favorably with Ernest Hemingway and noted of one of Tiptree's best-known stories, "The Women Men Don't See," that "it is a profoundly feminist story told in entirely masculine manner, and deserves close attention by those in the front lines of the wars of sexual liberation, male and female."[1] Despite the widespread recognition granted to Tiptree's work, however, the inclusion of one of his short stories in this anthology raises two significant questions. The first question, which some of the other contributors have also touched upon, is, What is feminist sf? The second question, which may be even more complex and difficult, is, Why Tiptree?

There is no easy or precise way to define feminist sf, in part because there are so many different answers to the question, What is feminism? Jenny Wolmark, however, makes the sensible assertion that feminist sf brings

> the politics of feminism into a genre with a solid tradition of ignoring or excluding women writers, and in doing so it has politicised our understanding of the fantasies of science fiction. To do so, it has drawn on feminist analysis of the criticism of gendered subjectivity in order to suggest possibilities for more plural and heterogeneous social relations, and to offer a powerful critique of the way in which existing social relations and power structures continue to marginalise women.[2]

Feminism, in Wolmark's description of feminist sf, is any system of analysis that identifies and seeks to understand how the ways in which humans beings think about and believe that they know themselves are always already marked by gender. In other words, at least in Euro-American cultures and possibly in virtually all contemporary cultures, it is impossible for human beings to think about themselves without immediately thinking about gender. The linkage of gender with cultural understandings of ontology — that is, of the ways in which humans can *be* in the world — is frequently so naturalized as to seem instinctive. Because humans can only exist inside culture, it is difficult for people to see the various ways in which culture shapes and gives meaning to human lives through gender.

Wolmark suggests two functions for feminist sf: to indicate alternative ways of being and knowing that do not take contemporary gender roles as a naturalized given; and to provide a means of critiquing the effects of cultural assumptions about gender on the ways in which people live, including the ways in which we, as humans, interact with knowledge, with social institutions, and with each other. Also important, as feminist sf writer and critic Gwyneth Jones points out in her article "Kairos," feminist science fiction involves repudiating women's role in sf not only as the alien (see, for example, feminist sf criticism by Jenny Wolmark, Robert Reid, Jacqueline Pearson, and so on, which examines the ways in which sf literalizes Simone de Beauvoir's insight that woman is the other, i.e., the alien), but also as the "alien dark," the amorphous natural cosmos awaiting *man's* conquest.[3]

Such feminist approaches *may*, but do not necessarily, involve introducing what some masculinist sf writers have been fond of calling "feminine" elements, the aspects of women's lives that men, throughout most of the twentieth century, have seen as peripheral to their own, such as domesticity, children, and relationships between women: the kind of focus that, for example, "Harry Harrison had derided as 'tears and Tampax sf.'"[4] As Lisa Yaszek points out, even contemporary critics like John Clute and Peter Nicholls (whose 1995 encyclopedia entry on women writing sf in the 1950s and 1960s insists that they produced only "sentimental stories dealing with . . . acceptable feminine concerns,") end up "reiterat[ing] many of the basic assumptions about the meaning and value of this fiction . . . , once again relegating it to the sidelines of the genre."[5]

Feminist sf may respond to some or all of these issues; it may also choose to find alternative focuses on gender precisely because, being science fiction, it is not intrinsically mimetic. Sf does not have to represent the contemporary world in an apparently naturalistic fashion, but can take alternative, often analogical or metaphorical, approaches to raising questions of gender and social construction. Thus Sarah Lefanu in the earliest book-length study of feminist science fiction, *In the Chinks of the World Machine*, concludes that the "stock conventions of science fiction — time travel, alternative worlds, entropy, relativism, the search for a unified field theory — can be used metaphorically and metonymically as powerful ways of exploring the construction of 'woman.' Feminist sf, then, is a part of science fiction while struggling against it."[6] I would add that feminist sf is as likely to use the stock conventions of sf to explore the construction of "man" as it is to explore ways of understanding what it means to be female. Feminist sf also raises similarly powerful questions about the naturalization of other identity formations, such as sexuality, race, and class.

When I ask, "Why Tiptree?" the most obvious answer, as some readers will know, is that in 1977, after almost a decade as an extremely successful male writer of sf (during which he was lauded as "the most masculine of writers,"), Tiptree was revealed to be a woman. Rather than arguing that there is a simple answer to the question, "Why Tiptree?" because Tiptree was "really" Alice Sheldon, a woman, and of course women can write feminist sf, I prefer to consider a number of complicating factors. First of all, Tiptree's biography—a childhood spent adventuring in Africa and India, World War II service in Army Air Force Intelligence, postwar years in the CIA, all of which appeared to the sf community at the time as absolute proof of Tiptree's masculinity—was also Alice Sheldon's.

Young Alice Hastings Bradley accompanied her parents on their trips across Africa and, to a lesser extent, India. As an adult, Bradley volunteered for Army Air Force Intelligence in the United States before joining the CIA, which she later left abruptly, reinventing herself as a student of psychology and eventually gaining a Ph.D. in the field. In the 1960s, Sheldon invented Tiptree and began to write and publish science fiction in his name.[7]

"Tiptree" was more than just a pseudonym for Sheldon. He was a recluse whom no one ever met, who had a voluminous correspondence with editors, other writers, and fans and took part in a variety of sf-related events, such as the symposium on women in science fiction printed in the fanzine *Khatru*.[8] Tiptree had a textual existence in a way that many other pseudonymous writers did not; in many cases, the "real" identities behind the pseudonyms were well known.

Tiptree's existence or lack of it, as well as the effect of readerly assumptions about gender, brings into question simplistic notions about male versus female style. For example, Tiptree's success as a male writer forces readers and critics to rethink whether gender is really the defining impetus behind the predisposition to write certain kinds of stories—such as the assumption that men write "hard" (i.e., technological science fiction) whereas women write "soft" (i.e., social science fiction)? Is gender alone the conclusive factor that inclines readers and critics to identify particular works as feminist or otherwise? If so, where does the reader place Tiptree's work? Is it "really" male? Or is it "really" female?

The common critical approach to the problem of Tiptree's identity, particularly among feminist sf critics, has been to examine the psychological dynamics involved in Sheldon's assumption of Tiptree's "male persona," as feminist critic Sarah Lefanu puts it. Lefanu even titles her chapter on Tiptree and "her" work "Who is Tiptree, What is She?"[9] This title raises a number of potentially unanswerable questions, especially as Alice Sheldon/James Tiptree is no longer alive to be quizzed on her/his motivations.[10] Was Tiptree simply a pseudonymous entree into a male-dominated publishing business, along the lines of Alice Norton's adoption of the male first name Andre or C. L. Moore's choice to use her initials, rather than publishing as Catherine Moore? Was Tiptree an adopted persona, a form of masquerade, that Sheldon undertook with both considerable effort and success — sufficient to get "himself" ejected from the *Khatru* symposium (mentioned above) by the female participants because, as Lefanu suggests, "the women found her male persona too irritating to deal with"?[11] Or was Tiptree an alternative identity for Sheldon, someone who actually — or perhaps that should be "virtually" — existed?

This last is the suggestion that Amanda Boulter makes in her excellent essay "Alice James Raccoona Tiptree Sheldon Jr: Textual Personas in the Short Fiction of Alice Sheldon." Boulter begins her article by saying that from 1968 to 1977, "Alice Sheldon . . . successfully masqueraded as a man."[12] Boulter's argument, however, becomes considerably more nuanced in terms of the issues of gender and identity that Tiptree/Sheldon invokes. Boulter points out that "when Sheldon writes as Tiptree this is no more an imitation (of gender) than when she writes as Raccoona," Sheldon's other, in this case female, sf-writing pseudonym.[13] Both Boulter and Justine Larbalestier conclude that Alice/Raccoona/James's multiple existences can best be understood, through the works of such feminist critics as Judith Butler and Sue Ellen Case, as performative: "Sheldon plays at being both Raccoona but also at being Alice Sheldon. They are all performances."[14]

In such a view, Alice Sheldon — like you and I — has no more permanent reality than does Tiptree himself. Unlike our own lives, however, which are so naturalized as to be opaque to us, Sheldon's "performance" of Tiptree (and of Raccoona and of Alice) makes the performative aspects of subjectivity and identity more visible than is normally the case. Because the reader sees Tiptree performing both masculinity in general and "Tiptreeness" in specific, their own performances of gender and identity become more visible.

The performance of gender cannot be understood as simple, willful playacting. Rather, as Judith Butler notes, our performances of gender are "compulsory performances, ones which none of us choose, but which each of us is forced to negotiate."[15] Every human being is required to negotiate these performances in terms of the gender expectations and concomitant anxieties of her or his particular culture(s) — and the reader should remember that the requirements of Tiptree's culture, at an earlier and perhaps less complex feminist moment, were not precisely the requirements of middle-class American culture today.

(Un)Gendering Writing?

All of these questions hinge on the idea that Sheldon's "invention" or "pretense" of being James Tiptree has to be explained. What becomes obscured when the critical focus is so firmly on the author is that for many readers, encountering Tiptree's work in a library or a secondhand bookstore, Tiptree remains Tiptree.

In other words, the revelation that Tiptree was "really" Sheldon, while it permeated the sf community at the time, is not necessarily known to the contemporary reader who comes across Tiptree's earlier work without any reference to the later revelation and subsequent controversy.[16] For some readers the experience of reading Tiptree remains the experience of reading an "obviously" male writer, not a feminist subverter of masculinist (and, in fact, of some feminist) assumptions about the inherently gendered nature of writing — nor as some of the sourer male critics have retrospectively observed, of encountering "a stylistic sham reflecting a counterfeit masculinity."[17]

Of course, this backlash raises other questions about the nature of gender itself: Is masculinity an inherent trait of males? Or is there, as Judith Halberstam so powerfully argues, a type (or types) of female masculinity? Halberstam claims in her introduction to *Female Masculinity* that "female masculinities are framed as the rejected scraps of dominant masculinity in order that male masculinity may appear to be the real thing."[18] This comment is particularly forceful in the wake of some of the retrospective backstabbing brought about within the sf community by the revelation of Tiptree's "real" identity as a woman. The double claim that Tiptree was a sham and that the claimant always, however unprovably, *knew* "her" to be a sham appeared to some male sf writers and readers as the necessary tactics for assuring both their own and sf's identity as "the real thing." Sheldon herself noted this reaction, claiming, for example that

> There were the male writers who had seemed to take my work quite seriously, but who now began discovering that it was really the enigma of Tip's identity which had lent a spurious interest, and began finding various more-or-less subtle ways of saying so. (Oh, how well we know and love that pretentiously amiable tone, beneath which hides the furtive nastiness). I'd been warned against it, but it was still a shock coming from certain writers. The one thing I admire about that type of male hatred is its strategic agility. They soon get their ranks closed. Only here the timing was so damned funny, the perfect unison of their "reevaluation" of poor old Tip.[19]

Indeed, the revelation that Tiptree was "really" Alice Sheldon not only produced all sorts of "reevaluation," both well- and ill-intentioned; it has also allowed some interesting critical investigations both into the nature of gender itself and into assumptions about female and male reading and writing. The ambiguity of Tiptree/Sheldon's identity has forced readers and critics at least to think about, if not actually to revise, their assumptions about supposedly masculine and supposedly feminine stylistic and reading practices. In his postscript to his introduction to *Warm Worlds and Otherwise*, Robert Silverberg ruefully notes that, after "upholding [in print] the ineluctable masculinity of Tiptree's writing," he discovered that Tiptree was also Sheldon. He adds: "She fooled me beautifully, along with everyone else, and called into question the entire notion of what is 'masculine' or 'feminine' in fiction."[20]

As Joanna Russ points out in *How to Suppress Women's Writing*, it has traditionally been believed that women and men write differently — or rather, that men write "great" literature about important and universal topics, while women's work is of limited literary value and confined to "feminine" topics of little importance or interest. Russ quotes, among many other examples, Robert Southey's 1837 correspondence with the novelist Charlotte Brontë in which he insisted that "literature cannot be the business of a woman's life and ought not to be."[21] In all forms of literary endeavor, the belief that male writing has universal themes and literary worth while female writing does not has remained in some form of circulation, whether through university or high school curricula, the institution of literary awards, or other types of canon formation. Ironically, Ursula Le Guin points out, in "Award and Gender," while the Hugo and Nebula Awards have a less equal ratio of male to female winners than the Booker Prize (2 : 1), they have a lower ratio of male winners than more traditionally literary awards, such as the Pulitzer Prize (5 : 1) or the American Book Award (6 : 1).[22]

If, as Joanna Russ demonstrates, it has been traditional to assume that men and women write differently and that men write (or at least write sf) better, some feminist critics have used the Tiptree story to support an equally essentialist platform concerning the positive values of women's writing.[23] Both sets of assumptions have been applied to Tiptree's writing. Lefanu notes, ruefully, that, following the revelation of Sheldon as the woman behind Tiptree, the "question of the writer's gender becomes extremely significant, much more significant to me than I would like to admit."[24] And yet Lefanu goes on to discuss "The Screwfly Solution" as if it were by Tiptree and not by Raccoona Sheldon, despite acknowledging that Alice Sheldon chose to publish certain, more "female" oriented stories, under Raccoona's name. But then, is the gender that matters here a question of textuality or biology? Tiptree is textually male, Raccoona textually female; yet insofar as both are embodied in Alice Sheldon, they are both, in a sense, biologically female.

Now You See (Gender), Now You Don't

"And I Awoke" is a very short story that simply consists of a conversation between two men at the Big Junction space station. The first-person narrator is an eager young human male news reporter in space for the first time; his interlocutor is a slightly drunken redheaded human male employee of the station. During their conversation, as the journalist casts about eagerly for a glimpse of an alien, the redheaded man tells him a story. This story is cast as an "Awful Warning," which, of course, the young narrator promptly ignores. The redheaded man's narrative explains his own seduction by the human sexual obsession with aliens, from his first contact in a sleazy Earth bar named Little Junction to his eventual employment on the space station, where, despite two degrees in engineering, he works as a swabber.

After describing the psychological and physiological damage that can be caused by encounters with both alien anatomies and alien sexual cultures, the redheaded man speculates as to why humans, unlike most alien species, are obsessed by sex with the Other and attempts to warn not only the journalist but the rest of humanity about what amounts to the willing destruction of the human race. The story finishes when the redhead's wife appears and the journalist, despite identifying her as the damaged woman in the redhead's story, ignores her as well to run off in search of his own first encounter with an alien.

This synopsis of the story indicates the extent to which, although identified as a hard-bitten masculine space adventure, it is actually not plot-driven at all. Its futuristic setting — spaceships, the space station, the aliens — operates only as a barely sketched background to the redheaded man's narrative. While the journalist wants to hear about the wonderful strangeness of aliens, the redheaded man can barely stand the reminder of his own past, when he was a naive youngster who would do anything for a moment of alien attention. Not only does the redhead no longer share the naive journalist's enthusiasm for the topic of aliens, he calls him a "consummated fool" and warns him to "go home and make babies. While you still can." (Tiptree, 161)

This is not, as the reporter thinks, a reference to Gamma Radiation, but an introduction to the problem of human desire, at least when that desire is focused on the other, the alien. It is not radiation damage but the impossibility of desiring a merely human woman that prevents the redheaded man from making babies himself. Nothing happens in the story; its focus is on both past and future. Indeed, the redhead tells the story of his past only as a warning about the journalist's — and thus humanity's — probable future. The story is primarily a meditation on the nature of human desire and human sexuality; its quality of "Awful Warning" is about the impossibility of knowing the other through heterosexual desire (as women are the Other, warning the journalist about the dangers of sex with the other becomes both a cautionary tale about alien sex and about heterosexuality) as well as about the dangers of desiring what is different. The language and attitude of the characters, however, allies it with the more action-driven hard-bitten sf that was associated, at the time, with male writers. Even at the level of the story's construction, assumptions about the gendered nature of science fiction are being brought into question, particularly for the reader widely read in sf who can associate "And I Awoke" with stories by other male writers that rely on similar effects.

Reading the beginning of the story on the most superficial level of gender, the two central characters are coded as masculine in stereotypical ways: the innocent abroad and the hard-bitten and cynically experienced space-dog. But Tiptree immediately rings the changes on at least the latter character; rather than a tale of conquest, whether sexual or spatial, the redheaded man's narrative is one of failure, of the destruction of the soul. As a hard-bitten masculine hero, the storyteller simply doesn't cut it.

It is not so much that he lacks the phallic drive that Gwyneth Jones identifies as underlying traditionally male sf — "what we're *always*, *really* talking about is how Man gets out there to the edge of the known, grabs hold of a chunk of that alien dark, and pumps it full of his seed" — as that this same drive, which he names "exogamous," has turned on him.[25] It is the very desire to seize "a chunk of that alien dark" that the redheaded storyteller believes has led to his own destruction and is leading to the dissolution of the human race as an autonomous entity. In order to gain access to aliens, even to be near them, humans are pillaging the Earth for materials that they can exchange for a little bit of alien attention, alien goods. Likening contemporary humans to the "poor damned Polynesians" in Earth's own colonial history, the storyteller insists that the desire for alien goodies (whether material or sexual) is always a mistake: "Read history. *Ballpoint pens and bicycles.*"

To the storyteller, what was given up by Indigenous peoples to trade for European goods was inherently unequal. The Europeans saw land, furs, slaves, and minerals as intrinsically valuable and believed the natives uneducated fools for trading them for minor items, like bicycles, or apparently worthless ones, like ballpoint pens. What lurks behind the redhead's indignation and fear, however, is the realization that the real imbalance is not in material goods, but in ways of life or even in life itself. To the redhead it seems as if, overwhelmed by the desire not simply for European products but for some essence of being itself, the Indigenous peoples traded away not merely their resources, but their very cultures.[26]

After listening to the redhead's description of his first encounter with aliens at the Little Junction Bar back on Earth and the awful, abject obsession the knowledge of alien existence created in him, the journalist attempts to rationalize the problem of humans exchanging Earth's resources for useless alien junk with a bland comment about the balance of trade. This angers the redhead, who retorts, "Balance of trade — balance of *life*, man. I don't know if our birth rate is going, that's not the point. Our soul is leaking out. We're bleeding to death!" But it is not only the trade in material goods that he blames for the abjection of the human race before the marvelous, technologically superior aliens; it's also the nature of human desire:

> What I'm trying to tell you, this is a trap. We've hit the supernormal stimulus.[27] Man is exogamous — all our history is one long drive to find and impregnate the stranger. Or get impregnated by him; it works for women too. Anything different-colored, different nose, ass, anything, man *has* to fuck it or die trying. That's a drive, y'know, it's built in. Because it works fine as long as the stranger is human. For millions of years that kept the genes circulating. But now we've met aliens we can't screw, and we're about to die trying. . . . Do you think I can touch my wife?"[28] (Tiptree, 166)

"Man," in the redhead's masculinist discourse, is supposedly humanity; however, he has to add that "it works for women too" in order to anticipate the narrator's and/or the reader's assumption that "man" really only refers to men and to emphasize that this is not purely about the phallic drive. At the precise level at which the storyteller proclaims the Truth behind his story, Tiptree continually, but subtly, upsets the gendered apple cart. The hero's vaunted sex drive has let him down, to the point where he can no longer touch, let alone impregnate, his wife. At the same time, the very malaise that afflicts him, a malaise that should discursively be a product of his masculinity, his desire to grab that alien dark and inject his seed into it, turns out not to be specific to his gender at all.

Ironically, in her discussion of the storyteller's viewpoint in "And I Awoke," Sarah Lefanu argues that it is, to some extent, Tiptree's handling of male desire that made his writing persuasively masculine to the unknowing reader: "Tiptree's descriptions of hard-ons amongst the male of the species have a convincingly misogynist specificity."[29] Yet, as this quote indicates, the apparent discussion of a masculine desire to "dream outward," with its thrusting, phallic implications is really much more ambiguous than it may seem at first glance. Similarly, when the redheaded man identifies his youthful past with the phrase "before you had hair in your pants," (Tiptree, ooo) the masculine specificity of this is actually a form of trompe l'oeil: girls also develop pubic hair and were known, even in 1972 when the story was first published, to wear pants.

Lefanu herself points out that such descriptive passages in Tiptree's work often contain "an element of ridicule" and cites the scene in "Houston, Houston, Do You Read?" where the women astronauts in the all-female future subvert and, in the end, control an attempted rape by the twentieth-century misogynist, Bud, for the sake of adding the genetic material in his sperm to their radically depleted gene pool.[30]

It is up to each reader to decide whether such work is a feminist subversion of the more stereotypical elements associated with masculine writing. Is it proof that male and female styles are, at most, cultural constructs that may not even exist? Does it suggest that a masculine style of writing does actually exist because Tiptree is able, apparently, to internalize and reproduce it so well — whether subversively mocking it at the same time, or not?

Postcolonial Fairy Tale?

At the same time it may be a mistake to specify gender by itself as paramount in Tiptree's fiction. As Adam Roberts has pointed out, "And I Awoke" can be read "as a postcolonial fable."[31] However, in arguing that it "might be more illuminating . . . reading Tiptree in terms not of feminist but rather post-colonial theory," Roberts both brings to the work a useful alternative perspective and fails to account for the extent to which sex and gender are already implicated in the colonial and the postcolonial.

The two coalesce, as Leela Gandhi points out, in the specter of the "Third World woman."[32] The Third World woman, in Gayatri Chakravarty Spivak's famous formulation, is the subaltern who cannot speak. She can only be spoken about or for by others. This figure of the woman silenced by gender, race, and colonization is a specter that also haunts Tiptree's story—the mute woman confined to the periphery of the tale, less significant even than the human male who has so far fallen from his status as supreme being in his own small world[33]—as much as she does the juncture of postcolonial and feminist theory. But the significant giveaway in "And I Awoke" is precisely the factor that Roberts neglects to reconcile in terms of his use of postcoloniality: the human obsession with the aliens is depicted by Tiptree as specifically a *sexual* obsession. It is this sexual obsession that the storyteller understands as the root of humanity's downfall and that he continually warns the journalist/narrator against. The issue of sexuality is thus linked to colonialism in the story in a remarkably clear way—a way whose clarity has its roots in the colonial situations the young Alice Bradley witnessed in Africa.

The situation in "And I Awoke," in which humans are clearly at the low end of the galactic totem pole, reproduces the colonial experience from the point of view of the colonized. And Tiptree has the redhead point this out: "Everything going out, nothing coming back. Like the poor damned Polynesians. We're gutting Earth, to begin with. Swapping raw resources for junk. Alien status symbols. Tape decks, Coca-Cola, Mickey Mouse watches." (Tiptree, 165)

The storyteller compares the relationship between aliens and humans to the historical situation between Polynesians and Europeans, calling it "some cargo-cult of the soul" and insisting that, while the destructive obsession with aliens is a product of the exogamous human sex drive, "sex is only part of it." (Tiptree, 166) The comparison to the twentieth-century phenomenon of the cargo cult locates the story firmly in the realm of the (post)colonial and also suggests that what seems at first to be purely sexual is also a product of the ways in which religion may provide consolations based on an apparent misunderstanding of the actual situation.[34]

The so-called cargo cults arose in Polynesia and Melanesia during the colonial period and became the subject of anthropological and ethnographic studies from the mid-1960s onward. In many cases, especially after air bases were abandoned at the end of World War II, native populations went to extraordinary lengths, creating landing strips and full-sized model aircraft, in the attempt to entice the gods into continuing to deliver material goods. Native agricultural practices were disrupted or even abandoned in favor of Western foods, leaving indigenous peoples in straitened circumstances after the war and seeming, from the perspective of Western anthropology, to cause a variety of attempts to placate the gods whose favor was so suddenly withdrawn. Cargo cults are also associated with millenarianism and eschatological beliefs in general; they arose, in part, because of the overlaying of Christianity onto traditional religious beliefs along with the appearance of a sometimes incomprehensible new order issued in by materially wealthy European colonizers and missionaries.

Tiptree may have been familiar with early research on cargo cults as religious and political movements that destroyed traditional customs and economies in anticipation of the delivery of Western material goods. Anthropologists in the 1960s considered the development of cargo cults to be a sign of the incomprehensibility of technologically advanced Western culture to the recently colonized.[35] Tiptree clearly uses the metaphor of the cargo cult to suggest the weakness of the colonized, overawed by the technological superiority and material wealth of the arriving foreigners and thus willingly trading their own immemorial culture for Coca-Cola and Mickey Mouse watches. Adam Roberts suggests that Tiptree "sees that too often the colonised people collaborate . . . in their own oppression, accepting and even welcoming degradation in the hope of money, or more nebulously in the hope of some *flavour* or *aspect* of the dominant culture."[36]

Is the intended target of Tiptree's irony the colonizer or the colonized — or both? Perhaps what is at issue here is the moral impossibility of imperialism itself. In taking such an ambiguous stance, one in which it seems that humans (standing in for the colonized everywhere) are at least partially to blame for their own capitulation to the colonial situation, Tiptree's emphasis on human exogamy and on the sexual abjection of the storyteller and his wife introduces a further and yet more complicated element.

Reading "And I Awoke" today, in the light of postcolonialism, readers are faced with the difficulty postcolonial theory has had in addressing issues of sexuality. Sexual issues have been largely ignored in favor of the study of race and gender in most postcolonial critiques, although clearly all three issues are deeply and complexly interwoven. Roberts's inability to integrate issues of colonialism with issues of sexuality makes his timely attempt to introduce a postcolonial approach to Tiptree's work somewhat less than convincing. Roberts refers the reader back to the story's title, which is a line from John Keats's poem "La Belle Dame sans Merci," in which the reason for the knight's pale loitering is his sexual encounter with the world of "faery." Lured into the faery maiden's "elfin grot," he sees "pale kings and princes too" who cry to him, "La Belle Dame sans Merci/Hath thee in thrall!" When he awakens, he finds himself no longer in the land of faery, but alone "On the cold hill side." Roberts refers briefly to the sexual overtones of Keats's poem, but concludes that Tiptree's real theme is power and money, not sex.

By contrast, reinforcing the point I made earlier about Tiptree's conflation of the pain of desiring the alien with the problems of heterosexuality, sf critic Veronica Hollinger argues that all of Tiptree's feminist stories are "extrapolations of some of the more dismal exigencies of a naturalized heterosexuality, (re)constructed as a kind of inescapable heterosexual bind." Referring briefly to "And I Awoke," Hollinger insists that "human (hetero)sexuality is both instinct and damnation. Human sexual desire for the 'other' results only in pain, as our objects of desire become increasingly, and sometimes literally, alien to us. Sexuality is the failed attempt to know the irreducibly alien. From this perspective, Tiptree's stories are modern tragedies of gender difference."[37] For Hollinger, the story's deployment of sexuality can be read, as indeed Keats's poem can, as a lamentation for the impossibility of knowing the (heterosexual) beloved across the divide of gender. Of course, this interpretation may vary for the contemporary reader of Keats, to whom the world of "faery" is less familiar than the slang use of "fairy" to disparage gay men; for this reader, Keats's poem may seem somewhat queerer (as is also true of Tiptree, as I will explain below).

It is fairly obvious that Tiptree borrowed the plot, such as it is, from Keats's poem, as well as some of its elegiac atmosphere. Both poem and story emphasize the sexual power of the alien: that of the faery woman in the poem and of the literal aliens in the story. Furthermore, while Keats sets his poem between two traditional elements of English folklore — the lone knight and the faery woman — Tiptree sets his in an alien future in which aliens are, even more clearly than in Anglo-Celtic myth, the indifferent masters of humanity. In other words, while the knight's encounter undoes him, so that he finds no satisfaction in human life, the storyteller's encounter is posed as representative of the undoing of humanity as a whole. And that undoing is indeed sexual, as all human sexual acculturation is set aside: not only is the storyteller willingly dominated by the female alien he adores, he tells the journalist of his first encounter with a Yyeir:

> The first Yyeir I saw, I dropped everything and started walking after it like a starving hound, just breathing. You've seen the pix of course. Like lost dreams. *Man is in love and loves what vanishes.* . . . It's the scent, you can't guess that. I followed until I ran into a slammed port. I spent half a cycle's credits sending the creature the wine they call stars' tears. . . . Later I found out it was a male. That made no difference at all. (Tiptree, 165)

In the early seventies, when this story was first published, the idea that a human might be indifferent to the biological sex of his object of desire was radical, almost nonsensical. Just a few years after the gay liberation movement began to make the decriminalization of homosexuality an issue, the distinction between homosexuality and heterosexuality and the assumed morality of the latter were very much taken for granted. Yet it is not the ambisexuality of the human encounter with the alien that is foregrounded here, however startling it may have seemed or still seems to the reader that our apparently macho hero could spend half his wages courting a male alien. What is at the forefront of the story is the question of abjection. It is precisely the abjection of humanity in the face of the indifferent imperialism of the alien that links the feminist critique of gender to the queer critique of sexuality to the postcolonial critique of the colonized condition.

One of the conditions of being, as Gwyneth Jones puts it, "the alien dark," is that the alien dark is perennially assigned the abject role in any set of relationships; the alien dark is not even the subject of its own desire, but can only be desired by the penetrating Man who will "grab hold of a chunk of [it] and pump it full of his seed." In "And I Awoke," however, Man, as much as woman, has lost the potential to be the subject of his own desire. He desires, but his desire is irrelevant, self-destructive, utterly abject — of no more interest to the masters of the New Galactic Order than the desires of women are to Man, the supposed master of both the New and Old Worlds here on Earth.

So indifferent are the aliens that humanity is not an object of desire to any but the oddest alien pervert. The storyteller points out, "You can see it here at Big Junction, always the same. Outside of the Procya, it's humans with aliens, right? Very seldom aliens with other aliens. Never aliens with humans. It's the humans who want in." (Tiptree, 164). In desiring admission to alien culture and life within the very terms set by the aliens themselves, Tiptree suggests that humans, like Pacific Islanders, create cargo cults as substitutes for the lost meaning of their own lives and cultures; humanity as a whole becomes the alien dark, a position previously occupied only by those who were subaltern, or abjected, within the human race: women, homosexuals, the colonized. As Barbara Creed has noted, "The place of the abject is where meaning collapses, the place where I am not. The abject threatens life, it must be radically excluded from the place of the living subject, propelled away from the body and deposited on the other side of an imaginary border which separates the self from that which threatens the self."[38]

Becoming Alien, Becoming Abject

At stake in "And I Awoke," is the loss of human subjectivity — a position long assumed to be the birthright of white, heterosexual males. Women, the abjected "alien dark," have historically been regarded as the objects, not the subjects, of the human story; history, culture, art, and indeed life itself — all have been taken as comprehensible only through the male "universal" perspective. This supposedly "universal" perspective is really that of straight white middle-class men. The viewpoints and knowledges of lesbians and gay people and of people of color are relegated to the peripheries, categorized as uninteresting to anyone else, and thus incomprehensible to "ordinary" people.

Roberts argues that the alien/human relationship in Tiptree's story is akin to the contemporary problems of Third World sweatshops and sex tourism, noting that he's "not merely trying to rehearse western liberal outrage at these unpalatable facts of the world today. . . , except to say that it is power and money that drives the sex tourism trade in the first place. Sex is really only a secondary consideration."[39] It is true that capitalism has become a primary means of organizing desire (and not only in the West), but that only means that narratives about money and power are always also narratives about sex and desire. Indeed, anthropologist Monty Lindstrom makes the same connection in his discussion of the salience of cargo cults in Western imaginations: being organized around a fascination with the other, "they supply late capitalist narratives of desire."[40] Thus Roberts's argument needs to be nuanced by the recognition that power and money cannot be given primacy over desire, but are part of a web of connections among knowledge, desire, and ways of being in the world.

Roberts's reading of the story may seem as compelling to some readers as an interpretation that focuses on gender. I believe that what makes this barely ten-page story so particularly brilliant is the very precise way it captures the interweaving of science fiction's woman-as-alien with queer theory's denaturalization of heteronormativity with postcolonialism's revelation of the colonial condition. By clarifying the linkages between Othernesses, Tiptree illuminates the need to find ways of making life meaningful that do not involve re-creating some group or other as the abjected "alien dark" against which all meaning must be asserted.

Women are figured as alien in science fiction in at least two ways. On the one hand, women are uncritically presented as aliens in a society in which men are assumed to be the norm — as is still the case in most Western societies. On the other hand, feminist critiques of sf attempt to expose this construction, where other sf does not see it because it takes its conditions (man = normal, woman = other) for granted. This exposure allows conscious understanding and criticism of both the analogy (woman = alien) itself and the social conditions that create it. Sf always responds, in one way or another, to the society in which it is produced.

As I noted above, however, gender is already implicated in other forms of critical and theoretical work. If postcolonial theory ignores questions of gender, then it is forced to assume that the experience of colonialism is the same both for the colonizers and the colonized. European women experienced colonialism differently from European men because they were allowed different, and generally more restricted, roles in European society; similarly, men and women experienced being colonized differently and in ways that were often complexly doubled by the gender expectations of the European colonizers overlaid on the gender expectations of their own cultures. In Alice Bradley's experience of Africa, the gender differences produced and exacerbated by colonialism were showcased, particularly in the distrust of African male sexuality exhibited by European men (for a fuller discussion of this issue, see L. Timmel Duchamp's essay in this volume "Something Rich and Strange: Karen Joy Fowler's 'What I Didn't See.'"

Race, gender, and sexuality are all aligned in complex ways through the discourses of colonialism. The focus on the production of white babies meant that European women were valued only for their reproductive potential, while homosexual behavior, which could only diminish the procreative possibilities of the supposedly superior white race, was increasingly stigmatized as a type of racial treachery. As Tim McCaskell argues, in his article "A History of Race/ism,"

> This preoccupation with [racially "pure" and eugenically beneficial] reproduction also resulted in an obsession with sex. Only properly regulated "heterosexual" behaviour could guarantee racial survival. Traditionally, improper sexual activity had been considered a matter of morality and sin.. . . But now, in a world where *race* was the primary concern, homosexuality or any non-reproductive sexual activity was akin to treason, since it wasted and exhausted the "germ plasm" that carried the strength and abilities of the race. Racial purity went hand in hand with sexual hygiene.[41]

It is impossible to separate the ways in which gender functioned in the colonial period from its relationship to both sexuality and race. All three of these issues, which today are considered largely in terms of identity, function to produce not merely the possibility of subjectivity for any given individual, but also to delineate the individual's position on the binary hierarchy of normal/different. To be white is to be normal, which leaves people of color in the position of aliens. To be male is to be normal, which positions women as the "alien dark." To be heterosexual is to be normal, which constructs homosexuals as the abjected other. The colonizer is the norm, the colonized is not; the colonizer speaks and is listened to, the colonized does not and is not.

In "And I Awoke," Tiptree literalizes the question of whose speech counts. The redheaded man speaks, but the narrator, even though he is also human, does not listen. Humans in this alien world, like Third World women in globalized economies, are too abject to be audible, even to other humans. They have no subjectivity; in essence, although the redheaded man speaks, his words register only for the audience on the outside of the story—and the words the audience registers are Tiptree's.

Feminist theories of abjection suggest that people must exclude whatever is understood as abject from their own sense of selfhood, or subjectivity; thus, for example, masculinity must exclude femininity, which is its abject other. Adam Roberts claims that Tiptree's story asks, *"why are people slaves?"* According to Roberts, the answer is not that the slaves, the colonized, lack the strength to throw off the oppressor, but rather that "part of the truth lies in the uncomfortable fact that human beings too often fall in love with that which oppresses and degrades them. That is what Tiptree's story tells us." But Roberts's interpretation here does not explain *why* this is the case, beyond the argument that "at the heart of the tale is a model of 'desire' that sees it as being fundamentally unrealisable."[42]

I would rather ask what, in the confluence of feminist, postcolonial, and queer theory (which is still the strongest theoretical approach to understanding human sexuality), offers an explanation for the problem of human abjection that Tiptree poses in "And I Awoke."[43] One possible answer is that Tiptree is not trying to create a comprehensive explanation for human desire and abjection, but rather that the story might be read as an analogy: speaking to the presumptive male reader of science fiction, the story puts the male in the position of the abject, the alien dark; it makes him *feel*, in every iota of his being, what it is like to be on the other side of the gender divide. The human has become the abjected "alien dark" before the colonizing indifference of the superior aliens; it is the human that is now the alien, the other. That male reader may never know consciously what it is he has experienced, but experienced it he has, nonetheless. This makes "And I Awoke" a profoundly feminist story as much as a postcolonial one. It also suggests that Tiptree's performance of masculinity is essential to the story's construction, a necessary element in the trap he sets for the reader, particularly the straight white male reader.

If, Tiptree seems to be saying, I can only be "I" at the cost of making someone else into the alien dark, then my subjectivity rests on very shaky grounds indeed: I risk always the abjection of my "I" should someone else come along who holds the power to reduce me from my role as impregnator of the universe to the amorphous and abject position of the one who cannot desire because the desiring self is dissolved into the new colonial hierarchy. Perhaps there are better ways of being male, of being heterosexual, and of being white that do not necessitate dehumanizing and abjecting others. Tiptree does not suggest what these methods might be, but he does demonstrate what abjection costs both the "normal" and the abjected.

NOTES

1. Robert Silverberg, "Who is Tiptree, What is He?" introduction to *Warm Worlds and Otherwise*, by James Tiptree Jr. (New York: Ballantine Books, 1975), xvi.

2. Jenny Wolmark, *Aliens and Others: Science Fiction, Feminism and Postmodernism* (London: Harvester Wheatsheaf, 1993), 1–2.

3. Gwyneth Jones, "Kairos," in *Edging into the Future: Science Fiction and Contemporary Cultural Transformation* eds. Veronica Hollinger and Joan Gordon (Philadelphia: University of Pennsylvania Press, 2003), 180.

While sf often literalizes *aliens* as beings from elsewhere, difference is implicit in the word itself, which comes from the Latin word "alienus," meaning other, different, strange.

4. Josephine Saxton, "'Goodbye to all that . . . ,'" in *Where No Man Has Gone Before: Women and Science Fiction*, ed. Lucie Armitt (New York: Routledge, 1991), 212.

5. Lisa Yaszek, "Unhappy Housewife Heroines, Galactic Suburbia, and Nuclear War: A New History of Midcentury Women's Science Fiction," *Extrapolation* 44, no. 1 (Spring 2003): 99.

6. Sarah Lefanu, *In the Chinks of the World Machine* (London: The Women's Press, 1988), 5.

7. Somewhat later, Sheldon invented her third persona, Raccoona Tiptree, who published sf stories that, according to later interviews with Alice Sheldon, allowed her to say "some things impossible to a male persona"; quoted in Lefanu, *In the Chinks of the World Machine*, 122.

8. See Lefanu's discussion of Tiptree's participation in the feminist sf symposium in issues 3 & 4 of Jeffrey Smith's fanzine *Khatru*, 105–106. The particpants were Suzy McKee Charnas, Virginia Kidd, Ursula Le Guin, Vonda McIntyre, Raylyn Moore, Kate Wilhelm and Chelsea Quinn Yarbro, along with Samuel Delany and *Khatru* editor Jeffrey Smith.

9. Lefanu's title is, of course, a play on the title of Robert Silverberg's now infamous introduction to *Warm Worlds and Otherwise*, titled "Who is Tiptree, What is He?" in which Silverberg both raises and dismisses the possibility that the reclusive writer might be a woman: "there is to me something ineluctably masculine about Tiptree's writing" (xii).

10. For the rest of this article, I shall refer to Alice Sheldon and Raccoona Sheldon both as "she" and to James Tiptree as "he." There is little consensus on the use of pronouns to refer to Tiptree; Adam Frisch and Sarah Lefanu, for example, both

call Tiptree "she," whereas Amanda Boulter and Justine Larbalestier refer to Tiptree as "he." Because I am arguing that the Tiptree persona was more than a simple pseudonym, I adhere to the latter practice.

11. Lefanu, *In the Chinks of the World Machine*, 105.

12. Amanda Boulter, "Alice James Raccoona Tiptree Sheldon Jr: Textual Personas in the Short Fiction of Alice Sheldon," *Foundation* 63 (Spring 1995): 5.

13. Raccoona Sheldon is the name that appeared on some short stories that appear to have a more female perspective — and sometimes a female protagonist — than is the case with Tiptree's writing. Notably, Raccoona Sheldon had difficulty getting her stories published until she began sending them to editors along with a testimonial by Tiptree, thus proving a point about the masculine bias inherent in the sf publishing business at the time. Somewhat problematically, in the first major consideration of Tiptree's work, *In the Chinks of the World Machine*, Sarah Lefanu considers a number of stories by Raccoona Sheldon, but under the rubric of Tiptree's name even though Alice Sheldon had clearly chosen to differentiate the Raccoona stories from the Tiptree stories. Boulter, "Alice James," 14.

14. Justine Larbalestier, *The Battle of the Sexes in Science Fiction* (Middletown, Conn.: Wesleyan University Press, 2002), 202.

15. Judith Butler, *Bodies that Matter: On the Discursive Limits of Sex* (New York: Routledge, 1993), 237.

16. I have met a number of readers in the last decade who have been unaware of Tiptree's double identity, in some cases despite its revelation in the introduction to the anthology they happen to be reading.

17. Both Boulter and Larbalestier have done a good job of pointing out the problems with the retrospective knowingness of those who claim never to have been fooled, as well as the backlash among some of the fooled, who then rushed to attempt to discredit Tiptree's work as impoverished and fraudulent. Boulter, "Alice James," 15.

18. Judith Halberstam, *Female Masculinity* (Durham: Duke University Press, 1998), 1. Halberstam begins with the obvious point that our culture has always acknowledged the possibility of male femininity (often through the derogatory term *effeminacy*) but has no coherent means of recognizing the variety of ways in which women can be masculine. However, the question of Tiptree's masculinity remains unresolved: was he the textual expression of Sheldon's own female masculinity or did he possess some form of (male) masculinity in his own right?

19. Quoted in Larbalestier, *Battle of the Sexes*, 197–198.

20. Silverberg, "Who is Tiptree," xviii.

21. Quoted in Joanna Russ, *How to Suppress Women's Writing* (London: The Women's Press, 1984), 11.

22. Ursula K. Le Guin, "Award and Gender," in her *The Wave in the Mind: Talks and Essays on the Writer, the Reader, and the Imagination* (Boston: Shambhala, 2004), 145.

23. This topic is too large to be dealt with in detail here, other than to note that many feminist approaches to women's writing take gendered difference for granted and understand it as empowering alternative approaches to meaning-making. A quick library catalogue search on the category "Authorship — Sex Differences" will reveal many critical works dealing with the subject. In the context of science

fiction, see particularly Russ, *How to Suppress Women's Writing*, and Larbalestier, *Battle of the Sexes*.

24. Lefanu, *In the Chinks of the World Machine*, 106.

25. Jones, "Kairos," 180. "Exogamy" refers to the custom of marrying outside the tribe, clan, or other unit of kinship and is generally assumed to have the purpose of increasing the spread and diversity of genetic material and avoiding interbreeding between close kin.

26. Many of the redhead's assumptions about the relationship between Indigenous and European peoples are problematic from the perspective of historical critiques of colonial practice: they treat trade as an option that the natives could have refused, ignoring the fact that the European presence in most colonized lands was enforced at gunpoint and facilitated by the introduction of diseases (particularly smallpox) and vices (like alcohol) that in combination devastated native populations. The redheaded man's anthropological perspective on indigenousness and cargo cults is drawn from work done in the 1960s, much of which has been superseded in anthropological circles today. For a discussion of this problem, see the special issue on anthropological approaches to cargo cults in *Oceania* 70, no. 4 (June 2000).

27. *Supernormal stimulus* is a term from psychology and ethnology for any stimulus that works by exaggerating the effects of a normal stimulus. Some birds, for example, will ignore their own egg if a larger or more brightly colored fake egg is introduced into the nest. The supernormal stimulus is thus one that the individual responds to *more* than to the normal stimulus.

28. The problem of racial hierarchies created through colonization and the proscription against racial interbreeding that governed much sexual behavior until well into the 1960s is simply elided by the redheaded man's argument. Theoretically, it appears that racism functions to prevent interracial relationships in much the same way as homophobia works to discourage homosexual relations. Tiptree's story erases racial tensions by rewriting humanity as a single race with a universal approach to the organization of desire, one that leaves humans intrinsically vulnerable to their galactic colonizers.

29. Lefanu, *In the Chinks of the World Machine*, 107.

30. Ibid.

31. Adam Roberts, "James Tiptree Jr.'s 'And I Awoke and Found Me Here on the Cold Hill's Side' as Neocolonialist Fable," *Alien Online* (April 2003), <http://www.thealienonline.net/columns/rcsf_tiptree_apr03.asp?tid=7&scid=55&iid=1591> (cited February 12, 2004).

32. Leela Gandhi, *Postcolonial Theory: A Critical Introduction* (St. Leonards, New South Wales: Allen & Unwin, 1998), esp. chap. 5.

33. Ironically, the storyteller's an American in a story written in 1972, a time when the Vietnam War was read by critics inside and outside the United States as an expression of U.S. imperialism.

34. There is considerable disagreement about "whether to locate these phenomena [of the cargo cults] in the cultures of the Melanesians or the concepts and concerns of Western anthropologists"; Doug Dalton, "Introduction," *Oceania* 70, no. 4 (June 2000): 285. In other words, assuming that cargo cults are cultlike and ineffectual responses to the encounter with colonialism (resulting from ignorance

of the "real" situation) says as much about Western assumptions about the nature of knowledge, religion, and the importance of rationalism as it does about Melanesian cultures.

35. More recent scholarship has tended to emphasize both the millennial and the anticolonial, political aspects of various cargo cult movements. Dalton notes: "No one could disagree today that the term 'cargo cult' was used by colonial authorities to de-legitimize and criminalize the behavior of their subjects that it designated" (ibid., 286).

36. Roberts, "James Tiptree Jr.'s 'And I Awoke.'"

37. Veronica Hollinger, "(Re)reading Queerly: Science Fiction, Feminism, and the Defamiliarization of Gender," *Science Fiction Studies* 26, no. 1 (March 1999): 27.

38. Barbara Creed, *Horror and the Monstrous Feminine: An Imaginary Abjection* (London: Routledge, 1993), 65.

39. Roberts, "James Tiptree Jr.'s 'And I Awoke.'"

40. Quoted in Dalton, "Introduction," 285.

41. Tim McCaskell, "A History of Race/ism," Toronto Board of Education, 1994, http://www3.sympatico.ca/twshreve/Inclusive/HistoryRacism.htm (20 July 2000).

42. Roberts, "James Tiptree Jr.'s 'And I Awoke.'"

43. For good discussions of queer theory, see particularly Nikki Sullivan's *A Critical Introduction to Queer Theory* (Edinburgh: University of Edinburgh Press, 2003) and William B. Turner's *A Genealogy of Queer Theory* (Philadelphia: Temple University Press, 2000). The central insight of queer theory is that the ways in which we understand sexuality are not innate or natural, but products of culture. Different cultures assign different meanings to sexual choices, sexual acts, and even to what counts as sexual.

Wives

Freedom from men they experienced during war time

LISA TUTTLE

First published in The Magazine of Fantasy and Science Fiction, *December 1979*

A smell of sulphur in the air on a morning when the men had gone, and the wives, in their beds, smiled in their sleep, breathed more easily, and burrowed deeper into dreams.

Jack's wife woke, her eyes open and her little nose flaring, smelling something beneath the sulphur smell. One of those smells she was used to not noticing, when the men were around. But it was all right, now. Wives could do as they pleased, so long as they cleaned up and were back on their proper places when the men returned.

Jack's wife — who was called Susie — got out of bed too quickly and grimaced as the skintight punished her muscles. She caught sight of herself in the mirror over the dressing table: her sharp teeth were bared, and she looked like a wild animal, bound and struggling. She grinned at that, because she could easily free herself.

She cut the skintight apart with scissors, cutting and ripping carelessly. It didn't matter that it was ruined — skintights were plentiful. She had a whole boxful, herself, in the hall closet behind the Christmas decorations. And she didn't have the patience to try soaking it off slowly in a hot bath, as the older wives recommended. So her muscles would be sore and her skintight a tattered rag — she would be free that much sooner.

She looked down at her dead-white body, feeling distaste. She felt despair at the sight of her small arms, hanging limp, thin and useless in the hollow below her ribs. She tried to flex them but could not make them move. She began to massage them with her primary fingers, and after several minutes the pain began, and she knew they weren't dead yet.

She bathed and massaged her newly uncovered body with oil. She felt terrifyingly free, naked and rather dangerous, with the skintight removed. She sniffed the air again and that familiar scent, musky and alluring, aroused her.

She ran through the house — noticing, in passing, that Jack's pet spider was eating the living room sofa. It was the time for building nests and co-

coons, she thought happily, time for laying eggs and planting seeds; the spider was driven by the same force that drove her.

Outside the dusty ground was hard and cold beneath her bare feet. She felt the dust all over her body, raised by the wind and clinging to her momentary warmth. She was coated in the soft yellow dust by the time she reached the house next door — the house where the magical scent came from, the house which held a wife in heat, longing for someone to mate with.

Susie tossed her head, shaking the dust out in a little cloud around her head. She stared up at the milky sky and around at all the houses, alien artefacts constructed by men. She saw movement in the window of the house across the street and waved — the figure watching her waved back.

Poor old Maggie, thought Susie. Old, bulging and ugly; unloved and nobody's wife. She was only housekeeper to two men who were, rather unfortunately Susie thought, in love with each other.

But she didn't want to waste time by thinking of wives and men, or by feeling pity, now. Boldly, like a man, Susie pounded at the door.

It opened. "Ooooh, Susie!"

Susie grinned and looked the startled wife up and down. You'd never know from looking at her that the men were gone and she could relax — this wife, called Doris, was as dolled up as some eager-to-please newlywed and looked, Susie thought, more like a real woman than any woman had ever looked.

Over her skintight (which was bound more tightly than Susie's had been) Doris wore a low-cut dress, her three breasts carefully bound and positioned to achieve the proper, double-breasted effect. Gaily patterned and textured stockings covered her silicone-injected legs, and she tottered on heels three centimetres high. Her face was carefully painted, and she wore gold bands on neck, wrists and fingers.

Then Susie ignored what she looked like because her nose told her so much more. The smell was so powerful now that she could feel her pouch swelling in lonely response.

Doris must have noticed, for her eyes rolled, seeking some safe view.

"What's the matter?" Susie asked, her voice louder and bolder than it ever was when the men were around. "Didn't your man go off to war with the others? He stay home sick in bed?"

Doris giggled. "Ooooh, I wish he would, sometimes! No, he was out of here before it was light."

Off to see his mistress before leaving, Susie thought. She knew that Doris was nervous about being displaced by one of the other wives, her man was always fooling around with — there were always more wives than there were men, and her man had a roving eye.

"Calm down, Doris. Your man can't see you now, you know." She stroked one of Doris's hands. "Why don't you take off that silly dress and your skintight. I know how constricted you must be feeling. Why not relax with me?"

She saw Doris's face darken with emotion beneath the heavy make-up, and she grasped her hand more tightly when Doris tried to pull away.

"Please don't," Doris said.

"Come on," Susie murmured, caressing Doris's face and feeling the thick paint slide beneath her fingers.

"No, don't . . . please . . . I've tried to control myself, truly I have. But the exercises don't work, and the perfume doesn't cover the smell well enough — he won't even sleep with me when I'm like this. He thinks it's disgusting, and it is. I'm so afraid he'll leave me."

"But he's gone now, Doris. You can let yourself go. You don't have to worry about him when he's not around! It's safe, it's all right, you can do as you please now — we can do anything we like and no one will know." She could feel Doris trembling.

"Doris," she whispered and rubbed her face demandingly against hers.

At that, the other wife gave in, and collapsed in her arms.

Susie helped Doris out of her clothes, tearing at them with hands and teeth, throwing shoes and jewellery high into the air and festooning the yard with tags of dress, stockings and undergarment.

But when Doris, too, was naked, Susie suddenly felt shy and a little frightened. It would be wrong to mate here in the settlement built by man, wrong and dangerous. They must go somewhere else, somewhere they could be something other than wives for a little while, and follow their own natures without reproach.

They went to a place of stone on the far northern edge of the human settlement. It was a very old place, although whether it had been built by the wives in the distant time before they were wives or whether it was natural, neither Susie nor Doris could say. They both felt it was a holy place, and it seemed right to mate there, in the shadow of one of the huge, black, standing stones.

It was a feast, an orgy of life after a season of death. They found pleasure in exploring the bodies which seemed so similar to men but which they knew to be miraculously different, each from the other, in scent, texture and taste. They forgot that they had ever been creatures known as wives. They lost their names and forgot the language of men as they lay entwined.

There were no skintights imprisoning their bodies now, barring them from sensation, freedom and pleasure, and they were partners, not strangers, as they explored and exulted in their flesh. This was no mockery of the sexual act — brutishly painful and brief as it was with the men but the true act in all its meaning.

They were still joined at sundown, and it was not until long after the three moons began their nightly waltz through the clouds that the two lovers fell asleep at last.

"In three months," Susie said dreamily. "We can . . ."

"In three months we won't do anything."

"Why not? If the men are away . . ."

"I'm hungry," said Doris. She wrapped her primary arms around herself. "And I'm cold, and I ache all over. Let's go back."

"Stay here with me, Doris. Let's plan."

"There's nothing to plan."

"But in three months we must get together and fertilize it."

"Are you crazy? Who would carry it then? One of us would have to go without a skintight, and do you think either of our husbands would let us slop around for four months without a skintight? And then when it's born how could we hide it? Men don't have babies, and they don't want anyone else to. Men kill babies, just as they kill all their enemies."

Susie knew that what Doris was saying was true, but she was reluctant to give up her new dream. "Still, we might be able to keep it hidden," she said. "It's not so hard to hide things from a man . . ."

"Don't be so stupid," Doris said scornfully. Susie noticed that she still had smears of make-up on her face. Some smears had transferred themselves to Susie in the night. They looked like bruises or bloody wounds. "Come back with me now," Doris said, her voice gentle again. "Forget this, about the baby. The old ways are gone — we're wives now, and we don't have a place in our lives for babies."

"But some day the war may end," Susie said. "And the men will all go back to Earth and leave us here."

"If that happens," said Doris, "then we would make new lives for ourselves. Perhaps we would have babies again."

"If it's not too late then," Susie said. "If it ever happens." She stared past Doris at the horizon.

"Come back with me."

Susie shook her head. "I have to think. You go. I'll be all right."

She realized when Doris had gone that she, too, was tired, hungry and sore, but she was not sorry she had remained in the place of stone. She needed to stay a while longer in one of the old places, away from the distractions of the settlement. She felt that she was on the verge of remembering something very important.

A large, dust-coloured lizard crawled out of a hole in the side of a fallen rock, and Susie rolled over and clapped her hands on it. But it wriggled out of her clutches like air or water or the wind blown dust and disappeared somewhere. Susie felt a sharp pang of disappointment — she had a sudden memory of how that lizard would have tasted, how the skin of its throat would have felt, tearing between her teeth. She licked her dry lips and sat up. In the old days, she thought, I caught many such lizards. But the old days were gone, and with them the old knowledge and the old abilities.

I'm not what I used to be, she thought. I'm something else now, a "wife," created by man in the image of something I have never seen, something called "woman."

She thought about going back to her house in the settlement and of wrapping herself in a new skintight and then selecting the proper dress and shoes to make a good impression on the returning Jack; she thought about painting her face and putting rings on her fingers. She thought about boiling and burning good food to turn it into the unappetizing messes Jack favoured, and about killing the wide-eyed "coffee fish" to get the oil to make the mildly addictive drink the men called "coffee." She thought about watching Jack, and listening to him, always alert for what he might want, what he might ask, what he might do. Trying to anticipate him, to earn his praise and avoid his blows and harsh words. She thought about letting him "screw" her and about the ugly jewellery and noisome perfumes he brought her.

Susie began to cry, and the dust drank her tears as they fell. She didn't understand how this had all begun, how or why she had become a wife, but she could bear it no longer.

She wanted to be what she had been born to be — but she could not remember what that was. She only knew that she could be Susie no longer. She would be no man's wife.

"I remembered my name this morning," Susie said with quiet triumph. She looked around the room. Doris was staring down at her hands, twisting them in her lap. Maggie looked half asleep, and the other two wives — Susie didn't remember their names; she had simply gathered them up when she found them on the street — looked both bored and nervous.

"Don't you see?" Susie persisted. "If I could remember that, I'm sure I can remember other things, in time. All of us can."

Maggie opened her eyes all the way. "And what good would that do," she asked, "except make us discontented and restless, as you are?"

"What *good* . . . why, if we all began to remember, we could live our lives again — our *own* lives. We wouldn't have to be wives, we could be . . . ourselves."

"Could we?" said Maggie sourly. "And do you think the men would watch us go? Do you think they'd let us walk out of their houses and out of their lives without stopping us? Don't you — you who talk about remembering — don't you remember how it was when the men came? Don't you remember the slaughter? Don't you remember just who became wives, and why? We, the survivors, became wives because the men wouldn't kill us then, not if we kept them happy and believing we weren't the enemy. If we try to leave or change, they'll kill us like they've killed almost everything else in the world."

The others were silent, but Susie suspected they were letting Maggie speak for them.

"But we'll die," she said. "We'll die like this, as wives. We've lost our identities, but we can have them back. We can have the world back, and our lives, only if we take them. We're dying as a race and as a world, now. Being a wife is a living death, just a postponement of the end, that's all."

"Yes," said Maggie, irony hanging heavily from the word. "So?"

"So why do we have to let them do this to us? We can hide — we can run far away from the settlement and hide. Or, if we have to, we can fight back."

"That's not our way," said Maggie.

"Then what *is* our way?" Susie demanded. "Is it our way to let ourselves be destroyed? They've already killed our culture and our past — we have no "way" anymore — we can't claim we do. All we are now is imitations, creatures moulded by the men. And when the men leave — *if* the men leave — it will be the end for us. We'll have nothing left, and it will be too late to try to remember who we were."

"It's already too late," Maggie said. Susie was suddenly impressed by the way she spoke and held herself, and wondered if Maggie, this elderly and unloved wife she had once pitied, had once been a leader of her people.

"Can you remember why we did not fight or hide before?" Maggie asked. "Can you remember why we decided that the best thing for us was to change our ways, to do what you are now asking us to undo?"

Susie shook her head.

"Then go and try to remember. Remember that we made a choice when the men came, and now we must live with that choice. Remember that there was a good reason for what we did, a reason of survival. It is too late to change again. The old way is not waiting for our return, it is dead. Our world had been changed, and we could not stop it. The past is dead, but that is as it should be. We have new lives now. Forget our restlessness and go home. Be a good wife to Jack — he loves you in his way. Go home, and be thankful for that."

"I can't," she said. She looked around the room, noticing how the eyes of the others fell before hers, so few of them had wanted to listen to her, so few had dared venture out of their homes. Susie looked at Maggie as she spoke, meaning her words for all the wives. "They're killing us slowly," she said. "But we'll be just as dead in the end, I would rather die fighting, and take some of them with us."

"You may be ready to die now, but the rest of us are not," Maggie said. "But if you fought them, you would get not only your own death, but the death of us all. If they see you snarling and violent, they will wake up and turn new eyes on the rest of us and see us not as their loving wives but as beasts, strangers, dangerous wild animals to be destroyed. They forget that we are different from them; they are willing to forget and let us live as long as we keep them comfortable and act as wives should act."

"I can't fight them alone, I know that," Susie said. "But if you'll all join with me, we have a chance. We could take them by surprise, we could use their weapons against them. Why not? They don't expect a fight from us — we could win. Some of us would die, of course, but many of us would survive. More than that — we'd have our own lives, our own world, back again."

"You think your arguments are new," said Maggie. There was a trace of impatience in her usually calm voice. "But I can remember the old days, even if you can't. I remember what happened when the men first came, and I know what would happen if we angered them. Even if we managed somehow to kill all the men here, more men would come in their ships from the sky. And they would come to kill us for daring to fight them. Perhaps they would simply drop fire on us, this time being sure to burn out all of us and all life on our world. Do you seriously ask us to bring about this certain destruction?"

Susie stared at her, feeling dim memories stir in response to her words. Fire from the sky, the burning, the killing. . . . But she couldn't be certain she remembered, and she would rather risk destruction than go back to playing wife again.

"We could hide," she said, pleading. "We could run away and hide in the wilderness. The men might think we had died — they'd forget about us soon, I'm certain. Even if they looked for us at first, we could hide. It's our world, and we know it as they don't. Soon we could live again as we used to, and forget the men."

"Stop this dreaming," Maggie said. "We can never live the way we used to — the old ways are gone, the old world is gone, and even your memories are gone, that's obvious. The only way we know how to live now is with the men, as their wives. Everything else is gone. We'd die of hunger and exposure if the men didn't track us down and kill us first."

"I may have forgotten the old ways, but you haven't. You could teach us."

"I remember enough to know that what is gone, is gone. To know that we can't go back. Believe me. Think about it, Susie. Try—"

"Don't call me that!"

Her shout echoed in the silence. No one spoke. Susie felt the last of her hope drain out of her as she looked at them. They did not feel what she felt, and she would not be able to convince them. In silence, still, she left them, and went back to her own house.

She waited for them there, for them to come and kill her.

She knew that they would come; she knew she had to die. It was as Maggie had said: one renegade endangered them all. If one wife turned on one man, all the wives would be made to suffer. The look of love on their faces would change to a look of hatred, and the slaughter would begin again.

Susie felt no desire to try to escape, to hide from the other wives as she had suggested they all hide from the men. She had no wish to live alone; for good or ill she was a part of her people, and she did not wish to endanger them nor to break away from them.

When they came, they came together, all the wives of the settlement, coming to act in concert so none should bear the guilt alone. They did not hate Susie, nor did she hate them, but the deadly work had to be done.

Susie walked outside, to make it easier for them. By offering not the slightest resistance, she felt herself to be acting with them. She presented the weakest parts of her body to their hands and teeth, that her death should come more quickly. And as she died, feeling her body pressed, pounded and torn by the other wives, Susie did not mind the pain. She felt herself a part of them all, and she died content.

After her death, one of the extra wives took on Susie's name and moved into her house. She got rid of the spider's gigantic egg-case first thing — Jack might like his football-sized pet, but he wouldn't be pleased by the hundreds of pebble-sized babies that would come spilling out of the egg-case in a few months. Then she began to clean in earnest: a man deserved a clean house to come home to.

When, a few days later, the men returned from their fighting, Susie's man Jack found a spotless house, filled with the smells of his favourite foods cooking, and a smiling, sexily-dressed wife.

"Would you like some dinner, dear?" she asked.

"Put it on hold," he said, grinning wolfishly. "Right now I'll take a cup of coffee — in bed — with you on the side."

She fluttered her false eyelashes and moved a little closer, so he could put his arm around her if he liked.

"Three tits and the best coffee in the universe," he said with satisfaction, squeezing one of the bound lumps of flesh on her chest. "With this to come home to, it kind of makes the whole war-thing worthwhile."

The Universal Wife: Exploring 1970s Feminism with Lisa Tuttle's "Wives"

Cathy Hawkins

Lisa Tuttle was born in 1952 in Austin, Texas. She began writing stories as a child and, by her teens, had discovered science fiction and fantasy. From age fifteen she was writing what she describes as "odd, subtle horror stories," science fiction, and other short tales.[1] She submitted these to a range of magazines, from *The Magazine of Fantasy and Science Fiction* to *Seventeen* and the *New Yorker* and was rejected by them all. Instead, she found a home for her writing in her local Texas fan community and in nonprofessional fan-produced journals (or fanzines).

In 1971, aged nineteen, Tuttle enrolled in the Clarion Science Fiction Writers' Workshop, held at Tulane University, Louisiana.[2] The Clarion Workshops are science fiction's training ground for up-and-coming writers, a six-week intensive residential writing course with a different tutor each week. Lisa Tuttle is one of many well-known Clarion graduates; others include Octavia Butler, Nalo Hopkinson, and Kim Stanley Robinson.[3] The Clarion experience allowed Tuttle to met successful female writers such as Kate Wilhelm, Joanna Russ, and Ursula Le Guin. Clarion also gave Tuttle the confidence to consider herself a professional in her field. She remarks that "for six weeks I'd been treated like a writer, surrounded by other writers, in a world where the written word . . . was the most important thing."[4]

She also forged important contacts in the community of professional science fiction writers, and attributes breakthroughs in her career to the help of people such as Harlan Ellison and Samuel R. Delany.

The Clarion workshop also led to Tuttle's first professional sale: "Stranger in the House" to the anthology *Clarion II* (1972) edited by Robin Scott Wilson.[5] Two years later she received the John W. Campbell Award for best new science fiction writer. Tuttle has since published dozens of short stories, as well as several novels and edited collections. She has been nominated for many writing awards, and has won four for short fiction.[6] The Lisa Tuttle Collection — a compilation of her manuscripts and papers — was opened in 2004 at Texas A&M University. Her nonfiction works include the *Encyclopedia of Feminism* and *Writing Fantasy and Science Fiction*.[7]

Publishing "Wives"

Tuttle wrote the first draft of "Wives" in December 1976, shortly after graduating with a degree in English and creative writing.[8] This was the time when second-wave feminism was beginning to make its revolutionary presence felt across the Western world. The term "second wave" had been coined by columnist Martha Lear in 1968 to describe the revival of interest in feminism that began in the 1960s, and was also known as the women's movement or women's liberation.[9] During that decade many women took part in civil rights causes, and while doing so began to identify and discuss the oppression of women as a class. They saw signs of female subjugation in everyday life, such as domestic servitude and male violence. They also perceived larger patterns of patriarchal dominance in world events, like the escalating war in Vietnam.[10] Armed with the new insights of feminist philosophy and practice, many science fiction writers in the 1960s and 1970s — of which Tuttle was one — sought to recast the basic sexist assumptions of the genre. They responded critically to the genre's history of demeaning depictions of female characters, and rejected the assumption that males were the naturally superior sex.

Feminism is fundamental to Tuttle's short story. In its narrative a wife is an alien being with a foreign biology. She has a secret past, with only the dimmest memory of her own name. Through the enforced wearing of corseted skintights, a wife must assume the guise of a "woman," a creature she has never seen. A wife lives an uncertain, fear-filled existence at the behest of violent, selfish beings called men. Wives have no control over their bodies or their lives. They are not allowed to reproduce. They must express no needs of their own. They have no escape: the only alternative to being a wife is being dead.

The very name of the story, "Wives," invokes the feminist critique of female disempowerment. In 1974 feminist Lee Comer began *Wedlocked Women*, her book on female domestic oppression, with a Russian saying: "I thought I saw two persons coming down the road but it was only a man and his wife."[11] This patriarchal vision, overlooking the individual wife, and classifying her as the property of a man, is one of the story's key ideas. Early second-wave feminism saw housewives as embodiments of system in which women become exploited domestic chattels, available to their husbands as unpaid servants and sexual playthings. By performing domestic tasks, pleasing her man sexually, and adopting an ultrafeminine physical appearance, the story's extraterrestrial wives can be exploited just like the human women they are forced to copy. In setting the story on another world peopled with aliens, Tuttle shows that the role of wife is a constructed one rather than a "natural" feminine function.

After revising her new short story full of these feminist perceptions, Tuttle sought a publisher. In mid-1977, science fiction editor David Hartwell accepted the story for inclusion in a new science fiction magazine *Cosmos* but the journal folded before the story appeared:

> I'd heard that a new magazine was soon to be launched — this was to be *Omni* — and that Ben Bova (whom I knew, and had sold to before at *Analog*) would be the fiction editor, so I promptly sent the [manuscript] off to him. . . . As I recall it, the rejection [note] was very short . . . [and] rather sniffy, something along the lines of Thanks for thinking of us, but we're not THAT sort of magazine.[12]

Omni was an American hybrid science and science fiction magazine published between 1978 and 1995. It featured popular science articles, glossy artwork, and up to five science fiction stories per issue. It also ran a science fiction book column. *Omni* was owned by Bob Guccione (who also controlled the men's magazine *Penthouse*) and was published under the directorship of his wife, Kathy Keeton. *Omni* became the highest paying magazine dedicated to the publication of science fiction stories.

In the magazine's early years, Guccione's association with *Penthouse* caused some literary agents and writers to misinterpret what kinds of stories *Omni* would publish. Many submitted sexually explicit, *Penthouse*-type manuscripts to the science fiction journal. They were rejected out of hand. Tuttle thinks that "Wives" was "misunderstood and misidentified" by *Omni* as "one of those" kinds of stories.[13]

If so, this was a remarkable reading of a story that is not gratuitously sexy. Perhaps the opening description of a wife in heat misled the magazine's staff into thinking it was inappropriate: "She was coated in the soft yellow dust by the time she reached the house next door — the house where the magical scent came from, the house which held a wife in heat, longing for someone to mate with." (Tuttle, 191) Tuttle was bemused by the form of the rejection but did not link it to any explicit sexism. She recalls that "everybody else I knew was also getting rejections from *Omni* — whenever a new magazine appeared on the scene all the writers dug out their unsold stories to try again."[14] It is not unusual for an author to approach several publishers before finding one interested in a particular manuscript. Yet the rejection of "Wives" as inappropriate for a science fiction magazine might just as easily have been read against a backdrop of sexist exclusion, a process to which feminist writers and readers were becoming attuned. In the early 1970s writer and editor Pamela Sargent was seeking a publisher for *Women of Wonder*, a collection of women's science fiction. Sargent recalls: "Some editors found the idea absurd, a couple doubted whether I could find enough good stories to fill the book, and one editor didn't think there was a large enough audience."[15] Rather than an absurd anomaly with no market, *Women of Wonder* (1974) sold well enough to be followed quickly by *More Women of Wonder* (1976) and *New Women of Wonder* (1978).[16]

Three years after it was written, "Wives" was finally published by Edward Ferman in the December 1979 issue of *The Magazine of Fantasy and Science Fiction*, alongside work of prominent writers such as Joanna Russ, Jane Yolen, Robert Silverberg, and Orson Scott Card.

"Wives" and Feminist Science Fiction

In 1972 science fiction critic Sam Moskowitz observed that the genre had a history of depicting the sexes locked in perpetual conflict, as if they were "two completely different species."[17] In the influential essay "*Amor Vincit Fœminam*: The Battle of the Sexes in Science Fiction," feminist author Joanna Russ took up Moskowitz's criticism, and examined ten science fiction stories written by men between the years 1926 and 1973.[18] Each narrative dealt with a war between males and females. Russ found that all the stories portrayed men as natural rulers. They also showed how uprisings by women are doomed to failure because females eventually succumb to feminine weaknesses (from incompetence to unfulfilled sexual desires that only a he-man can satisfy).

This notion of a gender war is one of the key science fictional ideas of "Wives" and thus the story can be situated in a battle-of-the-sexes history of the genre. Moreover, its gender conflict was not limited to the fictional world. Following its initial publication, some male readers attacked "Wives," calling Tuttle a "man-hater." The epithet "man-hating women's libbers" was a patriarchal jibe directed at feminists in the 1970s, and was particularly used in the tabloid media. Yet rather than hatred, science fiction by women in the 1970s often revealed fear of masculinity, a dread of what Alice Sheldon called "the sky-darkening presence of the patriarchy."[19]

"Wives" describes men as very frightening creatures, illustrated by Susie's fearful awareness of her man's every need: "She thought about watching Jack, and listening to him, always alert for what he might want, what he might ask, what he might do. Trying to anticipate him, to earn his praise and avoid his blows and harsh words. (Tuttle, 194) Far from the natural leaders and intellectually superior sex of traditional science fiction tales, these men need sex and physical comforts after bouts of violence. Their outlook is summed up by Jack's final words: "Three tits and the best coffee in the universe . . ." Men are cruel and sexually greedy rather than reasoning, rational beings: they live to fight and to fornicate. If men do not get what they want, if ever the mask of the wives should slip, they will have their revenge. Alice Sheldon illustrated a similar mistrust of masculinity in "The Screwfly Solution" (first published in 1977). Writing as Raccoona Sheldon, the story tells of invading aliens who manipulate the men of Earth into killing females until whole tracts of land become cleansed, "liberated" of women. In order to colonize the planet, the aliens simply exploit the preexisting patriarchal violence of men.[20]

"Wives" depicts how alien creatures have been forcibly shaped by male battle-of-the-sexes oppression. In so doing it reflects the ideas of anthropologist Gayle Rubin. In a key feminist essay of the 1970s, "The Traffic in Women: Notes on the 'Political Economy' of Sex," Rubin posed the rhetorical question "What is a domesticated woman?" describing what she called the sex-gender system as "a systematic social apparatus which takes up females as raw materials and fashions domesticated women as products."[21] Tuttle takes this idea further by proposing that there might be a "universal" domesticated product, one constructed by the sex-gender system from local "raw materials" to comfort the human male wherever he goes in the cosmos. This wife doesn't need to be human at all.

Feminist writers in the 1970s knew that the genre's fictionalized gender battle was often played out on the domestic front. In 1971, Joanna Russ painted a scathing picture of what she called the "Intergalactic Suburbia" found in the stories of many (mostly) male writers:

> What is most striking about these stories is what they leave out: the characters' personal and erotic relations are not described; child-bearing arrangements . . . are never described; and the women who appear in these stories are either young and childless or middle-aged, with their children safely grown up. This is, the real problems of a society without gender-role differentiation are not faced.[22]

In 1975 Pamela Sargent also observed that male-authored science fiction stories set on far-flung planets often simply transferred the traditional domestic roles of "bearing and caring for children and the home" into outer space. [23]

"Wives" counteracts the fiction of a childless transplanted suburbia and replaces it with complex social and gender relationships unique to the planet of the wives. In their previous existence, the wives evolved in a world without males. Susie and Doris are same-sexed creatures whose mating will generate an egg: they use parthenogenesis, or one-sex reproduction. To a patriarchal society this is an untenable situation, and it is little wonder that the men utterly destroy the wives' way of life. Justine Larbalestier has noted that many male-authored battle-of-the-sexes stories enacted such fantasies of male sexual dominance and female submission, and often depicted males sweeping away unnatural matriarchal societies. In particular, these tales showed how "matriarchal women must be incorporated into the heterosexual economy."[24] Male battle-of-the-sexes narratives also embrace the notion that women in all-female societies are waiting to be "taken" by a real man.[25] In Russ's terms, such male characters (and their male creators) merely see themselves restoring "the natural order of things."[26]

By adopting the standpoint of the vanquished aliens, however, "Wives" shows that the masculine "natural order" is a myth. In place of the wives' original way of life, the men impose a mix of passive femininity and sex-kittenish exaggeration: "Doris wore a low-cut dress, her three breasts carefully bound and positioned to achieve the proper, double-breasted effect. Gaily patterned and textured stockings covered her silicone-injected legs, and she tottered on heels three centimetres high. Her face was carefully painted, and she wore gold bands on neck, wrists and fingers." (Tuttle, 191) The wives are forced to endure an overdetermined, compulsory heterosexuality, from the "thick paint" of their made-up faces, to the "painful and brief" sex they have to endure with the men. The only "natural order" in this battle-of-the-sexes story is patriarchal brutality.

"Wives" and 1970s Feminist Theory

In its feminist vision, "Wives" uses some of the key political ideas of the early second wave. Like many young women of the time, it was in her years at university that Lisa Tuttle first encountered feminist activism and theory. Excited by feminist political ideas, Tuttle became involved in the local chapter of the National Organization for Women and began organizing for feminist causes. She remarks: "I read a lot of the important second wave texts . . . among many others, Kate Millett, [and] Shulamith Firestone."[27] These writers were two of the leading feminist theorists of the era. Millett's *Sexual Politics* and Firestone's *The Dialectic of Sex: The Case for Feminist Revolution* were both published in 1970, and had a profound influence on feminist thought. "Wives" explores several of their key ideas.

Kate Millett is credited with introducing the term "patriarchy" to modern feminist theory. In *Sexual Politics* she argued that female oppression is socially constructed, and formed by the repressive politics of male-identified "power-structured relationships."[28] She asserted that these structures of male domination formed the fundamental oppression experienced by all women, in all societies, and at all times. Millett was concerned with the way in which patriarchy shaped social institutions — such as the family and government — in order to bring about (and then to continue) the oppression of women. She saw this as the method by which patriarchy established and perpetuated sexual difference by creating the fiction of femininity: "The image of woman as we know it is an image created by men and fashioned to suit their needs. . . . The male has already set himself as the human norm, the subject and referent to which the female is "other" or alien."[29] "Wives" is built on this account of patriarchal oppression. In the world of the wives, the human men deliberately reproduce the patriarchal family based on sexual difference, domestic isolation, dependence, and sexual availability. It is these repressive power structures that create universal wives to serve the needs of the Earth men.

Unlike Millett, Shulamith Firestone located women's oppression in female biology. At the time "Wives" was written:

> [Firestone's] radical feminism made a HUGE impact on me. . . . [I] was forced to think differently about the "naturalness" of all sorts of social constructs and even such biological "givens" as childbirth, motherhood, etc. . . . I was particularly intrigued by notions of some ancient, matriarchal culture which might have existed before being suppressed by the universal Patriarchy.[30]

In *The Dialectic of Sex*, Firestone famously argued that all women are oppressed by their enslavement to childbearing and child rearing, by the "biological contingencies of the human family." Only by taking charge of reproduction and *rejecting* it as a biological role, could women ever hope to be free of the self-perpetuating sex-class system.[31] She hoped that reproductive technology would be used in the service of women to entirely eliminate the need for childbirth.[32] Denise Thompson argues in her reappraisal of the radical feminism of the 1970s, that this assertion is one of the key difficulties in Firestone's thesis. Creating life and giving birth are not naturally exploitive processes. Oppression is not reproduction itself but rather a "consequence of [reproduction] happening under conditions of male domination."[33]

Engaging in these feminist dialogues, "Wives" challenges the givens of human biology. The story suggests that the wives are not enslaved simply because they have babies and become parents. In their ancient world, procreation was a mutual agreement among equals with no division between the sexes. The wives are not enslaved by the mere fact that they reproduce, but because men do not allow them to control the practices or rituals of their own biology. Like Jack's pet spider, their patriarchal conquerors reject the reproductive ability of the wives; unfettered, it might overrun the colonizers. Doris says: "Men don't have babies. . . . Men kill babies, just as they kill all their enemies." (Tuttle, 193). In this "universal Patriarchy" babies are a threat to sterile domestic bliss.

As in feminist science fiction of the era, the fear of men also underlined a great deal of 1970s feminist polemic. In Susan Brownmiller's *Against Our Will: Men, Women and Rape*, she famously asserted that rape was "a conscious process of intimidation by which *all men* keep *all women* in a state of fear."[34] Brownmiller argued that rape was, and always had been, an instrument of systemic patriarchal oppression rather than arbitrary acts of sexual violence. "Wives" draws together these connections. Sex with the soldier Jack is coercive and hurtful, a "screw" to use his own words. For the wives, rape is indistinguishable from ordinary sexual relations with men. Brownmiller also used examples of rape in wartime to exemplify the nexus between sex and conquest: "When men are men, slugging it out among themselves, conquering new land, subjecting new people, driving on toward victory, *unquestioningly* there shall be some raping."[35] Like some 1970s feminist theorists, Brownmiller's position is both ahistorical and essentialist. It does, nevertheless, forcefully articulate how feminists were connecting violence, militarism, and colonialism with the sexual oppression of patriarchy. This link between the extreme masculinity of wartime and the oppression of women extends to the "othering" of colonized peoples.

"Wives" and War

Tuttle wrote "Wives" about "war and conquest and imperialism. . . . My feelings about America's role in Vietnam — and American foreign policy in general — was a major, conscious source of the story."[36] During the 1960s, anti-Vietnam war posters proclaimed "Join the Army . . . travel to exotic and distant lands; meet exciting, unusual people and kill them."[37] This sums up the actions of the men in "Wives."

According to the *Encyclopedia of Science Fiction*, war is "one of the principal imaginative stimuli to futuristic and scientific speculation."[38] The *Encyclopedia* argues that the technological possibilities of warfare have fired the imagination of the genre from its beginnings. In his essay

"The Vietnam War as American Science Fiction and Fantasy," cultural historian H. Bruce Franklin goes further. He contends that ideals of American technological and moral superiority, of "manly and military virtue," had been developing within U.S. science fiction and fantasy for some decades.[39] By the postwar era, these ideas had become part of the country's popular and political imaginary. He persuasively argues that American involvement in the conflict in Indochina was supported by national "fantasies of techno-wonders and of superheroes."[40] These fantasies in turn influenced the way in which the U.S. entered and carried out the war in South-East Asia.

The spectacular violence remembered by the wives recalls the real-world events of that conflict. Prior to human invasion, the wives lived by subsistence, responding to the same natural rhythms that lead Susie (and the spider) to seek a mate and reproduce. Yet Maggie and Susie recall "the slaughter" and "fire from the sky, the burning, the killing" that marked the arrival of the invaders. The attacks were so thorough that they "killed almost everything else in the world" except those who would become the wives. In Southeast Asia, the United States and its allies used advanced military technology to drop millions of tons of conventional bombs, napalm, and defoliants (such as the infamous Agent Orange) onto homes, farms, villages, and jungles. Massive amounts of firepower were used fighting a fundamentally agrarian culture. Whole communities and landscapes were destroyed, and huge numbers of civilian casualties were inflicted in Vietnam, Laos, and Cambodia.[41] The context of the Vietnam War also adds a dimension to Doris's claim that "men kill babies, just as they kill all their enemies." One of the more chilling events of the war took place in the small village of My Lai in 1967, where American servicemen committed atrocities against women and girls before murdering them along with their babies and children. [42] The men in "Wives" belong to a military system that conducts a merciless slaughter against similarly unprotected people.

After the onslaught the wives became prisoners — a "pacified" population — lacking the means or will to resist their conquerors. Their planet is now a home base or recreation centre for battle-weary soldiers. Like the "rest and recreation" or "R&R" centers provided for servicemen during the Vietnam War. American soldiers changed "R&R" to "I&I" for "intercourse and intoxication," and took advantage of U.S. government–funded brothels provided in Thailand. Jill Steans, theorist on gender and international relations, points out that women have always been utilized by state military systems to support male personnel as wives or workers.[43] In Tuttle's story, the wives are the sexual payoff for soldiers needing to make "the whole war-thing worthwhile."

The connections between oppression and patriarchy that Tuttle explores in "Wives" were also questioned by other feminist science fiction writers of the era. In "American SF and The Other," from the essay collection *Language of the Night* (1982), Ursula Le Guin pointed to the implicit authoritarianism in much American science fiction in the 1970s. She observed that anyone who did not share in the dominant values of a male military hierarchy became stylized as aliens. She placed "the poor, the undereducated, the faceless masses and all the women" at the bottom strata of an order created out of the masculinist values of the 1970's military/industrial complex.[44] Agreeing with Le Guin's stance against science fiction's love of militarism, Hilary Rose observes: "Sf seemed to be part and parcel of the genocidic war the US was waging in South East Asia, where an all powerful science and technology harnessed to imperialistic ends was seeking to crush and erase people and nature alike. . . . There was always another planet, another third world country, out there."[45]

"*Other*" Wives

In Simone de Beauvoir's landmark feminist text *The Second Sex*, she described women "living in a world where men compel her to assume the status of the Other," one in which females are constructed as foreigners surviving in an all-male world.[46] By assuming that the male is the standard from which other beings vary, this process called female Othering takes place. In Tuttle's story the soldiers cannot be fully human men — they cannot be conquerors — without their opposite, without their defeated wives to give their conquest meaning. They assign the creatures they vanquish to a recognizably different category, and control their movements and appearance in a male-defined world. This idea also underpins the well-known short story "The Women Men Don't See" by James Tiptree Jr. A female character tells Tiptree's male chauvinist narrator that women survive in a world of patriarchal oppression as outsiders, squeezing through the "*the chinks in your world machine.*"[47]

In a colonialist context, an understanding of Othering needs also to encompass understandings of racial difference. Despite its interest in war and the colonization of other worlds, science fiction has remained ill-informed about race. *The Encyclopedia of Science Fiction*, for example, makes no direct comment on the subject, and under the heading of "racial conflict" refers the reader to "politics." Race itself does not seem to be a topic of interest.[48] This omission reflects a range of assumptions about the *Encyclopedia*'s readership, as well as how the genre as a whole engages with the issue of racial difference.

Writing in the early 1980s, literary critic Sandra Govan notes that from an African American perspective "in most of the vast expanse of science fiction's recorded universe, black folk are not present. They are gone."[49] Govan points to instances where the race of the story's protagonist has been the basis for rejection by publishers, including Samuel R. Delany's *Nova*.[50] This incident is described in more detail by Delaney in his essay "Racism and Science Fiction."[51] In 1967 he submitted his novel *Nova* to well-known science fiction editor John W. Campbell Jr., for serialization in *Analog*. Campbell told Delaney that he had to reject the story not because of any racist feeling on his own part, but because he felt the magazine's readership would not welcome a black protagonist. Delaney calls this "the slippery and always commercialized form of liberal American prejudice."[52] Another example is offered by Michelle Erica Green when discussing the work of feminist African American writer Octavia Butler. Butler experienced problems with the cover illustration of *Dawn* (the first novel in her *Xenogenesis* trilogy). Although the book features black protagonist Lilith Iyapo, an athletic woman in her twenties, the cover showed

> a slender white girl apprehensively unwrapping what looks like a blanket from the body of a naked white woman. The girl is Lilith, here young, fair-skinned and delicate, peering shyly . . . because she cannot look with eagerness at a naked woman.[53]

As Green illustrates, this one image manages to employ ageism, sexism, racism, *and* homophobia.[54]

Given such examples, critic Sandra Govan is skeptical when some science fiction commentators claim that the genre has a liberal attitude toward race. She quotes critic Robert Scholes, who wrote in 1977 that science fiction commonly saw racial difference as irrelevant in its imagined future worlds, a relic of past intolerance.[55] This glibness is problematic for two important reasons. First, white Western culture often overlooks the fact that "whiteness" is itself a racial category, one that assigns to itself a superior position within systems of power and domination. In this sense, no text is immune from its raced context. Authors and readers draw on culturally implicit (as well as explicit) assumptions and expectations and these in turn have cultural and political ramifications. The second issue to arise from the genre's lack of direct engagement with race is that it overlooks the extent to which the alien is used as a metaphor for the racialized (as well as the gendered) Other. In *Aliens and Others: Science Fiction, Feminism and Postmodernism*, cultural theorist Jenny Wolmark observes that many science fiction writers have used the figure of the alien to duplicate existing race and gender relations rather than challenge them. Wolmark quotes Octavia Butler: "Many of the same science fiction writers who started us thinking about the possibility of extraterrestrial life did nothing to make us think about here-at-home variation — women, blacks, Indians, Asians, Hispanics, etc."[56] As long as extraterrestrials can be read as alien *races*, then the supposed "invisibility" of race is not a positive feature of the genre.

While "Wives" does not directly mention race in human terms, it suggests that racial difference can be coded through the bodies and behavior of the wives. The story has several references to the captivity of the wives, so that Susie sees herself in the mirror "like a wild animal, bound and struggling." Not only is she physically repressed (enslaved): she defines herself as animal in relation to male human standards. This defining has resonance with the construction of racialized Others. By white imperialist standards, nonwhite bodies have long been viewed as less human, more bestial, than white ones. The tribal nature of the wives' original society and their "uncivilized" ways (such as the taste of raw lizard Susie remembers, and the smells of their "primitive" pungent bodies) draw on ideas of the brutish, racialized alien — alien, that is, to the (implicitly white) world of the men. The wives are even forced to squeeze inside ill-fitting false skins (the skintights) as a way to mask their physical differences. The universal wife has her own cultural, sexual, and racial markings removed by men who police the boundaries of the Other in all its forms.[57]

Like Tuttle, Ursula Le Guin also addressed racial and gendered Othering in the context of the Vietnam War. Her novella *The Word for World is Forest* (originally published in 1972) is set on Athshe, a planet in the process of being colonized by male humans. Its inhabitants are treated as racialized slave labor, little better than beasts, while their sophisticated culture remains invisible to humans. As in "Wives," there are parallels between this interplanetary invasion and the war in Southeast Asia. Just as the defoliants used in Vietnam destroyed that country's landscape, the colonialists devastate the wives' world and level Athshe's ancient forests. Unlike the indigenous inhabitants in "Wives," those on Athshe do achieve their freedom. They live out Susie's vision of rebellion. Asthsheans destroy property and kill (male) military personal. They also slay a group of human women, the "212 buxom beddable breasty little figures" delivered as wives and sex workers for the planet's all-male colonizers.[58] In "Wives," however, a similar act of destruction is turned upon one of their own, and inscribes Susie's struggle against oppression as ultimately hopeless.

Sisterhood and "Wives"

"Sisterhood is Powerful" was a catchphrase of women's liberation. It represented a revolutionary desire to free all women from sexist tyranny through unified self-determination. When Tuttle's protagonist realizes that "she could be Susie no longer. She would be no man's wife," her desire for liberty resonates with the rhetoric of the women's movement in the 1960s and 1970s.

One of the key ways in which women organized at this time was by forming consciousness raising (or CR) groups; while a student in Austin, Tuttle herself was part of the CR movement. Small groups would gather to discuss patriarchal oppression in their lives, often meeting in one another's homes. In *Contemporary Feminist Thought*, Hester Eisenstein explains that CR groups were a "way of heightening one's awareness, becoming attuned to the evidence of male domination to which previously one paid little attention."[59] Women also used CR groups to plan feminist political activities such as marches and other protests.

The meeting Susie arranges in her house with the other wives resembles a CR group. She asks the wives to consider their position under the domination of the men. She wants them to fight for their liberation. They won't. Susie is finally silenced not by the men, but by the other wives. If sisterhood is *fatal*, how can the outcome of "Wives" be consistent with a 1970s feminist outlook?

In *Sexual Politics*, Kate Millett argued that patriarchy was vitally interested in producing a myth of the feminine. She used the term *interior colonization* to describe part of this process.[60] Indifferent to who individual women are or might want to become, Millet said, patriarchy imposes itself on the body and psychological makeup of females. Using the device of the skintight, the story neatly combines both the sexist and the racialized oppression of the wives. The skintight holds the real self in, hiding the vast differences between the creatures the wives once were, and the image to which they must conform. The skintight robs the wives of "sensation, freedom and pleasure." Yet Doris continues to wear the garment long after her man has left. The men also try to conceal the smell of the wife in heat with perfume. When Doris knows she is releasing these telltale odors, she exclaims, "he won't sleep with me when I'm like this. He thinks it's disgusting, and it is." (Tuttle, 192). She denigrates her own body, describing herself through his eyes. The process of interior colonization dictates the conduct of the wives even in the absence of their men.

On the planet of the wives men do not have to go on killing to control their conquered wives, who live with memories of slaughter and must keep their men "happy and believing we weren't the enemy" in order to survive. In a ritual of terrible self-regulation, the wives embrace bloodshed and turn it inward upon one of their own, an "unnatural" wife. They have no path to, or hope of, liberation.

Of course "Wives" *was* written in an atmosphere of sisterhood. It is a 1970s feminist science fiction allegory about unchecked patriarchy, war, and imperialist oppression. While the creatures in "Wives" are not human women, there are direct parallels between their experiences and the real-world concerns of early second-wave feminism. The invading men turn Susie and her people into idealized wives in order to colonize and re-create a sexist vision of human society on an alien world. Tuttle uses the every-day term *wife* to stand for the enslavement of an entire people. This allows her to take apart the traditional meanings of the word — with notions of domestic tasks, commitment to the home, and to the intimacy of martial relationships — to reveal their sinister patriarchal potential.

NOTES

1. Tuttle, e-mail message to author, June 29, 2004. Throughout this chapter, I quote from personal correspondence between myself and Lisa Tuttle that took place between November 2003 and June 2004.

2. In 1971 there were two venues for the Clarion Workshop, Clarion East at Tulane University in New Orleans, and Clarion West at the University of Washington in Seattle. Tuttle and several classmates also attended the Seattle Clarion the following year. There are now three Clarion Workshops annually: Clarion East is based at Michigan State University; Clarion West, in Seattle; and Clarion South, in Brisbane, Australia. Clarion East's future funding is currently in doubt.

3. More information on the Clarion Science Fiction Writers' Workshop, as well as a longer list of famous alumni, can be found on the organization's website: http://www.msu.edu/~clarion/workshop/workshopinfo.html.

4. E-mail correspondence with Lisa Tuttle, June 29, 2004.

5. *Clarion II: An Anthology of Speculative Fiction and Criticism* (New York: Signet, 1972).

6. Tuttle's short fiction awards are the Locus Poll Award for "The Storms of Windhaven" (with George R. R. Martin) in 1975; the Nebula for "The Bone Flute" in 1981 (which she declined); and the Analog Award for "One-Wing" (also with Martin) in 1980. In 1990 she was the first woman to win the British Science Fiction Award, for the story "In Translation." A fuller (but not complete) bibliography

of Tuttle's short fiction is available on the Internet Speculative Fiction Database
<http://isfdb/tamu/edu>.

7. *Encyclopedia of Feminism* (Harlow: Longman, 1986); *Writing Fantasy and Science Fiction* (London: A & C Black, 2001).

8. Tuttle, e-mail message to author, October 11, 2003.

9. Martha Weinman Lear, "What do these women want? The second feminist wave," *New York Times Magazine* (March 10, 1968). The "first wave" of feminism refers to women's suffrage movements that developed during the latter half of the nineteenth century. These women's rights campaigners remained active as an organized political force into the 1920s. Their main concerns focused on votes for women, contraception, support for mothers and children, and better wages for working women. Such activists were often dubbed suffragettes. While the British suffrage movement employed this name themselves, in an American context "suffragette" tended to be a scornful term. It was used in much the same way as "women's lib" and "women's libbers" became negative media shorthand for the women's movement and its supporters in the late 1960s and 1970s.

10. For background on second-wave feminism, see for example Jane Gerhard's *Desiring Revolution: Second-Wave Feminism and the Rewriting of American Sexual Thought 1920 to 1982* (New York: Columbia University Press, 2001), and Denise Thompson's *Radical Feminism Today* (London: SAGE, 2001). The online resource "Source Works of the Second Wave of Feminism: International Archives of the Second Wave of Feminism" holds some of the important documents of this early stage of the movement: <http://home.att.net/~celesten/2w_bibl.html>. Robin Morgan's edited volume *Sisterhood is Powerful* (New York: Vintage, 1970) also illustrates some of the issues of second-wave feminism.

11. Lee Comer, *Wedlocked Women* (Leeds, U.K.: Feminist Books, 1974), i.

12. E-mail correspondence with Lisa Tuttle, October 11, 2003.

13. Ibid.

14. Ibid.

15. Pamela Sargent, "Introduction" in her *Women of Wonder, The Classic Years: Science Fiction by Women from the 1940s to the 1970s* (Orlando: Harcourt Brace, 1995), 1.

16. All three volumes were published by Vintage. The phenomenon continued into the 1990s with two further collections: *Women of Wonder, The Classic Years: Science Fiction by Women from the 1940s to the 1970s*, and *Women of Wonder, The Contemporary Years: SF by Women from 1970s to the 1990s*, both published by Harcourt Brace in 1995.

17. See the introduction to Sam Moskowitz's anthology *When Women Rule* (New York: Walker, 1972), 26.

18. Russ, "*Amor Vincit Fœminam*," in *To Write Like a Woman: Essays in Feminism and Science Fiction* (Bloomington: Indiana University Press, 1995): 47. The essay was first published in *Science-Fiction Studies* 7, no. 1 (March 1980): 2–15.

19. Alice Sheldon, "A Woman Writing Science Fiction and Fantasy," in *Women of Vision*, ed. Denise Du Pont (New York: St Martin's, 1988), 43.

20. Raccoona Sheldon, "The Screwfly Solution" *Analog* (June 1977).

21. Gayle Rubin, "The Traffic in Women: Notes on the 'Political Economy' of Sex," in *Towards a Cultural Anthropology of Women*, ed. Rayna R. Reiter (New York: Monthly Review Press, 1975), 158.

22. Russ, "The Image of Women in Science Fiction," in *Images of Women in Fiction: Feminist Perspectives*, ed. Susan Koppleman Cornillion (Bowling Green: Bowling Green University Popular Press, 1973), 81. Russ's position has itself received critique, as she seems to suggest that the work of some midcentury women writers does not measure up in terms of gendered writing. For discussions of these debates, see Lisa Yaszek's "Unhappy housewife heroines, galactic suburbia, and nuclear war: a new history of midcentury women's science fiction," *Extrapolation* 44, no. 1 (Spring 2003): 97–103, and Justine Larbalestier and Helen Merrick, "The Revolting Housewife: Women and Science Fiction in the 1950s," *Paradoxa* 18 (2003) 136–156.

23. Pamela Sargent, introduction to *Women of Wonder: Science Fiction Stories by Women about Women* (New York: Vintage, 1974), 37–38.

24. Justine Larbalestier, *The Battle of the Sexes in Science Fiction* (Middletown, Conn.: Wesleyan University Press, 2002), 40.

25. Russ offers the unpalatable example of Edmund Cooper's *Gender Genocide*, where multiple rapes and other physical assaults lead to the victim falling in love with her assailant. Russ, "Amor Vincit Fœminam," 49–52.

26. Ibid., 42.

27. E-mail correspondence with Lisa Tuttle, October, 24 2003.

28. Kate Millett, *Sexual Politics* (London: Abacus, 1972), 23.

29. Ibid., 46.

30. Email correspondence with Lisa Tuttle, October 24, 2003.

31. Shulamith Firestone, *Dialectic of Sex: The Case for Feminist Revolution.* (London: Paladin, 1972), 17; italics in original.

32. Ibid., 193.

33. Thompson, *Radical Feminism Today*, 117.

34. Susan Brownmiller, *Against Our Will: Men, Women and Rape* (Harmondsworth, Eng.: Penguin, 1976), 15. Italics in original.

35. Ibid., 31. Italics in original.

36. E-mail correspondence with Lisa Tuttle, October 24, 2003.

37. Robin Gerster, "A bit of the other: Touring Vietnam," in *Gender and War: Australians at War in the Twentieth Century*, ed. Joy Damousi and Marilyn Lake (Cambridge: Cambridge University Press, 1995), 223.

38. John Clute and Peter Nicholls, eds., *The Encyclopedia of Science Fiction* Revised Edition. (New York: St. Martin's, 1995), 1296.

39. H. Bruce Franklin, *Vietnam and Other American Fantasies* (Amherst: University of Massachusetts Press, 2000), 152. An earlier version of Franklin's essay on the Vietnam War and science fiction was published in *Science-Fiction Studies* 17, no. 3 (November 1990): 341–359.

40. Ibid., 151.

41. For more information, see also Marvin E. Gettleman et al., eds., *Vietnam and America: A Documented History*, expanded ed. (New York: Grove/Atlantic, 1995).

42. For more, see Franklin, *Vietnam*, 161–162.

43. Jill Steans, *Gender and International Relations: An Introduction* (Cambridge: Polity Press, 1998), 90–91.

44. Ursula K. Le Guin, *Language of the Night: Essays on Fantasy and Science Fiction* (New York: Berkley Books, 1982), 99.

45. Hilary Rose, "Dreaming the Future," *Hypatia* 3, no. 1 (1988): 120.

46. *The Second Sex*, Penguin Modern Classics Series (Harmondsworth, Eng.: Penguin, [1949] 1983), 29. See particularly the introduction for a summary of this argument.

47. James Tiptree Jr. [1973], "The Women Men Don't See," in *Warm Worlds and Otherwise* (New York: Del Rey, 1975), 163–164, italics in original. For further discussion of Tiptree see also the essays by L. Timmel Duchamp and Wendy Pearson in this volume.

48. Clute and Nicholls, *Encyclopedia of Science Fiction*, 988, 947. I am not the first to notice this omission. In 1984, Sandra Y. Govan noted that there was no listing for race in Peter Nicholls's original edition of *The Encyclopedia of Science Fiction* (St Albans: Granada, 1979). See Govan's "The Insistent Presence of Black Folk in the Novels of Samuel R. Delany," in *Black American Literature Forum* 18, no. 2 (1984): 48. The current edition of the *Encyclopedia*'s entry "colonization of other worlds" is worth noting. Its main focus is on stories where humans are the colonizers and, except for a few sentences, mostly overlooks texts dealing with the experience of the colonized and invaded (244–246). For further discussion of gender, race, and colonialism, see also the essays by Jane Donawerth and Wendy Pearson in this volume.

49. Govan, "Insistent Presence," 43.

50. Ibid., 44.

51. First published in 1999, Delany's essay is reprinted in Sheree R. Thomas's edited volume, *Dark Matter: A Century of Speculative Fiction from the African Diaspora* (New York: Aspect/Warner Books, 2000). In 2004 Thomas published a companion volume, *Dark Matter: Reading the Bones*, also published by Aspect/Warner.

52. Delany, "Racism and Science Fiction," 387.

53. Michelle Erica Green, "'There Goes the Neighborhood': Octavia Butler's Demand for Diversity in Utopias," in *Utopian and SF by Women: Worlds of Difference*, ed. Jane L. Donawerth and Carol A. Kolmerton (Syracuse: Syracuse University Press, 1994), 166. For more on Butler and the raced contexts of science fiction, see Andrea Hairston's essay in this volume. Hairston also draws attention to the genre's reticence to show non-Anglo characters both in print and on the screen.

54. Ibid.

55. Govan, "Insistent Presence," 44.

56. Jenny Wolmark, *Aliens and Others: Science Fiction, Feminism and Postmodernism* (Hemel Hempstead, Eng.: Harvester Wheatsheaf, 1994), 28.

57. For more about race and second-wave feminism, see Angela Davis's *Women, Race and Class* (New York, Random House, 1981) and *This Bridge Called My Back; Writings by Radical Women of Color*, ed. Cherríe Moraga and Gloria Anzaldúa (Watertown, Mass.: Persephone, 1981).

58. Ursula K. Le Guin, *The Word for World is Forest* in *Eye of the Heron and The Word for World is Forest* (London: VGSF, 1991), 173.

59. Hester Eisenstein, *Contemporary Feminist Thought* (London and Sydney: Unwin, 1984), 35. For a fuller description of CR groups, see chapter 4 of Eisenstein's book, as well as Joan Cassell's *A Group Called Women: Sisterhood and Symbolism in the Feminist Movement* (New York: David McKay, 1977), 35–37.

60. Millett, *Sexual Politics*, 25.

Rachel in Love

PAT MURPHY

First published in Isaac Asimov's Science Fiction Magazine, April 1987

It is a Sunday morning in summer and a small brown chimpanzee named Rachel sits on the living room floor of a remote ranch house on the edge of the Painted Desert. She is watching a Tarzan movie on television. Her hairy arms are wrapped around her knees and she rocks back and forth with suppressed excitement. She knows that her father would say that she's too old for such childish amusements — but since Aaron is still sleeping, he can't chastise her.

On the television, Tarzan has been trapped in a bamboo cage by a band of wicked Pygmies. Rachel is afraid that he won't escape in time to save Jane from the ivory smugglers who hold her captive. The movie cuts to Jane, who is tied up in the back of a jeep, and Rachel whimpers softly to herself. She knows better than to howl: she peeked into her father's bedroom earlier, and he was still in bed. Aaron doesn't like her to howl when he is sleeping.

When the movie breaks for a commercial, Rachel goes to her father's room. She is ready for breakfast and she wants him to get up. She tiptoes to the bed to see if he is awake.

His eyes are open and he is staring at nothing. His face is pale and his lips are a purplish color. Dr. Aaron Jacobs, the man Rachel calls father, is not asleep. He is dead, having died in the night of a heart attack.

When Rachel shakes him, his head rocks back and forth in time with her shaking, but his eyes do not blink and he does not breathe. She places his hand on her head, nudging him so that he will waken and stroke her. He does not move. When she leans toward him, his hand falls limply to dangle over the edge of the bed.

In the breeze from the open bedroom window, the fine wisps of grey hair that he had carefully combed over his bald spot each morning shift and flutter, exposing the naked scalp. In the other room, elephants trumpet as they stampede across the jungle to rescue Tarzan. Rachel whimpers softly, but her father does not move.

Rachel backs away from her father's body. In the living room, Tarzan is swinging across the jungle on vines, going to save Jane. Rachel ignores the television. She prowls through the house as if searching for comfort — stepping into her own small bedroom, wandering through her father's laboratory. From the cages that line the walls, white rats stare at her with hot red eyes. A rabbit hops across its cage, making a series of slow dull thumps, like a feather pillow tumbling down a flight of stairs.

She thinks that perhaps she made a mistake. Perhaps her father is just sleeping. She returns to the bedroom, but nothing has changed. Her father lies open-eyed on the bed. For a long time, she huddles beside his body, clinging to his hand.

He is the only person she has ever known. He is her father, her teacher, her friend. She cannot leave him alone.

The afternoon sun blazes through the window, and still Aaron does not move. The room grows dark, but Rachel does not turn on the lights. She is waiting for Aaron to wake up. When the moon rises, its silver light shines through the window to cast a bright rectangle on the far wall.

Outside, somewhere in the barren rocky land surrounding the ranch house, a coyote lifts its head to the rising moon and wails, a thin sound that is as lonely as a train whistling through an abandoned station. Rachel joins in with a desolate howl of loneliness and grief. Aaron lies still and Rachel knows that he is dead.

When Rachel was younger, she had a favorite bedtime story. — Where did I come from? she would ask Aaron, using the abbreviated gestures of ASL, American Sign Language. — Tell me again.

"You're too old for bedtime stories," Aaron said.

Please, she signed. — Tell me the story.

In the end, he always relented and told her. "Once upon a time, there was a little girl named Rachel," he said. "She was a pretty girl, with long golden hair like a princess in a fairy tale. She lived with her father and her mother and they were all very happy."

Rachel would snuggle contentedly beneath her blankets. The story, like any good fairy tale, had elements of tragedy. In the story, Rachel's father worked at a university, studying the workings of the brain and charting the electric fields that the nervous impulses that an active brain produced. But the other researchers at the university didn't understand Rachel's father; they distrusted his research and cut off his funding. (During this portion of the story, Aaron's voice took on a bitter edge.) So he left the university and took his wife and daughter to the desert, where he could work in peace.

He continued his research and determined that each individual brain produced its own unique pattern of fields, as characteristic as a fingerprint. (Rachel found this part of the story quite dull, but Aaron insisted on including it.) The shape of this "Electric Mind," as he called it, was determined by habitual patterns of thoughts and emotions. Record the Electric Mind, he postulated, and you could capture an individual's personality.

Then one sunny day, the doctor's wife and beautiful daughter went for a drive. A truck barrelling down a winding cliffside road lost its brakes and met the car head-on, killing both the girl and her mother. (Rachel clung to Aaron's hand during this part of the story, frightened by the sudden evil twist of fortune.)

But though Rachel's body had died, all was not lost. In his desert lab, the doctor had recorded the electrical patterns produced by his daughter's brain. The doctor had been experimenting with the use of external magnetic fields to impose the patterns from one animal onto the brain of another. From an animal supply house, he obtained a young chimpanzee. He used a mixture of norepinephrin-based transmitter substances to boost the speed of neural processing in the chimp's brain, and then he imposed the pattern of his daughter's mind upon the brain of this young chimp, combining the two after his own fashion, saving his daughter in his own way. In the chimp's brain was all that remained of Rachel Jacobs.

The doctor named the chimp Rachel and raised her as his own daughter. Since the limitations of the chimpanzee larynx made speech very difficult, he instructed her in ASL. He taught her to read and to write. They were good friends, the best of companions.

By this point in the story, Rachel was usually asleep. But it didn't matter — she knew the ending. The doctor, whose name was Aaron Jacobs, and the chimp named Rachel lived happily ever after.

Rachel likes fairy tales and she likes happy endings. She has the mind of a teenage girl, but the innocent heart of a young chimp.

Sometimes, when Rachel looks at her gnarled brown fingers, they seem alien, wrong, out of place. She remembers having small, pale, delicate hands. Memories lie upon memories, layers upon layers, like the sedimentary rocks of the desert buttes.

Rachel remembers a blonde-haired fair-skinned woman who smelled sweetly of perfume. On a Halloween long ago, this woman (who was, in these memories, Rachel's mother) painted Rachel's fingernails bright red because Rachel was dressed as a gypsy and gypsies liked red. Rachel remembers the woman's hands: white hands with faintly blue veins hidden just beneath the skin, neatly clipped nails painted rose pink.

But Rachel also remembers another mother and another time. Her mother was dark and hairy and smelled sweetly of overripe fruit. She and Rachel lived in a wire cage in a room filled with chimps and she hugged Rachel to her hairy breast whenever any people came into the room. Rachel's mother groomed Rachel constantly, picking delicately through her fur in search of lice that she never found.

Memories upon memories: jumbled and confused, like random pictures clipped from magazines, a bright collage that makes no sense. Rachel remembers cages: cold wire mesh beneath her feet, the smell of fear around her. A man in a white lab coat took her from the arms of her hairy mother and pricked her with needles. She could hear her mother howling, but she could not escape from the man.

Rachel remembers a junior high school dance where she wore a new dress: she stood in a dark corner of the gym for hours, pretending to admire the crepe paper decorations because she felt too shy to search among the crowd for her friends.

She remembers when she was a young chimp: she huddled with five other adolescent chimps in the stuffy freight compartment of a train, frightened by the alien smells and sounds.

She remembers gym class: gray lockers and ugly gym suits that revealed her skinny legs. The teacher made everyone play softball, even Rachel who was unathletic and painfully shy. Rachel at bat, standing at the plate, was terrified to be the center of attention. "Easy out," said the catcher, a hard-edged girl who ran with the wrong crowd and always smelled of cigarette smoke. When Rachel swung at the ball and missed, the outfielders filled the air with malicious laughter.

Rachel's memories are as delicate and elusive as the dusty moths and butterflies that dance among the rabbit brush and sage. Memories of her girlhood never linger; they land for an instant, then take flight, leaving Rachel feeling abandoned and alone.

Rachel leaves Aaron's body where it is, but closes his eyes and pulls the sheet up over his head. She does not know what else to do. Each day she waters the garden and picks some greens for the rabbits. Each day, she cares for the rats and the rabbits, bringing them food and refilling their water bottles. The weather is cool, and Aaron's body does not smell too bad, though by the end of the week, a wide line of ants runs from the bed to the open window.

At the end of the first week, on a moonlit evening, Rachel decides to let the animals go free. She releases the rabbits one by one, climbing on a stepladder to reach down into the cage and lift each placid bunny out. She carries each one to the back door, holding it for a moment and stroking the soft warm fur. Then she sets the animal down and nudges it in the direction of the green grass that grows around the perimeter of the fenced garden.

The rats are more difficult to deal with. She manages to wrestle the large rat cage off the shelf, but it is heavier than she thought it would be. Though she slows its fall, it lands on the floor with a crash and the rats scurry to and fro within. She shoves the cage across the linoleum floor, sliding it down the hall, over the doorsill, and onto the back patio. When she opens the cage door, rats burst out like popcorn from a popper, white in the moonlight and dashing in all directions.

Once, while Aaron was taking a nap, Rachel walked along the dirt track that led to the main highway. She hadn't planned on going far. She just wanted to see what the highway looked like, maybe hide near the mailbox and watch a car drive past. She was curious about the outside world and her fleeting fragmentary memories did not satisfy that curiosity.

She was halfway to the mailbox when Aaron came roaring up in his old jeep. "Get in the car," he shouted at her. "Right now!" Rachel had never seen him so angry. She cowered in the jeep's passenger seat, covered with dust from the road, unhappy that Aaron was so upset. He didn't speak until they got back to the ranch house, and then he spoke in a low voice, filled with bitterness and suppressed rage.

"You don't want to go out there," he said. "You wouldn't like it out there. The world is filled with petty, narrow-minded, stupid people. They wouldn't understand you. And anyone they don't understand, they want to hurt. They hate anyone who's different. If they know that you're different, they punish you, hurt you. They'd lock you up and never let you go."

He looked straight ahead, staring through the dirty windshield. "It's not like the shows on TV, Rachel," he said in a softer tone. "It's not like the stories in books."

He looked at her then and she gestured frantically. — I'm sorry. I'm sorry.

"I can't protect you out there," he said. "I can't keep you safe."

Rachel took his hand in both of hers. He relented then, stroking her head. "Never do that again," he said. "Never."

Aaron's fear was contagious. Rachel never again walked along the dirt track and sometimes she had dreams about bad people who wanted to lock her in a cage.

Two weeks after Aaron's death, a black-and-white police car drives slowly up to the house. When the policemen knock on the door, Rachel hides behind the couch in the living room. They knock again, try the knob, then open the door, which she had left unlocked.

Suddenly frightened, Rachel bolts from behind the couch, bounding toward the back door. Behind her, she hears one man yell, "My God! It's a gorilla!"

By the time he pulls his gun, Rachel has run out the back door and away into the hills. From the hills she watches as an ambulance drives up and two men in white take Aaron's body away. Even after the ambulance and the police car drive away, Rachel is afraid to go back to the house. Only after sunset does she return.

Just before dawn the next morning, she wakens to the sound of a truck jouncing down the dirt road. She peers out the window to see a pale green pickup. Sloppily stenciled in white on the door are the words: PRIMATE RE-SEARCH CENTER. Rachel hesitates as the truck pulls up in front of the house. By the time she has decided to flee, two men are getting out of the truck. One of them carries a rifle.

She runs out the back door and heads for the hills, but she is only halfway to hiding when she hears a sound like a sharp intake of breath and feels a painful jolt in her shoulder. Suddenly, her legs give way and she is tumbling backward down the sandy slope, dust coating her red-brown fur, her howl becoming a whimper, then fading to nothing at all. She falls into the blackness of sleep.

The sun is up. Rachel lies in a cage in the back of the pickup truck. She is partially conscious and she feels a tingling in her hands and feet. Nausea grips her stomach and bowels. Her body aches.

Rachel can blink, but otherwise she can't move. From where she lies, she can see only the wire mesh of the cage and the side of the truck. When she tries to turn her head, the burning in her skin intensifies. She lies still, wanting to cry out, but unable to make a sound. She can only blink slowly, trying to close out the pain. But the burning and nausea stay.

The truck jounces down a dirt road, then stops. It rocks as the men get out. The doors slam. Rachel hears the tailgate open.

A woman's voice: "Is that the animal the County Sheriff wanted us to pick up?" A woman peers into the cage. She wears a white lab coat and her brown hair is tied back in a single braid. Around her eyes, Rachel can see small wrinkles, etched by years of living in the desert. The woman doesn't look evil. Rachel hopes that the woman will save her from the men in the truck.

"Yeah. It should be knocked out for at least another half hour. Where do you want it?"

"Bring it into the lab where we had the rhesus monkeys. I'll keep it there until I have an empty cage in the breeding area."

Rachel's cage scrapes across the bed of the pickup. She feels each bump and jar as a new pain. The man swings the cage onto a cart and the woman pushes the cart down a concrete corridor. Rachel watches the walls pass just a few inches from her nose.

The lab contains rows of cages in which small animals sleepily move. In the sudden stark light of the overhead fluorescent bulbs, the eyes of white rats gleam red.

With the help of one of the men from the truck, the woman manhandles Rachel onto a lab table. The metal surface is cold and hard, painful against Rachel's skin. Rachel's body is not under her control; her limbs will not respond. She is still frozen by the tranquilizer, able to watch, but that is all. She cannot protest or plead for mercy.

Rachel watches with growing terror as the woman pulls on rubber gloves and fills a hypodermic needle with a clear solution. "Mark down that I'm giving her the standard test for tuberculosis; this eyelid should be checked before she's moved in with the others. I'll add thiabendazole to her feed for the next few days to clean out any intestinal worms. And I suppose we might as well de-flea her as well," the woman says. The man grunts in response.

Expertly, the woman closes one of Rachel's eyes. With her open eye, Rachel watches the hypodermic needle approach. She feels a sharp pain in her eyelid. In her mind, she is howling, but the only sound she can manage is a breathy sigh.

The woman sets the hypodermic aside and begins methodically spraying Rachel's fur with a cold, foul-smelling liquid. A drop strikes Rachel's eye and burns. Rachel blinks, but she cannot lift a hand to rub her eye. The woman treats Rachel with casual indifference, chatting with the man as she spreads Rachel's legs and sprays her genitals. "Looks healthy enough. Good breeding stock."

Rachel moans, but neither person notices. At last, they finish their torture, put her in a cage, and leave the room. She closes her eyes, and the darkness returns.

Rachel dreams. She is back at home in the ranch house. It is night and she is alone. Outside, coyotes yip and howl. The coyote is the voice of the desert, wailing as the wind wails when it stretches itself thin to squeeze through a crack between two boulders. The people native to this land tell tales of Coyote, a god who was a trickster, unreliable, changeable, mercurial.

Rachel is restless, anxious, unnerved by the howling of the coyotes. She is looking for Aaron. In the dream, she knows he is not dead, and she searches the house for him, wandering from his cluttered bedroom to her small room to the linoleum-tiled lab.

She is in the lab when she hears something tapping: a small dry scratching, like a wind-blown branch against the window, though no tree grows near the house and the night is still. Cautiously, she lifts the curtain to look out.

She looks into her own reflection: a pale oval face, long blonde hair. The hand that holds the curtain aside is smooth and white with carefully clipped fingernails. But something is wrong. Superimposed on the reflection is another face peering through the glass: a pair of dark brown eyes, a chimp face with red-brown hair and jug-handle ears. She sees her own reflection and she sees the outsider; the two images merge and blur. She is afraid, but she can't drop the curtain and shut the ape face out.

She is a chimp looking in through the cold, bright windowpane; she is a girl looking out; she is a girl looking in; she is an ape looking out. She is afraid and the coyotes are howling all around.

Rachel opens her eyes and blinks until the world comes into focus. The pain and tingling has retreated, but she still feels a little sick. Her left eye aches. When she rubs it, she feels a raised lump on the eyelid where the woman pricked her. She lies on the floor of a wire mesh cage. The room is hot and the air is thick with the smell of animals.

In the cage beside her is another chimp, an older animal with scruffy dark brown fur. He sits with his arms wrapped around his knees, rocking back and forth, back and forth. His head is down. As he rocks, he murmurs to himself, a meaningless cooing that goes on and on. On his scalp, Rachel can see a gleam of metal: a permanently implanted electrode protrudes from a shaven patch. Rachel makes a soft questioning sound, but the other chimp will not look up.

Rachel's own cage is just a few feet square. In one corner is a bowl of monkey pellets. A water bottle hangs on the side of the cage. Rachel ignores the food, but drinks thirstily.

Sunlight streams through the windows, sliced into small sections by the wire mesh that covers the glass. She tests her cage door, rattling it gently at first, then harder. It is securely latched. The gaps in the mesh are too small to admit her hand. She can't reach out to work the latch.

The other chimp continues to rock back and forth. When Rachel rattles the mesh of her cage and howls, he lifts his head wearily and looks at her. His red-rimmed eyes are unfocused; she can't be sure he sees her.

Hello, she gestures tentatively. —What's wrong?

He blinks at her in the dim light. —Hurt, he signs in ASL. He reaches up to touch the electrode, fingering skin that is already raw from repeated rubbing.

Who hurt you? she asks. He stares at her blankly and she repeats the question. —Who?

Men, he signs.

As if on cue, there is the click of a latch and the door to the lab opens. A bearded man in a white coat steps in, followed by a clean-shaven man in a suit. The bearded man seems to be showing the other man around the lab. ". . . only preliminary testing, so far," the bearded man is saying. "We've been hampered by a shortage of chimps trained in ASL." The two men stop in front of the old chimp's cage. "This old fellow is from the Oregon center. Funding for the language program was cut back and some of the animals were dispersed to other programs." The old chimp huddles at the back of the cage, eying the bearded man with suspicion.

Hungry? the bearded man signs to the old chimp. He holds up an orange where the old chimp can see it.

Give orange, the old chimp gestures. He holds out his hand, but comes no nearer to the wire mesh than he must to reach the orange. With the fruit in hand, he retreats to the back of his cage.

The bearded man continues, "This project will provide us with the first solid data on neural activity during use of sign language. But we really need greater access to chimps with advanced language skills. People are so damn protective of their animals."

"Is this one of yours?" the clean-shaven man asks, pointing to Rachel. She cowers in the back of the cage, as far from the wire mesh as she can get.

"No, not mine. She was someone's household pet, apparently. The county sheriff had us pick her up." The bearded man peers into her cage. Rachel does not move; she is terrified that he will somehow guess that she knows ASL. She stares at his hands and thinks about those hands putting an electrode through her skull. "I think she'll be put in breeding stock," the man says as he turns away.

Rachel watches them go, wondering at what terrible people these are. Aaron was right: they want to punish her, put an electrode in her head.

After the men are gone, she tries to draw the old chimp into conversation, but he will not reply. He ignores her as he eats his orange. Then he returns to his former posture, hiding his head and rocking himself back and forth.

Rachel, hungry despite herself, samples one of the food pellets. It has a strange medicinal taste, and she puts it back in the bowl. She needs to pee, but there is no toilet and she cannot escape the cage. At last, unable to hold it, she pees in one corner of the cage. The urine flows through the wire mesh to soak the litter below, and the smell of warm piss fills her cage. Humiliated, frightened, her head aching, her skin itchy from the flea spray, Rachel watches as the sunlight creeps across the room.

The day wears on. Rachel samples her food again, but rejects it, preferring hunger to the strange taste. A black man comes and cleans the cages of the rabbits and rats. Rachel cowers in her cage and watches him warily, afraid that he will hurt her too.

When night comes, she is not tired. Outside, coyotes howl. Moonlight filters in through the high windows. She draws her legs up toward her body, then rests with her arms wrapped around her knees. Her father is dead, and she is a captive in a strange place. For a time, she whimpers softly, hoping to awaken from this nightmare and find herself at home in bed. When she hears the click of a key in the door to the room, she hugs herself more tightly.

A man in green coveralls pushes a cart filled with cleaning supplies into the room. He takes a broom from the cart, and begins sweeping the concrete floor. Over the rows of cages, she can see the top of his head bobbing in time with his sweeping. He works slowly and methodically, bending down to sweep carefully under each row of cages, making a neat pile of dust, dung, and food scraps in the center of the aisle.

The janitor's name is Jake. He is a middle-aged deaf man who has been employed by the Primate Research Center for the past seven years. He works night shift. The personnel director at the Primate Research Center likes Jake because he fills the federal quota for handicapped employees, and because he has not asked for a raise in five years. There have been some complaints about Jake — his work is often sloppy — but never enough to merit firing the man.

Jake is an unambitious, somewhat slow-witted man. He likes the Primate Research Center because he works alone, which allows him to drink on the job. He is an easy-going man, and he likes the animals. Sometimes, he brings treats for them. Once, a lab assistant caught him feeding an apple to a pregnant rhesus monkey. The monkey was part of an experiment on the effect of dietary restrictions on fetal brain development, and the lab assistant warned Jake that he would be fired if he was ever caught interfering with the animals again. Jake still feeds the animals, but he is more careful about when he does it, and he has never been caught again.

As Rachel watches, the old chimp gestures to Jake. — Give banana, the chimp signs. — Please banana. Jake stops sweeping for a minute and reaches down to the bottom shelf of his cleaning cart. He returns with a banana and offers it to the old chimp. The chimp accepts the banana and leans against the mesh while Jake scratches his fur.

When Jake turns back to his sweeping, he catches sight of Rachel and sees that she is watching him. Emboldened by his kindness to the old chimp, Rachel timidly gestures to him. — Help me.

Jake hesitates, then peers at her more closely. Both his eyes are shot with a fine lacework of red. His nose displays the broken blood vessels of someone who has been friends with the bottle for too many years. He needs a shave. But when he leans close, Rachel catches the scent of whiskey and tobacco. The smells remind her of Aaron and give her courage.

Please help me, Rachel signs. — I don't belong here.

For the last hour, Jake has been drinking steadily. His view of the world is somewhat fuzzy. He stares at her blearily.

Rachel's fear that he will hurt her is replaced by the fear that he will leave her locked up and alone. Desperately she signs again. — Please please please. Help me. I don't belong here. Please help me go home.

He watches her, considering the situation. Rachel does not move. She is afraid that any movement will make him leave. With a majestic speed dictated by his inebriation, Jake leans his broom on the row of cages behind him and steps toward Rachel's cage again. — You talk? he signs.

I talk, she signs.

Where did you come from?

From my father's house, she signs. — Two men came and shot me and put me here. I don't know why. I don't know why they locked me in jail.

Jake looks around, willing to be sympathetic, but puzzled by her talk of jail. — This isn't jail, he signs. — This is a place where scientists raise monkeys.

Rachel is indignant. — I am not a monkey, she signs. — I am a girl.

Jake studies her hairy body and her jug-handle ears. — You look like a monkey.

Rachel shakes her head. — No. I am a girl.

Rachel runs her hands back over her head, a very human gesture of annoyance and unhappiness. She signs sadly, — I don't belong here. Please let me out.

Jake shifts his weight from foot to foot, wondering what to do. — I can't let you out. I'll get in big trouble.

Just for a little while? Please?

Jake glances at his cart of supplies. He has to finish off this room and two corridors of offices before he can relax for the night.

Don't go, Rachel signs, guessing his thoughts.

I have work to do.

She looks at the cart, then suggests eagerly, — Let me out and I'll help you work.

Jake frowns. — If I let you out, you will run away.

No, I won't run. I will help. Please let me out.

You promise to go back?

Rachel nods.

Warily he unlatches the cage. Rachel bounds out, grabs a whisk broom from the cart, and begins industriously sweeping bits of food and droppings from beneath the row of cages. — Come on, she signs to Jake from the end of the aisle. — I will help.

When Jake pushes the cart from the room filled with cages, Rachel follows him closely. The rubber wheels of the cleaning cart rumble softly on the linoleum floor. They pass through a metal door into a corridor where the floor is carpeted and the air smells of chalk dust and paper.

Offices let off the corridor, each one a small room furnished with a desk, bookshelves, and a blackboard. Jake shows Rachel how to empty the wastebaskets into a garbage bag. While he cleans the blackboards, she wanders from office to office, trailing the trash-filled garbage bag.

At first, Jake keeps a close eye on Rachel. But after cleaning each blackboard, he pauses to sip whiskey from a paper cup. At the end of the corridor, he stops to refill the cup from the whiskey bottle that he keeps wedged between the Saniflush and the window cleaner. By the time he is halfway through the second cup, he is treating her like an old friend, telling her to hurry up so that they can eat dinner.

Rachel works quickly, but she stops sometimes to gaze out the office windows. Outside, moonlight shines on a sandy plain, dotted here and there with scrubby clumps of rabbit brush.

At the end of the corridor is a larger room in which there are several desks and typewriters. In one of the wastebaskets, buried beneath memos and candy-bar wrappers, she finds a magazine. The title is *Love Confessions* and the cover has a picture of a man and woman kissing. Rachel studies the cover, then takes the magazine, tucking it on the bottom shelf of the cart.

Jake pours himself another cup of whiskey and pushes the cart to another hallway. Jake is working slower now, and as he works he makes humming noises, tuneless sounds that he feels only as pleasant vibrations. The last few blackboards are sloppily done, and Rachel, finished with the wastebaskets, cleans the places that Jake missed.

They eat dinner in the janitor's storeroom, a stuffy windowless room furnished with an ancient grease-stained couch, a battered black-and-white television, and shelves of cleaning supplies. From a shelf, Jake takes the paper bag that holds his lunch: a baloney sandwich, a bag of barbequed potato chips, and a box of vanilla wafers. From behind the gallon jugs of liquid cleanser, he takes a magazine. He lights a cigarette, pours himself another cup of whiskey, and settles down on the couch. After a moment's hesitation, he offers Rachel a drink, pouring a shot of whiskey into a chipped ceramic cup.

Aaron never let Rachel drink whiskey, and she samples it carefully. At first the smell makes her sneeze, but she is fascinated by the way that the drink warms her throat, and she sips some more.

As they drink, Rachel tells Jake about the men who shot her and the woman who pricked her with a needle, and he nods. —The people here are crazy, he signs.

I know, she says, thinking of the old chimp with the electrode in his head. —You won't tell them I can talk, will you?

Jake nods. —I won't tell them anything.

They treat me like I'm not real, Rachel signs sadly. Then she hugs her knees, frightened at the thought of being held captive by crazy people. She considers planning her escape: she is out of the cage and she is sure she could outrun Jake. As she wonders about it, she finishes her cup of whiskey. The alcohol takes the edge off her fear. She sits close beside Jake on the couch, and the smell of his cigarette smoke reminds her of Aaron. For the first time since Aaron's death she feels warm and happy.

She shares Jake's cookies and potato chips and looks at the *Love Confessions* magazine that she took from the trash. The first story that she reads is about a woman named Alice. The headline reads: "I became a Go-go dancer to pay off my husband's gambling debts, and now he wants me to sell my body."

Rachel sympathizes with Alice's loneliness and suffering. Alice, like Rachel, is alone and misunderstood. As Rachel slowly reads, she sips her second cup of whiskey. The story reminds her of a fairy tale: the nice man who rescues Alice from her terrible husband replaces the handsome prince who rescued the princess. Rachel glances at Jake and wonders if he will rescue her from the wicked people who locked her in the cage.

She has finished the second cup of whiskey and eaten half Jake's cookies when Jake says that she must go back to her cage. She goes reluctantly, taking the magazine with her. He promises that he will come for her again the next night, and with that she must be content. She puts the magazine in one corner of the cage and curls up to sleep.

She wakes early in the afternoon. A man in a white coat is wheeling a low cart into the lab.

Rachel's head aches with hangover and she feels sick. As she crouches in one corner of her cage, he stops the cart beside her cage and then locks the wheels. "Hold on there," he mutters to her, then slides her cage onto the cart.

The man wheels her through long corridors, where the walls are cement blocks, painted institutional green. Rachel huddles unhappily in the cage, wondering where she is going and whether Jake will ever be able to find her.

At the end of a long corridor, the man opens a thick metal door and a wave of warm air strikes Rachel. It stinks of chimpanzees, excrement, and rotting food. On either side of the corridor are metal bars and wire mesh. Behind the mesh, Rachel can see dark hairy shadows. In one cage, five adolescent chimps swing and play. In another, two females huddle together, grooming each other. The man slows as he passes a cage in which a big male is banging on the wire with his fist, making the mesh rattle and ring.

"Now, Johnson," says the man. "Cool it. Be nice. I'm bringing you a new little girlfriend."

With a series of hooks, the man links Rachel's cage with the cage next to Johnson's and opens the doors. "Go on, girl," he says. "See the nice fruit." In the new cage is a bowl of sliced apples with an attendant swarm of fruit flies.

At first, Rachel will not move into the new cage. She crouches in the cage on the cart, hoping that the man will decide to take her back to the lab. She watches him get a hose and attach it to a water faucet. But she does not understand his intention until he turns the stream of water on her. A cold blast strikes her on the back and she howls, fleeing into the new cage to avoid the cold water. Then the man closes the doors, unhooks the cage, and hurries away.

The floor is bare cement. Her cage is at one end of the corridor and two walls are cement block. A door in one of the cement block walls leads to an outside run. The other two walls are wire mesh: one facing the corridor; the other, Johnson's cage.

Johnson, quiet now that the man has left, is sniffing around the door in the wire mesh wall that joins their cages. Rachel watches him anxiously. Her memories of other chimps are distant, softened by time. She remembers her mother; she vaguely remembers playing with other chimps her age. But she does not know how to react to Johnson when he stares at her with great intensity and makes a loud huffing sound. She gestures to him in ASL, but he only stares harder and huffs again. Beyond Johnson, she can see other cages and other chimps, so many that the wire mesh blurs her vision and she cannot see the other end of the corridor.

To escape Johnson's scrutiny, she ducks through the door into the outside run, a wire mesh cage on a white concrete foundation. Outside there is barren ground and rabbit brush. The afternoon sun is hot and all the other runs are deserted until Johnson appears in the run beside hers. His attention disturbs her and she goes back inside.

She retreats to the side of the cage farthest from Johnson. A crudely built wooden platform provides her with a place to sit. Wrapping her arms around her knees, she tries to relax and ignore Johnson. She dozes off for a while, but wakes to a commotion across the corridor.

In the cage across the way is a female chimp in heat. Rachel recognizes the smell from her own times in heat. Two keepers are opening the door that separates the female's cage from the adjoining cage, where a male stands, watching with great interest. Johnson is shaking the wire mesh and howling as he watches.

"Mike here is a virgin, but Susie knows what she's doing," one keeper was saying to the other. "So it should go smoothly. But keep the hose ready."

"Yeah?"

"Sometimes they fight. We only use the hose to break it up if it gets real bad. Generally, they do okay."

Mike stalks into Susie's cage. The keepers lower the cage door, trapping both chimps in the same cage. Susie seems unalarmed. She continues eating a slice of orange while Mike sniffs at her genitals with every indication of great interest. She bends over to let Mike finger her pink bottom, the sign of estrus.

Rachel finds herself standing at the wire mesh, making low moaning noises. She can see Mike's erection, hear his grunting cries. He squats on the floor of Susie's cage, gesturing to the female. Rachel's feelings are mixed: she is fascinated, fearful, confused. She keeps thinking of the description of sex in the *Love Confessions* story: When Alice feels Danny's lips on hers, she is swept away by the passion of the moment. He takes her in his arms and her skin tingles as if she were consumed by an inner fire.

Susie bends down and Mike penetrates her with a loud grunt, thrusting violently with his hips. Susie cries out shrilly and suddenly leaps up, knocking Mike away. Rachel watches, overcome with fascination. Mike, his penis now limp, follows Susie slowly to the corner of the cage, where he begins grooming her carefully. Rachel finds that the wire mesh has cut her hands where she gripped it too tightly.

It is night, and the door at the end of the corridor creaks open. Rachel is immediately alert, peering through the wire mesh and trying to see down to the end of the corridor. She bangs on the wire mesh. As Jake comes closer, she waves a greeting.

When Jake reaches for the lever that will raise the door to Rachel's cage, Johnson charges toward him, howling and waving his arms above his head. He hammers on the wire mesh with his fists, howling and grimacing at Jake. Rachel ignores Johnson and hurries after Jake.

Again Rachel helps Jake clean. In the laboratory, she greets the old chimp, but the animal is more interested in the banana that Jake has brought than in conversation. The chimp will not reply to her questions, and after several tries, she gives up.

While Jake vacuums the carpeted corridors, Rachel empties the trash, finding a magazine called *Modern Romance* in the same wastebasket that had provided *Love Confessions*.

Later, in the janitor's lounge, Jake smokes a cigarette, sips whiskey, and flips through one of his own magazines. Rachel reads love stories in *Modern Romance*.

Every once in a while, she looks over Jake's shoulder at grainy pictures of naked women with their legs spread wide apart. Jake looks for a long time at a picture of a blonde woman with big breasts, red fingernails, and purple-painted eyelids. The woman lies on her back and smiles as she strokes the pinkness between her legs. The picture on the next page shows her caressing her own breasts, pinching the dark nipples. The final picture shows her looking back over her shoulder. She is in the position that Susie took when she was ready to be mounted.

Rachel looks over Jake's shoulder at the magazine, but she does not ask questions. Jake's smell began to change as soon as he opened the magazine; the scent of nervous sweat mingles with the aromas of tobacco and whiskey. Rachel suspects that questions would not be welcome just now.

At Jake's insistence, she goes back to her cage before dawn.

Over the next week, she listens to the conversations of the men who come and go, bringing food and hosing out the cages. From the men's conversation, she learns that the Primate Research Center is primarily a breeding facility that supplies researchers with domestically bred apes and monkeys of several species. It also maintains its own research staff. In indifferent tones, the men talk of horrible things. The adolescent chimps at the end of the corridor are being fed a diet high in cholesterol to determine cholesterol's effects on the circulatory system. A group of pregnant females are being injected with male hormones to determine how that will affect the female offspring. A group of infants is being fed a low protein diet to determine adverse effects on their brain development.

The men look through her as if she were not real, as if she were a part of the wall, as if she were no one at all. She cannot speak to them; she cannot trust them.

Each night, Jake lets her out of her cage and she helps him clean. He brings treats: barbequed potato chips, fresh fruit, chocolate bars, and cookies. He treats her fondly, as one would treat a precocious child. And he talks to her.

At night, when she is with Jake, Rachel can almost forget the terror of the cage, the anxiety of watching Johnson pace to and fro, the sense of unreality that accompanies the simplest act. She would be content to stay with Jake forever, eating snack food and reading confessions magazines. He seems to like her company. But each morning, Jake insists that she must go back to the cage and the terror. By the end of first week, she has begun plotting her escape.

Whenever Jake falls asleep over his whiskey, something that happens three nights out of five, Rachel prowls the center alone, surreptitiously gathering things that she will need to survive in the desert: a plastic jug filled with water, a plastic bag of food pellets, a large beach towel that will serve as a blanket on the cool desert nights, a discarded plastic shopping bag in which she can carry the other things. Her best find is a road map on which the Primate Center is marked in red. She knows the address of Aaron's ranch and finds it on the map. She studies the roads and plots a route home. Cross country, assuming that she does not get lost, she will have to travel about fifty miles to reach the ranch. She hides these things behind one of the shelves in the janitor's storeroom.

Her plans to run away and go home are disrupted by the idea that she is in love with Jake, a notion that comes to her slowly, fed by the stories in the confessions magazines. When Jake absent-mindedly strokes her, she is filled with a strange excitement. She longs for his company and misses him on the weekends when he is away. She is happy only when she is with him, following him through the halls of the center, sniffing the aroma of tobacco and whiskey that is his own perfume. She steals a cigarette from his pack and hides it in her cage, where she can savor the smell of it at her leisure.

She loves him, but she does not know how to make him love her back. Rachel knows little about love: she remembers a high school crush where she mooned after a boy with a locker near hers, but that came to nothing. She reads the confessions magazines and Ann Landers' column in the newspaper that Jake brings with him each night, and from these sources, she learns about romance. One night, after Jake falls asleep, she types a badly punctuated, ungrammatical letter to Ann. In the letter, she explains her situation and asks for advice on how to make Jake love her. She slips the letter into a sack labelled "Outgoing Mail," and for the next week she reads Ann's column with increased interest. But her letter never appears.

Rachel searches for answers in the magazine pictures that seem to fascinate Jake. She studies the naked women, especially the big-breasted woman with the purple smudges around her eyes.

One night, in a secretary's desk, she finds a plastic case of eyeshadow. She steals it and takes it back to her cage. The next evening, as soon as the Center is quiet, she upturns her metal food dish and regards her reflection in the shiny bottom. Squatting, she balances the eye shadow case on one knee and examines its contents: a tiny makeup brush and three shades of eye shadow — INDIAN BLUE, FOREST GREEN, and WILDLY VIOLET. Rachel chooses the shade labeled WILDLY VIOLET.

Using one finger to hold her right eye closed, she dabs her eyelid carefully with the makeup brush, leaving a gaudy orchid-colored smudge on her brown skin. She studies the smudge critically, then adds to it, smearing the color beyond the corner of her eyelid until it disappears in her brown fur. The color gives her eye a carnival brightness, a lunatic gaiety. Working with great care, she matches the effect on the other side, then smiles at herself in the glass, blinking coquettishly.

In the other cage, Johnson bares his teeth and shakes the mesh. She ignores him.

When Jake comes to let her out, he frowns at her eyes. — Did you hurt yourself? he asks.

No, she says. Then, after a pause, — Don't you like it?

Jake squats beside her and stares at her eyes. Rachel puts a hand on his knee and her heart pounds at her own boldness. — You are a very strange monkey, he signs.

Rachel is afraid to move. Her hand on his knee closes into a fist; her face folds in on itself, puckering around the eyes.

Then, straightening up, he signs, — I liked your eyes better before.

He likes her eyes. She nods without taking her eyes from his face. Later, she washes her face in the women's restroom, leaving dark smudges the color of bruises on a series of paper towels.

Rachel is dreaming. She is walking through the Painted Desert with her hairy brown mother, following a red rock canyon that Rachel somehow knows will lead her to the Primate Research Center. Her mother is lagging behind: she does not want to go to the Center; she is afraid. In the shadow of a rock outcropping, Rachel stops to explain to her mother that they must go to the Center because Jake is at the Center.

Rachel's mother does not understand sign language. She watches Rachel with mournful eyes, then scrambles up the canyon wall, leaving Rachel behind. Rachel climbs after her mother, pulling herself over the edge in time to see the other chimp loping away across the wind-blown red cinder-rock and sand.

Rachel bounds after her mother, and as she runs she howls like an abandoned infant chimp, wailing her distress. The figure of her mother wavers in the distance, shimmering in the heat that rises from the sand. The figure changes. Running away across the red sands is a pale blonde woman wearing a purple sweatsuit and jogging shoes, the sweet-smelling mother that Rachel remembers. The woman looks back and smiles at Rachel. "Don't howl like an ape, daughter," she calls. "Say Mama."

Rachel runs silently, dream running that takes her nowhere. The sand burns her feet and the sun beats down on her head. The blonde woman vanishes in the distance, and Rachel is alone. She collapses on the sand, whimpering because she is alone and afraid.

She feels the gentle touch of fingers grooming her fur, and for a moment, still half asleep, she believes that her hairy mother has returned to her. In the dream, she opens her eyes and looks into a pair of dark brown eyes, separated from her by wire mesh. Johnson. He has reached through a gap in the fence to groom her. As he sorts through her fur, he makes soft cooing sounds, gentle comforting noises.

Still half asleep, she gazes at him and wonders why she was so fearful. He does not seem so bad. He grooms her for a time, and then sits nearby, watching her through the mesh. She brings a slice of apple from her dish of food and offers it to him. With her free hand, she makes the sign for apple. When he takes it, she signs again: apple. He is not a particularly quick student, but she has time and many slices of apple.

All Rachel's preparations are done, but she cannot bring herself to leave the Center. Leaving the Center means leaving Jake, leaving potato chips and whiskey, leaving security. To Rachel, the thought of love is always accompanied by the warm taste of whiskey and potato chips.

Some nights, after Jake is asleep, she goes to the big glass doors that lead to the outside. She opens the doors and stands on the steps, looking down into the desert. Sometimes a jackrabbit sits on its haunches in the rectangles of light that shine through the glass doors. Sometimes she sees kangaroo rats, hopping through the moonlight like rubber balls bouncing on hard pavement. Once, a coyote trots by, casting a contemptuous glance in her direction.

The desert is a lonely place. Empty. Cold. She thinks of Jake snoring softly in the janitor's lounge. And always she closes the door and returns to him.

Rachel leads a double life: janitor's assistant by night, prisoner and teacher by day. She spends her afternoons drowsing in the sun and teaching Johnson new signs.

On a warm afternoon, Rachel sits in the outside run, basking in the sunlight. Johnson is inside, and the other chimps are quiet. She can almost imagine she is back at her father's ranch, sitting in her own yard. She naps and dreams of Jake.

She dreams that she is sitting in his lap on the battered old couch. Her hand is on his chest: a smooth pale hand with red-painted fingernails. When she looks at the dark screen of the television set, she can see her reflection. She is a thin teenager with blonde hair and blue eyes. She is naked.

Jake is looking at her and smiling. He runs a hand down her back and she closes her eyes in ecstasy.

But something changes when she closes her eyes. Jake is grooming her as her mother used to groom her, sorting through her hair in search of fleas. She opens her eyes and sees Johnson, his diligent fingers searching through her fur, his intent brown eyes watching her. The reflection on the television screen shows two chimps, tangled in each other's arms.

Rachel wakes to find that she is in heat for the first time since she came to the Center. The skin surrounding her genitals is swollen and pink.

For the rest of the day, she is restless, pacing to and fro in her cage. On his side of the wire mesh wall, Johnson is equally restless, following her when she goes outside, sniffing long and hard at the edge of the barrier that separates him from her.

That night, Rachel goes eagerly to help Jake clean. She follows him closely, never letting him get far from her. When he is sweeping, she trots after him with the dustpan and he almost trips over her twice. She keeps waiting for him to notice her condition, but he seems oblivious.

As she works, she sips from a cup of whiskey. Excited, she drinks more than usual, finishing two full cups. The liquor leaves her a little disoriented, and she sways as she follows Jake to the janitor's lounge. She curls up close beside him on the couch. He relaxes with his arms resting on the back of the couch, his legs stretching out before him. She moves so that she pressed against him.

He stretches, yawns, and rubs the back of his neck as if trying to rub away stiffness. Rachel reaches around behind him and begins to gently rub his neck, reveling in the feel of his skin, his hair against the backs of her hands. The thoughts that hop and skip though her mind are confusing. Sometimes it seems that the hair that tickles her hands is Johnson's; sometimes, she knows it is Jake's. And sometimes it doesn't seem to matter. Are they really so different? They are not so different.

She rubs his neck, not knowing what to do next. In the confessions magazines, this is where the man crushes the woman in his arms. Rachel climbs into Jake's lap and hugs him, waiting for him to crush her in his arms. He blinks at her sleepily. Half asleep, he strokes her, and his moving hand brushes near her genitals. She presses herself against him, making a soft sound in her throat. She rubs her hip against his crotch, aware now of a slight change in his smell, in the tempo of his breathing. He blinks at her again, a little more awake now. She bares her teeth in a smile and tilts her head back to lick his neck. She can feel his hands on her shoulders, pushing her away, and she knows what he wants. She slides from his lap and turns, presenting him with her pink genitals, ready to be mounted, ready to have him penetrate her. She moans in anticipation, a low inviting sound.

He does not come to her. She looks over her shoulder and he is still sitting on the couch, watching her through half-closed eyes. He reaches over and picks up a magazine filled with pictures of naked women. His other hand drops to his crotch and he is lost in his own world.

Rachel howls like an infant who has lost its mother, but he does not look up. He is staring at the picture of the blonde woman.

Rachel runs down dark corridors to her cage, the only home she has. When she reaches the corridor, she is breathing hard and making small lonely whimpering noises. In the dimly lit corridor, she hesitates for a moment, staring into Johnson's cage. The male chimp is asleep. She remembers the touch of his hands when he groomed her.

From the corridor, she lifts the gate that leads into Johnson's cage and enters. He wakes at the sound of the door and sniffs the air. When he sees Rachel, he stalks toward her, sniffing eagerly. She lets him finger her genitals, sniff deeply of her scent. His penis is erect and he grunts in excitement. She turns and presents herself to him and he mounts her, thrusting deep inside. As he penetrates, she thinks, for a moment, of Jake and of the thin blonde teenage girl named Rachel, but then the moment passes. Almost against her will she cries out, a shrill exclamation of welcoming and loss.

After he withdraws his penis, Johnson grooms her gently, sniffing her genitals and softly stroking her fur. She is sleepy and content, but she knows that they cannot delay.

Johnson is reluctant to leave his cage, but Rachel takes him by the hand and leads him to the janitor's lounge. His presence gives her courage. She listens at the door and hears Jake's soft breathing. Leaving Johnson in the hall, she slips into the room. Jake is lying on the couch, the magazine draped over his legs. Rachel takes the equipment that she has gathered and stands for a moment, staring at the sleeping man. His baseball cap hangs on the arm of a broken chair, and she takes that to remember him by.

Rachel leads Johnson through the empty halls. A kangaroo rat, collecting seeds in the dried grass near the glass doors, looks up curiously as Rachel leads Johnson down the steps. Rachel carries the plastic shopping bag slung over her shoulder. Somewhere in the distance, a coyote howls, a long yapping wail. His cry is joined by others, a chorus in the moonlight.

Rachel takes Johnson by the hand and leads him into the desert.

. . .

A cocktail waitress, driving from her job in Flagstaff to her home in Winslow, sees two apes dart across the road, hurrying away from the bright beams of her headlights. After wrestling with her conscience (she does not want to be accused of drinking on the job), she notifies the county sheriff.

A local newspaper reporter, an eager young man fresh out of journalism school, picks up the story from the police report and interviews the waitress. Flattered by his enthusiasm for her story and delighted to find a receptive ear, she tells him details that she failed to mention to the police: one of the apes was wearing a baseball cap and carrying what looked like a shopping bag.

The reporter writes up a quick humorous story for the morning edition, and begins researching a feature article to be run later in the week. He knows that the newspaper, eager for news in a slow season, will play a human-interest story up big—kind of Lassie, Come Home with chimps.

Just before dawn, a light rain begins to fall, the first rain of spring. Rachel searches for shelter and finds a small cave formed by three tumbled boulders. It will keep off the rain and hide them from casual observers. She shares her food and water with Johnson. He has followed her closely all night, seemingly intimidated by the darkness and the howling of distant coyotes. She feels protective toward him. At the same time, having him with her gives her courage. He knows only a few gestures in ASL, but he does not need to speak. His presence is comfort enough.

Johnson curls up in the back of the cave and falls asleep quickly. Rachel sits in the opening and watches dawnlight wash the stars from the sky. The rain rattles against the sand, a comforting sound. She thinks about Jake. The baseball cap on her head still smells of his cigarettes, but she does not miss him. Not really. She fingers the cap and wonders why she thought she loved Jake.

The rain lets up. The clouds rise like fairy castles in the distance and the rising sun tints them pink and gold and gives them flaming red banners. Rachel remembers when she was younger and Aaron read her the story of Pinocchio, the little puppet who wanted to be a real boy. At the end of his adventures, Pinocchio, who has been brave and kind, gets his wish. He becomes a real boy.

Rachel had cried at the end of the story and when Aaron asked why, she had rubbed her eyes on the backs of her hairy hands. —I want to be a real girl, she signed to him. —A real girl.

"You are a real girl," Aaron had told her, but somehow she had never believed him.

The sun rises higher and illuminates the broken rock turrets of the desert. There is a magic in this barren land of unassuming grandeur. Some cultures send their young people to the desert to seek visions and guidance, searching for true thinking spawned by the openness of the place, the loneliness, the beauty of emptiness.

Rachel drowses in the warm sun and dreams a vision that has the clarity of truth. In the dream, her father comes to her. "Rachel," he says to her, "it doesn't matter what anyone thinks of you. You're my daughter."

I want to be a real girl, she signs.

"You are real," her father says. "And you don't need some two-bit drunken janitor to prove it to you." She knows she is dreaming, but she also knows that her father speaks the truth. She is warm and happy and she doesn't need Jake at all. The sunlight warms her and a lizard watches her from a rock, scurrying for cover when she moves. She picks up a bit of loose rock that lies on the floor of the cave. Idly, she scratches on the dark red sandstone wall of the cave. A lopsided heart shape. Within it, awkwardly printed: Rachel and Johnson. Between them, a plus sign. She goes over the letters again and again, leaving scores of fine lines on the smooth rock surface. Then, late in the morning, soothed by the warmth of the day, she sleeps.

Shortly after dark, an elderly rancher in a pickup truck spots two apes in a remote corner of his ranch. They run away and lose him in the rocks, but not until he has a good look at them. He calls the police, the newspaper, and the Primate Center.

The reporter arrives first thing the next morning, interviews the rancher, and follows the men from the Primate Research Center as they search for evidence of the chimps. They find monkey shit near the cave, confirming that the runaways were indeed nearby. The news reporter, an eager and curious young man, squirms on his belly into the cave and finds the names scratched on the cave wall. He peers at it. He might have dismissed them as the idle scratchings of kids, except that the names match the names of the missing chimps. "Hey," he called to his photographer, "Take a look at this."

The next morning's newspaper displays Rachel's crudely scratched letters. In a brief interview, the rancher mentioned that the chimps were carrying bags. "Looked like supplies," he said. "They looked like they were in for the long haul."

. . .

On the third day, Rachel's water runs out. She heads toward a small town, marked on the map. They reach it in the early morning — thirst forces them to travel by day. Beside an isolated ranch house, she finds a faucet. She is filling her bottle when Johnson grunts in alarm.

A dark-haired woman watches from the porch of the house. She does not move toward the apes, and Rachel continues filling the bottle. "It's all right, Rachel," the woman, who has been following the story in the papers, calls out. "Drink all you want."

Startled, but still suspicious, Rachel caps the bottle and, keeping her eyes on the woman, drinks from the faucet. The woman steps back into the house. Rachel motions Johnson to do the same, signaling for him to hurry and drink. She turns off the faucet when he is done.

They are turning to go when the woman emerges from the house carrying a plate of tortillas and a bowl of apples. She sets them on the edge of the porch and says, "These are for you."

The woman watches through the window as Rachel packs the food into her bag. Rachel puts away the last apple and gestures her thanks to the woman. When the woman fails to respond to the sign language, Rachel picks up a stick and writes in the sand of the yard. "THANK YOU," Rachel scratches, then waves good-bye and sets out across the desert. She is puzzled, but happy.

The next morning's newspaper includes an interview with the dark-haired woman. She describes how Rachel turned on the faucet and turned it off when she was through, how the chimp packed the apples neatly in her bag and wrote in the dirt with a stick.

The reporter also interviews the director of the Primate Research Center. "These are animals," the director explains angrily. "But people want to treat them like they're small hairy people." He describes the Center as "primarily a breeding center with some facilities for medical research." The reporter asks some pointed questions about their acquisition of Rachel.

But the biggest story is an investigative piece. The reporter reveals that he has tracked down Aaron Jacobs lawyer and learned that Jacobs' left a will. In this will, he bequeathed all his possessions — including his house and surrounding land — to "Rachel, the chimp I acknowledge as my daughter."

The reporter makes friends with one of the young women in the typing pool at the research center, and she tells him the office scuttlebutt: people suspect that the chimps may have been released by a deaf and drunken janitor, who was subsequently fired for negligence. The reporter, accompanied by a friend who can communicate in sign language, finds Jake in his apartment in downtown Flagstaff.

Jake, who has been drinking steadily since he was fired, feels betrayed by Rachel, by the Primate Center, by the world. He complains at length about Rachel: they had been friends, and then she took his baseball cap and ran away. He just didn't understand why she had run away like that.

"You mean she could talk?" the reporter asks through his interpreter.

Of course she can talk, Jake signs impatiently. — She is a smart monkey.

The headlines read: "Intelligent chimp inherits fortune!" Of course, Aaron's bequest isn't really a fortune and she isn't just a chimp, but close enough. Animal rights activists rise up in Rachel's defense. The case is discussed on the national news. Ann Landers reports receiving a letter from a chimp named Rachel; she had thought it was a hoax perpetrated by the boys at Yale. The American Civil Liberties Union assigns a lawyer to the case.

By day, Rachel and Johnson sleep in whatever hiding places they can find: a cave; a shelter built for range cattle; the shell of an abandoned car, rusted from long years in a desert gully. Sometimes Rachel dreams of jungle darkness, and the coyotes in the distance become a part of her dreams, their howling becomes the cries of fellow apes.

The desert and the journey have changed her. She is wiser, having passed through the white-hot love of adolescence and emerged on the other side. She dreams, one day, of the ranch house. In the dream, she has long blonde hair and pale white skin. Her eyes are red from crying and she wanders the house restlessly, searching for something that she has lost. When she hears coyotes howling, she looks through a window at the darkness outside. The face that looks in at her has jug-handle ears and shaggy hair. When she sees the face, she cries out in recognition and opens the window to let herself in.

By night, they travel. The rocks and sands are cool beneath Rachel's feet as she walks toward her ranch. On television, scientists and politicians discuss the ramifications of her case, describe the technology uncovered by investigation of Aaron Jacobs' files. Their debates do not affect her steady progress toward her ranch or the stars that sprinkle the sky above her.

It is night when Rachel and Johnson approach the ranch house. Rachel sniffs the wind and smells automobile exhaust and strange humans. From the hills, she can see a small camp beside a white van marked with the name of a local television station. She hesitates, considering returning to the safety of the desert. Then she takes Johnson by the hand and starts down the hill. Rachel is going home.

Simians, Cyborgs, and Women in "Rachel in Love"

Joan Haran

"Rachel in Love" was first published in *Isaac Asimov's Science Fiction Magazine* in April 1987. It won a Nebula, the Isaac Asimov Reader's Award, and the Theodore Sturgeon Memorial Award, and has since been reprinted repeatedly in collections that showcase the very best science fiction.[1]

"Rachel in Love" was also produced as an audiotape by Durkin Hayes, served as the inspiration for a multimedia artwork by Diana Thater, was published as a stand-alone short story paperback by Pulphouse, and has been translated into Hungarian and French. Despite the evident popularity and quality of the story, the story has received little detailed critical attention to date.

As Susan Faludi documented in *Backlash*, in the 1980s there was "a powerful counter-assault on women's rights, a backlash, an attempt to retract the handful of small and hard-won victories that the feminist movement did manage to win for women."[2] In "An Open Letter to Joanna Russ," Jeanne Gomoll suggested that the rhapsodic rhetoric about the cyberpunks of the late 1980s was part of the backlash, yet another strategy to suppress women's writing. Joanna Russ, of course, had already detailed an extensive range of such strategies in her inimitable witty and biting fashion in *How to Suppress Women's Writing*. For Jeanne Gomoll the following paragraph from Bruce Sterling's preface to *Burning Chrome*, an anthology of stories by William Gibson, was a punch in the stomach: "The sad truth of the matter is that SF has not been much fun of late. All forms of pop culture go through the doldrums: they catch cold when society sneezes. If SF in the late Seventies was confused, self-involved, and stale, it was scarcely a cause for wonder."[3]

Gomoll suggests that such statements can be taken up by those "made nervous or bored or threatened by the explosion of women's writing and issues" as a code for what they really mean: "The women writers of the '70s bored me because I didn't care about their ideas; I felt left out. 'They wrote it but it was a *boring* fad.'"[4] Gomoll concluded her open letter by suggesting that the obvious solution to the problem of erasing women writers and fans from science fictional history was for her and other women like her to redress the balance: "We should all keep up critical pressure for balanced retrospectives, anthologies and reprints (fannish and professional). If we ourselves forget, why should we expect new generations of readers and fans to dig up the truth about what really happened?"[5]

With the advantage of hindsight, it is a striking counterpoint to Gomoll's unease about the potential erasure of women from the official history of sf in the 1980s, that it was the very decade in which Pat Murphy began to publish regularly and successfully. She rapidly made her mark on the field as an outstanding writer who evaded easy labeling. Her work combines serious attention to "women's issues" with wit and humor, often of a very dark hue. In 1987, she won a Nebula for her novel *The Falling Woman* in addition to the multiple awards for "Rachel in Love." Another Nebula winner in the same year was Kate Wilhelm, one of the women writers who had paved the way for feminist science fiction of the 1970s. Wilhelm and Anne McCaffrey were the first women Nebula award-winners in 1968, and the same year McCaffrey was the first woman to win a Hugo award in a professional rather than a fan capacity.[6] Both appeared in Pamela Sargent's landmark first *Women of Wonder* collection in 1974. So the 1980s could also be viewed as a period of consolidation and the mainstreaming of *some* women writers.

As one of the many award-winning feminist sf writers who emerged in the 1970s, Pat Murphy has combated attempts to suppress or sideline women's writing, not just in her own fiction, but through the creation of the James Tiptree, Jr. Award in collaboration with Karen Joy Fowler. Launched in 1991 at WisCon, a feminist science fiction convention, the Tiptree Award is an annual literary prize for science fiction or fantasy that expands or explores understandings of gender.[7]

Debbie Notkin, a member of the Tiptree Award's Motherboard, recalls the panic that ensued in the science fiction community in 1975 when the author James Tiptree, Jr. (whose writing was described by Robert Silverberg as "ineluctably masculine") was revealed to be Alice Sheldon. It was Tiptree's own exploration and expansion of gender understanding that made her "unmasking" so symbolic in a decade when women (lesbian and heterosexual) and gay men were becoming a more visible presence in the community of science fiction writers.[8] So naming a new science fiction award specifically to recall this iconic moment of sf history was an inspired response by Pat Murphy to Jeanne Gomoll's call to action. Just as inspired was the suggestion to fund the award from the proceeds of bake sales. Jeanne Gomoll was one of many in the audience at WisCon waving her hand and volunteering to help with fundraising. Fundraising Tiptree Bake Sales and Tiptree Auctions fronted by the irrepressible Ellen Klages, sf short fiction writer and member of the Tiptree Motherboard, are now a regular feature of many science fiction conventions, keeping awareness of the prize high within the sf community.

In discussing its success in bringing writers, fans, and academics together, I should mention that WisCon was my own introduction to the feminist sf community as a group of real people, rather than an imagined community in which I participated through reading great fiction. An Australian feminist sf scholar, Helen Merrick, and I met on a panel at a Women's Studies conference in the United Kingdom in 1996 and she told me about WisCon: a convention that filled a hotel with about seven hundred people discussing feminism and science fiction (by 2005 that number had grown to almost 900).

Two years later I gave my first academic presentation at WisCon and I have returned many times since. I've seen the Tiptree Award presented, and I've even chaired the judging panel. At the turn of the twenty-first century, I am confident that women writers of the twentieth century will continue to be remembered and read as central to science fiction thanks to Gomoll's strategy of speaking out about the witting and unwitting erasure of women's contribution to the genre and the clever activism of the Tiptree Award. Indeed, the success has been such that it has been suggested that there is no longer a need for the award. I disagree: the backlash in the 1980s that Faludi documented and the erasure that Gomoll noted were real phenomena that had to be challenged; it is not clear that they have become chimeras.

The Cyberpunk Landscape

For example, in the 1980s, cyberpunk and the critical acclaim it garnered did seem to account for a disproportionate amount of the attention given to sf both within and outside the field of science fiction. For many academics and cultural commentators, this subgenre did seem to capture the spirit of the age and the future they could envisage emerging from the proliferation of information technology and the global mobility of capital. While William Gibson's *Neuromancer* is its iconic exemplar, the term "has acquired such cultural resonance that it has since been applied to a far wider range of cultural products, and unconscious traces of cyberpunk are now seen everywhere, particularly in films such as *Blade Runner* and *Brazil*."[9]

Cyberpunk as it was represented in Bruce Sterling's *Mirrorshades: The Cyberpunk Anthology* was a male-dominated subgenre, with Pat Cadigan the honorable female exception. Indeed, Sterling claimed: "Cyberpunk comes from the realm where the computer hacker and the rocker overlap, a cultural Petri dish where writhing gene lines splice."[10] These two subcultures are typically dominated by young white males. Sterling went on to identify central themes in cyberpunk: "the theme of body invasion: prosthetic limbs, implanted circuitry, cosmetic surgery, genetic alteration. The even more powerful theme of mind invasion: brain-computer interfaces, artificial intelligence, neurochemistry — techniques radically redefining the nature of humanity, the nature of the self."[11]

Cyberpunks do not hold the copyright on exploration of these themes, as "Rachel in Love" demonstrates. Tom Maddox suggests that *Neuromancer* and *Blade Runner* "together set the boundary conditions for emerging cyberpunk: a hard-boiled combination of hi tech and low life."[12] So it is both the imminent horizon of the hi-tech future and a particular prose style that characterizes cyberpunk.

Sterling offers a vivid description of what he calls the "crammed" prose of cyberpunk: rapid, dizzying bursts of novel information, sensory overload that submerges the reader in the literary equivalent of the hard-rock "wall of sound."[13] "Rachel in Love" is very different stylistically from this. The story is a deceptively simple third-person narrative, written in the present tense from a single point of view, albeit that of a small brown chimpanzee with trace memories of an adolescent human female. Rachel is not a hard-boiled ironic protagonist. It is only in the course of the story that she comes to full self-consciousness and takes responsibility for herself. Thematically, however, the novelette shares similar preoccupations with cyberpunk: "the . . . powerful theme of mind invasion . . . and the nature of the self," but Pat Murphy's choice of protagonist as well as the geography in which that protagonist is located decenters the experience of the white urban male and thus produces a text that is much more clearly ambivalent and ambiguous about the pleasures and dangers of science and technology. Rachel does not have the global mobility of cyberpunk protagonists. Until the death of Aaron Jacobs, in fact, she has barely left the confines of the fenced garden around her ranch house. Although he claimed that this was for her safety, as he would be unable to protect her in the outside world, his tirade is rather more expressive of the judgment passed on him by the scientific researchers who distrusted his work and cut off his funding: "You wouldn't like it out there. The world is filled with petty, narrow-minded, stupid people. They wouldn't understand you. And anyone they don't understand, they want to hurt. They hurt anyone who's different. If they know that you're different, they punish you, hurt you. They'd lock you up and never let you go." (Murphy, 221)

Rachel is a keen TV viewer but she does not have the relatively empowered access to technology experienced by the cyberpunk (anti)heroes who can directly interface with cyberspace. She may inhabit a gritty environment, but it is barren rocky land on the edge of the Painted Desert, not a polluted and overcrowded megalopolis. Murphy's prose is as redolent of the arid western landscape, and its historical associations, as Gibson's is of urban sprawl and the end of history: "Rachel dreams. She is back at home in the ranch house. It is night and she is alone. Outside, coyotes yip and howl. The coyote is the voice of the desert, wailing as the wind will when it stretches itself thin to squeeze through a crack between two boulders. The people native to this land tell tales of Coyote, a god who was a trickster, unreliable, changeable, mercurial." (Murphy, 224)

The revolutionary cutting edge of 1980s contemporary culture that formed the backdrop for the cultural diffusion of cyberpunk has become the taken-for-granted of the early twenty-first century. Preschool children in the West play games on PCs before they learn to read, and virtual reality has made it into the arcades. But computers were not quite so mundane in the 1980s, a decade that saw a massive burgeoning of information technology in the affluent parts of the globe. The market penetration of arcade video games and the introduction of games consoles for the home gave some users a new understanding of the pleasurable possibilities of the human/machine interface. Computers began to move out of their hermetically sealed machine rooms and onto desktops. Predictions about the future this ubiquity of silicon offered included great hopes for the development of genuine artificial intelligence, as well as fantasies about the merging of humans and machines. These fantasies were not new; what was new was that they spread far beyond their original audience base of information scientists and hardcore sf fans to become the stuff of blockbuster movies like *Blade Runner* (1982), *The Terminator* (1984), *Robocop* (1987), and *Total Recall* (1990), and the stock-in-trade of the cyberpunks.

Since 1987, of course, the term *cyberpunk* and the sets of texts to which it has been applied have been hotly debated both by critics and by sf authors, many of whom have destabilized the boundaries that Sterling tried to define. I read "Rachel in Love" as one of the texts that contributes to that destabilization. Investing in Rachel's point of view, I find it much harder to be seduced by any promise of using technology to transcend my fleshiness. The detailed attention to the pain attendant on "body invasion" in this text gives me much pause for thought:

> Rachel can blink, but otherwise she can't move. From where she lies, she can see only the wire mesh of the cage and the side of the truck. When she tries to turn her head, the burning in her skin intensifies. She lies still, wanting to cry out, but unable to make a sound. She can only blink slowly, trying to close out the pain. But the burning and nausea stay. (Murphy, 222)

Reading this, I am reminded that mind and body invasion have been practiced on nonhuman animals and on poor women and black women during the development of new technologies. Because Rachel is depicted as a chimpanzee whose consciousness has been melded with that of a young woman, I am excruciatingly conscious, *qua* Haraway, of the potential permeability of the species boundary, and the way the boundary has been blurred historically by the powerful white Western men who have dominated science. Women — assumed to be white — and black people have been conceptualized in Western science as being closer to nature, more animal-like than rational white men. Such concepts have been implicated in scientific research that we would now consider to be unethical, like the Tuskegee syphilis experiment with poor black men; or at the very least exploitative of people's lack of economic power, such as the involuntary sterilization of women of color in exchange for free health care, an abuse famously fictionalized in Marge Piercy's *Woman on the Edge of Time*.[14]

Feminist Science Studies and Cyberculture

Paradoxically, by focusing on the merging of two female minds across a species divide, "Rachel in Love" makes itself comprehensible to readers who are not habitual consumers of science fiction, and thus may entice new readers to the genre, those who might have felt alienated by having to learn the specific reading conventions of cyberpunk. Reading practices and affiliations outside sf can enable a pleasurable and productive encounter with this story. For example, I cannot read feminist science fiction without thinking about feminist critiques of science by authors like Evelyn Fox Keller, Donna Haraway, Sandra Harding, and Carolyn Merchant amongst others. These feminist science critics often draw on feminist science fiction for inspiration or illustrations of their critiques, so I know I am not alone in finding my reading of each genre enriched by the other.[15]

For readers of this anthology not familiar with that other genre, feminist science studies provides a critical perspective on scientific ideology and practice that takes account of the ways in which gender, class, and "race" shape the questions that scientists ask, and the projects they undertake. In this context, reading "Rachel in Love" together with Donna Haraway's essay, "A Cyborg Manifesto," produces an extremely illuminating dialogue.

The "Manifesto" was first published in 1985, but was revised and reprinted in several versions throughout the decade, being made available to an increasingly wide readership, much as "Rachel in Love" was. Haraway's "ironic political myth" about the breakdown of boundaries between humans and other animals, and between humans and machines is an obvious counterpart to this story of a chimpanzee who shares her consciousness with that of a dead child.

Haraway's manifesto has been enormously influential in feminist science studies, feminist cultural studies, and in studies of cyberculture more generally. As much a call to action as a critique, the essay argues that it is imperative that feminists attend to the social relations of science and technology.[16] Haraway argues that the myths and meanings that structure our imaginations of science require feminist scrutiny and intervention just as much as the material practices of science. That is, just as it is important to get more women working in laboratories and defining the questions to be addressed, so it is important to craft feminist science fictions that enable us to think differently about science. The figure of the cyborg, "a cybernetic organism, a hybrid of machine and organism, a creature of social reality as well as a creature of fiction," was to be used to take pleasure in the confusion of boundaries and responsibility for their destruction.[17]

The three crucial boundary breakdowns that Haraway identified as the social and historical context for this figure were the boundary between human and animal, the "leaky distinction" between animal-human (organism) and machine, and the boundary between physical and nonphysical, machines that are "nothing but signals, electromagnetic waves, a section of a spectrum."[18] We, as feminists engaging in this collective project of using science fiction to interrogate the social relations of technoscience, might identify each of these boundary breakdowns in Murphy's story, and ask therefore how we might read it as feminists who are interested in the systems of myths and meanings that structure our imaginations about science and technology.

Haraway's essay is an inaugural moment in socialist feminism's turn toward poststructuralism and postmodernism, and sees enormous promise, as well as massive jeopardy, in the possibilities for boundary confusion and boundary transgression opened up for feminists and other critical interest groups by technoscience. For example, one of the science fictions that Haraway discusses in her essay is "Anne McCaffrey's pre-feminist *The Ship Who Sang* [which] explored the consciousness of a cyborg, hybrid of girl's brain and complex machinery, formed after the birth of a severely handicapped child."[19] This novel could be read as offering liberatory possibilities, but might also be read as devaluing the distinctive subjectivity of those who do not conform to an able-bodied norm.

Information Theory and the Scientific Imagination

I am not suggesting that "A Cyborg Manifesto" inspired "Rachel in Love" (indeed, Pat Murphy told me she has not read the Haraway essay) but some of the common themes are very striking. This coincidence can be traced back, I would suggest, to their shared preoccupation with science as it has been practiced in the United States, particularly in the aftermath of World War II. Katherine Hayles, a professor of English, who has published extensively on literature and science, describes some of the key elements of this emergent technoscientific culture in *How We Became PostHuman*. She tells three interrelated stories: "*how information lost its body*," "*how the cyborg was created as a technological artifact and cultural icon*," and "*how the human is giving way to a different construction called the posthuman*."[20]

Resonating with Haraway's earlier essay, Hayles provides an illuminating insight into the scientific imagination that forms the context of "Rachel in Love." She discusses the rise of information theory, which perhaps reached its apotheosis in Hans Moravec's assertion that it would soon be possible to download human consciousness into a computer. Moravec was not the originator of such a notion; Norbert Wiener, one of the founders of cybernetics, claimed it was theoretically possible to telegraph a human being, as early as the 1950s, drawing on the same assumptions as Moravec.[21]

Hayles sets out a genealogy that documents the processes through which information has come to be thought of as separate/separable from the material through which it is communicated. She refers to the Turing test, initially proposed by Turing in his paper "Computer Machinery and Intelligence" (1950) and made globally famous through the film *Blade Runner*'s spin on it. Turing's original scenario invited an investigator to determine, solely from typed responses to questions received on computer terminals, which remote entity was a human and which was a machine.[22] Turing argued that should the investigator fail to distinguish between the verbal performances of a human and a machine, this would prove that machines could think. Hayles claims that the effect of Turing's thought experiment was that "at the inaugural moment of the computer age, the erasure of embodiment (was) performed so that 'intelligence' becomes a property of the formal manipulation of symbols rather than enaction in the human lifeworld."[23]

To elaborate, by understanding intelligence as a set of information communication processes that might not be unique to human beings, the distinctiveness of human embodiment is downplayed to the point where it appears to become immaterial in both senses of the word. This, Hayles argues, set the agenda for three decades of research on artificial intelligence. So the kernel that sets Murphy's story in motion — the imprinting of the patterns of a human mind on a chimpanzee's brain — has much in common with the imaginings of both cyberneticists and cyberpunks. By erasing or diminishing embodiment in the way that Hayles describes — albeit for the purpose of thought-experiments — information scientists and cyberneticists set the stage for thinking about human identity as just a particular pattern of information. Moravec's fantasy scenario, as described by Hayles, discards the body in its pursuit of information:

> a robot surgeon purees the human brain in a kind of cranial liposuction, reading the information in each molecular layer as it is stripped away and transferring the information into a computer. At the end of the operation, the cranial cavity is empty, and the patient, now inhabiting the metallic body of the computer, wakens to find his consciousness exactly the same as it was before.[24]

In her blurb for How We Became PostHuman, Haraway claims that the book "is a powerful prophylactic against our most likely alien abduction scenario — to be raptured out of the bodies that matter in the lust for information." Similarly, I would argue that "Rachel in Love" provides the same check on the headier (pun intended) fantasies of cyberpunk. The cyborg boundary that Murphy examines is not that between human and machine, in the robotic lab of Moravec's fantasy, or in the gritty margins of the kind of futuristic corporate dystopia seen in Blade Runner and William Gibson's Neuromancer. Rather, it is the boundary between human and animal (or, more properly, nonhuman animal). As Rachel herself remarks, "Are they really so different? They are not so different." (Murphy, 237) Nor is the disembodiment of the human mind so radical in this tale, achieved as it is with the assistance of a rather unusual form of information technology, a combination of chemical stimulation and electrical patterning that reembodies that mind in another fleshy body. In his Science Fiction Encyclopedia entry on Pat Murphy, John Clute refers to this as displacement across the gulf of species, but my reading of "Rachel in Love" would read "proximity" where he reads "gulf." That this story of boundary confusion is located in the present rather than the future is much more in sympathy with Haraway's take on the cyborg than the noir cyberspace hackers of Gibson et al. In the mid-1980s Haraway saw cyborgs as creatures of contemporary social reality that were a useful resource for thinking about the ways that bodies are being remade in the context of late technoscientific capitalism.

In "A Cyborg Manifesto" Haraway cautioned against nostalgia for the organic, but her concern was with people insisting on purity and static boundaries; she did not want to transcend "the meat" altogether.[25] In her more recent manifesto, however, she suggests that "companion species" (dogs, in particular) might offer more useful figures for contemporary engagements with technoscience than cyborgs. Reading between the lines, it appears that cyborgs have been more recalcitrant than Haraway had hoped, more faithful to their emergence from militarism and patriarchal capitalism than she had imagined. To take just one example, in cyberpunk, the sf genre most lauded for its preoccupation with cybernetic organisms, the feminist socialist myth she attempted to craft was largely absent in a field saturated with masculinist liberal individualism.[26]

Disappearing Bodies

Feminists have been very critical of the legacies of Cartesian thinking, which sees the body as no more than a container for the mind. And, indeed, it is consciousness that is privileged in this worldview, our thoughts and our capacity to think them. The late twentieth century offered an extreme version of Cartesian dualism, imagining mind as separable even from the fleshly human brain. This logical extreme of mind-body dualism arose in the United States in when the information theory paradigm spread throughout the life and social sciences.[27] The postmodern and poststructuralist focus on narratives and discourses in the humanities and the social sciences can be seen as a parallel development, because the focus is on the knowledge that is produced rather than the ability of individuals to construct that knowledge. In fact, this supposition that *all* objects of knowledge are mediated and constructed through language also called into question previously assumed boundaries between reality and representation (ultimately making it extremely difficult within certain academic circles to think about the physical or the material at all).

This poststructuralist assumption — that any knowledge we can communicate linguistically is a product of language and not verifiable outside language — has created a challenging balancing act for feminist theorists. On the one hand, they want to take full account of their grasp on the materiality and specificity of bodies, particularly women's bodies. On the other hand, they recognize that if "reality" is a continual process of construction, then they cannot rely on timeless or universal understandings of what a "woman" or a "body" is. To clarify: for many centuries in the West, our discourse has conceptualized human bodies as being produced in just two sexes (latterly, genders), so we have understood bodies as either male or female. More recently, with the discovery of other chromosomal combinations than XX and XY, it has been argued that it would be more accurate to think of humans as coming in five sexes. It is likely that these chromosomal variants have always existed, but before that knowledge became exchangeable through discourse, XYY bodies, for example, could only be understood as deviant males. We might argue that the possibility of constructing such knowledge is due to the critiques of gender and sexuality offered by feminists and gay and lesbian activists expanding what it is possible to think and say.

Feminists engaged in empirical research, on the other hand, particularly those who deal with pain and suffering, have found other ways to engage with the postmodern. These focus less on the production of embodiment through discourse and more on the ways in which different interest groups have produced different stories about embodiment to effect particular power relationships. So, for example, feminists engaged with medical technoscience have noted the ways that women's bodies are erased or made transparent in the rhetoric and visual imagery used by fetal rights advocates, with material effects on the choices that women can make about abortion. Some anti-abortion activists refer to fetuses, or even embryos, as *babies*, equating a cluster of cells with a born child. Images captured through ultrasound photography (and now video) make it look as if the fetus is free-floating rather than inhabiting a woman's body.

A story like "Rachel in Love" takes full account of the fleshy brains and bodies in which memories and subjectivities are produced. The story presents a more nuanced version of cybernetics and the relationship between mind and environment than stories or theories that equate information and/or consciousness with transcendence of the flesh.

One of Pat Murphy's undergraduate classes was taught by Gregory Bateson, the author of *Steps Towards an Ecology of Mind.* Murphy remembers Bateson's classes because of the ways in which he apparently jumped from topic to topic, leaving his students to figure out the relationships between their subject matter. She recalls her Eureka! moment when she figured out that he was intentionally allowing his students to make the connections. In writing "Rachel in Love" she did not deliberately draw on these classes, but acknowledges that they provoked ideas that, despite seeming ephemeral, left traces that might be incorporated into a story.

Bateson was an important figure in the development and dissemination of the information paradigm by way of cybernetics, a field that attempted — as Hayles points out — to initiate new ways of thinking about boundaries:

> Gregory Bateson brought the point home when he puzzled his graduate students with a question koanlike in its simplicity, asking if a blind man's cane is part of the man. . . . Seen from the cybernetic perspective coalescing into awareness during and after World War II, however, cybernetic systems are constituted by flows of information. In this viewpoint, cane and man join in a single system, for the cane funnels to the man essential information about his environment.[28]

This question suggests that rather than disembodying humanity, Bateson instead extended embodiment into the tools that humans use to make sense of their environment. As Donna Haraway inquires: "Why should our bodies end at the skin, or include at best other beings encapsulated by skin?"[29] "Rachel in Love," therefore, can be read both as being influenced by the cybernetic worldview, but also as resistant to the degree that its author wishes to explore the interaction between information and its body: the human or animal body that gets left behind in the systems-thinking that evacuates individual agency from the picture. Murphy's insistence on the importance of Rachel's development of self-consciousness through painful and pleasurable experiences, as well as through her acquisition of language, drives this point home.

In Dialogue with the Author

Before my lengthy telephone conversation with Pat Murphy about the novella, I sent her a number of questions to consider, and she began by telling me that the question she'd found most interesting was one about the different levels of story circulating in "Rachel in Love." The character uses stories told to her by her "father" and stories she reads (and views) herself to make sense of the world and her place in it. The setting of the story draws on tropes from westerns, romances, coming-of-age stories, and tales of animals finding their own way home. For me it also resonates with the critical stories told by feminist science scholars.

Growing up, Pat Murphy was an avid reader of science fiction and fantasy, but like many other female readers she found no place for herself in these stories. Her solution was to reimagine them, to retell the stories so that there was a space for a fourth-grade girl: "I spent all my time reimagining stories and shoehorning myself into them, but when I first started writing, I wrote the type of stories I had *read*, not those I had retold myself. Once I realized that, I started writing stories with a place for me in them."[30] Pat's most recent novels, *There and Back Again, by Max Merriwell, Wild Angel*, and *Adventures in Time and Space with Max Merriwell*, are self-conscious examples of this rewriting of stories.[31] Until I asked her, however, Pat hadn't realized how much she was already using the device of retelling stories in "Rachel in Love." Pat explains that the story originated when

> [I] worked as a features writer for a time, writing human interest stories, and for one of the features I interviewed a woman who wrote for the *True Confessions* type of magazine. In preparation for the interview, I had been reading some of the magazines and thought I had spotted their formula. It goes something like — there's a woman, she's in love with the wrong man, he isn't good for her, and in the background there is another man who is a good friend, and in the end she realizes he is the one for her. I checked this out with the writer, and she confirmed my observation. So that was a kernel around which the story grew. . .[32]

Of course, the "right man" for Rachel is Johnson, and she makes a conscious decision to take him as her partner when she realizes that she can have neither a romance nor a sexual relationship with Jake. It is her desire to be touched that leads her to this choice, however much she has wanted to be "a real girl."

Stories, Memory, and Subjectivity

"Rachel in Love" explores the relationship between stories and memory and between memory and subjectivity. I have already mentioned Rachel's captivation by a Tarzan movie, in which she appears to be taking Tarzan's part: "On the television, Tarzan has been trapped in a bamboo cage by a band of wicked pygmies. Rachel is afraid that he won't escape in time to save Jane from the ivory smugglers who hold her captive. The movie cuts to Jane who is tied up in the back of a Jeep, and Rachel whimpers to herself." (Murphy, 217)

Edgar Rice Burroughs's portrayal of a noble white hero, beset by evil black tribesmen is a deeply racist vision that emerged from the Western project of colonial conquest and its self-justifying narratives of white superiority and scientific progress. Juxtaposing the passage above with the passage about Rachel's first experience of captivity emphasizes that a similar worldview underpins the scientific imagination that both views the great apes as our nearest relatives and subjects them to painful *and* invasive research:

> Her mother was dark and hairy and smelled sweetly of overripe fruit. She and Rachel lived in a wiry cage in a room filled with chips and she hugged Rachel to her hairy breast whenever any people came into the room. Rachel's mother groomed Rachel constantly, picking delicately through her fur in search of the lice that she never found.
>
> Memories upon memories: jumbled and confused, like random pictures clipped from magazines, a bright collage that makes no sense. Rachel remembers cages: cold wire mesh beneath her feet, the smell of fear around her. A man in a white lab coat took her from the arms of her hairy mother and pricked her with needles. She could hear her mother howling, but she could not escape from the man (Murphy, 220).

Again, there are obvious parallels between Aaron Jacobs's experimentation on a young chimpanzee when he "imposes" the pattern of his dead daughter's mind upon her brain, and the activities of the Primate Research Center, particularly as both Jacobs and the PRC attempt to deprive Rachel of self-determination and of her place within a larger community of chimpanzees for their own purposes. However, by instructing her in sign language (ASL), teaching her to read and write, and enabling her to understand herself as the subject of her own story, Jacobs does provide her with the resources to empower herself. Rachel has a favorite story, the story of her origin: " — Where did I come from? she would ask Aaron, using the abbreviated gestures of ASL, American Sign Language. — Tell me again." (Murphy, 218) She compares Aaron's narrative to that of a fairy tale, suggesting a complex relationship between those stories that are "true" and those that are "just for entertainment." Rachel identifies with the heroines in fairy tales and this is sometimes consoling and sometimes troubling when she attempts to integrate her dissonant memories, particularly in her dreams:

> She looks into her own reflection: a pale oval face, long blond hair. The hand that holds the curtain aside is smooth and white with carefully clipped fingernails. But something is wrong. Superimposed on the reflection is another face peering through the glass: a pair of dark brown eyes, a chimp face with redbrown hair and jug-handle ears. She sees her own reflection and she sees the outsider; the two images merge and blur. She is afraid, but she can't drop the curtain and shut the ape face out.

> She is a chimp looking in through the cold, bright windowpane; she is a girl looking out; she is a girl looking in; she is an ape looking out. She is afraid and the coyotes are howling all around (Murphy, 224).

When Rachel is taken to the Primate Research Center, she cannot understand why she has been locked in jail as she hasn't done anything wrong. She is sensitive to the call of the coyote, the quintessential western call of the wild. Is this because of her own animal nature or because she is so conscious of wilderness tropes from her education as an American "girl" that the symbolic resonance cannot escape her? Even Rachel's dreams evoke associations with *Through the Looking Glass and What Alice Found There* and Catherine Earnshaw at the window in *Wuthering Heights*.

Romance, Pornography, and Sexuality

In order to assuage her loneliness following her father's death and her incarceration in the Primate Research Center (PRC), Rachel becomes friends with the janitor, Jake, and a male chimpanzee, Johnson. She is unsure how to behave with either the male human or the male chimp and strives to understand her relationships with them in terms of the stories about love and romance, and the visual images from romance and pornographic magazines, as well as from her limited observation of chimpanzee behavior in the PRC:

> Rachel knows little about love: she remembers a high-school crush where she mooned after a boy with a locker near hers, but that came to nothing. She reads the confessions magazines and Ann Landers' column in the newspaper that Jake brings with him each night, and from these sources, she learns about romance. (Murphy, 234)

Rachel's struggles to understand relationship rules and roles are like those of any young woman attempting to come to terms with herself and her social world through the confusing collage of popular culture, peer interaction, and parental control, with the added complication that although she has the memories and remembered desires of a young human female, she also has the memories and desires of a female chimpanzee:

> Mike stalks into Susie's cage. The keepers lower the cage door, trapping both chimps in the same cage. Susie seems unalarmed. She continues eating a slice of orange while Mike sniffs at her genitals with every indication of great interest. She bends over to let Mike finger her pink bottom, the sign of estrus.
> Rachel finds herself standing at the wire mesh, making low moaning noises.

She can see Mike's erection, hear his grunting cries. He squats on the floor of Susie's cage, gesturing to the female. Rachel's feelings are mixed: she is fascinated, fearful, confused. She keeps thinking of the description of sex in the *Love Confessions* story: When Alice feels Danny's lips on hers, she is swept away by the passion of the moment. He takes her in his arms and her skin tingles as if she were consumed by an inner fire (Murphy, 232).

Reading this story and thinking about the feminist historical context of its production, the poignant representations of the uses to which Rachel puts pornography and romance magazines recall another flashpoint for feminism in the 1980s, the so-called sex wars. In her "Manifesto" Haraway alludes to the problems posed for feminists by an insistence on victimhood, taking as a case in point "Catherine MacKinnon's version of radical feminism." MacKinnon is notorious, along with Andrea Dworkin, for drafting civil rights legislation that attempted to give women the right to seek damages from the producers or distributors of pornography on the ground that they had been harmed by it. Opponents of the position taken up by MacKinnon and Dworkin argued that a simplistic equation was being drawn between the publication of pornography and violence against women. They also believed that MacKinnon and Dworkin's analysis belittled the ability of women to make choices about sexuality, including the choice to participate in erotic play around dominance and submission. They warned that banning pornography was opening the door to a kind of censorship that would be used against feminists and people whose sexuality was outside the married heterosexual norm.

In Murphy's tale, Rachel attempts to understand her own sexuality and desire, as well as that of Jake and Johnson through the textual and visual narratives of pornography and romance magazines, as well as through close observation of their behavior. Rachel, the "small brown chimp," has sensory advantages over Rachel, the "pretty girl, with long golden hair," as she can derive meaning from scent. Rachel's active attempts to initiate sex — in the pursuit of intimacy as well as to assuage the physical symptoms of her desire — are at odds with any reading of her as submissive or objectified, despite accounts by some feminists that view pornography as only a site of women's oppression. Rachel mimics the postures in the magazines so that *she* will arouse Jake.

Murphy's representation of Rachel's desire invites many questions about the "nature" of sexuality and the extent to which it is instinctual or else constructed or mediated through narratives. Is Rachel a dupe of patriarchal and romantic ideology? Or does viewing her thus disparage her active sexuality? Is sexual intercourse simply a behavior that humans share with animals? Are the stories told about sex in the context of romance merely edifices built to give sex meaning beyond "animal lusts"? Are all the stories of romance fantasies constructed to make human behavior seem unique and special? Certainly, Murphy reports that the explicit descriptions of sexual behavior in the story troubled some readers. But, as she points out, sexuality is of vital interest to adolescents and chimpanzees alike and to explore the subjectivity of a young woman/young chimpanzee without dealing with sexuality would neglect a crucial aspect of her developing sense of identity.

The Science in Science Fiction

Despite John Clute's assertion that "nothing in the tale, with the exception of Rachel's cognitively enhanced responses, is in any sense sf, or even unlikely," the novella is clearly sf.[33] Murphy points out that she had the idea for the story shortly after taking a university course in neurology and the chemistry of neurological impulses. Cross-fertilize this with her physics courses on electricity and magnetism, and the use of primates as surrogates for humans in experimentation and you have the germ of Aaron Jacobs's research.

Whether or not this experiment is a likely technoscientific intervention I could debate with Clute, but if the cyberpunk heroes who upload their consciousness onto the Net are legitimate sf, then a chimp with the downloaded neurological impulses of an adolescent girl must be. The entire story encourages the reader to ask searching questions about the ethics of scientific research while at the same time empathizing with Rachel, whose very identity is dependent on a dubious application of science.

According to Pat Murphy, Rachel's search for who she really is and her coming to terms with herself, drove the way the story unfolded. Murphy believes that it is this focus on character and subjective experience that might lead some readers to question the tale's genre status. She argues that this kind of judgment is a misunderstanding of what science fiction is: "science is the core of the problem."[34]

Scientific Experimentation and Animal Rights

I have already mentioned "true romance" and the fictional professor's experiment with neurological patterning as providing structural and thematic elements for this story. In addition, Murphy realized that the narrative required Rachel to be in some jeopardy, hence the introduction of Rachel's incarceration in the Primate Research Center. I am sure that, having read "Rachel in Love," you will find it unimaginable that this story would be the same without the compelling drama of this episode. Murphy reveals, however, that there were two prior complete drafts of the story that imagined Rachel's romance in very different situations and explored the same themes about identity and communication. Yet without the obstacles experienced in this final version of the story, Rachel could not develop fully.

When writers of fiction discuss the organic process by which they evolve their work, it undercuts any simple assumptions that might be made about the relationship between the authors' intentions and the meaning readers make of the end-product. Literary theorists have proclaimed the death of the author, but I would argue that the science fiction genre foregrounds the debate between author and reader. Pat Murphy is quite clear that "Rachel in Love" is not simply a cautionary tale *about* the horrors of animal experimentation, but many readers have read it as written with an animal rights agenda. Pat Murphy again: "A number of readers asked whether animal rights were the 'reason' for 'Rachel in Love.' I can see how you might see that as the impetus, but it is actually much more complicated. This is not an essay or an article. Once I understood that jeopardy was required for the story, I went back and did the research on primate experiments. I remembered reading about chimps that had learned American Sign Language (ASL) and then ended up back in the general chimp population. But that was in the back of my head and not the reason for the story."[35]

Nonetheless, the story works through an extended thought-experiment about how particular scientific interventions are experienced by their subjects. Rachel's agency is so convincing — she is no passive victim — and what she learns and remembers is entirely dependent on experiences that might cause the reader ethical discomfort. Murphy points out that she didn't need to invent any of the research projects or methods described in her portrayal of the Primate Research Center; they were all written up in the scientific literature she consulted. Yet she wasn't trying to persuade people that animal research was intrinsically wrong: "I didn't make up anything more horrible than actually goes on. In terms of animal testing, I think for most of us it's a fuzzy area. I mean, I can do without eye makeup, but I'd like the vaccine, please. These are judgment calls and I don't claim to have the answer. When I'm writing a story, I'm writing about a question."[36]

"Rachel in Love" does not invite the reader to take the moral high ground or occupy any fixed points of view about animal experimentation. Rather, readers are able to empathize with Rachel's predicament as a contemporary thinking subject who cannot be purified of her dubious origins, but who can rework the story of her future by active reworking of a patchwork of origin stories and trace memories. This active reworking requires ongoing struggle and close attention to networks of power, particularly those authorized by technoscience; that is the same work that Donna Haraway identified as necessary for feminists in her "Cyborg Manifesto."

In empathizing with Rachel, then, perhaps it is possible to think again about what feminists can do in the twenty-first century. Rachel could not have come into being without the Frankensteinian actions of her "father," but having read "Rachel in Love" and seen her character develop(ed) would any reader want to stop him taking those actions? Science fiction readers are probably, at the very least, sympathetic to the liberatory potential of technoscience. With Haraway and Rachel, then, it is possible to think of how to seize that potential.

NOTES

1. "Rachel in Love" has been reprinted in the following edited collections: Michael Bishop, ed. *Nebula Awards 23*, (San Diego, Harcourt Brace Jovanovich, 1989); Charles N. Brown and Jonathan Strahan, eds. *The Locus Awards: Thirty Years of the Best in Science Fiction and Fantasy*, (New York, Eos, 2004); Orson Scott Card, ed. *Future on Fire*, (New York, Tor Books, 1991); Gardner Dozois, ed. *The Year's Best Science Fiction: Fifth Annual Collection* (New York, Bluejay, 1988); David Garnett, ed. *Orbit SF Yearbook*, (London, Orbit, 1987); Pat Murphy, *Points of Departure*, (New York, Spectra, 1990); Pamela Sargent, ed. *Women of Wonder: The Contemporary Years*, (San Diego, Harcourt Brace, 1995); Sheila Williams, ed. *Hugo and Nebula Winners from Asimov's Science Fiction Magazine*, (New York, Random House, 1995); Connie Willis and Sheila Williams, eds. *A Women's Liberation*, (New York, Warner Aspect, 2001); Donald A. Wollheim, ed. *World's Best SF 1988*, (New York, DAW, 1988).

2. Susan Faludi, *Backlash*, (London: Vintage, 1992), 12.

3. Bruce Sterling, quoted in Jeanne Gomoll, "An Open Letter to Joanna Russ" <http://www.geocities.com/Athens/8720/letter.htm>.

4. Jeanne Gomoll, "An Open Letter to Joanna Russ," <http://www.geocities.com/Athens/8720/letter.htm>.

5. Ibid.

6. Debbie Notkin, "Why Have a Tiptree Award?" in *Flying Cups and Saucers: Gender Explorations in Science Fiction and Fantasy*, ed. Debbie Notkin and the Secret Feminist Cabal (Cambridge, Mass.: Edgewood, 1998), x.

7. WisCon has taken place annually since 1976 in Madison, Wisconsin. An auction is held there each year to raise funds to support the Tiptree Award. Jeanne Gomoll is a Madison fan. In 2005, at WisCon 29, the Carl Brandon Society announced the creation of two annual juried fiction awards, each with a prize of U.S. $1000: one for speculative fiction dealing with issues of race and ethnicity, and one

for the best work of speculative fiction by an author of color. The first award is modelled on the Tiptree Award. See http://www.sf3.org/wiscon/about.html for more on the world's first feminist science fiction convention, http://www/tiptree.org for more on the Tiptree Award, and http://www.carlbrandon.org/ for more on the Carl Brandon Society and its awards.

8. Notkin, "Why Have a Tiptree Award?" xii–xiii.

9. Jenny Wolmark, *Aliens and Others: Science Fiction, Feminism and Postmodernism* (London and Harvester Wheatsheaf, 1993), 108. According to Gibson, both he and Ridley Scott were inspired by the work of the French artist Moebius, which may account for the similarity of the aesthetic between Gibson's novel and Scott's film. See <http://www.brmovie.com/FAQs/BR_FAQ_BR_Influence.htm> for "The Blade Runner FAQ."

10. Bruce Sterling, *Mirrorshades: The Cyberpunk Anthology.* (London: HarperCollins, 1994), xi.

11. Ibid.

12. Tom Maddox, "After the Deluge: Cyberpunk in the '80s and '90s," in *Thinking Robots, an Aware Internet, and Cyberpunk Librarians,* ed. R. Bruce Miller and Milton T. Wolf. (Chicago: Library and Information Technology Association, 1992), 2.

13. Sterling, *Mirrorshades,* xiii.

14. Between 1932 and 1972, some 399 black men with syphilis were subject to a medical experiment without their informed consent. They were not told what disease they were suffering from, and treatment, once available, was withheld. See James Jones, "'The Tuskegee Syphilis Experiment': A Moral Astigmatism" in *The Racial Economy of Science,* edited by Sandra Harding (Bloomington: Indiana University Press, 1993) and the following websites for more details: http://www.infoplease.com/spot/bhmtuskegee1.html and http://www.cdc.gov/nchstp/od/tuskegee/time.htm.

15. Donna Haraway, Sandra Harding, and Hilary Rose are just three examples of feminist science critics who have pointed out the important critical work carried out in feminist sf.

16. Donna Haraway, "A Cyborg Manifesto: Science, Technology, and Socialist-Feminism in the Late Twentieth Century," in *Simians, Cyborgs and Women: The Reinvention of Nature* (London: Free Association Books, 1991), 149.

17. Ibid., 152–153.

18. Ibid., 178.

19. N. Katherine Hayles, *How We Became Posthuman* (Chicago: University of Chicago Press, 1999), 2; italics in original.

20. Ibid., 1.

21. Although Hayles points out that this was only one of the "imitation games" proposed by Turing. He also suggested trying the same exercise with a man and a woman providing the responses to the two terminals.

22. Hayles, *How We Became Post Human,* xi.

23. Ibid., i.

24. Cf. this short extract from *Neuromancer* for the gendered, Cartesian use of this phrase and its biblical associations: "For Case, who'd lived for the bodiless exultation of cyberspace, it was the Fall. In the bars he'd frequented as a cowboy hot-

shot, the elite stance involved a certain relaxed contempt for the flesh. The body was meat. Case fell into the prison of his own flesh." William Gibson, *Neuromancer* (London: HarperCollins, 1993), 12.

25. Although see the work of Melissa Scott for a corrective to this; e.g., Melissa Scott, *Trouble and Her Friends* (New York: Tor, 1994).

26. Lily E Kay, *Who Wrote the Book of Life?* (Stanford: Stanford University Press, 2000).

27. Hayles, *How We Became Post Human*, 84.

28. Haraway, "A Cyborg Manifesto," 178.

29. Phone conversation with Pat Murphy, March 13, 2004.

30. *There and Back Again* is *The Hobbit* retold as space opera by Max Merriwell. Max Merriwell is a pseudonym of Pat Murphy's and a prolific sf writer in an alternate world. Mary Maxwell, a pseudonym of both Murphy and Merriwell, is the "author" of *Wild Angels*, Tarzan of the Apes with a female protagonist relocated to the period of the gold rush in California. *Adventures in Time and Space* deals with the nature of fiction and identity and is Pat Murphy writing about Max Merriwell.

31. Phone conversation with Pat Murphy, March 13, 2004.

32. John Clute and Peter Nicholls, eds. *The Encyclopedia of Science Fiction* (New York: St. Martin's, 1995), 839.

33. Phone conversation with Pat Murphy, March 13, 2004.

34. Ibid.

35. Ibid.

9

The Evening and the Morning and the Night

OCTAVIA E. BUTLER

First published in Omni, May 1987

When I was fifteen and trying to show my independence by getting care-less with my diet, my parents took me to a Duryea-Gode disease ward. They wanted me to see, they said, where I was headed if I wasn't careful. In fact, it was where I was headed, no matter what. It was only a matter of when: now or later. My parents were putting in their vote for later.

I won't describe the ward. It's enough to say that when they brought me home, I cut my wrists. I did a thorough job of it, old Roman style in a bath-tub of warm water. Almost made it. My father dislocated his shoulder breaking down the bathroom door. He and I never forgave each other for that day.

The disease got him almost three years later — just before I went off to college. It was sudden. It doesn't happen that way often. Most people no-tice themselves beginning to drift — or their relatives notice — and they make arrangements with their chosen institution. People who are noticed and who resist going in can be locked up for a week's observation. I don't doubt that observation breaks up a few families. Sending someone away for what turns out to be a false alarm. . . . Well, it isn't the sort of thing the victim is likely to forgive or forget. On the other hand, not sending someone away in time — missing the signs or having a person go off suddenly without signs — is inevitably dangerous for the victim. I've never heard of it going as badly, though, as it did in my family. People normally injure only them-selves when their time comes — unless someone is stupid enough to try to handle them without the necessary drugs or restraints.

My father killed my mother, then killed himself. I wasn't home when it happened. I had stayed at school later than usual, rehearsing gradua-tion exercises. By the time I got home, there were cops everywhere. There was an ambulance, and two attendants were wheeling someone out on a stretcher — someone covered. More than covered. Almost . . . bagged.

The cops wouldn't let me in. I didn't find out until later exactly what had happened. I wish I'd never found out. Dad had killed Mom, then skinned her completely. At least that's how I hope it happened. I mean I hope he killed her first. He broke some of her ribs, damaged her heart. Digging.

Then he began tearing at himself, through skin and bone, digging. He had managed to reach his own heart before he died. It was an especially bad example of the kind of thing that makes people afraid of us. It gets some of us into trouble for picking at a pimple or even for daydreaming. It has inspired restrictive laws, created problems with jobs, housing, schools. . . . The Duryea-Gode Disease Foundation has spent millions telling the world that people like my father don't exist.

A long time later, when I had gotten myself together as best I could, I went to college — to the University of Southern California — on a Dilg scholarship. Dilg is the retreat you try to send your out-of-control DGD relatives to. It's run by controlled DGDs like me, like my parents while they lived. God knows how any controlled DGD stands it. Anyway, the place has a waiting list miles long. My parents put me on it after my suicide attempt, but chances were, I'd be dead by the time my name came up.

I can't say why I went to college — except that I had been going to school all my life and didn't know what else to do. I didn't go with any particular hope. Hell, I knew what I was in for eventually. I was just marking time. Whatever I did was just marking time. If people were willing to pay me to go to school and mark time, why not do it?

The weird part was, I worked hard, got top grades. If you work hard enough at something that doesn't matter, you can forget for a while about the things that do.

Sometimes I thought about trying suicide again. How was it I'd had the courage when I was fifteen but didn't have it now? Two DGD parents — both religious, both as opposed to abortion as they were to suicide. So they had trusted God and the promises of modern medicine and had a child. But how could I look at what had happened to them and trust anything?

I majored in biology. Non-DGDs say something about our disease makes us good at the sciences — genetics, molecular biology, biochemistry. . . . That something was terror. Terror and a kind of driving hopelessness. Some of us went bad and became destructive before we had to — yes, we did produce more than our share of criminals. And some of us went good — spectacularly — and made scientific and medical history. These last kept the doors at least partly open for the rest of us. They made discoveries in genetics, found cures for a couple of rare diseases, made advances against other diseases that weren't so rare — including, ironically, some forms of cancer. But they'd found nothing to help themselves. There had been nothing since the latest improvements in the diet, and those came just before I was born. They, like the original diet, gave more DGDs the courage to have children. They were supposed to do for DGDs what insulin had done for diabetics — give us a normal or nearly normal life span. Maybe they had worked for someone somewhere. They hadn't worked for anyone I knew.

Biology school was a pain in the usual ways. I didn't eat in public anymore, didn't like the way people stared at my biscuits — cleverly dubbed "dog biscuits" in every school I'd ever attended. You'd think university students would be more creative. I didn't like the way people edged away from me when they caught sight of my emblem. I'd begun wearing it on a chain around my neck and putting it down inside my blouse, but people managed to notice it anyway. People who don't eat in public, who drink nothing more interesting than water, who smoke nothing at all — people like that are suspicious. Or rather, they make others suspicious. Sooner or later, one of those others, finding my fingers and wrists bare, would fake an interest in my chain. That would be that. I couldn't hide the emblem in my purse. If anything happened to me, medical people had to see it in time to avoid giving me the medication they might use on a normal person. It isn't just ordinary food we have to avoid, but about a quarter of a *Physician's Desk Reference* of widely used drugs. Every now and then there are news stories about people who have stopped carrying their emblems — probably trying to pass as normal. Then they have an accident. By the time anyone realizes there is anything wrong, it's too late. So I wore my emblem. And one way or another, people got a look at it or got the word from someone who had. "She *is!*" Yeah.

At the beginning of my third year, four other DGDs and I decided to rent a house together. We'd all had enough of being lepers twenty-four hours a day. There was an English major. He wanted to be a writer and tell our story from the inside — which had only been done thirty or forty times before. There was a special-education major who hoped the handicapped would accept her more readily than the able-bodied, a premed who planned to go into research, and a chemistry major who didn't really know what she wanted to do.

Two men plus three women. All we had in common was our disease, plus a weird combination of stubborn intensity about whatever we happened to be doing and hopeless cynicism about everything else. Healthy people say no one can concentrate like a DGD. Healthy people have all the time in the world for stupid generalizations and short attention spans.

We did our work, came up for air now and then, ate our biscuits, and attended class. Our only problem was the housecleaning. We worked out a schedule of who would clean what when, who would deal with the yard, whatever. We all agreed on it; then, except for me, everyone seemed to forget about it. I found myself going around reminding people to vacuum, clean the bathroom, mow the lawn. . . . I figured they'd all hate me in no time, but I wasn't going to be their maid, and I wasn't going to live in filth. Nobody complained. Nobody even seemed annoyed. They just came out of their academic daze, cleaned, mopped, mowed, and went back to it. I got into the habit of running around in the evening reminding people. It didn't bother me if it didn't bother them.

"How'd you get to be housemother?" a visiting DGD asked.

I shrugged. "Who cares? The house works." It did. It worked so well that this new guy wanted to move in. He was a friend of one of the others, and another premed. Not bad looking.

"So do I get in or don't I?" he asked.

"As far as I'm concerned, you do," I said. I did what his friend should have done — introduced him around, then, after he left, talked to the others to make sure no one had any real objections. He seemed to fit right in. He forgot to clean the toilet or mow the lawn, just like the others. His name was Alan Chi. I thought Chi was a Chinese name and I wondered. But he told me his father was Nigerian and that in Ibo the word meant a kind of guardian angel or personal God. He said his own personal God hadn't been looking out for him too well to let him be born to two DGD parents. Him too.

I don't think it was much more than that similarity that drew us together at first. Sure, I liked the way he looked, but I was used to liking someone's looks and having him run like hell when he found out what I was. It took me a while to get used to the fact that Alan wasn't going anywhere.

I told him about my visit to the DGD ward when I was fifteen — and my suicide attempt afterward. I had never told anyone else. I was surprised at how relieved it made me feel to tell him. And somehow his reaction didn't surprise me.

"Why didn't you try again?" he asked. We were alone in the living room.

"At first, because of my parents," I said. "My father in particular. I couldn't do that to him again."

"And after him?"

"Fear. Inertia."

He nodded. "When I do it, there'll be no half measures. No being rescued, no waking up in a hospital later."

"You mean to do it?"

"The day I realize I've started to drift. Thank God we get some warning."

"Not necessarily."

"Yes, we do. I've done a lot of reading. Even talked to a couple of doctors. Don't believe the rumors non-DGDs invent."

I looked away, stared into the scarred, empty fireplace. I told him exactly how my father had died — something else I'd never voluntarily told anyone.

He sighed. "Jesus!"

We looked at each other.

"What are you going to do?" he asked.

"I don't know."

He extended a dark, square hand, and I took it and moved closer to him. He was a dark, square man — my height, half again my weight, and none of it fat. He was so bitter sometimes, he scared me.

"My mother started to drift when I was three," he said. "My father only lasted a few months longer. I heard he died a couple of years after he went into the hospital. If the two of them had had any sense, they would have had me aborted the minute my mother realized she was pregnant. But she wanted a kid no matter what. And she was Catholic." He shook his head. "Hell, they should pass a law to sterilize the lot of us."

"They?" I said.

"You want kids?"

"No, but—"

"More like us to wind up chewing their fingers off in some DGD ward."

"I don't want kids, but I don't want someone else telling me I can't have any."

He stared at me until I began to feel stupid and defensive. I moved away from him.

"Do you want someone else telling you what to do with your body?" I asked.

"No need," he said. "I had that taken care of as soon as I was old enough."

This left me staring. I'd thought about sterilization. What DGD hasn't? But I didn't know anyone else our age who had actually gone through with it. That would be like killing part of yourself — even though it wasn't a part of yourself you intended to use. Killing a part of yourself when so much of you was already dead.

"The damned disease could be wiped out in one generation," he said, "but people are still animals when it comes to breeding. Still following mindless urges, like dogs and cats."

My impulse was to get up and go away, leave him to wallow in his bitterness and depression alone. But I stayed. He seemed to want to live even less than I did. I wondered how he'd made it this far.

"Are you looking forward to doing research?" I probed. "Do you believe you'll be able to—"

"No."

I blinked. The word was as cold and dead a sound as I'd ever heard.

"I don't believe in anything," he said.

I took him to bed. He was the only other double DGD I had ever met, and if nobody did anything for him, he wouldn't last much longer. I couldn't just let him slip away. For a while, maybe we could be each other's reasons for staying alive.

He was a good student—for the same reason I was. And he seemed to shed some of his bitterness as time passed. Being around him helped me understand why, against all sanity, two DGDs would lock in on each other and start talking about marriage. Who else would have us?

We probably wouldn't last very long, anyway. These days, most DGDs make it to forty, at least. But then, most of them don't have two DGD parents. As bright as Alan was, he might not get into medical school because of his double inheritance. No one would tell him his bad genes were keeping him out, of course, but we both knew what his chances were. Better to train doctors who were likely to live long enough to put their training to use.

Alan's mother had been sent to Dilg. He hadn't seen her or been able to get any information about her from his grandparents while he was at home. By the time he left for college, he'd stopped asking questions. Maybe it was hearing about my parents that made him start again. I was with him when he called Dilg. Until that moment, he hadn't even know whether his mother was still alive. Surprisingly, she was. "Dilg must be good," I said when he hung up. "People don't usually . . . I mean . . ."

"Yeah, I know," he said. "People don't usually live long once they're out of control. Dilg is different." We had gone to my room, where he turned a chair backward and sat down. "Dilg is what the others ought to be, if you can believe the literature."

"Dilg is a giant DGD ward," I said. "It's richer—probably better at sucking in the donations—and it's run by people who can expect to become patients eventually. Apart from that, what's different?"

"I've read about it," he said. "So should you. They've got some new treatment. They don't just shut people away to die the way the others do."

"What else is there to do with them? With us."

"I don't know. It sounded like they have some kind of . . . sheltered workshop. They've got patients doing things."

"A new drug to control the self-destructiveness?"

"I don't think so. We would have heard about that."

"What else could it be?"

"I'm going up to find out. Will you come with me?"

"You're going to see your mother."

He took a ragged breath. "Yeah. Will you come with me?"

I went to one of my windows and stared out at the weeds. We let them thrive in the backyard. In the front we mowed them, along with the few patches of grass.

"I told you my DGD-ward experience."

"You're not fifteen now. And Dilg isn't some zoo of a ward."

"It's got to be, no matter what they tell the public. And I'm not sure I can stand it."

He got up, came to stand next to me. "Will you try?"

I didn't say anything. I focused on our reflections in the window glass — the two of us together. It looked right, felt right. He put his arm around me, and I leaned back against him. Our being together had been as good for me as it seemed to have been for him. It had given me something to go on besides inertia and fear. I knew I would go with him. It felt like the right thing to do.

"I can't say how I'll act when we get there," I said.

"I can't say how I'll act, either," he admitted. "Especially . . . when I see her."

He made the appointment for the next Saturday afternoon. You make appointments to go to Dilg unless you're a government inspector of some kind. That is the custom, and Dilg gets away with it.

We left L.A. in the rain early Saturday morning. Rain followed us off and on up the coast as far as Santa Barbara. Dilg was hidden away in the hills not far from San Jose. We could have reached it faster by driving up I-5, but neither of us was in the mood for all that bleakness. As it was, we arrived at one P.M. to be met by two armed gate guards. One of these phoned the main building and verified our appointment. Then the other took the wheel from Alan.

"Sorry," he said. "But no one is permitted inside without an escort. We'll meet your guide at the garage."

None of this surprised me. Dilg is a place where not only the patients but much of the staff has DGD. A maximum security prison wouldn't have been as potentially dangerous. On the other hand, I'd never heard of anyone getting chewed up here. Hospital and rest homes had accidents. Dilg didn't.

It was beautiful — an old estate. One that didn't make sense in these days of high taxes. It had been owned by the Dilg family. Oil, chemicals, pharmaceuticals. Ironically, they had even owned part of the late, unlamented Hedeon Laboratories. They'd had a briefly profitable interest in Hedeonco: the magic bullet, the cure for a large percentage of the world's cancer and a number of serious viral diseases — and the cause of Duryea-Gode disease. If one of your parents was treated with Hedeonco and you were conceived after the treatments, you had DGD. If you had kids, you passed it on to them. Not everyone was equally affected. They didn't all commit suicide or murder, but they all mutilated themselves to some degree if they could. And they all drifted — went off into a world of their own and stopped responding to their surroundings.

Anyway, the only Dilg son of his generation had had his life saved by Hedeonco. Then he had watched four of his children die before Doctors Kenneth Duryea and Jan Gode came up with a decent understanding of the problem and a partial solution: the diet. They gave Richard Dilg a way of keeping his next two children alive. He gave the big, cumbersome estate over to the care of DGD patients.

So the main building was an elaborate old mansion. There were other, newer buildings, more like guest houses than institutional buildings. And there were wooded hills all around. Nice country. Green. The ocean wasn't far away. There was an old garage and a small parking lot. Waiting in the lot was a tall, old woman. Our guard pulled up near her, let us out, then parked the car in the half-empty garage.

"Hello," the woman said, extending her hand. "I'm Beatrice Alcantara." The hand was cool and dry and startlingly strong. I thought the woman was DGD, but her age threw me. She appeared to be about sixty, and I had never seen a DGD that old. I wasn't sure why I thought she was DGD. If she was, she must have been an experimental model — one of the first to survive.

"Is it Doctor or Ms.?" Alan asked.

"It's Beatrice," she said. "I am a doctor, but we don't use titles much here."

I glanced at Alan, was surprised to see him smiling at her. He tended to go a long time between smiles. I looked at Beatrice and couldn't see anything to smile about. As we introduced ourselves, I realize I didn't like her. I couldn't see any reason for that either, but my feelings were my feelings. I didn't like her.

"I assume neither of you has been here before," she said, smiling down at us. She was at least six feet tall, and straight.

We shook our heads. "Let's go in the front way, then. I want to prepare you for what we do here. I don't want you to believe you've come to a hospital."

I frowned at her, wondering what else there was to believe. Dilg was called a retreat, but what difference did names make?

The house close up looked like one of the old-style public buildings — massive, baroque front with a single domed tower reaching three stories above the three-story house. Wings of the house stretched for some distance to the right and left of the tower, then cornered and stretched back twice as far. The front doors were huge — one set of wrought iron and one of heavy wood. Neither appeared to be locked. Beatrice pulled open the iron door, pushed the wooden one, and gestured us in.

Inside, the house was an art museum — huge, high ceilinged, tile floored. There were marble columns and niches in which sculptures stood or paintings hung. There were other sculptures displayed around the rooms. At one end of the rooms there was a broad staircase leading up to a gallery that went around the rooms. There more art was displayed. "All this was made here," Beatrice said. "Some of it is even sold from here. Most goes to galleries in the Bay Area or down around L.A. Our only problem is turning out too much of it."

"You mean the patients do this?" I asked.

The old woman nodded. "This and much more. Our people work instead of tearing at themselves or staring into space. One of them invented the p.v. locks that protect this place. Though I almost wish he hadn't. It's gotten us more government attention than we like."

"What kind of locks?" I asked.

"Sorry. Palmprint-voiceprint. The first and the best. We have the patent." She looked at Alan. "Would you like to see what your mother does?"

"Wait a minute," he said. "You're telling us out-of-control DGDs create art and invent things?"

"And that lock," I said. "I've never heard of anything like that. I didn't even see a lock."

"The lock is new," she said. "There have been a few news stories about it. It's not the kind of thing most people would buy for their homes. Too expensive. So it's of limited interest. People tend to look at what's done at Dilg in the way they look at the efforts of idiot savants. Interesting, incomprehensible, but not really important. Those likely to be interested in the lock and able to afford it know about it." She took a deep breath, faced Alan again. "Oh, yes, DGDs create things. At least they do here."

"Out-of-control DGDs."

"Yes."

"I expected to find them weaving baskets or something — at best. I know what DGD wards are like."

"So do I," she said. "I know what they're like in hospitals, and I know what it's like here." She waved a hand toward an abstract painting that looked like a photo I'd once seen of the Orion Nebula. Darkness broken by a great cloud of light and color. "Here we can help them channel their energies. They can create something beautiful, useful, even something worthless. But they create. They don't destroy."

"Why?" Alan demanded. "It can't be some drug. We would have heard."

"It's not a drug."

"Then what is it? Why haven't other hospitals — ?"

"Alan," she said. "Wait."

He stood frowning at her.

"Do you want to see your mother?"

"Of course I want to see her!"

"Good. Come with me. Things will sort themselves out."

She led us to a corridor past offices where people talked to one another, waved to Beatrice, worked with computers. . . . They could have been anywhere. I wondered how many of them were controlled DGDs. I also wondered what kind of game the old woman was playing with her secrets. We passed through rooms so beautiful and perfectly kept it was obvious they were rarely used. Then at a broad, heavy door, she stopped us.

"Look at anything you like as we go on," she said. "But don't touch anything or anyone. And remember that some of the people you'll see injured themselves before they came to us. They still bear the scars of those injuries. Some of those scars may be difficult to look at, but you'll be in no danger. Keep that in mind. No one here will harm you." She pushed the door open and gestured us in

Scars didn't bother me much. Disability didn't bother me. It was the act of self-mutilation that scared me. It was someone attacking her own arm as though it was a wild animal. It was someone who had torn at himself and been restrained and drugged off and on for so long that he barely had a recognizable human feature left, but he was still trying with what he did have to dig into his own flesh. Those are a couple of the things I saw at the DGD ward when I was fifteen. Even then I could have stood it better if I hadn't felt I wasn't looking into a kind of temporal mirror.

I wasn't aware of walking through that doorway. I wouldn't have thought I could do it. The old woman said something, though, and I found myself on the other side of the door with the door closing behind me. I turned to stare at her.

She put her hand on my arm. "It's all right," she said quietly. "That door looks like a wall to a great many people."

I backed away from her, out of her reach, repelled by her touch. Shaking hands had been enough, for god's sake.

Something in her seemed to come to attention as she watched me. It made her even straighter. Deliberately, but for no apparent reason, she stepped toward Alan, touched him the way people sometimes do when they brush past — a kind of tactile "Excuse me." In that wide, empty corridor, it was totally unnecessary. For some reason, she wanted to touch him and wanted me to see. What did she think she was doing? Flirting at her age? I glared at her, found myself suppressing an irrational urge to shove her away from him. The violence of the urge amazed me.

Beatrice smiled and turned away. "This way," she said. Alan put his arm around me and tried to lead me after her.

"Wait a minute," I said, not moving.

Beatrice glanced around.

"What just happened?" I asked. I was ready for her to lie — to say nothing happened, pretend not to know what I was talking about.

"Are you planning to study medicine?" she asked.

"What? What does that have to do — ?"

"Study medicine. You may be able to do a great deal of good." She strode away, taking long steps so that we had to hurry to keep up. She led us through a room in which some people worked at computer terminals and others with pencils and paper. It would have been an ordinary scene except that some people had half their faces ruined or had only one hand or leg or had other obvious scars. But they were all in control now. They were working. They were intent but not intent on self-destruction. Not one was digging into or tearing away flesh. When we had passed through this room and into a small, ornate sitting room, Alan grasped Beatrice's arm.

"What is it?" he demanded. "What do you do for them?"

She patted his hand, setting my teeth on edge. "I will tell you," she said. "I want you to know. But I want you to see your mother first." To my surprise, he nodded, let it go at that.

"Sit a moment," she said to us.

We sat in comfortable, matching upholstered chairs — Alan looking reasonably relaxed. What was it about the old lady that relaxed him but put me on edge? Maybe she reminded him of his grandmother or something.

She didn't remind me of anyone. And what was that nonsense about study-ing medicine?

"I wanted you to pass through at least one workroom before we talked about your mother — and about the two of you." She turned to face me. "You've had a bad experience at a hospital or rest home?"

I looked away from her, not wanting to think about it. Hadn't the people in that mock office been enough of a reminder? Horror film office. Night-mare office.

"It's all right," she said. "You don't have to go into detail. Just outline it for me."

I obeyed slowly, against my will, all the while wondering why I was doing it.

She nodded, unsurprised. "Harsh, loving people, your parents. Are they still alive?"

"No."

"Were they both DGD?"

"Yes, but . . . yes."

"Of course, aside from the obvious ugliness of your hospital experience and its implications for the future, what impressed you about the people in the ward?"

I didn't know what to answer. What did she want? Why did she want anything from me? She should have been concerned with Alan and his mother.

"Did you see people unrestrained?"

"Yes," I whispered. "One woman. I don't know how it happened that she was free. She ran up to us and slammed into my father without moving him. He was a big man. She bounced off, fell, and . . . began tearing at herself. She bit her own arm and . . . swallowed the flesh she'd bitten away. She tore at the wound she'd made with the nails of her other hand. She . . . I screamed at her to stop." I hugged myself, remembering the young woman, bloody, cannibalizing herself as she lay at our feet, digging into her own flesh. Digging. "They try so hard, fight so hard to get out."

"Out of what?" Alan demanded.

I looked at him, hardly seeing him.

"Lynn," he said gently. "Out of what?"

I shook my head. "Their restraints, their disease, the ward, their bodies . . ."

He glanced at Beatrice, then spoke to me again. "Did the girl talk?"

"No. She screamed."

He turned away from me uncomfortably. "Is this important?" he asked Beatrice.

"Very," she said.

"Well . . . can we talk about it after I see my mother?"

"Then and now." She spoke to me. "Did the girl stop what she was doing when you told her to?"

"The nurses had her a moment later. It didn't matter."

"It mattered. Did she stop?"

"Yes."

"According to the literature, they rarely respond to anyone," Alan said.

"True." Beatrice gave him a sad smile. "Your mother will probably respond to you, though."

"Is she? . . ." He glanced back at the nightmare office. "Is she as controlled as those people?"

"Yes, though she hasn't always been. Your mother works with clay now. She loves shapes and textures and — "

"She's blind," Alan said, voicing the suspicion as though it were fact. Beatrice's words had sent my thoughts in the same direction. Beatrice hesitated. "Yes," she said finally. "And for . . . the usual reason. I had intended to prepare you slowly."

"I've done a lot of reading."

I hadn't done much reading, but I knew what the usual reason was. The woman had gouged, ripped, or otherwise destroyed her eyes. She would be badly scarred. I got up, went over to sit on the arm of Alan's chair. I rested my hand on his shoulder, and he reached up and held it there.

"Can we see her now?" he asked.

Beatrice got up. "This way," she said.

We passed through more workrooms. People painted, assembled machinery; sculpted in wood, stone; even composed and played music. Almost no one noticed us. The patients were true to their disease in that respect. They weren't ignoring us. They clearly didn't know we existed. Only the few controlled DGD guards gave themselves away by waving or speaking to Beatrice. I watched a woman work quickly, knowledgeably, with a power saw. She obviously understood the perimeters of her body, was not so dissociated as to perceive herself as trapped in something she needed to dig her way out of. What had Dilg done for these people that other hospitals did not do? And how could Dilg withhold its treatment from the others?

"Over there we make our own diet foods," Beatrice said, pointing through a window toward one of the guest houses. "We permit more variety and make fewer mistakes than the commercial preparers. No ordinary person can concentrate on work the way our people can."

I turned to face her. "What are you saying? That the bigots are right? That we have some special gift?"

"Yes," she said. "It's hardly a bad characteristic, is it?"

"It's what people say whenever one of us does well at something. It's their way of denying us credit for our work."

"Yes. But people occasionally come to the right conclusions for the wrong reasons." I shrugged, not interested in arguing with her about it.

"Alan?" she said. He looked at her.

"Your mother is in the next room."

He swallowed, nodded. We both followed her into the room.

Naomi Chi was a small woman, hair still dark, fingers long and thin, graceful as they shaped the clay. Her face was a ruin. Not only her eyes but most of her nose and one ear were gone. What was left was badly scarred. "Her parents were poor," Beatrice said. "I don't know how much they told you, Alan, but they went through all the money they had, trying to keep her at a decent place. Her mother felt so guilty, you know. She was the one who had cancer and took the drug. . . . Eventually, they had to put Naomi in one of those state-approved, custodial-care places. You know the kind. For a while, it was all the government would pay for. Places like that . . . well, sometimes if patients were really troublesome — especially the ones who kept breaking free — they'd put them in a bare room and let them finish themselves. The only things those places took good care of were the maggots, the cockroaches, and the rats."

I shuddered. "I've heard there are still places like that."

"There are," Beatrice said, "kept open by greed and indifference." She looked at Alan. "Your mother survived for three months in one of those places. I took her from it myself. Later I was instrumental in having that particular place closed."

"You took her?" I asked.

"Dilg didn't exist then, but I was working with a group of controlled DGDs in L.A. Naomi's parents heard about us and asked us to take her. A lot of people didn't trust us then. Only a few of us were medically trained. All of us were young, idealistic, and ignorant. We began in an old frame house with a leaky roof. Naomi's parents were grabbing at straws. So were we. And by pure luck, we grabbed a good one. We were able to prove ourselves to the Dilg family and take over these quarters."

"Prove what?" I asked.

She turned to look at Alan and his mother. Alan was staring at Naomi's ruined face, at the ropy, discolored scar tissue. The gaunt, lined face of the old woman was remarkably vivid — detailed in a way that seemed impossible for a blind sculptress.

Naomi seemed unaware of us. Her total attention remained on her work. Alan forgot about what Beatrice had told us and reached out to touch the scarred face.

Beatrice let it happen. Naomi did not seem to notice. "If I get her attention for you," Beatrice said, "we'll be breaking her routine. We'll have to stay with her until she gets back into it without hurting herself. About half an hour."

"You can get her attention?" he asked.

"Yes."

"Can she? . . . " Alan swallowed. "I've never heard of anything like this. Can she talk?"

"Yes. She may not choose to, though. And if she does, she'll do it very slowly."

"Do it. Get her attention."

"She'll want to touch you."

"That's all right. Do it."

Beatrice took Naomi's hands and held them still, away from the wet clay. For a few seconds Naomi tugged at her captive hands, as though unable to understand why they did not move as she wished.

Beatrice stepped closer and spoke quietly. "Stop, Naomi." And Naomi was still, blind face turned toward Beatrice in an attitude of attentive waiting. Totally focused waiting.

"Company, Naomi."

After a few seconds, Naomi made a wordless sound.

Beatrice gestured Alan to her side, gave Naomi one of his hands. It didn't bother me this time when she touched him. I was too interested in what was happening. Naomi examined Alan's hand minutely, then followed the arm up to the shoulders, the neck, the face. Holding his face between her hands, she made a sound. It may have been a word, but I couldn't understand it. All I could think of was the danger of those hands. I thought of my father's hands.

"His name is Alan Chi, Naomi. He's your son." Several seconds passed.

"Son?" she said. This time the word was quite distinct, though her lips had split in many places and healed badly. "Son?" she repeated anxiously. "Here?"

"He's all right, Naomi. He's come to visit."

"Mother?" he said.

She reexamined his face. He had been three when she started to drift. It didn't seem possible that she could find anything in his face that she could remember. I wondered whether she remembered she had a son.

"Alan?" she said. She found his tears and paused at them. She touched her own face where there should have been an eye, then she reached back toward his eyes. An instant before I would have grabbed her hand, Beatrice did it.

"No!" Beatrice said firmly.

The hand fell limply back to Naomi's side. Her face turned toward Beatrice like an antique weather vane swinging around. Beatrice stroked her hair, and Naomi said something I almost understood. Beatrice looked at Alan, who was frowning and wiping away tears.

"Hug your son," Beatrice said softly.

Naomi turned, groping, and Alan seized her in a tight, long hug. Her arms went around him slowly. She spoke words blurred by her ruined mouth but just understandable.

"Parents?" she said. "Did my parents . . . care for you?" Alan looked at her, clearly not understanding.

"She wants to know whether her parents took care of you," I said.

He glanced at me doubtfully, then looked at Beatrice.

"Yes," Beatrice said. "She just wants to know that they cared for you."

"They did," he said. "They kept their promise to you, Mother."

Several seconds passed. Naomi made sounds that even Alan took to be weeping, and he tried to comfort her.

"Who else is here?" she said finally.

This time Alan looked at me. I repeated what she had said.

"Her name is Lynn Mortimer," he said. "I'm . . ." He paused awkwardly. "She and I are going to be married."

After a time, she moved back from him and said my name. My first impulse was to go to her. I wasn't afraid or repelled by her now, but for no reason I could explain, I looked at Beatrice. "Go," she said. "But you and I will have to talk later."

I went to Naomi, took her hand.

"Bea?" she said.

"I'm Lynn," I said softly.

She drew a quick breath. "No," she said. "No, you're . . ."

"I'm Lynn. Do you want Bea? She's here."

She said nothing. She put her hand to my face, explored it slowly. I let her do it, confident that I could stop her if she turned violent. But first one hand, then both, went over me very gently.

"You'll marry my son?" she said finally.

"Yes."

"Good. You'll keep him safe."

As much as possible, we'll keep each other safe. "Yes," I said.

"Good. No one will close him away from himself. No one will tie him or cage him." Her hand wandered to her own face again, nails biting in slightly.

"No," I said softly, catching the hand. "I want you to be safe, too."

The mouth moved. I think it smiled. "Son?" she said.

He understood her, took her hand.

"Clay," she said. Lynn and Alan in clay. "Bea?"

"Of course," Beatrice said. "Do you have an impression?"

"No!" It was the fastest that Naomi had answered anything. Then, almost childlike, she whispered. "Yes."

Beatrice laughed. "Touch them again if you like, Naomi. They don't mind."

We didn't. Alan closed his eyes, trusting her gentleness in a way I could not. I had no trouble accepting her touch, even so near my eyes, but I did not delude myself about her. Her gentleness could turn in an instant. Naomi's fingers twitched near Alan's eyes, and I spoke up at once, out of fear for him.

"Just touch him, Naomi. Only touch."

She froze, made a soft, interrogative sound.

"She's all right," Alan said.

"I know," I said, not believing it. He would be all right, though, as long as someone watched her very carefully, nipped any dangerous impulses in the bud.

"Son!" she said, happily possessive. When she let him go, she demanded clay, wouldn't touch her old-woman sculpture again. Beatrice got new clay for her, leaving us to soothe her and ease her impatience. Alan began to recognize signs of impending destructive behavior. Twice he caught her hands and said no. She struggled against him until I spoke to her. As Beatrice returned, it happened again, and Beatrice said, "No, Naomi." Obediently, Naomi let her hands fall to her sides.

"What is it?" Alan demanded later when we had left Naomi safely, totally focused on her new work — clay sculptures of us. "Does she only listen to women or something?"

Beatrice took us back to the sitting room, sat us both down, but did not sit herself. She went to a window and stared out. "Naomi only obeys certain women," she said. "And she's sometimes slow to obey. She's worse than most—probably because of the damage she managed to do to herself before I got her." Beatrice faced us, stood biting her lip and frowning. "I haven't had to give this particular speech for a while," she said. "Most DGDs have the sense not to marry each other and produce children. I hope you two aren't planning to have any—in spite of our need." She took a deep breath. "It's a pheromone. A scent. And it's sex-linked. Men who inherit the disease from their fathers have no trace of the scent. They also tend to have an easier time with the disease. But they're useless to us as staff here. Men who inherit from their mothers have as much of the scent as men get. They can be useful here because DGDs can at least be made to notice them. The same for women who inherit from their mothers but not their fathers. It's only when two irresponsible DGDs get together and produce girl children like me or Lynn that you get someone who can really do some good in a place like this." She looked at me. "We are very rare commodities, you and I. When you finish school you'll have a very well-paying job waiting for you."

"Here?" I asked.

"For training, perhaps. Beyond that, I don't know. You'll probably help start a retreat in some other part of the country. Others are badly needed." She smiled humorlessly. "People like us don't get along well together. You must realize that I don't like you any more than you like me."

I swallowed, saw her through a kind of haze for a moment. Hated her mindlessly—just for a moment.

"Sit back," she said. "Relax your body. It helps."

I obeyed, not really wanting to obey her but unable to think of anything else to do. Unable to think at all. "We seem," she said, "to be very territorial. Dilg is a haven for me because I'm the only one of my kind here. When I'm not, it's a prison."

"All it looks like to me is an unbelievable amount of work," Alan said.

She nodded. "Almost too much." She smiled to herself. "I was one of the first double DGDs to be born. When I was old enough to understand, I thought I didn't have much time. First I tried to kill myself. Failing that, I tried to cram all the living I could into the small amount of time I assumed I had. When I got into this project, I worked as hard as I could to get it into shape before I started to drift. By now I wouldn't know what to do with myself if I weren't working."

"Why haven't you . . . drifted?" I asked.

"I don't know. There aren't enough of our kind to know what's normal for us."

"Drifting is normal for every DGD sooner or later."

"Later, then."

"Why hasn't the scent been synthesized?" Alan asked. "Why are there still concentration-camp rest homes and hospital wards?"

"There have been people trying to synthesize it since I proved what I could do with it. No one has succeeded so far. All we've been able to do is keep our eyes open for people like Lynn." She looked at me. "Dilg scholarship, right?"

"Yeah. Offered out of the blue."

"My people do a good job of keeping track. You would have been contacted just before you graduated or if you dropped out."

"Is it possible," Alan said, staring at me, "that she's already doing it? Already using the scent to . . . influence people?"

"You?" Beatrice asked.

"All of us. A group of DGDs. We all live together. We're all controlled, of course, but . . ." Beatrice smiled. "It's probably the quietest house full of kids that anyone's ever seen."

I looked at Alan, and he looked away. "I'm not doing anything to them," I said. "I remind them of work they've already promised to do. That's all."

"You put them at ease," Beatrice said. "You're there. You . . . well, you leave your scent around the house. You speak to them individually. Without knowing why, they no doubt find that very comforting. Don't you, Alan?"

"I don't know," he said. "I suppose I must have. From my first visit to the house, I knew I wanted to move in. And when I first saw Lynn, I . . ." He shook his head. "Funny, I thought all that was my idea."

"Will you work with us, Alan?"

"Me? You want Lynn."

"I want you both. You have no idea how many people take one look at a workshop here and turn and run. You may be the kind of young people who ought to eventually take charge of a place like Dilg."

"Whether we want to or not, eh?" he said.

Frightened, I tried to take his hand, but he moved it away. "Alan, this works," I said. "It's only a stopgap, I know. Genetic engineering will probably give us the final answers, but for God's sake, this is something we can do now!"

"It's something *you* can do. Play queen bee in a retreat full of workers. I've never had any ambition to be a drone."

"A physician isn't likely to be a drone," Beatrice said.

"Would you marry one of your patients?" he demanded. "That's what Lynn would be doing if she married me — whether I become a doctor or not."

She looked away from him, stared across the room. "My husband is here," she said softly. "He's been a patient here for almost a decade. What better place for him . . . when his time came?"

"Shit!" Alan muttered. He glanced at me. "Let's get out of here!" He got up and strode across the room to the door, pulling at it, then realized it was locked. He turned to face Beatrice, his body language demanding she let him out. She went to him, took him by the shoulder, and turned him to face the door. 'Try it once more," she said quietly. "You can't break it. Try."

Surprisingly, some of the hostility seemed to go out of him. "This is one of those p.v. locks?" he asked.

"Yes."

I set my teeth and looked away. Let her work. She knew how to use this thing she and I both had. And for the moment, she was on my side.

I heard him make some effort with the door. The door didn't even rattle. Beatrice took his hand from it, and with her own hand flat against what appeared to be a large brass knob, she pushed the door open.

"The man who created that lock is nobody in particular," she said. "He doesn't have an unusually high I.Q., didn't even finish college. But sometime in his life he read a science-fiction story in which palmprint locks were a given. He went that story one better by creating one that responded to voice or palm. It took him years, but we were able to give him those years. The people of Dilg are problem solvers, Alan. Think of the problems you could solve!"

He looked as though he were beginning to think, beginning to understand. "I don't see how biological research can be done that way," he said. "Not with everyone acting on his own, not even aware of other researchers and their work."

"It *is* being done," she said, "and not in isolation. Our retreat in Colorado specializes in it and has — just barely — enough trained, controlled DGDs to see that no one really works in isolation. Our patients can still read and write — those who haven't damaged themselves too badly. They can take each other's work into account if reports are made available to them. And they can read material that comes in from the outside. They're working, Alan. The disease hasn't stopped them, *won't* stop them."

He stared at her, seemed to be caught by her intensity — or her scent. He spoke as though his words were a strain, as though they hurt his throat. "I won't be a puppet. I won't be controlled . . . by a goddamn smell!"

"Alan —"

"I won't be what my mother is. I'd rather be dead!"

"There's no reason for you to become what your mother is."

He drew back in obvious disbelief.

"Your mother is brain damaged — thanks to the three months she spent in that custodial-care toilet. She had no speech at all when I met her. She's improved more than you can imagine. None of that has to happen to you. Work with us, and we'll see that none of it happens to you."

He hesitated, seemed less sure of himself. Even that much flexibility in him was surprising. "I'll be under your control or Lynn's," he said.

She shook her head. "Not even your mother is under my control. She's aware of me. She's able to take direction from me. She trusts me the way any blind person would trust her guide."

"There's more to it than that."

"Not here. Not at any of our retreats."

"I don't believe you."

"Then you don't understand how much individuality our people retain. They know they need help, but they have minds of their own. If you want to see the abuse of power you're worried about, go to a DGD ward."

"You're better than that, I admit. Hell is probably better than that. But . . ."

"But you don't trust us."

He shrugged.

"You do, you know." She smiled. "You don't want to, but you do. That's what worries you, and it leaves you with work to do. Look into what I've said. See for yourself. We offer DGDs a chance to live and do whatever they decide is important to them. What do you have, what can you realistically hope for that's better than that?"

Silence. "I don't know what to think," he said finally.

"Go home," she said. "Decide what to think. It's the most important decision you'll ever make."

He looked at me. I went to him, not sure how he'd react, not sure he'd want me no matter what he decided.

"What are you going to do?" he asked.

The question startled me. "You have a choice," I said. "I don't. If she's right . . . how could I not wind up running a retreat?"

"Do you want to?"

I swallowed. I hadn't really faced that question yet. Did I want to spend my life in something that was basically a refined DGD ward?

"No!"

"But you will."

" . . . Yes." I thought for a moment, hunted for the right words. "You'd do it."

"What?"

"If the pheromone were something only men had, you would do it."

That silence again. After a time he took my hand, and we followed Beatrice out to the car. Before I could get in with him and our guard-escort, she caught my arm. I jerked away reflexively. By the time I caught myself, I had swung around as though I meant to hit her. Hell, I did mean to hit her, but I stopped myself in time. "Sorry," I said with no attempt at sincerity.

She held out a card until I took it. "My private number," she said. "Before seven or after nine, usually. You and I will communicate best by phone."

I resisted the impulse to throw the card away. God, she brought out the child in me.

Inside the car, Alan said something to the guard. I couldn't hear what it was, but the sound of his voice reminded me of him arguing with her — her logic and her scent. She had all but won him for me, and I couldn't manage even token gratitude. I spoke to her, low voiced.

"He never really had a chance, did he?"

She looked surprised. "That's up to you. You can keep him or drive him away. I assure you, you *can* drive him away."

"How?"

"By imagining that he doesn't have a chance." She smiled faintly. "Phone me from your territory. We have a great deal to say to each other, and I'd rather we didn't say it as enemies."

She had lived with meeting people like me for decades. She had good control. I, on the other hand, was at the end of my control. All I could do is scramble into the car and floor my own phantom accelerator as the guard drove us to the gate. I couldn't look back at her. Until we were well away from the house, until we'd left the guard at the gate and gone off the property, I couldn't make myself look back. For long, irrational minutes, I was convinced that somehow if I turned, I would see myself standing there, gray and old, growing small in the distance, vanishing.

Octavia Butler — Praise Song to a Prophetic Artist

Andrea Hairston

Prophets needn't offer a vision of the actual future, an answer to current problems, or even the salvation of an afterlife. With historical insight and a fluent grasp of tradition, prophets illuminate the immanent possibilities of the here and now. They shake our minds loose from the iron grip of the indicative case. By substituting *might be* or *would be* for *is*, prophets allow us the subjunctive flight of fancy that prefigures transformation and ushers in a brand new day.

Octavia Butler is a prophetic artist.

The World: Current Condition.

Whenever I agonize about how hard it is to get anything done in this world, how even small change seems impossible; when I whine about the backlash, the backsliding, the men and women who believe that we have long since arrived at the Promised Land and that all the "isms" — sexism, racism, classism, heterosexism — are way behind us now in our multicultural egalitarian utopia;[1] when I turn off the TV because liberation is a jeweled thong on *Sex in the City* and bold profit junkies brag about drilling holes in the Alaskan wilderness while sending more young people to kill and die in the desert for the oil there; when I despair because choice is one thousand channels owned by the same two companies, because PR wizards have convinced us that toxic sludge really *is* good for us and it is environmental crackpots and feminasties who are actually to blame for declining productivity;[2] as babies all over the world are too hungry to make it to their first birthday and today's front page in the local newspaper proclaims, "World's women worse off than ten years ago";[3] as statistics on black people and people of color indicate that, despite the flashy photogenic celebrities and multimillion dollar ghetto-chic distractions, we're still getting ground down amidst the bounty and magic of this technological wonderland . . . I mean, when it looks as if the future's been mortgaged, several futures in fact, and it's getting grimmer than grim, I pick up an Octavia Butler novel or story and find hope.

What could be more entertaining than hope?

Octavia Butler declares:

> I'm a 56-year-old writer who can remember being a 10-year-old writer and who expects some day to be an 80-year-old writer. I'm comfortably asocial—a hermit living in a large city—a pessimist if I'm not careful; a student, endlessly curious; a feminist; an African American; a former Baptist; and an oil and water combination of ambition, laziness, insecurity, certainty, and drive.[4]

As a prophetic feminist artist looking back at the past, looking hard at the present, Butler foretells what might be. She is an impossibility specialist, a conjurer whose wizard words call forth our humanity in the midst of holocaust, of apocalypse wrought by our biology and culture. She never lets us forget that we are all agents of change. Reading her stories and novels challenges the inertia of our spirits. With transparent, undecorated prose, she renders the banality, brutality, and insanity of human nature and society in chilling detail. Always writing her way to characters who make something out of less than nothing, she re-envisions past devastation and invents parables of the not-too-distant future, insisting there is no *deus ex machina* coming to the rescue, no magic bullet cure for what ails us. We are the change we've been waiting for. As Beatrice Alcantara, the head of the alternative institute for treating DGD, tells Alan Chi in "The Evening And The Morning And The Night," "The people of Dilg are problem solvers, Alan. Think of the problems you could solve!" (Butler, 284)

A Brief History

Like the heroines in her stories, Butler is one of those black women who wasn't meant to be. Finding no cultural space for her voice and vision, she changed the limitations of her historical moment and redefined black literature, SF and F, and feminist literature. She created a space not only for herself and her particular imaginative genius, but also inspired a generation of new writers, literary and social theorists, fans, and casual readers with her meditations on agency and change.

With her groundbreaking research and *Dark Matter* anthologies Sheree R. Thomas has demonstrated that writers from the African Diaspora have been creating speculative fiction since the mid-nineteenth century. Martin Delany in *Blake, Or the Huts of America* (1857 or 1859) imagined a successful slave uprising; Pauline Hopkins in *Of One Blood* (1879) envisions an African American discovering a lost African empire; in *Imperium in Imperio* (1899) by Sutton E. Griggs, a secret society of black men creates an all black nation in Texas; a white woman and black man are the only New Yorkers who survive the Earth's passage through a comet's tail in W. E. B. Du Bois' "The Comet" (1920); and a Negro doctor can change black people to white people in three days in George S. Shulyler's *Black No More* (1931).[5]

Despites these and other speculative meditations on history and culture by black artists, from the 1920s on, science fiction has been dominated and defined in the public mind by white males — authors, critics, and readers. Until recently, publishers feared that black writers, "black" themes, or even the appearance of black characters in a story would put off (white) SF and F readers. A character's "blackness" distracted from the blissful sense of wonder that enveloped a good SF story. Butler recounts an anecdote in which a magazine editor told her:

> that he didn't think blacks should be included in science fiction stories because they changed the character of the stories; that if you put in a black, all of a sudden the focus is on this person. He stated that if you were going to write about some sort of racial problem, that would be absolutely the only reason he could see for including a black.[6]

In other words, to deal with universal human themes, to speculate on human possibility, writers should use characters not "burdened" with race.

The myth that black folks weren't/aren't SF and F writers or fans, and the realities that engendered this myth, also limited the reception and development of black SF writers from the 1920s to the present. Urging black authors to write science fiction in an essay for *Dark Matter — a Century of Speculative Fiction from the African Diaspora*, Charles R. Saunders mused on the history of black readers and writers of SF and F:

> When I wrote "Why Blacks Don't Read Science Fiction," [1978] I believed most blacks shunned sf and fantasy because there was little for us to identify with in the content . . . A literature that offered mainstream readers an escape route into the imagination and, at its best, a window to the future could not bestow a similar experience for blacks and other minority readers. . . .
> At the time [late '70s], science fiction was still in the process of freeing itself from the grasp of its so-called Golden Age in the 1930s–1950s, when hard science was a king whose court was closed to blacks. And fantasy was still frozen in an amber of Celtic and Arthurian themes.[7]

Reviewing Octavia Butler's Xenogenesis series in 1989, Adele S. Newman wrote:

> It is a widespread myth that Blacks don't write or read science fiction. The myth is fed by the notion that they cannot afford to indulge in fantasy.[8]

In 1998 Jeffrey Allen Tucker, Ph.D., a Samuel Delany scholar, confessed:

> When I tell people that my most recent research has been on works of African-American Science Fiction, I often get responses that range from incredulous — "You mean, there is such a thing?" — to the ridiculous: "You mean like Homeboys in Outer Space or Dionne Warwick's Psychic Friends Network, right?"[9]

In the utilitarian Puritan cultural landscape of the United States, where the practice and enjoyment of art is suspect, "escaping into the imagination" is sinful at worst, frivolous at best; "indulging in fantasy" is a prerogative of the privileged, not an essential aspect of shared humanity. In the early and mid-twentieth century, the African American artist's major labor was to correct the damage, the devastation of a blackface minstrel past. Blues People cut off from history didn't dabble in the future. They left that to the white folks and spent their precious time throwing off oppression.

In the minds of many readers, writers, and critics, the mimetic realism of so-called literary fiction held out the best opportunity for blacks to reclaim borrowed or stolen history, re-create a positive group identity from shared experiences, and uplift the race. The "serious" artistry of literary fiction allowed black artists to battle the science fiction and fantasy of white supremacy. The experience/story of the slave trade, colonization of Africa, and the Jim Crow laws and violent repression in the United States reads like an SF and F dystopic narrative. Supported by religious apologists on the hunt for benighted souls and a pseudoscientific doctrine of racial hierarchy, the real-life "aliens" that violated black bodies, twisted their histories, and despoiled the future also got to tell their stories. This on-going struggle over representation has circumscribed African American cultural production. "Serious" literature could set the record straight. Instead of the coons, Jezebels, bucks, and mammies strutting across screen, stage, page, or hanging in the American/world imagination, realist black narratives could show who we *actually* were. Black artists could thereby rupture minstrel fantasies and define *authentic* black men and women.[10]

Authenticity is the problem child of pseudo-science, commodity culture, and anxious nostalgia for a mono-cultural identity. In a relentlessly multicultural, pluralistic society, authenticity and other essentialist notions of identity and community help to maintain the power status quo. Conjuring the *authentic* black character, while often a mighty attempt to free the African American image from white racist control, was/is a (racist) trap of its own. Despite shared experiences, racism doesn't magically erase differences and make all black people the same. Nor is racism the only concern or obligatory obsession of black folks. The complexity hidden by the minstrel mask, by the Harlem Renaissance's New Negro visage, or the '60's Black Revolutionary power stance would not be contained. Variations in class, gender, age, ethnicity, sexuality, etc. made a monolithic performance of race impossible. Authenticity would not save us from exploitation and oppression and in fact made self determination/self definition more difficult. As Audre Lorde famously said, "the master's tools will never dismantle the master's house."[11]

Not Just Tearing Down the House

Samuel R. Delany and Octavia Butler were the first celebrated African American SF writers of the twentieth century. Very different writers, drawn by the freedom and potential of the genre, neither were simply engaged in the re-appropriation and redefinition of images of blackness. They weren't just tearing down the master's house; rather, they meditated on our humanity, on who we all might become. To the frequent challenge, "What good is science fiction to Black people?" which implicitly demanded a justification for abandoning the honorable labor of racial uplift, Butler replied:

> What good is any form of literature to Black people? What good is science fiction's thinking about the present, the future, and the past? What good is its tendency to warn or to consider alternative ways of thinking and doing? What good is its examination of the possible effects of science and technology, or social organization and political direction? At its best, science fiction stimulates imagination and creativity. It gets reader and writer off the beaten track, off the narrow, narrow footpath of what "everyone" is saying, doing, thinking — whoever "everyone" happens to be this year.
> And what good is all this to Black people?[12]

As Octavia Butler declared herself a feminist and wrote her early novels — SF and F works that interrupted essentialist notions of race, class, gender, etcetera, while investigating complex humanity — radical feminists of color such as Audre Lorde, bell hooks, Cherríe Moraga, Alice Walker, Gloria Anzaldúa, Toni Morrison, Pearl Cleage, Michelle Wallace, and Maxine Hong Kingston were, to paraphrase Kingston, all learning to make their minds large, as the universe is large, with room for paradoxes.[13] These warrior women expanded the limited agenda of the male-dominated Civil Rights movement and also challenged the narrowness of (white middle-class) feminism.

Since Sojourner Truth, black women have critiqued a narrowly defined feminism that would universalize the particular experiences of one group of woman and signify the experiences of "other" women as marginal or aberrant. Gender as a category of difference like race cannot magically confine or predict the protean identities and complex experiences of the people it purports to describe. Many feminist SF and F writers vigorously challenge the social construction of gender while discounting, repressing, or sidelining other differences.[14]

In the struggle for black liberation, gender issues (along with sexuality and class issues) were/are often viewed as side issues, distractions from the "real" black struggle. In the late '70s and early '80s Ntozake Shange, Michelle Wallace, Alice Walker, and other black feminists were accused of being race traitors for airing dirty laundry, for challenging the sexism of black men and black culture and politics in public. Shange's play *for colored girls who have considered suicide when the rainbow is enuf*, Walker's novel, *The Color Purple*, and Wallace's critical text, *Black Macho and the Myth of the Superwoman* resulted in a storm of controversy about black male bashing that is ongoing. Interestingly, black men who harass, oppress, marginalize, and brutalize black women were/are not viewed as race traitors.[15] In fact strong black women were/are seen as pathological matriarchs, as obstacles impeding black men from attaining their manhood.[16] Feminism was/is often characterized as a white, middle class, trivial movement and not part of the "uplift the race" agenda. Thus Butler faced a public questioning not only "what good was science fiction to black people," but a black nationalist agenda that questioned "what good was feminism to black people."

Falling Out of the Margins

Many mid-twentieth-century radical feminists of color used fantastical, speculative elements in their work as did earlier writers. For example, Lorraine Hansberry invented an African nation for *Les Blancs*, as did Alice Walker for *The Color Purple* and *Possessing the Secret of Joy*. Toni Morrison's *Beloved* is a ghost story, and Pearl Cleage's *In the Time Before the Men Came* is alternative history. Yet, no matter how anti-realist their work, these authors remained in the literary fiction bins. And although an early novel, *Kindred*, was turned down by SF presses and published by a mainstream house, Butler named herself a science fiction writer.

SF and F as a form of meta-literature poses difficulties for a feminist author riffing on, among other things, "black" idioms and story repertoire. An author extrapolating on a past or present social reality requires an audience fluent in that social reality, an audience aware of the characters, experiences, values, gestures, and nuances that inspire the extrapolation. Any author whose references fall outside the margins of the mainstream must struggle with the false universalism of the dominant stories, must face down publishers and critics who confuse their cultural ignorance with the author's supposed artistic failings. Critics and publishers who devalue the significance of women's experience often label works centering on women's lives as trivial, insisting that their evaluation is purely aesthetic, "all about craft." Authors dealing in so-called women's trivia or black particularity simply aren't good enough to know what makes a well-crafted story, a rollicking good blockbuster narrative.[17]

Octavia Butler's narratives fall out of a lot of margins (Mainstream, African American, Feminist, SF and F). However, she artfully educates her audience in the motifs she riffs on. Using black women heroines to meditate on humanity — not as the ultimate universal subjects but as particular agents of change in whose stories we might find hope — Butler decenters the presumed white male reader of SF and F, looking for geeky entertainment. She also doesn't write Doris Day Blues — tales of a middle-class housewife languishing in alienated suburbs, trapped in nuclear-family hell, servicing a predator-capitalist husband (whose dreams of adventure have soured in the workaday world), driving her children here, there, and everywhere, but getting nowhere herself. Rescuing women from domestic bondage, from the prison of family, from an essentialized, obligatory motherhood is/was not a trivial concern.[18] However Butler's approach to family and motherhood is from a different angle. Her heroines reinvent family and create community as a way to rescue and redefine humanity. Lynn Mortimer, the narrator in "The Evening and the Morning and the Night" observes:

> I watched a woman work quickly, knowledgeably, with a power saw. She obviously understood the perimeters of her body, was not so dissociated as to perceive herself as trapped in something she needed to dig her way out of. What had Dilg done for these people that other hospitals did not do? (Butler, 277)

Dilg is a constructed family, a community guided by a visionary woman who works to redefine the diseased bodies of DGDs as productive and creative. In fact, allowing DGD sufferers access to their creativity allows them to heal. In much of her work, Butler gives a "domestic" sensibility to the "public" discourse of liberation and survival.

In addition to being abstract cultural constructs, Butler's characters refer to body-based beings in a cultural/historical context where the performance of identity and the nature of community have a profound impact on everyone's survival. Individual agency within a strong community network heads off annihilation. Even when family members are oppressive, Butler's heroines sacrifice themselves to save their families, their communities, their people, their species from total destruction. They are prophets witnessing for the future.

Not Being Able To Stop

Who was I anyway? Why should anyone pay attention to what I had to say? Did I have anything to say? I was writing science fiction and fantasy for God's sake. At that time nearly all the professional science-fiction writers were white men. As much as I loved science fiction and fantasy, what was I doing? Well, whatever it was I couldn't stop. Positive obsession is about not being able to stop just because you're afraid and full of doubts. Positive obsession is dangerous. It's about not being able to stop at all.[19]

A casual search through literary, feminist, African American, and SF journals and publications reveals a staggering amount of criticism devoted to analyzing, celebrating, pondering, and fussing with Butler's work. All concur that she has had a profound impact on the SF genre and black and feminist literature. In 1995, Butler received a MacArthur "Genius" Award, and in October 2000, she received the Lifetime Achievement Award in writing from PEN.

Starting in 1976 with *Patternmaster*, Octavia Butler has published eleven novels. *Kindred* (1979), a time traveling epic, features a twentieth-century black woman snatched into the antebellum South to save the life of her white slave master ancestor. The fantasy novel was an international bestseller and has sold 250,000 copies to date. As mentioned earlier, despite eventual popularity, Butler had difficulty finding an SF and F publisher for her decidedly non-Celtic, non-Arthurian *Kindred*, so it came out as mainstream fiction from Doubleday.

With *Kindred* and *Wildseed* (1980), Butler reinvented the slave narrative as speculative fiction. Her artistry has been compared to Toni Morrison's *Beloved*. Butler had heard too many voices in the black consciousness movement dismissing the efforts of previous generations as a betrayal of a hip, revolutionary present. The cavalier contempt contemporary black people displayed for the slaves who accommodated their masters to survive spurred Butler to write the present into the past.[20] Showing what black people in the early 1800s had endured, so that folks in the twentieth century could strut their stuff, Butler restored cultural memory. The sacrifices and accommodations that characters are asked to make in "The Evening and the Morning and the Night" are similar in nature. In *Kindred* and *Wildseed*, Butler honors the clarity of vision and the mundane, backbreaking heroics that laid the ground for who black people could be today.

In the Xenogenesis trilogy of *Dawn* (1987), *Adult Rites* (1988), and *Imago* (1989), the warmongers have blown up the world and most of the people with it. The only hope for humanity is assimilation. Survivors of the nuclear holocaust must integrate on a genetic level with the alien Oankali. The Xenogenesis trilogy, like "The Evening and the Morning and the Night," explores the connection between biology and agency. The cover of *Dawn* featured a white heroine as opposed to the black one found in the story. In the late '80s, a black protagonist on the face of an SF novel was still too scary.[21]

In *Parable of the Sower* (1995) and *Parable of the Talents* (2000), Butler speculates on the implications of late model capitalism. In these books, the cutthroat, commodity culture values of transnational corporations and patriarchal militarism ravish and rend asunder the human fabric of life. Extrapolating from Los Angeles in the 1990s, Butler centers on those who do not have the resources to insulate themselves from vicious urban violence and decay. The majority of the population, who cannot afford a gated community protected by thugs for hire, become homeless wanderers — not unlike the "Okies" running from the over-farmed dustbowls and the depression-depleted cities of the 1930s. Floundering in the throes of corporate fascism, abandoned by a complicit military and an ineffectual democracy, Butler's characters reinvent community in order to rescue the future. They are led by a black woman empath who feels the actual pain of those around her. She is an embodiment of *communitas* — the individual resonating collective identity — and the antithesis of the rugged individualist who doesn't even feel his own pain. *Parable of the Talents* won the 2000 Nebula award for best novel.

Prophetic Artist

An avid science fiction reader and dear friend told me once that Octavia Butler's work, although excellent, was unrelentingly bleak and brutal. As noted earlier, Butler herself claims to be pessimistic (if not careful) and resists any attempts by readers and critics to label her fiction utopian. So why do I find this self-proclaimed pessimist so hopeful?

Cornel West says to hope is "to go beyond the evidence to make new possibilities based on visions that become contagious to allow us to engage in heroic actions always against the odds."[22] In *Prophetic Thought in Post-modern Times,* West argues that postmodern prophets must be discerning, empathetic, humble, and hopeful in order to deal with the material and spiritual crises of the late twentieth century. For him, hope in the face of atrocity may be the most difficult to manage, but it's a necessity.

> To talk about human hope is to engage in an audacious attempt to galvanize and energize, to inspire and to invigorate world-weary people. Because that is what we are. We are world-weary; we are tired . . . we have given up on the capacity of human beings to do *anything* right. The capacity of human communities to solve any problem.
>
> We must face that skeleton as a challenge, not a conclusion. Be honest about it. Weary, but keep alive the notion that history is incomplete, that the world is unfinished, that the future is open-ended and that what we think and what we do can make a difference.[23]

Without a shred of optimism, Octavia Butler writes stories from the last outposts of humanity that are a bridge to the future. In her work, humanity teeters at the edge of extinction, but never falls in. A motley crew of opportunistic heroes — that is, heroes who seize the moment — struggle against the odds and transform what it means to be human. Through the changes they imagine and realize, we continue. History reaches into the future. Butler has no truck with arrested development or romanticized museum humans. Her hope is hard edged.

In "The Evening and the Night and the Morning" when the magic bullet cancer cure has caused a violent degenerative (fatal) disease, Butler, as usual, celebrates the faith and spirit of women who find themselves in impossible, horrific circumstances. Despite the extremity of the situations and their seeming powerlessness, Butler's heroines struggle to act — against or in the face of enormous loss; against the persistence of the old regime in themselves and others; against the despair and hostility that can impede change. Butler's women confront the horrific reality and their own conflicting desires and come to believe, not just in their individual moments, in their ephemeral personal freedom, but in collective possibilities across generations. Their faith is a time-traveling, space-faring spirituality.

"The Evening and the Morning and the Night" is vintage Butler.

> "What are you going to do?" he asked.
>
> The question startled me. "You have a choice," I said. "I don't. If she's right . . . how could I not wind up running a retreat?"

"Do you want to?"

I swallowed. I hadn't really faced that question yet. Did I want to spend my life in something that was basically a refined DGD ward? "No!"

"But you will."

". . . Yes." I thought for a moment, hunted for the right words. "You'd do it."

"What?"

"If the pheromone was something only men had, you would do it." (Butler, 285)

Butler's characters value community over individual success. Or better, individual success is defined in terms of community. Her questions are: what do *we* do to survive? How must *we* change if we are not to be wiped out by the others, by ourselves? Her stories focus on those who make the compromises, those who do not have the power to determine their place in society, those who are forced to live lives defined by more powerful beings/ forces. However, confronting alien invaders and thug democracies, dealing with biological imperatives — genes and pheromones that could lead to violence — there is always the possibility of community, of cultural intervention.

In "The Evening and the Morning and the Night," despite her genetically based bodily response, despite irrational, violent revulsion, Lynn doesn't attack Beatrice; Beatrice, who has the same powerfully negative urges, mentors Lynn, offers her a future. Dilg residents don't gouge out their eyes or mutilate their bodies. They are guided by their community "to live and do whatever they decide is important to them. What do you have, what can you realistically hope for that's better than that?" (Butler, 285)

Butler's stories are about the dispossessed — those whose identity, subjectivity, and agency are circumscribed; whose humanity is under siege; whose extinction is a distinct possibility — yet her heroines call to the future with incredible acts of compromise and imagination.

Some critics insist that her stories, like "Bloodchild," are SF slavery parables; Butler denies that was her intention.[24] The disjunction between her intention and readings of her work is complex. Significant is what she's not doing — she admits to not writing the British Empire in Space, to not writing another *Star Trek*.[25] She does not investigate the frequent (but not exclusively) white male heroic fantasy of conquering the final frontiers, but instead focuses on the "accommodations" we have to make when we strike out into the unknown and encounter difference or when it lands on our shores or drops from the sky onto our deserts and the power differential is not in our favor. Accommodation smacks of defeat, of women sacrificing their individuality for husbands and offspring, of slaves betraying the revolutionary spirit to survive. It has become difficult to imagine as heroes those who would rather stay alive as slaves than find freedom in death. How can they be our heroes if they "agree" to being slaves? Yet Butler insists on revising our memories of this sort of terrible agreement, this sort of compromise with oppressive forces. To revise the memory is to heal a wounded past.

When a man, a captain, sacrifices himself to get the passengers and crew ashore, and goes down with his ship, freely choosing death, this is a classic heroic gesture, a cornerstone of the celebrated warrior tradition. A woman, who sacrifices herself so that the ship of life doesn't go down, who accommodates the "enemy" so her biological children or invented family might take another breath, is not a glorious hero, but an average mom and suspect feminist. Yet Butler celebrates these black-power mothers who embody communal values and sacrifice themselves to define the future.

Unfinished Business

In "The Evening and the Morning and the Night," Butler thrusts her characters into an impossibly bleak, hopeless setting. A miracle drug cancer cure turns the user's children into violent, self-mutilating zombies. Inevitably digging and drifting, DGDs become alienated from their own bodies and the bodies of other people. The disease cuts DGDs off from identity and community, from the past and the future, and from the possibility of being human. Lynn Mortimer as a double DGD has no hope, no faith, no trust.

DGD transforms disparate individuals into a collective, marginal group. The disease obliterates differences — DGD is a monolithic type in the eyes of the healthy world, yet of course differences abound.[26] Seeing her suicidal fatalism mirrored in Alan, Lynn "takes him to bed." And, although saving him saves her, companionship and personal pleasure do not alone offer them hope or a full sense of humanity.

Traveling to the Dilg retreat tests Lynn and Alan's identities, as well as their relationship, their position in the world. Dilg offers DGDs a life possibility, not a cure back to "normal" again, not a happy-ever-after life in the suburbs. Rather, Dilg offers DGDs an alternative to the inevitable zombie-subhuman narrative that Alan, Lynn, and the rest of the world believe in. Still bearing the scars of their injuries, of hospital warehousing, still capable of violence, DGDs at Dilg create, invent, solve problems, and integrate themselves in human society. They do not self-destruct. Butler offers a cultural, experiential/relational cure for a genetic malfunction. Beatrice explains, "Here we can help them channel their energies. They can create something beautiful, useful, even something worthless. But they create. They don't destroy." (Butler, 274)

For Butler, humanity is not merely an individual or essentially biological phenomenon but is constituted in our relations to others and to ourselves. Certainly Butler is fascinated by the extent to which our personal characters and social realities are determined by our genetic makeup. However, human beings aren't biological blank slates to be written on by culture. Admitting to the urges, tendencies, pathologies, bounties of our biological makeup, Butler still insists on culture's capacity to offer us choices, interventions, and communal solutions to what is negative in our heritage and enhancements for what is wonderful. We can and do culturally enhance the ugly, destructive aspects of our nature, but Butler has faith in those cultural practices that call to our best selves. Beatrice grabs Naomi Chi's hands, before she gouges out her son's eyes, and guides her to embracing him. Later Lynn and Alan recognize when Naomi is straying and help guide her back.

Difference is terrifying.

If we are different, we might not be equal or even equivalent. Difference has been used to oppress. Lynn asks Beatrice: "What are you saying? That the bigots are right? That we have some special gift?" (Butler, 278) A genetic basis for difference is also terrifying. Does that prove the bigots right? Does that mean we have no choice in who and what we are? Is human tragedy written in our genes? "I won't be controlled . . . by a goddamn smell!" Alan growls in defiance. Butler insists that human variability, genetic or cultural, is a resource and human agency is a given. Beatrice illuminates this for Lynn when she questions the older woman about Alan's agency:

> "He never really had a chance, did he?"
> She looked surprised. "That's up to you. You can keep him or drive him away. I assure you, you can drive him away."
> "How?"
> "By imagining that he doesn't have a chance." (Butler, 286)

Butler does a careful dance around freedom, responsibility, alienation, choice, and manipulation. Her heroines rarely live for themselves alone. They are impossibility specialists, high priestesses of the God of change.

> All that you touch
> You Change.
>
> All that you Change
> Changes you.

> The only lasting truth
> is Change
>
> God
> is Change.[27]

Working in community, Butler's characters do not hold onto a past world that has been blown up or snatched away from them. They may try suicide as in "The Evening and the Morning and the Night," but with the support of community they go on to create a possible future.

Feminists have brilliantly critiqued "biology as destiny," demonstrating that gender is to a large degree a cultural construct. It is biology and culture that define the roles a woman plays in her society, her family, her relationships. Although some critique Butler's work for being essentialist, she interrupts the notion of biology as destiny again and again.[28] As agents of change, her characters in "The Evening and the Morning and the Night" work with their genetic makeup, their human community, their historical context to create new identities and fashion their destiny.

Some feminist critics, like Dorothy Allison, find the motherly sacrifices of her feminist heroines for the future of the community maddening.

> I love Octavia Butler's women even when they make me want to scream with frustration. . . . What drives me crazy is their attitude: the decisions they make, the things they do in order to protect their children — and the assumption that children and family come first.
>
> Butler's nine books are exceptional not only because she is that rarity, a black woman writing science fiction, but because she advocates motherhood as the humanizing element in society (not a notion I have ever taken too seriously).[29]

For Butler, Motherhood is defining a community, nurturing a nation. Mothers define the material and spiritual future. It is not all that women are born to do, but it is how they can choose to keep hope alive. Butler's mothers redefine the public and the private sphere and in their visionary way alter the gender relations and role possibilities. Turning their backs on the limitations of tyranny, they give birth to tomorrow. Butler does not jettison Motherhood, but carefully negotiates the space between freedom, alienation, and extinction. When facing genocide, the literal or figurative erasure of the people who have named the cosmos, nurtured your being, and offered you identity — the sacrifices of Motherhood — do not constitute a loss of individuality. The right to abortion may not be your primary issue when you face forced sterilization. Despite the deadly consequences — all children born of DGD parents will be DGD — and despite human beings' ferocious sexual drive — copulating and the future be damned — Lynn defends her right to choose. She will not kill part of herself when so much is already dead.

Butler investigates the heroic significance of mothering the next generation, when you were not meant to survive. If identity is a community, a performance, a dance with the other, then a woman's *choice* to sacrifice for her children in the face of extinction is a hopeful one. Such a woman has a dream of the future, when the future seems destroyed and hopeless. The vision, the hope of a better future defined by her actions in the present, make unbearable choices bearable. If there's been a nuclear holocaust or if somebody has snatched you out of your home to work sugar cane and cotton in an alien world, if your parents took a drug that modified your genes so that violent self-mutilation and madness look inevitable, there's no going back to the past and making it present with a magical cure. When the future is the only dream you can have, you act to save it in the present.

In the Georgia Sea Islands, Gullah and Geechie black folk tell the story/ myth of Ibo Landing. On every island there is a sheltered cove where a slave ship supposedly pulled into shore and unloaded its human cargo. Walking ashore, the Ibos felt the weight of the place in their bones and souls. They looked into the faces of the white sailors and slave masters and glimpsed what was in store for them. Seeing this horror-future, they turned around and went back into the water, preferring to die rather than endure slavery. Some say they didn't drown in the waves despite being weighted down by heavy chains. They flew away to Africa or walked across the ocean to the motherland.

Octavia Butler tells stories of the people who stepped on shore, glimpsed a grim future, but couldn't walk on water or fly through the clouds. Yet despite suicidal despair, perhaps even after a failed attempt to walk their grief to the bottom of the sea, these world-weary ancestors came to believe where there is life, there is hope. They saw an alternate future beyond the slavers and inspired themselves and others to take another breath. These ancestors survived to tell the story of the freedom-loving Ibos. The telling and retelling of this mythic defiance nourished their spirits. Speculating on a glorious past offered a bridge to a glorious future.

Butler names as heroes the world-weary ancestors who accommodated and compromised. They faced the devastation of personal dreams and hopes, of their gods and children, and yet, like the Ibos flying home, they loved freedom. With their sacrifices, they offered freedom they could only remember or imagine to the future as a precious gift. These world-weary ancestors dreamt of us, survive in us, are who we are now. Octavia Butler, a prophetic artist, an agent of change, declares history unfinished business. Rehearsing the possible in the face of catastrophe, she calls us all to action.

NOTES

1. Well, perhaps there is less denial about the persistence of heterosexism. Despite *Queer Eye for the Straight Guy* and the *L Word*, the flak over gay marriage registers as a solid indication of how far we still are from a queer Promised Land.

2. See *Toxic Sludge is Good for You: Lies, Damn Lies and the Public Relations Industry* by John C. Stauber and Sheldon Rampton. Monroe Maine: Common Courage Press, 1995.

3. *Daily Hampshire Gazette*, March 4, 2005. June Zeitlin of Women's Environment and Development was quoted under the headline: "What we see are powerful trends — growing poverty, inequality, growing militarization, and fundamentalist opposition to women's rights. These trends are harming millions of women worldwide."

4. Interview with Octavia Butler, sfwa.org/members/Butler/Autobiography.html.

5. Conversation with Sheree R. Thomas, April 14, 2005. See also *Dark Matter — a Century of Speculative Fiction from the African Diaspora*, ed. Sheree R. Thomas, (New York: Warner Books, 2000).

6. Octavia Butler interview with Frances M. Beal, "Black Women and the Science Fiction Genre," in *Black Scholar*, vol. 17, no. 2, March/April, 1986, 18. See Samuel Delany's "Racism in Science Fiction" in *Dark Matter* for other examples.

7. Charles R. Saunders, "Why Blacks Should Read (And Write) Science Fiction," *Dark Matter — A Century of Speculative Fiction from the African Diaspora*, ed. Sheree R. Thomas, (New York: Warner Books, 2000), 398–399.

8. A review of *Dawn* and *Adult Rites* in *Black American Literature Forum* vol. 23, no. 2, Summer, 1989, 389–396.

9. "Studying the Works of Samuel R. Delany," Jeffrey Allen Tucker in *Ohio University College of Arts and Science Forum* vol. 15, Spring 1998.

10. For example, Francis Ellen Watkins Harper countered negative stereotypes and sanitized plantation mythology in *Iola Leroy* or *Shadows Uplifted* (1892). Harper showcased middle-class African Americans working to "uplift the race" from poverty and oppression. This would become a dominant approach in the twentieth century. Charles Chestnut critiqued white supremacy in *The Marrow of Tradition* (1901). His thorough examinations of African American experience in the context of oppression laid a literary foundation for the writers that followed. Richard Wright presented black men twisting in the noose of Jim Crow in *Uncle Tom's Children* (1938) and *Native Son* (1940) and defined black literature as urban realism. Playwrights such as Langston Hughes (*Mulatto*, 1938), Alice Childress (*Trouble in Mind*, 1955), Lorraine Hansberry (*Raisin in the Sun*, 1959), James Baldwin (*Blues for Mr. Charlie*, 1964) also worked to set the record straight.

11. Audre Lord, a black lesbian feminist poet and critical thinker, made these comments at "The Personal and the Political Panel (Second Sex Conference, October 29, 1979).

12. Octavia Butler, *Bloodchild and Other Stories*, (New York: Seven Stories Press, 1996), 134–135.

13. Maxine Hong Kingston, *The Woman Warrior*, (New York: Vintage Books, 1977), 35.

14. See in this volume: "The Conquest of Gola," "Created He Them," "The Fate of the Poseidonia."

15. A notorious example: Clarence Thomas complained of a high-tech lynching when Anita Hill accused him of sexual harassment in the hearings on his nomination to the Supreme Court. The specter of "lynching" black men falsely accused of raping white women, confused the debate. The "lynching" metaphor vilified Hill and demanded simplistic racial solidarity in support of Thomas. See *Race-ing Justice, En-gendering Power: Essays on Anita Hill, Clarence Thomas, and the Construction of Social Reality*, ed., Toni Morrison (New York: Pantheon, 1992) or "Clarity on Clarence" in *Deals with the Devil and Other Reasons to Riot*, Pearl Cleage (New York: Ballantine Books, 1993).

16. The stereotype of the evil-tempered, ball-busting black woman with weapons grade attitude and machine gun mouth has been anxiously performed throughout the twentieth and into the twenty-first century. In addition to artistic portrayals of pathological dominatrixes ruining black men, Daniel Patrick Moynihan justified the image with science in *The Negro Family: The Case for National Action*, (1965). Shahrazad Ali wrote *The Blackman's Guide to Understanding the Black Woman* in 1989, urging black male violence to bring black women in line. Radical black feminists such as Pearl Cleage, who wrote *Mad at Miles: A Blackwoman's Guide To Truth*, have mounted an on-going response to Ali's and other anti-woman, anti-feminist stances in African-American public discourse, yet the stereotype remains entrenched.

17. Of course, Minstrel Shows (difference contained and controlled in ethnic/gender caricature) are still one of Americas most popular (and longest running) forms of entertainment. See *Big Mama's House* (2000), *Meet the Fockers* (2004), and *Beauty Shop* (2005). Such Minstrel Show stories can be told ad nauseum with abandon and confidence.

18. See "Created He Them" in this anthology.

19. Octavia Butler, *Bloodchild and Other Stories*, (New York: Seven Stories Press, 1996), 133.

20. Octavia Butler interview with Frances M. Beal, "Black Women and the Science Fiction Genre," in *Black Scholar*, vol. 17, no. 2, March/April, 1986, pp 14–15.

21. Butler's book covers now feature black women as do the covers of Nalo Hopkinson's *Brown Girl in the Ring*, Sheree R. Thomas's *Dark Matter*, etcetera. However we are not quite out of the woods. Ursula K. Le Guin complains of the persistence of anxiety at colored faces in SF&F. See "A Whitewashed Earthsea: How the Sci Fi Channel Wrecked My Books." (http://slate.msn.com/id/2111107/) posted Dec. 16, 2004 for a discussion of how her multicultural, colored *Earthsea* was whitewashed for the TV audience. Terror in the bookstore has abated or perhaps migrated to the screen.

22. In Anna D. Smith's play, *Twilight Los Angeles*, 1992.

23. Cornel West, *Prophetic Thought in Postmodern Times*, (Monroe, Main: Common Courage Press, 1993), 6.

24. In a 1990 interview quoted by Elyce Rae Helford in "'Would You Really Rather Die Than Bear My Young?': The Construction of Gender, Race, and Species in Octavia E. Butler's 'Bloodchild,' " Butler responds to the notion that all her work explores forms of slavery and domination with: "I know some people think that, but I don't agree, although this may depend on what you mean by "slavery." In the story "Bloodchild," for example, some people assume I'm talking about slavery when what I am really talking about is symbiosis . . . " (*African American Review*, vol. 28, no. 2, Summer, 1994, p. 256).

25. See *Bloodchild*, pp. 31–32 for Butler's discussion of her intentions.

26. Ethnicity is mentioned only once in the story. Discussion of Alan's heritage elegantly interrupts a reader's possible assumption about the race/ethnicity of any of the characters.

27. Octavia Butler, *Parable of the Sower* (New York: Four Walls Eight Windows, 1993), 3.

28. See for example: Elyce Rae Helford in "'Would You Really Rather Die Than Bear My Young?': The Construction of Gender, Race, and Species in Octavia E. Butler's *Bloodchild*," *African American Review*, vol. 28, no. 2 (Summer, 1994), 259–271; Michelle Erica Green, "There Goes The Neighborhood: Octavia Butler's Demand for Diversity in Utopias," *Utopian and Science Fiction by Women: Worlds of Difference*, ed. Jane L Donawerth, Carol A. Kolmerten, and Susan Gubnar, Syracuse: Syracuse University Press, (1994), 166–189; Hoda M. Zaki, "Utopia, Dystopia, and Ideology in the Science Fiction of Octavia Butler," *Science Fiction Studies* 17 (1990): p239–251.

29. Dorothy Allison, "The Future of Female: Octavia Butler's Mother Lode," *Reading Black Reading Feminist*, ed. Henry Louis Gates, Jr. (New York: Meridian, 1990) 471.

Balinese Dancer

GWYNETH JONES

First published in Asimov's Science Fiction Magazine, *September 1997*

There comes a day when the road . . . the road that has served you so willingly and well, unfolding an endless absorbing game across the landscape,
throwing up donjons on secret hills, meadows and forests, river beaches,
sun-barred avenues that steadily rise and fall like the heart-beat of the summer, suddenly loses its charm. The baked verges sicken, the flowers have
all turned to straw, the air stinks of diesel fumes. The ribbon of grey flying
ahead of you up hills and down dales is no longer magically empty, like a
road in paradise. It is snarled with traffic: and even when you escape the
traffic everything seems spoiled and dead.

The cassette machine was playing one of Spence's ancient compilations.
The machine was itself an aged relic, its repertoire growing smaller as the
tapes decayed, sagged and snapped and could not be replaced. They'd
been singing along to this one merrily, from Avignon to Haut Vienne. Now
Anna endured in silence while Spence stared dead ahead, beating time on
the steering wheel and defiantly muttering scraps of lyric under his breath.
They hadn't spoken to each other for hours. Jake lay in the back seat sweating, his bare and dirty feet thrust into a collapsed tower of camping gear.
He was watching *The Witches* on his headband, his soft little face disfig-
ured by the glossy bar across his eyes; his lips moving as he repeated under
his breath the Roald Dahl dialogue they all knew by heart. Anna watched
him in her mirror. Eyeless, her child looked as if he was dead. Or like an
inadequately protected witness, a disguised criminal giving evidence.

"Got one!" barked Spence.

They were looking for a campsite.

It was late afternoon, the grey and brassy August sky had begun to fade.
Spence had been following minor roads at random since that incident, in
the middle of the day, on the crowded *route nationale*, when Anna had
been driving. They had escaped death but the debriefing had been inadequate — corticosterone levels rising; the terrible underlying ever present

stress of being on the road had come up fighting, shredding through their myths and legends of vagabond ease. Spence, in his wife's silence, swung the wheel around: circled the war memorial, cruised through a pretty village, passed the ancient church and the norman keep, took the left turn by the *piscine.*

"Swimming!" piped up Jake, always easily pleased. He had emerged from tv heaven and was clutching the back of the driver's seat.

But the site was full of *gens de voyage,* a polite French term for the armies of homeless persons with huge battered mobile homes, swarms of equally battered and despairing kids, and packs of savage dogs, that were becoming such a feature of rural holidays in La Belle France. They usually kept to their own interstices of the road-world: the cindered truckstop laybys and the desolate service areas where they hung their washing between eviscerated domestic hardware and burned-out auto wrecks. But if a bunch of them decided to infest a tourist campsite, it seemed that nothing could be done. Spence completed a circuit and stopped the car by the entrance, just upwind of a bonfire of old tyres.

"Well, it seems a popular neighbourhood. Shall we move in?"

Some hours ago Anna had vowed that she was sick to death of this pointless, endless driving. She had threatened to get out of the car and *simply walk away,* if they didn't stop at the next possible site. No matter what. She kept silent.

"They shouldn't be here," complained Jake. "They're not on holiday, are they?"

"No, kid, I guess they're not."

Spence waited, maliciously.

"Do whatever you want," she muttered.

Anna when angry turned extra-English, clipped and tart. In half conscious, half helpless retaliation Spence reverted to the mid-west. He heard himself turning into that ersatz urban cowboy, someone Anna hated.

"Gee, I don't know, babe. Frankly, right now I don't care if I live or die."

The bruised kids, and their older brothers, were gathering. Spence waited.

"Drive on," she snapped, glowering in defeat.

So they drove on, to a drab little settlement about twenty klicks further along, where they found a municipal campsite laid out under the eaves of a wood. It had no swimming pool, but there was a playground with a trapeze. Jake, who believed that all his parents' sorrows on this extended holiday were occasioned by the lack of ponies, mini-golf or a bar in some otherwise ideal setting, pointed this out with exaggerated joy. The huge rhino-jeep and trailer combo that they'd been following for the last few miles had arrived just ahead of them. Otherwise there was no one about. Anna and Spence set up the yurt, each signalling by terse but courteously functional remarks that if acceptable terms could be agreed, peace might be restored. Each of them tried to get Jake to go away and play. But the child believed that his reluctance to help with the chores was another great cause of sorrow, so of course he stayed. Formal negotiations, which would inevitably have broken up in rancour, were therefore unable to commence. Peace returned in silence, led home by solitude; by the lingering heat and dusty haze of evening and the intermittent song of a blackbird.

While they were setting up, a cat appeared. It squeezed its way through the branches of the beech hedge at the back of their pitch, announcing itself before it could be seen in a loud, querulous oriental voice. It was a long-haired cat with a round face, small ears, blue eyes and the colouring of a seal-point Siamese, except that its four dark brown feet seemed to have been dipped in cream. Spence thought he knew cats. He pronounced it a Balinese, a long haired Siamese variant well known in the States.

"No," said Anna. "It's a Birman, a Burmese Temple Cat. Look, see the white tips to its paws. They're supposed to be descended from a breed of cats that were used as oracles in Burma, ages ago. Maybe it belongs to the people with the big trailer."

The cat was insistently friendly, but distracted. Alternately it made up to them, purring and gabbing on in its raucous Siamese voice: then broke off to sit in the middle of their pitch, fluffy dark tail curled around its white toes, staring from side to side as if looking for someone.

Spence, Jake and Anna went for a walk in the gloaming. They inspected the sanitaires, and saw the middle aged couple from the trailer walking towards the little town, probably in search of somewhere to eat. They studied the interactive guide to their locality that had been installed beside the toilet block. As usual, the parents stood at gaze while the child poked and touched, finding everything that was clickable and obediently reading all the text. There was a utility room with a washer-drier, sinks, and a card-in-the-slot multimedia screen, so you could watch a movie or video-phone *maman* while your socks were going round. Everything was new, bare and cheap. Everything was waiting for the inexorable tide of tourism to arrive even here, even on this empty shore.

"Since everywhere interesting is either horribly crowded or destroyed already," said Anna, "obviously hordes of people will be driven to visit totally uninteresting places instead. One can see the logic."

"The *gens de voyage* will move in first," decided Spence.

Beyond the lower terrace of pitches they found a small lake, the still surface of the water glazed peach-colour by the sunset. Green wrought-iron
benches stood beside a gravel path. Purple and yellow loosestrife grew in
the long grass at the water's edge; dragonflies hovered. The hayfields beyond had been cut down to sonorous insect-laden turf; and in the distance
a little round windmill stood up against the red glistening orb of the sun.

"Well, hey: this isn't so bad," Spence felt the shredded fabric coming together. They would be happy again.

"Lost in France," murmured Anna, smiling at last. "That's all we ask."

"What's that silver stuff in the water?" wondered Jake.

"It's just a reflection."

When they came closer they saw that the water margin was bobbing
with dead fish.

Jake made cheerful retching noises. "What a stink!"

They retreated to the wood, where they discovered before long a deep
dell among the trees that had been turned into the town dump. Part of it
was smouldering. A little stream ran out from under the garbage, prattling
merrily as it tripped down to pollute the lake. The dim but pervasive stink
of rot, smoke and farm chemicals pursued them until the woodland path
emerged at a crossroads on the edge of town.

"Typical gallic economy," grumbled Spence, trying to see some humour
in the situation. "Put the dump by the campsite. Why not? Those tourists
are only passing through."

Anna said nothing, but her smile had vanished.

The town was a miniature ribbon development, apparently without a centre. There was no sign of life, the two bars and the single restaurant were
firmly shuttered. They turned back, keeping to the road this time. Spence
put together a meal of paté and bread and wine; *fatigue* salad from lunch
in a plastic box. Anna took Jake to play on the trapeze. Unable to decide who
had won the short straw on this occasion, Spence moved about the beech-
hedge pitch, fixing things the way he liked them and making friends with the
long-haired cat, which was still hanging around. He named it the Balinese
Dancer, from an old Chuck Prophet song that was going around in his head,
about a guy who had a Balinese dancer tattooed across his chest, like something, someone he couldn't quite recall in a Bogart movie. . . . He couldn't
remember what the point of the song was, either — probably something
about having an amenable girlfriend who'd dance for you any time —; but it
gave him an excuse to restore his own name for the cat. Anna's inexhaustible
fund of general knowledge annoyed him. Why couldn't she be ignorant: or
even *pretend* to be ignorant, just once in a while? It was thin as a rail under

the deceptive thickness of its coat, and though it obviously strove to keep up appearances its fur was full of hidden burrs and tangles. He looked across the empty pitches to the playground and saw his wife hanging upside down on the trapeze, showing her white knickers: a lovely sight in the quiet evening. If only she could take things more easily, he thought. A few dead fish, what the hell. It doesn't have to ruin your life. The middle aged couple from the trailer were standing by their beefy hunk of four wheel drive, heads together, talking hard. They looked as if they were saying things that they wouldn't want anyone to overhear. Probably having a filthy row thought Spence, with satisfaction. He meditated going over to improve their camping-trip-hell by asking them why they didn't take better care of their cat. But refrained. The Balinese Dancer was still with him when Anna and Jake came back. It had reverted to its sentry duty, sitting alert and upright in the middle of the pitch.

"He's a lost cat," said Jake. "Can we keep him?"

"I thought we decided he belonged to those guys over there," Spence pointed out.

"No he doesn't."

"It doesn't," Anna confirmed. "Jake asked them. They have no cat."

"I think he was left behind. Did you notice, our pitch is the only one on this terrace that people have used recently? There was a caravan and a tent here. About a week ago by the look of the marks on the grass. They went and left without him. That's what I think."

Over his head, young Sherlock's parents exchanged an agreement to block any further moves towards an adoption application.

"No, I bet he comes from that place up on the road." Spence pointed to a red-roofed ranchero that they could see over their hedge, the last house of the town. "He's probably discovered that tourists are a soft touch, and comes here on the scrounge."

"Can I go and ask them?"

"No!" snapped Anna and Spence together. Jake shrugged, and gave the cat some paté. It didn't have the manners of a beggar. It ate a little, as if for politeness' sake, and resumed its eager watchfulness.

The child was put to bed and finally slept, having failed to persuade the cat to join him inside the yurt. The parents stayed outside. The air was so still that Anna brought out candles, to save the big lamp. They lay wrapped in rugs, reading and talking softly; and made a list for the next hypermarché: where, it was to be hoped, there'd be cooking gas cylinders in stock again at last. And batteries for Jake's headband tv, the single most necessary luxury in their lives. The cat came to visit them, peering sweetly into their faces and inviting them to play. It showed no sign of returning to the red-roofed ranch.

"You know," said Anna, "Jake could be right. It's weird for a fancy cat like that to be wandering around on the loose, like any old moggie. It's a tom, did you notice?"

"I thought toms were supposed to roam."

"Cat breeders keep their studs banged-up. They spend their lives in solitary, except when they're on the job. An inferior male kitten sold for a pet gets castrated. Let's take a closer look."

The Burmese Temple Cat was a young entire male, very thin but otherwise in good health. He had once worn a collar. He now had no identifying marks. He suffered their examination with good-tempered patience, stayed to play for a little longer and then resumed his vigil: staring hopefully into the night.

"He's waiting for someone," said Anna, finishing her wine. "Poor little bugger. He must have gone off exploring, and they left without him. Pity he's not tattooed."

"Libertarians are everywhere," Spence reminded her. "That's probably why he still has his balls, too. No castration for me, no castration for my cat. I can see that."

"What can we do? I suppose we could leave a message at the gendarmerie, if there is one. Any one who lost a cat like that's bound to have reported him missing."

"We can tell the *gardienne* in the morning, when she comes to collect the rent."

Next day started slowly. After lunch Spence and Jake walked into town to look for the Post Office. Spence needed to despatch the proofs of *The Coast Of Coromandel*, latest of the adventures of a renowned female pirate captain: who, with her dashing young mate Jake and the rest of the desperate crew, had been keeping Patrick Spencer Meade in gainful employment for some years. The postmistress greeted them with disdain and pity, as if tourists were an endangered species too far gone to be worth your sympathy. She examined his laptop, and refused to admit that her establishment possessed a phone jack that he could plug into. She told him he could use the telephone in a normal manner, but she was afraid that connections with England and the United States were impossible at present. She told him to go to Paris. Or Lyons.

Or just get the hell out of here.

Spence's understanding of French was adequate but not subtle. He was always missing the point on small details. He'd learned to smile and nod and pass for normal, it had never failed so far. He accepted the woman's

hostility without complaint, and wondered what had caused the latest telecoms melt. Urban terrorism? Surprise right-wing coup brings down the Paris
government? Whole population of the UK succumbs to food-poisoning? It
was almost enough to send him in search of an English language newspaper, or drive him to reconnect the broadband receiver in the car. But not
quite. They were on holiday. Lost in France, and planning to stay lost for
as long as the market would bear. He paid for a mass of stamps and handed
over the package containing the printed copy, which his publishers rou-
tinely required to back up anything sent down the wire. Andrea would be
happy. His editor was an elderly young lady with a deep contempt for all
things cyberspatial. She'd have loved it if Spence turned in his books written in longhand on reams of parchment. He collected Jake from the phi-
lately counter, and they left.

They wandered on up the single street, which was hardly less deathly
still than it had been the evening before. They bought bread, and for want
of anything else to explore went into the ugly yellow church, that stood by
the war memorial in a walled yard paved with gravestones.

The interior had a crumbling nineteenth-century mariolatory decor: sky
blue heavens, madonna lilies, silver ribbons. The structure was much older.
Spence traced a course of ancient stone, revealed where a long chunk of
painted plaster had fallen away. It was cool and damp to the touch, and still
marked by the blows of its maker who had been dead for a thousand years.
He sat on the front bench in the lady chapel, holding his laptop on his
knees. Jake went to investigate a dusty Easter Garden in the children's corner: Christ's sepulchre done in papier-mâché and florist's moss; a match-
wood cross draped in a swag of white.

Spence was glad of a chance to sit and stare; a chance to think about the
situation. For some reason his thoughts today took the form of considering
their different ethnicities. Anna the European: *so old a ship, so old . . .*
Spence the American. He had been brought up to believe, (along with an
improbably large percentage of the U.S. population), that he was of almost
pure Irish descent, with a smattering of West African (tribe unspecified);
and a soupçon of Cherokee. Anna had informed him that in fact what distinguishes United States citizens is a genetic inheritance extra-weighted towards callous survival. Spence's ancestors were people who quit England
because they could not stand the idea of religious tolerance; people who
escaped from hellish conditions in nineteenth century Europe rather than
staying to fight for a better society. People who, given the real and immediate physical choice, had preferred slavery to death. Americans are descended
from those who refused to suffer; or if they had to suffer they refused to die.

Could he correct that inheritance, could he become more like Anna? He imagined himself taken up from the nine-inch board in that stinking hold, extricated from his neighbours, his chains struck off. Over the side, a sack of spoiled meat. He saw himself fall into grace, loose limbs flapping: down into the green water, silver bubbles rising as the body slowly tumbles, into the deep, the very deep. . . . But it was too late. Can't turn back the hand of time. Spence lived, and would have to keep this thick-skinned hardiness: this spirit, wherever it came from, that would not be mortified.

At least he could claim to be a permanent exile. Spence could never go home, not for more than a week or so at a time, not so long as his wife and his mother both lived. The whole United States wasn't big enough to contain the iron-hard territoriality of those two females. This didn't bother him. It only surprised him occasionally, when he realised how solidly his marriage confirmed a choice that he'd made for himself long before. He preferred America this way: preserved from one brief visit to the next in his voice, in his tastes, in his childhood memories. Yet displacement breeds displacement. They had travelled a great deal, in Europe and beyond: always going further and staying away longer than other people. They'd have taken longer and wilder trips still, except for Anna's commitment to her work.

Now Anna's job was gone. There was nothing to go back for. No drag, no tie, no limit. They were no longer locked into that damned university laboratory academic year, miserable crowded August holidays. She's mine now, he thought. She's all my own. Instantly he was punished by a vision of Anna's hands. Anna moving round a clothes shop like a blind woman, assessing the fabric as if she's reading braille: smoothing a shoulder seam, judging the cut and the fall of the cloth with those animate fingers, those living creatures imbued with genius. Anna removing and cleaning her contact lenses, nights in the past, so smashed she could hardly *breathe*, the deft economy of her gestures serenely undisturbed. Those hands rendered useless, unable to practice the subtle art that he only knew in its faint, mundane echoes? Oh no. He thought of Marie Curie, the exacting drudgery of women scientists; it comes naturally to them. Delicacy and endurance, backed by a brain the size of Jupiter. She can't have lost all that. . . . Recent memory, from those last extraordinary weeks in England, cast up a red-faced drunken old man at a publishers' party, shouting *"your wife has destroyed the fabric of society!"* One of the more bizarre incidents in his career as a scientist's spouse.

He could not take her disaster seriously, and therefore he was free to indulge his fantasy. Of course she'd get another job, but they didn't have to go home yet. They could stay away for the whole of September, mellow empty

September in the French countryside. We can afford it, he thought, glowing a little. Easy. Could go south again, over to Italy, move into hotels if the weather gives out (but they all three loved to live outdoors). I may be a mere kiddies' entertainer, but I can put food on the family table. She practically had a breakdown, she's still fragile, depressed, not herself: she needs space.

But what would it be like to live with Anna, without her career? What about sex? There'd be no more foreign conferences, no more jokes about over-sexed sex biologists. No more of those sparky professional friendships that had to make him suspicious, damn it, though he'd persistently denied it. He could be sure of her now. . . . That made him uneasy. What would happen to desire, if the little goad of fear was removed? Spence had been trained by his wife to believe that animal behaviour invariably has an end in view, however twisted; however bent out of shape. What if sex with his best beloved (since they weren't making babies, and it was no longer the forever inadequate confirmation that she belonged to him), began to seem unnecessary, a pointless exercise, a meaningless pleasure? An awful pang, as if the loss was real and already irrevocable, broke him out of his reverie.

He stood up. "Let's go, kid."

Jake was reluctant to leave the empty tomb, which was surrounded by a phalanx of home-made fake sunflowers, each with a photograph of a child's face in the centre. He admired the whole ensemble greatly: because, Spence guessed, he could imagine doing something like that himself. The greatest art in Europe had left Jake unimpressed, since he felt he had no stake in the enterprise.

"Can we take a picture of it?"

"'Fraid not. We didn't bring the camera."

"Can we come back with the camera, later?"

"Maybe."

"Maybe means no," muttered Jake under his breath, "Why not call a spade a spade?"

They went in search of the *gardienne*. She hadn't turned up to claim their rent in the morning. The manager of a municipal campsite usually operated out of the town hall, but this one had a house near that crossroads where the path through the wood came out. They were permitted to enter a stiff, funereal parlour. The registration form was filled in, with immense labour, by the skinny old lady and a very fat man, either her husband or her son, who was squelched immovable into a wheelback armchair at the parlour table. Jake made friends with a little dog. Spence stared at a huge ornate clock that seemed on the point of plunging to its death from the top shelf of an oak dresser laden with ugly china.

She didn't know anything about the Balinese Dancer. There was no such cat in the village. No such cat had been reported missing by any campers. She could not recall when pitch 16 had last been used, and rejected the suggestion that she might consult her records. She supposed he might report this lost cat to the police, but she saw no reason why he should give himself the trouble. The police here knew their business, they would not be interested in his story.

Spence began to get very strange vibes.

He changed the subject. They chatted a little about the political situation, always a safe topic for non-specific head-shaking and sighing. Spence paid for two nights' camping and recovered his passport. "Let's go back through the woods," he said, when they were outside.

"We haven't finished exploring,"

"Your Mom's been alone long enough."

Sitting on the floor in the sanitaires, Anna scrubbed her legs with an emery paper glove. She blew away a dust of powdered hair from the page of Ramone Holyrod's essays, keeping the book open with the balls of her feet.

> . . . like the civil rights movement, feminism has achieved certain goals at a wholly destructive price. It has created an aspirational female middle class whose interests are totally at odds with the interests of the female masses, and with the original aim of the movement. Successful women trade on their femininity. They have no desire to see difference between the sexes eroded, they foster and elaborate that same difference which condemns millions of other women . . .

Anna was catching up. She'd once known Ramone personally, but she'd never had time to read books like this. She worked moisturising lotion into the newly smooth bare skin and removed a vagrant drop, the colour of melted chocolate ice cream, from the text. Feminist rage, she decided, had not changed much since she last looked. She turned Prefutural Tension face down and went to the mirror above the sinks; took her kohl pencil from the family washbag, stretched the skin of her left upper eyelid taut by applying a firm fingertip to the outer corner, and drew a fine solid line along the base of her lashes. Mirrors had begun to be haunted by the ghost of Anna's middle age, by whispers from magazines saying *don't drink and go to bed early*. But what good did it do if you couldn't sleep? There was always something to prevent her. Last night, the faint smell of that dump . . .

The campsite was completely quiet. The couple with the big trailer had left at dawn. If they were intent on skipping the rent they needn't have bothered. The gardienne here obviously wasn't the conscientious kind. Anna turned a soft brush in a palette of eye-shadow, a shade of yellow that was nearly gold, and dusted it across the whole area of her eyes: to lift and brighten the natural tone of her tanned skin, and correct the slightly too-deep sockets.

Ramone had a nerve. A professional feminist, and accusing other people of trading on their feminine identity. Maquillage, she thought (carefully stroking the mascara wand upwards, under her lower lashes) is not a female trait. I can give you chapter and verse on that, Ramone my dear. It's a male sexual gesture. As you well know. The public world is male, and to deal with it we all have to adopt male behaviour. You and me both, Ramone, we have to display: strut our stuff or perish, publish or be damned. It's not your fault or mine, sister. It's simply a question of whose head is on the coin. You want to work for the company, you wear the uniform. Where do you get off, claiming that you can speak from some *female* parade ground, where competition and challenge are unknown? Balls to that.

She gazed at the face of Caesar in the mirror. Wide brow, pointed chin, black eyes, golden brown skin: Anna Senoz. *Yes, I'm married. No, I didn't change my name. Why didn't you change your name? Because I didn't want to. Next question.* . . . She thought of her ancestors, Spanish jews, pragmatic converts to Christianity. Discreet, tolerated aliens. I should have strutted my two-fisted stuff more, and used less eyeliner. Ramone's right. Power dressing is a short term solution, but in the end a female who paints *"I am sexually available"* all over herself is offering submission, not issuing a challenge. That's the animal truth, and it can't be subverted. I was giving hopelessly confused signals all these years, and now I pay the price. She had collected suitors, not subordinates. She had been envied, desired, but never feared. And when she needed to fight she had none of the right responses. It's Spence's fault, she thought. Before Spence, I liked sex and I hoped I was attractive enough to get my share, but I had no more paranoia about my personal appearance than if I was Albert Einstein. He told me I was beautiful. He got me hooked on femininity, and it's done me no good at all.

Anna was not a professional feminist, but she wasn't a political moron. She had known there would be trouble. She had known that her team's paper (along with the simultaneous presentation on superjanet) would be challenged, questioned; angrily dismissed in some quarters. The erosion of difference between the sexes, though it might not interest Ramone's *aspirational female middle class*, had been a hot topic in Anna's world for several years. At the molecular level, that is. Anna knew that she'd made an extraordinary proposition. She'd even joked that the news might hit the tabloids. It had never occurred to her that she could lose her job.

She remembered the room, her boss's office. It was May time, but it had been raining and the sky was grey. Outside his floor length windows wet tassels of sycamore flower littered the Biology car-park. Across uncut grass, starred with buttercups and daisies, the small patch of woodland beside Material Sciences was brilliant with new leaf. She could not understand what she'd done wrong. *But it isn't a scare story,* she protested. *What I'm saying is that this isn't like global warming or holes in the ozone layer. It's not a punishment, it's not an awful warning. Something is happening, that's all. It's just evolution.* She was floundering. She had prepared the wrong script. She had been expecting to discuss tactics: how can we use this notoriety, how can we make it work for us? But he was furious. *What does it matter?* she begged. *It's not as if anything's going to change overnight. This is not something any one will consciously experience. This will be like . . . coming down from the trees.*

Anna had demonstrated that the future belongs neither to women nor to men but to some new creature, now inexorably on its way. She had spoken this as fact, she had nothing to defend. Suddenly she was fighting for her life, but she couldn't concentrate. She had found herself staring over his shoulder at the green world outside, trying to hear the birds in the little wood. There would be blackbirds, robins, perhaps a wren. The chorus was sadly depleted. Did he say *your views are not welcome in this department?* I don't have any "views" protested Anna. . . . Did he say he *will not be renewing your contract?* She was thinking of the songthrush and the cuckoo, those sweet and homely voices forever stilled. *Don't you see that the house is on fire? Our house is on fire, the little ones are dead. How can you jabber on about these ridiculous trivialities?* Now she was crying. He gave her a paper tissue from a box he kept in his desk drawer. "I'm sorry," he said. "I'm sorry, but . . ."

The door of the sanitaires creaked, and in walked the lost cat. He glanced around, and came to question Anna with a diffident *mrrrow?* She wiped her eyes. Of course I reacted as stupidly as possible. It was bitter to think how her loss had made her into even more of a woman. Waiting here, grooming herself for comfort, doing the domestic, while Spence went out in public to deal with the world. "I'll be taking to the veil next," she told the cat gloomily. And indeed, there'd been times in the last months when she'd have been glad to hide her head, to retire under a big thick blanket and never come out.

The yurt was too hot and the campsite was too empty. Neither of them offered any secure shelter. She took Ramone's essays next door to the utility room, where their washing was still going round, and sat on the cool tiled floor to read. The Burmese Temple Cat came with her, but couldn't settle. He paced and cried. "Poor thing," Anna sympathised. "Poor thing. They let you down didn't they. They abandoned you, and you haven't an idea what you did wrong. Never mind, maybe we'll find them."

But his grief disturbed her. It was too close to her own.

Spence and Jake walked through the woods. Spence was wondering what the hell *is* the approved *Académie Française* term for "modem", anyhow? For God's sake, even the Vatican accepts "modem". If it's good enough for the Pope. . . . He'd have to ask Anna. But he wasn't sure there had been any misunderstanding at the Post Office. It was possible the postmistress really had been telling him, *don't hang around.* He was still getting very strange vibes from that conversation with the gardienne. Maybe something final and terrible had happened at last. France and England had declared war on each other, and tourists were liable to be rounded up as undesirable aliens. He wasn't sure that war between two states of the European Union was technically possible. It would have to be a civil war. No problem with that: a very popular global sport. In fact, he wouldn't be a bit surprised. The only problem would be for the French and English governments to handle anything so *organised.* Have to get the telecoms to work again first . . .

They had reached the dump. That smell surrounded them. Crowds of flies hummed and muttered, and the surface of the wide, garbage filled hollow drew Spence's eyes. He was looking for something that he had seen last night in the twilight, seen and not quite registered. The flies buzzed. He had stopped walking. Jake was looking up at him, wrinkling his nose: puzzled that an adult could be so indifferent to the ripe stink.

He handed over his laptop; Jake was already carrying the bread. "Go on back. I'll be along in a minute. I want to check something." "But I want to see what you find!" "I'm not going to find anything. I'm just going to take a leak." "I want a wee too." "No you don't. Get going. Tell Anna I won't be long."

Spence waited until he was sure the child wasn't going to turn back. Then he went to investigate the buried wreckage. He found the remains of a caravan. It had been burned out, quite recently, having been stripped first (as far as he could tell) of any identification. He crouched on the flank of a big plastic drum that had once contained fertiliser, and pondered. Someone had rolled a wrecked mobile home into this landfill, having removed the plates; and covered it over. What did that prove? It didn't prove anything, except that he was letting himself get spooked. "I'm overtired" he said aloud, scowling. "Been on the road too long." But the garbage had shifted when he was clambering over it, and the dump refused to let him cling to his innocence. He climbed down from his perch, and discovered that the suggestive-looking bunch of twigs that he'd spotted really was a human hand.

It had been a woman's hand, and not young. It was filthy and the rats had been at it, but he could still see lumpy knuckles and the paler indentations left by her rings. He found a stick and pried at the surrounding layers of junk until he had uncovered her face. There wasn't very much left of that. He squatted, looking down: remembering Father Moynihan in his coffin, like something carved out of yellow wax. His own father too, but he had no memory of that dead body. He'd been too young: not allowed to look.

"What did you do?" he whispered. "Too rich, too funny-looking? Wrong kind of car? Did you support the wrong football team?"

The flies buzzed. Around him, beyond the thin woodland, stretched the great emptiness, all the parched, desolate rural heartlands of Europe, where life was strained and desperate as in any foundering city. All the lost little towns starved of hope, where people turned into monsters without anything showing on the outside.

Anna groped for potatoes in the sack in the back of the car, brought out another that was too green to eat and chucked it aside. He knows nothing. He hasn't a clue about the backbiting, the betrayals, all the internal politics. Spence admires my work in a romantic way, but in the end it's just something that keeps me away from home. Maybe he's my wife. She felt the descant of male to female, the slipping and sliding between identities that had been natural and understood surely by most people, for years and years. It was Anna's boss who was crazy. How could anyone be *angry* about an arrangement of chemicals? The sack was nearly empty. *What's happening to my french beans? The lettuces will all be shot.* She was pining for her garden. It was so difficult to get hold of good fresh vegetables on the road. The prepacked stuff in the hypermarkets was an insult, but the farmers' markets weren't much better. Not when you were a stranger and didn't know your way around. We'll go home. I'll pull myself together, start fighting my corner the way I should have done at the start. We'll have to go back soon, she assured herself, knowing Spence's silent resistance. Jake has to go to school. She saw him come out of the wood. He went straight to the sanitaires, vanished for several minutes and slowly came towards her. He sat on the rim of the hatchback. There were drops of water in his hair, and his hands were wet.

"Where's Jake?"

"In the playground. What's the matter? You look sick."

"I found a body in the dump."

They both stared at the distant figure of the child. He was climbing on the knotted rope, singing a song from a french tv commercial. Anna felt claws of shock dig into her spine, as if something expected but ridiculously forgotten had jumped out, *Boo!* from behind a door.

"You mean a human body?"

"Yes. I could only find one, but I think there must be two." He imagined a couple, a middle-aged early-retirement couple, modestly well heeled, children if any long ago departed. Spending the summer en plein air, the way the French love to do: with their cat. "I covered it over again. I was afraid to root around, but there's a caravan too. I'm not joking. It's true."

"You'd better show me."

Spence gasped, and shook his head. "I can't."

"Why not?"

"Because we can't let Jake see that, and we can't leave him alone."

Anna nodded. She went to the front of the car, and started searching under the seats and in the door pockets.

"What are you looking for?"

"The camera." She brought it out. "I'll take pictures. Will it be easy for me to find?"

It was about the same time of day as it had been when they arrived. Shortly, Jake noticed that his father had returned, and came running over. The Balinese Dancer ran along beside him. "Where's Mummy?"

"She's gone to check something."

Jake's eyes narrowed. "Her too?" Spence had forgotten he'd used the exact same words at the dump, when he sent the kid on alone. "Is it something about my cat?"

Balinese Dancer looked up. Spence had a terrible, irrational feeling that the cat knew. He knew what Spence had seen; and that there was no hope any more.

"Don't start getting ideas."

For most of the time that Anna was away it didn't cross his mind that she was in danger. Then it did and he spent a very unhappy quarter of an hour, playing Scrabble with Jake while racking his brains to recover every word he'd spoken in that town, especially in his rash interview with the *gardienne*: praying to God he'd said nothing to rouse anyone's suspicions. They washed the potatoes. Spence cut them up, chopped an onion and some garlic, opened a can of tomatoes and one of chickpeas. He put olives in a bowl and spread the picnic table-cloth. He didn't light the stove until everything was ready, because they were running out of gas. At last Anna came out of that grisly wood.

"Shall I start cooking?"

"I'm going to have a shower," she said.

While Anna put Jake to bed Spence did the washing up, and stored away the almost untouched potato stew. He checked the car over, and gathered a few stray belongings from the shrivelled grass. Their camp was compact. One modest green hatchback, UK plates, anonymous middle class brand. One mushroom shaped tent dwelling. No bicycles, no surf-boards. No tv aerial dish, no patio furniture. The sky was overcast, blurred with moon silver in the east. How often had they camped like this beside some still and secret little town? That place in Italy on the hilltop, most certainly a haunt of vampires . . .

The cat wove at his ankles, and followed him indoors. Inside, the yurt was a single conical space that could be divided by cunning foldaway partitions. It was furnished with nomad simplicity and comfort: their bed, rugs, books; small useful items of gear. There was no mere decoration, no more than if they'd been travelling on the steppes with Ghengis Khan. Spence set down the wine bottle, two glasses and the rest of the bread. Anna stepped out of Jake's section and sealed it behind her. They sat on the floor with the lamp turned low, and looked at the pictures she had taken. She'd uncovered the body further and taken several shots of the head and torso, the hands and wrists; and then the whole ensemble, the wrecked caravan. She hadn't looked for another corpse, but she thought Spence was right. It was probably there.

"You think it was locals?" she asked.

Spence told her about the postmistress, and the *gardienne*. A one street town wrapped in guilty silence: and the behaviour of the other campers, the ones who had left at dawn, so quickly and quietly. "I'm sure they know about it. Maybe someone had an accident. Someone ran into them and wrecked them, found they were dead and got scared . . ."

"And took the woman's rings. And gouged out her eyes. And tied her up."

Anna touched the preview screen, advancing from shot to shot until she found the woman's face. She moved it into close-up, but their camera was not equal to this kind of work. The image blurred into a drab hallowe'en mask: crumpled plastic; black eye holes.

"Well," said Spence, "It's been all around us. We finally managed to run right into it. The town that eats tourists. Of course in the good old U S of A we're cool about this kind of thing. Vampire towns, ghoul towns, whole counties run by serial-killer aliens. We take it for granted. Poor Balinese Dancer, I'm afraid your people definitely aren't coming back."

"You can't call him that," she said. "He's not a Balinese. He's a Birman. Don't you believe me? Hook up the cd drive and we can look him up in Jake's encyclopedia—"

"I believe you. But why can't I *call* him Balinese?"

"*Because you're doing it to annoy me.* And . . . we don't need that."

In the direct look she gave him, the hostilities that had rumbled under their un-negotiated peace finally came to an end. Spence sighed. "Oh, okay. I won't."

"Is there any wine left?" asked Anna. He handed her the bottle. She poured some into their glasses, broke a chunk of bread and ate it.

"So what are we going to do? Report our finds to the gendarmes?"

"Don't be stupid," said Anna.

"Not here, definitely not. But in Lyons maybe."

"They wouldn't do anything. You know they wouldn't. City flics don't come looking for trouble in the *deserte rural.*"

The rural desert. That was what the French called their prairie band. Mile upon mile of wheat and maize and sunflowers: all of it on death row as an economic activity, having lived just long enough to kill off most of the previous ecology. And destroy a lot of human lives.

"Okay, then we could stick around here and do a little investigation for ourselves."

The cat was sitting diffidently outside the circle of lamplight, his eyes moving from face to face. Spence's heart went out to him. "Try to find out who the cat's folks were, where they came from, why this happened to them. Uncover some fetid tale or other, maybe get one or other of ourselves tortured and killed as well; or maybe Jake—"

Anna grimaced wryly. "No thanks."

"Or we could do what they never do in the movies. Stop the thrilling plot before it starts. Walk on by."

She switched off the camera and stayed for a long time staring at the grey floor of the yurt, elbows on her knees and chin in her hands. She had turned the dead face from side to side, without flinching from her task. *This is the truth. It must be examined, described.* "Spence, I have a terrible feeling. It's about my paper. I started thinking this when I was looking at her, when I was recording her death. Suppose . . . Suppose the tabloids aren't loopy and my boss isn't deranged. Suppose I really did do something appalling by publishing that. And while we've been away, while we've been cut off from all the news, the world has finally been going over the edge, because of what I did?"

"The whole place was going mad before you published, kid. The end of the world as we know it started a long time ago."

"Yes, Spence dear. Exactly. That's what my paper says."

Spence took a slug from the wine bottle, neglecting the glass that was poured for him. That sweet tone of invincible intellectual superiority, *when it was friendly*, always made him go weak at the knees.

"Would you like to do sex?" he hazarded, across the tremulous lamplight.

"Like plague victims," said Anna huskily. "Rutting in the streets, death all around."

"Okay, but would you?"

Flash of white knickers in the twilight. Nothing's sure. Every time could be the last.

"Yes."

When they were both done, both satisfied, Spence managed to fall asleep. He dreamed he was clinging to the side of a runaway train, that was racing downhill in the dark. Anna was in his arms and Jake held between them. He knew he had to leap from this train before it smashed, holding his family in his arms. But he was too terrified to let go.

They had pitched the yurt at dusk, in a service area campsite. The great road thundered by the scrubby expanse of red grit, where tents and trucks and vans stood cheek by jowl, without a tree or a blade of grass in sight. The clientele was mixed. There were gens de voyage, with their pitches staked out in the traditional, aggressive washing lines; colourful new age travellers trying to look like visitors from the stone age, respectable itinerant workers in their tidy camper vans; truckdrivers asleep in their cabs. Among them were quite a few people like Anna and Jake and Spence, turned back from the channel ports by the fishing-dispute blockade; who had wisely moved inland from the beaches.

Spence was removing the cassette player from the car, so he could re-fit the broadband receiver that would give them access to the great big world again. The dusk was no problem, as this campsite was lit by enormous gangling floodlights, that seemed to have been bought second hand from a football stadium. But of course the player had turned obstinate. He was lying on his back, legs in the yard and face squished in the leg space under the dashboard, getting rusty metal dust in his eyes and struggling with some tiny recalcitrant screws. Chuck, ever fascinated and helpful when there was work going on, did his best to assist by sitting on the passenger seat and patting the screws that *had* come out into the crack at the back of the cushion. Something thumped near his head. He wriggled out. Anna had returned from her mission with a lumpy burlap sack.

"What's in there?"

"Potatoes, courgettes-I-mean-zucchini and string beans. But the beans are pure string."

"Still, that's pretty good. What did you have to do?"

The channel tunnel had been down, so to speak, for most of the summer. This new interruption of the ferry services had compounded everyone's problems. Hypermarchés along the coast had turned traitor, closing their doors to all but the local population. The more enterprising of the stranded travellers were resorting to barter.

"Nothing too difficult. First aid. Dietary advice to an incipient diabetic, she needs an implant but diet will help; and I'm attending to a septic cut."

"This is weird. You can't practice medicine You're a molecular biologist."

Anna rubbed her bare brown shoulder, where the sack had galled her; and shrugged. "Let me see. *First do no harm.* Well, I have no antibiotics, no antimalarials, genecarrier viruses or steroids, so that's all right. I have aspirin, I know how to reduce a fracture, and I wash my hands a lot. What more can you ask?"

"My God." He groped for the smaller screwdriver, which had escaped into camping-trip-morass. "Could you give me some assistance for a moment. Since you're here?"

"No, because I don't want you to do that."

"But I'm doing it anyway."

"Good luck to you," she said, without rancour. "It's mostly pure noise, in my opinion."

At bedtime Anna listened while Jake read to her the story of the Burmese Temple cat called Sinh, who was an oracle. He lived with a priest called

Mun-Ha, and they were both very miserable because Burma was being invaded. When Mun-Ha died, the goddess Tsun-Kyankse transfused Mun-Ha's spirit into Sinh. His eyes turned blue as sapphires, his nose and feet and tail turned dark as the sacred earth and the rest of him turned gold, except for the tips of his paws — which were touching Mun-Ha's white hair at the moment the priest died. Then Sinh transfused his power into the rest of the priests, and they went and saved Burma.

"Do you know what an oracle is?"

"Yeah," he answered drowsily. "It's a little boat."

Spence finished up, and repaired to the bar. He ordered two *pression* and took them to a table by the doors that he already thought of as his and Anna's table, because that was where they'd sat when they came in for a drink before setting up. It was a large and comfortable establishment, rather dimly lit; with absolutely no pretensions. Baby-foot in the games room, pizzas and frites and sandwiches readily available. Yes, he thought. We could live here. The room was crowded, but not oppressively stuffed. The raucous clatter of conversation, mostly French, soon blended into a soothing, encompassing roar like the sound of the ocean: laughter or the clink of glassware occasionally spurting up like spray.

We *could* live here, he fantasized. In this twilight . . . imagining the blockade stretching into months and years; imagining the actual no-kidding disintegration had begun. Which of course was nonsense. Anna with her home-medicine manual could become a quack doctor. Maybe I could sell information? He dallied with the idea of describing Anna as a *wisewoman*, but rejected it. Call a spade a spade. This is not the dawning of the magical, nurturing female future. This is the same road we've been travelling for so long: going down into the dark. Chuck had followed him from the car and was sitting on the chair next to Spence, looking around, taking it all in with his usual assured and gentle gaze. The young woman from the bar came by with a tray of glasses. Spence had a moment's anxiety, in case his companion was going to get thrown out. He was respectably vaccinated and tattooed now. They'd managed to get this done in the same town where they'd despatched (this was the compromise they'd reached) an anonymous tip-off, and prints of Anna's photographs, to the police in the regional capital. However, he might not be welcome in the bar.

But she'd only stopped to admire. "What do you call him?" she asked.

"Chuck Prophet."

The girl laughed, effortlessly balancing her tray on one thin muscular arm, and bending to rub the Birman's delectably soft, ruffled throat. "That's an unusual name for a cat."

"He's an unusual cat," explained Spence.

She moved on. Chuck had accepted her caress the way he took any kind of attention: sweetly, but a little distracted, a little disappointed at the touch of a hand that was not the hand he waited for. The moment she was gone he resumed his eager study of the crowd, his silver-blue eyes searching hopefully: ears alert for a voice and a step that he would never hear again. Still keeping the faith: confident that soon normal service would be restored.

"Prefutural Tension": Gwyneth Jones's Gradual Apocalypse

Veronica Hollinger

1.

I could argue that [science fiction] is the only fiction about the present, everything else is historical romance. But at this particular moment in time, reality and science fiction are moving into such close conjunction that science fiction is no longer the strange reflection and artistic elaboration of current preoccupations: the mirror and the actuality have almost become one.[1]

Gwyneth Jones, born in Manchester, England, in 1952, is a successful full-time writer who has been publishing adult science fiction more or less steadily since the mid-1980s. She pursues an even more prolific career as Ann Halam, writer of sf, fantasy, and horror novels for young readers. Jones's science fiction is widely admired for its intensity and its complex intelligence, as well as for its creation of highly original imagined worlds.

Jones is one of the most significant genre writers working in England today — and this at a time when British science fiction is enjoying what many enthusiasts are referring to as a "Boom."[2] While it is probably inaccurate to identify Jones as a "Boom" writer, her career certainly intersects that of many of the writers — including China Miéville, M. John Harrison, Justina Robson, Stephen Baxter, Jon Courtenay Grimwood, and Ken MacLeod — who are closely associated with the current resurgence. Given both the quality and quantity of Jones's writing over the past two decades, it is a safe assumption that she will continue to produce important genre work even if the current "Boom" should go bust.[3]

Since the early 1990s, Jones's writing has been recognized by a variety of awards and award nominations, including two World Fantasy Awards for her collection *Seven Tales and a Fable* (1995) and the Dracula Society's Children of the Night Award for *The Fear Man* (as Ann Halam, 1995). Her novel *White Queen*, a complex and challenging story about first contact and gender politics — and the first of a trilogy that includes *North Wind* (1994) and *Phoenix Café* (1997) — was nominated in 1991 for Britain's Arthur C. Clarke Award. Jones won this prestigious award in 2001 for *Bold As Love*, the first in a projected five-volume series of hybrid sf/fantasy novels set in a near-future United Kingdom in the process of political dissolution. At the time of writing, this series also includes *Castles Made of Sand* (2002) and *Midnight Lamp* (2003); and *Band of Gypsies* (2005); a fifth novel, *Stone Free*, will eventually complete the sequence. In a 2002 interview, Jones described the series — somewhat facetiously — as "a Human Comedy of the near future, a global political romance (based in England) with science-fictional and fantasy elements."[4] *Life* (2004) won the 2005 Philip K. Dick Award.

In 1991 *White Queen* was also cowinner — with Eleanor Arnason's *A Woman of the Iron People*, another brilliantly revisionary tale of alien contact and gender difference — of the first James Tiptree, Jr. Award for science fiction and fantasy that explores and expands our understanding of gender. Jones's work has continued to attract Tiptree Award attention. She was shortlisted for *North Wind* in 1994, for "Balinese Dancer" in 1997, and for "La Cenerentola" in 1998. "Balinese Dancer" was reprinted in the fifteenth (1998) edition of Gardner Dozois's *The Year's Best Science Fiction*.

Jones is one of a small group of influential sf and speculative writers — including Joanna Russ, Samuel R. Delany, and Ursula K. Le Guin — who also publish as theorists, critics, and reviewers of the field.[5] Her thoughtful and informed pieces have appeared in a range of venues, including *Foundation: The International Review of Science Fiction, Science Fiction Studies*, and the *New York Review of Science Fiction*. In addition, she has participated several times as guest writer at scholarly conferences, such as the 1995 "Virtual Futures" conference at Warwick University and the 2001 "Celebration of British Science Fiction" conference at the University of Liverpool. Her nonfiction collection *Deconstructing the Starships: Science, Fiction and Reality* (1999) demonstrates the range and and diversity of her interests in both literary and scientific theories, as well as in the fortunes of both feminism and science fiction. In her review of *Deconstructing the Starships*, Wendy Pearson notes its consistent attention to gender politics "in the context of a coherent feminist analysis of science fiction as a genre."[6]

2.

Everything is *not* all right. The Bomb has not exterminated us, nor has the Virus; aliens have not landed. . . . And yet, unspeakable and portentous events have occurred, are occurring, as we were looking the other way, or even watching directly.[7]

"Balinese Dancer" appeared originally in the November 1997 issue of *Asimov's Science Fiction Magazine,* an American venue that confers an imprimatur of sf authenticity. Set in a very ordinary world that almost exactly mirrors this one, the story is rigorously realist in its depiction of the psychological and emotional drama of its characters; in the context of a fictional scientific discovery of cataclysmic, if immaterial, proportions, it both comments on current environmental issues and raises some complex questions about human sex and gender difference.

Very few signs in the world of "Balinese Dancer" signify "the future": Jake's "headband tv," is — at least in sf terms — an already rather outdated piece of (fictional) technology and it is the only unfamiliar techno-artifact mentioned in the story. Spence listens to music on an obsolete tape machine described as "an aged relic," and the family tent — a yurt — is positively primitive. This is, after all, the story of an ordinary family camping trip. On the surface, nothing much seems to differentiate this family's world from our own, except, perhaps, that certain economic and environmental problems appear to have worsened. At the same time, Anna's discovery that human sexual difference is slowly and quietly fading away is news that, for many people, threatens the very bedrock of humanity's understanding of itself.

In keeping with issues of growing concern over the past few decades, one strand of "Balinese Dancer" dramatizes the increasingly catastrophic consequences of environmental degradation. As Jones argues in one of her reviews, "No invention is necessary [to end the world.] . . . [T]he pressure of so many lives of the kind we live now will provide the wars . . . the degraded farmland, everything. It needs nothing else. Nothing complicated, nothing weird."[8] Like much late-twentieth-century science fiction — including feminist novels such as Octavia Butler's apocalyptic *Parable of the Sower* (1992), set in an environmentally devastated California, and Marge Piercy's *He, She and It* (1992), a novel that incorporates Donna Haraway's cyborg-feminist politics into a cyberpunk-inflected future where the planet has become almost uninhabitable — "Balinese Dancer" is a story about the terrible fragility of the natural world.[9]

In the story's opening scenes, Anna and Spence must abandon their plans to stay at a particular campsite because "the site was full of *gens de voyage,* a polite French term for the armies of homeless persons with huge battered mobile homes, swarms of equally battered and despairing kids, and packs of savage dogs, that were becoming such a feature of rural holidays in La Belle France." The disturbing signs of increasing social unrest render the characters' deep appreciation of the simple pleasures of camping and countryside particularly poignant:

Beyond the lower terrace of pitches they found a small lake, the still surface of the water glazed peach-colour by the sunset. Green wrought-iron benches stood beside a gravel path. Purple and yellow loosestrife grew in the long grass at the water's edge; dragonflies hovered. The hayfields beyond had been cut down to sonorous insect-laden turf; and in the distance a little round windmill stood up against the red glistening orb of the sun. (Jones, 308)

But the lake reeks of dead fish; there is passing reference to "the latest telecoms melt"; and the family's return home is delayed because of "the fishing-dispute blockade" that has paralyzed travel between French and English ports. These features of the fictional world provide a muted but significant backdrop to Anna's and Spence's attempts to deal with her traumatic job loss. More or less in the background as well is their horrific discovery, in the campsite dump, of two dead travelers and their burned-out trailer.

The uneasy lack of concern about or interest in these grisly murders on the part of the local people constitutes another dismal thread in the weave of gradual social decline that characterizes this future: "Around [Spence], beyond the thin woodland, stretched the great emptiness, all the parched, desolate rural heartlands of Europe, where life was strained and desperate as in any foundering city. All the lost little towns starved of hope, where people turned into monsters without anything showing on the outside."

Even as Anna experiences the dislocation of losing her job because of her "sensational" scientific discovery, she realizes that her boss's panicked response is completely misplaced:

Did he say *your views are not welcome in this department?* I don't have any "views" protested Anna. . . . She was thinking of the songthrush and the cuckoo, those sweet and homely voices forever stilled. *Don't you see that the house is on fire? Our house is on fire, the little ones are dead. How can you jabber on about these ridiculous trivialities?* (Jones, 316)

Jones is a self-described political writer, "more in sympathy with the ancient maniacs of the past, truffle-hunting for Utopia in the dirt of sf's lies, damned lies and sugared political indoctrination, than with the majority of my cool, hep-cat, morally neutral contemporaries."[10]

It is a nice irony that "Balinese Dancer" was published in the same year that Tony Blair's New Labour party was elected to power in Great Britain. In his analysis of the current fortunes of British science fiction, Roger Luckhurst maps the increasingly apolitical stance of the British cultural establishment over the past two decades. Most recently, this apathy has been encouraged by New Labour's operations of "cultural governance," that is, by the increasing involvement of government in shaping and regulating cultural policy. In Luckhurst's view, the result has been the "mainstreaming of oppositional culture"[11] in its increasing "conformity to the ideological vision of the political centre."[12]

For Luckhurst, many genre writers such as Jones, situated as they are on the margins of dominant culture, have more readily avoided this kind of co-optation and have sustained the kind of involvement in feminist/left/environmental politics that has been all but abandoned by artists working in the cultural mainstream. Luckhurst concludes that

> the genres undergoing inventive hybridization and regenerative "implosion" — Gothic, sf, and fantasy — experienced such a revitalization in the 1990s because genres could still find spaces outside the general de-differentiation or "mainstreaming" effect sought by the strategy of cultural governance. The low value accorded to the Gothic-sf-fantasy continuum allowed these genres to flourish largely below the radar of a cultural establishment often complicit, in complex ways, with this method of governance.[13]

In the course of his analysis, Luckhurst includes an appreciative reading of the first volumes of Jones's *Bold as Love* series, noting that "the ways in which the characters [who are musicians and artists] agonize over questions of compromise and resistance, incorporation and rejection, [makes] this work centrally engaged with the problems of cultural governance in a way few others outside sf/fantasy have addressed."[14]

3.

If gender is the social construction of sex, and if there is no access to this "sex" except by means of its construction, then it appears not only that sex is absorbed by gender, but that "sex" becomes something like a fiction, perhaps a fantasy.[15]

There is another and more subtle apocalypse at work in the world of "Balinese Dancer," the gender apocalypse of Anna's discovery that "the future belongs neither to women nor to men but to some new creature, now inexorably on its way." In her article "Sex: The Brains of Female Hyena Twins," Jones notes "the received wisdom" that "regards human gender as a given: one of the pillars of the universe."[16] While science has demonstrated that sex difference is "malleable" but "unambiguous,"[17] overwhelming evidence suggests that it is gender, not sex, that forms the basis of the social behaviors that are expected of individual women and men.[18] In Brian Attebery's ironic terms, "sexual differentiation is enforced with the special vigilance reserved for instilling what a culture believes to be natural."[19]

So deeply does gender permeate a person's sense of being human, however, that Anna's discovery is popularly read as a sign that humanity itself is undergoing a kind of gradual extinction. And while the conflicted history of gender relations might well suggest that this is an extinction devoutly to be desired, it nevertheless poses a radical threat to received ideas about what it means to be human. Anna's discovery is not, of course, about "just evolution." The gendered roles of women and men have always been constructed upon the conviction of direct, natural, and stable relations among physical/biological sex (embodiment), gender (the range of feminine and masculine behaviors performed in the sociocultural sphere), and sexual desire (an individual's particular orientation to a range of possible objects of desire — as a rule, all but heterosexual object choices are discouraged). The real impact of Anna's discovery lies in the implication that sexual difference, one of the foundations of human life, is transitory.

"Balinese Dancer" dramatizes two mutually exclusive interpretations of Anna's discovery. From her perspective as a microbiologist, it is the sign of a natural and neutral evolutionary process, one that is in stark contrast to the "unnatural" environmental disaster currently overtaking the world: "*Something is happening, that's all. It's just evolution*" (Jones, 316). This is a philosophical apocalypse with no immediate consequences; as Anna tells her supervisor, who is appalled by her discovery, "*It's not as if anything's going to change overnight. This is not something any one will consciously experience. This will be like . . . coming down from the trees*" (Jones, 316).

While Anna's science is concerned only with questions of biological sex, feminist studies such as Judith Butler's influential analyses of gender and performance have argued that the oppositional positions of women and men in almost every human culture are the result, not of sex (physical embodiment), but of the social and cultural valuations and expectations that have become attached to physical bodies. It is crucial to appreciate the force of social and cultural expectations in the construction of individual identities, to realize how deeply people's sense of themselves as individual subjects who are either "women" or "men" is informed by gender. For Jones, this is the real crux of the situation:

> If sexual behaviour and function are malleable, and yet sexual identity, *difference*, remains obstinately intact — which is what the science predicts and what we see happening around us — then we don't have two complementary sexes any more, each safe in its own niche. All there is left is gender: an us and them situ-

ation. Two tribes, separated by millennia upon millennia of grievances and bitterness, occupying the same territory and squabbling over the same diminished supply of resources.[20]

Jones has always written about the thorny entanglements of sex and gender. Her Tiptree Award–winning novel, White Queen (1991), published several years before "Balinese Dancer," provides a rich, although quite different, treatment of this "us and them situation." The action in White Queen is set against the backdrop of the "gender wars," one of a number of conflicts (including political and economic rivalries, and ethnic and religious hostilities) that have fragmented its near-future world. The arrival of the alien — and hermaphroditic — Aleutians poses a radical challenge to the gendered perspectives of the human characters of this world and threatens to destabilize its already fragile political and economic balance.

For readers of the novel, the Aleutians' comically skewed views on gender difference — in all their apparent illogicality and contingency — strongly suggest the same lack of logic and necessity in the constructions of human gender. In other words, White Queen dramatizes Jones's conviction that gender owes at least as much to social and cultural conditioning, in all its potential variations, as it does to anything like a predetermined "human nature." Not surprisingly, given that the Aleutians are hermaphroditic, their ideas about gender have nothing to do with sexed bodies; in fact, one of the aliens considers how differentiation by gender is "an idle, gossipy game":

> Feminine people . . . are the people who'd rather work through the night in the dark than call someone who can fix the light. . . . The kind of people who can't live without being needed but refuse to need anything from anyone. Masculine people, on the other hand, can never leave well enough alone, break things by way of improving them, will do absolutely anything for a kiss and a kind word. (121)[21]

Not surprisingly, the Aleutians have great difficulty appreciating the basis of human gender difference. The Aleutian Clavel tries to explain it in this way to his companions ("< >" indicates Aleutian nonverbal communication):

> <There are two nations. . . . One bears the others' children for them. They get called "Feminine"; and the obligate-parasites "Masculine." . . . >
>
> A division into parasites and childbearers was another peculiarity to add to their obsession with religion, their promiscuous mingling of formal and informal language, their horrid food. But the variation of human traits is wild and wide, even within a single nation.[22]

Jones also makes use of her Aleutians to imaginatively revise the (gendered) history of colonial power politics; it is no accident that much of the action in the novel takes place in Africa and Asia. In her article "Aliens in the Fourth Dimension," she remarks that she deliberately gave the Aleutians — inadvertent invaders and accidental colonizers — many of the features conventionally associated with the not-male, the not-Western, the not-victorious:

> I planned to give my alien conquerors the characteristics, all the supposed deficiencies, that Europeans came to see in their subject races in darkest Africa and the mystic East — "animal" nature, irrationality, intuition; mechanical incompetence, indifference to time, helpless aversion to theory and measurement: and I planned to have them win the territorial battle this time. It was no coincidence, for my purposes, that the same list of qualities or deficiencies — a nature closer to the animal, intuitive communication skills and all the rest of it — were and still are routinely awarded to *women*, the defeated natives, supplanted rulers of men, in cultures north and south, west and east, white and non-white, the human world over.[23]

In "Balinese Dancer," Anna and Spence lead lives that are proof both of the inaccuracies of simple gender binarism and of the indelible marks it leaves on individual identity. She is a physical scientist, while he is a writer of books for children; both are nurturing parents; each is intelligent, selfish, and giving. Like all of us, they are also complicit in the sex/gender system, enjoying its various advantages even as they recognize and decry its limitations and injustices. Spence takes pride in his ability to support the family through his writing; he secretly enjoys his occasional bouts of possessive jealousy. Anna finds psychological comfort in feminizing herself and has developed an emotional dependence on Spence's appreciation of her beauty. At the same time, she resents the specifically feminine way in which she has responded to her ruined career: "It was bitter to think how her loss had made her into even more of a woman. Waiting here, grooming herself for comfort, doing the domestic, while Spence went out in public to deal with the world."

"Balinese Dancer" directly addresses the conflicted situation of contemporary feminist politics when Anna considers passages from *Prefutural Tension*, the perfectly titled collection of essays by the fictional Ramone Holyrod. Holyrod's attack is aimed at professional women just like Anna: "Successful women trade on their femininity. They have no desire to see difference between the sexes eroded, they foster and elaborate that same difference which condemns millions of other women" (Jones, 314). Anna's response is an equally angry rebuttal of Holyrod's position: "The public world is male, and to deal with it we all have to adopt male behaviour. You and me both, Ramone, we have to display: strut our stuff or perish, publish or be damned. It's not your fault or mine, sister. It's simply a question of whose head is on the coin" (Jones, 315)

In answer to a question about how she came to write "Balinese Dancer," Jones explains:

> "Balinese Dancer" is associated with a novel I've written, a fictional biography of a woman scientist of genius (that's Anna); for which I've never found a publisher.[24] The tension in the novel is between Anna's detemination not to be defined as a feminist (she knows it would be poison to her career); her experience, which brings her up against all the gender-based disadvantages a woman in science can suffer; and her big idea — which, unfortunately for Anna, is embedded in sex science, and bound to stir up the kind of trouble she's avoided all her life. So . . . the fantasy-science is saying: women who resist gender stereotyping, who want to be regarded *primarily* as scientists, artists, whatever, will find their work itself keeps forcing them back to their sex . . . because the world doesn't have a "neutral" setting.[25]

Meanwhile, in "Balinese Dancer," a more pressing apocalyptic threat is looming for the populations of Europe, detailed in the gloomy descriptions of wasted nature and collapsing economies. According to Jones, in answer to the same question, "it's impossible to know if the gathering collapse of civilisation — suggested in the story — is in any sense directly caused by the DNA changes [discovered by Anna]; or if it's purely a cultural response; or if it's just co-incidentally the end of the road for the old way of doing things. I meant to leave the question open."[26] The fact that this is indeed a story about "the end of the road for the old way of doing things" leads to the deep irony in the final image of Chuck the cat, "ears alert for a voice and a step that he would never hear again. Still keeping the faith: confident that soon normal service would be restored" (Jones, 325).

4.

Masculine and feminine are correlatives which involve one another. I am sure of that — the quality and its negation are locked in necessity. But what the nature of masculine and the nature of feminine might be, whether they involve male and female . . . that I do not know. Though I have been both man and woman, still I do not know the answer to these questions.[27]

"Balinese Dancer" is one of an important body of feminist science fiction stories that directly addresses the tangled complexities of the sex/gender system, the same complexities that drive Angela Carter's transsexual "new Eve" to her helpless declaration: "What the nature of masculine and feminine might be . . . that I do not know." Even before the unprecedented entry of large numbers of women into the sf field in the 1970s, writers like C. L. Moore were challenging conventional ideas about the "natural" links between sex and gender; her Golden Age story, "No Woman Born" (1941), constructs a very early version of the female cyborg that suggests the possibility of a new posthuman way of moving beyond the strictures of gender. Charlotte Perkins Gilman's even earlier utopian fiction, *Herland* (1915), anticipated many later stories — for example, Joanna Russ's "When It Changed" (1972) and Suzy McKee Charnas's *Motherlines* (1978) — that imagine separatist worlds where women, no longer defined merely as "the opposite sex," can live fully human lives.[28]

In a minority of cases, feminist sf writers ground their stories in a bedrock belief in biological difference, somewhat like Anna's boss, who becomes "furious" when that bedrock proves to be — however gradually — in the process of eroding away. A classic example is Sally Miller Gearhart's lesbian-feminist *The Wanderground: Tales of the Hill Women* (1979), which espouses the "essential fundamental knowledge"[29] that women and men are virtually different species, and that men are inherently violent and destructive. Sheri Tepper offers a more nuanced treatment of this same position in her satirical utopia *The Gate to Women's Country* (1988), which recounts the history of a large-scale attempt to breed out male violence through a secret eugenics program.

Most feminist sf writers have tended to denaturalize the links between sex and gender, however, and to emphasize instead the ways that sociocultural forces shape female and male individuals into appropriately feminine women and appropriately masculine men.[30] Joanna Russ's great sf satire, *The Female Man* (1975), calls ironic attention to the powers and privileges inherent in the position "man" and the simultaneous disadvantages of the position "woman" when her narrator Joanna very sensibly decides that she too will inhabit the more powerful of the two roles:

> there is one and only one way to possess that in which we are defective, therefore that which we need, therefore that which we want.
>
> Become it.
>
> . . . I think I am a Man; I think you had better call me a Man; I think that you will write about me as a Man from now on and speak of me as a Man and employ me as a Man and recognize child-rearing as a Man's business; you will think

of me as a Man and treat me as a Man until it enters your . . . head that *I am a man.* (And you are a woman.) . . .

If you don't, by God and all the Saints, *I'll break your neck.*[31]

"Balinese Dancer" invites readers to think of a human subject even more impossible than Russ's female man, a subject for whom sexual difference will have become irrelevant. From this perspective, the story — as well as the novels in Jones's *White Queen* trilogy — shares some ground with a number of earlier stories that use the figure of the androgyne to highlight how deeply the binary perspective of gender marks people's deepest understandings about themselves and about the world.

Ursula K. Le Guin's *The Left Hand of Darkness* (1969) and Marge Piercy's *Woman on the Edge of Time* (1976) are two of the best known of these: Le Guin's alien Gethenians spend most — although not all — of their lives as ungendered subjects, and Piercy's future utopians have all but obliterated human gender differences, not least through the technologization of human reproduction.[32] Jones's "new creature, now inexorably on its way" is not dissimilar to Le Guin's androgynous Gethenians — although, even more so than they, it will have to be conceived as outside the feminine/masculine binary altogether; the categories themselves will have become extinct.

When asked to comment on the idea of androgyny in the context of her story, Jones notes that

> when you remove the gender divide you don't get people who are "both sexes at once" or people who are "neither men nor women." What you've removed is the either/or, the binary opposition, so it's *gone*, it's no longer an issue. The science I studied for ["Balinese Dancer"] . . . left me feeling that sexuality, left to itself so to speak, is more of a mosaic. Maybe my sexual-politics utopia would be a place where the *mosaic* of human sexuality was the accepted background theory, in place of the Great Divide.[33]

"Balinese Dancer" invites us to imagine an unimaginable human future. If, as Jones has remarked, "Once we start taking something of this order apart, we never manage to fit the pieces together again, quite the way they were before,"[34] then it is worth considering how the story itself participates in the most radical of deconstructions. The biological foundations of humanity are not static and sexual difference has its own evolutionary history, just as gender difference has its history in culture. History assures us that the present is different from the past. Science fiction assumes that the only certainty about the future is that it too will be different. And feminism is a politics of change.

NOTES

1. Gwyneth Jones, *Deconstructing the Starships: Science, Fiction and Reality* (Liverpool: University of Liverpool Press, 1999), vii.

2. The term "Boom" began to circulate a few years ago among British sf readers and scholars to mark a perceived resurgence of creativity and productivity on the part of a new generation of British sf writers, most of whom came to prominence during the 1980s and 1990s. As Istvan Csicsery-Ronay Jr. notes, "Not since the New Wave have British writers held such a commanding position in the genre." Istvan Csicsery-Ronay Jr., "Editorial Introduction: The British SF Boom," *Science Fiction Studies* 30 (November 2003): 353.

3. Few women writers are associated with the current British sf "Boom," in part, because many are writing fantasy rather than science fiction, while others are producing work for young readers (as does Jones in her alternate career as Ann Halam). Mark Bould also suggests that this situation reflects "a perennial problem in sf that has been exacerbated by the collapse of overtly feminist sf publishing and the failure of mainstream sf publishing to provide adequate replacement venues. . . . And then there is the Angela Carter Effect: many of the best contemporary women writers find that they either do not need sf or can achieve sf effects without recourse to genre publishing." Mark Bould, "Bould on the Boom," *Science Fiction Studies* 29 (July 2002): 310.

4. Andrew M. Butler, "Going Uphill: An Interview with Gwyneth Jones," *Femspec* 5.1 (2004): 242.

5. See, for example, Russ's *To Write Like a Woman: Essays in Feminism and Science Fiction* (Bloomington: Indiana University Press, 1995); Delany's *Silent Interviews: On Language, Race, Sex, Science Fiction, and Some Comics* (Hanover, N.H.: Wesleyan University Press, 1994); and Le Guin's *Dancing at the Edge of the World: Thoughts on Words, Women, Places* (New York: Grove, 1989).

6. Wendy Pearson, "Taking Apart SF: Gwyneth Jones's *Deconstructing the Starships: Science, Fiction and Reality*," *Strange Horizons* (10 September 2001), <http://www.strangehorizons.com/2001/20010910/taking_apart_SF.shtml> (3 January 2005). Pearson concludes on a note of high praise: "Anyone who is interested in SF, in what it is and how it works and in how sf writers think and write about their own field, will find *Deconstructing the Starships* an invaluable addition to their collection. It is a book which combines the best traditions of informed critical thought and engagement with the ideas of academic criticism, especially postmodernism, with a readable, trenchant and witty style."

7. James Berger, *After the End: Representations of Post-Apocalypse* (Minneapolis: University of Minnesota Press, 1999), 217.

8. Jones, *Deconstructing the Starships*, 176.

9. *Parable of the Sower* and *He, She and It* are also significant for their sophisticated attention to issues of race and ethnicity, especially in terms of how racial and ethnic politics are interwoven with gender politics in the construction of individual subjects. Butler, one of the very few African American women who works full-time as an sf writer, has produced a body of work strongly committed to examining how race intersects with gender to produce both character and conflict.

Although Piercy is probably better known for her poetry and for her realist novels than for her occasional forays into the sf field, she has long been interested in exploring both Jewish and Latina ethnicities in her fiction. While "Balinese Dancer" does not directly touch on these issues, Jones's awareness of and interest in questions of racial and cultural diversity in the context of increasing globalization is apparent in novels such as *White Queen*, to which I shall return below.

10. Jones, *Deconstructing the Starships*, 23.

11. Roger Luckhurst, "Cultural Governance, New Labour, and the British SF Boom," *Science Fiction Studies* 30 (November 2003): 420.

12. Ibid., 419. Luckhurst acknowledges that "political protest has revived and proliferated in diverse forms in post-1997 Britain" even as it has all but disappeared within the increasingly co-opted sphere of the culture industries (422).

13. Ibid., 423.

14. Ibid., 428.

15. Judith Butler, *Bodies That Matter: On the Discursive Limits of "Sex"* (New York: Routledge, 1993), 5.

16. Jones, *Deconstructing the Starships*, 99.

17. Ibid., 105.

18. In very broad terms, "gender" here refers to the specific social category (feminine, masculine) that is assigned to a human individual on the basis of her/his prior assignment to a specific biological category or "sex" (female, male). The result of these twin assignments is the production of human subjects who are either "women" or "men." Traditional understandings of sex and gender assume a direct and necessary link between, for example, the female body and that set of social behaviors, emotional investments, and physical stylizations identified as "feminine." In the past several decades, however, many feminist and queer theorists have mounted convincing arguments against any such simplistic conflation of anatomical sex and socially inscribed gender. See, for example, Barbara L. Marshall's detailed study, *Configuring Gender: Explorations in Theory and Politics* (Peterborough, Ont.: Broadview, 2000), in which she describes gender as "a marker of the social and cultural elaboration of sexual difference" (8). From this perspective, "woman" and "man" are terms that refer both to bodies and to social positions.

19. Brian Attebery, *Decoding Gender in Science Fiction* (New York: Routledge, 2002), 130.

20. Jones, *Deconstructing the Starships*, 107.

21. Gwyneth Jones, *White Queen* (London: Victor Gollancz, [1991] 1992), 121.

22. Ibid., 117.

23. Jones, *Deconstructing the Starships*, 110. Note Istvan Csicsery-Ronay Jr's very astute assessment of the role of the aliens in *White Queen*: "the alien transposes — displaces — the problems of the triangulation of desire from the human social sphere to the ontological. In an age of radical egalitarianism, individualism and materialism, the alien reveals human beings to be a single species. If it reveals sexual, racial, and other differences within the species, these are not trivial differences, but constitutive. We are a species that is not one"; "The Lost Child: Notes on *White Queen*," *Femspec* 5.1 (2004): 242.

24. Aqueduct Press in Seattle published this novel in late 2004. Its original title, *Differences*, has been changed to *Life*. The book is the winner of the 2005 Philip K. Dick Award.

25. E-mail correspondence with Gwyneth Jones, September 22, 2003.

26. Ibid.

27. Angela Carter, *The Passion of New Eve* (London: Virago, [1977] 1982), 149–150.

28. See Russ's essay, *"Amor Vincent Fœminam:* The Battle of the Sexes in Science Fiction," *Science Fiction Studies* 7 (March 1980): 2–15, for a witty and biting overview of the misogynist "battle-of-the-sexes" tradition in science-fiction stories written by men; these feminist stories pose a powerful challenge to that quite pernicious tradition.

29. Sally Miller Gearhart, *The Wanderground: Tales of the Hill Women* (Watertown, Mass.: Persephone, 1979), 115.

30. Examples of such stories include Ursula K. Le Guin's *The Left Hand of Darkness* (1969), James Tiptree, Jr.'s "The Girl Who Was Plugged In" (1973), Margaret Atwood's *The Handmaid's Tale* (1984), Amy Thomson's *Virtual Girl* (1993), and Shariann Lewitt's "A Real Girl" (1998).

31. Joanna Russ, *The Female Man* (New York: Bantam, 1975), 139–140.

32. As Caroline Heilbrun writes of this figure in her highly influential study *Toward a Recognition of Androgyny* (New York: Knopf, 1973), "This ancient Greek word ... defines a condition under which the characteristics of the sexes, and the human impulses expressed by men and women, are not rigidly assigned. Androgyny seeks to liberate the individual from the confines of the appropriate" (x). Piercy's version of sex/gender equality is also directly inspired by Shulamith Firestone's radical-feminist manifesto *The Dialectic of Sex* (1970), which calls for both biological and social revolution. Piercy's most effective erasure of difference in *Woman on the Edge of Time* is performed at the level of language: Mattapoisett's community uses neologistic pronouns — such as "per" in place of both "she" and "he" — that indicate nothing of the sex/gender of the individuals to whom they refer.

33. E-mail correspondence with Gwyneth Jones, September 22, 2003. Despite theoretical reservations about the efficacy of the concept of androgyny for a feminist politics, Brian Attebery argues for its function as a constantly transformative sign of difference: "What can't be pinned down to a single meaning can be redirected indefinitely, can continue to challenge assumptions about meaning and identity"; *Decoding Gender in Science Fiction*, 133. See Attebery's chapter, "Androgyny as Difference," which concludes with a brief discussion of "Balinese Dancer," 129–150.

34. Jones, *Deconstructing the Starships*, 105.

What I Didn't See

KAREN JOY FOWLER

First published in scifiction, *July 2002*

I saw Archibald Murray's obituary in the Tribune a couple of days ago. It was a long notice, because of all those furbelows he had after his name, and dredged up that old business of ours, which can't have pleased his children. I, myself, have never spoken up before, as I've always felt that nothing I saw sheds any light, but now I'm the last of us. Even Wilmet is gone, though I always picture him such a boy. And there is something to be said for having the last word, which I am surely having.

I still go to the jungle sometimes when I sleep. The sound of the clock turns to a million insects all chewing at once, water dripping onto leaves, the hum inside your head when you run a fever. Sooner or later Eddie comes, in his silly hat and boots up to his knees. He puts his arms around me in the way he did when he meant business and I wake up too hot, too old, and all alone.

You're never alone in the jungle. You can't see through the twist of roots and leaves and vines, the streakish, tricky light, but you've always got a sense of being seen. You make too much noise when you walk.

At the same time, you understand that you don't matter. You're small and stuck on the ground. The ghosts of paths weren't made for you. If you get bitten by a snake, it's your own damn fault, not the snake's, and if someone doesn't drag you out you'll turn to mulch just like anything else would and show up next as mold or moss, ferns, leeches, ants, millipedes, butterflies, beetles. The jungle is a jammed-alive place, which means that something is always dying there.

Eddie had this idea once that defects of character could be treated with doses of landscape: the ocean for the histrionic, mountains for the domineering, and so forth. I forget the desert, but the jungle was the place to send the self-centered.

We seven went into the jungle with guns in our hands and love in our hearts. I say so now when there is no one left to contradict me.

. . .

Archer organized us. He was working at the time for the Louisville Museum of Natural History and he had a stipend from Collections for skins and bones. The rest of us were amateur enthusiasts and paid our own way just for the adventure. Archer asked Eddie (arachnids) to go along and Russell MacNamara (chimps), and Trenton Cox (butterflies), who couldn't or wouldn't, and Wilmet Siebert (big game), and Merion Cowper (tropical medicine), and also Merion's wife, only he turned out to be between wives by the time we left, so he was the one who brought Beverly Kriss.

I came with Eddie to help with his nets, pooters, and kill jars. I was never the sort to scream over bugs, but if I had been, twenty-eight years of marriage to Eddie would have cured me. The more legs a creature had, the better Eddie thought of it. Up to point. Up to eight.

In fact Archer was anxious there be some women and had specially invited me, though Eddie didn't tell me so. This was smart; I would have suspected I was along to do the dishes (though of course there were the natives for this) and for nursing the sick, which we did end up at a bit, Beverly and I, when the matter was too small or too nasty for Merion. I might not have come at all if I'd known I was wanted. As it was, I learned to bake a passable bread on campfire coals with a native beer for yeast, but it was my own choice to do so and I ate as much of the bread myself as I wished.

I pass over the various boats on which we sailed, though these trips were not without incident. Wilmet turned out to have a nervous stomach; it started to trouble him on the ocean and then stuck around when we hit dry land again. Russell was a drinker, and not the good sort, unlucky and suspicious, a man who thought he loved a game of cards, but should have never been allowed to play. Beverly was a modern girl in 1928 and could chew gum, smoke, and wipe the lipstick off her mouth and onto yours all at the same time. She and Merion were frisky for Archer's taste and he tried to shift this off onto me, saying I was being made uncomfortable, when I didn't care one way or the other. I worried that it would be a pattern and every time one of the men was tired on the trail they'd say we had to stop on my account. I told Eddie right away I wouldn't like it if this was to happen. So by the time we were geared up and walking in, we already thought we knew each other pretty well and we didn't entirely like what we knew. Still, I guessed we'd get along fine when there was more to occupy us. Even during those long days it took to reach the mountains — the endless trains, motor cars, donkeys, mules, and finally our very own feet — things went smoothly enough.

By the time we reached the Lulenga Mission, we'd seen a fair bit of Africa — low and high, hot and cold, black and white. I've learned some things in the years since, so there's a strong temptation now to pretend that I felt the things I should have felt, knew the things I might have known. The truth is otherwise. My attitudes toward the natives, in particular, were not what they might have been. The men who helped us interested me little and impressed me not at all. Many of them had their teeth filed and were only ten years or so from cannibalism, or so we were informed. No one, ourselves included, was clean, but Beverly and I would have tried, only we couldn't bathe without the nuisance of being spied on. Whether this was to see if we looked good or only good to eat, I did not wish to know.

The fathers at the mission told us that slaves used to be led through the villages in ropes so that people could draw on their bodies the cuts of meat they were buying before the slaves were butchered, and with that my mind was set. I never did acknowledge any beauty or kindness in the people we met, though Eddie saw much of both.

We spent three nights in Lulenga, which gave us each a bed, good food, and a chance to wash our hair and clothes in some privacy. Beverly and I shared a room, there not being sufficient number for her to have her own. She was quarreling with Merion at the time though I forget about what. They were a tempest, those two, always shouting, sulking, and then turning on the heat again. A tiresome sport for spectators, but surely invigorating for the players. So Eddie was bunked up with Russell, which put me out, because I liked to wake up with him.

We were joined at dinner the first night by a Belgian administrator who treated us to real wine and whose name I no longer remember though I can picture him yet — a bald, hefty man in his sixties with a white beard. I recall how he joked that his hair had migrated from his head to his chin and then settled in where the food was plentiful.

Eddie was in high spirits and talking more than usual. The spiders in Africa are exhilaratingly aggressive. Many of them have fangs and nocturnal habits. We'd already shipped home dozens of button spiders with red hourglasses on their backs, and some beautiful golden violin spiders with long delicate legs and dark chevrons underneath. But that evening Eddie was most excited about a small jumping spider, which seemed not to spin her own web, but to lurk instead in the web of another. She had no beautiful markings; when he'd first seen one, he'd thought she was a bit of dirt blown into the silken strands. Then she grew legs and, as we watched, stalked and killed the web's owner and all with a startling cunning.

"Working together, a thousand spiders can tie up a lion," the Belgian told us. Apparently it was a local saying. "But then they don't work together, do they? The blacks haven't noticed. Science is observation and Africa produces no scientists."

In those days all gorilla hunts began at Lulenga, so it took no great discernment to guess that the rest of our party was not after spiders. The Belgian told us that only six weeks past, a troupe of gorilla males had attacked a tribal village. The food stores had been broken into and a woman carried off. Her bracelets were found the next day, but she'd not yet returned and the Belgian feared she never would. It was such a sustained siege that the whole village had to be abandoned.

"The seizure of the woman I dismiss as superstition and exaggeration," Archer said. He had a formal way of speaking; you'd never guess he was from Kentucky. Not so grand to look at — inch-thick glasses that made his eyes pop, unkempt hair, filthy shirt cuffs. He poured more of the Belgian's wine around, and I recall his being especially generous to his own glass. Isn't it funny, the things you remember? "But the rest of your story interests me. If any gorilla was taken I'd pay for the skin, assuming it wasn't spoiled in the peeling."

The Belgian said he would inquire. And then he persisted with his main point, very serious and deliberate. "As to the woman, I've heard these tales too often to discard them so quickly as you. I've heard of native women subjected to degradations far worse than death. May I ask you as a favor then, in deference to my greater experience and longer time here, to leave your women at the mission when you go gorilla hunting?"

It was courteously done and obviously cost Archer to refuse. Yet he did, saying to my astonishment that it would defeat his whole purpose to leave me and Beverly behind. He then gave the Belgian his own thinking, which we seven had already heard over several repetitions — that gorillas were harmless and gentle, if oversized and over-muscled. Sweet-natured vegetarians. He based this entirely on the wear on their teeth; he'd read a paper on it from some university in London.

Archer then characterized the famous Du Chaillu description — glaring eyes, yellow incisors, hellish dream creatures — as a slick and dangerous form of self aggrandizement. It was an account tailored to bring big game hunters on the run and so had to be quickly countered for the gorillas' own protection. Archer was out to prove Du Chaillu wrong and he needed me and Beverly to help. "If one of the girls should bring down a large male," he said, "it will seem as exciting as shooting a cow. No man will cross a continent merely to do something a pair of girls has already done."

He never did ask us, because that wasn't his way. He just raised it as our Christian duty and then left us to worry it over in our minds.

Of course we were all carrying rifles. Eddie and I had practiced on bottles and such in preparation for the trip. On the way over I'd gotten pretty good at clay pigeons off the deck of our ship. But I wasn't eager to kill a gentle vegetarian—a nightmare from hell would have suited me a good deal better (if scared me a great deal more.) Beverly too, I'm guessing.

Not that she said anything about it that night. Wilmet, our youngest at twenty-five years and also shortest by a whole head—blond hair, pink cheeks, and little rat's eyes—had been lugging a tin of British biscuits about the whole trip and finishing every dinner by eating one while we watched. He was always explaining why they couldn't be shared when no one was asking. They kept his stomach settled; he couldn't afford to run out and so on; his very life might depend on them if he were sick and nothing else would stay down and so forth. We wouldn't have noticed if he hadn't persisted in bringing it up.

But suddenly he and Beverly had their heads close together, whispering, and he was giving her one of his precious biscuits. She took it without so much as a glance at Merion, even when he leaned in to say he'd like one, too. Wilmet answered that there were too few to share with everyone so Merion upset a water glass into the tin and spoiled all the biscuits that remained. Wilmet left the table and didn't return and the subject of the all-girl gorilla hunt passed by in the unpleasantness.

That night I woke under the gauze of the mosquito net in such a heat I thought I had malaria. Merion had given us all quinine and I meant to take it regularly, but I didn't always remember. There are worse fevers in the jungle, especially if you've been collecting spiders, so it was cheerful of me to fix on malaria. My skin was burning from the inside out, especially my hands and feet, and I was sweating like butter on a hot day. I thought to wake Beverly, but by the time I stood up the fit had already passed and anyway her bed was empty.

In the morning she was back. I planned to talk to her then, get her thoughts on gorilla hunting, but I woke early and she slept late.

I breakfasted alone and went for a stroll around the mission grounds. It was cool with little noise beyond the wind and birds. To the west, a dark trio of mountains, two of which smoked. Furrowed fields below me, banana plantations, and trellises of roses, curving into archways that led to the church. How often we grow a garden around our houses of worship. We march ourselves through Eden to get to God.

Merion joined me in the graveyard where I'd just counted three deaths by lion, British names all. I was thinking how outlandish it was, how sadly unlikely that all the prams and nannies and public schools should come to this, and even the bodies pinned under stones so hyenas wouldn't come for them. I was hoping for a more modern sort of death myself, a death at home, a death from American causes, when Merion cleared his throat behind me.

He didn't look like my idea of a doctor, but I believe he was a good one. Well-paid, that's for sure and certain. As to appearances, he reminded me of the villain in some Lillian Gish film, meaty and needing a shave, but handsome enough when cleaned up. He swung his arms when he walked so he took up more space than he needed. There was something to this confidence I admired, though it irritated me on principle. I often liked him least of all and I'm betting he was sharp enough to know it. "I trust you slept well," he said. He looked at me slant-wise, looked away again. *I trust you slept well.* I trust you were in no way disturbed by Beverly sneaking out to meet me in the middle of the night.

Or maybe — I trust Beverly didn't sneak out last night.

Or maybe just I trust you slept well. It wasn't a question, which saved me the nuisance of figuring the answer.

"So," he said next, "what do you think of this gorilla scheme of Archer's?" and then gave me no time to respond. "The fathers tell me a party from Manchester went up just last month and brought back seventeen. Four of them youngsters — lovely little family group for the British museum. I only hope they left us a few." And then, lowering his voice, "I'm glad for the chance to discuss things with you privately."

There turned out to be a detail to the Belgian's story judged too delicate for the dinnertable, but Merion, being a doctor and maybe more of a man's man than Archer, a man who could be appealed to on behalf of women, had heard it. The woman carried away from the village had been menstruating. This at least the Belgian hoped, that we'd not to go up the mountain with our female affliction in full flower.

And because he was a doctor I told Merion straight out that I'd been light and occasional; I credited this to the upset of travel. I thought to set his mind at ease, but I should have guessed I wasn't his first concern.

"Beverly's too headstrong to listen to me," he said. "Too young and reckless. She'll take her cue from you. A solid, sensible, mature woman like you could rein her in a bit. For her own good."

A woman unlikely to inflame the passions of jungle apes was what I heard. Even in my prime I'd never been the sort of woman poems are written about, but this seemed to place me low indeed. An hour later I saw the humor in it, and Eddie surely laughed at me quickly enough when I confessed it, but at the time I was sincerely insulted. How sensible, how mature was that?

I was further provoked by the way he expected me to give in. Archer was certain I'd agree to save the gorillas and Merion was certain I'd agree to save Beverly. I had a moment's outrage over these men who planned to run me by appealing to what they imagined was my weakness.

Merion more than Archer. How smug he was, and how I detested his calm acceptance of every advantage that came to him, as if it were no more than his due. No white woman in all the world had seen the wild gorillas yet — we were to be the first — but I was to step aside from it just because he asked me.

"I haven't walked all this way to miss out on the gorillas," I told him, as politely as I could. "The only question is whether I'm looking or shooting at them." And then I left him, because my own feelings were no credit to me and I didn't mean to have them anymore. I went to look for Eddie and spent the rest of the day emptying kill jars, pinning and labeling the occupants.

The next morning Beverly announced, in deference to Merion's wishes, that she'd be staying behind at the mission when we went on. Quick as could be, Wilmet said his stomach was in such an uproar that he would stay behind as well. This took us all by surprise as he was the only real hunter among us. And it put Merion in an awful bind — we'd more likely need a doctor on the mountain than at the mission, but I guessed he'd sooner see Beverly taken by gorillas than by Wilmet. He fussed and sweated over a bunch of details that didn't matter to anyone and all the while the day passed in secret conferences — Merion with Archer, Archer with Beverly, Russell with Wilmet, Eddie with Beverly. By dinnertime Beverly said she'd changed her mind and Wilmet had undergone a wonderful recovery. When we left next morning we were at full complement, but pretty tightly strung.

It took almost two hundred porters to get our little band of seven up Mount Mikeno. It was a hard track with no path, hoisting ourselves over roots, cutting and crawling our way through tightly woven bamboo. There were long slides of mud on which it was impossible to get a grip. And always sharp uphill. My heart and my lungs worked as hard or harder than my legs and though it wasn't hot I had to wipe my face and neck continually. As the altitude rose I gasped for breath like a fish in a net.

We women were placed in the middle of the pack with gun-bearers both ahead and behind. I slid back many times and had to be caught and set upright again. Eddie was in a torment over the webs we walked through with no pause as to architect and Russell over the bearers who, he guaranteed, would bolt with our guns at the first sign of danger. But we wouldn't make camp if we stopped for spiders and couldn't stay the course without our hands free. Soon Beverly sang out for a gorilla to come and carry her the rest of the way.

Then we were all too winded and climbed for hours without speaking, breaking whenever we came suddenly into the sun, sustaining ourselves with chocolate and crackers.

Still our mood was excellent. We saw elephant tracks, large, sunken bowls in the mud, half-filled with water. We saw glades of wild carrots and an extravagance of pink and purple orchids. Grasses in greens so delicate they seemed to be melting. I revised my notions of Eden, leaving the roses behind and choosing instead these remote forests where the gorillas lived — foggy rains, the crooked hagenia trees strung with vines, golden mosses, silver lichen; the rattle and buzz of flies and beetles; the smell of catnip as we stepped into it.

At last we stopped. Our porters set up which gave us a chance to rest. My feet were swollen and my knees stiffening, but I had a great appetite for dinner and a great weariness for bed; I was asleep before sundown. And then I was awake again. The temperature, which had been pleasant all day, plunged. Eddie and I wrapped ourselves in coats and sweaters and each other. He worried about our porters, who didn't have the blankets we had, although they were free to keep a fire up as high as they liked. At daybreak, they came complaining to Archer. He raised their pay a dime apiece since they had surely suffered during the night, but almost fifty of them left us anyway.

We spent that morning sitting around the camp, nursing our blisters and scrapes, some of us looking for spiders, some of us practicing our marksmanship. There was a stream about five minutes walk away with a pool where Beverly and I dropped our feet. No mosquitoes, no sweat bees, no flies, and that alone made it paradise. But no sooner did I have this thought and a wave of malarial heat came on me, drenching the back of my shirt.

When I came to myself again, Beverly was in the middle of something and I hadn't heard the beginning. She might have told me Merion's former wife had been unfaithful to him. Later this seemed like something I'd once been told, but maybe only because it made sense. "Now he seems to think the apes will leave me alone if only I don't go tempting them," she said. "Lord!"

"He says they're drawn to menstrual blood."

"Then I've got no problem. Anyway Russell says that Burunga says we'll never see them, dressed as we're dressed. Our clothes make too much noise when we walk. He told Russell we must hunt them naked. I haven't passed that on to Merion yet. I'm saving it for a special occasion."

I had no idea who Burunga was. Not the cook and not our chief guide, which were the only names I'd bothered with. I was, at least (and I do see now, how very least it is) embarrassed to learn that Beverly had done otherwise. "Are you planning to shoot an ape?" I asked. It came over me all of sudden that I wanted a particular answer, but I couldn't unearth what answer that was.

"I'm not really a killer," she said. "More a sweet-natured vegetarian. Of the meat-eating variety. But Archer says he'll put my picture up in the museum. You know the sort of thing — rifle on shoulder, foot on body, eyes to the horizon. Wouldn't that be something to take the kiddies to?"

Eddie and I had no kiddies; Beverly might have realized it was a sore spot. And Archer had made no such representations to me. She sat in a spill of sunlight. Her hair was short and heavy and fell in a neat cap over her ears. Brown until the sun made it golden. She wasn't a pretty woman so much as she just drew your eye and kept it. "Merion keeps on about how he paid my way here. Like he hasn't gotten his money's worth." She kicked her feet and water beaded up on her bare legs. "You're so lucky. Eddie's the best."

Which he was, and any woman could see it. I never met a better man than my Eddie and in our whole forty-three years together there were only three times I wished I hadn't married him. I say this now, because we're coming up on one of those times. I wouldn't want someone thinking less of Eddie because of anything I said.

"You're still in love with him, aren't you?" Beverly asked. "After so many years of marriage."

I admitted as much.

Beverly shook her golden head. "Then you'd best keep with him," she told me.

Or did she? What did she say to me? I've been over the conversation so many times I no longer remember it at all.

In contrast, this next bit is perfectly clear. Beverly said she was tired and went to her tent to lie down. I found the men playing bridge, taking turns at watching. I was bullied into playing, because Russell didn't like his cards and thought to change his luck by putting some empty space between hands. So it was me and Wilmet opposite Eddie and Russell, with Merion and Archer in the vicinity, smoking and looking on. On the other side of the tents the laughter of our porters.

I would have liked to team with Eddie, but Russell said bridge was too dangerous a game when husbands and wives partnered up and there was a ready access to guns. He was joking, of course, but you couldn't have told by his face.

While we played Russell talked about chimpanzees and how they ran their lives. Back in those days no one had looked at chimps yet so it was all only guesswork. Topped by guessing that gorillas would be pretty much the same. There was a natural order to things, Russell said, and you could reason it out; it was simple Darwinism.

I didn't think you could reason out spiders; I didn't buy that you could reason out chimps. So I didn't listen. I played my cards and every so often a word would fall in. Male this, male that. Blah, blah, dominance. Survival of the fittest, blah, blah. Natural selection, nature red in tooth and claw. Blah and blah. There was an argument then as to whether by simple Darwinism we could expect a social arrangement of monogamous married couples or whether the males would all have harems. There were points to be made either way and I didn't care for any of those points.

Wilmet opened with one heart and soon we were up to three. I mentioned how Beverly had said she'd get her picture in the Louisville Museum if she killed an ape. "It's not entirely my decision," Archer said. "But, yes, part of my plan is that there will be pictures. And interviews. Possibly in magazines, certainly in the museum. The whole object is that people be told." And this began a discussion over whether, for the purposes of saving gorilla lives, it would work best if Beverly was to kill one or if it should be me. There was some general concern that the sight of Beverly in a pith helmet might be, somehow, stirring, whereas if I were the one, it wouldn't be cute in the least. If Archer really wished to put people off gorilla-hunting, then, the men agreed, I was his girl. Of course it was not as bald as that, but that was the gist.

Wilmet lost a trick he'd hoped to finesse. We were going down and I suddenly saw that he'd opened with only four hearts, which, though they were pretty enough, an ace and a king included, was a witless thing to do. I still think so.

"I expected more support," he said to me, "when you took us to two," as if it were my fault.

"Length is strength," I said right back and then I burst into tears, because he was so short it was an awful thing to say. It took me more by surprise than anyone and most surprising of all, I didn't seem to care about the crying. I got up from the table and walked off. I could hear Eddie apologizing behind me as if I was the one who'd opened with four hearts. "Change of life," I heard him saying. It was so like Eddie to know what was happening to me even before I did.

It was so unlike him to apologize for me. At that moment I hated him with all the rest. I went to our tent and fetched some water and my rifle. We weren't any of us to go into the jungle alone so no one imagined this was what I was doing.

The sky had begun to cloud up and soon the weather was colder. There was no clear track to follow, only antelope trails. Of course I got lost. I had thought to take every possible turn to the right and then reverse this coming back, but the plan didn't suit the landscape nor achieve the end desired. I had a whistle, but was angry enough not to use it. I counted on Eddie to find me eventually as he always did.

I believe I walked for more than four hours. Twice it rained, intensifying all the green smells of the jungle. Occasionally the sun was out and the mosses and leaves overlaid with silvered water. I saw a cat print that made me move my rifle off of safe to ready and then often had to set it aside as the track took me over roots and under hollow trees. The path was unstable and sometimes slid out from under me.

Once I put my hand on a spider's web. It was a domed web over an orb, intricate and a beautiful pale yellow in color. I never touched a silk so strong. The spider was big and black with yellow spots at the undersides of her legs and, judging by the corpses, she carried all her victims to the web's center before wrapping them. I would have brought her back, but I had nothing to keep her in. It seemed a betrayal of Eddie to let her be, but that sort of evened our score.

Next thing I put my hand on was a soft looking leaf. I pulled it away full of nettles.

Although the way back to camp was clearly downhill, I began to go up. I thought to find a vista, see the mountains, orient myself. I was less angry by now and suffered more from the climbing as a result. The rain began again and I picked out a sheltered spot to sit and tend my stinging hand. I should have been cold and frightened, but I wasn't either. The pain in my hand was subsiding. The jungle was beautiful and the sound of rain a lullaby. I remember wishing that this was where I belonged, that I lived here. Then the heat came on me so hard I couldn't wish at all.

A noise brought me out of it—a crashing in the bamboo. Turning, I saw the movement of leaves and the backside of something rather like a large black bear. A gorilla has a strange way of walking—on the hind feet and the knuckles, but with arms so long their backs are hardly bent. I had one clear look and then the creature was gone. But I could still hear it and I was determined to see it again.

I knew I'd never have another chance; even if we did see one later the men would take it over. I was still too hot. My shirt was drenched from sweat and rain; my pants, too, and making a noise whenever I bent my knees. So I removed everything and put back only my socks and boots. I left the rest of my clothes folded on the spot where I'd been sitting, picked up my rifle, and went into the bamboo.

Around a rock, under a log, over a root, behind a tree was the prettiest open meadow you'd ever hope to see. Three gorillas were in it, one male, two female. It might have been a harem. It might have been a family—a father, mother and daughter. The sun came out. One female combed the other with her hands, the two of them blinking in the sun. The male was seated in a patch of wild carrots, pulling and eating them with no particular ardor. I could see his profile and the gray in his fur. He twitched his fingers a bit, like a man listening to music. There were flowers—pink and white—in concentric circles where some pond had been and now wasn't. One lone tree. I stood and looked for a good long time.

Then I raised the barrel of my gun. The movement brought the eyes of the male to me. He stood. He was bigger than I could ever have imagined. In the leather of his face I saw surprise, curiosity, caution. Something else, too. Something so human it made me feel like an old woman with no clothes on. I might have shot him just for that, but I knew it wasn't right— to kill him merely because he was more human than I anticipated. He thumped his chest, a rhythmic beat that made the women look to him. He showed me his teeth. Then he turned and took the women away.

I watched it all through the sight of my gun. I might have hit him several times—spared the women, freed the women. But I couldn't see that they wanted freeing and Eddie had told me never to shoot a gun angry. The gorillas faded from the meadow. I was cold then and I went for my clothes.

Russell had beaten me to them. He stood with two of our guides, staring down at my neatly folded pants. Nothing for it but to walk up beside him and pick them up, shake them for ants, put them on. He turned his back as I dressed and he couldn't manage a word. I was even more embarrassed. "Eddie must be frantic," I said to break the awkwardness.

"All of us, completely beside ourselves. Did you find any sign of her?"

Which was how I learned that Beverly had disappeared.

.   .   .

We were closer to camp than I'd feared if farther than I'd hoped. While we walked I did my best to recount my final conversation with Beverly to Russell. I was, apparently, the last to have seen her. The card game had broken up soon after I left and the men gone their separate ways. A couple of hours later, Merion began looking for Beverly who was no longer in her tent. No one was alarmed, at first, but by now they were.

I was made to repeat everything she'd said again and again and questioned over it, too, though there was nothing useful in it and soon I began to feel I'd made up every word. Archer asked our guides to look over the ground about the pool and around her tent. He had some cowboy scene in his mind, I suppose, the primitive who can read a broken branch, a footprint, a bit of fur and piece it all together. Our guides looked with great seriousness, but found nothing. We searched and called and sent up signaling shots until night came over us.

"She was taken by the gorillas," Merion told us. "Just as I said she'd be." I tried to read his face in the red of the firelight, but couldn't. Nor catch his tone of voice.

"No prints," our chief guide repeated. "No sign."

That night our cook refused to make us dinner. The natives were talking a great deal amongst themselves, very quiet. To us they said as little as possible. Archer demanded an explanation, but got nothing but dodge and evasion.

"They're scared," Eddie said, but I didn't see this.

A night even more bitter than the last and Beverly not dressed for it. In the morning the porters came to Archer to say they were going back. No measure of arguing or threatening or bribing changed their minds. We could come or stay as we chose; it was clearly of no moment to them. I, of course, was given no choice, but was sent back to the mission with the rest of the gear excepting what the men kept behind.

At Lulenga one of the porters tried to speak with me. He had no English and I followed none of it except Beverly's name. I told him to wait while I fetched one of the fathers to translate, but he misunderstood or else he refused. When we returned he was gone and I never did see him again.

The men stayed eight more days on Mount Mikeno and never found so much as a bracelet.

Because I'm a woman I wasn't there for the parts you want most to hear. The waiting and the not-knowing were, in my view of things, as hard or harder than the searching, but you don't make stories out of that. Something happened to Beverly, but I can't tell you what. Something happened on the mountain after I left, something that brought Eddie back to me so altered in spirit I felt I hardly knew him, but I wasn't there to see what it was. Eddie and I departed Africa immediately and not in the company of the other men in our party. We didn't even pack up all our spiders.

For months after, I wished to talk about Beverly, to put together this possibility and that possibility and settle on something I could live with. I felt the need most strongly at night. But Eddie couldn't hear her name. He'd sunk so deep into himself, he rarely looked out. He stopped sleeping and wept from time to time and these were things he did his best to hide from me. I tried to talk to him about it, I tried to be patient and loving, I tried to be kind. I failed in all these things.

A year, two more passed, and he began to resemble himself again, but never in full. My full, true Eddie never did come back from the jungle.

Then one day, at breakfast, with nothing particular to prompt it, he told me there'd been a massacre. That after I left for Lulenga the men had spent the days hunting and killing gorillas. He didn't describe it to me at all, yet it sprang bright and terrible into my mind, my own little family group lying in their blood in the meadow.

Forty or more, Eddie said. Probably more. Over several days. Babies, too. They couldn't even bring the bodies back; it looked so bad to be collecting when Beverly was gone. They'd slaughtered the gorillas as if they were cows.

Eddie was dressed in his old plaid robe, his gray hair in uncombed bunches, crying into his fried eggs. I wasn't talking, but he put his hands over his ears in case I did. He was shaking all over from weeping, his head trembling on his neck. "It felt like murder," he said. "Just exactly like murder."

I took his hands down from his head and held on hard. "I expect it was mostly Merion."

"No," he said. "It was mostly me."

At first, Eddie told me, Merion was certain the gorillas had taken Beverly. But later, he began to comment on the strange behavior of the porters. How they wouldn't talk to us, but whispered to each other. How they left so quickly. "I was afraid," Eddie told me. "So upset about Beverly and then terribly afraid. Russell and Merion, they were so angry I could smell it. I thought at any moment one of them would say something that couldn't be unsaid, something that would get to the Belgians. And then I wouldn't be able to stop it anymore. So I kept us stuck on the gorillas. I kept us going after them. I kept us angry until we had killed so very many and were all so ashamed, there would be no way to turn and accuse someone new."

I still didn't quite understand. "Do you think one of the porters killed Beverly?" It was a possibility that had occurred to me, too; I admit it.

"No," said Eddie. "That's my point. But you saw how the blacks were treated back at Lulenga. You saw the chains and the beatings. I couldn't let them be suspected." His voice was so clogged I could hardly make out the words. "I need you to tell me I did the right thing."

So I told him. I told him he was the best man I ever knew. "Thank you," he said. And with that he shook off my hands, dried his eyes, and left the table.

That night I tried to talk to him again. I tried to say that there was nothing he could do that I wouldn't forgive. "You've always been too easy on me," he answered. And the next time I brought it up, "If you love me, we'll never talk about this again."

Eddie died three years later without another word on the subject passing between us. In the end, to be honest, I suppose I found that silence rather unforgivable. His death even more so. I have never liked being alone.

As every day I more surely am; it's the blessing of a long life. Just me left now, the first white woman to see the wild gorillas and the one who saw nothing else — not the chains, not the beatings, not the massacre. I can't help worrying over it all again, now I know Archer's dead and only me to tell it, though no way of telling puts it to rest.

Since my eyes went, a girl comes to read to me twice a week. For the longest time I wanted nothing to do with gorillas, but now I have her scouting out articles as we're finally starting to really see how they live. The thinking still seems to be harems, but with the females slipping off from time to time to be with whomever they wish.

And what I notice most in the articles is not the apes. My attention is caught instead by these young women who'd sooner live in the jungle with the chimpanzees or the orangutans or the great mountain gorillas. These women who freely choose it — the Goodalls and the Galdikas and the Fosseys. And I think to myself how there is nothing new under the sun, and maybe all those women carried off by gorillas in those old stories, maybe they all freely chose it.

When I am tired and have thought too much about it all, Beverly's last words come back to me. Mostly I put them straight out of my head, think about anything else. Who remembers what she said? Who knows what she meant?

But there are other times when I let them in. Turn them over. Then they become, not a threat as I originally heard them, but an invitation. On those days I can pretend that she's still there in the jungle, dipping her feet, eating wild carrots, and waiting for me. I can pretend that I'll be joining her whenever I wish and just as soon as I please.

Something Rich and Strange: Karen Joy Fowler's "What I Didn't See"

L. Timmel Duchamp

Thirty Years of Feminist SF

When Don Fenton, the narrator of "The Women Men Don't See," observes to Ruth Parsons that because women like her are the "backbone of the system," they could bring the country "to a screeching halt before lunch" if they chose, Ruth Parsons replies, "Women don't work that way. We're a toothless world. . . . What women do is survive. We live by ones and twos in the chinks of the world-machine."[1] Fenton, who's getting paranoid about this woman he's been taking for granted, responds, "Sounds like a guerilla operation." Ruth Parsons dismisses this: "Guerillas have something to hope for."[2] All that *women* can hope for, she tells him, is for whatever "rights" men will allow them.[3]

"The Women Men Don't See," a story by James Tiptree Jr. (a pseudonym of Alice Sheldon) first appeared in 1973, the year the U.S. Supreme Court issued the landmark *Roe* v. *Wade* ruling. Fenton cites "the feminists'" "getting that equal rights bill" as a sign that women's lib is not "doomed" — as Ruth says that it is. While in real life U.S. feminists never did get "that equal rights bill," feminist activism accomplished so much in the course of the 1970s that the pessimism of Tiptree's Ruth Parsons surely represents a minority view in feminist sf of the 1970s and the early 1980s.[4] And yet the backlash against feminism was well under way by the time of Alice Sheldon's death in 1987 and enough (though by no means the most important) of the second wave's advances were on their way to being undone that I can imagine her sadly thinking, "Yes, just as I feared. Ruth Parsons's perspective was all too correct." Although a few feminist sf dystopias published in the 1980s envisage a retreat to pre–first-wave conditions,[5] the mainstream version of the backlash has largely taken the form of proclamations that male privilege no longer exists and that therefore feminism is no longer necessary. Young women now often adopt this posture of disavowal, reminiscent of Nixon and Kissinger's 1972 declaration of victory as they ordered the withdrawal of all U.S. troops from Vietnam.[6]

The reality of life in the early twenty-first-century United States is a mixed bag for feminists: neither victory nor defeat. And the reality for feminists writing sf is equally complex. For accomplished, conscious writers who have been feminists for thirty years, feminism is the water they swim in.[7] The difference that "swimming" in the water of feminism makes to their work does not hinge on assessments of progress (or retreat); nor does it require feminist sf to continually reinvent the wheel of feminist sf or give lessons in Feminism 101. Rather, thirty years of feminist sf have created a context in which feminists may write with subtlety and in constant conversation with the canonical feminist sf texts they assume their readers will know well. This difference, necessary for the continuing expansion of feminist consciousness and thinking, also means that readers who have not been swimming in that water often fail to understand feminist sf texts and misread them.

Karen Joy Fowler's Nebula Award–winning story, "What I Didn't See," offers a superb example of the kind of subtle, sophisticated sf that thirty years of unbroken feminist consciousness has made possible, fiction that those lacking that consciousness often do not "get."[8] The title's reference to "The Women Men Don't See" at once cues the experienced feminist sf reader that the story is in dialogue with the Tiptree story and, as a result, that it will probably have something to do with male and female humans and some kind of relation to aliens. Such readers on beginning the story will at once pick up on its strong biographical reference to Tiptree/Sheldon's childhood experiences and will recall that Sheldon's mother, Mary Hastings Bradley, contributed substantially to the genre of travel and hunter-explorer writing in the 1920s.[9] They will understand, at the very least, that the text bears a genealogical relationship to the earlier Tiptree story and likely builds on its themes, tropes, and narrative conventions.

Nonfeminist readers familiar with the earlier story, however, are apparently unable to perceive the story's genealogical relationship to the earlier Tiptree story. Hundreds of posts — made to the SFF.net listserv by science fiction professionals shortly after "What I Didn't See," appeared at SciFiction.com in July 2002 — bear witness to this inability. Many of the story's readers assumed that the relationship to the Tiptree story was either spurious or superficial, regardless of whether they praised or condemned it.

"The Women Men Don't See" has been accounted Alice Sheldon's most famous story.[10] It is a story that has always been read through the perceived gender of the author.[11] As "Tiptree," someone known to have traveled widely, hunted, had military and other government-work experience, residing in McLean, Virginia, not far from CIA headquarters, the author was a figure of mystery.

"The Women Men Don't See" furnished its male narrator, Don Fenton, with a similar background, but ornamented this background with the trappings of Hemingwayesque manliness to the point of parody. At the time the story was first published, feminists hailed it as an extraordinarily perceptive work of feminism by a male writer (implicitly critiquing its narrator's explicitly masculinist point of view). Male readers accepted its credibility precisely because they regarded "Tiptree" as the epitome of a man's man. When the story was nominated for both a Hugo and a Nebula, Sheldon withdrew it from consideration because, as she said later, "I thought too many women were rewarding a man for being so insightful, and that wasn't fair."[12]

While the idea that a male writer could be so perceptive about gender politics excited and encouraged the story's admirers, its author, in fact a woman, had found the depiction of Don Fenton her greatest challenge in writing the story—a depiction that readers took for absolute granted (particularly in light of all the stories about Tiptree's personal history then in circulation).[13] Later, after Tiptree was revealed to be Alice Sheldon, many men ceased to find Tiptree worth their notice. Sheldon wrote, of the revelation, "My secret world had been invaded, and the attractive figure of Tiptree—he *did* strike several people as attractive—was revealed as nothing but an old lady in Virginia."[14] She noted that "as Tiptree," her understanding was "insight," but "as Alli Sheldon, it is merely the heavy center of my soul."[15] How "The Women Men Don't See" has been read, in short, has depended profoundly on its readers' perception of its author's gender.

Inscriptions of Difference

"Women in disguise as aliens or aliens in disguise as 'women' turn up in SF written by women quite interestingly," wrote Joanna Russ in a letter to Sarah Lefanu.[16] Alice Sheldon, however, questions Russ's observation that in women's sf women are aliens (to men):

> I see here the interesting question about whether it is man or woman who can be seen as the alien, the Other. Yet it seems obvious: From my viewpoint, it is the male who is the alien. It is understandable that women could view themselves as alien to male society—a viewpoint of despair, I think. But if you take what you are as the normal Human, as any self-respecting person is bound to do, then it is clear that to a woman writer men are very abnormal indeed.[17]

Sheldon characterizes "The Women Men Don't See" as a "man-as-alien" narrative.[18] When their plane crash-lands in a swamp in Belize, Ruth and Althea Parsons do not see themselves as making a choice between remaining on earth and living with humans or leaving earth with the aliens they have just encountered, which is how the narrator, Don Fenton presents the case; rather, they see themselves as choosing to go off with *another* set of aliens. In her discussion of the story, Lefanu suggests that men and women have become "alien" to one another because their relations have been affected by the power that men exercise over women. "'The alien' is *difference* personified," she quotes Judith Hanna. "Aliens are the Other, feared, loathed, longed for. In Tiptree's work aliens serve as a metaphor for women in relation to men and for men in relation to women; they are also a metaphor for the alienated part of the self and, in particular, the divided self forced on women by male hegemony."[19]

"Difference" may be described as the inscription of characteristics (such as class, race, gender, age, sexual orientation, [dis]ability, and so forth) that mark an individual as not comforming to a socially and linguistically imagined norm (most often white, heterosexual, middle-class, able-bodied male).[20] In daily life, individuals marked by difference learn to adapt themselves to the norm through a variety of strategies, such as disavowing difference or internalizing it as the sign of their own innate inferiority. Such strategies create what Hanna calls the "divided self," in which individuals identify with the norm and project their differences from the norm onto an "alienated part of the self." Hanna, in other words, suggests that Tiptree's aliens are a metaphorical representation of those characteristics of women that do not fit the (male-defined) norm for human.

"What I Didn't See" takes this recognition of "*difference* personified" far beyond the gender polarity at the heart of Ruth Parsons's perception of man-as-alien and complicates it.[21] The moral crisis that lies at the heart of the story is triggered when Beverly disappears, perhaps having chosen to run off and live with gorillas just as Ruth and Althea Parsons choose to run off and live with extraterrestrials. The case Fowler presents is complicated by two intertwined moral knots that have plagued Western study of primates in Africa. The narrator depicts herself as having been completely unconscious of these moral knots at the time the story she relates was unfolding, but Fowler arranges the narrative such that one cannot understand the narrator's tale without acknowledging the play of these other *differences* that are inscribed in the characters' discourse as binary relations, as I shall show below.[22]

The tale's denouement, in fact, hinges on two terrible, interlocked ironies: on the one hand, the head of the expedition, Archer, plans to have a woman shoot a large, healthy male in order to put an end to the hunting of gorillas in the wild; on the other hand, Eddie, the narrator's husband, instigates a slaughter of gorillas in order to prevent a massacre of Africans. In both cases, a particular form of killing is seen as offering a means for preventing a worse form of killing. And the conceptualization behind each notion of preventive killing rests upon the relentless operation of the binary inscription of these differences.

The two moral issues at stake in the story are (1) colonial-era white racism as practiced by the Belgians at the Lulenga Mission, with which the members of Archer's expedition are to varying degrees complicitous; and (2) the treatment and conceptualization of the gorillas by the scholars and hunters who have targeted them.

The relations among white primatologists, Africans, and primates have always been vexed, from the beginning of white interest in primates in the nineteenth century up to the present day.[23] From the postcolonial African point of view, the white primatologists who set up camp to study primates in their natural habitat tend to assign the local inhabitants the role of assistants to their high and noble calling and assume that the interests of the humans sharing space with the primates should in every case yield to the imperative to preserve the jungle and its (nonhuman) inhabitants as a laboratory for their studies. The primatologists, for their part, see themselves as occupying the moral high ground, advocating environmental responsibility and the (altruistic) preservation of threatened species without acknowledging the history, needs, and traditions of the human inhabitants, toward whose welfare they remain largely indifferent.[24]

But as Donna Haraway demonstrates at thorough and explicit length, primatologists have always practiced a version of what Edward Said calls Orientalist discourse ("simian orientalist discourse," Haraway names it) by constructing a series of binary pairs intended to inscribe a set of differences between humans and primates, thereby allowing humans to distinguish themselves as not occupying the inferior side of the binary they assign to the primates they study. To take the most common example, in the simian orientalist discourse primates are to nature as humans are to culture. Many of the same dualisms characteristic of simian orientalist discourse have appeared in the discourses of race and gender: for example, man is to culture as woman is to nature, and European is to culture as African is to nature. Binary inscriptions of difference always serve, first and foremost, to define the superior term of a binary through its negative relation to the inferior term.

"What I Didn't See" subtly draws attention to the operations of racist and simian orientalist dualisms that have the effect of sometimes (though not always) shifting white women to the culture side of the culture/nature dualism. The fathers at the Belgian mission tell the Archer party that "slaves used to be led through the villages in ropes so that people could draw on their bodies the cuts of meat they were buying before the slaves were butchered." The narrator observes that on hearing that, "my mind was set. I never did acknowledge any beauty or kindness in the people we met, though Eddie saw much of both." (Fowler, 342). The narrator thus positions herself on the superior side of a binary that inscribes differences between white Europeans and Americans on the one side and "the natives" on the other. To the extent that she is able to foreground this "difference" between herself and the Africans, she is able to locate herself on the "culture" rather than the "nature" side of the binary, where women are usually placed in the binary relation that inscribes gender differences.

By contrast, Beverly's (presumptive) choice to join gorilla society signifies her either refusing to acknowledge the nature/culture binary or else aligning herself with the nature position with a vengeance. The characters' intermittent discussion about how menstruating women attract (male) gorillas exemplifies the linkage the characters make between women and nature (and therefore primates). Although all information about Beverly's consciousness of the operations of these three binary dualisms comes filtered through the narrator's observations, it seems likely that her consciousness is at the very least a great deal more acute than the narrator's at the time of the events she relates. The narrator, after all, remarks ruefully that Beverly knew who Burunga was, while she herself had not bothered to learn the names of any of the Africans but the cook and chief guide.

But another linkage — between Africans and primates — lurks between the lines of the story, understood though unspoken. This linkage is such a commonplace racist stereotype that the narrator has no need even to mention it. "Man," Jack says to Bigger Thomas in Richard Wright's *Native Son*, "if them folks saw you they'd run. They'd think a gorilla broke loose from the zoo and put on a tuxedo."[25] Jack and Bigger Thomas are talking about rich white society people in a movie called *The Gay Woman*. They sexually fantasize about the lead white female character and Bigger says he'd "like to be invited to a place like that just to find out what it feels like"[26] — which is when Jack reminds his friend that people like that think of black men as being like gorillas. A white woman from the United States traveling in early twentieth-century Africa would certainly be as aware of the stereotype as the African American men in Wright's novel, and so would the narrator of Fowler's story.

Much of what the narrator says that she "didn't see" includes not only the constant presence of European racism and its ever-threatening attending violence, but also the discursive dualisms (i.e., the gender, race, and species binaries) framing the perceptions and choices of the story's main characters. Don Fenton, Tiptree's narrator, also is oblivious to his own subjection to these dualisms; unlike Fowler's narrator, however, because he remains unconscious of them, he never does understand the story he recounts.

"I've learned some things in the years since, so there's a strong temptation now to pretend that I felt the things I should have felt, knew the things I might have known." (Fowler, 342). The narrator is referring here mostly to her racist indifference to the welfare of the Africans upon which the hunting party so heavily depend — and her failure to see them as human. "It took almost two hundred porters to get our little band of seven up Mount Mikeno." (Fowler, 346). When the party halts, the whites, exhausted, see it as a chance to rest — even as the porters continue to work, setting up camp, preparing and serving a meal. The narrator notes that her husband, Eddie, "worried about our porters, who didn't have the blankets we had, although they were free to keep a fire up as high as they liked." (Fowler, 347). When the porters complain about the cold to Archer, he raises their pay a dime apiece, but "almost fifty of them left us anyway."

Although the narrator "did not feel what she ought to have felt" about the porters' hardships, she did at least "see" it. What she did *not* see, though, was the risk to which Beverly's disappearance exposed all African males in the vicinity — "not the chains, not the beatings, not the massacre." (Fowler, 354). She also did not *hear* it, when one of the porters at Lulenga tried to tell her. "He had no English and I followed none of it except Beverly's name." (Fowler, 352). The narrator misunderstands the porters' refusal to stay to help search for Beverly. "No measure of arguing or threatening or bribing changed their minds. We could come and stay as we chose; it was clearly of no moment to them." She tells us that Eddie told her they were scared, "but I didn't see this." (Fowler, 352).

Although she is unable to see, hear, and comprehend the constant, threatening presence of European racism in herself and other Americans and Europeans, the narrator seems to be slightly more aware of the simian orientalism pervading the expedition's mission and discourse. She sharply distinguishes her own view of "the chimps" from the men's views when she describes their discussion of "chimpanzees and how they ran their lives" during a game of bridge. Russell, asserting "simple Darwinism," says there is a "natural order to things" in explaining that "gorillas would be pretty much the same" as chimps. The narrator is scornful: "I didn't buy that you could reason out chimps. So I didn't listen. I played my cards and every so often a word would fall in. Male this, male that. Blah, blah, dominance. Survival of the fittest, blah, blah. Natural selection, nature red in tooth and claw. Blah and blah." (Fowler, 349).

Not long after this conversation, (which stokes in the narrator a generalized anger against all the men, including her husband), the narrator wanders off on her own with her rifle and catches sight of a gorilla, strips off her clothes, and tracks it. Soon she comes upon one male and two females in "the prettiest open meadow you'd ever hope to see." The male is pulling carrots and eating them, while one of the females is grooming the other. The narrator watches "for a good long time" and then raises the barrel of her gun (Fowler, 351).

Up until this point in the story, we have been led to perceive the party's chief purpose as that of killing a large healthy male specimen for skinning. Archer has deliberately included two women in the party with the idea that if one of them does the shooting, white big-game hunters will lose interest in killing any more of them, since once a woman had brought down a large male, killing gorillas would cease to be a sign of masculine prowess. Part of the narrator's anger has to do with the men's discussion during the bridge game about how it would be more likely to "put people off gorilla-hunting" if the narrator rather than Beverly were to shoot the gorilla because Beverly would look "stirring" in a pith helmet, while the narrator "wouldn't be cute in the least" (Fowler, 349).

Presumably all of this is in the narrator's mind when she raises the barrel of her gun. But when the gorilla looks at her, the narrator sees "surprise, curiosity, caution. Something else, too. Something so human it made me feel like an old woman with no clothes on. I might have shot him just for that, but I knew it wasn't right — to kill him merely because he was more human than I anticipated" (Fowler, 351). More human — and thus more like the men who had discussed how the narrator in a pith helmet "wouldn't be cute in the least." The narrator then says, "I might have hit him several times — spared the women, freed the women. But I couldn't see that they wanted freeing and Eddie had told me never to shoot a gun angry" (Fowler, 351). Not only has the narrator here included the male gorilla within the group of males with whom she is angry, but she finds herself projecting onto the *females* the possibility of something like emancipation — even as she acknowledges that she *couldn't see* "that they wanted freeing" — a move that brackets the human/primate binary in favor of the male/female binary.

The narrator's bracketing of the human/primate binary in favor of the male/female binary is particularly interesting in relation to Beverly's presumptive choice to leave human society in favor of gorilla society. The narrator never offers a clear indication of all that was said in her last conversation with Beverly. "When I'm tired and have thought too much about it all, Beverly's last words come back to me." The last words she attributes to Beverly in her narration are "Then you'd best keep with him" — referring to Eddie (Fowler, 348).

The narrator describes Beverly as fed up with the pressure her partner, Merion, has been exerting on her, fed up with just about all the white males in the party but Eddie. "Merion," she says, "keeps on about how he paid my way here. Like he hasn't gotten his money's worth" (Fowler, ooo). Beverly talks to the narrator about how Merion "seems to think the apes will leave me alone if only I don't go tempting them" and about how Burunga told Russell that the apes must be hunted naked and that Beverly said she hadn't yet told Merion that, that she was "saving it for a special occasion" (Fowler, 348).

The narrator hints that Beverly may be sleeping with other men in the party besides the alpha male, Merion. In the last paragraph of the story the narrator says that sometimes she turns over Beverly's "last words" and "then they become, not a threat as I originally heard them, but an invitation" (Fowler, 355). Resentful of Beverly's sexual freedom and youth, the narrator apparently hears Beverly telling her that if she isn't careful, she'll take Eddie from her.

But in a belated riposte to Beverly's telling the narrator to "keep with" Eddie, because he's "the best," the narrator ends the story by saying, "I can pretend that she's still there in the jungle, dipping her feet, eating wild carrots, and waiting for me. I can pretend that I'll be joining her whenever I wish and just as soon as I please." The narrator says that she has been thinking about all the women primatologists "who'd sooner live in the jungle with the chimpanzees or the orangutans or the great mountain gorillas."

Now that she knows there is no one left to contradict her, she puts aside her resentment of Beverly and forgets Beverly's male-identified behavior and transforms her image of Beverly from that of aggressive sexual competitor to one of feminist sisterhood. She imagines Beverly choosing the gorilla society over human society for similar reasons to those she attributes to the women primatologists — and she imagines herself, all these years later, doing so as well. She does not, however, imagine the missing African woman, said at the mission to have been abducted by gorillas, as having made such a choice, likely because *that* particular case of a woman gone missing never registered significantly enough to engage her imagination, so taken with the Belgian Fathers' racist tales of cannibalism as to erase her consciousness of the woman's subjectivity entirely.

Reading the Story of Beverly's Disappearance

On first reading the story, I was still reeling with the shock of Eddie's revelation when I encountered the narrator's admission that she sometimes imagines joining Beverly, the women primatologists, and primate society in the jungle. This grace note of a fantasy instantly captivated me, drawing me into an ecstatic construction of the familiar topos of feminist utopian fantasy. The feminist utopian topos tends to be associated with a white middle-class feminism that fails to see its own exclusionary whiteness; thus to the extent that Fowler constructs "the jungle" as a site for utopian fantasy, her grace note is silently complicitous with primatologists' long-standing refusal to acknowledge the local politics and history of Central Africa. This complicitousness is confirmed by the narrator's exclusion of another woman in the story said to have disappeared: the nameless villager who leaves behind her bracelets and is presumed to have been carried off by gorillas. And yet, the story's grace note sounded and felt absolutely right to my ear, resonating as it does with the denouement of "The Women Men Don't See" and with "all those old stories" of women "carried off by gorillas."

For all that the grace note rings in perfect harmony with a song that can be found in every longtime white feminist reader's repertoire, on rereading, I realized that the shock I felt the first time through had kept me from picking up on *how* the narrative manages to end on that note. Although the story frequently resonates with "The Women Men Don't See" — which itself gestures toward the idea of women escaping gender oppression through an act of deliberate separatism — it nevertheless has been developing the latter story's theme with respect to the operations of difference as described above and not as a story of women running from human, male-dominated society. In other words, in its very last sentences, "What I Didn't See" moves in one great leap from being a story critiquing 1970s-style cultural feminism to celebrating one of that same feminism's cherished fantasies. The net effect of this leap is not to erase the story's critique of second-wave feminism, but to insist that such a critique does not negate the insights of 1970s-style feminism: rather, it complicates them fruitfully.

In trying to understand how the story could make such a seemingly radical shift in its last sentences and still make sense to the feminist reader, two questions in particular need to be raised. First: when did the narrator become such a feminist, that she could plausibly end the story with a fantasy of feminist utopian community? Although she portrays herself as quick to notice and resent the uses the men put her to in order to protect their masculine egos, she does not give the impression of having been particularly sympathetic to Beverly's situation or reactions at the time of the story's events. Was she some sort of feminist all along, or did she become a feminist later (just as she only later began to "see" the operations of racism)? A closer examination of the text suggests that my failure to perceive her feminism at first sight might have been as much a result of what the narrator doesn't say as a matter of my own tendency to read the characters and their situation through the prism of an early twenty-first-century mind-set.

Consider, first, what the narrator doesn't say.

The main events of the story coincide with an otherwise unrelated crisis in the narrator's life: her need to come to terms with others' (particularly *male* others') changing perceptions of her as a middle-aged woman and to accept the fact that she will never bear a child, a crisis that in this story neatly dovetails with the onset of perimenopausal symptoms. She describes behavior and actions that are inflected by this crisis but offers no feminist analysis of it. Obviously if she had offered such analysis she would not have been able to focus so relentlessly on the larger events she wishes to relate. And she would also have had to articulate her resentment of Beverly and the threat Beverly posed to her marriage. In the context, such an analysis would have not only been painful to the narrator and distracting from the story the narrator sets out to tell (the "last word," as she calls it, since she is now the sole survivor of the party), but also would have laid the narrator open to the suspicion of being at the least self-centered and at the worst self-serving. A feminist analysis of the narrator's crisis, therefore, must be provided by the reader.

Next: how much does my impression that the narrator wasn't particularly feminist at the time of the events she relates have to do with her portraying Eddie as the sensitive male, as the one who is always aware of what is going on, while the narrator portrays herself as virtually blind? Eddie knows she's begun menopause and that she is suffering from hot flashes, not malarial fever. Eddie understands Beverly's situation. Eddie is acutely aware of just how threatening racism is to the Africans. Eddie is, as Beverly says, "the best."

But consider: Eddie is as familiar a figure to feminist readers of 2002 as Don Fenton was to feminist readers of 1973. Many of us have Eddies in our lives, as friends, partners, coworkers — or even fathers and brothers. Turn-of-the-twenty-first-century readers may be likely to take Eddie's sensitivity for granted. But the events of the story are not, in fact, set in 2002. The narrator provides 1928 as a date.[27] As older feminists will know well, during and prior to early second-wave feminism, "sensitive" males with feminist values had to be taught and trained to see the world differently from their male peers: they did not simply do so on their own through an innate sensitivity.

Who, then, taught Eddie to be so sensitive? A second look at the story suggests that the narrator did this herself. Early in the story, the narrator writes: "I worried that it would be a pattern and every time one of the men was tired on the trail they'd say we had to stop on my account. I told Eddie right away I wouldn't like it if this was to happen" (Fowler, 341). It is the narrator in this passage who recognizes the operations of gender, and it is the narrator who cues Eddie to see them as well. The inference to be drawn is that it is the narrator who taught Eddie to "see" the operations of gender (even as he apparently taught her — long after the events of the story — to see the operations of race). The narrator, then, may very well be an example of what Sheldon calls "a feminist of a far earlier vintage, where we worked through a lot of the first stages by our lonesomes")[28] — in which case, imagining a collective society of women and primates is an amazing (though certainly not impossible) departure from the isolated position of, say, a Ruth Parsons.

Having answered the question of whether the narrator was a feminist all along, I can now address my second question: how does the narrator leap-frog from Beverly's disappearance to those "old stories" of women being carried off by gorillas and so to her collective feminist fantasy? My exploration of the first question suggests that the two questions are linked.

The narrator's reference to "the old stories" conjures for the experienced feminist reader not only the old pulp stories in which primates and other large, hairy males carry off women, but also more recent feminist stories in which women become the lovers of nonhuman animals whom they prefer to their husbands. In Rachel Ingalls's *Mrs. Caliban*, Dorothy takes Larry, an escaped "giant lizard-like animal," for her lover.[29] In Carol Emshwiller's "Yukon," a woman leaves her husband (hoping at first that he'll come after her) and goes into the mountains and lives with a bear in his cave; it is the bear who leaves her, not she the bear: "When the bear stays out six days in a row, she suspects she's made the same old mistake . . . same kind of destructive relationship she's always had before."[30] And in Peter Høeg's *The Woman and the Ape*, the wife of an animal researcher takes Erasmus, a highly intelligent 300-pound ape with a political agenda, as her lover.[31] In every example of this subgenre I know of, a single woman becomes involved with a nonhuman male, usually because her human partner is in some way unsatisfactory.

While Beverly shows every indication of finding Merion unsatisfactory, her discontent seems to be as much with the entire scene as with him as a partner. Importantly, the reader can be confident that she did not become intimate with any *particular* gorilla before her departure. So if Beverly *did* choose to leave human society for gorilla society, it could only have been for the same reasons that Ruth and Althea Parsons choose to leave human society for an unknown alien society. The narrative subtly reinforces this point by intimating that Beverly may be pregnant, just as the Parsons women seem to want to arrange Althea's getting pregnant as they prepare to leave human society.[32] And so the narrator's fantasy extrapolation cannot be adequately explained in the terms offered by these male/female cross-species romances, but must include the larger social and political frame of reference that "The Women Men Don't See" so powerfully established.[33]

Reading Beverly's disappearance through the lens of "The Women Men Don't See," then, almost fills the gap between the cross-species romance stories and the narrator's fantasy. *Almost*. But something has changed in the temporal space lying between Tiptree's story and Fowler's. There is a difference between these stories beyond the theoretical sophistication and more supple narrative structures unavailable to Sheldon in 1973 that Fowler uses so adeptly in 2002. That difference, I believe, is a product of thirty years of feminist sf.

Something Rich and Strange

ARIEL'S SONG
Full fathom five thy father lies;
Of his bones are coral made;
Those are pearls that were his eyes;
Nothing of him that doth fade
But doth suffer a sea-change
Into something rich and strange.
Sea nymphs hourly ring his knell.[34]

"We live by ones and twos in the world-machine," Ruth Parsons says in "The Women Men Don't See."[35] That, she notes, is the reason that feminism can't succeed. And so when Ruth Parsons leaves human society, it is with only one other woman. If women can't be imagined to "live" (and act politically) with other women except singly or in pairs, they certainly can't be imagined escaping to an alternate society except singly or in pairs, either. And this surely must have been the logic behind Sheldon's designating "Message No. 2" as "the bleak future for feminism."[36]

In all the feminist discussion of "The Women Men Don't See," critics never try to imagine the kind of life Ruth and Althea will face — much less imagine other women choosing to join them. Don Fenton describes one of the aliens as "eight feet of snowy rippling horror," its face "a black horror," "metallic, like a big glimmering distributor head," its body possessing a "long white rubbery arm with black worms." The narrative's emphasis is on escape, not on the promising possibilities of an alternative life. The view is Fenton's, after all. Yet one can't help but be conscious that Ruth and Althea are so physically different from the aliens they run off with that they are likely to always remain outsiders — aliens — in this other society.[37] So although the difference between Tiptree's and Fowler's treatment of the image might be attributable to the respective difference in their narrators' gender, I am not persuaded that that particular difference accounts for it.

Assessments of the progress of feminism typically focus on changes in the effects of gender in the economic, political, and social circumstances of individual women's lives. I propose to recognize another kind of change, a change not just in how women think about their lives and what might be possible to them in the future, but a feminism-driven change in how our imaginations work.

Alice Sheldon's imagination conceived of a pair of women first surviving within and then escaping the "world machine." Sheldon had little hope that women would be able to negotiate their differences sufficiently to forge a solidarity powerful enough to enable a collective, feminist agency; the power of her story's image of escape lies in what it tells the reader about the alienation inherent in very ordinary, even tolerable passing.[38]

Karen Joy Fowler's imagination, however, takes what had been an image of escape and transforms it into the hope of joy and community.[39] "Ariel's Song," quoted above, evokes this fabulous transformation. As the sea transforms bones to coral and eyes to pearl, the body of the father to "something rich and strange," just so after thirty years in the sea of feminist sf Sheldon's image of survival and escape has been transformed. Thirty years of feminist sf have generated far-flung explorations of separatism, of assertions of feminist agency, of women living and working in alien societies, of women cooperating openly in communities rather than collaborating privately in pairs. Thirty years of feminist sf have brought many of us face-to-face with differences and taught us to think about the politics of those differences. And finally, perhaps most important, thirty years of feminist sf have educated the feminist imagination in the delight and pleasure of empowering play.

And so in Fowler's hands "the Goodalls, the Galdikas and the Fosseys" become more than examples found in the real world; they become material
for imaginative expansion, for allowing feminist readers to see beyond the
conceptual limitations of ordinary, nonfeminist reality.[40]

Postscript: But Is "What I Didn't See" Science Fiction?

Although "What I Didn't See" later won the 2003 Nebula Award, a storm
of controversy attended its debut on the SciFiction.com site. Dozens of
people, most of them professional sf writers and editors, made hundreds of
posts in July and August 2002 to *Tangent Online*'s SFF.net mailing list. The
controversy focused on the issue of whether the story should have been
published in a science fiction venue.[41] In a favorable review of the story,
Brenda Cooper alludes to this controversy: "In the end, the heart of the
story is unresolved and haunting, and perhaps this sense of the mysterious
is why it was published at *SCI FICTION*. It is not science fiction or fantasy as I understand them; it is a very well done literary story. Regardless,
I'm glad that Ellen Datlow chose it. If you like literary fiction, you are very
likely to appreciate this offering."[42]

Judging by the posts made to the SFF.net listserv, few of the story's
readers — including its defenders — read the story as science fiction. Even
fewer readers comprehended the story's relationship to "The Women Men
Don't See." There were almost as many theories about what the story was
about (and even what the basic events of the story were) as there were
posters. And almost none of the posters understood the story's relation to
the history of feminist science fiction.

My discussion of "What I Didn't See" has hinged on reading it not only
as science fiction, but also as understandable as such only with reference
to its feminist sf genealogy. Such a reading does not share Cooper's sense
that "the heart of the story is unresolved."

What exactly is "the heart of the story"? What haunts Eddie? Why does
he need the narrator to tell him he did the right thing? Is there anything at
all "mysterious" about the heart of the story?

Cooper, I believe, places Beverly's disappearance at the heart of the
story and apparently finds this disappearance "unresolved and haunting."
Granted, it is *mysterious*, in the sense that neither the narrator nor the
reader can know for certain what lay behind Beverly's disappearance. "My
full, true Eddie never did come back from the jungle," the narrator says
(Fowler, 353). But it is not Beverly's disappearance that haunts Eddie and
keeps him from sleeping (though he cannot bear the sound of her name,

presumably because it reminds him of everything he is desperate to forget) or that motivates the narrator to tell the story, now that she is the last one alive who knows it. And it is not Beverly's disappearance that gives the story its title.

Eddie says, of the slaughter of forty or more gorillas, "It felt like murder. Just exactly like murder" (Fowler, 353). And it was a "murder" that he himself instigated, in order to prevent his colleagues from saying "something that couldn't be unsaid, something that would get to the Belgians." He says, "I kept us angry until we had killed so very many and were all so ashamed, there would be no way to turn and accuse someone new" (Fowler, 354).

He is haunted by what "felt like murder" and by urging his peers into such an excess of killing that they would be too ashamed to accuse anyone else — even an African — of being a killer. He is haunted by his sense that there might have been a better way to have protected the porters from hysterical, racist violence. And reading between the lines of the story, he may very well be haunted, too, by the suspicion that Merion killed Beverly, provoked by Beverly's sleeping around — not only with Willet, but with himself, which would implicate him in contributing to Beverly's death.[43] What *I* find haunting about this story is the way in which it lays bare the violence, inherent in the operations of racism and simian orientalism, that results when the white men in the story lose control of a situation involving a white woman they consider theirs.

"Something happened to Beverly, but I can't tell you what," the narrator says. She, like Eddie, doesn't believe that Beverly was killed by a porter. Beverly's lover at first says that he believes she was carried off by gorillas. Eight days of searching reveals no trace of Beverly — not even a bracelet (referring to the bracelets said to have been left behind when a village woman was supposedly abducted by gorillas). The narrator remarks that Beverly hadn't been dressed for the extreme cold of the nights. On the basis of what the narrator reveals, I think the presumption must be that either Merion murdered Beverly, or Beverly went off by herself (the way the narrator did) because she wanted a break from the men and then either had an accident (and thus probably died of exposure) or, like the narrator, came upon a group of gorillas. If the latter occurred, then she, unlike the narrator, who raised the barrel of her gun at the male in the group, joined them.

If one reads the story as "literary fiction" and refuses the story's science-fictional allusions, one must assume that either Beverly got lost, had an accident, and died of exposure or she was murdered by her lover. But if one reads the story as feminist sf, the story's relationship to "The Women Men Don't See" as well the narrator's fascination with "these young women who'd sooner live in the jungle with the chimpanzees or the orangutans or the great mountain gorillas" would bring what Ruth and Althea Parsons did in the jungle in Belize into prominence. Moreover, if one reads the story in relation to "The Women Men Don't See," one must also attend to the story's genealogy in the childhood experience of Alice Sheldon and so find oneself up against another reason for not taking the story as "literary" (in the sense of being mimetic).

Donna Haraway's text, which Fowler read in advance of writing "What I Didn't See," makes plain the strong connection between Alice Sheldon's childhood experience and certain details of the story.

> Tucked in the margins and endnotes of "Teddy Bear Patriarchy" was a little white girl in Brightest Africa in the early 1920s. Little Alice Hastings Bradley was brought there by Carl Akeley, the father of the game, on his scientific hunt for the gorilla, in the hope that her golden-haired presence would transform the ethic of hunting into the ethic of conservation and survival, as "man" and his surrogates, sucked into decadence, stood at the brink of extinction.[44]

Fowler's stand-in for Akeley, Archer, invites two women to join the hunt with the idea of arranging for one of them to shoot the gorilla rather than relying on the mere presence of the little girl her mother fictionalized in a children's series called *Alice in Jungleland*.[45] But the reasoning and the stated goal of Akeley and Archer are unmistakably the same.

In her "Biographical Sketch," Sheldon dates the expedition that Fowler fictionalizes: "*1919/1920*, Bradleys with Carl Akeley on successful final quest for legendary Central African Mountain Gorilla."[46] Donna Haraway describes a photograph from the expedition now located in the American Museum film archive:

> Carl Akeley, Herbert Bradley [Sheldon's father], and Mary Hastings Bradley [Sheldon's mother] holding up the gorilla head and corpse to be recorded by the camera is an unforgettable image. The face of the dead giant evokes Bosch's conception of pain, and the lower jaw hangs slack, held up by Akeley's hand. The body looks bloated and utterly heavy. Mary Bradley gazes smilingly at the faces of the male hunters, her own eyes averted from the camera. Akeley and Herbert Bradley look directly at the camera in unshuttered acceptance of their act. Two Africans, a young boy and a young man, perch in a tree above the scene, one looking at the camera, one at the hunting party.[47]

Fowler sets her fantastic version of the Akeley hunt for the "legendary Central African Mountain Gorilla" in 1928, that is, after Akeley's death and at a time when the Bradleys happened to be absent from the African continent. Haraway tells us that Akeley hoped to debunk DuChaillu's account of gorillas and replace the big-game hunting with the photographing of gorillas — *after* he had acquired a healthy male specimen for a museum diorama. As mentioned above, the presence of the little white girl, Alice, was intended to further advance the point. Fowler's Archer wishes to do the same — but by having the narrator or Beverly do the shooting. Fowler uses accounts of the Akeley expedition (of which the very young Alice Sheldon was a member) not as the basis for producing a mimetic historical fiction but to science-fictionally complicate and update "The Women Men Don't See" through the analytic lens of Haraway's history of primate science.

Fowler's nonmimetic treatment of the material allows her to put gender, race, and simian orientalism at the heart of the story. Her depiction of the historic hunt not only insists that gender and race politics are intertwined, it also reminds us that any fantasy that feminists might entertain about women escaping gender politics by going off with aliens (or wild primate species) will necessarily be implicated with the politics of race: something that the Goodalls and the Fosseys failed to understand (in one case with fatal consequences).[48] And it gently insists on inserting into the story an awareness of what divides women, even as the story's narrator suspends that awareness when fantasizing a feminist utopia.

Reading the story as "literary fiction" must obviously change its meaning. The reader then must wonder, for instance, about how the narrator could so happily fantasize about joining Beverly in the jungle (many decades later), or draw a connection to the Goodalls et al. — and then perhaps "explain" this fantasy as a symptom of senility and therefore extraneous to the story (which, if not science fiction, would then be one in which a woman disappeared into the jungle and the men who were with her went briefly, collectively insane as a result). This would not be a feminist story, but a tragic story about a decent white man, Eddie, trying to do the right thing in terrible circumstances.[49] The title would then refer more to how the narrator's failure to see or understand what was going on right under her nose resulted in her failure to be a supportive wife to this good man caught up in a terrible situation than to white feminists' history of not seeing that the politics of race are inextricable from the politics of gender. This alternative reading, in my view, impoverishes the story, even as it makes it more comfortable fare, more sympathetic to decent white liberals like Eddie trying to do the right thing.

Read as feminist sf, "What I Didn't See" embraces the transformation of the feminist imagination wrought through thirty years of feminist consciousness. At the same time it brings into the story told in "The Women

Men Don't See" the Women Men Do See and the Men [that white] Women Don't See (Beverly and the porters respectively) without ignoring or minimizing the painful, continuing contradictions with which other oppressions, most especially those of race, necessarily complicate feminist politics.[50] As such, "What I Didn't See" offers a powerful expression of the state of feminist sf in the first decade of the twenty-first century.

As if to say: and so the struggle continues.

NOTES

1. James Tiptree Jr., "The Women Men Don't See," in *Warm Worlds and Otherwise* (New York: Ballantine Books, 1975), 154.

2. Ibid.

3. Ibid., 153.

4. There has been much talk among feminists about pessimism in Alice Sheldon's fiction; my own impression, however, is that although Sheldon never lost sight of the terrible things human beings are capable of, she also believed humans capable of significant change. Sheldon described herself as "a feminist of a far earlier vintage, where we worked through a lot of the first stages by our lonesomes." See "Everything But the Signature is Me," in *Meet Me at Infinity: The Uncollected Tiptree: Fiction and Nonfiction* (New York: Tor Books, 2000), 313. She also, however, characterized "Message No. 2" of "The Women Men Don't See" as the "bleak future for feminism" in her (unpublished) summary of the story; quoted courtesy of Julie Phillips in *The Battle of the Sexes in Science Fiction*, by Justine Larbalestier (Middletown, Conn.: Wesleyan University Press, 2002), 145. Until I read that Sheldon herself considered one of the two "messages" of the story to be that of pessimism for the future of feminism, I had assumed that Ruth Parsons could be taken as an example of a woman who had chosen not to be a feminist because she considered feminism hopelessly idealistic.

5. The most notable are Margaret Atwood's *The Handmaid's Tale* (1986) and Suzette Haden Elgin's *Native Tongue* series (1984, 1987, 1994).

6. See Misha Kavka, "Feminism, Ethics, and History; or, What Is the 'Post' in 'Postfeminism'?" *Tulsa Studies in Women's Literature* 21, no. 1 (Spring 2002): 29–44, at 32. I've more than once been told by younger women (usually in response to comments I've made on panels in public forums) that because their mothers (and the other feminists of their mothers' generation — women like me, that is) fought the battles of feminism, it's now a waste of time to be thinking about gender at all. Academic friends who have taught women's studies courses report more hostile and critical remarks, to the effect that second-wave feminists either succumbed to believing they were victims (following Kate Roiphe's invidious line of argument) or that they simply didn't know how to get along with men. Joanna Russ describes a slightly different phenomenon, in which young women call themselves "feminists" but (quoting a letter written to her by a colleague in women's studies) "had a very limited concept of what feminism was all about. Almost no one saw feminism as the impetus to a radical reordering of society." Joanna Russ, *What Are We*

Fighting For? Sex, Race, Class, and the Future of Feminism (New York: St. Martin's, 1998), 7–8.

7. Karen Joy Fowler used this metaphor in a discussion (September 2003) about the current state of feminist sf.

8. Karen Joy Fowler, "What I Didn't See," posted at scifiction.com, July 2002. Scifiction.com, edited by Ellen Datlow, is not only the highest-paying market for sf stories, but also offers them via the Internet to readers without charge. Sales to the site are therefore highly coveted by sf writers, which helped fuel the outrage against Datlow's choosing Fowler's story for the site.

9. See Alice Sheldon's "Biographical Sketch for *Contemporary Authors*" in *Meet Me At Infinity*, 334–347. "From age 4 to 15, Alice Sheldon's childhood was dominated by the experience of accompanying her parents on all their (widely reported) explorations and trips," Sheldon writes. "She found herself interacting with adults of every color, size, shape, and condition — lepers, black royalty in lionskins, white royalty in tweeds, Arab slavers, functional saints and madmen in power, poets, killers, and collared eunuchs, world-famous actors with head-colds, blacks who ate their enemies and a white who had eaten his friends" (336–337).

10. John Clute, "James Tiptree, Jr.," in *The Encyclopedia of Science Fiction*, ed. John Clute and Peter Nicholls (New York: St. Martin's, 1995), 1231.

11. A number of critics discuss the story at length and enjoy talking about how Sheldon fooled Robert Silverberg (among others). Larbalestier closely examines the difference the author's perceived gender made to the way in which the story was read. See Larbalestier, *Battle of the Sexes*, 144–148, and 192–202. Larbalestier's chapter "I'm Too Big But I Love to Play" maps the pitfalls in naively assuming that Sheldon's female "Raccoona Sheldon" pseudonym was identical with her Alice Sheldon identity while the "James Tiptree, Jr." pseudonym allowed her to develop an alter ego. Sheldon herself made contradictory and ambivalent statements concerning her gendered pseudonyms. One of the best documented changes in attitude toward Sheldon and the texts she produced as Tiptree is to be found in the annotations of the reprinted historic *Khatru* (1975, issues 3 & 4) in *Symposium: Women in Science Fiction*, ed. Jeffrey D. Smith (Madison, Wis.: SF3, 1993). Tiptree (along with the two other participants known to be male, Jeffrey D. Smith and Samuel R. Delany) were asked to leave the *Symposium*. Some of the comments made in the early 1990s interpreted this naively, as showing that sex prejudice had been at work. But Gwyneth Jones astutely insists on reading Tiptree's contributions to the *Symposium* not as a woman writing under a masculine label, but as a certain kind of *performance* of gender. Jones refers to the "three men" participating, and then writes, "Did I say *three* men? Yes I did, because the male impersonator has to be counted among them. I was surprised — although I shouldn't have been — at how poorly 'James Tiptree, Jr.'s' contribution reads. And not at all surprised it had several women participants (going to call them 'parts' from now on) gnashing teeth and tearing hair. I reckon this is inevitable. A male impersonator is no better than a female impersonator, after all: basically a sham. And it *sounds* sham — this 'clumsy-ignorant' male's paean to motherhood, how hollow, overdone, sentimental. And the pseudo-science! You can see him, big, burly chap in tweeds with leather elbow patches: shy smile, doggy-sincere eyes, pompous rather old-fashioned manner. Longs to open doors for you but doesn't dare, calls you 'dear lady' when he for-

gets himself, which is frequently. . . . It would have been better, I can't help feeling, if Alice Sheldon had simply played the male, straight. A male-feminist impersonator comes over as . . . guilty and smug, smug and guilty." 132. Jones, by the way, sees Smith and Delany as performing as male-feminist impersonators, too.

12. "A Woman Writing Science Fiction," in *Meet Me at Infinity*, 391. There were men for whom the feminist significance of the story hinged entirely upon its being written by a male. Terry Carr, praising the story, said that a woman "writing a profoundly feminist story" would not be such a revelation (Larbalestier, *Battle of the Sexes*, 147).

13. In "Who Is Tiptree, What Is He?" (the introduction to *Warm Worlds and Otherwise*), Robert Silverberg observes (immediately after characterizing Tiptree's writing as "inelectuably masculine" [xii]): "Because Tiptree lives just a few miles from the Pentagon, or at least uses a mailing address in that vicinity, and because in his letters he often reports himself as about to take off for some remote part of the planet, the rumor constantly circulates that in 'real' life he is some sort of government agent involved in high-security work. His obviously first-hand acquaintance with the world of airports and bureaucrats, as demonstrated in such stories as 'The Women Men Don't See,' gives some support to this notion, just as his equally keen knowledge of the world of hunters and fisherman, in the same story, would appear to prove him male" (xii).

14. "A Woman Writing Science Fiction," 390–391. In "Biographical Sketch," Sheldon writes that after her "unmasking," "only the feminist world remained excited, but on a different basis, having nothing to do with the stories. . . . The more vulnerable males discovered simultaneously that Tiptree had been much overrated, and sullenly retired to practice patronizing smiles" (346). In her "*Contemporary Authors* Interview," in *Meet Me at Infinity* (348–370), Tiptree attributes disappointment to her SF friends, postrevelation (353–354), when hearing her voice on the phone, and says that her correspondence all but ceased, because "Alice Sheldon" (as opposed to "Tiptree") had no "epistolary style." She even suggests that her usefulness to other female writers ceased, as she could no longer play the old boys' system on their behalf — or use her male courtliness to help them "brace up" ("A Woman Writing Science Fiction," 314).

15. "Zero at the Bone," in *Meet Me at Infinity*, 382. "After the revelation, quite a few male writers who had been, I thought, my friends and called themselves my admirers, suddenly found it necessary to adopt a condescending, patronizing tone, or break off altogether, as if I no longer interested them" ("A Woman Writing Science Fiction," 391).

16. "A Woman Writing Science Fiction," 389.

17. Ibid.

18. Sarah Lefanu, *Feminism and Science Fiction* (Bloomington: University of Indiana Press, 1989), 127.

19. Ibid., 18.

20. See Audre Lorde, "Age, Race, Class, and Sex: Women Redefining Difference," in *Sister Outsider: Essays and Speeches* (Trumansburg, N.Y.: Crossing Press, 1984), 114–123.

21. Sylvia Kelso notes that for feminist theorist Judith Butler, "it is no longer enough to list 'gender, sexuality, race, class' as separate axes in the constitution of

a subject. To her, they are rather 'vectors of power' that can only be articulated through each other; that is, race is not an addition, but a founding component of both gender and sexuality." See Sylvia Kelso, "These are Not the Aliens You're Looking For: Reflections on Race, Theory and Writing in Recent SF," in *Flashes of the Fantastic: Selected Essays from the War of the Worlds Centennial, Nineteenth International Conference of the Fantastic in the Arts*, ed. David Ketterer (Bowling Green, Ohio: Greenwood, 1998). The continual shifting of the narrator's position with respect to the gender, race, and simian orientalist binaries throughout "What I Didn't See" demonstrates the fluidity of white women's position with respect to these "vectors of power."

22. For an extensive elaboration of these intertwined issues, see Donna Haraway, *Primate Visions: Gender, Race, and Nature in the World of Modern Science* (New York: Routledge, 1989). When asked if she had read Haraway's book before writing the story, Karen Joy Fowler said that she had.

23. Haraway discusses this throughout her book. She notes, for instance that Jane and Vanne Goodall, delayed by the successful revolution in the Congo in 1960, fixed two thousand Spam sandwiches for the fleeing Belgians but that later, in her book, *In the Shadow of Man*, Goodall did not even mention the fact that fifteen African nations achieved independence in 1960; she wrote, simply, that "violence and bloodshed had erupted in the Congo" and that "it was necessary to wait and find out how the local Kigoma district Africans would react to the tales of rioting and disorder in the Congo" (164–165).

24. See, for instance, Haraway's description and analysis of a National Geographic TV special, *Gorilla*, which focuses on the pressure of human population on the gorilla habitat (265–266).

25. Richard Wright, *Native Son* (New York: Harper & Row, 1966), 33.

26. Ibid.

27. The date of the actual expedition on which this one is modeled was 1919–1920. See Alice Sheldon's "Biographical Sketch for *Contemporary Authors*" in *Meet Me At Infinity*, 333–334. Traveling with her parents, Alice Sheldon spent the first half of the decade in Africa and the second half in India and Southeast Asia; she returned to Africa with them for a final expedition in 1929–1930. The author's decision to set the story in 1928 accomplishes two things: it establishes the nonhistorical and therefore nonmimetic character of the story, freeing readers to theorize it as having occurred in an alternate branch of history than our own; and it allows the possibility for the narrator, who was already middle-aged at the time of the expedition, to live long enough to follow the women primatologists in the news.

28. "Everything But the Signature," 313.

29. Rachel Ingalls, *Mrs. Caliban* (Harvard and Boston: The Harvard Common Press, 1983).

30. Carol Emswhiller, "Yukon," in *Verging on the Pertinent* (Minneapolis, Minn.: Coffee House Press, 1989), 1–7. Marian Engel's feminist novel, *Bear* (1976) also envisions a woman living with a bear.

31. Peter Høeg, *The Woman and the Ape*, trans. Barbara Haveland (New York: Penguin Books, 1997).

32. When Beverly and the narrator are talking about the gorillas supposedly being drawn to menstrual blood, Beverly says, "Then I've got no problem." In an

e-mail to me (November 3, 2003) discussing the contrast between the cooperative pairing of the Parsons mother-daughter team and the faintly hostile relationship between the narrator and male-identifying Beverly, Fowler writes: "In the Tiptree story the women work together to get the younger woman pregnant; there is no jealousy, no difficulties over making the sexual overtures work as planned. I think, if women really worked together, like the Tiptree story, the situation for women would not be as dark as Tiptree then goes on to suggest." Fowler notes of her own story, "There is also, as per the Tiptree story, a hint that Beverly may be pregnant. The narrator cannot admit having heard this, but it is largely responsible for her bad mood during the bridge game and her storming off alone."

33. Molly Gloss's *Wild Life* (New York: Simon and Schuster, 2000) may also be apropos; its protagonist, Charlotte Bridger Drummond, gets lost in an early twentieth-century Pacific Northwest wilderness and lives for a time with a tribe of mysterious beasts.

34. William Shakespeare, *The Tempest*, ed. Northrop Frye, act 1, scene 2, lines 397–403, in *The Complete Works*, ed. Alfred Harbage (Baltimore: Penguin Books, 1969), 1378.

35. "The Women Men Don't See," 154.

36. Sheldon describes the main message of the story as "total misunderstanding of woman's motivations by narrator, who relates everything to self" (Larbalestier, *Battle of the Sexes*, 145).

37. The physical (and presumably social) differences between human and primate societies are much less stark. And one can't help noting that any human woman would always find it easy to position herself on the "culture" side of the nature/culture binary in all her dealings with primates, which would likely not be true with a culture that has achieved interstellar travel. The differences between the societies to which Tiptree's and Fowler's women escape obviously were chosen very deliberately by their authors and only underscores the differences in what they are able to imagine.

38. *Passing* is a strategy that individuals use to disguise difference, either by letting others think that they are not different (as when a light-skinned African American *passes* for white, or when a woman dresses, lives, and identifies herself to others as male), or by effacing their difference from the norm so thoroughly as to make it invisible to people who do not share the difference in question (as secretaries and servants have traditionally done).

39. And yet Fowler also insists on what is missing from Tiptree's story: the women men *do* see and the men women *don't* see (exemplified by Beverly and the porters, respectively). In her November 3, 2003, e-mail to me, Fowler writes "If every woman made her commitment to other women instead of the family unit or the church or whatever, sexism would have to end or end in gender war. . . . But in fact women are divided and complicit, so I made my women divided and complicit."

40. This difference that thirty years of feminist sf has made carries a certain irony. Although Sheldon's imagination was limited to the desperate escape of a mother and daughter into an unknown, likely difficult situation and Fowler's imagination can conjure up a community of women living comfortably with primates in the wild, Sheldon shows her characters actually *performing* the escape, while Fowler's narrator only imagines a utopian community. That Fowler's narrator set-

tles for an imaginary solution for taking away the pain of the destruction of her marriage seems apropos, given the current state of white, middle-class feminism in the United States in 2002.

41. A small but vocal segment of the sf field perennially complain that "literary" stories deprive the genre of space for supposedly simpler, more entertaining stories espousing the more "traditional" values of the genre (which, as is usually the case with "traditional values," have at any time been universally agreed upon). About half a dozen of the people who posted about "What I Didn't See" argued that the story's publication in such a prestigious venue as scifi.com prevented worthier stories from being published and would have the effect of further demoralizing writers who were writing traditional adventure stories, thereby shrinking the pool of "good" sf even further. A panel at WisCon 28 revisited the controversy again in May 2004. Interestingly, one of the story's admirers, John Kessel, said that he did not think the story was science fiction; he also read it as a tragedy.

42. Brenda Cooper, review of "What I Didn't See," posted on July 10, 2002, <http://tangentonline.com/reviews/magazine.php3?review=668>.

43. In the author's e-mail to me, she puts it this way: "I wanted there to be three alternatives to what happened to Beverly — (1) she wandered off and was accidentally killed by the jungle; (2) she ran off and joined the gorillas; (3) one of the men murdered her because she is sexually out of control. When Eddie spurs the killing spree, he is horribly aware of that possibility. He thinks that Merion may have killed Beverly. So it's an even nastier bargain in Eddie's mind, that Merion may be looking for a patsy and what Eddie offers, without a word being spoken either way, is that Merion won't accuse the porters and Eddie won't accuse Merion. It's a bargain he can't, actually, live with."

44. Haraway, *Primate Visions*, 377.

45. For more about *Alice in Jungleland*, see Larbalestier's chapter "I'm Too Big but I Love to Play."

46. "Biographical Sketch," 337–338.

47. Haraway, *Primate Visions*, 34.

48. Dian Fossey was murdered in Rwanda in late 1985. Haraway writes that "Fossey used controversial direct action tactics to deter local poachers who harassed, trapped, and killed gorillas. She bitterly opposed the schemes to protect the gorillas through making them a foreign tourist resource. Her intense efforts to protect and to be 'alone' with personally named, wild gorillas in what was for her, and for the west before her, a dream land gave way to painful political difficulties, as well as to a different organization of scientific research." Although it is most likely that Fossey was murdered by the poachers she fought, a U.S. graduate student, Wayne McGuire, studying paternal care among the gorillas, was tried and convicted for her murder *in absentia* and sentenced to death by firing squad. Haraway, *Primate Visions*, 265–267.

49. This was in fact how several of the story's defenders in the discussion on the sff.publishing list read the story.

50. In the author's e-mail, she writes that she conceptualized Tiptree's characters in a Venn diagram, with two quadrants left out; the expressions "The Women Men Do See" and "The Men Women Don't See" are hers. Although this Venn diagram brings African men into visibility, it silently elides the presence of African

women, perhaps because the "seeing" and "not seeing" of Tiptree's and Fowler's stories refer inherently to vision that is raced white in the binary-based schematic that typically renders women of color unrepresentable. Where, in such a diagram, would the African woman who disappears from her village (leaving behind her bracelets) fit? She is someone the narrator forgets when she's envisioning a community of women living with gorillas in the jungle. Does she belong with the "Men Women Don't See"? Or with the "Women Men Don't See" that Tiptree describes as existing by ones and twos in the world-machine? The difficulty of representing this woman exemplifies the inadequacy of binary dualisms (even when they are portrayed as interlocking) to structure our comprehension of the world we live in.

Works Consulted

Abramson, Albert. "The Invention of Television." In *Television: An International History*, edited by Anthony Smith, 9–22. 2nd ed. Oxford: Oxford University Press, 1998.

Aldiss, Brian W. Foreword to "The Heat Death of the Universe." In *The Mirror of Infinity: A Critics' Anthology of Science Fiction*, edited by Robert Silverberg, 267–273. New York: Harper & Row, 1970.

Aldiss, Brian W., and Harry Harrison, eds. *Decade The 1960s*. London: Macmillan London Limited, 1977.

Allison, Dorothy. "The Future of Female: Octavia Butler's Mother Lode." In *Reading Black Reading Feminist*, edited by Henry Louis Gates, Jr. 471–478. New York: Meridian, 1990.

Asimov, Isaac. "The Mule." *Astounding Science Fiction* pt. 1 (Nov. 1945): 7–53, 139–144; pt 2 (Dec. 1945): 60–97, 148–168.

———. "Profession." *Astounding Science Fiction* (July 1957): 8–56.

Attebery, Brian. *Decoding Gender in Science Fiction*. New York: Routledge, 2002.

Atwood, Margaret. *The Handmaid's Tale*. London: J. Cape, 1986.

Bainbridge, William Sims. *Dimensions of Science Fiction*. Cambridge, Mass.: Harvard University Press, 1986.

Beal, Frances M. with Octavia Butler. "Black Women and the Science Fiction Genre." *Black Scholar*, 17, no. 2. (March/April, 1986): 14–18.

Benjamin, Walter. "The Work of Art in the Age of Mechanical Reproduction." 1936. In *The Critical Tradition: Classic Texts and Contemporary Trends*, edited by David H. Richter, 571–588. New York: St. Martin's, 1989.

Berger, James. *After the End: Representations of Post-Apocalypse*. Minneapolis: University of Minnesota Press, 1999.

Bishop, Michael, ed. *Nebula Awards 23*. San Diego: Harcourt Brace Jovanovich, 1989.

Boucher, Anthony, ed. *Best from Fantasy & Science Fiction, Fifth Series*. New York: Doubleday, 1956.

Bould, Mark. "Bould on the Boom." *Science Fiction Studies* 29 (July 2002): 307–310.

Boulter, Amanda. "Alice James Raccoona Tiptree Sheldon Jr: Textual Personas in the Short Fiction of Alice Sheldon." *Foundation* 63 (Spring 1995): 5–31.

Britt, Alan. Letter to the Editor. *Amazing Stories* (February 1937), 135.

Brownmiller, Susan. *Against Our Will: Men, Women and Rape*. Harmondsworth, Eng.: Penguin, [1975] 1976.

Brown, Charles N., and Jonathan Strahan, eds. *The Locus Awards: Thirty Years of the Best in Science Fiction and Fantasy*. New York: Eos, 2004.

Butler, Andrew M. "Going Uphill: An Interview with Gwyneth Jones." *Femspec* 5.1 (2004): 216–233.

Butler, Judith. *Bodies that Matter: On the Discursive Limits of "Sex."* New York: Routledge, 1993.

Butler, Octavia. *Bloodchild and Other Stories*. New York: Seven Stories Press, 1996.

———. *Parable of the Sower*. New York: Four Walls Eight Windows, 1993.

Card, Orson Scott, ed. *Future on Fire*. New York: Tor Books, 1991.

Carter, Angela. *The Passion of New Eve*. London: Virago, [1977] 1982.

Cassell, Joan. *A Group Called Women: Sisterhood and Symbolism in the Feminist Movement*. New York: David McKay, 1977.

Charnas, Suzy McKee. *Motherlines*. New York: Berkley Books, 1978.

Clarion Science Fiction Writers' Workshop. http://www.msu.edu/~clarion/workshop/workshopinfo.html.

Clute, John. "James Tiptree, Jr." In *The Encyclopedia of Science Fiction*, edited by John Clute and Peter Nicholls, 1230–1231. 2nd ed. New York: St. Martin's, 1993

———. "Pat Murphy." In *The Encyclopedia of Science Fiction*, edited by John Clute and Peter Nicholls, 839. 2nd ed. New York: St. Martin's, 1993.

———. "The Golden Age of SF." In *The Encyclopedia of Science Fiction*, edited by John Clute and Peter Nicholls, 506–07. 2nd ed. New York: St. Martin's, 1993.

Comer, Lee. *Wedlocked Women*. Leeds, UK: Feminist Books, 1974.

Conklin, Groff, ed. *The Best of Science Fiction*. New York: Crown, 1946.

Connell, R. W. *Masculinities*. Berkeley and Los Angeles: University of California Press, 1995.

Contento, William. *Index to Science Fiction Anthologies and Collections*. Boston: G.K. Hall, 1978.

Conway, Michael, Roberto DiFazio, and Francois Bonneville. "Sex, Sex Roles, and Response Styles for Negative Affect: Selectivity in a Free Recall Task." *Sex Roles* 25 (1991): 687–700.

Coontz, Stephanie. *The Way We Never Were: American Families and the Nostalgia Trap*. New York, Basic Books, 1992.

Cooper, Brenda. Review of "What I Didn't See." *Tangent Online* (July 2002).

Cranny-Francis, Anne. *Feminist Fiction: Feminist Uses of Generic Fiction*. New York: St. Martin's, 1990.

Creed, Barbara. *Horror and the Monstrous Feminine: An Imaginary Abjection*. London: Routledge, 1993.

Cridge, Annie Denton. Excerpt from *Man's Rights; or, How Would You Like It? In Future Perfect: American Science Fiction of the Nineteenth Century*, edited by Bruce Franklin, 317–336. New Brunswick: Rutgers University Press, 1995.

Csicsery-Ronay, Jr., Istvan. "Editorial Introduction: The British SF Boom." *Science Fiction Studies* 29 (November 2003): 353–354.

———. "The Lost Child: Notes on *White Queen*." *Femspec* 5.1 (2004): 234–253.

Cuordileone, K. A. "'Politics in an Age of Anxiety': Cold War Political Culture and the Crisis in American Masculinity, 1949–1960," *Journal of American History* 87 (2000): 515–545.

Daily Hampshire Gazette, March 4, 2005.

Davis, Angela. *Women. Race and Class*. New York: Random House, 1981.

Davis, Chandler. "Critique and Proposals — 1949." Reprinted in *Pseudopodium*, edited by Ray Davis http://www.pseudopodium.org/repress/chandler-davis/critique-1949.html.

Davis, Flora. *Moving the Mountain: The Women's Movement in America Since 1960*. New York: Simon & Schuster, 1991.

Dean, Robert D. "Masculinity as Ideology: John F. Kennedy and the Domestic Politics of Foreign Policy." *Diplomatic History* 22 (1998): 29–62.

De Beauvoir, Simone. *The Second Sex*. Penguin Modern Classics Series. Harmondsworth, Eng.: Penguin, [1949] 1983.

Delany, Samuel R. "Racism and Science Fiction." In *Dark Matter: A Century of Speculative Fiction from the African Diaspora*, edited by Sheree R. Thomas, 383–397 New York: Aspect/Warner Books, [1999] 2000.

———. *Silent Interviews: On Language, Race, Sex, Science Fiction, and Some Comics*. Hanover, N.H.: Wesleyan University Press, 1994.

Dick, Philip K. *Clans of the Alphane Moon*. 1964. New York: Carroll & Graf, 1988.

Disch, Thomas M., and Charles Naylor, eds. *Strangeness: A Collection of Curious Tales*. New York: Scribner's, 1977.

Dixon, Robert. *Writing the Colonial Adventure: Gender, Race, and Nation in Anglo-Australian Popular Fiction, 1875–1914*. New York: Cambridge University Press, 1995.

"Documents from the Women's Liberation Movement: An On-line Archival Collection." n.d. Special Collections Library, Duke University. http://scriptorium.lib.duke.edu/wlm.

Donawerth, Jane. *Frankenstein's Daughters: Women Writing Science Fiction*. Urbana: University of Illinois Press, 1997.

———. "Science Fiction." In *The Oxford Companion to Women's Writing in the United States*, edited by Cathy N. Davidson and Linda Wagner-Martin, 780–782. New York: Oxford University Press, 1995.

———. "Science Fiction by Women in the Early Pulps, 1926–1930." In *Utopian and Science Fiction by Women*, edited by Jane L. Donawerth and Carol A. Kolmerten, 137–152. Syracuse: Syracuse University Press, 1994.

Douglas, Ann. "Periodizing the American Century: Modernism, Postmodernism, and Postcolonialism in the Cold War Context." *Modernism/Modernity* 5 (1998): 71–98.

Disch, Thomas. "The Astounding Pamela Zoline." In *The Heat Death of the Universe and Other Stories by Pamela Zoline*, 7–9. Kingston, N.Y.: McPherson, 1988.

Dray, Philip. *At the Hands of Persons Unknown: The Lynching of Black Americans*. New York: Random House, 2002.

DuPlessis, Rachel Blau. *Writing Beyond the Ending: Narrative Strategies of Twentieth-Century Women Writers*. Bloomington: Indiana University Press, 1985.

Eisenstein, Hester. *Contemporary Feminist Thought*. London: Unwin, 1984.

Emshwiller, Carol. "Day at the Beach." In *SF: The Best of the Best*, edited by Judith Merril, 274–284. New York: Delacourt, [1959] 1967.

———. "Yukon." *Verging on the Pertinent*. Minneapolis, Minn.: Coffee House Press, 1989.

Faludi, Susan. *Backlash*. London: Vintage, 1992.

Firestone, Shulamith. *Dialectic of Sex: The Case for Feminist Revolution*. London: Paladin, [1970] 1972.

Fowler, Karen Joy. "What I Didn't See." Scifiction.com (July 2002).

Fox, George R. "The Electronic Wall." *Amazing Stories* 2, no. 3 (June 1927): 234–244.

Frank, Janrae, Jean Stine, and Forrest J. Ackerman, eds. *New Eves: Science Fiction about the Extraordinary Women of Today and Tomorrow.* Stamford, Conn.: Longmeadow, 1994.

Franklin, H. Bruce. *Robert A. Heinlein: America as Science Fiction.* New York: Oxford University Press, 1980.

———. "Vietnam and Other American Fantasies." *Science-Fiction Studies* 17, no. 3 (November 1990): 341–359.

———. *Vietnam and Other American Fantasies.* Amherst: University of Massachusetts Press, 2000.

Friedan, Betty. *The Feminine Mystique.* New York: Norton, 1963.

———. *The Feminine Mystique.* New York: Dell, [1963] 1984.

Gamble, Sarah. "'Shambleau . . . and others': The Role of the Female in the Fiction of C. L. Moore." In *Where No Man Has Gone Before*, edited by Lucie Armitt, 29–49. New York: Routledge, 1991.

Garnett, David, ed. *Orbit SF Yearbook.* London: Orbit, 1987.

Gearhart, Sally Miller. *The Wanderground: Tales of the Hill Women.* Watertown, Mass.: Persephone, 1979.

Gerhard, Jane. *Desiring Revolution : Second-Wave Feminism and the Rewriting of American Sexual Thought 1920 to 1982.* New York: Columbia University Press, 2001.

Gernsback, Hugo. "$500 Prize Story Contest." *Amazing Stories* 1, no. 9 (December 1926): 733.

———. "The $500 Cover Prize Contest." *Amazing Stories* 2, no. 3 (June 1927): 213.

———. Inset introduction to George R. Fox, "The Electronic Wall." *Amazing Stories* 2, no. 3 (June 1927): 234.

———. Inset introduction to Clare Winger Harris, "The Fate of the Poseidonia." *Amazing Stories* 2, no. 3 (June 1927): 245.

———. Inset introduction to Cyril G. Wates, "The Visitation." *Amazing Stories* 2, no. 3 (June 1927): 214.

———. "The Wonders of Creation." *Wonder Stories* (April 1931): 1209.

Gerster, Robin. "A bit of the other: Touring Vietnam." In *Gender and War: Australians at War in the Twentieth Century*, edited by Joy Damousi and Marilyn Lake, 223–235. Cambridge: Cambridge University Press, 1995.

Gettleman, Marvin E., Jane Franklin, Marilyn B. Young, H. Bruce Franklin, eds. *Vietnam and America: A Documented History.* Expanded ed. New York: Grove/Atlantic, 1995.

Gibson, William. *Neuromancer.* London: HarperCollins, [1984] 1993.

Gledhill, Christine. "Pleasurable Negotiations." In *Cultural Theory and Popular Culture*, edited by John Storey, 241–254. New York: Harvester/Wheatsheaf, 1994.

Gloss, Molly. *Wild Life.* New York: Simon and Schuster, 2000.

Gomoll, Jeanne. "An Open Letter to Joanna Russ." Reprinted from *Six Shooter* by Jeanne Gomoll, Linda Pickersgill, and Pam West. 1987. <http://www.geocities.com/Athens/8720/letter.htm2004>.

Govan, Sandra Y. "The Insistent Presence of Black Folk in the Novels of Samuel R. Delany." *Black American Literature Forum* 18, no. 2, (1984): 43–48.

Green, Michelle Erica. "'There Goes the Neighborhood': Octavia Butler's Demand for Diversity in Utopias." In *Utopian and SF by Women: Worlds of Dif-*

ference, edited by Jane L. Donawerth and Carol A. Kolmerton, 166–189. Syracuse N.Y.: Syracuse University Press, 1994.

Gubar, Susan. "C. L. Moore and the Conventions of Women's Science Fiction." *Science Fiction Studies* 7 (1980): 16–27.

Gunn, James E., ed. *The Road to Science Fiction #4*. N.P.: Mentor, 1982.

Haining, Peter, ed. *The Fantastic Pulps*. New York: Vintage Books, 1975.

Halberstam, Judith. *Female Masculinity*. Durham: Duke University Press, 1998.

Hamilton, Edmond. "The Man Who Evolved." *Wonder Stories* (April 1931): 1266–1277.

Haraway, Donna. "A Cyborg Manifesto: Science, Technology, and Socialist-Feminism in the Late Twentieth Century." In *Simians, Cyborgs and Women: The Reinvention of Nature*, 149–181. London: Free Association Books, 1991.

——. *Primate Visions: Gender, Race, and Nature in the World of Modern Science*. New York: Routledge. 1989.

Harris, Clare Winger. "The Artificial Man." *Science Wonder Quarterly* 1, no. 1 (Fall 1929): 78–83.

——. *Away from the Here and Now: Stories in Pseudo-Science*. Philadelphia: Dorrance, 1947.

——. "The Fate of the Poseidonia." *Amazing Stories* 2, no. 3 (June 1927): 245–52 and 267.

——. "The Fifth Dimension." *Amazing Stories* 3, no. 9 (December 1928): 823–825, 850.

——. "The Menace from Mars." *Amazing Stories* 3, no. 7 (October 1928): 582–597.

Harris, Rose Flores. "Zoline, Pamela A." In *Twentieth-Century Science-Fiction Writers*, edited by Curtis C. Smith, 610. New York: St. Martin's, 1981.

Harvey, Brett. *The Fifties: A Women's Oral History*. New York: HarperCollins, 1993.

Hayles, N. Katherine. *How We Became Posthuman: Virtual Bodies in Cybernetics*. Chicago: University of Chicago Press, 1999.

Heilbrun, Caroline G. *Toward a Recognition of Androgyny*. New York: Knopf, 1973.

Helford, Elyce Rae. "'Would You Really Rather Die Than Bear My Young?': The Construction of Gender, Race, and Species in Octavia E. Butler's 'Bloodchild.'" *African American Review* 28, no. 2, Summer, 1994. 259-71. http://www.sfwa.org/members/Butler/Autobiography.html.

Hoberek, Andrew P. "Sociology as Science Fiction." *Paradoxa: Studies in World Literary Genres* 18 (2003): 81–98.

Hochschild, Arlie Russell. *The Managed Heart: Commercialization of Human Feeling*. Berkeley and Los Angeles: University of California Press, 1983.

Hollinger, Veronica. "(Re)reading Queerly: Science Fiction, Feminism, and the Defamiliarization of Gender." *Science Fiction Studies* 26, no. 1 (March 1999): 23–40.

Høeg, Peter. *The Woman and the Ape*. Translated by Barbara Haveland. New York: Penguin Books, 1997.

Ingalls, Rachel. *Mrs. Caliban*. Harvard and Boston: Harvard Common Press, 1983.

Internet Speculative Fiction DataBase. The Cushing Library Science Fiction and Fantasy Research Collection and Institute for Scientific Computation. Texas A&M University: http://www.isfdb.org/sfdbase.html.

James, Edward. *Science Fiction in the Twentieth Century.* Oxford: Oxford University Press, 1994.

Jones, Alice Eleanor. "Created He Them." *The Magazine of Fantasy and Science Fiction* 8, no. 6, (June 1955): 29–37.

——. "The Happy Clown." *If* (December 1955): 105–115.

——. "The Honeymoon." *Redbook* (June 1957): 31, 88–91.

——. "How to Give Advice and Take It." *The Writer* 71 (December 1958): 12–13.

——. "How to Sell an Offbeat Story." *The Writer* 75 (March 1962): 18–20.

——. "If You Want to Know, Ask." *The Writer* 73 (August 1960): 16–18.

——. "Jenny Kissed Me." *Ladies' Home Journal* (November 1955): 93, 167–171.

——. "Life, Incorporated." *Fantastic Universe* (April 1955): 59–74.

——. "Miss Quatro." *Fantastic Universe* (June 1955): 55–63.

——. "Morning Watch." *Redbook* (November 1958): 42–43, 111–115.

——. "One Shattering Weekend." *Redbook* (July 1960): 40, 72–76.

——. "Ones That Got Away." *The Writer* 78 (May 1965): 17–18, 46.

——. "The Real Me." *Redbook* (October 1962): 62–63, 137–140.

——. "Recruiting Officer." *Fantastic* (October 1955): 87–101.

Jones, Gwyneth. "Balinese Dancer." *Asimov's Science Fiction* 21, no. 9 (September 1997): 54–74.

——. *Deconstructing the Star Ships: Science, Fiction and Reality.* Liverpool: University of Liverpool Press, 1999.

——. "Kairos: the Enchanted Loom." In *Edging into the Future: Science Fiction and Contemporary Cultural Transformation*, edited by Veronica Hollinger and Joan Gordon, 175–189. Philadelphia: University of Pennsylvania Press, 2003.

——. *White Queen.* London: Victor Gollancz, [1991] 1992.

Jones, James. "The Tuskegee Syphilis Experiment: 'A Moral Astigmatism.'" In *The 'Racial' Economy of Science*, edited by Sandra Harding, 275–286. Bloomington: Indiana University Press, 1993.

Kaledin, Eugenia. *Mothers and More: American Women in the 1950s.* Boston: Twayne, 1984.

Kaufmann, Sue. *The Diary of a Mad Housewife.* New York: Random House, 1967.

Kavka, Misha. "Feminism, Ethics, and History; or, What Is the 'Post' in 'Post-feminism'?" *Tulsa Studies in Women's Literature* 21, no. 1 (Spring 2002): 29–44.

Kay, Lily E. *Who Wrote the Book of Life?* Stanford: Stanford University Press, 2000.

Kelly, William P. "Catherine L. Moore." *Twentieth-Century American Science Fiction Writers, Part 2: M–Z.* Vol. 8 of *Dictionary of Literary Biography*, edited by David Cowart and Thomas L. Wymer, 30–34. Detroit, Mich.: Gale Research, 1981.

Kelso, Sylvia. "These are Not the Aliens You're Looking For: Reflections on Race, Theory and Writing in Recent SF." In *Flashes of the Fantastic: Selected Essays from the War of the Worlds Centennial, Nineteenth International Conference of the Fantastic in the Arts*, edited by David Ketterer 65–76. Bowling Green, Ohio: Greenwood, 1998.

Kennedy, John F. Freedom of Communications: Final Report on the Committee of Commerce, United States Senate: Part 1, The Speeches, Remarks, Press Conferences, and Statements of Senator John F. Kennedy, August 1 through November 7, 1960. Washington, D.C., 1961.

Ketterer, David. *New Worlds for Old: The Apocalyptic Imagination, Science Fiction, and American Literature.* Garden City, N.Y.: Anchor, 1974.

Kingston, Maxine Hong. *The Woman Warrior.* New York: Vintage Books, 1977.

Komter, Aafke. "Hidden Power in Marriage." *Gender and Society* 13 (1989): 187–216.

Landon, Brooks. *Science Fiction after 1900: From the Steam Man to the Stars.* New York: Twayne, 1997.

Larbalestier, Justine. *The Battle of the Sexes in Science Fiction.* Middleton, Conn.: Wesleyan University Press, 2002.

Larbalestier, Justine, and Helen Merrick. "The Revolting Housewife: Women and Science Fiction in the 1950s." *Paradoxa* 18 (2003): 136–156.

Lear, Martha Weinman. "What do these women want? The second feminist wave." *New York Times Magazine* (10 March 1968): 24–25, 50–62.

Lefanu, Sarah. *Feminism and Science Fiction.* Bloomington: University of Indiana Press, 1989.

———. *In the Chinks of the World Machine.* London: Women's Press, 1988.

Le Guin, Ursula K. *Dancing at the Edge of the World: Thoughts on Words, Women, Places.* New York: Grove, 1989.

———. *Eye of the Heron and The Word for World Is Forest.* London: VGSF, [1972] 1991.

———. *Language of the Night: Essays on Fantasy and Science Fiction.* New York: Berkley Books, 1982.

———. *The Left Hand of Darkness.* New York: Ace Books, 1969.

———. *The Wave in the Mind: Talks and Essays on the Writer, the Reader, and the Imagination.* Boston: Shambhala, 2004.

Levin, Ira. *The Stepford Wives.* New York: Random House, 1972.

Levine, Lena, and David Loth. *The Emotional Sex: Why Women Are the Way They Are Today.* New York: Morrow, 1964.

Lorde, Audre. "The Master's Tools Will Never Dismantle the Master's House." In *This Bridge Called My Back,* edited by Cherríe Moraga and Gloria Anzaldúa, 98–101. Watertown, Mass.: Persephone Press, 1981.

———. "Age, Race, Class, and Sex: Women Redefining Difference." In *Sister Outsider: Essays and Speeches.* Trumansburg, N.Y.: Crossing Press, 1984: 114–128.

Lorraine, Lilith. "Into the 28th Century." *Science Wonder Quarterly* 1, no. 2 (Winter 1930): 250–262 and 276.

Luckhurst, Roger. "Cultural Governance, New Labour, and the British SF Boom." *Science Fiction Studies* 30 (November 2003): 417–435.

McCaskell, Tim. "A History of Race/ism." Toronto Board of Education, 1994. <http://www3.sympatico.ca/twshreve/Inclusive/HistoryRacism.htm> (20 July 2000).

McHale, Brian. "Review of Monsters, Mushroom Clouds, and the Cold War." *Paradoxa: Studies in World Literary Genres* 18 (2003): 366–372.

Maddox, Tom. "After the Deluge: Cyberpunk in the '80s and '90s." In *Thinking Robots, an Aware Internet, and Cyberpunk Librarians,* edited by R. Bruce Miller and Milton T. Wolf. Chicago: Library and Information Technology Association, 1992.

Madle, Robert A. Letter to the Editor. *Amazing Stories* (February 1937), 137.

Mailer, Norman. *The Presidential Papers.* New York: Putnam, 1963.

Marshall, Barbara L. *Configuring Gender: Explorations in Theory and Politics.* Peterborough, Ont.: Broadview, 2000.

May, Elaine Tyler. *Homeward Bound: American Families in the Cold War Era.* New York: Basic Books, 1988.

Mendlesohn, Farah. "Gender, Power, and Conflict Resolution: 'Subcommittee' by Zenna Henderson." *Extrapolation* 35, no. 2 (1994): 120–129.

Merrick, Helen. "'Fantastic Dialogues': Critical Stories About Feminism and Science Fiction." In *Speaking Science Fiction: Dialogues and Interpretations,* edited by Andy Walker and David Seed, 52–68. Liverpool: Liverpool University Press, 2000.

Merril, Judith, ed. *England Swings SF: Stories of Speculative Fiction.* Garden City, N.Y.: Doubleday, 1968.

——. "That Only a Mother." In *Science Fiction Hall of Fame.* Edited by Robert Silverberg, 344–354. New York: Avon, [1948] 1970.

Merril, Judith, and Emily Pohl-Weary. *Better to Have Loved: The Life of Judith Merril.* Toronto, Canada: Between the Lines, 2002.

Meyerowitz, Joanne. "Beyond the Feminine Mystique: A Reassessment of Postwar Mass Culture, 1946–1958." In *Not June Cleaver: Women and Gender in Postwar America, 1945–1960,* edited by Joanne Meyerowitz, 229–262. Philadelphia: Temple University Press, 1994.

Miller, Stephen T., and William G. Contento. *The Locus Index to Science Fiction, Fantasy, and Weird Magazine Index (1890–2001).* CD-ROM. Oakland, Calif.: Locus, 2002.

Millett, Kate. *Sexual Politics.* London: Abacus, [1970] 1972.

Modleski, Tania. *Loving with a Vengeance: Mass-Produced Fantasies for Women.* New York: Routledge, 1996.

"Moorcock, Michael." In *England Swings SF: Stories of Speculative Fiction,* edited by Judith Merril 343–349. Garden City, N.Y.: Doubleday, 1968.

Moorcock, Michael, ed. *Best SF Stories from New Worlds 3.* New York: Berkley Publishing, 1968.

——. Introduction to *Best SF Stories from New Worlds 3,* 7–8. New York: Berkley Publishing, 1968.

——, ed. *New Worlds: An Anthology.* N.P.: Fontana Flamingo, 1983.

Moraga, Cherrie, and Gloria Anzaldúa, eds. *This Bridge Called My Back: Writings by Radical Women of Color.* Watertown, Mass.: Persephone, 1981.

Morgan, Robin. "Goodbye to All That." 1970. *Going Too Far: The Personal Chronicle of a Feminist.* New York: Vintage, 1978.

——. *Sisterhood is Powerful: An Anthology of Writings from the Women's Liberation Movement.* New York: Vintage, 1970.

Moskowitz, Sam. *The Immortal Storm: A History of Science Fiction Fandom.* Westport, Conn.: Hyperion Press, 1974.

——. "The Origins of Science Fiction Fandom: A Reconstruction." *Science Fiction Fandom.* Edited by Joe Sanders, 17–36. Westport, Conn.: Greenwood Press, 1994.

——. *When Women Rule.* New York: Walker, 1972.

Murphy, Pat. *Points of Departure.* New York: Spectra, 1990.

National Writers' Union. Report on Pay Rates for Freelance Journalists, 2002. http://www.nwu.org/journ/minrate.htm>, 7 July 2004.

New, Caroline. "Man Bad, Woman Good? Essentialisms and Ecofeminisms." *New Left Review* 219 (1996): 79–93.

———. "Oppressed and Oppressors? The Systematic Mistreatment of Men," *Sociology* 35 (2001): 729–748.

Newson, Adele S. "A review of *Dawn* and *Adult Rites*." *Black American Literature Forum* 23, no. 2 (Summer , 1989): 389–396.

Nicholls, Peter, ed. 1979. *The Encyclopedia of Science Fiction*. St. Albans, Eng.: Granada.

———. *The Science Fiction Encyclopedia*. Garden City, N.Y.: Doubleday, 1979.

Nies, Betsy L. *Eugenic Fantasies: Racial Ideology in the Literature and Popular Culture of the 1920s*. New York: Routledge, 2002.

Notkin, Debbie. "Why Have a Tiptree Award?" In *Flying Cups and Saucers*, edited by Debbie Notkin and the Secret Feminist Cabal, ix–xiii. Cambridge, Mass.: Edgewood, 1998.

"P. A. Zoline . . ." In *England Swings SF: Stories of Speculative Fiction*, edited by Judith Merril, 329–330. Garden City, N.Y.: Doubleday, 1968.

Paglia, Camille. *Sexual Personae: Art and Decadence from Nefertiti to Emily Dickinson*. New Haven: Yale University Press, 1990.

Papke, Mary. "What Do Women Want?" *Context: A Forum for Literary Arts and Culture* 11 (Fall 2002): 12–13.

Pearson, Wendy. "Taking Apart SF: Gwyneth Jones's *Deconstructing the Starships: Science, Fiction and Reality*." *Strange Horizons* (10 September 2001). <http://www.strangehorizons.com/2001/20010910/taking_apart_SF.shtml> [26 September 2003].

Piercy, Marge. *Woman on the Edge of Time*. New York: Knopf; London: The Women's Press, 1976.

Piper, H. Beam. "Omnilingual." *Astounding Science Fiction* (February 1957): 8–46.

Platt, Charles. "The Rape of Science Fiction." *Science Fiction Eye* 1, no. 5 (July 1989): 45–49.

Pohl, Frederik. *The Way the Future Was: A Memoir*. New York: Del Rey, 1978.

Powell, Thomas. *The Persistence of Racism in America*. Lanham, Md: University Press of America, 1992.

Rabkin, Eric S. "Science Fiction Women Before Liberation." In *Future Females: A Critical Anthology*, edited by by Marleen S. Barr, 9–25. Bowling Green, Ohio: Bowling Green State University Popular Press, 1981.

Radway, Janice A. *Reading the Romance: Women, Patriarchy, and Popular Literature*. Chapel Hill: University of North Carolina Press, [1984] 1991.

Reed, Kit. "To Lift a Ship." *The Magazine of Fantasy and Science Fiction* (April 1962): 68–76.

Rice, Louise, and Tonjoroff-Roberts. "The Astounding Enemy." *Amazing Stories Quarterly* 3, no. 1 (Winter 1930): 78–103.

Richards, Alfred H. Fan letter. *Amazing Stories* 2, no. 6 (September 1927): 610.

Roberts, Adam. "James Tiptree Jr's 'And I Awoke and Found Me Here on the Cold Hill's Side' as Neocolonialist Fable." *The Alien Online*. April 2003. <http://www.thealienonline.net/columns/rcsf_tiptree_apr03.asp?tid=7&scid=55&iid=1591> (February 12, 2004).

Roberts, Garyn G., ed. *The Prentice Hall Anthology of Science Fiction and Fantasy.* Upper Saddle River, N.J.: Prentice Hall, 2001.

Roberts, Robin. *A New Species: Gender and Science in Science Fiction.* Urbana: University of Illinois Press, 1993.

Rose, Hilary. "Dreaming the Future," *Hypatia* 3, no. 1, (1988): 119–138.

Rosen, Ruth. *The World Split Open: How the Modern Women's Movement Changed America.* New York: Viking Penguin, 2000.

Rubin, Gayle. "The Traffic in Women: Notes on the 'Political Economy' of Sex." In *Towards a Cultural Anthropology of Women,* ed. Rayna R. Reiter, 157–210. New York: Monthly Review Press, 1975.

Russ, Joanna. "Amor Vincit Fœminam: The Battle of the Sexes in Science Fiction." *Science-Fiction Studies* 7 (March 1980): 2–15. Reprinted in *To Write Like a Woman: Essays in Feminism and Science Fiction.* Bloomington: Indiana University Press, 1995, 41–59.

——. *The Female Man.* New York: Bantam, 1975; Boston: Beacon, 1986.

——. *How to Suppress Women's Writing.* London: Women's Press, [1983] 1984.

——. "The Image of Women in Science Fiction." In *Images of Women in Fiction: Feminist Persepectives,* edited by Susan Koppelman Cornillon, 79–94. Bowling Green, Ohio: Bowling Green University Popular Press, [1971] 1973.

——. *Picnic on Paradise.* New York: Ace, 1968.

——. *To Write Like a Woman: Essays in Feminism and Science Fiction.* Bloomington: Indiana University Press, 1995.

——. *What Are We Fighting For? Sex, Race, Class, and the Future of Feminism.* New York: St. Martin's, 1998.

——. "When It Changed." In *The Road to Science Fiction.* Vol. 3, *From Heinlein to Here,* edited by James Gunn, 490–496. Clarkson, Calif.: White Wolf, [1972] 1979.

St. Clair, Margaret. *Signs of the Labrys.* New York: Bantam, 1963.

Sanders, Scott. "Women As Nature in Science Fiction." In *Future Females: A Critical Anthology,* edited by Marleen S. Barr, 42–59. Bowling Green, Ohio: Bowling Green State University Popular Press, 1981.

Sargent, Pamela. Introduction to *The New Women of Wonder,* xiii–xxxiv. New York: Vintage, 1978.

——. "Introduction: Women and Science Fiction." In *Women of Wonder: Science Fiction Stories by Women about Women,* edited by Pamela Sargent, xiii–lxiv. New York: Vintage, 1975.

——, ed. *More Women of Wonder.* New York: Vintage, 1976.

——, ed. *New Women of Wonder: Recent Science Fiction Stories by Women about Women.* New York: Vintage Books, 1978.

——, ed. *Women of Wonder: Science Fiction Stories by Women about Women.* New York: Vintage Books, 1975.

——, ed. *Women of Wonder, The Classic Years: Science Fiction by Women from the 1940s to the 1970s.* Orlando, Fla.: Harcourt Brace, 1995.

——, ed. *Women of Wonder, The Contemporary Years: Science Fiction by Women from the 1970s to the 1990s.* Orlando, Fla.: Harcourt Brace, 1995.

Sauer, Rob, ed. *Voyages: Scenarios for a Ship Called Earth.* N.P.: Ballantine, 1971.

Saunders, Charles R. "Why Blacks Should Read (and Write) Science Fiction." In *Dark Matter—A Century of Speculative Fiction from the African Diaspora*, edited by Sheree Renee Thomas, 398–404. New York: Warner Books, 2000.

Saxton, Josephine. "Goodbye to all that . . ." In *Where No Man Has Gone Before: Women and Science Fiction*, edited by Lucie Armitt, 205–217. London: Routledge, 1991.

Schlesinger, Arthur M., Jr. "The Crisis of American Masculinity." November 1958. In *The Politics of Hope*. Cambridge, Mass.: Riverside, 1962.

———. "The New Mood in Politics." January 1960. In *The Politics of Hope*. Cambridge, Mass.: Riverside, 1962.

———. *The Vital Center: Our Purposes and Perils on the Tightrope of American Liberalism*. Boston: Houghton Mifflin, 1949.

Scott, Melissa. *Trouble and Her Friends*. New York: Tor, 1994.

Seed, David. *American Science Fiction and the Cold War: Literature and Film*. Chicago: Fitzroy Dearborn, 1999.

Shakespeare, William. *The Tempest*. Edited by Northrop Frye. In *The Complete Works*, edited by Alfred Harbage. Baltimore: Penguin Books, 1969.

Sheldon, Alice. "Biographical Sketch for *Contemporary Authors*." In *Meet Me at Infinity: The Uncollected Tiptree: Fiction and Nonfiction*. New York.: Tor Books, 2000.

———. "A Woman Writing Science Fiction and Fantasy". In *Women of Vision*, edited by Denise Du Pont, 43–58. New York: St Martin's, 1988.

Sheldon, Raccoona. "The Screwfly Solution." *Analog* (June 1977): 54–73.

Siegel, Mark. *Hugo Gernsback: Father of Modern Science Fiction*. San Bernardino, Calif.: Borgo, 1988.

Silverberg, Robert, ed. *The Mirror of Infinity: A Critics' Anthology of Science Fiction*. New York: Harper & Row, 1973.

———. "Who Is Tiptree, What Is He?" Introduction to *Warm Worlds and Otherwise* by James Tiptree Jr., ix–xviii. New York: Ballantine Books, 1975.

Smith, Anna D. *Twilight Los Angeles, 1992*. New York: Doubleday, 1994.

———. *House Arrest and Piano*. New York: Anchor Books, 2004.

Smith, Anthony, ed. Introduction to *Television: An International History*, 1–6. 2nd ed. Oxford: Oxford University Press, 1998.

Smith, Curtis C., ed. *Twentieth-Century Science-Fiction Writers*. 2nd ed. Chicago: St. James, 1986.

Smith, Jeffrey D., ed. "Symposium: Women in Science Fiction." In *Khatru 3 & 4*. 1975; expanded second printing, edited by Jeanne Gomoll. May 1993.

"Source Works of the Second Wave of Feminism: International Archives of the Second Wave of Feminism." International Archives of the Second Wave of Feminism, Berkeley, California: <http://home.att.net/~celesten/2w_bibl.html>.

Stauber, John C., and Sheldon Rampton. *Toxic Sludge is Good for You: Lies, Damn Lies and the Public Relations Industry*. Monroe, Maine: Common Courage Press. 1995.

Steans, Jill. *Gender and International Relations: An Introduction*. Cambridge: Polity, 1998.

Sterling, Bruce, ed. *Mirrorshades: The Cyberpunk Anthology*. London: HarperCollins, 1994.

Stone, Leslie F. "The Conquest of Gola." *Wonder Stories* (April 1931): 1278–1287.

———. "Day of the Pulps." *Fantasy Commentator* 9, no. 50, part 2 (Fall 1997): 100–103, 152.

———. "The Great Ones." *Astounding Stories* (July 1937): 75–89.

———. "Men with Wings."*Air Wonder Stories* (July 1929): 58–87.

———. "Out of the Void." *Amazing Stories* (August 1929): 440–455; and (September 1929): 544–565.

———. "Women with Wings." *Air Wonder Stories* (May 1930): 985–1003.

Sullivan, Nikki. *A Critical Introduction to Queer Theory*. Edinburgh: University of Edinburgh Press, 2003.

Sutin, Lawrence. *Divine Invasions: A Life of Philip K. Dick*. 1989; New York: Citadel, 1991.

Tanner, Tony. Introduction to *Villette*. London: Penguin, 1979.

Thomas, Sheree R., ed. *Dark Matter: A Century of Speculative Fiction from the African Diaspora*. New York: Aspect/Warner Books, 2000.

———. *Dark Matter: Reading the Bones*. New York: Aspect/Warner Books, 2004.

———. Personal interview. March 7, 2005.

Thompson, Denise. *Radical Feminism Today*. London: SAGE, 2001.

Tiptree, James, Jr. "Everything but the Signature Is Me." In *Meet Me at Infinity: The Uncollected Tiptree: Fiction and Nonfiction*. New York: Tor Books, 2000.

———. *Meet Me at Infinity: The Uncollected Tiptree: Fiction and Nonfiction*. New York: Tor Books, 2000.

———. "A Woman Writing Science Fiction." *Meet Me at Infinity: The Uncollected Tiptree: Fiction and Nonfiction*. New York: Tor Books, 2000.

———. "The Women Men Don't See." *Warm Worlds and Otherwise*, 131–164. New York: Ballantine Books, 1975.

———. "Zero at the Bone." *Meet Me at Infinity: The Uncollected Tiptree: Fiction and Nonfiction*. New York: Tor Books, 2000.

"The James Tiptree, Jr. Award," *http://www.tiptree.org* (accessed July 3, 2004).

Tucker, Jeffrey Allen. "Studying the Works of Samuel R. Delany." *Ohio University College of Arts and Science Forum* 15 (Spring 1998).

Turner, William B. *A Genealogy of Queer Theory*. Philadelphia: Temple University Press, 2000.

Tuttle, Lisa. "The Bone Flute." *The Magazine of Fantasy and Science Fiction* (May 1981): 114–128.

———. *Encyclopedia of Feminism*. Harlow, Eng.: Longman, 1986.

———. "In Translation." In. *Zenith: The Best in New British Science Fiction*, edited by David Garnett, 7–32. London: Sphere, 1989.

———. "Stranger in the House." In *Clarion II: An Anthology of Speculative Fiction and Criticism*, edited by Robin Scott Wilson, 233–239. New York: Signet, 1972.

———. "Wives." *The Magazine of Fantasy and Science Fiction* 57, no. 6 (December 1979): 6–13.

———. "Women SF Writers." In *The Encyclopedia of Science Fiction*, edited by John Clute and Peter Nicholls, 1344–1345. New York: St. Martin's Griffin, 1993.

——. "Women SF Writers." In *The Encyclopedia of Science Fiction*, edited by John Clute and Peter Nicholls, 1344–1345.

——. *Writing Fantasy and Science Fiction*, London: A & C Black, 2001.

Tuttle, Lisa, and George R. R. Martin. "One-Wing." *Analog*, pt. I (January 1980), 12–64; pt. II (February 1980), 48–99.

——. "The Storms of Windhaven." *Analog* (May 1975): 12–65.

Wates, Cyril G. "The Visitation." *Amazing Stories* 2, no. 3 (June 1927): 214–233.

Weinbaum, Batya. "Leslie F. Stone as a Case of Author-Reader Responding." *Foundation* 80 (Autumn 2000): 40–51.

——. "Sex-Role Reversal in the Thirties: Leslie F. Stone's 'The Conquest of Gola.'" *Science-Fiction Studies* 73 (November 1997): 471–482.

Wells, H. G. "The Star." 1899; reprinted in *Science Fiction: A Historical Anthology*, edited by Eric S. Rabkin, 222–233. New York: Oxford University Press, 1983.

West, Cornell. *Prophetic Thought in Postmodern Times*. Monroe, Maine: Common Courage Press, 1993.

Westfahl, Gary. *The Mechanics of Wonder: The Creation of the Idea of Science Fiction*. Liverpool: Liverpool University Press, 1998.

Westlake, Donald. "Don't Call Me, I'll Call You," 1961. Reprinted in *Mystery Scene* 78 (Winter 2003).

Wilhelm, Kate. "The Chosen." In *Orbit 6*. edited by Damon Knight, 92–114. New York: Putman, 1970.

——. "The Last Days of the Captain." *The Mile-Long Spaceship*. New York: Berkley, 1963.

——. "When the Moon Was Red." *The Downstairs Room and Other Speculative Fiction*. New York: Doubleday, 1968.

——. "Windsong." *The Downstairs Room and Other Speculative Fiction*. New York: Doubleday, 1968.

Williams, Sheila, ed. *Hugo and Nebula Winners from Asimov's Science Fiction Magazine*. New York: Random House, 1995.

Williamson, Jack. Letter to the editor. *Astounding Stories* (June 1937): 157.

Willis, Connie, and Sheila Williams, eds. *A Women's Liberation*. New York: Warner Aspect, 2001.

Wollheim, Donald A. *World's Best SF 1988*. New York: DAW, 1988.

Wolmark, Jenny. *Aliens and Others: Science Fiction, Feminism and Postmodernism*. London: Harvester Wheatsheaf, 1993.

Wood, Susan. "Kate Wilhelm Is a Writer," *Starship* 17 (1980): 7–16.

Wright, Richard. *Native Son*. New York: Harper & Row, 1966.

Yaszek, Lisa. "Media Landscapes and Social Satire in Postwar Women's Science Fiction." *Foundation: The International Review of Science Fiction*, 95, forthcoming 2005.

——. "Unhappy Housewife Heroines, Galactic Suburbia, and Nuclear War: A New History of Midcentury Women's Science Fiction." *Extrapolation* 44, no. 1 (2003): 97–111.

Zangrando, Robert L. *The NAACP Campaign Against Lynching, 1909–1950*. Philadelphia: Temple University Press, 1980.

Zoline, Pamela. *Annika and the Wolves: A Fairy Tale*. With drawings by the author. West Branch, Iowa: Hot Chocolate Books, Coffee House Press, 1985.

———. *Busy About the Tree of Life*. London: The Women's Press, 1988.

———. "The Heat Death of the Universe." *New Worlds* 51, no. 173 (July 1967): 32–39.

———. *The Heat Death of the Universe and Other Stories*. With an introduction by Thomas M. Disch. Kingston, N.Y.: McPherson, 1988.

List of Contributors

Brian Attebery, the author of *Decoding Gender in Science Fiction* and many other critical works, also coedited, with Ursula K. Le Guin and Karen Joy Fowler, *The Norton Book of Science Fiction*. When not directing the graduate program in English at Idaho State University, he moonlights as a teacher and performer on the cello. He is married to folklorist Jennifer Eastman Attebery.

Jane Donawerth, professor of English and affiliate in Women's Studies at the University of Maryland, has published books on Shakespeare and early modern women writers, and the history of rhetorical theory, as well as science fiction by women. She has won seven teaching awards and two NEH Fellowships. She is currently working on a critical study of history of rhetorical theory by women and an anthology of Golden Age science fiction by women in the pulps.

L. Timmel Duchamp is the author of *The Grand Conversation* (2004), a collection of essays; *Love's Body, Dancing in Time* (2004), a collection of short fiction; and *Alanya to Alanya* (2005), a novel. She has been a finalist for the Sturgeon, Homer, and Nebula awards and has been short-listed several times for the James Tiptree, Jr. Memorial Award. She is also the founder and editor of Aqueduct Press, which has published Gwyneth Jones's Philip K. Dick Award–winning novel, *Life,* and Nicola Griffith's Lambda Award–nominated collection, *With Her Body.* An ample selection of her critical writing as well as a few of her stories can be found at <ltimmel.home.mindspring.com>.

Andrea Hairston is Professor of Theatre and Afro American Studies at Smith College. She is the artistic director of Chrysalis Theatre and her plays have been produced at Yale Rep, Rites and Reason, the Kennedy Center, StageWest, and on Public Radio and Public Television. She is the author of *Mindscape* (2006), a speculative novel published by Aqueduct Press. "Griots of the Galaxy," a short story, appears in *So Long Been Dreaming: Postcolonial Visions of the Future* (2004). Andrea has received many awards for her writing from the National Endowment for the Arts, the Rockefeller Foundation, and the Ford Foundation.

Joan Haran is a Research Associate at the University of Cardiff in the ESRC Centre for Economic and Social Aspects of Genomics (CESAGen). She has a Ph.D. in Sociology from the University of Warwick; her thesis on feminist science fiction was entitled "Re-Visioning Feminist Futures: Literature as Social Theory." Joan's work on science fiction is part of a broader research program in feminist cultural studies with a particular focus on gender, technology, and representation. Joan has had essays on sf published in the journals *Extrapolation* and *Foundation,* and in the edited collections *Science Fiction: Critical Frontiers* and *Gender, Health and Healing: The Public/Private Divide.* She is also conducting ethnographic research on WisCon, the Madison-based feminist science fiction convention.

Cathy Hawkins is the assistant editor of *Australian Feminist Studies.* Her doctoral thesis, entitled "The Woman Who Saved the World: Re-imagining the Female Hero in 1950s Science Fiction Films," allowed her to explore her love of science fiction and cinema history. Other research interests include the female body and popular culture. Her paper "The Monster Body of Myra Hindley" is published online in *Scan* 1:4 (2004) <www.scan.net.au>. Cathy was part of the organizing committee for "Body Modification: Changing Bodies, Changing Selves" held in 2003 at Macquarie University in Sydney, Australia. She is coeditor of a 2005 special edition of the journal *Women's Studies* based on papers from the conference. She has taught women's studies and cultural studies. Cathy lives in Sydney with her partner and four aliens cleverly disguised as domestic cats.

Veronica Hollinger is Professor of Cultural Studies and Director of the Centre for Theory, Culture and Politics at Trent University in Peterborough, Ontario. She has published many articles on science fiction, with particular attention to feminist sf. Since 1990 she has been a coeditor of *Science Fiction Studies*; she is also coeditor, with Joan Gordon, of two scholarly collections, *Blood Read: The Vampire as Metaphor in Contemporary Culture* (University of Pennsylvania Press, 1997) and *Edging into the Future: Science Fiction and Contemporary Cultural Transformation* (University of Pennsylvania Press, 2002). She is a past winner of the Science Fiction Research Association's Pioneer Award.

Josh Lukin was born in Youngstown, Ohio, and attended Youngstown State University and State University of New York, Buffalo. He is the editor, with Samuel R. Delany, of *Paradoxa 18: Fifties Fictions.* His critical work has addressed authors as diverse as Walt Whitman, Oscar Wilde, Grant Morrison, Philip K. Dick, and Patricia Highsmith; he has also published extended interviews with L. Timmel Duchamp, William Tenn, and Chandler Davis. His acclaimed presentation at the 2002 convention of the Modern Language Association, "Feminist Science Fiction and the New Realism of the Body," was his first foray into feminist sf criticism. As of this writing, Dr. Lukin teaches in the English Department of Temple University, where he and novelist Don Belton occasionally bemuse the staff with their renditions of classic show tunes.

Mary E. Papke is Professor of English and Associate Dean of Graduate Studies at the University of Tennessee. She is the author of *Verging on the Abyss: The Social Fiction of Kate Chopin and Edith Wharton* (1990) and *Susan Glaspell: A Research and Production Sourcebook* (1993), and the editor of *Twisted from the Ordinary: Essays on American Literary Naturalism* (2003). In addition, she has published essays on feminist theory, postmodern women writers, the unpublished drama of Evelyn Scott, the political theater of Sean O'Casey, and Marxist literary criticism in early twentieth-century America, among other topics. All of these projects have focused significantly on issues of gender and class ideologies as well as the process of ethical and aesthetic evaluation.

Wendy Pearson holds a postdoctoral fellowship at the University of Western Ontario, where she is working on a project dealing with indigenous performativity in Canada and Australia, as well as teaching in Film Studies. She has published a number of articles in the areas of science fiction, sexuality, and queer theory, and Canadian literature and film. In 2000, she was awarded the Pioneer Award by the Science Fiction Research Association.

Lisa Yaszek is assistant professor in the School of Literature, Communication, and Culture at the Georgia Institute of Technology, where she also serves as literary administrator for the Bud Foote Science Fiction Collection. Her research interests include postmodern literature, gender studies, and science fiction. Yaszek's work appears in journals including *Rethinking History, electronic book review, Extrapolation,* and *Signs: Journal of Women in Culture and Society.* Her book *The Self Wired: Technology and Subjectivity in Contemporary Narrative* is available from Routledge Press.